. *Leading Lady* .

By the same author

When the Boat Comes In (Books I, II and III)
A Woman to Be Loved (Book I) ⎫
An Impossible Woman (Book II) ⎬ in the same series

JAMES   MITCHELL

. *Leading Lady* .

SINCLAIR-STEVENSON

For Peter and Gillian

First published in Great Britain in 1993
by Sinclair-Stevenson
an imprint of Reed Consumer Books Ltd
Michelin House, 81 Fulham Road, London SW3 6RB
and Auckland, Melbourne, Singapore and Toronto

A CIP catalogue record for this book
is available at the British Library
ISBN 1 85619 213 X

Typeset by ROM-Data Corp. Ltd, Falmouth, Cornwall, England
Printed and bound in Great Britain
by Clays Ltd, St Ives PLC

. 1 .

The field was a big one; seventeen horses at least, but there was no doubt who her money was on: the big chestnut mare, Bridget O'Dowd, was a devil to go and increasing its lead with every stride. Funny thing though. All the other jockeys wore racing silks, as was only right and proper, but the one riding her Bridget was in khaki, and old-fashioned khaki at that: the uniform of an infantry officer of fifteen years ago; the time of Passchendaele and Ypres.

And another funny thing: the way the horses moved: not a gallop, not even a hard trot, but a kind of rhythmic bounding as if they had some kind of clockwork spring inside them. She could even hear it: a steady, pulsing sound like a clock ticking. Bridget's spring must be stronger than anybody else's, she thought. The old girl was moving like a clockwork Bentley, khaki rider and all, moving so fast that she was almost out of sight when her rider turned to look back and touched the peak of his cap with the swagger stick he was using instead of a whip, and then it all made sense. Bridget's rider was John Patterson, a captain in the Royal Northumbrians, and the man she had been engaged to; the man who had been shot dead at La Bassée Canal on the 10th of November, 1918. Of course it made sense: the sort of sense that dreams make.

Jane Whitcomb stretched and woke up. There were no horses and no race course. She was coiled in a deck chair by the Blagdon Hall tennis court, watching, or rather preparing to swear that she had watched, a doubles game: her own Charles Lovell and John Patterson's brother Bob battling hard against Jay Bower and Piers Hilyard. Gracious how they all hated to lose. But at least the combat explained one thing: the swift tick tock of the horses was the sound of tennis ball meeting racket. She looked at the table

1

beside her. Someone had put a jug of lemonade and glasses on it: ice too, because for once the Northern sun was strong and Charles rather tended to demand value for what he paid for, in servants as in everything else. Bankers, he insisted, were like that. . . . Bob sneaked one past Bower, who chased it of course, but wasn't quite fast enough.

'Two games all,' Piers Hilyard said. Well at least she knew what the score was.

Lovell faced Bower, and served an ace. No doubt it was all very gratifying and all that – Charles was well past forty after all, – but really there was no need to look quite so pleased about it. On the other hand Charles detested Jay Bower, even though he usually went to enormous pains to pretend he didn't. . . . Charles served to Piers, who got it back, but Bob picked up the return and once again sneaked it past Bower. If anything Charles looked even happier. She really would have to speak to him.

Or would she? Speaking to someone in that way meant being married to them – like Mummy and her major – and she had no intention of being married to Charles, even if it were possible, no matter how pleasant it was to sleep with him. On the other hand she was very fond of him, and it hurt her to see him so schoolboyish.

She pulled down the brim of her hat to shade her face. Charles didn't like her to get too brown, and indeed it looked silly when one dressed for dinner: brown face and neck and lily white from there on, and with this year's fashions there on was rather a long way. Better to stay lily white, until one went to Cannes or Monte Carlo or somewhere. All the other women were lily whites too, except the ones who hunted a lot, but where on earth were they all – and their men for that matter? And then she remembered. There was racing at Hexham, which no doubt explained her dream. It certainly explained why she was all alone, except for the four combatants. Already Jay Bower had a sort of Dying Gladiator look about him.

Had their hostess gone to the races too? she wondered. Lovell's cousin Mrs Chandler-Spicer, pretty and plump and widowed, had come up from Maidenhead, where she lived in some style in a house Charles owned: sort of a grace and favour house. She was really awfully good at being a hostess, but she did rather worry about it,

2

thought Jane, and pretty, plump ladies shouldn't worry, or at least not show it.

Then Catherine Bower, Jay's wife, came over to join her. Sweet little dress – Hartnell by the look of it, but she was as miserable as Jay: sort of a Dying Gladiator's Mate. Please God, thought Jane, not advice to the lovelorn. Not here. Catherine came over to the deck chair next to hers, and behind her came Lovell's spaniel bitch Rosie, determined not to do anything so foolish as scamper on such a hot day.

'Who's winning?' Catherine asked.

'Charles and Bob,' said Jane.

The news cheered Catherine for two reasons, thought Jane. Bob was winning and Bower was losing.

'They do go at it,' she said aloud. 'You'd think it was a war.'

'They all hate to be beaten,' Catherine said. 'Especially – ' she hesitated. 'Especially Piers,' she said at last.

Piers Hilyard was her brother: a career soldier who hated being beaten at anything, even snakes and ladders, but he wasn't the one she had meant. Of the four of them the one who most hated to lose, the acknowledged champion, was her husband, Jay. Even Charles was a mere runner-up.

'I wish I'd gone racing,' Catherine said, and poured lemonade.

'Why didn't you?'

'I can't stand the women.'

Jane looked at her. 'None of them?'

'Not one,' Catherine said. 'They're all so bloody worthy.'

'They're supposed to be,' said Jane. 'They're all good works and things, or MPs' wives, or maybe both. That's why Charles invited them.'

'Is that why he invited me, too?'

'I rather think,' said Jane, 'that he thought you might be company for me.'

'Oh God,' Catherine said, 'I'm sorry.'

They watched in silence for a while. Bob and Charles were leading, four games to two, but Rosie, who found the game foolish – nothing was shot; there was nothing to retrieve – came to sit beside Jane.

'You see,' said Catherine, 'I bore even the bloody dogs.'

3

'Nonsense,' said Jane. 'Rosie likes the way I pull her ears, don't you my love?' She pulled one delicately, and the spaniel sighed.

'You never did that to Foch,' said Catherine.

'Foch's ears simply weren't designed for pulling,' said Jane, surprised as always to discover how much it hurt to pronounce her Scottie's name, even though he had been dead for so long.

'What Foch liked,' she continued, 'was to have his back scratched at a particular point which he couldn't reach himself. For that he would have forgone chocolate biscuits.'

'You really loved him, didn't you?'

The question was kindly meant, so she answered it truthfully. 'Every day of our lives.'

'Like a child, you mean?'

Like a dog, you idiot, thought Jane. What do I know about loving a child? Aloud she said, 'More like a grandfather half the time. Foch was a very stern moralist. All that Scots Calvinism, I expect.'

Catherine hadn't heard a word.

'I'd like a child,' she said. 'But not Jay's. Definitely not Jay's.'

Jane said nothing. Short of getting up and walking away, there was nothing else she could do. Rosie nudged her, and Jane began to pull at her other ear as Catherine said, 'We're going to split, you know.'

'Divorce?'

'Nothing else for it,' Catherine said. 'He's hopeless in bed.'

Say nothing, Jane told herself. This is none of your business.

'I doubt if he could give me a baby even if I wanted him to,' said Catherine, then broke off to applaud as a backhand return from Charles floated, just out of reach, past Bower, and her brother looked at her husband with a sort of wellbred despair.

'Divorce seems the only possible answer,' Catherine continued. 'At least when I'm rid of him I might meet some chap who knows how to go about it.' Her eyes were on Bob. A lot of women's eyes were, from time to time. It never seemed to do them any good: any lasting good, thought Jane.

'Does Piers know?' Jane asked. Piers was Catherine's twin, and there wasn't a lot he didn't know about her.

'Suspects, of course. Naturally,' said Catherine. 'But he doesn't pry. We don't, you know. When the time comes I'll tell him.'

'And your parents? And Lady Mangan?'

'Mummy and Daddy will be horrified,' said Catherine. 'Then they'll take another cruise and forget about it. As for Granny – she may not even know.'

Lady Mangan had had a stroke after seeing her house in County Meath burned down by Irish terrorists.

'She's ill again?' Jane asked.

'Another stroke,' Catherine said. 'Not so bad as the first one, but bad enough. After all her hard work. Learning to think again, to speak, to read. She's back to where she started. You remember the fun she had – even after the first one? Flying all over the place, Egypt for the winter, bossing us all right, left and centre. It's all over. Finis. All she can do is lie there. She can't even tell us what she's thinking – *if* she's thinking, that is.'

'But why on earth didn't you tell me?' asked Jane.

'You're not the easiest person to catch up with these days,' Catherine said. 'And not all that easy to talk to when I do catch up with you.' Jane stiffened. 'I think it's because you're so contented with your life,' Catherine said. 'When you're the way I am, it isn't all that easy to talk with the happy ones.'

Jane relaxed. The wail in Catherine's voice was like that of a child seeking comfort that no grown-up will offer, and yet Jane felt sorry. There was nothing on earth that she could do, but she could at least feel sorry.

The men on the court were gathering up tennis balls, restoring racquets to their presses before they walked over to where the women sat.

'Good game?' Jane asked.

'Six two,' said Bob. 'To us. Just the one set. It's too hot to play any more.'

'Just as well,' Piers Hilyard said. 'One thrashing's enough for one day.'

Bower went up to his wife. 'These Limeys were too good for me,' he said in his best American accent. 'Maybe your old man's getting too old for this game.'

'Maybe,' said Catherine, and Bower flinched.

More softly she added, 'But I don't think so. There'll be a next time, you'll see.'

5

And just what does she think she's playing at? Jane wondered. Nasty then nice like teasing a dog. Snatch the bone away then fling it straight to its jaws. Or was it because Bob was watching? She rose to her feet. Time to go indoors and drink tea. At least it was cool indoors. Bob Patterson walked with her towards the house.

'You'll know our Andy's getting married?' he said.

'Certainly,' said Jane. 'My invitation arrived before I left London.'

'I'm best man,' said Bob.

'So I should hope,' said Jane. 'Are you after a lift in my Bentley?'

'Be a treat, that would.'

'I shan't let you drive.'

'I'll just have to get one of my own then,' said Bob. 'All the same, I wouldn't say no to a lift.'

He smiled at her, and hurried ahead. Was it totally by chance that Catherine moved into him as he did so, obliging him to reach out to her and steady her on her feet?

What to wear at dinner. A problem, as so often it was, but not insoluble. God knows she had brought enough frocks. All the same it would be as well to have her mind made up, before the arrival of the maid Charles had assigned to her, the maid who bore such a startling resemblance to Lord Blagdon, from whom Charles had bought the house. A large and occasionally clumsy woman, Hepscott, though surprisingly deft at doing up buttons and tying tapes. It was being kept waiting for decisions that brought on the clumsiness. Better to make up one's mind in advance. The house telephone rang and she picked it up at once. It could only be Charles.

'Yes?' she said.

'There are some figures I'd like to go over with you,' he said. 'Is now a convenient time?'

'Perfectly,' she said. 'Hepscott won't be coming to help me dress for at least twenty minutes.'

'Oh,' said Charles. Once again she pondered the fact that love, desire, need, whatever it was, could make even a very intelligent man transparently obvious. After a moment he said, 'I'll come at once then.'

Come he did, with a file with figures in it, just in case he happened to run into someone: one of the thirty servants perhaps,

6

or the fifteen other house-guests. All the same the first thing he did was kiss her, and very satisfactory that was; not just because he kissed very well, but because the woman he held with such urgent need was well into her thirties and trying and failing to stick to a diet. She freed herself at last. Her lipstick would need repairs before Hepscott arrived.

'The figures?' she said.

'There's only one,' he said, touching it until she backed away. Charles could be very persuasive.

'All the same I do want to talk to you. About Felston.' She sat down and lit a cigarette. He was serious at last.

'The Depression's just about hit the bottom,' he said, 'and Felston's taking it worse than most.'

'As usual,' she said.

'Of course,' he said. 'It's entirely the wrong sort of town for 1932.'

'How on earth can a town be the wrong sort?'

'The wrong sort of industries,' said Charles. 'Coal, shipping, heavy engineering – and that means the wrong sort of skills. All over the industrialised world there's too much coal and shipping and heavy engineering – and most of them can do it cheaper than Felston.'

'The people there aren't lazy,' she said.

'I'm not suggesting they are. But their yards and factories are old. Out of date. And there are too many. The only things that will save Felston are new industries – and modernisation of the old ones. Some of them anyway.'

'And the rest of them?'

'They'll have to close,' said Charles. 'There's no other way.' She looked away. 'Damn it – most of them have been closed for years. On my advice among others. At least if we act now we might save something.'

'Jay Bower will back you?'

'Delighted,' said Lovell. 'Bower's always believed that Felston sells his newspapers – even before you organised their Hunger March for them.'

The *Daily World*, Bower's paper, had done very well out of that Hunger March of Felston's, which meant that she and Charles had

7

done well out of it too. They both owned a piece of the *Daily World*. But for neither of them was profit a motive this time. Jane loved the place because the first man she loved had lived there; because his grandmother, whom she had adored, had lived and died there, and because the whole town needed her for her skill in coaxing money and sympathy from those who had it to give. She was the only source of supply for a never-ending demand, she thought, and so I coax and wheedle and beg; and Charles helps me because he loves me, and I exploit the fact, but at least I'm grateful.

'Depressed Area, Distressed Area,' Charles was saying. 'They've got all sorts of names for the place, but all it means is malnutrition and tuberculosis and children with rickets.'

'And that's why you're giving this little party,' she said. 'Romanée Conti and Krug and smoked salmon and pâté de foie gras. Because people are poor.'

'Because some are rich,' he said, 'and if we stuff them like geese it'll be easier to get our hands on their money.'

'Did you have to ask Bob Patterson to your party?'

'Of course,' said Lovell. 'He's Felston's Dick Whittington. Went off to London and made his fortune.'

'And half of Mayfair's pussy cats are trotting after him.'

'He's living proof it can be done,' said Lovell, and then: 'Pussy cats?'

'Oh Charles,' she said. 'Don't pretend you don't know.'

'Of course I know,' said Lovell. 'He's my partner after all, and it isn't as if he tried to keep it a secret. But the women here aren't exactly –' He broke off. 'You don't mean Catherine Bower?' She nodded. 'But I thought that was over ages ago.'

'Bob thinks that, too. Catherine doesn't.'

'Oh dear God,' said Lovell. 'Does Bower know?'

'He must have some idea,' said Jane. 'Catherine's a rotten actress. I doubt if she's even bothered to try.'

'But I need Bower,' Lovell said. 'I need them both. What on earth are we to do?'

'Pray,' she said. 'That's about all that's left.'

Then Hepscott tapped at the door, Charles gathered up his papers, and Jane announced in a firm, clear voice that she had decided on the Lanvin dress.

8

. 2 .

'It's pretty,' Catherine said.

'Thank you.' And indeed that particular shade of green was the only one that was kind to her skin, as well as the perfect background for Charles's emeralds.

'You're looking quite delicious,' she said. Catherine's dress was of a subtle pink that set off her dark beauty in all its fulfilment, and yet hinted at the maiden she had been not so very long ago: looking back without regret, but rather with delight at what had taken the maiden's place. 'Paris?'

'Chanel,' said Catherine. 'I'm glad you like it. But I didn't come here to talk clothes.'

She looked round at Jane's sitting room: elegant, luxurious, and as impersonal as if it had been designed for a hotel. Jane poured champagne and offered Catherine a glass. From the moment the younger woman had telephoned she had sensed their conversation might be difficult. The champagne should make things easier. It almost always did.

'Where's Jay?' she asked.

'He changed early,' said Catherine. 'It seems Charles wanted a word with him. That's why –' Jane waited. 'Why I asked for a word with you.' She gulped at the champagne, then its flavour reached her taste buds and she looked at the glass, then sipped instead.

'What I said to you at the tennis court is all true,' she said. 'Jay *is* a hopeless lover, and I do want a divorce.'

'But why tell me?' said Jane.

'Because I'm a bitch, I suppose. I had to tell somebody, and there's only you. You're the one I can tell things to. You always were.' She hurried on: 'What's tricky is –'

'Yes?'

9

'Money,' said Catherine. 'How's that for squalor? If I leave him all I'll have to live on will be what I can gouge out of Granny, and the way she is now that could be nothing at all. Jay's been very generous, always, which makes it all the harder to leave him.'

'You're saying it's his fault?'

'Oh no,' said Catherine. Really she sounded quite shocked. 'In many ways he's made my life –' her hand flew up – 'almost perfect. He really does love me.'

'I've always thought so.'

'But I don't love him. I can't just be a pekinese on a silk cushion, eating truffles instead of dog biscuits.'

'It seems to me,' said Jane, 'that what you're saying is you can't be a lap dog and you can't not be a lap dog – so what on earth can you be?'

Catherine stood up. 'I'm sorry to have wasted your time,' she said. 'I know how valuable it is.'

'Oh for heaven's sake sit down and finish your champagne,' Jane said.

Catherine sat and picked up her glass. 'I'd forgotten how ruthless you can be,' she said.

'Ruthless?' said Jane. 'If I'd put my arms around you and said you poor darling how ghastly your life must be but what on earth can we *do*? – then pushed you out of the door – that would have been ruthless.'

Reluctantly Catherine smiled. 'Are you saying you're on my side?' she asked.

'There aren't any sides,' said Jane. 'There are only problems. And just for now yours is rather a little one.'

'Oh dear God,' Catherine said, 'we're not back to Felston again, are we? That's all Jay can talk about.'

'I'm afraid we are,' said Jane. 'That's why everyone is here, including you and me dressed out in our finery. We've done it before.'

'A charity concert, years ago,' Catherine said.

'And now we're going to do it again.' The younger woman tried to interrupt. 'No, listen to me,' said Jane. 'Just listen. In the war –'

'Oh God,' Catherine said.

'I said listen.' The words cut like whips, and Catherine was silent.

'When I drove that ambulance,' Jane continued, 'I picked up all sorts. Officers, other ranks, old sweats, boys who'd been out less than a week. One I remember was a battery sergeant major in the Royal Artillery. He had more than twenty years in. Time expired ages ago. He had no business being in France – and yet he was there. He'd got a bad one – in the leg. Gas gangrene. They took his leg off and he survived – he was as tough as old boots – and I used to look in and see him when I got a chance.

'What he liked to talk about was the army before the war: "the proper army" he called it, and the way he used to train the new recruits. "I used to line them up," he told me, "and I'd put it to them straight. In the Royal Artillery there's two ways of doing things – the hard way and the easy way. The easy way ain't easy and the hard way's ruddy hard. Now then."

'Darling, those last two words were like a door slamming shut on those recruits' entire civilian lives. From that time on there was only the Royal Artillery. Now I'm not telling you that from now on there's only Felston, but for the next two days that's all there can be – and after that we'll talk about you. So what's it going to be – the hard way or the easy way?'

'Whatever you say,' said Catherine. 'There's no point in fighting, because you always get your own way in the end. Funny, I've only just realised that after all these years.' She finished her champagne. 'What do I have to do?'

'Be pretty and agreeable,' said Jane. 'Flutter your eyelashes a lot, and make all those big, strong men realise that Felston is the cause most dear to your heart.' She put her arm round Catherine's shoulders. 'It should be pie for you,' she said.

Piers Hilyard savoured his port. It was a port at least as good as Granny's best, but then Charles Lovell had even more money than Granny. Beside him a fully paid-up bore was telling him all about his latest holiday in Germany, which seemed to be all castles and hock, but all he had to do was say 'Really?' and 'Oh I say' from time to time, which left his mind free to think about that story of Jane Whitcomb's that his sister had told him.

Very Jane, that story: spot on for detail and with a tacit goodwill towards soldiers he had sensed from the moment he met her. He wondered if the sergeant major of his own company used the expression. Probably not, he thought. The Rifle Brigade were the most colossal snobs. His CSM wouldn't borrow a phrase from the Guards, never mind the Royal Artillery.

But Jane, now. What a wonderful woman she was. Pity he didn't see more of her. He smiled, then. The bore appeared to think he had made a joke. Something about getting schlossed. Oh dear. Come to think of it he'd better not try to see more of Jane Whitcomb, because if he did he would fall in love with her and that would never do. Better to go on being the sporting mad nephew to her jolly young aunt, and try to wheedle a ride or two on one of her hunters when the season came round.

She must have a lover, anyway. For her not to be loved was unthinkable: waste of a wonderful woman. No doubt he could work out who it was if he wanted to: not that he would. None of his damn business. . . . Did Catherine have a lover, that was more to the point. She kept saying she'd finished with Bob Patterson, but she never said she was glad of it. He wouldn't have believed her if she had. He was her twin, and he knew. Her marriage was a mess, that was obvious. And poor old Bower giving rather a lot of stick to the port, and the claret before that, and no doubt the whisky before that. Trouble was he liked Bower. He was a Yank of course, and therefore totally incomprehensible, but all the same he liked him. There were times when he didn't like Catherine one bit – but she was his twin. On his other side the bishop who had said grace began to talk about the Beatitudes, but that was all right. That was what bishops were for.

Charles Lovell flicked another glance at Bower. Still holding it, but having to fight for control, as if alcohol were a fresh young horse that he could only just manage. Damn the man, this was neither the time nor the place. He'd have to make a move, and the timing for that was wrong. He knew it was. All his guests together, men and women, and Bower and Jane telling the sad story of Felston with Bob there to act as living proof, but not yet. The time wasn't right. He'd survived too many board meetings to be mistaken. This lot simply weren't ready to risk large sums of money. Not yet. There was a sudden silence, and Bower's voice boomed out in it: 'Babe Ruth's a goddam baseball player. And now I suppose you're going to ask me what baseball is. Cricket gone wrong I guess you'd call it. Only we play it to win.'

'Shall we join the ladies?' said Lovell.

The ladies were drinking coffee under the eye of Mrs Chandler-Spicer when the gentlemen came in, and Mrs Chandler-Spicer saw at once that Bower was tipsy. (Mr Chandler-Spicer had frequently been so.) Bower's wife saw it too and at once made room for him on the sofa she had occupied. He sat rather heavily, but said no more about baseball or anything else, as the other men moved into the drawing room. Piers, who unlike his sister had not needed to be told why he was invited, went at once to the bishop's wife and began to make himself agreeable by telling her about the Beatitudes, and Bob went to sit beside Jane, which just went to prove, thought Piers, that Bob had no pretensions to being a gentleman: absolutely none.

Mrs Chandler-Spicer poured coffee. 'Miss Whitcomb has been telling us all about her adventures,' she said. Somehow Charles Lovell's hand remained steady as he accepted a cup and saucer.

'Indeed?' he said.

'Hardly that,' said Jane. 'Somehow we got on to the subject of the Felston March – and I know it must sound strange, but I was remembering what fun it was.'

'Fun?' said the bishop.

'Oh, not the marchers. They were half-starved, and they walked every foot of the way – more than three hundred miles.'

'But how could they?' one of the men asked. 'If they were in such a state –'

'Pride, mostly,' said Jane, and looked at the bishop. 'I don't think it was a sinful pride – just a determination to show that they would work, and work hard, if somebody would only give them a chance. Work as hard as they marched, in fact.'

'No fun in that,' said Bob.

'Precisely,' said Jane. 'That was just something admirable and self-sacrificing, courageous even. The fun came in the things we did on the way: the concerts and sing-songs and picnics on the roadside – and the places where we rested at night. It might be a tent or a drill hall – or it could even be a house as grand as this. And the stunts we organised. Or rather the *Daily World* organised.'

13

'No,' said Bower. 'The stunts were your department. The "*World*" just provided the back up.' He was drinking black coffee now, and his voice was under control, his wife was close beside him.

'Stunts?' said the bishop's wife. She sounded wary, ready for combat.

'The people who marched with us. A couple of opera singers I remember, and the entire cast of a London show. Brass bands every other day, and Bonny Lad, the horse that won the Derby that year.' Her mother's second husband, Major Routledge, racing tipster for the *Daily World*, had arranged that one.

'Then of course there was Georgina Payne,' she said.

'The actress?' said Mrs Chandler-Spicer.

'The film star?' said the bishop's wife.

'The very same,' said Jane, and looked at Bower. 'She marched with every rank I remember, so that every man there could say they marched with her.'

'But what on earth was she doing here?' the bishop's wife asked. 'Surely she spends her life in Hollywood.'

If only she didn't make it sound quite so much like Gomorrah, thought Jane: but then according to Georgie quite often it is.

'She was preparing for a film called *The Angel of No Man's Land*,' said Bower. 'It was about a lady ambulance driver in the war. The lady in question was Miss Whitcomb here.'

'Good heavens,' the bishop said. 'I saw that film. Very moving. Very moving indeed. And you say it was about you?'

'Some of it, anyway,' said Jane. 'I also wrote the screenplay. A bit of luck for me.'

'She means a bit of luck for Felston,' said Bower. 'Every penny she earned went to Felston.'

Too soon, thought Lovell. Drunk or sober, Bower, you're rushing it.

But already Jane was saying, 'That's quite enough about me. I didn't come here to bore you all with my life story.'

Good girl, thought Lovell. She knows exactly when to ease off. He stood up and offered brandy, and Bower asked for more coffee, and his wife smiled.

People began to move around and talk to each other, and Jane

14

found herself confronted by a tall and elegant man a little younger than Charles perhaps, with the unmistakable mark of wealth about him. He might as well have it stencilled on his shirt front, she thought: 'I'm rolling in the stuff.'

'Miss Whitcomb,' he said, 'I just wanted to tell you that what you had to say was fascinating.'

'About Georgie?' she said.

'You call her Georgie? Georgina Payne?'

'We've been friends for years.'

'Oh I see. Well of course – any man who is a man would find her fascinating. Even a bishop.'

I do not like you, thought Jane. I do not like you *at all*, and smiled at him sweetly.

'But I was thinking more about those poor chaps on the Hunger March,' the tall, elegant man said. 'My name's Crawley by the way. Justin Crawley.' He waited.

'How do you do?' she said, and no more.

'You haven't heard of me then?'

'I'm sorry,' she said, 'Should I – ?'

Of course she'd heard of him. He'd been in 'This Wicked World', the *Daily World*'s gossip column, almost as often as she had herself. Mostly it was because he was rich, and because he had the ability to become engaged without the tiresome aftermath of marriage. Four times was it? Five? Certainly he had that air about him. He was looking at her now like a fat man considering a plate of oysters and reaching for the lemon.

'I would very much like to talk a little more with you about Felston,' he said. 'I know how dear the place is to your heart.' He was looking at where her heart was as he spoke, and she found herself wishing that her gown was not quite so décolleté.

'Perhaps tomorrow morning?' he said. 'We could go for a stroll?'

'But the bishop's preaching at Morning Prayer in the village church tomorrow,' she said. 'Surely you hadn't forgotten?'

'Do you know I believe I had,' he said. 'How wicked of me.'

The words were lightly spoken and he smiled, but there could be no doubt that he was furious. This was a man who found refusal difficult, if not incomprehensible. 'Perhaps after church?' he said at last.

'Why not? If there's time before lunch, that is. The bishop does tend to go on a bit, I'm told.'

Bob came over to her, a glass of cognac in his hand. He does enjoy the good life, thought Jane, pleased for him as always, as if he were a little boy with a brand-new box of soldiers.

'You serious about that lift to Andy's wedding?' he asked.

'Provided you don't ask to drive.'

'I'll see you tomorrow then,' said Crawley, still smiling, but the smile was now close to a snarl.

When he left them Bob said, 'Will you? See him tomorrow?'

'I'll see everybody tomorrow,' she said. 'Why not him?'

'Not a nice man,' said Bob. 'Not a nice man at all.'

'Naughty?' asked Jane.

'Every chance he gets,' said Bob. And then, before she could start referring to pots and kettles he added, 'But not nice. Not like me. Now you just watch out for him, our Jane.'

With the last sentence his accent broadened. He was reminding her that she had almost married into the Patterson clan, and that whether she had or not it was his business to look after her as a brother should.

'I'll watch out,' said Jane.

. 3 .

Charles Lovell came to her bed at one thirty that morning, just as she had turned out her light.

'What a delightful surprise,' she said.

'No it isn't,' said Lovell. 'You told me to come here.'

'Asked,' said Jane. 'I never *tell* you. Any more than you tell me.'

He got into bed beside her and unbuttoned the top of her pyjamas to feel her skin against his.

'It isn't going well,' he said.

'One does one's poor best,' she said. 'But after all you are getting on a bit, Charles.'

He slapped her bottom and she yelled discreetly.

'I was talking about Felston and you know it,' he said.

'They don't want to play?'

'They don't want to damn well pay,' Charles said. 'You sensed it too. When you were talking about the March.'

'Are we doing it wrong?'

'No,' Lovell said. 'It isn't that. They'll give a cheque for Stobbs's Clinic when you put the squeeze on them – which I've no doubt you will –'

'Of course.'

'But that'll be just like a weekend at Deauville – or bridge debts. Nothing we can use to make jobs.'

'There's my money,' she said.

He sighed his Why-Won't-Women-Ever-Listen? sigh.

'No,' he said. 'There's not. In the first place it's ungetatable – that relative who left it to you saw to that.'

'Aunt Pen,' said Jane. 'My uncle did the same to her.'

'Just as well,' said Lovell. 'And even if you did control your own money, I wouldn't let you give it to Felston –'

17

'But you want to give some of yours – and what you can get out of the rest of them.'

'That's different,' said Lovell. 'This lot love their money. They love playing with it and using it and making it do things. If I can show them they won't lose any of it – or at any rate not much – and they're in with a chance for a knighthood or a CBE or something – they might take a chance. But they'd still be in control of *their* money. And quite right too. It's *theirs*. But you – you'd just give it all to Felston and hope for the best.'

'If we do get it out of them – what then?'

'I talk to a man I know who makes bicycles – we try to persuade Bob to start making his own wireless sets, things like that. New industries for Felston. Then we go to the government and ask for more money. But we have to show them the colour of ours first.'

'Crawley might give me some,' said Jane.

'You keep away from Crawley,' said Lovell.

'That's what Bob said.'

'Bob's a sensible young fellow,' said Lovell.

'Bob's as randy as a stoat,' said Jane, 'but at least he fights fair.'

But Lovell had lost interest in everything and everybody but the woman he touched.

'La sir,' said Jane. 'What would the bishop say?'

Lovell told her his plans for the bishop.

'I'd sooner do it with you,' said Jane.

Catherine Bower reached out to the other bed and shook her husband as hard as she could, and at last he snorted and sat up.

'What?' he said. 'What was –?'

'You were snoring,' Catherine said. 'Again.' She switched on the bedside light to find matches and cigarettes.

'Sorry,' said Bower. 'Very sorry. Honest.' She blew out a plume of smoke, not quite in his face.

'God I feel awful,' Bower said.

'You were drunk.'

'Which of course explains it,' said Bower. 'One of the advantages of your Oxford education, right? It taught you all about cause and effect.'

She smoked in silence.

18

'I married this great kid,' said Bower. 'Debutante, Oxford graduate, daughter of an earl, best seat on a horse in the Quorn or the Pytchley, and so lovely my heart turns over every time she comes into the room. I still feel awful.'

'Isn't there some stuff you can take?'

'Bromo Seltzer. It's in the bathroom.'

'Shall I get it for you?'

'No,' said Bower. 'I'll get it. The walk will do me good.'

He padded off to the bathroom, not quite swaying. He was reasonably under control, she thought, considering the amount he'd taken. Everybody had seen that he was drunk, of course, but it hadn't made all that much difference. So many Americans *were* drunk, especially since Prohibition. Bower came back into the room, the stuff he took fizzing in his glass, and lifted the glass to her.

'Cheers,' he said.

'Oh for God's *sake*,' said Catherine.

'You shouldn't say that,' said Bower. 'That's wrong. Taking the name of the Lord in vain is wrong. I took it in vain myself today, so I know.'

'When?' said Catherine. 'When did you?'

'Over the port,' said Bower. 'Between my third and fourth glass. Some jerk who couldn't find his ass with both hands asked me who Babe Ruth was. Babe Ruth! . . . It's like asking who Pontius Pilate was – or Jesus Christ for that matter. But for an American I have the makings of a gentleman, and I told him. "Babe Ruth," I cried. "Babe Ruth's a goddam ball player." Taking His Name in vain, you see.'

'And I suppose everybody heard you.'

'Every single one,' said Bower.

'Including the bishop?'

'He was sitting next to the jerk who'd lost his ass.'

To his amazement she burst out laughing; that low and rippling gurgle of laughter that he had always found so exciting. That her laughter was genuine he had no doubt, any more than he doubted her indifference to him. He had simply turned for the moment from a dull and rather difficult older man to an older man with an unexpected talent to amuse.

'I'm glad I can still make you laugh,' he said, and at once the laughter died. He reached out his hands, and pulled down the shoulder straps of her nightgown to look at her naked breasts.

'What the hell do you think you're playing at?' she said.

'Just looking,' he said. 'That's all I'm capable of right now.'

He got into his bed and at once she turned her back to him and pulled up the straps of her nightgown before switching off the light. In the darkness he could hear the sound of her crying. From laughter to tears in under a minute, he thought. You should be proud of yourself, Bower. It's your fastest yet.

They had 'Bright The Vision That Delighted' and 'The Church's One Foundation', all sorts of prayers and a rather long collect, and now it was the bishop's turn. Today he had decided to have a go at St Paul: Corinthians 13:13, 'And now abideth faith, hope, charity, these three; but the greatest of these is charity.' He paused after he had read it, and then read out the whole magnificent passage that his predecessors had translated over three hundred years before, from 'Though I speak with the tongues of men and of angels'. Silently Jane recited them too: she had known them for a quarter of a century, ever since Vinny, her governess, had made her learn them by heart, – then where St Paul finished, the bishop began, and told them what charity really was.

Not just flag days, he admonished them sternly: not just putting your hand in your pocket for a singer in the street. Charity was love. He paused there, as if waiting for an astonished gasp at such a daring deduction. None came. But what kind of love? he asked, rather pettishly, Jane thought. Certainly not the kind portrayed by the cinema, or the circulating libraries, or the twopenny magazines that housemaids read. And how do you know what housemaids read? Jane wondered. I had a housemaid who read modern languages at London University, and now she's a translator at the League of Nations.

St Paul had little time for that aspect of love, said the bishop, calling her to order. He had written to those same Corinthians on that very subject: Your body is the temple of the Holy Ghost, he had told them, and the only encouragement he had offered was that it was better to marry than burn. Cold comfort you may say, said the bishop, and Jane Whitcomb, spinster, agreed with him. Far greater comfort was to be found in the knowledge and love of God, and for God: for that was the true meaning of charity.

There was a lot more of the same, and Jane allowed her mind to wander. The old boy was letting her down badly, and she wondered if it were on purpose. To love God, or to try to, of *course*. And to love one's neighbour too, even if one's neighbour were Charles Lovell, with a crazy wife in Switzerland. She knew something about being crazy: she'd done a bit in that line herself. And come to think of it that had been because of loving one's neighbours – only those neighbours were wounded men: Tommies for the most part, but Australians too, Canadians, Americans, French, even Germans. Whoever lay on a stretcher qualified for a ride in her ambulance, and she'd driven them for nearly two years, and when at last she cracked it hadn't been because of the sight of wounded men; legs blown off, the side of a face opened as if with a cleaver – it had been the sight of the horses: maimed and blasted like their masters, bodies smashed and opened like the toys of a destructive giant child. That and the death of her darling John – the day before it all came to an end.

But if going off her rocker had been God's will, putting her back on it must have been His doing, too, and her psychiatrist, J. A. B. Lockhart, His instrument. It had taken poor old Jabber simply ages, but in the end he had done it, and between them they'd earned a place in the medical text books. Dear, sweet Jabber. There was a man who really did know about charity.

What the bishop knew about was going on too long – even his wife, sitting next to Jane, was sneaking a look at her watch – and missing the point. He knew quite a bit about that, too. The point about charity wasn't just God: it was man. And woman too. Men and women who wanted to work and couldn't: who hated to see their children go hungry, yet had to see it every day. To put that right wasn't to buy a flag on a pin, or disgorge a sixpence to give to a beggar: to put that right was sacrifice, and that was what the bishop should have been going on about. But the bishop was saying 'And now to God the Father, God the Son and God the Holy Ghost' in the abrupt, sneaky way some clerics had, telling the congregation that the sermon was over, but wrong-footing them so to speak, so that they were still scrambling to their feet while the bishop sailed back to his stall.

'Onward Christian Soldiers' followed. An odd choice, after all that charity. Perhaps it was one of the bishop's favourites. He had been a chaplain in the war, according to Charles. She had told him she didn't know much about chaplains, not having carried one in her ambulance. . . . After that the blessing, and they were free to go out into the sunshine and birdsong, with that sense of release that children have when school is over. She shook hands with the vicar and breathed in the warm, sweet air – more like the Côte d'Azur than the North East of England – and found that Justin Crawley was waiting for her.

'I do hope you haven't forgotten our walk?' he said roguishly.

'How could I possibly?' said Jane.

Suddenly Bob was beside them, like a soul released from a nearby grave. 'Walk?' he said. 'Grand idea. Just the thing to give us an appetite for lunch.'

'Couldn't agree more,' said Piers, who appeared to have been released from the next grave but one. It would seem that she had acquired a bodyguard. Once again Crawley reacted with his own extraordinary version of rage pretending to be good humour.

'Surely you chaps have other things to do,' he said, laughing and snarling at once.

'That's just it,' said Piers. 'In England on a Sunday there's nothing else *to* do except go for a walk – unless it's the pub, and we could hardly take Miss Whitcomb there.'

'No fear,' said Bob. 'The beer's all right, but I shouldn't think they'd manage a cocktail.'

'Then why don't you go there and drink beer?' said Crawley.

'Look here,' said Bob, 'you can't monopolise Miss Whitcomb, you know. She and I have things to talk about.'

'Oh have you?' said Crawley.

'My brother's wedding,' said Bob. 'We're both going.'

'And I want a word about a horse of hers,' said Piers. 'So you see you can't expect to have her all to yourself – not unless you're a very selfish fellow.'

'Of course not,' said Crawley, yelping with fury, and led them off on a very short walk indeed, stamping away when it was over, like a man, as Piers said, in urgent need of a dog to kick. She turned to her two bodyguards and laughed out loud.

'Gracious what chivalry,' she said. 'But I can look after myself, you know.'

'Of course you can,' said Bob. 'It's just that – '

'He clings,' said Piers. 'Like tar to one's shoes. Almost impossible to get rid of.'

'Someone you know?' Piers nodded.

Brenda Coupland, she thought. Brenda isn't exactly famous for putting large quantities of money to flight. Crawley must be ghastly.

'The wedding's fixed,' she said to Bob. 'I told you I'll drive you. Let's go back to the house and try for a dry martini – and you can tell me about my horse, Piers.'

'Martinis? With a bishop and his wife there?' Bob said.

'He's lunching at the vicarage. So's she,' said Piers. 'Mrs bishop told me last night when I was having a little chat with her.'

'In that case I'll make them,' said Jane. 'If the butler will let me.'

The butler was happy to oblige. He didn't approve of cocktails. Bob and Piers sipped and approved.

'Better than beer in a pub,' said Bob.

'I'd forgotten how good you were at these things,' said Piers. 'Even Granny used to like them when you made them.'

'Tell me about the horse.'

'Just talk, really. Keeping the dreaded Crawley at bay. Except I'll be in England all through the hunting season and I wondered –'

'Not Bridget's Boy,' said Jane. 'Any of the others, but not him.'

'But Jane, he's absolutely the best.'

'Of course he is, but I'm racing him,' said Jane. 'Or rather Major Routledge is – my stepfather. He thinks he may even be right for the Gold Cup.'

'Cheltenham?' Piers, for once, seemed awestruck. 'Oh well in that case I'll take whatever you can spare – if that's all right.'

'Of course it is,' said Jane.

'You'll trust me?'

'Don't I always?' said Jane, and Lovell came over and asked if he could have a martini too. The two young men faded away as she poured: Charles, it seemed, had none of the tarry qualities of

23

Mr Crawley. She told him what had happened and Lovell laughed out loud.

'You didn't put them up to it then?' she asked.

'All their own initiative. Bob's idea probably – he was the one who knew – but I don't suppose he'd have much trouble recruiting Piers.'

'None whatsoever,' said Jane, and then: 'I don't mean to boast, but it's a jolly satisfying feeling having two young knights in armour to guard me at my age.'

'You've got three at least and you know it,' said Lovell, 'and your age will always be perfect, whatever it is.'

'Later for that sort of talk if you please,' she said. 'I don't want to be caught blushing by your other guests – so later. But then lots of it.'

He offered cigarettes and lit them for them both.

'Let's be serious then,' he said, and drew in smoke. 'This party isn't going to work.'

'I rather think so too,' said Jane. 'It occurred to me in church –'

'I could have killed that bloody bishop,' said Lovell, then broke off, horrified. 'Good God,' he said at last. 'What a perfectly dreadful thing to say.'

'Not at all,' said Jane. 'I could have held him while you did it.'

'Not a word about giving,' said Lovell. 'Not a word about Felston, after you spent half last night priming him. – And I'll bet he has the gall to pass *his* hat to me for the Cathedral Restoration Fund.'

'More likely to send his wife,' said Jane.

'I wouldn't give much for her chances.'

'Do you think he passed us by on the other side on purpose?'

'A bishop has no business to be a pharisee,' said Lovell, and brooded. 'Hard to say,' he said at last. 'He isn't here to give, after all. He's here to twist arms and he knows it – and after all it isn't as if it would be bad for him as a public man.'

'Of course not,' said Jane. 'Bower would give him a pretty fair spread for a start.'

'So it can't be that. But our bishop's a social animal as well as a public one. He likes weekends at places like this, sitting on committees to denounce modern manners, giving little talks on the BBC

24

'– and for that he needs to stay friends with the kind of bloated plutocrats I've invited here.'

'Friends with Crawley,' she said. 'Talk about God and Mammon.'

'He's the worst, I agree,' said Lovell, 'but they're all out of the same mould, women and men. I just thought I might be able to persuade them to risk a bit of it, – with your help, and Bob's, and the bishop's, in return for a puff in the *Daily World* or the chance of a K, but the bishop's obviously got the feeling that now is not the time, and I rather think he's right.'

'But why is it not the time?'

'Because 1932's the bottom of the trough, as I said. This Depression's got the country on its knees – and not just to pray to God. We're half way through the hiding of a lifetime – and so are the Germans and the French and the Yanks – maybe the Yanks most of all.'

'Half way through?' said Jane.

'It isn't anything like over,' said Lovell, 'and if there's one thing we filthy rich know, it's that. So my guests aren't in the mood to listen to bishops. They're far too busy battening down hatches, getting out of industrials, buying gold. They don't want to risk money on good works, no matter how good they are. They don't want to risk *that*.' He snapped his fingers. 'Oh – they might find a sixpence for a beggar, if they didn't happen to have a threepenny piece. But only if someone is watching.'

She fitted another cigarette into her holder, the long jade holder she had bought from Cartier's years ago. Andy Patterson had always thought its opulence indecent, but one didn't change the world by switching to cork-tipped cigarettes.

'This thing has really upset you,' she said.

'I hate to lose,' said Lovell. 'But that isn't it. Not all of it anyway.'

'What then?'

'It's you,' said Lovell. 'You've corrupted me.'

'I've *what*?'

'Well not corrupted exactly,' Lovell said. 'It's more like corruption in reverse – given me this terrible urge to do good.' She was silent, and he hurried on. 'I don't mean I'm doing it to curry favour, force an obligation on you. In the first place it wouldn't work – not

25

with you – and in the second place it wouldn't be true. I want to help Felston. You could almost say I need to help Felston, and I think I'm going to let Felston down.'

Then a man who owned fifteen cargo steamers came in and demanded that he too have one of Miss Whitcomb's cocktails. Just as well to be interrupted, thought Jane. She had just been about to say something that she might regret.

It was a long and boring lunch and Jane toyed with the idea of ringing Lionel and arranging to go dancing the next night. After all that, she deserved a treat.

. 4 .

When at last the wretched meal was over Charles took Jay Bower
off, doubtless to tell him his new running feature would have to be
postponed, and Piers took Catherine away. Jane scurried past Bob,
who had planted himself in front of Crawley and was asking him
if he had enjoyed his walk. Definitely time to telephone Lionel, she
thought, but she was interrupted by a tap at the door before she
could pick up the telephone. Jane called 'Come in' and found that
she was being visited by Mrs Chandler-Spicer.

'I just thought I'd look in to make sure that you have everything
you want,' Mrs Chandler-Spicer said. Now this was nonsense. Mrs
Chandler-Spicer was the hostess, not the housekeeper, and in any
case just before one left was not the time to ask such a question.

'Fine, thanks,' said Jane. 'Do sit down,' and sought in her
handbag for cigarettes, lighter and Cartier holder. Mrs Chandler-
Spicer sat in silence until she had found them.

'Dear Charles always likes to be sure his guests are comfortable,'
Mrs Chandler-Spicer said.

'Does he indeed?' said Jane. 'Well I must say that's jolly thoughtful of him.'

'Yes,' said Mrs Chandler-Spicer, 'isn't it?' There was another,
rather longer silence.

'He's a very kind man,' said Mrs Chandler-Spicer, but her voice
was far too loud to express such a sentiment.

Jane looked at her more closely. Surely Mrs Chandler-Spicer
wasn't drunk?

'We work on the same charity committee,' she said aloud. 'For
Felston, you know. So yes, I have noticed it rather.'

'That's a very pretty cigarette holder,' Mrs Chandler-Spicer
said.

What on earth had that to do with the agenda? And what was the agenda anyway?

'Cartier,' said Jane.

'It must have been jolly expensive.'

'It was,' said Jane.

Mrs Chandler-Spicer ceased to be a pouter pigeon and became an enraged robin fighting to defend its garden patch.

'I should think one would have to be very rich to buy such a thing,' Mrs Chandler-Spicer said, 'but then I've never been rich, you see.'

Jane waited.

'Bernard – Mr Chandler-Spicer,' the robin continued, 'always gave the impression that he was rich, despite the fact that he went to Repton. But really he wasn't. Oh not at all. In fact not to put too fine a point on it he was quite poor.'

Drunk as an owl, thought Jane; then, really I must stop these ornithological similes.

'How ghastly for you,' she said aloud.

'Well it was,' said Mrs Chandler-Spicer, 'but then I rather feel that married life *is* ghastly, even if one is well-off. Have *you* ever – ?'

'Never,' said Jane, and despite what she had just said, Mrs Chandler-Spicer seemed to find Jane's answer pleasing.

'Bernard never worked,' she continued. 'Not ever. He used to maintain that work formed no part of a gentleman's existence. And then he had never been to the university, or even the Inns of Court, so that he lacked any kind of qualifications. The only kind of work for which he was fitted would have been that of clerk in a not-too-demanding office, or the person who delivers the coal. And that of course was unthinkable.'

'But how on earth did you live?'

'I've often wondered,' Mrs Chandler-Spicer said.

Then silence returned for a while, and a damned uncomfortable silence it was, thought Jane, but I can hardly ask the woman to leave. At last Mrs Chandler-Spicer summoned up what was left of her courage.

'How on earth do *you* live?' she said.

'I'm rich,' said Jane. 'I thought we'd established that.' She waved her cigarette holder at Mrs Chandler-Spicer. 'Cartier and all that. Remember?'

28

'I don't think you'll be at all happy in Maidenhead,' Mrs Chandler-Spicer said.

'I've no intention of living in Maidenhead,' said Jane.

'But it's where my little house is,' said Mrs Chandler-Spicer, and then, as Jane continued to look bewildered: 'You don't understand, do you?'

'No,' said Jane, 'I don't.'

'Then I'd better explain,' Mrs Chandler-Spicer said, and settled herself more comfortably.

'Bernard died, you know,' she said. 'At least he managed that. Fell under a bus after an Old Boys' Dinner. It's impossible for me to explain what a relief that was – except that all he left me was bills and we lived in rooms and the rent wasn't paid. He hadn't even paid for the Old Boys' Dinner. Then dear Charles came along and found me in tears because I just couldn't cope – nobody had ever taught me how to cope, you see. And then he paid my debts.'

'Charles did?'

'Every penny,' said Mrs Chandler-Spicer. 'And it was *hundreds*. I'm not sure it didn't run to –' her voice sank to a whisper '– four figures, by the time he'd settled the undertaker and everything. And then he asked me if I'd like to live in Maidenhead and showed me his dear little house there and said I could live in it. He even arranged an annuity for me and ever since I've been so happy.' Then Mrs Chandler-Spicer proved it by bursting into tears.

Jane said, 'Well I'm glad it all had a happy ending, honestly I am, but I don't see what it has to do with me.'

'You're not listening,' said Mrs Chandler-Spicer. 'I said he lets me live in the house. I don't own it. Charles said it would be better if I didn't because there'd be expenses and things and I wouldn't cope because I can't, so he does it all – but I asked him how long I could stay there and he said until he found somebody he liked better and then I saw the two of you together before lunch, but if you've got all that money why should you live in my house?'

'I don't want to live in your house,' said Jane. 'I don't want to live anywhere near Maidenhead. I've a perfectly good house of my own and what's more –' She broke off. Gently she admonished herself. Kindly. This good lady is drunk and terrified because Charles once made a bad joke, so just you be nice, Jane Whitcomb.

29

'Mr Lovell and I were talking about Felston,' she said. 'We often do. Charity work, as I say. . . . Mrs Chandler-Spicer, did it never occur to you that when he said that about somebody he liked better – he was making a joke?'

'A joke? But Charles is a banker,' said Mrs Chandler-Spicer.

'What he was saying,' said Jane desperately, 'was that you could stay there as long as you like, because there's nobody he'd like better to live in that house in Maidenhead.'

Mrs Chandler-Spicer approached this proposition cautiously, circled round it so to speak, then gave it a tentative prod.

'You think so?' she said.

'I'm certain of it,' said Jane, meaning every word.

'Charles is married,' Mrs Chandler-Spicer said. 'Did you know that?'

'I've heard it mentioned,' said Jane. 'His wife is an invalid, I believe.'

'Tact,' said Mrs Chandler-Spicer. 'I've always said it was a gift of God,' and promptly fell asleep. Still no chance of telephoning Lionel. Instead Jane found her pen and began a letter to Georgie. Twenty minutes later Mrs Chandler-Spicer said, 'I did so enjoy our little chat.'

'I too,' said Jane, and put down her pen.

'But I really must go,' said Mrs Chandler-Spicer, as if her twenty minute nap had never happened. 'Just one thing, my dear. What we've told each other is confidential, I take it?'

'Of course,' said Jane.

'Splendid,' said Mrs Chandler-Spicer, still making no attempt to leave. They endured another of her silences, until she said at last, 'I looked up his name in the dictionary.'

'Bernard?' Jane asked.

'Chandler-Spicer. Spicer means grocer, from the French epicier, you know.'

'Really?' said Jane.

'Oh yes. And chandler is even worse. It's a sort of catch-all word for a dealer, especially one who dealt in candles. Unfortunately I only found out about it after he'd died. How Bernard would have hated it if he'd known. Such vulgar occupations.' She got to her feet. 'I really must go,' she said, as if Jane were begging her to stay.

'There's so much to do here – and for some reason I seem to have rather a headache.' She put her finger to her lips. 'You won't forget, will you? Our little secret?' And then she was gone.

So I've given my word, thought Jane, and that means I can't tell Charles to stop making inappropriate jokes. Not that he does. – Well, not all that often. And anyway he'd never dream of turning her out into the snows of Maidenhead, shivering beneath her ragged shawl. But at least she'd learned one thing. Put the two of them together and their feelings for each other were obvious to the meanest intelligences, such as Mrs Chandler-Spicer's. On the other hand that lady's perceptions had been honed to a fine edge by terror. Jane could only hope that alcohol had dulled them again. She picked up her pen, and then looked once more at the telephone. Two such darling friends: the luxury of choice. Another tap at the door.

'Come in,' she called. 'It isn't locked.'

Catherine did as she was bid. 'Goodness,' she said. 'How stern you sound.'

'There are limits,' said Jane. 'I think you're approaching them.'

'What on earth have I done?' said Catherine.

'Nothing,' Jane said at once. 'Nothing at all. Forgive me. It's just that the weekend's been a flop, that's all.'

'You too?' Catherine said.

'I'm talking about Felston,' said Jane. 'At one point I thought we were going to get somewhere, and now I'm quite sure we're not.'

'Oh yes, Felston,' Catherine said. She made it sound like a Merovingian king her tutor had referred to just once at university.

Patience yet again, thought Jane, and waited. Catherine waited too. 'I take it Felston isn't what you came to talk to me about?' Jane said at last.

'Well no,' Catherine said. 'I just wish it were. I mean such a worthy cause and all that. But as a matter of fact I came to talk about me if you can spare a couple of minutes. Not worthy at all, I know – but I did do my best to look pretty, and I fluttered my eyelashes all over the place.'

'So you did,' said Jane, 'and Felston and I are grateful. What about you?'

31

'Not wishing to be rude or anything,' Catherine said, 'but you haven't been having a word with Piers about me?'

'Certainly not,' said Jane.

'No of course not, but I didn't mean did you speak to him, I meant did he speak to you if you follow me.'

'The answer's still the same.'

'Jolly good.' And indeed she really did look relieved. 'Then it's all the twin thing. That's all it can be. . . . Piers suggested we go to have a look at the stables,' she explained, 'and I must say Charles Lovell's got some pretty mouth-watering stuff, and while we were there he started nagging me.'

'Nagging you?'

'About Jay,' said Catherine. 'Was I being true to him, and I said yes of course and I *am*. I mean chance would be a fine thing. But I don't mean to take up your time about all that –'

'You don't take up my time,' said Jane. 'How could you possibly?'

'What a darling you are,' Catherine said. 'But what I meant was I did promise yesterday – no more about me for the next couple of days. I just wanted to make sure that Piers is keeping it in the family.'

'I'm absolutely certain he is.'

'If he hasn't told you then he must be.' Suddenly she had the intensely vulnerable look of a fourteen-year-old. 'Am I in the way?' she asked. 'Or can I stay for a minute or two?'

'Of course you can,' said Jane. 'Sit down and have a cigarette.'

'Bless you.' Catherine took a cigarette from the case Jane offered. 'I know people sunk in gloom are absolute pests to everybody else,' she said. 'I've run a mile to escape them myself in my time. It's just –' Jane waited. 'We don't mean it, you know, and we can't help it, and if I can't be with you now I'll start to cry, and I shan't be able to stop for a week.'

'We can't have that,' said Jane. 'Shall I send for tea?'

'Just company,' said Catherine. 'May I just say one thing about all this?'

'Say as much as you like.'

'Piers doesn't think it's Jay's fault.'

'He blames you?'

32

'He doesn't blame anybody,' Catherine said. 'He says it's just one of those things that happen – and all one can do is put up with it and hang on and hope that things will change.'

Somewhere Piers seemed to have acquired the beginnings of wisdom.

'Things often do change,' said Jane.

'They won't for Granny – except she'll probably get worse. Oh God, Jane, I miss her so.'

Because she always kissed it better, whatever it was? But nobody can kiss this better. Only you and Jay.

'He mauled me last night,' Catherine said.

But there were limits: there had to be.

'You have no business to tell me, and I have no business to listen,' said Jane.

'Sorry.'

'Did you tell Piers?' Catherine shook her head. 'Why not? Afraid he'd challenge Jay to a duel?'

'He'd more probably have laughed,' Catherine said. 'I wonder if I were to take a holiday – go off somewhere –'

'On your own?'

'You could come with me.'

'Aren't you forgetting that Jay and I have been friends for years? Hardly a tactful thing to do, wouldn't you say?'

Especially as we were once lovers too, she thought, and oh please God I hope you never find out.

'I could ask somebody else,' said Catherine. 'Bunty Fairweather, maybe.' Jane said nothing. 'You don't approve?'

'That isn't the point,' said Jane. 'Whatever you do is your decision. I can listen – I *am* listening, but I can't make up your mind for you.'

Catherine said, 'You've been far more patient than I deserve. Let's talk about something else.'

But of course they didn't, because for Catherine nothing but her marriage had any real existence except for Bob, and mercifully she didn't talk about Bob. It was all Jay and Catherine, round and round like two goldfish in a bowl, while the cigarette stubs piled up in the ashtray and Jane did her best not to yawn, until at last it was possible to suggest that they ought to change for dinner, but when Catherine left Jane went at once to the telephone. Pott, Lionel's parlourmaid, told her that Lionel was out and she had no idea when he would be back, and Jane hung up before using the sort of language one should never use within earshot of parlourmaids. Lionel had no business to be out, not when she wanted to speak to him. Then reluctantly she grinned. That was as bad as Catherine, if not worse. At least Catherine had reason for her woes. Hepscott came to her, and Jane said at once: 'The Mainbocher. The blue and silver,' and went off to her bath wishing there were more like Hepscott, who showed not the slightest need to tell her troubles.

. 5 .

Dinner was as dull as lunch, but it had an apologetic flavour too. The bishop and his wife were back from the vicarage, and ate largely of everything, as if lunch with the vicar had not been all that good, and it was the bishop as much as anyone who sounded the note of apology. He hadn't come across, as Jay Bower would say, and the others hadn't come across either. All that slaughtering of beef and lamb and ducks, uprooting of asparagus, premier cru claret sloshing in every glass, and not a penny had been offered: hence the note of regret. Well a penny will be offered, thought Jane, if it's only for Dr Stobbs's Felston clinic, and a pretty penny it will be.

She started on the women when they left the men to their port. Asking for money to help Felston clinic wasn't exactly a novelty for her, and she no longer felt any of that to-beg-I-am-ashamed nonsense. The money was needed, and so she asked for it implacably, as if refusal were unthinkable, as indeed it was with all that apology in the air.

First she told them about the clinic itself, and the vast old brute of an Armstrong-Siddeley she had once driven for it: her very last ambulance, and called on Catherine to vouch for what she said. Then she told them about Dr Stobbs, his rudeness, his ruthlessness, and his utter devotion to the poor wretches he served: then she told them about Canon Messeter, gentler, kinder than Stobbs, but equally devoted, to the point where that devotion was now killing him. His heart, Stobbs told her, could not be expected to beat much longer. Then the clinic itself and its insatiable need for medicines, and even food: the cheap and healthy food that fuelled its soup kitchen.

They paid up, every one of them, some because they were

35

trapped and knew it, some because Jane had done her work well, and some – Mrs Chandler-Spicer, Jane was sure, was among them – because they wanted to. As Jane watched an MP's wife scribble out a cheque the men came in, and Catherine looked to Bower, and saw at once that he was perfectly sober.

She said to Jane, 'You must tell it all again.'

'Do you really think so?' said Jane, who had every intention of telling it all again. The women gave a kind of chorus of insistence, none more loudly than the bishop's wife, who saw the chances of the Cathedral Restoration Fund diminish by the second.

So Jane told it again, and the women watched their men grimly, to make sure that they were moved by it all, as they, the women, had been. When she got to the bit about Canon Messeter's imminent death every woman in the place was looking at the bishop, as if he might be responsible: and although it was all true, and unutterably sad, Jane found it hard not to smile, because she knew that if she had the chance to tell Canon Messeter he would laugh out loud.

Again her success was total. She had feared a certain resistance from Crawley, but Catherine was with her when she gathered in the cheques, and he wrote one without visible distress, then made a beeline for Catherine. Jane looked about her. Bob and Piers were both watching Crawley. How happy he'll be to leave this place, thought Jane.

The evening yawned on. No possibility of dancing, or even bridge: not with a bishop present. Jane went to sit beside Jay Bower.

'So we've lost,' she said.

'You've been talking to Charles?'

Jane shrugged. 'I didn't have to. I know when we've lost.'

'Well yeah,' he said. 'But I notice you can still draw blood – even in defeat.'

She smiled. 'Not nearly enough,' she said. 'Not enough to put Felston to work – or a headline for the *World*.'

'Not a headline,' he said, 'but a par or two for "This Wicked World". How the rich and famous sat spellbound as Jane Witcomb told her tragic tale.'

'Rich and *famous*?'

'Well maybe just rich, but our readers like it better if they're famous as well. After all, you're famous.'

'But famous for what? I mean – a bishop can be famous for being a bishop – I grant you that – but Crawley for instance. What's he famous for?'

Bower looked to where Crawley hovered beside his wife. 'For being very rich indeed,' he said at last. 'I hope the cheque he gave you was adequate.'

'More than.'

'He can afford it. . . . Have you enjoyed your weekend?'

'No,' said Jane. 'Losing isn't my idea of fun.'

'Me neither,' said Bower. 'I didn't win a thing this weekend. Not a damn thing. Not even a game of tennis.'

'You weren't supposed to come here tonight,' she said.

'Do you mind?'

'Oh no,' she said. 'I wanted you here so much. It was just a bit of a surprise, that's all.'

'I could hardly ring you at this hour and say I wanted to discuss investments.'

'What made you come?'

'The way we talked this morning.'

The way we talked and your cousin watched and found us out at once, she thought: but she couldn't say so. She'd promised.

'After that I thought it would be rather nice to be together.'

'It's wonderful.'

'I also wanted to congratulate you.'

'Whatever for?'

'Passing the hat,' he said. 'How much did you get?'

'Four hundred and seventy-five quid,' she said. 'How much were we after?'

'About a hundred thousand.'

'Not exactly a triumph, is it?'

She leaned into him, easy, relaxing, feeling her disappointment fade to its true perspective. It had never been more than a possibility after all.

'You feel good here,' she said.

'I most certainly do. It's where I belong.' She let it go. It might even be true.

'You go back by train tomorrow?'

'With Bob,' she said. 'Catherine and Jay and Piers are driving.'

'Catherine and Jay,' he said.

'Rather a mess, I agree. Was he very disappointed – about Felston, I mean?'

'A bit. But not as much as us. There are always other headlines. . . . When will I see you again?'

'When you come back to town.'

'Wednesday,' he said. 'I'll be back to town on Wednesday.'

'Will I see you then?'

'It will be a privilege and a pleasure.'

'Such sweet things you say,' she said, and her arms came round him. 'Such very sweet things.'

Tips for Hepscott and the butler, and the footman who came to carry her luggage down to the Daimler that would take her to the station, and a formal goodbye to her host before Mrs Chandler-Spicer came up to her.

'Goodbye, my dear,' she said. 'I hope you'll come up to see us again.'

'I hope so too,' said Jane.

'Oh *good*,' Mrs Chandler-Spicer said. 'Perhaps when you do we can find time for a little chat. I'd like that. This time of course I was far too busy – as indeed were you – but next time we really must make the effort.'

As far as Jane could see she meant every word.

'Justin Crawley?' said Lionel. 'Is he allowed in civilised society still?'

'He seemed to know which knives and forks to use,' said Jane.

'There are other crimes,' said Lionel severely, and then: 'Well well well. Creepy Crawley.'

'Is that what they call him?'

'It's what I call him.'

'Darling how clever you are,' said Jane. 'It suits him perfectly.'

The band played 'Embraceable You' and they got up at once, his arms came round her, as impersonal as a sister's. Such a waste, she thought, but he was always a joy to be with.

'How old would you say Crawley was?' he asked.

'About your age,' she said, 'but he shows it far more, and I bet he doesn't dance half as well as you do.'

'What makes you think so?'

'Nobody does,' she said.

'You are far and away my most favourite lady,' said Lionel, 'and always will be.' He looked about him as they circled the floor. 'This place is dead tonight,' he said.

More than two thirds full, and champagne at every other table.

'It used to be such fun here,' Lionel said.

Melancholy, it would seem, was à la mode.

'Why so depressed darling?' said Jane. 'Crossed in love again?'

'All my sailors are at sea,' said Lionel, 'which I must say is a bit hard when you consider how many ships aren't sailing at all.'

The music stopped, and he led Jane back to their table.

'It's just the way the world is,' he said, as the waiter poured champagne. 'I mean the Depression. All that. Oh I know you and I are all right – and all our chums – but it's awful to think about the ones who aren't. I mean you can't wear funny hats and throw streamers at people when half the country's starving and there isn't a damn thing one can do about it.'

'We did try,' said Jane. 'To do something about it, I mean.'

'Who did?'

'Charles. Me. Jay Bower too.'

Lionel knew about Charles, and approved, which was a relief. Jane valued Lionel's approval. She told him about the weekend at Blagdon.

'At least you tried,' said Lionel. 'Crawley was to be one of the subscribers, I take it?'

'He turned us down flat like the others.'

'Well of course he would,' said Lionel.

She looked at him more closely. 'Why do you say that?'

'He's interested in politics,' said Lionel.

'Crawley wants to be an MP?' Jane was incredulous.

'No no,' said Lionel. 'Not that sort of politics.'

'What then?'

'He's a Fascist,' Lionel said.

'You mean he wants to be the British Mussolini?' Jane sounded more incredulous still.

'Not exactly,' said Lionel. 'He's more keen on that new chap. The one in Germany.' He snapped his fingers. 'Hitler. That's the one.'

'Jackboots and uniforms, and beating the people you don't like.'

'Think about it,' said Lionel. 'Is it really so surprising?'

Jane thought about it. It wasn't surprising at all. 'Good God,' she said.

The band played 'Always'.

'Shall we?' Lionel asked, and she stood up at once. Nobody waltzed quite so well as Lionel.

Andy Patterson hadn't meant to go to the market place that night, but his Branch Meeting had finished early and Norah would still be at the hospital seeing her mother. By midweek a walk was all the entertainment he could afford and so he went to Felston market. The stalls would all have been cleared long ago, but there was a chance that the Salvation Army might be playing hymns, or somebody making a speech for the Liberals or the Tories, somebody he could heckle.

He reached the corner of Queen Victoria Street, where the one-armed man with the medal ribbons stood by an old and battered gramophone mounted on a pram that was even older. The record he played had been used so often that it was hard to distinguish the tune, and Andy hurried past him. He had nothing to give.

In the market place there was one platform, holding a group of chaps he had never seen before. Young chaps, most of them: big and hard, and for the most part well fed, by the look of them, and that *was* surprising. Bob would say 'In that case they must be strangers.' But Bob would make a joke about anything. Andy edged a little closer. They'd got a fair old crowd for a Wednesday. Every single man of them on the platform wore a black shirt, dark trousers and brightly polished boots, and one chap was holding a Union Jack. Bang in the middle was the only older man, a man of forty or so, but not bad looking, wearing the same outfit as the others, but of much more expensive cut. Andy stopped dead.

Good God! he thought. These chaps must be the Fascists he'd read about. But what are they doing *here*? This is a Socialist town.

40

This lot belongs in London, surely. But then he remembered more of what he'd read: the Fascists liked to hold their meetings in Whitechapel and Lambeth, and they were every bit as Socialist as Felston.

'No work, no money, not enough to eat and you're sick of it,' the speaker was shouting. 'Isn't that right ?' The crowd was silent. 'Well isn't it?' This time the crowd muttered assent. Every word the speaker had said was true. 'Well of course it is,' the speaker said. 'You're sick of it, these lads are sick of it' – his arm swung back towards the watching men in black – 'and I'm sick of it too. Only these lads and me, we're going to do something about it.'

'You're going to get work?' called a voice from the crowd. 'In Felston? The days of miracles is over, man.'

The crowd laughed then, and the speaker cut in quickly.

'No,' he said. 'It's not. For you, maybe, but not for me. If you believe what I believe then there'll be work and well-paid work, even here in Felston.'

He seemed so certain that the crowd surged forward. 'Tell us how then,' a woman called. But he made them wait for it.

This lad's good, thought Andy. This lad's really good. Not from round here, by his accent, but not from all that far off either.

At exactly the right moment the speaker said: 'We lived in a country that was once great. A country that conquered half the world and made it our own. A strong country. A proud country. A great country. Every other nation envied us – and they would envy us still if we hadn't allowed ourselves to be corrupted, cankered and tainted to the point where we threw away our greatness and tossed aside what we should have held most dear: the purity of our lives, our faith, our blood.'

His voice had taken on an almost liturgical quality. This man, Andy thought, had once been very close to the priesthood.

'We defiled our birthright,' the voice thundered. 'We defiled our blood. We defiled our sacred land. You in Felston are as guilty of it as the rest of us. I look about me here and what do I see? Arabs, Communists, Jews, walking about as if they owned the place. Wogs and Reds and Yids.'

There was a gasp from the crowd. Words spoken only in anger, or in drink, had been shouted aloud in the town's most public place.

Arabs yes, thought Andy. Lascar seamen for the most part, and as hard-up and in need of work as the rest of us. A few Communists, perhaps a couple of dozen, no more. Even he wasn't a Party member, but then the Party hadn't wanted him to join. Jews too, but again not many. Enough to support one synagogue, and that was about it. Not much in the way of defilement, even if you believed it was defilement, for a town of a hundred thousand people.

'You let them stay here. Live here.' The voice was booming now. 'You let them strut about as if they owned the place. *Our* place. The home of the free, pure, Anglo-Saxon race – until in come the blackies and the bomb throwers and the greasy kikes.'

Now we're getting to it, Andy thought.

'And do you throw them out? Do you even tell them to go back to where they came from? No. Not you. Come in, you say. Pull up a chair by the fire. Let me get you a sandwich – only make sure it isn't ham.' He began to rub his hands together like a bad actor playing Shylock. 'Oh my life, they say. Such goodness. Such kindness. How grateful I am already.' Someone in the crowd laughed, and Andy winced.

'I'll show you how grateful they are,' the voice boomed on. 'How many of you pay rent to a Jew, work for a Jew, pay money to a Jew?' The crowd was silent.

'Too frightened to speak,' the voice boomed on. 'Too frightened to as much as raise your hands. Still I can't say I blame you. I was scared of them myself until I joined the Fascists – and I'll tell you why I was scared. Because they don't fight fair. Not the Yids, oh dear me no. They don't come and face you like a man. Not the Yids. No honest combat and Queensberry rules. Not them. They don't hit you with their fists. They hit you with the sack and eviction and law courts and solicitors. With lies and starvation and prison. Haven't you seen them at it? *Haven't* you? And that's not all they do, by God it's not. You down there with pretty wives, pretty daughters, you know what I'm talking about. You owe a Yid money and he'll have his pound of flesh one way or another, won't he? *Won't he?*'

The crowd looked at each other and murmured, until the well-dressed man in the middle said: 'There's a Jew down there in the front. He's holding a stone or something. I think he's going to throw it.'

Four men leaped from the platform and into the crowd. Suddenly there was a high-pitched scream of pain. Andy moved forward, and a hand grasped his arm. He spun round, and found that he was confronting a police-inspector.

'Better leave it to us, councillor,' the inspector said. 'We don't want the council involved.'

'Then for God's sake get on with it,' said Andy.

The inspector moved into the crowd, and a sergeant and two constables followed. Andy looked at his hands and found that they were shaking. He doubled them into fists.

. 6 .

'Bernstein,' Andy said. 'His father owns that tailor's shop in Candlish Street.'

'He altered a coat for me once,' said Norah.

'They claimed he had half a brick he was going to throw,' Andy said. 'Though God knows where he would find half a brick in the market place, and if he took it there on purpose how come nobody else even noticed?'

'What happened?' Norah asked.

'They knocked him down and kicked him, that's what happened,' Andy said. 'Face and body. Gave him a proper leathering.'

'I thought you said the police were there.'

'So they were,' said Andy. 'But it all happened so quick.'

'Did they arrest those chaps then?'

Andy shook his head. 'Nobody saw anything,' he said. 'Nobody saw a bloody thing.' And then: 'I'm sorry.'

'Oh drink your tea,' said Norah. 'No harm in a man swearing when he's angry. Specially if it's my man.'

To herself she thought: Just as well I looked in on the way back from seeing my mother. He's in a right old state. Heaven knows what he'd have got up to if he'd been on his own.

'What did you do then?' she asked.

'Saw young Bernstein into an ambulance then came back here. He was in a right mess, poor lad. His face – '

'Don't fret yourself pet,' she said. 'There's nothing you can do.'

'There must be,' said Andy. 'There has to be.'

She looked at him more sharply then. The words were like a battle cry. 'Were they local – the chaps that did it?'

'Not from Felston,' said Andy. 'The one that said Bernstein had the brick was a posh chap. Loads of money by the look of him. It

44

seems the Fascists are making a tour of the North East. You would think it was a travelling theatre. Felston was their opening night.' He paused. 'Somebody fetched Bernstein's father before the ambulance came,' he said at last. The old man looked at his son, but he didn't cry, not at first. He just turned to me as if I was his best friend. I don't know him from Adam. "For this I left Russia," he said. "Who would believe it would be waiting for me in Felston?" I tell you, Norah – ' But for once the words didn't come.

She got up and drew him to his feet, put her arms about him, held him close. 'It's over,' she said. 'You did what you could.'

'I did nothing,' Andy said.

'You stayed with the boy,' she said. 'You cared. And I bet his father knows it.' Her arms came round his neck. 'Do you love me?'

'You know I do.'

'Then show me,' she said, but all he did was hold her.

'Crawley telephoned me from Manchester,' said Lovell.

'Creepy Crawley,' said Jane.

Charles laughed. 'Your name for him?'

'Lionel's.'

'Apt as ever.'

'What's the Creeper doing in Manchester?'

'Attending rallies. He was in Felston last night.'

'He makes speeches?'

'He watches other people make speeches. What he likes to do is sit on a platform in the middle of a bunch of thugs.'

'Charles, he can't have told you that,' said Jane.

'Of course not,' said Lovell. 'I've been making enquiries.' He hesitated. 'Somebody was hurt in Felston.'

Jane stiffened. 'Anyone I know?'

'I don't think so,' said Lovell. 'A young Jew called Bernstein. From what I hear Crawley virtually ordered his thugs to assault the poor chap – and they did. Put him in the hospital.'

'Who told you all this?'

'Bower.'

Of course, she thought, and then: Because darling Charles still has a hold on him, and so do I.

'The *World*'s stringer phoned in with the story.' said Lovell, 'but there wasn't enough evidence for Bower to print it. Besides – '

'Besides, what?'

'A lot of people don't like Jews,' Lovell said. 'That's why Crawley and his cohorts get away with it.'

'What did he phone you about?'

'He made me an offer – or rather he made us an offer. You and me. About Felston.'

'I'm listening.'

'He said he'd finance the whole thing. The whole of the town's redevelopment. One hundred thousand pounds' worth.'

'*What?*'

'There were conditions, however.'

'I somehow thought there would be.'

'He said he'd give us it all in one cheque, and we were to have a completely free hand, provided we announced to all and sundry that the Felston Development Plan was financed and sponsored by the British Union of Fascists.'

'How dare he – '

'Let me finish,' said Lovell. 'You and I have both to promise that we will give press interviews saying how lovely his playmates are – '

'Not the bishop?' said Jane. 'Not the bishop's mate?'

'He didn't seem to think they were important. But you have also to write an article about what a good idea Fascism is, and we're to arrange for the *Daily World* to print it.'

'What makes him think Jay Bower would do such a thing?'

'He considers that we may have some influence in that quarter.'

'He does his homework, doesn't he?'

'Yes,' said Lovell. 'He does. Damn him.'

'He couldn't renege if we did our share?'

'I doubt it. Not the way I'd tie it up,' said Lovell. 'If I did it Houdini wouldn't get out of it. But – '

'This is absolutely the most terrible decision I've had to make in my entire life,' said Jane. 'What an utterly bloody man. All the same, there's only one possible answer.'

'Which is?'

'Don't you know?' Jane asked.

'I know what I think,' said Lovell. 'I want to know what you think.'

'It just isn't on,' she said. 'It can't be.'

'You're absolutely right,' he said. 'Now tell me why.'

'Oh darling,' she said. 'I somehow knew you'd agree with me. As for why – it's because it wouldn't be for Felston. Not the whole of Felston. Not for the likes of poor Bernstein for instance, or the likes of Andy, either. I know Crawley offered you a free hand, but we couldn't tell him to keep his mouth shut – not if he's paying out that sort of money.'

'On the contrary,' said Lovell, 'he'd be yelling his head off.'

'And can he really cough up a hundred thousand just to finance this hobby of his?'

'Hobby?'

'Well what else can you call it?' said Jane. 'If he takes pleasure in seeing other people being hurt – and he obviously does – then that's his hobby, disgusting though it is. He must enjoy it an awful lot to shell out that kind of money.'

'I've no doubt he does,' said Lovell, 'but it won't be just him. There'll be other men – groups and organisations for that matter – adding their little mite.'

'They can't all be sadists, surely?'

'Of course not,' said Lovell. 'They're rich, and they want to stay rich. They've seen what's happened in Italy – Mussolini walloping the workers all over the place, and if Hitler gets to power he'll do even more walloping.'

'Like poor Bernstein. But a lot of Jews have money too.'

'If Crawley and his cohorts get their way, *they'll* get all the Jewish money, and then they'll be richer than ever.'

'I feel like getting tight,' said Jane. 'So tight I can't remember what you've just told me.'

'But you'd remember in the morning,' Lovell said, 'and you'd have a hangover as well.'

'Oh you,' said Jane. 'Always so sensible.'

'One of us has to be.'

'Then if that's so, answer me this. Must we have serious conversations only when we've got no clothes on?'

'What's wrong with that?'

She reached out to touch him. 'Other people seem to be able to manage it – talk seriously when they're dressed, I mean.'

'Other people are married,' said Lovell. 'Their lives are divided into compartments. Work. Dinner. Serious conversation. Love. We haven't the time for compartments – and besides – '

'Yes, Charles?'

'I need all of you I can get,' he said. 'And there are better ways of forgetting nasty things than getting drunk,' he said. 'Let's try one or two.'

Bob Patterson looked at her and thought: She was loved last night. Loved properly by a man who knew what he was doing: a man who cared for her. And she cares for him. You can tell just by looking at her: she's still glowing. All the same she parked the Bentley as neatly as if it were a baby Austin, and she's bang on time. He lugged his suitcase round to the boot, then she offered him her cheek to kiss. Even her skin glowed, and he thought: I'm happy for you, bonny lass, I really am, but try and turn it down before we get to Felston. Norah's the one who's getting married. The great car eased into the West End traffic. Like its owner, Bob thought, it was impatient for the Great North Road.

'How's business?' she asked.

'Booming,' said Bob. 'Folks seem to think the wireless takes their mind off their troubles. It never seems to occur to them they have to pay for it.' And if it's booming for me, he thought, it's coining it for that pal of yours. That Lovell. My senior partner. Sixty per cent of the equity. Not that he's any trouble – so long as I show a decent dividend. Could it be Lovell who sparked off all this glowing? he wondered. It didn't seem likely. Lovell was a serious chap: a banker. Dividends were more his line.

'Did you hear about Felston?' Jane asked.

'Sometimes I seem to hear about nowt else,' said Bob, 'but not recently. What's up?'

She told him about Bernstein and the Fascists.

'Andy won't like that,' said Bob.

'Do you?'

'Well of course not,' said Bob, 'but there's not a thing I can do about it, so where's the sense in worrying?'

The Bentley snarled its way to Highgate.

'What are you giving them?' Bob asked.

The Bentley was now on the road it liked best, and doing a steady seventy. 'Money,' said Jane, 'and shopping vouchers.' She named a department store in Newcastle: the best. 'And you?'

'Money – and a bedroom suite. That was Norah's idea. I told her to get whatever she wanted. – Our Andy won't like the idea of being given money.'

'Norah will,' said Jane. 'And after all – it's her day. And when the children come – '

'Good Lord,' said Bob. 'I never thought of that. Children … Our Andy a father.'

'It's what marriage is for, according to the Prayer Book,' said Jane.

'They'll stay on in John Bright Street,' Bob said. 'I offered them somewhere else but they wouldn't hear of it.'

'They'll be happy there,' said Jane. 'Why should they move?'

The Bentley shot past a bull-nosed Morris, almost with contempt. In this country, thought Bob, even the cars are class conscious.

'Will they be happy, do you think?' he asked.

Jane said, 'I've thought about it rather a lot, and so far as I can see I think they will. She's a strong woman – and it would need a strong woman to take Andy on. But she's also the one he chose.'

'You're one of us,' said Bob, 'so I can tell you this. He had to get married. – Not that she was pregnant or anything. I'm talking about politics. He won't get any further in that game till he's wed.'

'Well of course not,' said Jane.

When it comes to facing reality, thought Bob, women are far better than men.

'So you think they'll be happy?' he said.

'That's up to Andy,' said Jane, 'but I rather think the answer is yes.'

They stopped for lunch at a pub north of Grantham. Cold beef and salad, and lemonade for her, beer for him.

'What time will we get there?' he asked.

'If the traffic stays kind we'll be in time for a drink before dinner.'

'Are you going to see them tonight?'

'No,' she said. 'Tomorrow's Andy's stag night. I'll see Norah then. Better to let them have tonight with each other.'

49

'Andy's stag night,' said Bob. 'Who would have thought it?'

'No less likely than yours,' she said.

'Mine?' Bob smiled. 'That'll be the day. Mind you it was close a couple of times.'

Please don't let him talk about Catherine, she thought, but of course he didn't. In matters of sex at least Bob was a gentleman.

'Where is he having it?'

Bob finished his beer and offered her a cigarette.

'At first he didn't want to have one at all,' he said. 'Didn't see the point. But I wasn't having that. So he's got a few of his pals together and I've hired a room at the Labour Hall.'

'Lobsters and champagne and dancing girls?'

'Sandwiches and beer and a barmaid. Our Andy's not one to risk his future for a good night out.' Bob seemed to find the thought astounding.

'What will the reception be like?' asked Jane.

'I wanted to hold that in the Eldon Arms,' said Bob, 'but Andy wouldn't hear of it. I didn't mind paying – '

'Of course you didn't,' said Jane. 'But Andy's a councillor. A Labour councillor. He can't risk posh do's at the Eldon Arms.'

'That's what he told me,' said Bob. 'Not that the Eldon Arms is all that posh. I mean it's hardly the Savoy, is it?'

'Gracious,' said Jane. 'What a snob you've become.'

Bob grinned. 'Anyway,' he said, 'we're down for a knife-and-fork tea at the Labour Hall, but I'm in charge of the catering, so at least you and me'll get a decent drop of wine.'

'Grandma would have loved it,' said Jane.

'Aye,' said Bob. 'Da an' all. Not that he'd have touched the wine.'

Jane stubbed out her cigarette. 'Time to move,' she said.

Making that car do what she wanted was a passion with her, he thought. She was like a lion tamer whose only thought was to dominate lions. But at least she restricted her need to expensive machinery. If once she extended it to men she'd be – what was the phrase he'd heard in Hollywood? – oh aye. A real ball cutter. God help the poor bugger whose –

'Let's go straight on,' said Jane. 'Not bother about stopping for tea.'

'Anything you say,' said Bob.

50

. 7 .

The manager of the Eldon Arms was delighted to see them, as he always was, since his two best rooms were reserved for them, and this time they took dinner in the hotel too. Roast chicken. It always was. At its end Bob set out to meet Andy and arrange the plans for next day, and left Jane yawning over her coffee. An early night, she thought, and a long sleep, and then she was called to the phone.

Charles said, 'I hope this was a good time to call.'

'Perfect, bless you.'

'I just wanted to make sure you'd arrived safely. What are you doing?'

'Preparing for an early night.'

'Oddly enough so am I. When are you coming back?'

'Some time next week.'

'Could I interest you in a trip to America?'

'New York?'

'California too, and Mexico.'

'You could indeed,' said Jane. 'When do we start?'

'We'll talk about it when I see you,' said Lovell. 'But it's nice to give advance warning.'

'Coming from you that's bitter,' said Jane. He was still laughing when they hung up.

It would be nice to see Jane again, Norah thought, and then smiled at even the fact that she thought of her as Jane and not Miss Whitcomb. No respect, she told herself, but then Jane didn't want respect. She wanted friendship. When you got down to it what she really wanted was love, because she gave so much of it. There weren't that many had enough to lavish on a whole town. She looked around the front room where her wedding presents were on display. They were using her mother's flat in Redfern Street because it was bigger than Andy's: there was more space. Not that there was all that much to show, she thought, though mind you folks had been kind when they could, though there weren't many could give like Jane, or Bob. There weren't any, in fact.

Her mother fretted because she was laid up in hospital with bronchitis. Had visions of Andy flitting about the bedroom like a bee round a honeypot. Fat lot she knew. Andy wasn't the buzzing sort. Not like her first. A right buzzer Marty had been. Never let her alone – and she not more than twenty, and hardly knowing what she was supposed to do. Marty knew all right, and he'd hurt her at the beginning, till she got used to it. He could never get enough, not even during that final illness when the pneumonia got him. 1922 would it be? The pneumonia was due to him having spent a day and a night in the North Sea in 1918, after he'd been torpedoed, and it finally killed him four years later. Maybe he knew, she thought. Maybe that was what drove him to her like that. So little time. Still, he hadn't been a bad chap otherwise, and she'd have had a terrible time of it without the pension. War widow, that's what she was. But tomorrow she wouldn't be and the pension would stop. Suddenly she got up and went to her bedroom. There Marty was, on her mantelpiece: sailor's cap pushed back on his head, tab in his mouth, thumb cocked at the photographer so the world would know what a lad he was.

Aloud she said to him, 'I'm sorry Marty, but this is no place for you,' and took him into the scullery. There was an old chest there full of stuff she never used: a clock that wanted mending, tools that had belonged to her father, a vase she couldn't stand, and she tucked Marty at the bottom of the pile. But she bet his eyes were still laughing.

Andy didn't laugh much. But then if you looked at life like he did, there wasn't much to laugh about. He'd done six months in Durham Prison for being a conscientious objector while Marty was in the navy getting torpedoed, and by what she'd heard there wasn't much to choose between the two. And then he believed all that stuff he went on about: a just society; a living wage; a better world. No wonder he didn't laugh much. She'd have to do the laughing for both of them.

That was all right. She could usually manage a laugh, she thought, and went back to the bedroom to make sure there was nothing else of Marty's lying about – but that was daft. Even Marty couldn't get into her bed from where he was now.

Andy could. In fact Andy would have to. It was expected. His duty, you might say. Not that it should be all that much like hard work, she thought, and looked at the mirror. Getting on a bit, lass. Thirty-two. But your skin's still good and you've kept your figure. No bairns, that was why, though she'd wanted them so. Felt she'd earned them, you might say – there had to be some recompense for all that humping and grunting – but all she'd ever managed was two miscarriages. Better luck with Andy?

The trouble was that Andy was – shy? No. Shy sounded soft, and Andy wasn't soft. Good and kind, yes, but never soft. It was almost as if he were afraid of sex. The other night she'd almost *asked* him to do it with her – after all they'd be married before the week was out – but all he'd done was hold her. As if he were afraid to do it. Something had happened to him somewhere, she thought. It must have done to cause that fear, because Andy wasn't one that was easily scared.

His brother Bob, she thought. He wouldn't be scared any more than Marty, though he probably knew a lot more about doing it than Marty ever learned. And that's quite enough of that, she told herself. Thinking such thoughts the day before you get married.

Her mother didn't like Andy either, and the thought distressed her. Mostly it was because he'd been in prison: done time. No matter what the reasons, her mother could find no forgiveness for a man who'd done time. Been a gaolbird. Our family has always been respectable, she'd said. Over and over she'd said it. She didn't like his making speeches in the market place, either. Making an exhibition of himself, she called it. Being a councillor was all right, though. Councillors were respectable: could even end up becoming mayor. But how could a gaolbird end up mayor of Felston?

Somewhere at the back of Norah's mind the thought nagged that her mother was not too unhappy at being in hospital when her daughter was being married. The bronchitis was genuine enough, after all. The perfect excuse. She couldn't go because the doctors wouldn't let her.

53

Norah got up abruptly, and went to put the kettle on. Jane was due soon, and Bet after that, and you couldn't put two women together in Felston, never mind three, without making a pot of tea.

Jane stood in the doorway of the Eldon Arms that looked out on to Queen Victoria Street. Behind her the hotel porter stood poised ready to load boxes and parcels, but the taxi was late. Jane spotted an old acquaintance, a one-armed man with medals, pushing a pram that held a gramophone instead of a baby. Artlessly, apparently unaware that she was watching, he stopped the pram, put on the brake, and selected a record. For once it was a new one, and every word was clear.

> Look at the widow, crying her eyes out.
> Ain't it grand to be blooming well dead?
> Look at the coffin, blooming great handles.
> Ain't it grand to be blooming well dead?

The singer's voice was high pitched, rather thin, but indomitably cheerful.

> Look at the parson, [it sang] wearing his surplice.
> Ain't it grand to be blooming well dead?

Jane sought in her purse and found a shilling, her customary tribute. The appositeness of the song was appalling, because in Felston death was the only means of escape, and to hear it so cheerfully extolled, witty though it was, soon became unbearable. It was like that other song of fourteen, fifteen years ago, that so many officers, John Patterson among them, had tried in vain to stop the soldiers from singing:

> If you want to find the sergeant, I know where he is,
> I know where he is, I know where he is.
> If you want to find the sergeant, I know where he is,
> He's hanging on the old barbed wire.

What the soldiers were singing was: 'I know I'm going to be killed, but at least I'll sing about it first,' and from what John had told her they'd sung about it with an aching sweetness that made it even harder to bear, just as this record she heard greeted the release of death with a wit that somehow made it even more appalling.

Look at the flowers. Blooming great orchids.
Ain't it grand to be blooming well dead?

Bob appeared beside her. 'Enjoying the music?' he asked.
'Enjoying?'
But he continued unheeding. 'I bought it for him myself from the music shop up the road.'
'But why on earth – '
'All his others were so scratched you couldn't tell what they were. And this one seemed so absolutely right for Felston. Puts the place into what's the word – perspective?'
Jane opened her mouth, then shut it again. No point in arguing with Bob about his attitude to Felston. He was born here, after all. Might as well argue with a salmon about swimming upstream at spawning time. Instead she gave the one-armed man his shilling, and Bob gave him another, and the one-armed man moved on because two bob in three minutes wasn't going to happen again in a hurry.
'You off to Norah's?' Bob asked.
'Got a cab coming,' said Jane. 'Can I drop you anywhere?'
'No thanks,' said Bob. 'I'm going to Newcastle. There's some shops I want to look at.'
'Don't get too drunk tonight,' said Jane.
'With our Andy as guest of honour?' said Bob. 'Some hopes.'
He set off for the station, the cab turned up at last, the porter handed in the parcels, and Jane set off for Redfern Street.
'So much stuff,' said Norah, carrying the last parcel in, and then: 'But I've already spent the shopping vouchers. That's them. And that.' She nodded towards a pile of plates, saucers, cups, and a canteen of cutlery.
'These are just a few afterthoughts,' said Jane. 'Let's have a cup of tea and I'll tell you.'
'In the kitchen,' Norah said, and led the way.
'Where's Bet?' asked Jane.
'I asked her for later,' Norah said. 'I thought it would be nice if we had a bit of time on our own first.'

'Very nice indeed,' said Jane, and sipped at her tea that was mahogany brown and scalding hot: a real Felston brew.

'Mm. Delicious,' she said, and then quickly, before the lie became too obvious: 'All excited about tomorrow?'

'Well yes,' said Norah. 'It's a big thing, getting married.'

'You've got a good man in Andy,' said Jane.

'I know that,' said Norah. 'Honestly I do. But – '

'Goodness isn't always all that easy to live with?' Jane suggested, and Norah nodded. 'I found that out when I was engaged to his brother,' said Jane.

'It must have been dreadful for you,' Norah said. 'I mean the tenth of November. Just one more day . . .'

'Well yes it was,' said Jane, 'but it was a long time ago. Nearly fourteen years. And you're the one I've come to talk about. Not me. Let's go and take a look at the prezzies.'

'Prezzies?' said Norah.

'The presents,' said Jane. 'The afterthoughts.'

In the front room Norah said, 'I haven't said thank you for the money.'

'Please don't,' said Jane.

'And Bob gave me money too,' Norah said. 'As well as the bedroom suite. He was that funny about the bedroom suite.'

He would be, thought Jane. Aloud she said, 'Funny?'

'He took me to Newcastle and told me to pick the one I wanted – and I did, – but then he sent me back three times.'

'What on earth for?'

'He said I wasn't spending enough money.'

'I hope you got what you liked?' said Jane.

'Oh I did,' said Norah. 'It's lovely. And with the money – yours and Bob's – we thought we could afford a week in Scarborough – if that's all right.'

'Well of course it's all right,' said Jane. 'It's your honeymoon. Now let me show you the afterthoughts.' She sorted through her parcels. 'Something old, something new,' she said. 'Something borrowed, something blue.'

'I thought that was only what you read about in books,' Norah said.

'Well it's not,' said Jane. 'Let's have a look.'

She handed the parcels to Norah, who tore at them eagerly. Something old turned out to be a string of pearls.

'Oh I can't possibly,' Norah said. 'They'll be real, likely.'

'Well yes,' said Jane.

'Then how can I?'

'Because it's the custom,' said Jane. 'And I hardly ever wear pearls anyway. They don't suit me.' And I've got three better sets at home.

Something new was a pair of silk stockings. Real silk. Norah had never worn real silk stockings in her life, and handled them lovingly, wary of ladders. Some of the left-over money had gone on new underwear – her trousseau you might say – and if that and the stockings didn't do the trick then nothing would.

Something borrowed was a lipstick and powder compact.

'But I wouldn't know where to start,' Norah said. And what would her mother say?

'Then I'll come round and make you up myself,' said Jane.

That would be nice, Norah thought. She'd seen it done at the pictures. And Mother would just have to lump it. She didn't like Andy anyway.

Something blue for the last: a turquoise brooch set in gold.

'Oh dear God,' Norah said.

'The stones are the colour of your eyes,' said Jane. 'I couldn't resist them.'

This time Norah made no effort to refuse, but hugged Jane instead.

Now don't you stand there feeling like Lady Bountiful, Jane admonished herself. It cost you no more than your last day at the races. Then she relented towards herself.

But you didn't do it to make yourself look good, she thought. You did it to make Norah feel happy, and it has. She looked at the other woman, who was carefully trying on the jewels she had given her. The bride to be could only be described as radiant.

'May I see your wedding dress?' she asked.

'I'd love you to,' said Norah. 'I'll just go into the bedroom and slip it on.'

'I'll come with you,' said Jane.

'No!' Norah's voice was sharp. 'You wait here. I won't be a minute.'

57

Now what brought that on? Jane wondered. Shy of my seeing her in her underwear? Or ashamed of her underwear?

Rich people had no shame, thought Norah. No shame at all. She'd seen that at the pictures too, and it seemed it was true. Not that it made her love Jane any the less. It was just the way she was. Then suddenly it dawned on her. Jane had never been married, but she had a house of her own, lived her own life, and there could be no doubt that a man was part of that life. Perhaps more than one. There could be no doubt in other words that she had done it as well; not that Norah could possibly ask her, although she very much wanted to. It would give her a chance to talk about Andy, but of course it wasn't possible. Andy was *her* problem. She must tackle it on her own.

'But it's charming,' said Jane, and so it was: white cotton with a delicate pattern of blue to discount any suggestion of virginity. A dress as tactful as it was pretty.

'Where did you get it?' asked Jane.

Norah looked surprised. 'I made it myself,' she said.

'You didn't!'

Jane sounded incredulous. Honestly rich people were funny – queer, you might say. Even the nicest of them.

'How else could I manage a dress like this?' Norah said aloud. 'I wrote off for the pattern and bought the material at the remnant shop – and my cousin let us have her sewing machine while I did it.'

'It's lovely,' said Jane, 'and just right for that jewellery, too.'

Even so: 'If you don't mind,' Norah said, 'we won't say anything to Bet about the things you gave me.'

. 8 .

Bob walked from the station to look at the Newcastle shops. They were all nice and handy, and anyway it was a good idea to move on foot through shopping areas. It gave you the feel of a place somehow: let you see how things were, how much money there was about.

He looked at his watch: still a bit early for his last appointment. Just time for a whisky and soda in that elegant bar behind Eldon Square: cocktail barman in a white mess jacket, glasses with a good solid feel to them. They even had ice: and the barman left you alone when he saw you working at figures on the back of an envelope. Not that it took long. He'd been buying up shops for years now: knew to a fiver what they were worth – and how much to offer when the bidding started. He made up his mind how far to go. Nice to have them, but it wouldn't break his heart if the vendors wouldn't play. His business was doing well, and there were always more shops to be had.

He'd have to tell Lovell, whether he bought or not, but Lovell never interfered – not so long as he made money, he thought again, but then he always did make money. All the same it would be nice to be shot of Lovell, one of these fine days, be his own boss. But that fine day was not yet. A deal like that took time, and there was no sense in rushing things. He looked at the clock behind the bar. It was true, as he'd told Jane, that he'd come to Newcastle to look at shops, but he'd also come to have lunch with Mrs Sybil Hendry, and it was time to go.

Daughter of a general, widow of a – squire would you call him? – that was Mrs Hendry. The squire had owned seven thousand acres of the worst land in North East England, but there was coal under a fair bit of it. Game on it too, and a couple of trout streams.

59

Mrs Hendry had not been left destitute after Hendry had had his shooting accident. That was all it was, everybody hastened to assure each other. An accident. Well it stood to reason, didn't it? Tony had everything to live for. Money, fine house, lovely wife. It must have been an accident. The coroner had said so after all. The trouble was that Tony had been rather a dab hand with a twelve bore, – but after all anybody could have an accident. . . .

Mrs Hendry was already at the cocktail bar of the hotel by the theatre, punctual to the minute as a general's daughter should be. She was by herself, drinking a dry martini, and the barman was far too afraid of her to tell her that she couldn't; that it Wasn't The Policy Of The Hotel. But the fear she inspired had nothing to do with her being a general's daughter. It was due entirely to the fact that she was Sybil Hendry, and capable of a raging bitchiness that no mere barman could cope with. Bob went up to her, and the barman allowed himself to be a little less nervous.

'You're late,' she said. Her voice was a purr, but cats purr too before they scratch.

'Business,' said Bob.

'Before pleasure you mean?'

'Just this once,' said Bob, and ordered a whisky and soda.

'So it's not an invariable rule then? Only when you've arranged to give me lunch?'

The barman served Bob his whisky and soda and moved to the other end of the bar, where it was safer.

Bob looked at her. Huge eyes, little beak of a nose, black hair, pale skin, and a neatly rounded figure sheathed in a dress that even Jane would have found it hard to match. Worth making an effort for, this one, even if she did believe in making you suffer for the terrible sin of being male.

'How was I to know you'd be punctual?' he said. 'You're the only woman I've ever met who was.'

She laughed then. 'You've met a lot of women, I gather?' she said.

'A canny few.'

Again she laughed, and the barman looked at Bob with a kind of amazed respect.

'Do you do that deliberately?' she asked.

'Do what?'

'Talk like a miner or a dustman or whatever you're supposed to be.'

'A printer,' said Bob. 'I served me time right through. If folks ever get tired of listening to the wireless I can always go back to it.'

'Answer the question,' Sybil Hendry said. 'It's far too early for autobiography.'

'Do I do it on purpose?' said Bob. 'Sometimes. Some folks – people find it amusing. Sometimes I do it because I forget to talk posh.'

'You can talk posh then?'

'When I concentrate,' said Bob. 'I can't do the accent – not like you, but I can manage the grammar pretty well. Comes of being a printer.'

'I think I might find it amusing so long as you don't overdo it,' she said. 'I know it made me laugh at that party at – where was it?'

'Brenda Coupland's,' said Bob. 'It was her engagement party – to that chap Meldrum.'

'That ghastly fat man,' said Sybil Hendry. 'He couldn't keep his eyes off her, and she couldn't keep hers off that rifleman – '

'Piers Hilyard,' said Bob.

'Or her hands either,' said Sybil Hendry. 'And where did you meet a rifleman, printer – and an earl's son into the bargain?'

'General Strike,' said Bob. 'We were in a fight together.'

'How on earth – ' She stopped, then, 'No,' she said. 'Rules are rules – even one's own. Too early for autobiography, I said, and so it must be. Let's go to lunch instead.'

Lunch was consommé, salmon, and strawberries, and she noticed that he ate it deftly, and without fuss, and that the wine he chose, a Pouilly-Fuissé, was a perfect complement to the food. Moreover she noticed that he enjoyed his meal, not just because she was there but because it was good.

'Wireless sets,' she said when the coffee came. 'Is there money in wireless sets?'

'There is if you do it right.'

'And keeping a lady waiting while you look at shops – that's doing it right?'

61

'Exactly,' he said, as if pleased at her ready understanding.

'I was going to finish that martini and go,' she said. 'I'd had enough of the masterful male nonsense with that cocktail barman.'

'He didn't look all that masterful when I came in,' said Bob.

Sybil Hendry looked smug. 'No,' she said. 'He didn't, did he?'

'Have I been masterful?' said Bob.

She considered the question. 'Not yet,' she said, 'and you'd better not start if you want to buy me another lunch.' She took a cigarette from her case and he lit it for her.

'Are you in trade, would you say?' she asked.

'Well of course,' said Bob, and she smiled.

'What an honest little chap it is,' she said. "You're in trade because you sell things, I take it.'

'I don't even sell things,' said Bob. 'I rent them.'

'You don't find it boring?'

'If I did I'd be doing something else.'

'Yes you would, wouldn't you?' she said. 'You couldn't stand being bored any more than I can.' She flicked cigarette ash into an ashtray. 'My father would be appalled if he knew I was lunching here,' she said.

'He doesn't like the food?'

'He doesn't like you,' she said. 'Or he wouldn't if he knew of your existence, which I doubt he ever will.'

'Because I'm common?'

'Because you're awful,' she said. 'By his standards, that is. I mean look at you. Ex-printer. In trade. The sort of funny accent you hear at the music hall. Quite awful.'

'One does one's poor best,' said Bob, and she exploded with laughter, but in her mind she thought: No, not masterful, but witty and cunning, and that's far more dangerous. I'll have to watch myself with you, printer.

'I expect it's because my father was an officer,' she said. 'Finished up as a general, as a matter of fact. According to him chaps like you belong in the ranks.'

'Piers Hilyard's a pal of mine,' said Bob.

'He's not of my father's generation,' she said. 'The world's changing – even I accept that, but Daddy prefers it the way it was.' She stubbed out her cigarette. 'There's a flat in Gosforth I want to visit,' she said. 'Would you like to come with me?'

'Delighted.'

'I'm afraid there's nobody in it. Will that bother you?'

'Not in the least,' said Bob.

The child was enchanting, thought Jane. Gravely serious at first, because her parents had obviously told her that she must be on her best behaviour in the presence of Miss Whitcomb, from whom so many material blessings flowed. Seven, would she be? Certainly no more, and gratifyingly pretty. (Her brother, who wasn't pretty at all, was asleep in his pram in the front room.) Soon Bet and Norah were gossiping, and it was left to Jane to talk to her godchild, that new and fascinating younger Jane.

Like so many children, the young Jane possessed the ability to get straight to the point, to ask the questions that in their opinion at least were in urgent need of an answer.

'Miss Whitcomb,' the child said. 'Is it true you've got a car?'

'Well yes, it is,' said Jane. 'But I wish you wouldn't call me Miss Whitcomb. Call me Aunt Jane. It's so much more friendly.'

The child considered this. 'Well yes it is,' she said at last. 'But you don't look like an aunt.'

'Don't I?' said Jane. 'Well let's pretend I am for now, and see what happens.'

The child looked at her. Part of the enchantment, Jane saw at once, was that despite her cheap and rather ugly clothes, she was very pretty indeed, and in a way that tugged at her heart strings. She was, Jane was sure, an exact replica of what her great grandmother must have been at the same age; and she, Jane Whitcomb, had adored that old lady: John's, Andy's, Bob's, Bet's grandma, whose death still had the power to make her sad. She had something of Grandma's quickness too, and altogether Jane found it hard not to reach out and touch her, but such things must not be hurried.

'What sort of a car have you got?' the child asked.

'It's called a Bentley,' said Jane. 'Would you like a ride in it?'

'Oh yes,' the child said. 'Can I?' And then: 'Is it big?'

'Well yes,' said Jane. 'I suppose it is. Very big, as a matter of fact.'

The child went at once to her mother.

63

'Mam,' she said. 'Aunt Jane says her car's a big one. She says I can have a ride in it. Can I, Mam?'

'Don't bother Miss Whitcomb,' her mother said.

'She isn't bothering me,' said Jane. 'Honestly. And I really would like to take her for a ride in my car. You too, of course.'

'I'm afraid I can't,' said Bet. 'I have to get back home to start Frank's tea.'

Her husband Frank worked for the tramways, and still yearned to be an inspector, though he was now a driver of some seniority, and his tea, at the end of a day-shift, was something of a ritual feast.

'Can I go with Aunt Jane, Mam?' the child asked. 'Can I?'

'If you're sure it's no trouble,' her mother said.

'Of course not,' said Jane. 'I have a cab coming for me soon. We'll go back to my hotel, pick up the car and have a quick spin, then I'll drop her home. I remember very well where you live.' Suddenly her conscience nudged her, or was it her guardian angel? 'Would you like me to take young Frank as well?' she asked.

'No,' said Bet, a hint of alarm in her voice. 'Franky's far too young to be gadding about in cars. He's still in his push-chair. But it's kind of you to offer.' She turned to her daughter.

'And mind you say thank you for the treat,' she said.

'Oh yes, Mam.'

Bet turned back to Norah, and resumed the discussion on who should sit next to whom at tomorrow's wedding feast without causing offence, if not outrage. Young Jane produced a comic, and together she and her new aunt read it. Most of it seemed to concern the adventures of a group of animals: a fox, a dog, and what might have been a badger, in pullovers and shorts, and a cat and a mole in gym slips. Text and pictures alike were of an inanity beyond belief, and Jane was sure from the start that her godchild thought so too.

'Golly,' Sybil Hendry said. 'Did you learn all that behind the printing press?'

Bob grinned at her.

'Don't start being smug,' she said. 'I don't like it when men are smug.'

'Not smug,' said Bob. 'Just happy. And if it comes to that you've learned a few tricks yourself. Where was that? Behind the bike shed at Cheltenham Ladies' College?'

She struck out at him then, but he was too quick for her and caught her wrist, not hurting her, just holding.

'Touché,' she said, and he let her go at once. 'They wouldn't let me in,' she said, 'though my mother tried hard enough. Neither would Roedean – I had to make do with governesses, pour souls. But seriously – where did you learn?'

'Here and there,' he said. She pulled a face. 'Oh come off it,' said Bob. 'What do you expect me to say?'

'Quite right,' she said. 'Excuse the question. It's just – well you really are remarkable, you know.'

She rolled over on the bed to reach for her clothes, quite unconcerned that he could see her nakedness from so many angles as she did so. But then why should she be? he thought. She had a lovely little body. Not in Georgina Payne's class perhaps, or Lily Dunn's, but lovely all the same.

'Are there any more at home like you?' she asked.

'A sister,' said Bob, 'and one brother living. Your father would approve of our Bet. She knows her place.'

'But not your brother?' She wriggled into her girdle.

'Andy? No. Born rebel is Andy.'

'In what way?'

'Conscientious Objector during the war – he went to prison for it – active in the General Strike – and any other strike come to that – Labour Councillor.'

'Definitely not Daddy's type,' she said.

'Mind you he's got brains,' said Bob. 'He went to Cambridge for a bit.' He got up then, yawned and stretched, then he too began to dress.

'Worse and worse,' she said, and drew on a stocking, clipped it to a suspender, then looked up to find that he was watching her. 'Enjoying the view?' she asked.

'Well of course I am,' he said. 'Better than the pier end is that.'

'What a compliment.' She rolled on the other stocking. 'You did say one brother living?'

'Aye,' said Bob. 'Our John was killed in the war.'

'I'm sorry.'

'Me an' all,' said Bob. 'You would have liked our John.'

'Would Daddy?'

'I doubt it,' said Bob.

'Whyever not? If he was a soldier – '

'He was a captain,' said Bob.

'Good God!' she said, and then again, 'I'm sorry. I didn't mean – '

'Of course you didn't,' said Bob. 'There's nothing to apologise for. Very keen on what you might call self-improvement, our John. Before the war, even. Went to night school, got himself an education. English, shorthand, book-keeping, a bit of law. Even a bit of French. Then he moved on to Bradford.'

'What an odd place to go.'

He looked at her, but she seemed perfectly serious.

'Got himself an office job in the wool trade,' he said, 'then he set up for himself. Selling piece-goods. Doing well.'

'Just like you.'

'A bit of me, a bit of Andy,' said Bob. 'All that learning and education. Then the war came and he joined up first chance he got. Then from what he told me, a lot of the young officers got killed, more than the men even, if you worked it out in percentages – '

'Subalterns,' she said. 'They were the ones who led, and so the Germans shot them.'

'Makes sense, I suppose,' said Bob. 'If anything in a war makes sense. Anyway our John was well spoken, like I say, and he knew which knife and fork to use – '

'That's quite enough of that,' she said. '*You* know which knife and fork to use –'

'So they sent him off on a course somewhere and made him into an officer.'

'Which regiment?'

'The Royal Northumbrians. Fourth Battalion.'

'Good Lord,' she said. 'He was in Daddy's division.'

'Major-General Sir Archibald Lomax, KCVO.'

'Quite right,' she said, 'except that he's a lieutenant-general now. A retired one. But how did you know?'

'There's a letter from him in our house – what was our house. It's Andy's now.'

'From Daddy?'

66

'About our John. After he was killed.'

'Usually it was the colonel who wrote that kind of letter.'

'There's one from him, too. I think your dad wrote because of John's medals. He had a DSO and something called an MC and bar.'

'He must have been a remarkable man. When was he killed?'

'Tenth of November, 1918,' said Bob.

'How utterly ghastly,' Sybil Hendry said.

'Aye. It took a bit of getting used to. I'll tell you another thing about our John.'

'Please do.'

'He was engaged to Jane Whitcomb,' said Bob. 'That's why she works so hard for Felston.'

'Young Jane liked the Bentley,' Jane Whitcomb said.

Bob said, 'Of course she did. She's not daft.'

'Certainly she's not,' said Jane. 'She's a very bright little girl.'

'And anyway,' said Bob, 'that'll be the first Bentley she ever rode in.'

'Well of course.'

'And the last,' said Bob.

'That remains to be seen,' said Jane, and he looked down at her, then away. Now wasn't the time to go into whatever that implied. Perhaps there never would be a time to go into that.

'Did you buy lots of lovely shops?' Jane asked.

'Just the two,' said Bob. 'And anyway they're not for buying, they're for renting. It's all renting in my business.'

'Buying's too expensive?'

'Too permanent,' said Bob. 'For all I know the wireless could be just a fad. Folks could get bored. . . . I don't want to be landed with two hundred empty shops.'

'*Two hundred?*'

'So far,' said Bob.

'That's quite a craze,' said Jane. 'You *must* be rich.'

'Not yet,' said Bob. 'Doing canny. But not rich. Not yet anyway . . . I ran into someone you know when I was in Newcastle. Sybil Hendry. She was at Brenda Coupland's party. As a matter of fact we had lunch together.'

I thought you would,' said Jane.

'What's that supposed to mean?'

'Oh come off it,' said Jane. 'She's a very pretty girl. Nice lunch?'

'Delicious,' said Bob. 'We got to talking about my family.'

'She *must* be serious,' said Jane.

'Oh knock off,' said Bob. 'It was just talk, that's all. Only I happened to mention you were engaged to our John.' He looked at her face. 'I hope you don't mind?'

'Why on earth should I?' said Jane. 'It's true. Was she surprised?'

'A bit,' said Bob. 'Then she asked me when John was killed, and when I told her she was that sad –'

'It's a sad story,' said Jane, 'but it ended fourteen years ago.' But that was a lie. Even after madness, and Jay Bower, and Charles Lovell, John was still there. He walked into her dreams as if he had written the scripts himself, and perhaps he had.

'Is it serious?' she asked.

'You know me,' said Bob. 'It's never all that serious with me.'

Let's hope she knows your rules, Jane thought. To her Sybil Hendry had seemed a very determined person, perhaps ruthlessly so, and if even half the rumours about her were true, she was most certainly trouble.

'What time's the stag party?' she asked.

'As soon as the cab gets here.' He looked around the Eldon Arm's depressed and gloomy hall.

'God this place is dreary,' he said.

'Certainly not the place for a stag night,' she said. 'All the same Bob – taking a taxi to the Labour Hall, isn't that defying the gods just a little?'

He grinned. 'I like folks to know where I stand,' he said. 'And anyway, there's a few bottles I have to take over. I'd be in dead trouble if I dropped them.'

Then the cab arrived and he was gone.

Jane looked at her watch. Seven o'clock. Dr Stobbs's surgery would be over, and by the time she'd walked to the clinic he'd have washed, lit his pipe, and be writing up his case notes, but he wouldn't mind her interrupting him – not this time: not after she'd given him a cheque for four hundred and seventy-five pounds.

. 9 .

It was just as she had predicted: if Stobbs wasn't overjoyed to see her, the sight of her cheque was pleasing.

'Good,' he said. 'Very good . . . Needed, too.'

'It always is.'

He looked at her, suspicious as usual, but there had been no hint of irony, and he knew it.

'It gets worse,' he said. 'Like the Somme. On and on and on. That's Felston clinic. A Somme that never ends.'

He lay back in his chair, then yawned and stretched. He was still stocky, strong, combative, thought Jane, but for the first time he looked tired. Exhausted.

'You run the clinic on your own, now?'

'There's nobody else daft enough to come in with me,' he said. 'Nobody qualified, that is.'

Can he be warning me off? thought Jane. Can he still be worried that I may want to interfere – the one flamingo flaunting it among Felston's drab crows?

'How's Canon Messeter?' she asked.

'Good Lord!' Stobbs took his pipe from his mouth and looked at it suspiciously, as if it were about to explode, then reached for his matches.

'I've got a surprise for you,' he said. 'Messeter's here.'

'In Felston?'

'*Here,*' said Stobbs again. 'In his old room. In the clinic.'

'He can't possibly be working here,' said Jane.

'No,' said Stobbs. 'He's dying here.'

'But I thought he went to live in Hampshire – with a cousin or something.'

'Quite right,' said Stobbs, 'but the cousin or something had the urge to visit her brother in Canada and dumped poor old Messeter on me.'

'You don't mind, surely?'

'Well of course I mind. He takes up a lot of my time – and my nurses' time as well, but how could I turn him away?'

'How indeed? But if he's as ill as that, how on earth did he get here?'

'Will power mostly. He wasn't ready to die till he'd seen Felston again. Can you imagine anything more daft? Even death has to wait because he's homesick for Felston.'

'Death is so near?'

'Overdue,' said Stobbs. 'Would you like to see him?'

'I can do that?'

'If it's what he wants,' said Stobbs. 'One thing about being at death's door – you can do what the devil you like and damn the consequences.'

Not the ideal way to talk of the imminent demise of a priest, she thought, then remembered that Stobbs was an atheist. He got to his feet.

'Let's go and see him,' he said.

The canon was in a large and crumbling room that must once have been elegant: oak panelling, a stucco ceiling, sash windows that looked out on a garden: but the panelling was worm eaten, the stucco crumbling, and the garden had long since died of despair. Even so the room was spotless; scrubbed and dusted and with that whiff of carbolic that recalled a field hospital as nothing else could.

In the middle of it Messeter lay, in a small, neat bed – white sheets, red blankets – that might have been borrowed from the same field hospital. He looks skeletal, thought Jane, as if there were no flesh on him at all: just beautifully symmetrical bone and tight-stretched skin, and thick white hair that seemed to contain all his remaining strength, until he looked at her and she saw his eyes: the eyes too still had life left: eyes that were dark and piercing, and yet compassionate. The eyes of a kindly hawk.

'Jane,' the canon said, 'my dear.' He put down the book he had been reading. 'How very kind of you to call.'

Not so long ago, she thought, this man had walked from Felston to London in the front rank of the Felston Marchers, and then his heart had rebelled. Given in. But even then he didn't look as he did now. Now he looked as if a walk to the bedroom door would kill him.

She went up to him, took his hand and kissed his forehead. 'It's good to see you,' she said.

He sniffed. 'Delightful perfume,' he said.

'Chanel,' she said. 'Nothing but the best for you, my dear.'

He smiled. Before he took orders Messeter had been an army officer, and a great one for the ladies.

He turned to Stobbs. 'Be a good fellow,' he said. 'In the little fridge in your surgery you'll find a bottle of champagne –'

'That fridge is for medicines,' said Stobbs.

'Champagne *is* my medicine.' Messeter said. 'The only one I can swallow. Do fetch it, Stobbs. And three glasses.'

Stobbs went off obediently.

'My my,' said Jane. 'You bullying the good doctor. How brave of you.'

'Brave, fiddlesticks,' said Messeter. 'What on earth could I possibly be afraid of now?'

She was silent.

'Death? Is that what you're thinking?'

'No,' she said.

'Of course not,' said the canon. 'A blessed release. – Isn't that what they call it? Well so it is. But it's so much more.' He smiled. 'And soon I shall know what it is. So why shouldn't I bully Stobbs? I'd bully Mussolini if he had my champagne in his fridge.' He hesitated. 'Mussolini . . . Why does that ring a bell? Oh yes . . . Your friend Crawley.'

'He's not my friend,' said Jane.

'He stayed at Charles Lovell's house while you took money off him for the clinic.'

Really, thought Jane, the canon's intelligence service would have made the German General Staff envious.

'How on earth did you know?' she asked.

'One of the other guests was a relative of mine. I may be skint,' he added coarsely, 'but I'm still well connected. And the nobs love a good gossip. – You wanted rather more than a cheque for Felston, I gather.'

71

'I didn't get it.'

'Not yet. That doesn't mean you'll give up. Not you.' He brooded for a moment. 'Know why I mentioned Mussolini?'

'Crawley's a Fascist.'

'Quite right. I've been thinking a lot about Fascism – and praying, of course. I've come to the conclusion that it's the work of the devil.'

His voice was completely matter of fact, as a maths master would say that as far as circles were concerned $c = \pi D$.

'You must have no dealings with him whatsoever,' said Messeter. 'None.'

'Yessir,' said Jane, then added: 'Creepy Crawley.' Messeter yelped with laughter.

'Who called him that?' he said.

'A friend of mine.'

'Lionel Warley? No wonder he doesn't like him. Crawley and Warley. But it's a good name for him – and deserved. He's a very wicked man.'

'Bower knows him of course,' said Jane.

'Bound to.'

'And yet he didn't warn us – Charles and me.'

'Could have been misplaced altruism,' said the canon. 'Or it could have been –' She waited, and at last the canon said carefully, 'In these days maybe even Bower is not quite master of his own fate. How's Charles?'

'Very well. He sends his best wishes.'

'Are you still sinning?'

Every chance we get, she thought, but aloud she said, 'I'm afraid so.'

'I shall pray for the two of you,' he said, 'but not very much. It's a very unimportant sin.'

Stobbs came in with a bottle and three glasses. 'Vintage,' he said. 'You *do* do yourself well.'

'My cousin Frank,' said Messeter. 'He's got the best cellar in the North Riding. Let me feel that bottle, will you?' Stobbs held it out to him. 'Just right,' Messeter said. 'Let's have the cork out.'

Stobbs's hands were strong and deft, and the cork popped: the wine foamed into the glasses, and Stobbs handed one to Jane, then turned to Messeter, strangely hesitant for a man so purposeful. 'You shouldn't be having this,' he said.

'Nonsense,' Messeter said. 'How many more times do you suppose I'll blandish a pretty girl with champagne?' Then more gently, 'Please, Stobbs.'

Stobbs gave him the glass, then turned at once to Jane. 'I really am grateful for the cheque,' he said.

'There'll be others, I hope,' said Jane, 'but surely the canon told you that I was after rather more?'

'Well yes,' said Stobbs, 'he did. And God knows I'd have been grateful for that.'

'Atheists should not invoke the name of God,' said Messeter. 'It's not polite.'

Stobbs continued unheeding. 'But if you couldn't get the vaccine, at least I can say thank you for the bandages.' He drank off his champagne in two gulps.

'I have calls to make,' he said. 'I'll leave you to your blandishing.' He turned to Jane. 'Don't let him gossip for too long,' he said, 'though if you finish the bottle he won't need a sleeping draught. There's a nurse on duty, by the way. She's having a meal in the kitchen.'

He was gone then with his impatient, bustling walk: the walk that had no time to slow down for fools: not when people were dying.

Jane said, 'Why has he started being nice? It's not fair.'

'It's the times we live in,' said the canon. 'These terrible times. Even Stobbs has learned to be grateful for goodness when he sees it. Even to him it's no longer a right. In the past he automatically expected it in others because there's so much in himself. . . . Andy Patterson's to be married, I hear?'

'Yes.'

'He was handyman for the clinic once,' Messeter said. 'There seemed to be nothing he couldn't mend. I hope his bride to be is nice?'

'I like her very much,' said Jane.

'There's hope for her then. I'm told you'll be on your travels shortly – where will you go?'

'New York. California. Mexico.'

'God keep you safe,' he said. 'It doesn't seem as if I'll see you again. Please pour some more champagne.'

73

She did so, and said: 'I can stay on here for a while if you wish.'

'I?' Messeter smiled. 'My dear child, I shan't be staying on here much longer myself. No no. You be off on your travels. You always did enjoy them, didn't you?'

'Enormously.'

'I too. India before the war, with the regiment. Temples and the Red Fort, and the rice paddies that seemed to go on for ever. Shikar . . . Not just tigers, but duck by the dozen. Antelope. Even a couple of brown bears . . .' His voice faded and his eyes drooped. At last he said, 'Would you like my blessing?'

'Oh yes,' she said.

'Then kneel beside me.' Jane knelt, and he blessed her. 'Go and ask the nurse to come and tuck me in,' he said when he had done. 'Tell her she can have what's left of the champagne.'

'Can't I tuck you in?'

He looked at her, his eyes alight, and for a moment she was looking at Major Messeter, scourge of tigers, duck, antelope, bears, and of husbands too; for his blandishments, she was sure, had usually been effective.

'Certainly not,' he said. 'You're far too pretty. My chances of Paradise are no more than even money as it is. No no. Run along and fetch the nurse. And pray for me.'

'Of course,' she said, and bent to kiss him. That it was goodbye she had no doubt at all.

Bob looked around him. They'd hired the small room at the back of the hall, just right for the dozen men sitting there. Right for size, at any rate, but not for much else. Trestle table, collapsible chairs, uncovered floorboards – and for those who fancied a bit of art there was a photograph of Keir Hardie. Still at least there was beer, crates of the stuff, and lemonade for Andy to mix with his after the first pint, and whisky for the ones like him who didn't like beer, the ones for whom good Scotch was a treat. There was a gramophone, too, playing the kind of music someone had considered appropriate to a Stag Night. At the moment it was Harry Lauder singing 'Keep Right On To The End Of The Road'. Bob sipped his whisky and tried not to think of the Embassy, then sneaked a look at his watch. Ten o'clock. Far too early for the

Embassy: a good revue, then supper at the Caprice, and *then* the Embassy. Fat chance.

Joe Mason, the man beside him, said, 'Getting late, is it?'

'Nigh on ten,' said Bob.

'That's late when you knock on at eight o'clock.'

Bob turned to him. 'You're in work then?'

'One of the lucky ones, you mean?' The man's voice was mocking. 'I'm a fitter in the one yard still working. – One ship on the stocks. Two months left on her, if that – then –' He shrugged. 'We'll just have to see, won't we?'

Bob crossed his fingers and held them up.

'Aye,' said Mason. 'That's about all that's left. Are things as bad as this in London?'

'Nothing like,' said Bob.

'I don't mean for you,' Mason said. 'I mean everybody knows you've got on. – No offence, I hope?'

'Of course not,' said Bob. 'It's true.'

'I was thinking of chaps like me. The working men. How are they doing?'

'Fair to middling,' said Bob. 'There's black spots, but there's work as well. Chaps like you, chaps with a trade– they do all right. Why don't you try it?'

'Me? Leave Felston?' Mason sounded horrified.

'It's not that bad once you get used to it.'

'Me go to London?' Mason said. 'The wife would kill me.'

He may be joking, thought Bob, but I doubt it, and picked up his glass and walked over to where Andy was talking to Billy Caffrey, nice and handy to the whisky bottle. Not that Billy Caffrey was a shirker. Labour councillor, Billy was, noted orator, mayor of Felston when Andy led the march to London that Jane had organised. It was just that when there was a party Billy Caffrey liked his share of whatever was going. And why not? he admonished himself. You're that way yourself.

As he drew closer Andy drew an envelope and a pencil from his pocket, and began to do what looked like sums, and again Bob thought, Why not? There's far too many folks evicted in Felston as it is. All the same: *On his stag party night?* Bob remembered the last stag party he had been to. In Hollywood. The high point had been when a near-naked blonde had jumped out of a wedding cake. Just like the pictures, that had been. But then it turned out later the blonde had been on the pictures from time to time. Jumping out of wedding cakes was more of a hobby. Resting, she called it.

Andy said, 'Oh there you are, kidder. Having a good time?'

'Fantastic,' said Bob.

Billy Caffrey said, 'I'll leave you to it. There's a couple of chaps I want a word with.' He looked at the whisky bottle.

'After you,' said Bob.

Billy Caffrey topped up his glass, and Bob helped himself.

'You enjoying yourself?' he said.

'Me?' said Andy. 'I suppose so.'

'*Suppose?*'

'Well it's all a bit tribal, isn't it?' said Andy. 'Ritual drunkenness just because a chap's getting married.'

Not that Andy was drunk, or anywhere near it. A pint of beer to start with, then halves of shandy that got weaker and weaker as the night went on.

Bob let it lie. There just wasn't any point.

'When do they shout time in this place?' he asked. 'Not that I'm not enjoying meself. I'm just wondering if I should open another bottle of whisky.'

'Ten o'clock,' said Andy, and looked at the clock on the wall. 'Good Lord, it's nearly that now. Save your whisky for yourself.'

'We'll see it off tomorrow.'

Andy opened his mouth then shut it again. Bob would have bet money he'd been about to ask what whisky had to do with weddings.

'Thanks, Bob,' he said at last.

Bob said carefully, 'When we've finished here, is there anywhere else you'd like to go?' After all, he thought, Andy is my brother, and it's his last night of freedom, and even in Tyneside there were places: and one of them not bad, from what he'd been told.

'Go somewhere else at this time of night? It's near enough ten o'clock man,' said Andy. 'And anyway, we've got a busy day tomorrow.'

Bob looked at him. From what he could see his brother was perfectly serious.

. 10 .

Jane drove to Norah's house in the Bentley, decorated for the occasion with silk ribbons. At once a mob of children appeared, but she'd anticipated that. With her was her old friend ex-corporal Laidlaw, of the Royal Northumbrians, ex-Felston marcher come to that, acting as footman. He got out of the car, and the children took one look and scattered, as he walked round the Bentley to open the door for Jane. Wearing all his medals, Jane noticed, and quite right, too. Then as she rapped at the knocker: 'Good God what am I thinking of? Is a marriage a test of courage?' As the door swung open she decided that perhaps it was.

'I've brought all the stuff,' she said to Norah, but Norah was having second thoughts.

'I don't know,' she said. 'It doesn't seem right.'

'Doesn't it?' said Jane. 'I use it all the time.'

She sat Norah down and looked at her. Already the bride looked good. The dress really was right for her, mittens hid the roughness of her hands, and her hair had been brushed until it gleamed. Nothing remained but to gild the lily. She found a towel to protect the dress, then set to work: eyebrow tweezers – but easy with those: there would be some very sharp eyes in the chapel – face cream, rouge, lipstick. Easy with those, too. The eyes would stay sharp. But Norah must look her best. Patiently, carefully, she worked, then turned Norah at last to the room's one mirror.

'Well?' she asked. Norah stared long and hard.

'I don't think I'll ever wash my face again,' she said, and Jane chuckled.

The door knocker sounded and Jane went to answer its summons. Bet in all her finery, and young Jane in her finery too, but with eyes so intent on the Bentley that she had to be dragged inside.

77

Bet's eyes went at once to Jane's handiwork, but all she said was, 'My, you do look bonny.' Cautiously Norah kissed her.

'You too,' she said. 'I did tell you Jane's going to drive us to the chapel?'

'Oh *great*,' young Jane said.

'That'll do from you, my lady,' said her mother.

'There's a drop sherry,' Norah said. 'I know you don't usually – but seeing it's such a special day –' Bet bowed her head, as one submitting to penance.

Sweet as treacle, thought Jane, and about as thick; and then – For goodness sake stop that. This woman is facing the trickiest day of her life, and she's doing it with courage. She's even remembered to be hospitable. . . .

Jane lifted her glass. 'To your health and happiness, darling,' she said.

Mother and daughter looked astounded. They had never heard anyone addressed as darling before.

'Well I'm blessed,' said Andy.

Norah twisted a little to one side and looked up to him. 'Was it all right then?' she asked.

'*All right?* It was the most wonderful thing I – it was marvellous, and do you know I was dreading it? Shows you how daft I am.'

That makes two of us, she thought, because I was dreading it too, but she must never tell him.

'Do you know I'd never –'

'Sh!' She covered his mouth with her hand and the movement slipped the sheet from her shoulder. At once his hand moved out to touch it, to move down slowly, gently, to cup her breast.

'You don't mind?' he said.

Still cautious; still diffident. Still more wary of causing pain than creating pleasure.

'What's to mind?' she said. 'You're loving me.'

She pulled the sheet down further, and his arms came round her, but his hands still moved. This is mine, his hands seemed to say, and this, and this: like a miser fondling his treasure, and yet she loved it.

'I was that proud of you today,' he said.

'It was you made the speech.'

'Talk,' said Andy. 'The gift of the gab, that's all. I was proud of what you were.'

'And what was I?'

'Beautiful.'

Her hands explored in their turn.

'Hey,' he said, 'what on earth are you –'

'Sh!' she said again. 'You don't need the gift of the gab now. Not when you've got this.'

'The most extraordinary ceremony,' said Jane.

'In what way?' her mother asked.

They were taking tea together at her mother's house in Kensington: tea and cucumber sandwiches and a large plate of some special chocolate biscuits available only from Fortnum and Mason. Her mother adored those biscuits, Jane knew, but on her own resisted them. Jane's visit was an excuse to be exploited ruthlessly. A loving daughter, she took another, and her mother instantly followed suit.

'It was extraordinary in the way the service was conducted,' said Jane. 'There were hymns, of course, though not hymns one had ever heard of, but mostly it was the – minister I believe they called him. He harangued the congregation and the bride and groom. At one point he even seemed to be haranguing God. Extraordinary.'

'It was not Canon Messeter, I take it?'

'No no,' said Jane. 'This was a Congregational Chapel. Norah's mother insisted, it seems, though Norah herself looked a little bewildered from time to time.– And then her mother wasn't there after all.'

'Will they be happy?'

'That's rather up to him,' said Jane. 'If he remembers to kiss her from time to time and gives her a baby or two she'll be delirious.'

'Is he– in work? Isn't that the expression?'

'It is. He's with an engineering works on Felston Trading Estate. One of the few still going. He's also chairman of his union branch and a Labour Councillor.'

'Not much time for kissing – never mind making babies.'

'He'll just have to fit it in somehow,' said Jane.

Only a few years ago her mother would have left the room in outrage. Now she merely smiled, and then the smile faded.

'Tell me about the canon,' she said, and Jane told her.

When she had done her mother said, 'So he's chosen Felston to die in?'

'It's the place he loved best,' said Jane.

'It's the place that will have killed him,' said her mother.

'He doesn't mind dying, you know,' said Jane. 'Especially for Felston.'

'A remarkable man,' said her mother. 'I'm glad I met him, even although sanctity can be a little uncomfortable sometimes.'

'And how is my wicked stepfather?' said Jane.

'At Newmarket,' said her mother. 'Blithe and bonny so far as I know.'

'Still the scourge of the bookmakers?'

'We had five winners last week: one of them at a hundred to eight. If we do as well this week we shall approach the *Daily World* for an increase in salary.'

Major Routledge was the *Daily World*'s racing tipster, but the 'we' was quite justified. Her mother worked at the job every bit as hard as the major.

'I can just hear Jay Bower's yelps of agony,' said Jane.

'I think he will endure the pain,' her mother said, 'if only because we have received several flattering offers from other newspapers.'

'You're a wicked woman,' said Jane.

'At all events I am a successful one,' said her mother, 'and quite reasonably well off in these depressed times.– Though not of course as well off as my daughter.'

She smiled then: the merest echo of that malicious smile that had once had the power to wound even more than her malicious tongue. Smile and tongue alike were telling her: Don't go too far. Not even now. Or perhaps it was because she hadn't asked about Francis. Well Francis could jolly well wait a while. She looked at the chocolate biscuits, and the association of ideas was immediate.

'How is Miss Gwatkin?' she asked.

'Gwendolyn Gwatkin has now become obese,' said her mother, as if obesity was a religious cult of a rather dubious nature. 'From time to time she retires to a health clinic, the kind one visits in order

80

to lose weight, but she invariably contrives to escape within the first three days.'

'Still gossiping?'

'Almost as frequently as she eats. It's her passion, poor creature. She telephones me once a week. Mostly we talk about you.'

'Why me?' said Jane.

'You're the source of so much of her juiciest gossip, as you know,' said her mother, but with no intent to wound. 'Not that I ever tell her anything you would not want her to know.'

'Thank you, Mummy,' said Jane, then: 'And Francis . . . How is he?'

'Healthy, I gather,' said her mother.

'In Germany for the Long Vacation?'

'Why is it,' her mother asked, 'that homosexuals are so obsessed by Germany? They flock there like migratory birds.'

'Because it's permissive and it's cheap,' said Jane. 'He didn't get that fellowship at King's we all worked so hard for?'

'Miaow,' said her mother equably. 'No he did not. Though we were made to strive for it, were we not? Especially you.'

'Dances,' said Jane. 'Nightclubs. Hunt Balls. Le High Life. He was to have been known as the Dancing Don– and for a couple of weeks perhaps he was. He begged and yelled and pleaded for it – like a child that wants a new toy.'

'You're saying it was a matter of some importance?'

'Not to him,' said Jane. 'Obviously. But to me it was, and I told him so at the time. For reasons I'm still not sure of he wanted to be part of the Social Whirl, or whatever one calls it, and asked me to arrange it. And I did. But it wasn't easy. I had to draw on all the credit I had at the *Daily World*. Fortunately Jay Bower saw it as a good story– one that might run for a while– and decided to take a chance.'

Her mother nodded politely, but her scepticism was all too evident.

'Mummy,' said Jane. 'Listen to me. You know about racing. I know about gossip. – Far more than Gwendoline Gwatkin will ever learn. I'm a professional, like you. I've worked on "This Wicked World" gossip column for years– and I know this. Stories may just happen, but characters don't. They have to be created. And sometimes creating them costs money. It was just good luck that Jay liked the idea of the Dancing Don.'

'But how did it cost money?'

'Club membership fees,' said Jane. 'Subscriptions. Expenses. First Nights. One way and another Francis cost the *Daily World* rather a lot.'

'And you?'

'Towards the end, yes. When he accepted invitations then forgot to turn up, I could hardly expect the *Daily World* to pay for Francis's amnesia.'

'But whyever not?'

'Hard to say,' said Jane. 'The honour of the family, perhaps.'

'No perhaps about it,' her mother said. 'That's precisely what it was.'

'I don't grudge it,' said Jane. 'But I do grudge the fact that he never told the *Daily World* when he had no intention of attending a dance or whatever it was.'

'By then he didn't think it was important,' said their mother.

'It was important to him when he begged me to get up that May Ball party at his college and launch him into society.'

'Oh yes, then,' said her mother, 'but later on it wasn't what he needed, so it wasn't important at all. Ceased to exist, in fact.'

'My God,' said Jane, 'you really do make him seem to be four years old.'

'Outside of economics and homosexual adventures I think perhaps he is,' her mother said.

So that's why you love him so, thought Jane.

Aloud she said, 'Why did his social career cease to be important?'

'He wrote a book,' her mother said. 'Oh I know he's written four at least, but this one was popular. Not the Cambridge University Press sort of thing at all. Smart London publisher – smart London title, too. *Money for the Masses.* All inside a book jacket as yellow as custard. It sold thousands, so they tell me. Perhaps even tens of thousands. Like David in the Bible,' she ended vaguely.

'But what on earth has that got to do with his not going to dances?'

'Don't you see, child?' said her mother. 'In a small way now

Francis is famous. He can get his name in the papers without going to dances.'

So objective, thought Jane: so ironic. And yet she loves him as I have never loved anyone since John died.

Her mother said, 'At least this time he hasn't taken that dreadful Burrowes with him.'

'They've quarrelled?'

'Oh, I do hope so,' said her mother, 'but I suspect it's no more than a tiff.'

This part of Newcastle isn't like Felston at all, Andy thought. To begin with it was old, really old. A hundred years, some of it, and some of it more like a hundred and fifty. Moreover it was rich. The big town houses were all offices now: solicitors, accountants, architects; but the wealth remained: elegant stonework, mahogany doors, gleaming brass plates. The sort of house our Bob could end up in, he thought.

. 11 .

The Fitters' Union owned one of the houses. Now that was a pleasing thought, that men like him could own even a tiny piece of such a house, because a thousand other men like him did, too. Unity was strength, all right, though there hadn't been that much strength in the area meeting that night. Nothing to be strong about. No work for most of them: not even the chance of work. The Hardship Fund had been half of the agenda. Still, they'd been full of congratulations about his marriage and that was pleasing too, and now he was going home to Norah, and that was most pleasing of all.

Well, I'm blessed, he'd said that first time. The daftest thing he could have said, except that it was true. If an atheist could be blessed he was that atheist. . . . Was she pregnant? he wondered. She should be, the way they went at it– and she wanted a bairn. Needed one, you might say. He was her bairn for the moment, but that wouldn't last. Nor shouldn't.

She'd taught him so much, and not just about his body, though that had been good to learn. About caring, and being together, the feel of her next to him in what had once been the lonely hours, before he closed his eyes and sleep came back to him. One day he'd have to tell her about what they'd done to him in prison, but not yet, he told himself. Not while life's so good.

There was a sound of running feet behind him, and he turned and, atheist or not, he thought of the Book of Genesis. Every Eden had to have a serpent. He was looking at Burrowes. At Julian de Groot Burrowes.

'You stride out so manfully,' Burrowes said. 'I had to run to catch you. I hope I didn't frighten you with my twenty-yard dash?'

'No,' said Andy. 'I wasn't frightened.'

Nor had he been. There'd been a time when he'd have jumped

out of his skin, not because of physical fear – not of Burrowes – but because the sight of him meant that the Communist Party had sent him orders he almost certainly wouldn't want to obey: unpleasant things, perhaps even dangerous things: but those days were over.

'What's there to be frightened of?' he asked, and Burrowes scowled. He preferred Andy to be nervous.

'On your way to the station?' he asked.

'On my way home,' Andy said.

'Let's go to the station buffet first and I'll buy you a drink,' said Burrowes. 'They tell me you do celebrate nowadays from time to time – and you do have something to celebrate after all.'

For a clever man, thought Andy, he's a right bloody fool. The fact that the Party was still keeping an eye on him didn't surprise him – they kept an eye on everybody – but why did Burrowes have to tell him so?

'Thanks anyway,' he said, 'but if I don't get a move on I'll miss me train.'

'Impatient for the nuptial couch?' said Burrowes.

He'd been expecting it, of course. You could always rely on something nasty from Burrowes, but even so it was hard to remain impassive.

'Knocking-on time's half past seven,' he said. 'If I'm late they'll finish me.' He set off walking. Burrowes walked with him.

'I have to talk to you,' Burrowes said.

'And I have to get home,' said Andy. 'We can talk on the way to the station. You don't need me to help you drink whisky in the buffet.'

'How masterful you've become,' said Burrowes. 'Does the little woman enjoy it?'

Andy stopped dead. 'Is that what you've come to talk about?'

Burrowes looked at him. 'No,' he said at last. 'It's Jimmy Wagstaff I've come to talk about.' Felston's MP – and leading drunk.

'What's he done this time?'

'What he does every time,' said Burrowes. 'Finish the bottle. Fall down in the street. Get up and stagger on and hope the press don't get hold of it. Only this time –' he paused, knowing that the other man was avid to hear what he had to say.

'Well?'

'This time the press did get hold of it, and he's applied for the Chiltern Hundreds or whatever the jargon is.'

'You mean he's resigning?'

'Andy, Andy.' Burrowes's voice was reproachful. 'You don't use simple language like that in an effete and bourgeois establishment like the House of Commons.'

'*Is he?*'

'Yes,' said Burrowes. 'There may be a slight delay – some committee he's serving on – but this time he's being forced to resign.'

Andy turned from the spacious, elegant square into a back street that led down to the station: a nasty little street that would have fitted into Felston like a jig-saw piece into a puzzle.

'Why are you telling me this?' he asked.

'I don't know,' Burrowes said. 'Those aren't words I use often, as you know, but this time it's true. That was my message, and I've delivered it. Are you sure you won't have a drink?'

'I'm sure.'

'Not for old times' sake – I wouldn't presume on our acquaintance so far as that – but simply to toast the charming, I'm sure, and oh-so-recent Mrs Patterson. No?' Andy walked on.

'Do you know I really was surprised to learn that you'd done it,' he said. 'Until now I had always assumed you were a member of that merry band of deviants to which I have the honour to belong. Not in any practical way, of course – '

Andy had reached a railway bridge. Below him a locomotive and half a dozen wagons shunted backwards and forwards aimlessly, as if undecided which way to go. Burrowes watched Andy's stride lengthen. Not that way, he thought. You won't punish him that way. Not any more. And yet he must be punished, that was obvious. He'd been rude and not in the least subservient, and that cried out for punishment.

'Your bride is a widow, so they tell me,' he said. 'It must have made the wedding night quite exciting.'

He thought later that Andy didn't even break his stride. He was a pace ahead of him, then a second later he had swung round, grasped him by the lapels of his coat, and heaved him against the rail of the bridge, pressing hard. Burrowes could feel the pain of it, and as always, that brought its own excitement. Andy hoisted him a little higher.

'Look down,' he said.

Burrowes looked down. The railway line wasn't all that far away – twenty feet perhaps – but from where he was, it was far enough. Besides, immediately beneath him was an open truck, filled with what looked like lumps of rock.

Andy lifted him a little higher. He really was immensely strong, but then manual workers usually were – in their prime.

'I apologise,' said Burrowes. 'Now put me down.'

'I don't know,' said Andy.

'What do you mean you don't know?' Suddenly Burrowes's voice was shrill.

'It would be so easy,' Andy said. 'Lift you another foot, swing you sideways, and over you'd go.'

'Don't be a fool, man,' Burrowes said.

'But I am a fool,' said Andy. 'At least you always act as if I was.... So easy,' he said again, and then, 'Your breath stinks, you know that? And you a toff.'

'I eat garlic,' said Burrowes. 'It's good for me.' He turned his face away. 'Put me down. Please.'

'It's a bit late to start saying please,' said Andy, and lifted him further. Burrowes screamed as the engine's whistle hooted. He was now balanced against the handrail of the bridge – and the pain in his back was excruciating: the excitement long since gone.

The engine made up its mind at last, and backed away, tugging its waggon loads of stone. Below him the railway lines gleamed and waited.

'Andy *please*.' Burrowes yelled out the words.

The other man looked at him.

'Why you're frightened,' he said. 'What would the Party say? Tell you what. Let's see if your luck's in tonight.'

He opened his hands, and Burrowes screamed again, but his luck was in. He fell forward on to the bridge, and crouched there, sobbing.

'You're thinking you'll report me, I daresay?' Burrowes gave no answer. 'But just ask yourself this,' Andy continued. 'If you report me, who would believe you? My brother might have done it – in fact he would have done, and let you drop – but me? Andy Patterson who was that grateful for what he was taught at Cambridge? Andy Patterson that always does what he's told? Andy Patterson the pacifist?' He looked down at Burrowes's tear-streaked face.

'Ah stop bubbling,' he said. 'You make me ashamed to be a man.'

Then he was off, walking more briskly than ever. If he didn't hurry he would miss his train. Once on it he went over the whole thing again and discovered he wasn't bothered in the least, and the thought intrigued him. He'd gone to prison because he didn't want to kill people or even hurt them, and he'd almost done both. Not only that but he'd ignored whatever advantage he could expect from Jimmy Wagstaff's retirement. Not that Burrowes could influence that, he decided. Like he'd said himself, he was only the messenger. . . .

'Good meeting, pet?' Norah said.

'Canny.'

He watched as she fried bread and bacon to make him a sandwich. He was eating like a horse these days, and there was nowt surprising in that, he thought. She turned to look at him, knowing him so well that even his tone of voice was a give-away.

'Something wrong?' she asked.

'Not wrong, no,' he said. 'It was just – the Hardship Fund. The list was longer than ever. It's never easy to say no to folks in need, Norah. You know that.'

'Oh, I do,' she said, and then: 'There wasn't anything else?'

'Nothing that comes to mind,' said Andy.

Carlo's was in Soho: a small and cheerful Italian restaurant where the food was cheap and very good. Charles liked it because no one they knew went there – or even knew that it existed. Jane liked it because of the food. Over the spaghetti carbonara she had been describing the wedding yet again.

'Bob handled it all right?' said Charles.

Really, she thought, Bob might have been a promising young executive negotiating a merger, but then in a sense that was precisely what he had been.

'Read out the telegrams and so on?' Charles said.

'Telegrams? In Felston?'

'Oh dear,' said Charles, and poured more Bardolino. 'How foolish of me. And Messeter was too ill to be there, you say?'

'He's dying.'

The waiter brought their saltimbocca, and Charles waited. When the waiter had gone he said, 'I find that incredible.'

'That the canon's dying?'

'Mm … In the war he was my company commander. Then they gave him the battalion – after his predecessor had done his best to destroy it. A more alive man you never met. You know that in those days he was quite a lad for the ladies?'

'And now he's quite a lad for God,' said Jane. 'In fact my mother considers him to be a saint.' She ate a piece of veal. 'I shall miss him terribly.'

'I too,' said Charles. 'He had this trick – not just of being so alive himself, but of making you feel the same.'

'He's still got that,' said Jane. 'He'll have it till Dr Stobbs closes his eyes.' She drank some wine. 'I made a new friend when I was there.'

'Nice one?'

'I think so,' said Jane. 'I think you'd like her, too.'

'She's pretty, then?'

'Enchanting. Her name's Jane. She's my god-daughter.'

'But she's only seven.'

'Six actually,' said Jane, 'but we all have to start somewhere and she's very sound on Bentleys.'

'What are you up to?' said Lovell.

'I don't know, really.' For once Jane seemed almost furtive. 'I just thought I'd like to do something for her.'

'What could you possibly do for the daughter of an unemployed man in Felston?'

'He's not unemployed,' she said. 'He's a tram driver.'

'Even so,' said Lovell, 'I doubt if his pay would keep you in martinis.'

'I doubt it too,' said Jane, 'and I don't drink all that many.'

'I never said you did,' said Lovell, 'so stop trying to change the subject. Are you going to give the family some money? Is that it?'

'It's not the family,' she said. 'It's young Jane.'

She could visualise her now: the earnest miniature replica of Grandma.

'Bob thinks that if Frank – that's Jane's father – got his hands on money in any quantity he'd spend it. Not that he's a thief or anything. He just wouldn't be able to help himself.'

'Most thieves can't. Or so they say.'

'Well anyway Bob and I set up a trust fund for our god-child, and Frank and Bet can't touch it.'

'Didn't you say she has a brother?'

'Young Frank. He'll be about two, I suppose. Rather a disagreeable child.'

'Have you set up a trust fund for him, too?'

'Of course I haven't,' said Jane, then added quickly: 'He isn't my god-child.'

'So one day he'll still be poor when his sister becomes rich – by their standards at any rate.'

'You reduce every problem I've ever brought you to money,' she said, her irritation beginning to show.

'I'm a banker,' said Lovell, 'and anyway what else is a trust fund but money?'

Jane said, 'I could do other things besides give her money.'

'What things?'

'Take her about in London. Holidays too. The right clothes. The right education.'

'All of which cost money,' Lovell said, then added: 'You're talking about adoption.'

'Yes,' said Jane. 'I suppose I am.'

'You're also talking about taking somebody else's child from its natural parents.'

'I know, Charles,' she said, 'but oh! I wish you could see her.'

He opened his mouth then shut it again, dabbing at his lips with his napkin.

Covering up, she thought, and knew precisely what he had so very nearly said: I don't want you to adopt a child. I want you to bear my child. But he'd swallowed the words, and for that at least she was grateful.

'Have you discussed this with your mother?' he asked.

'No.'

'May one ask why?'

'Funked it,' she said.

'Then you must have some idea of what her reaction would be.'

'Damn you, Charles,' she said. 'Must you always be so bloody clever?' Suddenly her hand went to her mouth. 'Oh my God,' she said, 'I'm sorry.'

'It's all right.'

'No it's not,' she said. 'I had no right to take my frustrations out on you like that. No right at all.'

'I'm not upset,' he said. 'Honestly I'm not. I just happened to be nearest.'

Her hand reached out to take his. 'And dearest,' she said. 'I mean that, Charles. Honestly.'

For once Charles Lovell allowed her to hold hands without looking uncomfortable. 'That's all right then,' he said.

They walked through Soho towards Shaftesbury Avenue: tarts and flower girls, and theatres disgorging women in furs, men in tail coats.

'I wish I could come back with you tonight,' said Jane.

'I too. But Dodo would *not* approve.'

'Dodo?'

'My cousin. Dorothy Chandler-Spicer. In the family she's always been known as Dodo.'

'Oh the poor thing,' said Jane. 'That too,' then added: 'I'm hardly the model of tact tonight, am I? – But why is she staying with you, Charles?'

'She's brought a friend with her,' said Lovell. 'Most improper to stay with me on her own.'

'You should have given them dinner.'

'I offered it because I had to. Of course. But they wished to visit the opera and there I drew the line. When it comes to musical theatre I can just about cope with *The Student Prince*.'

'But *why* is she visiting you?'

'Her accounts are in a muddle as usual.'

'Couldn't one of your clerks unmuddle them for her?'

'She isn't quite – how did she put it – she isn't quite comfortable discussing her financial affairs with anyone except myself.'

Ten quid gone astray, thought Jane. Twenty at most. Really Charles was a much nicer person than he allowed himself to appear. That was the second time he'd proved it that night.

From Shaftesbury Avenue there came the sound of voices: a kind of rhythmic chanting that resembled that which the soldiers on the march had used sometimes.

> Left! Left!
> I had a good job and I left!

But if the rhythm was the same, the words were ominously different:

> Yids! Yids!
> We got to get rid of the Yids!

A group of men in black shirts, black trousers, black boots, marching in columns of twos and preceded by a Union Jack. In the front rank was Crawley, stern, square shouldered: the only one silent, and somehow therefore even more sinister.

'Good God,' said Jane. 'It's Creepy Crawley.'

Perhaps he heard her – he was certainly close enough – but if he did he gave no sign.

> Yids! Yids!
> We got to get rid of the Yids!

The column moved on and Lovell said, 'Let's get away from the theatre crowd and find a cab.' From further up the road there came the sound of breaking glass.

'Probably Goldman's,' said Lovell. 'That cigar shop on the corner of Denman Street.'

Jane moved towards the sound, but Lovell caught her arm. 'No, Jane,' he said. 'Let somebody else drive the ambulance this time. I'm taking you home.'

. 12 .

Andy thought: No need to be proud of yourself. You're twice as strong as he is, and you were sober after all. I doubt if he's been properly sober these last ten years. And you had anger on your side an' all. Now that was an interesting discovery. Even anger could work for you if you learned how to control it. Just as well he had learned: otherwise he could have killed the sod.

He shouldn't have gone for Norah like that, though. He has no idea how I feel about her, but even so he had no business getting at her like that. . . . Unless he thinks I married her to show I'm normal: to get ahead in politics, he thought. To be Felston's next MP. And maybe I did. All the way through the engagement, and the ceremony, and the reception. But not after the wedding night. Then she showed me I was wrong. Logical, but wrong. I married her because I love her, and I've never stopped being happy ever since. Of course I'd still like to be Felston's MP if it's offered, and I'd do a better than average job what's more. But chance is a fine thing, and if it's up to Burrowes I'll never be Felston's MP. On the other hand Norah will lie beside me every night in life, and that's not a bad swap. . . . His wife sighed in her sleep, and turned to him, and his arm went round her. She said something then, something incoherent, and Andy smiled, and his eyes closed as knocking-on time drew nearer.

There was really no reason to go dancing apart from the fact that Lionel wanted to go dancing, and that Charles, too, seemed to think it was a good idea.

'One lady with two gentlemen?' she'd asked him.

'Not at all. I shall bring Dodo.'

'And what about her friend?'

'She also has a friend,' Charles had told her. 'They are going to the ballet together at Sadler's Wells. When it comes to dancing it seems that she would rather watch.'

So Truett had laid out a Schiaparelli dress described for some reason as Napoleonic, and indeed, she thought, Josephine would have filled it admirably. White silk, high waisted, with a wide and flowing skirt. Bare arms, of course, but decorous enough in front. The back however was as bare as a back could be, to the point where it could only just be called a back. Still, Charles deserved a treat, and Lionel approved of her wearing dresses like that. The only man she knew who could view her body as if it were a piece of sculpture rather than something to be coveted, lusted for, possessed. Now now, she admonished herself. What about all the men who seemed unaware that you had a body at all?

Even so it was nice to see that the Schiaparelli still fitted after Mummy's chocolate biscuits, and that all in all it fitted a body that could still carry a Schiaparelli. It wouldn't be for all that much longer. She took out Charles's emeralds from her jewel box: the ones by Fabergé. Since the dress still fitted she deserved a treat too.

Lionel arrived prompt to the minute, and was loud in his praise.

'Far too good for a First Consul, my dear,' he said. 'Even Wellington would have to be on his best behaviour to deserve that.'

He mixed martinis and gave her one.

'But who,' he asked, 'is Mrs Chandler-Spicer? Can she dance?'

'She's Charles's cousin,' said Jane. 'A widow. From what Charles tells me she can go where she's pushed in time to the music.'

'But what a delightful prospect,' said Lionel, 'though she's Charles's cousin after all.'

'Lionel,' said Jane, 'you will do your duty by Dodo. Now promise me.'

'Oh very well,' said Lionel. 'Wax in your hands as usual.' And then he choked. 'Did you say Dodo?'

'Short for Dorothy it seems,' said Jane.

'Oh what bliss,' said Lionel, and swigged down his martini as if it were rum before a bayonet charge. 'Lead me to her.'

All in all it was a good thing to have Dodo there, thought Jane. Charles's cousin had taken one look at Lionel and decided that they must be lovers. So handsome, so elegant, so witty. Once she had danced with him she was convinced of it. That he was queer as well never crossed her mind. Lionel set himself to please, and the widow basked in a sophistication she only half comprehended. Looking charming, too, thought Jane, in a Victor Stiebel gown that was not in the least over-awed by the Savoy. How sweet Charles was. Not only kind, but thoughtful, too.

'Do you come to London often, Mrs Chandler-Spicer?' Lionel asked.

'Not so very often,' said Mrs Chandler-Spicer. 'Except for the day, you know. Matinées and things.' She looked at Lovell. 'This time it was business.'

'Pleasure too, I hope,' said Charles.

'Oh yes,' said his cousin.

'You should come up more often, Mrs Chandler-Spicer,' said Lionel. 'We tired old habitués need new blood, we really do.'

Mrs Chandler-Spicer blushed a not unpleasing pink.

'Oh please call me Dodo,' she said. 'All my friends do, don't they Charles?'

The band played 'I Got Rhythm'. It was Jane's turn for Lionel.

'Habitués indeed,' said Jane. 'More like vampires.'

'At least she said I could call her Dodo,' Lionel said smugly.

'And didn't you work hard for it?' said Jane. Lionel was unperturbed. He knew he was dancing as well as ever.

They went back to champagne. Dodo, Jane noticed, hardly touched hers. Alcohol it seemed was only for the defence of territory.

Mrs Chandler-Spicer was dancing with Lionel when Lovell, sitting out with Jane, glanced at the door.

'Oh Lord,' he said.

Jane followed his gaze. A group of people, preceded by the head waiter, was making its way towards them. Leading were Brenda Coupland and her fat fiancé, Meldrum, followed by Catherine and Piers, then Crawley with a young woman she didn't know, a rather pretty young woman. Jane glanced at Lionel, who nodded to show he'd seen them too, and continued to steer Dodo round the room as if she were a cabinet full of valuable china.

The head waiter brought the group to the table next to theirs, and there was a great deal of fuss about seating and the ordering

95

of champagne. Crawley, she noted, was particularly exigent, though it was obviously Meldrum's party.

Piers spotted them first. He smiled at Jane, who waved to him, then Catherine waved too, and Brenda Coupland. Meldrum still thumbed through the wine list, Crawley snapped at him as if telling him to get a move on, and the pretty stranger looked bored. And yet not quite a stranger, she thought. Somewhere or other they'd met.

'They'll come over here. I know they will,' said Charles.

'Not all at once,' said Jane. 'They can't. There isn't room. And I doubt if Creepers will come at all – unless it's to be rude, of course.'

'For God's sake keep your voice down,' Lovell said, and as he spoke Catherine stood up and came over to them.

'Darling, what bliss to see you,' she said. 'What a divine gown. Where did you get it?'

'Paris,' said Jane. 'You remember Charles Lovell of course?'

'Of course. How could I forget?'

She looked at him, wide eyed, the power turned on full, thought Jane. Who on earth was she trying to make jealous? Not her own brother, or Meldrum either, even if he weren't enmeshed in dear Brenda's toils. That left only Crawley. Hard to believe that any woman, let alone a young and attractive one, could fall for such a monster, she thought, but perhaps she was wrong. He was an elegant monster after all, and a rich one, and these days Catherine was rather obsessed by wealth.

'What fun that house-party of yours was,' Catherine said to Lovell. 'You really were an absolutely super host.'

The fact that Charles's jaw didn't drop indicated enormous self-control, thought Jane, then watched it tested again as Catherine sat down beside him.

'Such a pity that scheme of yours never came to anything,' she continued. 'I was so upset for those poor people in that terrible town that I cried. Honestly.'

'I expect Jay was upset, too,' said Jane.

'I expect he was,' Catherine said. 'Charles's idea would have sold masses of papers.'

There really was nothing to be said to that, particularly as Crawley chose that moment to come up to Catherine to demand the dance which she had promised him. He gave no sign that he

96

was aware of Jane's or Lovell's presence, and Catherine got up at once to go to the dance floor, but not without a backward glance at Lovell.

'Well really,' said Jane, but already Brenda Coupland was beckoning to them. She and Meldrum sat alone at her table.

What followed was like a weird parlour game, the rules of which were never quite explained: a sort of musical chairs with a dash of hopscotch. From time to time Jane danced, but when she sat out she was never quite sure who would sit with her, or even at which table.

But first it was Brenda Coupland.

'Darling, what a delicious surprise,' she said.

'Scrumptious,' said Jane. 'Do you know Charles Lovell?'

'We've met,' said Brenda Coupland. 'Here and there. How are you, Charles?'

'Very well, thank you.'

Meldrum emerged from some internal reverie.

'Good Lord,' he said. 'Charles Lovell. What brought you here?'

'Dancing,' said Lovell. 'What else?'

Meldrum turned to Jane. 'What I meant was Lovell's a banker. He looks after my money.'

'He does a very good job of it,' Brenda Coupland said.

Jane looked at the enormous solitaire diamond on her engagement ring finger and agreed with her.

'The thing is you see that we've been and gone and done it,' Meldrum said.

'Done what?' Lovell asked.

'Set the date for our wedding,' said Meldrum, and added helpfully: 'Hence our little party.'

Brenda's lover, thought Jane, Brenda's lover's sister, London's richest Fascist and a pretty unknown much younger than Brenda. For an engagement party the choice of guests might be considered eccentric.

'Not our official party, of course,' Brenda Coupland said hurriedly. 'You'll both receive invitations to that when the time comes. Of course. This is just a little spur of the moment thing, but rather fun, don't you think?'

Piers came back with the pretty stranger, and the introductions began.

'Mrs Hendry, Sybil,' said Piers, and began to name the others.

Of course. One saw her at parties. Bob's merry widow, thought Jane, but not because of champagne. Is she merry because she's attracted such a handsome young man, or because Brenda is trying so hard not to show that she resents the fact?

'I believe we have a friend in common,' Sybil Hendry said. 'Bob Patterson.'

'Good Lord,' said Piers. 'Do you know him too?'

Sybil Hendry had obviously expected annoyance or even sulks at the mention of so formidable a rival, and found Piers's enthusiasm disconcerting, although, Jane noted, Brenda rather enjoyed it.

'I don't know why it is,' said Piers, 'but every time I meet Bob we seem to get into a fight with some Leftwinger or other.'

'You do indeed,' said Brenda Coupland. 'Such fun.'

'You mean a real fight? Fists and things?' Sybil Hendry asked.

'Oh rather,' said Piers. 'Last time was at Cambridge.' He looked up and saw Crawley leading his sister back to their table.

'But don't let's go into that now,' he said.

'But I want to know,' said Sybil Hendry.

'And so you shall,' said Piers. 'Have dinner with me next week and I'll tell all.'

Jane looked at Charles, who was nodding approval. No point in setting Crawley off about Leftwingers, and Piers had realised it at once. Charles looked positively smug, but then he too had been in the Rifle Brigade.

'We'd better get back to our seats,' he said, and once again Catherine smiled, once again Crawley appeared to find them both invisible.

'A little abrupt, weren't you?' said Jane.

'We don't want Crawley sharing a table with Lionel,' said Lovell.

'You'd hardly call the poor darling a man of the Left.'

'He's on Crawley's list,' Lovell said.

'Queers too, you mean?'

'And blacks and browns, *and* gypsies,' said Lovell. 'Though I can't see that gypsies can be much of a threat to the British Empire.'

Dodo and Lionel came back to them.

'My dear,' Dodo said, 'what a wonderful dancer your friend is.'

'Isn't he, though?' said Jane. 'Usually we poor girls have to form a queue.'

Brenda Coupland was already sending out signals, but it was Jane that Lionel led out to the floor. Another foxtrot: 'Sweet Lorraine', played at a speed which allowed Lionel scope for that unfussed elegance of footwork that made dancing with him such a pleasure.

'You're very pensive for the Savoy,' he said. 'It can't have been the champagne.'

'Creepy Crawley,' she said.

'You were about to warn me?'

'You mean you already knew?'

'Of course,' he said, and added bitterly: 'One thing we Nancy-boys pride ourselves on is our sense of self-preservation.'

'Don't talk about yourself like that,' she said.

'I don't,' said Lionel. 'You know I don't. It's how Crawley talks about me.' He embarked on a more than usually tricky reverse spin, then added: 'I'm not afraid of him, you know.'

'Of course you're not,' said Jane. 'There isn't much you are afraid of.'

'Apart from losing my looks, such as they are,' Lionel said. 'Charles told you about the big match, I suppose?'

'Big match?'

'Fascists versus Fairies.'

'He seems to know an awful lot about it,' said Jane.

'I wish more people did,' said Lionel, and risked a glance at Meldrum's table. Crawley appeared to be delivering a monologue: everyone else looked bored.

'Would you like to leave early?' Jane asked.

'Run away, you mean,' said Lionel in reproof. 'No I wouldn't. The Royal Flying Corps never funked a dog-fight: not even us bitches.'

After that dance Jane went to the powder room. A long dance with Lionel was usually followed by running repairs. Ladies might glow rather than perspire, she thought, but I certainly need face powder. Brenda Coupland came in, sat before the next mirror and glanced warily about her. No one else was there.

'I expect you're wondering why I made up such an extraordinary party,' she said.

'Well yes,' said Jane.

'The answer is I didn't,' the other woman said. 'Hugo did.'

'Your fiancé?'

'Yes,' Brenda Coupland said. 'My fiancé. I do wish he wasn't, sometimes.'

'He doesn't have to be, surely?'

'Only a woman as rich as you could make a remark like that,' Brenda Coupland said. 'But please don't let's quarrel.'

'Very well.'

'I'm broke,' said Brenda Coupland. 'HRH used to like to see me in a different gown each night. Different jewels, too. It never seemed to occur to him somebody had to pay for them.'

In her heyday Brenda Coupland always referred to the Prince of Wales as The Little Man, Jane remembered. Now he was dismissed as HRH – but then poor Brenda had been dismissed, too.

'Hugo pays for everything,' said Brenda Coupland. 'I know it sounds mad – but that's what he likes best. Paying for me.'

'But what's wrong with that?'

'Don't you see – it means he's buying me. He knows Piers and I are lovers and he doesn't bloody care – not so long as he owns me.'

'And that's why he invited him tonight?' Brenda Coupland nodded. 'And the delectable Mrs Hendry? And Crawley?'

'We just happened to meet them in a restaurant. I think Piers is keen on her. So Hugo invited her.'

'Because Piers is keen on her?' If I sound incredulous, thought Jane, who can wonder?

'Because she was there,' said Brenda Coupland, 'and because he wanted to come here and show me off, and anyone half way presentable will do for the chorus.' She looked into the mirror as if the face that looked back at her was vaguely familiar.

'But he's really not all that bad,' she said, swept compact and lipstick into her handbag, and left.

Jane looked into the mirror at a face which, in these days, was becoming all too familiar, decided that no more could be done in the lily-gilding line, and lit a cigarette instead. As she did so Sybil Hendry came in and sat by the mirror that had reflected Brenda Coupland. Jane fitted her cigarette into the Cartier holder and waited.

'Bob really does seem awfully fond of you,' Sybil Hendry said at last.

'How sweet of him.'

'You don't feel the same?'

'Well of course I do,' said Jane. 'I'm fond of his brother Andy, too.' And Grandma, she could have added, and her son Stan, the father of John, Andy, Bob; but she didn't say it aloud, because then she would have to say that she was fond of Bet, too, and that would be a lie.

'Oh yes of course,' said Mrs Hendry. 'You were engaged to the other brother, weren't you? The one who was killed. – All those years ago.'

'John,' said Jane. 'Yes. He was killed at Waterloo. Or was it Agincourt? One forgets, you know, after all these years.'

Sybil Hendry looked at her, then threw back her head and laughed: a loud and happy guffaw.

'I must say you look well on it,' she said, 'and I take the point you're making.'

'Jolly good,' said Jane, and waited.

'My point is that I'm rather keen on Bob,' Sybil Hendry said, 'and it always helps to know what the competition is.'

'Well it isn't me.'

'So I gather. You're rather marvellous – but I expect you know that?' Again Jane waited. 'So elegant,' Sybil Hendry said. 'From top to toe. And that jade cigarette holder which has to be Cartier – just the teeniest bit old fashioned, but absolutely you.

'The thing is,' Sybil Hendry continued, 'is that Piers Hilyard appears to be quite potty about you, too. It's going to be a little bit tricky if I have to follow in the footsteps of all your admirers.'

'I'm their big sister,' said Jane. 'In Bob's case it was almost inevitable. I mean I *would* have been his big sister if John had lived. And in Piers's case I was sort of elected. Rather a privilege, really. Two remarkable young men.'

'They are, aren't they?' said Sybil Hendry. 'They're lucky, too.' Again Jane waited. 'Having you for a big sister,' said Sybil Hendry.

In the ballroom Charles was at last dancing with Dodo, Lionel with Brenda Coupland, and Piers was gossiping with friends at a table near the door. Meldrum waved to her and held up a glass of champagne. Reluctantly she went up to him, and Crawley at once swivelled in his chair so that his back was to her, and began talking in a loud voice about something called 'The Protocols of the Elders of Zion'. Jane sat, and Meldrum uttered a sound that sounded like 'Mm'.

'I beg your pardon?' said Jane.

'Mumm,' Meldrum said. 'The champagne, you know. Mumm. I hope it's all right?'

'Scrumptious,' said Jane.

'So glad,' Meldrum said. 'I'm rather fond of it myself.' He drank some, and then, 'I say? That chap who's dancing with Brenda. My fiancée.' Quite without warning he giggled. 'Quite extraordinary thing for *me* to say – my fiancée. Makes one seem really rather important, wouldn't you agree?'

'She's a really lovely girl,' said Jane.

'Indeed she is,' said Meldrum, 'but the point is she's *my* lovely girl.' He blushed. 'Rather lost the thread,' he said. 'Where were we?'

'The chap she's dancing with,' said Jane.

'Quite right,' said Meldrum. 'Well I don't know whether you know it or not, but he's the L.J.R. Warley who played in the Eton and Harrow match of 1910 – or maybe 1911.' Then to avoid any misconceptions, 'For Eton, of course.'

'Of course,' said Jane. Meldrum seemed to have drunk rather a lot of champagne, but then he must be used to it, waiting for Brenda to finish dancing with her latest man, and after all that practice at least he carried it well.

'L.J.R. Warley,' Meldrum said again. 'Made a half century.'

'Fifty three not out,' said Jane. 'He did rather well in the war, too. He was in the Royal Flying Corps.'

Meldrum thought about this, and said at last, 'You know him, do you?'

'Well of course I do,' said Jane. 'He was the one who introduced us – at an Eton and Harrow match, incidentally.'

'By jove yes,' said Meldrum. 'I remember. Brenda was with us. Eton lost.' He drank more champagne, then added: 'Not that I ever played for Eton, though I wish I had.'

'Perhaps it's because you're not a pansy,' said Crawley.

'Of course I'm not,' said Meldrum. 'I'm engaged to Brenda Coupland.'

'What Mr Crawley means,' said Jane helpfully, 'is that you'd have had more chance of playing for Eton if you were.' She looked at Crawley, who still seemed to find her invisible.

'Oh please,' Catherine said. 'Don't let's –'

But Meldrum, who had been pondering the implications of what Jane had said, for once forgot his manners and interrupted her.

'Do you mean to say that L.J.R. Warley's a pansy?'

'Of course he is,' Crawley said.

'Well I'm blessed,' said Meldrum, but he said it as one more astonished than horrified. Then he added as if by way of explanation, 'Fifty three not out.'

'The Royal Flying Corps doesn't seem to count,' said Jane.

'He's a jolly good dancer,' Meldrum said.

'Good God man, is that all you have to say?' said Crawley.

He's beginning to yelp again, thought Jane. It always seems to happen when he's thwarted.

'Well what do you expect me to say?' said Meldrum reasonably. 'Either he is or he isn't, and if he is he's far too old to change his habits now. Same as me. Not that I'm a pansy you understand. Can't be, can I? I'm engaged to Brenda.' He turned to Jane, as one he could rely on. 'What point am I making?' he asked.

He's far more drunk than he looks, bless him, thought Jane. Aloud she said, 'Set in your ways.' Brenda and Lionel were coming back to the table.

'Well so I am,' said Meldrum, 'and L.J.R. Warley's set in his.' He turned to Jane again. 'What is it the French say?'

Jane fought for control. If she laughed now, Crawley would explode. 'Chaqu'un à son goût,' she said.

'Exactly,' said Meldrum, as one who had scored a devastating point in debate.

'I thought my ears were burning,' said Lionel. 'You've been talking about me, you naughty things.'

'We were saying that you're a pansy,' said Crawley. 'Or rather I was.'

'But I thought everybody knew that,' said Lionel. 'I mean it's not as if I went to any trouble to hide it. Wouldn't you agree?' He turned to Brenda Coupland.

'Of course,' she said.

'Bless you, darling,' said Lionel.

He spoke with an airy archness that was deliberately effeminate, and yet Jane knew that he was furious, perhaps dangerously so. He'd explained it to her once. 'For a public school man I know some really awful dirty tricks,' he'd told her. 'You're bound to when you spend as much time with the Merchant Navy as I do.'

Now he turned back to Crawley. 'Let me come and sit by you and explain myself,' he said.

'Certainly not,' said Crawley.

'Oh don't be mean,' said Lionel. 'We belong together.'

'What on earth do you mean?' Crawley said.

'Warley and Crawley,' said Lionel. 'We sound like a turn on the music hall. Do let me sit by you.'

Crawley was so enraged he couldn't even yelp.

'I tell you what,' said Lionel. 'Why don't you dance with me instead? You can lead if you like.'

Crawley turned to Catherine. 'I promised your husband I'd take care of you this evening,' he said, 'which means I can't leave you any longer with this filth.' He stood up, and very reluctantly Catherine did so too.

'I'm most awfully sorry,' she said to Brenda Coupland.

'We have to go,' said Crawley, and led her away.

Lionel called after him, 'What an old spoilsport you are, ducky. Just when we were beginning to enjoy ourselves.'

Crawley kept going, but Catherine swerved away to speak to her twin, and Crawley began to yelp again. Behind Jane there was the sound of applause, and she turned. Sybil Hendry was clapping her hands, and smiling at Lionel.

'My God you were marvellous,' she said.

'You saw it, then?' Lionel said, and reached out for champagne, his hand trembling.

'Certainly I saw it,' said Sybil Hendry. 'What a man.'

'*Man?*'

It was hard to believe the bitterness that Lionel put into that one syllable, but Sybil Hendry made the only possible response: she ignored it. 'May I ask you a favour?' she said.

'Of course.'

'May I have this dance?'

Lionel put down his glass: his hand was steady again. 'My pleasure,' he said, and led her to the floor. The band were playing 'Sweet And Lovely'.

'Our tune,' Sybil Hendry said.

'Both our tunes,' said Lionel.

Piers Hilyard came back to the table, to watch the girl he loved – or was it just very polite lust? – giggling helplessly in Lionel's arms, and yet dancing far better than she ever danced with him.

'Have I missed anything?' he asked.

'Come and dance and I'll tell you,' said Brenda Coupland.

. 13 .

'A remarkable woman,' said Lovell.

'Remarkable indeed,' said Jane. 'Are you smitten, Charles?'

'No no,' said Lovell. 'One remarkable woman is quite enough.'

She settled her head on his shoulder.

'Thank you, kind sir,' she said, and then: 'I rather think Piers is. Smitten, I mean. The trouble is that if she's smitten at all it's with Bob.'

'Well well,' said Lovell.

'If you mean by that that she could give Bob a game you could be right. . . . Lionel likes her too. – '

'Of course he does, from what you've told me.'

' – And yet at the same time he's – how shall I put it? Wary. It's his opinion that if crossed she could be very volatile.'

'Mine too,' said Lovell, and began to stroke her. Jane thought: If he keeps this up I shall be purring soon – and why not.

'Crawley's volatile too,' said Lovell, 'and he knows some very volatile people. I had a word with Bower about it. Funny.'

'Funny?'

'Peculiar,' said Lovell. 'Not ha-ha. Definitely not ha-ha. What I meant was he hates to tell me things even if I do own a chunk of his paper. So do you, for that matter.'

'What things?'

'About Crawley. . . . It seems he likes to see people being hurt.'

'Humiliated, you mean?'

'I mean beaten,' said Lovell.

'Good God,' said Jane, and moved to get out of bed. 'I must phone Lionel at once.'

Lovell pushed her back. 'I already have,' he said. 'I warned him to stay away from dark alleys.'

'And?'

'He told me his favourite tramp steamer is due in any day. Once the crew have paid off, he's going to take them down every dark alley he can find.'

'Crawley had better not be at the end of one,' she said. 'Why have you stopped?'

'Sorry,' Lovell said. 'Your fault really. Wanting to use the phone.' The stroking resumed. 'I say?'

'Mm?'

'Why is your chum Catherine collecting millionaires? I mean she's got one already.'

'Bower? Is he still a millionaire?'

'Just about. If he doesn't do anything rash. The *World*'s been doing quite well recently.'

'She's gone off him,' said Jane. 'Ever since Bob.'

'Oh dear,' Lovell said.

'Absolutely,' said Jane. 'So she's looked around for another.'

'Crawley, you mean?'

'If she must,' said Jane. 'How could she be keen on Crawley? How could anybody? She'd much sooner put up with you.'

'Don't flatter me,' said Lovell. 'I'm not used to it.'

'Sorry,' said Jane. 'What I mean is it isn't love she wants, it's cash. Mountains of it.'

'You're not flattering me at all,' Lovell said.

'I am really,' said Jane. 'Otherwise I wouldn't be telling you.'

'Doesn't she know I'm married?'

'She doesn't even know we're lovers.' She touched his cheek. 'You don't want her to know, do you? You don't want anyone to know.' She moved in closer. 'Brenda Coupland sent me a wedding invitation today,' she said. 'I wrote back to tell her I'll be in New York at the time.'

'I got one too,' said Lovell.

'What did you say?'

'Thanks very much,' said Lovell.

'You don't mean you're going?'

'Of course not,' Lovell said. 'I'll be in New York too. I'll send her a telegram – and a wedding present of course. I thought of a silver tea service.'

'I shall send something splendid by Wedgwood,' said Jane. 'Not for Brenda. For darling Hugo.'

'Why on earth – ?'

'Because he routed Crawley without even knowing he'd done it,' said Jane. 'All he knew was that he was having a conversation with someone he didn't like very much, and Creepers was gobbling like a gander. Oh Charles, he was wonderful.' Her hand moved. 'Perhaps it's time we got down to serious business,' she said.

'More than time,' said Lovell.

'Do you have to go out tonight?' Norah asked.

Andy looked up from the boot he was polishing .'There's a talk on at the Labour Hall,' he said. 'Chap just back from Russia. I told Billy Caffrey I might look in.'

'If it's what you want to do – ' said Norah.

Andy thought about it. It wasn't what he wanted to do: it was what he had to do. Get yourself seen. Ask questions. Every chance you get. That had been Billy Caffrey's advice. That way people notice you, and you have to be noticed if you want to get on in politics.

'You could come with me,' he said.

'Me? Go to a talk about Russia? I bet there won't even be lantern slides.'

'You'd win,' said Andy.

'No,' Norah said. 'You get off to the talking shop. I'll listen to the wireless and get on with the mat.'

She nodded to where it stood waiting in its frame, a hook and a pile of clippings from discarded clothes beside it. Old socks, a sweater, a couple of vests, cotton stockings, cut up and ready to be hooked on to a canvas backing to make a mat that would last for ever.

'It's on account of politics, you see,' said Andy.

'Well of course,' Norah said. 'With you everything's on account of politics.'

'Except you,' said Andy.

'Where do you want to end up, Andy? she asked. 'Mayor of Felston? A funny sort of mayoress I'd make.'

'You'd be grand,' he said, 'but I'm looking a bit higher than mayor.'

Now you've done it, he thought. Now you're going to have to tell her, and anyway you love her, man. She's your wife. She has a right to be told.

'Don't be daft,' said Norah. 'You can't get higher than being mayor.'

'I could be Felston's MP,' said Andy, and to his amazement Norah laughed aloud.

'By that's a good un,' she said. 'Really rich, that is. We haven't got tuppence to rub together and we're off to London. You making laws and me opening bazaars.'

'The union would sponsor me if I got the nomination,' said Andy, and the laughter died.

'You're serious, aren't you?' she said.

'Aye,' said Andy. 'I am. . . . You don't like the idea?'

'If you want it that much I'll just have to lump it,' said Norah. 'But it scares me to death if you must know.'

'Why on earth should you be scared?'

'Because I've seen pictures in the papers of MP's wives, and they didn't look like me.'

'Jimmy Wagstaff's wife looked just like you, except she wasn't so bonny,' Andy said.

'Jimmy Wagstaff's wife died six months after he was elected.'

'She had cancer,' said Andy. 'It had nothing to do with – '

'With what?'

'Politics. Or being scared. It isn't that hard, pet. What you'd have to do.' He took her hand. 'Just be at the Hall when I've a speech to make, or on the platform in the market place. Drink a cup of tea with some of the wives mebbe, or be one of the judges at a Baby Show. You could handle that. Don't tell me you couldn't.'

His words were coaxing, no more than that, but she knew that he was begging her.

'I could try,' she said. 'I won't say I'd enjoy it, but I could always try.'

'That's all I ask,' he said. 'And if you can't manage it I promise I'll – '

Her hand covered his mouth.

'Don't say it,' she said. 'It might turn out to be a promise you can't keep. . . . You said *if* you got the nomination?' Andy nodded. 'Does that mean it isn't settled yet?'

'It hasn't even started,' said Andy. 'Jimmy Wagstaff hasn't retired yet, and when he does there'll be half a dozen chaps after it. I'd be one of them, that's all.'

Norah Patterson discovered that it was possible to long simultaneously for success and failure. 'There could be a bit of a complication when it comes to sitting on platforms,' she said at last.

'How d'you mean?' said Andy.

'Well,' his wife said, 'you haven't been exactly idle since we were married, any more than I have.' He still showed no sign of understanding. 'You daft thing,' she said. 'I'm expecting.'

'You're never,' said Andy.

'Well the way you and me's been carrying on we should get our money back if I wasn't,' Norah said, and then: 'You don't mind, do you?'

'Mind? Of course I don't mind,' Andy said. 'I think it's marvellous.'

He was shouting so loud she had to shush him before the neighbours downstairs shared the news.

'You're sure?' he asked her.

'I've missed twice,' she said, 'but I'll go and see Dr Stobbs on Monday just to be sure.'

'Stobbs? He's the best one?'

'He's the only one we can afford,' said Norah. 'You're not Prime Minister yet.'

'I could always ask our Bob for a sub.'

'No,' said Norah. 'He's offered before and we've said no before, and we're not going to start begging now. We'll keep our self-respect, thank you very much.'

'Yes, missus,' Andy said meekly, and she laughed again and aimed a mock blow at him.

There was a gurgle in her laughter as sensual as an embrace, but he embraced her anyway, pressing her to him, and then he remembered.

'Sorry,' he said. 'You'll have to keep reminding me.'

She pressed back against him. 'There's seven months to go yet,' she said, 'and I'm not made of bone china.' Her arms tightened, and she lifted her face to be kissed. At last she said, 'You'd better be off to that meeting of yours.'

'Bugger the meeting,' Andy said.

He really must be pleased she thought, for him to swear like that.

'What will you do then?' she asked.

'Give you a hand with that mat.'

Sybil Hendry came out from the bath, looked at herself in the glass and approved of what she saw. Still all smooth and firm and slender, despite all those martinis. Slender, not skinny, that was the point. So many people up here in the North were skinny – it was a word they used often – but they were skinny because they never had enough to eat, except for the poachers, and the ones who stole her sheep, and those miners who were still working: but she was slender despite the fact that she had too much to eat. She resisted temptation. Not that she wasn't sorry for those poor people with their ghastly complexions and terrible clothes: *of course* she was sorry. But what could she do? Give to charity? Well she did that. Rather a lot, really. But what else could she do?

She began to dress. Start with perfume. First thing you put on, last thing you take off, Bob had said. Printer, printer, where did you learn such things? Silk underwear and stockings (how could those poor women bear the touch of what they wore?) and a gown of green silk by Vionnet. She shopped at other couturiers too of course – all women did – but she always returned to Madeleine Vionnet, who could make her seem even smoother, firmer, more slender than she was. And all this, she thought, to dine with her father, who seemed to have decided that he would stay at Crag Fell indefinitely. No good appearing before her father looking frumpish. That would be like giving away three tricks before she'd even opened the bidding.

Not that the metaphor did the situation justice. This wasn't a card game: this was war. A siege if you like. Daddy had occupied Crag Fell, and she wanted him out; and Daddy wasn't an easy man to shift. Came of being a general, probably. All the same it wasn't his house, it was hers, and yet he acted as if it were his house: telling the head gardener what to plant, the butler which wine to serve;

111

shooting her game before he told her gamekeeper, if indeed he told him at all. Not that there was much to shoot at this time of year, but it still annoyed the gamekeeper, and how could she blame the poor man? He could hardly have a row with Mrs Hendry's father. None of them could.

The trouble was that Daddy was broke. Too many hope-filled nights at Monte Carlo and Deauville, and far too many mornings of regret. His excuse was that he had only a tiny flat in Knightsbridge to live in, but in fact it was the other way round. He only had a tiny flat because of his trips to Monte Carlo and Deauville, and so when he was broke he came to stay with his daughter in Northumberland. Keeping her company, he called it, but he kept her company when she was in London and he was still here.

It had been bad enough when Tony was alive, but now and then even poor Tony would put his foot down, drive him to Newcastle, and buy him a first class single to King's Cross: but now that Tony was dead, Daddy carried on as if he owned the place. Sometimes she thought that he believed he did. Oh he knew well enough that Tony had left it to her – he wasn't *batty* or anything – but he took the view that anything that belonged to his daughter automatically belonged to her father. *Anything*.

Tony ... She felt sorry for Tony. Not about him, but for him. She couldn't blame herself because he'd – had an accident. Might as well call it that, since everybody else did. Even her solicitor. Must have something to do with the money, she thought, and anyway it wouldn't have been very nice, an inquest telling half the county that Tony had blown his brains out, and so he'd had an accident. Even Daddy said so. All because she'd liked men. Well she'd liked Tony come to that, even before they'd married – and oh what a fuss he'd made when she'd said she wouldn't wear a white gown. Couldn't he see she was teasing? She was rather good at teasing. Even so she'd made him happy. Trouble was she'd made a few others happy, and so Tony had reached for his trusty twelve bore. It didn't make sense.

He hadn't altered his will though. That had surprised her. Despite Tim and Martin and Freddy – if he knew about Freddy – he had still left everything to her, and everything was rather a lot, even in these hard-up times. Awful land of course, but three pits still working. Lots and lots of coal which meant lots and lots of mun, and explained Daddy's presence. She wouldn't be surprised if he asked her for a cheque over dinner. He'd had a sort of Deauville look in his eye recently, and there was nothing left to shoot.

The trouble with Deauville was that once he'd been to the Casino and lost her cheque he'd be back to Crag Fell like a homing pigeon. He must really hate that flat in Knightsbridge, she thought. Well of course he does. Barely room to turn round, and utterly devoid of claret and salmon, VSOP cognac and Havana cigars. He should get married again, she thought: not come and guzzle hers all the time.

But suppose she did get rid of Daddy for a while at least, what would she do at Crag Fell? Ask Bob to stay? That really would set the neighbours talking, especially the dear Duchess, who seemed to have no objections to her second son marrying a widow, provided that she was wealthy. It was the wealthy widow who had the objections. Definitely not a second son. The heir was in the rudest of health.

Anyway Bob probably wouldn't come. Too busy selling wireless sets. Get yourself down to London and show us your perfume there, he'd tell her. The devil of it was she probably would. She put on the diamonds Tony had given her as an engagement present: ear-rings and the necklace, but not the bracelet. That would be overdoing it even for Daddy.

General Sir Archibald Lomax, KCVO, was drinking sherry in the drawing room: a pale fino, the kind she detested. He didn't even drink it cold. That night he was wearing a black tie, and the coat of a dining club he had once belonged to, and which had long since gone bankrupt. So many of the institutions he belonged to went bankrupt. He looked at his daughter.

'Very nice,' he said, and lifted the decanter. 'Sherry?'

'No thank you.'

'It's a good one,' said the general.

'I know, Daddy,' said Sybil Hendry. 'Tony always did choose good wine.'

She went to the drinks tray. Pettit, their butler, had left ice in the

113

bucket beside the gin and vermouth and the cocktail shaker. She began to mix a martini.

'I wish you wouldn't drink those things,' said the general.

'I know, Daddy,' she said again.

It was a struggle they engaged in every evening, combat as precise and ritual as an eighteenth-century siege, and she was bored with it. Daddy Must Go, she thought. There were worse slogans.

'I mean to say, spirits and wine in the same glass,' said her father. 'You're drinking spirits and wine in the same glass.'

'Sherry's different,' said her father. 'The spirit in sherry is brandy. Made from grapes. Same as the wine. What you've got is gin. Who on earth drinks gin – apart from charwomen?'

'Well I do for one,' said his daughter, 'and so do most of my friends.' He looked as if he were about to yell, then drank sherry instead.

'Well well,' he said at last. 'You young people have your preferences, and no reason why you shouldn't. Old duffers like me are too set in their ways.'

Sybil Hendry told herself: Darling, be very careful. Daddy is up to something, and it isn't something you're going to like.

She went to the fire and sat in a wing chair. Its bottle-green leather made the Vionnet gown glow. In front of her a log fire crackled gently. Tony had always been keen on log fires, and the house could be cold, sometimes, even in August. Her father sat in the chair opposite her and looked at her steadily. Preparing his plan of attack. What a handsome man he is, she thought. Distinguished, too, like a general in a play. Whatever good looks I have I owe to him. Mummy was quite plain, but she had all the money. – And now I have it all. But history won't repeat itself. He's not giving all my money to French croupiers.

'I've been thinking,' her father said.

'Yes, Daddy?'

'Well not thinking, exactly. More like wondering. Do I really need a flat in Knightsbridge? I mean I spend most of my life up here with you, or else at one of those French health resorts.'

He makes Deauville and Monte Carlo sound like spas, she thought, but that was a side alley. Better not venture down it just at the moment.

114

'Where would you stay in London?' she asked. 'At your club?'

'My club's well enough for the odd lunch,' said her father, 'but I wouldn't recommend the beds. Mattresses like sandbags. And damp more often than not.'

'But you really do need a place to stay in London,' Sybil Hendry said. 'You have to go there sometimes. And hotels are very expensive.'

Her father winced. Hotel bills played no part in his scheme.

'Not hotels,' he said. 'They're worse than the club, besides being a waste of money. Got to watch the pennies these days, Sybil.'

He said this severely, as if whatever it might be was all her fault.

'My point is this,' he said. 'You have a flat in Mayfair. In Bruton Street.'

Sybil Hendry suddenly found it very hard to appear relaxed. She got up instead, and went to the cocktail shaker.

I know what street my flat's in she thought as she filled up her glass, and the answer is no.

'Two flats in London,' said her father. 'Yours and mine. Eating their heads off, as you might say. Rates and electricity and gas and telephones and God knows what else. Now my idea is this. Why don't we consolidate?'

'Consolidate, Daddy?'

'Join forces, if you like. One of those flats is surplus to requirement, as we used to say in the army. We don't need it, not when there are just the two of us.'

His daughter said nothing.

'Of course,' her father said at last, 'I'm not suggesting you get rid of the Bruton Street flat. Good Lord no. You're probably very fond of it. But that little cupboard of mine – to tell you the truth I'll be glad to get rid of it for whatever it will fetch.'

Still his daughter didn't speak.

'Naturally,' her father said, 'whatever the wretched place fetches I shall make over to you. *Of course*. My contribution and so on. What do you say?'

At last his daughter spoke. 'I shall have to have a word with my lawyers first,' she said.

'Nonsense,' said her father. 'There isn't anything in my idea for them. Money's all lawyers ever think about. Just tell them what you intend to do and let them get on with it.'

'That's just it,' said Sybil Hendry, and thought to herself, Dear God, can't he see a bonfire when it's blazing at midnight, or is it that he won't?

'Don't see what you're driving at,' said her father.

Suddenly she realised why she wanted to send him away. It wasn't so that she could go romping with Bob; not here at any rate. It was because she *liked* living at Crag Fell: liked owning it and being the landed gentlewoman, and telling Pettit and the gardener and the gamekeeper what to do, without any help from her father. She would make him an allowance – he was her father after all – but that would be it. No more Crag Fell, and certainly no Bruton Street. He would just have to put up with his cupboard when he had no money for French health resorts.

'What I'm driving at is that this is *my* house, and Bruton Street is *my* flat,' she said.

'You're a very lucky young woman,' said her father.

'I may well be,' his daughter said, 'but that doesn't alter the fact that they belong to me. Don't you see, Daddy? If I'd wanted you to live with me I'd have asked you.'

'I don't see what that has to do with lawyers,' said the general.

'You're by no means a fool,' said his daughter, 'so don't try to pretend that you are.' The general blinked. Here was plain speaking indeed. 'This has nothing to do with lawyers and you know it. This has to do with you and me. The lawyers were just a way of postponing the decision. But you don't want that.'

'All I want is to be with you,' said the general. 'Nothing wrong with a chap wanting to be with his daughter, surely?'

'Maybe not for the chap,' said Sybil Hendry, 'but it might not be so wonderful for the daughter. The answer is no, Daddy. You must stick to your cupboard – and French health resorts.'

'But damn it, I introduced you to Tony,' said her father. 'If it wasn't for me you wouldn't *be* here.'

'You coaxed me into marrying him, come to that,' said Sybil Hendry, 'but only after you'd seen Crag Fell and the Bruton Street flat. Really Daddy, one could say you were living on your daughter's immoral earnings.'

'Now that's unkind,' said her father. 'Nothing immoral about marriage.'

'It's your motivation that might bother the clergy,' said his daughter. 'The answer's still no.'

Hard as nails, the general thought, not without pride. All the same it was a bit much.

'But I've been thinking too,' said his daughter.

'Nice thoughts, I hope.'

'I think you'll enjoy them. . . . The real reason you spend so much time here is that you can't afford to go to one of your resorts and lose money.'

'I wouldn't put it like that, exactly,' said her father.

'There's no other way to put it,' said his daughter. 'You're bored here, and you interfere in what doesn't concern you, and I start screeching at you, and it's bad for both of us. Now if I made you an allowance you could pop off to France from time to time and come up here by invitation only.'

'An allowance?'

'That's what I said.'

'How much?' His daughter laughed, as proud of him as he had been of her.

'You certainly get to the point, Daddy,' she said.

'You too. No doubt you get it from me. But so far as I'm concerned it's the only question that matters.'

'I can't answer you tonight. There are people I have to talk to – but it will be adequate, I promise you. What do you say?'

'What can I say?' said the general. 'You have all the big guns. . . . I accept.'

Pettit came in to announce dinner, and she told him to open champagne.

. 14 .

Jane chose the *Ile de France* because Lionel was adamant that a French ship with a rather naughty reputation would have no shortage of partners. How right he was. Her suite was the equivalent of a suite at the Ritz or the Crillon, her stewardess spoke excellent English and the steward identified her at once as the real-life heroine of *The Angel of No Man's Land*, the autobiographical movie which she had written and in which Georgina Payne had starred. It seemed he was a fan of Georgie's, but then the entire ship's complement were fans of Georgie's, crew and passengers alike. Her place at the captain's table was guaranteed. The ship itself was quite staggering: three lounges done with the kind of opulence that only the French could redeem from vulgarity, and a dining room decorated with three shades of marble which served the kind of food she had thought could be made only in Paris: sinful food that no amount of swimming, dancing and deck tennis could quite counteract. And parties every night: rooms crammed with people drinking Krug, and telling each other how poor they were.

Lionel had been right about the dancing, too, but then Lionel was never wrong about dancing. Positive queues of young men asking her to do the foxtrot, the quick step, the tango. Some of them asked her to do rather more, but though she found it flattering enough at her age, she turned them down at once. After all she had Charles for that sort of thing, she thought, and then Really! You make him sound like a gigolo or something, and he's much, much more than that. . . . Isn't he? But the band were playing 'These Foolish Things', and now was not the time for answering questions, particularly the ones she asked of herself.

Just before she fell asleep she thought of Charles again. He'd had to go to Germany, poor darling. Stuttgart, was it? Dusseldorf? His story was that he'd done it so as to avoid poor Brenda's wedding, at the same time making it clear that they weren't away together committing naughtiness, but Jane rather doubted it. If it were only that he'd have gone back to Blagdon Hall and shot grouse. Since it was Germany there had to be money in it too. Not that she blamed him. The trouble was it meant he'd have to come over on a German liner, probably the *Bremen*, and a German liner couldn't possibly be so much fun as the *Ile de France*. (Not that she wanted Charles to have too much fun.) All the same a German luxury liner sounded like a contradiction in terms: all physical exercises and health foods and quartettes by Honneger, and Cole Porter absolutely verboten.

When they docked at Pier 90 there was no Barry waiting. New York's equivalent of Lionel had long since disappeared, swallowed whole by the Depression. Instead Charles had wired his corresponding bank in New York, and there was a Cadillac there to meet her, and a junior executive awestruck by the presence of a lady so powerful that two banks had conferred across the Atlantic on how best to take her to her apartment: almost to the point of being struck dumb.

The fact didn't bother her. She was wearing a suit by Patou and a hat by Louise Bourbon, and looked good enough to be taken care of by three banks at least, and the silence gave her the chance to look at the city. New York seemed exhausted. The El still thundered by, there were still cars on the streets, but even so she could almost smell the sense of defeat, even from inside the most expensive car the Americans made. The poor, the unemployed were everywhere: singing and dancing for pennies, queuing outside a soup kitchen, trying to sell apples, or simply standing at a street corner and watching whatever there was to watch. A well-dressed woman in a Cadillac was a sight to be remembered all week, she thought. One day soon it might provide the inspiration for a lynch mob. In London too there were the poor, but only in certain districts. Here they were everywhere.

She said as much to Martha, who was helping her to unpack in her bedroom that looked out on Central Park. Martha was half of her domestic staff: the other half was her husband, George.

'Bad all over, Miss Whitcomb,' Martha said. 'From what I hear share-croppers in the South are just about starving to death.'

George and Martha were negroes: they knew all about the South.

'Worse for negroes?' said Jane.

'Worse for everybody,' Martha said. 'This Depression is for everybody – without distinction of colour, race or creed.'

'I beg your pardon?'

'My son Booker, he said that. He's a real educated boy, Miss Whitcomb.'

'Booker?'

Martha sighed. 'Sort of a joke in a way, but it's kind of difficult to explain,' Martha said. 'It was George's idea. He's smart too. He hasn't had an education like Booker, but he reads a lot. Knows a lot, too.'

'You see, miss, George and Martha were the given names of President Washington and his wife, so when we was – were courting we got all kinds of jokes about Mister President and his First Lady, so after we married and I had my son, George said one president's enough for any family, specially one from the South, and it was time for a change.'

'But why Booker?'

Martha sighed once more. 'I guess that's the joke,' she said. 'You see, miss, the blacks had a Washington, too. Not a president of course, being black, but a – well George calls him a learned man. Professor, principal of a college, stuff like that. And his given name was Booker. Booker Taliaferro Washington. – My Booker really likes it, him being a learned man himself. Booker Taliaferro Stanton, MD.'

'Your son's a doctor?'

Martha rapped on a chest of drawers with her knuckles. 'Knock on wood,' she said, and turned to Jane. 'Not yet. He's still got one more year to go. But he will be, Miss Whitcomb. He will be. I prayed for him so much God must be sick of all that pestering, but He's listening. I know He is. Besides, my Booker's real smart. Just like his pa.'

'I'll pray for him too, then,' said Jane. 'We'll always need smart doctors. Is he your only child?'

'Heavens no, Miss Whitcomb. We got a girl, too. Lucille.'

'And what does she do?'

'She's going to be a singer. Not jazz. Not Harlem nightclubs. That's not for Lucille.'

'What then?'

'She's at the conservatory,' Martha said. 'Going to be an opera singer. She won't be the first black girl to make it, but maybe she'll be the best.'

'Don't tell me you haven't got pictures of them,' said Jane.

Carefully Martha put down an armful of lingerie, left the room, and came back with a couple of photographs in a wrinkled frame of artificial leather, and Jane prepared to lie, but there was no need to lie. Both boy and girl were good looking and, if the camera couldn't lie, intelligent. Determined, too, thought Jane, but then to succeed in the professions they had chosen and be as black as they were, they had to be determined.

'I could say you've been blessed in your children,' she said.

'Amen,' said Martha.

'But I could equally say that they've been blessed in you,' said Jane. 'They must be costing you a fortune.'

'They work every chance they get,' Martha said, 'but there aren't all that many chances nowadays. It costs us plenty, sure it does, but how else should we spend our money?'

'You manage to stay in work then?'

'This is a mighty popular apartment,' Martha said, 'and we kind of go with it. We manage.' She began to place the lingerie in a drawer. Each scrap of hand-sewn silk, thought Jane, would support one of her children for a week, but Martha worked on placidly, even cheerfully, delighting in the elegance of what she handled.

'We're doing a sight better than those folks on the streets,' she said, and closed the drawer.

The subject, Jane gathered, was closed.

Charles was still on the high seas, she thought. Wheat germ and yoghurt and running on the spot. When he reached New York he'd want a little higher life than that: good lunches and dinners, well-behaved parties, rather stately dancing at El Morocco – or even the Cotton Club if it wasn't too rowdy. What he wouldn't want – would find it hard to forgive even her for thrusting upon him – would be the company of Leftwing lesbians in Greenwich

Village, and yet she had promised Jay Bower that she would call on his sister. Better, far better, to get the beastly business over before the *Bremen* docked. She reached out for the phone and dialled. It rang for some time.

At last a weary voice said, 'Jennifer Klein.' It was the sort of voice that went with tousled hair and not nearly enough sleep. Oh God! Jane thought. Not even Jay's sister: her girlfriend or boyfriend or whatever she is: and if she likes me she hides it well.

'Erika Bauer, please,' she said, making it as Teutonic as possible, because in America Bauer was how it was still pronounced.

'Who is this?'

'Jane Whitcomb.' There was a long pause.

'Hold the wire,' Jennifer Klein said at last. 'I'll see.'

Jane didn't have to wait long.

'What a nice surprise,' Erika's voice said. 'How long have you been here?'

'We docked this morning,' said Jane, and marvelled. Erika's voice sounded at least as tousled as her chum's, and yet it managed to convey a welcome.

'Sweet of you to call so soon,' she said. 'Can you come over for drinks? Just a few people, and maybe we'll go on to a restaurant afterwards. Nothing grand. Just a plate of spaghetti or something.'

'When?' asked Jane.

'Why, tonight. Say seven o'clock? Something like that?'

At least she would get it over with.

'I'll look forward to it,' she said.

'Oh great.' Erika hesitated for a moment, then said: 'We don't dress up, you know. For the restaurant, I mean.'

'Who does these days?' said Jane, and then to punish her just a little: 'Catherine and Jay are well and send their love.'

'Catherine?' said Erika, bewildered, and then: 'Oh Catherine. Yes of course.' Another pause, then, 'Oh damn it to hell. I never could do all that social stuff – but you will come, won't you?'

'About seven,' said Jane. 'See you then.'

She hung up, then as a reward for duty done she called Long Distance and asked for Georgie's number in Beverly Hills and was through in no time at all. Really the Americans were awfully good at telephones. She got first a butler, then a maid, and finally Georgie, who sounded almost as tousled as Messrs Klein and Bauer, but far more relaxed.

'Darling,' she said. 'How lovely. What time is it?'

'In New York it's half past three.'

'I mean what time is it here?'

'You work it out,' said Jane firmly. 'Or look at your watch or something. Have you been drinking?'

'Well of course,' said Georgie. 'The most divine party. It went on for days.'

'In the middle of a Depression?'

'Well that's just it,' Georgie said. 'We were all depressed, every one of us, so we decided that we might as well be depressed together. Where did you say you were?'

Jane decided to soldier on. Drunk or sober it was fun to talk to Georgie.

'I gather you've finished your latest movie,' she said.

'*Rather,*' George said.

'How was it?'

'Utter hell,' said Georgie. 'Nothing like *The Angel* at all.'

'Sweet of you,' said Jane. 'Lots of lovely men?'

'Not one,' said Georgie. 'The lovely ones are all queer – in Hollywood at any rate. I should know, shouldn't I? I married the loveliest of them all. I still haven't found them.'

'The ones who killed your Dan?'

'Yes.'

Jane could picture her, probably lying on her bed in an explosion of satin pillows, the lovely brow knitted, the lovely face stern, as she registered her determination on revenge, – and yet she meant it, too. Suddenly Georgie sighed a genuine sound of grief.

'He really was mine you know,' she said. 'Oh not in any sinful way – no *fun*, how could there be? And yet he really trusted me, relied on me even. I do miss him, Jane.' A rasping sound then. Match struck, cigarette lit. 'When are you coming out?'

'Soon. Depends on how quickly Charles concludes his deal.'

'Still the same nice chap?'

'The one and only.'

'How lucky you are,' Georgie said. 'How's Bob?'

'Well. Chasing another girl.'

'Of course,' said Georgie.

'This one's not a girl exactly,' said Jane. 'Well technically not. Not jeune fille anyway. She's a widow.'

'Merry?'

'I shouldn't *think* so,' Jane said cautiously. 'More lovely than merry, I'd say.'

'He'll survive,' said Georgie. 'Whatever happens. He survived me, after all.'

'How's Murray Fisch?' Jane asked.

'Meaning he survived me too? Well *he* thinks he has anyway, but I'm not so sure. I may have a little surprise for Murray.'

'Do tell.'

'When I see you,' Georgie said firmly. 'Telephones have ears. – In this town, anyway.' Another voice murmured briefly, then Georgie said, 'Sod it' very loudly, then: 'Sorry darling. Must fly. Party at Picfair.'

'At what?'

'Mary Pickford's and Douglas Fairbank's house. It's called Picfair.'

'Good Lord,' said Jane.

'Yes I know, but I really have to go. I'm not sure it isn't in my contract.'

'Will it be a good party?'

'Not specially,' Georgie said. 'Command performances never are.'

Erika's and darling Jennifer's didn't look a specially good party either, thought Jane. She had arrived in style, driven by George. (Minus points for a bourgeois capitalist car, plus points for employing a negro driver. Starting from scratch in fact.) Driving her there had been George's idea, after she had told him where the party was. She had intended to drive herself.

'Not to the village,' George had said. 'Greenwich Village is no place for a lady on her own. Not nowadays.'

'And who's going to attack me?' she had asked. 'Legs Diamond? Dutch Schultz?'

'Gutter trash more likely,' George had said, 'or maybe just ordinary men turned desperate because their children are starving.

Either way you shouldn't lead them into temptation.'

Right as usual, thought Jane. There was no one quite so adept as George at putting one in one's place. She had asked him if he were a good driver.

'Fair to middling,' George had said. 'Don't worry. I'll get you there. But I'm better at mixing martinis, and seeing you don't have to drive I can mix you one right now.'

If Booker were as clever as his father, she thought, he'd be a consultant surgeon at thirty.

George had been right on every point, she thought. Greenwich Village was no place for a lady: at least 73, Chestnut Street wasn't. Lesbians for the most part: dressed in fishermen's jerseys, collars and ties, workmen's overalls. One of them smoked a pipe, but the effect was rather spoiled by its smelling of opium rather than shag. Erika wore a jacket and trousers in a material that looked like linen, well-enough cut to flatter her heavy Teutonic prettiness. Darling Jennifer looked ravishing as usual, in the sort of dress one wore to play tennis, with, for some reason, a Spanish shawl tied round her waist. Also as usual she looked to be in a thoroughly bad temper.

There were men there too: some obviously homosexual, some not. Most of them wore red ties, as indeed did many of the lesbians, though the homosexuals were far more elegantly dressed. Crows and parakeets, she thought, and looked at her own blue day dress by Schiaparelli. What am I in all this? she wondered. A kingfisher? A homosexual handed her a drink, and began to talk about Kierkegaard. He does it rather well, thought Jane, if one is even remotely interested in Kierkegaard. She looked down at the floor. The stain on the carpet was the same one that she had seen when she was last here, years ago. She felt simultaneously pleased because of Jennifer and sad because of Erika.

'Of course Kierkegaard isn't everybody's cup of tea,' the homosexual said.

'By no means,' said Jane.

'Oo a witty one,' said the homosexual. 'An ironist.'

What was his name? Began with a D. Derek? No – one syllable. Dyke? – It couldn't be. Dirk, that was it. Dirk van Alder.

'Not like your dress,' said Dirk. 'Admired by all, that dress should be, though perhaps not by all here. Schiaparelli if I'm not mistaken?'

'Indeed it is,' said Jane. 'How clever of you.'

'In daytime, when I earn a crust,' said Dirk, 'I deal in such frivolities as yours.'

'Do you enjoy it?'

'Love it,' said Dirk, and sighed. 'I was born too late, I fear. I'm an extremely frivolous person.'

'Despite Kierkegaard?'

'My one party trick,' said Dirk. 'I'm afraid I bored you with it just to get a closer look at your dress. My dear, what are you doing here?'

'My duty,' said Jane. Jennifer was moving towards her, more furious than ever, it seemed, but Erika intercepted her and handed her an empty martini jug. For a moment Jane thought the row would begin there and then, but instead Jennifer snatched the jug and stamped towards the kitchen. Erika came up to them.

'Dirk, do you mind?' she said. 'It's ages since I spoke to Jane.'

'Of course not.' Dirk turned to Jane. 'You and the Italian lady go together very well,' he said, and took himself off.

'Cryptic,' said Erika.

'Mm,' said Jane. 'He's rather sweet.'

Erika looked severe. 'Aren't you being condescending?' she asked.

'Not consciously,' said Jane.

Erika thought about it, then said: 'Of course. You make jokes. I remember. But is this really the time to make jokes? Among such suffering. Such poverty.'

'It's the only alternative to weeping,' said Jane.

'You may think so,' Erika said, 'but – forgive me – you have not suffered.'

'Nonsense,' said Jane. 'Everybody's suffered at one time or another. Including you.'

Again that moment for thought. She was much more German than her brother, even in the phrasing of her English: but then in her father's house she had spoken only German.

'But you are rich,' she said at last.

'So I cried into a silk handkerchief,' said Jane, 'but I still cried.'

'You don't cry now?'

'No no,' said Jane. 'I'm happy – for now at least,' and then, anticipating the next accusation, 'but I do my best for those who aren't.' She told Erika about the Felston Hunger March. Erika was enchanted.

'*Three hundred miles?*' she said. Jane nodded. 'And *you* marched too, all the way?'

'I did indeed,' said Jane. 'I'll show you my corns if you like.'

This time a joke was permitted. 'You must write this,' she said. 'For the magazine.'

'We'll see,' said Jane, being diplomatic. 'The magazine' was called *Red Awakening*. It was jointly owned and edited by E. Bauer and J. Klein.

'But you must,' Erika said.

'It's possible your brother may have the copyright on what I write about Felston,' said Jane.

'I shall write to him tomorrow,' Erika said. 'Or perhaps telephone. He's well, you say?'

'Extremely.'

'And – Catherine you say she's called? She's well too, you said. But didn't she have an accident?'

'A car crash,' said Jane. 'She was pregnant at the time. She's well, but she lost her baby.'

'She must be so unhappy.'

Jane thought of Bob. 'Sometimes she is,' she said.

'Tell her I wish her well.'

'I'll be delighted,' said Jane, and reached out to touch Erika's hand. It was really no more than a sign that she must go and mingle. A pity that Jennifer came back with another jug of martinis as she did it. She came at them through the mob like a swan through a flock of ducks, thought Jane, and she didn't spill a drop.

'Erika *told* you we didn't dress up for the restaurant,' she said, her voice already a yell. The more tactful guests huddled and muttered; the more honest ones listened.

'But I didn't,' said Jane. Her voice, though low, had a carrying quality that was a great relief to the listeners.

'Not only a liar, but a lousy liar,' Jennifer yelled. 'Or don't you know what you're wearing?'

'A day dress,' said Jane. 'Normally by this time I'd be wearing something for the evening, but as you all go to such trouble to appear unconventional I thought I'd better do the same.'

Jennifer took a deep breath, and Erika went to her.

'Jennifer, please,' she said.

She too knows the meaning of suffering, thought Jane, and waited for the barrage. Only physical force could stop her soulmate now.

Out it all came. Patronising Britisher: half-educated show-off: rentier: sweater of seamstresses' brows, and of course bourgeois-capitalist bitch.

Jane tried to remember it all. Her mother would enjoy it enormously, though half-educated show-off was rather too close for comfort.

When the other woman paused for breath she said, 'Jennifer darling.' For a moment she thought she was about to be drenched in a quart of martinis, but Erika grabbed her friend's arm.

'Do listen,' said Jane. 'Just for a minute. I came here because I was invited. I wore this dress because all my dresses are like this. It wasn't a matter of choice: I just took the nearest. If I'd wanted to wear the sort of clothes you and your friends wear, I'd have had to go out and buy them, but I didn't because I much prefer my own.

'Now you must excuse me. I don't somehow feel in the mood for Italian food tonight, so I'll say toodle-pip, Jennifer darling. Bye-bye, Erika.'

Jennifer then delighted the company by dropping the jug of martinis, howling loudly, and reaching for the comfort of Erika's arms.

Better to leave now, thought Jane. There was a telephone in the hallway. She could phone George from there. As she left, the tongues were already wagging: delight slightly tempered by the fact that there were no more martinis. . . . In the hallway a young man was straightening his tie. He turned to face her: it was Timothy Jordan.

. 15 .

Timothy Jordan said, 'You wouldn't have liked the food at Luigi's anyway. It's disgusting.'

They were sitting in a restaurant off Times Square, eating steaks and drinking the house red wine, which the waiter had called Coca-Cola en carafe. Neither her dress nor his neat, lawyerlike suit seemed out of place.

'Then why do they eat there?' she asked.

'Luigi had to leave Italy on account of Mussolini,' he said, 'so they support him.'

'You mean he's a Communist?'

'It's possible,' he said. 'Either that or he's clever.' He began to brood, as he had so often done in Spain.

'I'll need more than that,' said Jane.

'Oh sorry,' he said. 'It's just – he has all the required words and phrases – the Leftist jargon. But that doesn't mean he believes it. Not necessarily. What he does believe in is that terrible restaurant of his. He owns it after all. They bought it for him.'

'Who did?'

'Oh – Erika, Jennifer, Dirk. – Half the people at the party.'

'But if the food's so awful his restaurant will fail,' she said.

'Of course it will – and he'll have to sell it. It's in a good location. It should make a few bucks even these days.'

'Oh,' she said.

'You think I'm just being cynical?'

'My guess is you're being realistic,' she said. 'There weren't too many realists at that party. Did you give money?'

'I offered a loan,' he said, 'but they thought a loan was uncaring. Cruel, even, because it implied criticism. So I pulled out.'

She looked at him with respect. This was not the Tim she had

129

known in Spain, who had burned to sell everything that everybody had and give it to the poor, with a more-than-early-Christian zeal.

'Are you working in New York?' she asked.

He nodded. 'Perkiss, Maberley, Bronstein and Fitt. Wall Street. Capitalism's innermost citadel. Imagine it, Jane. Me a Wall Street lawyer. How can I do it?'

'You must enjoy it,' she said.

'Not the system,' he said. 'I hate the system as much as ever I did – but the problem solving. That's something else. That I enjoy.'

'And I've no doubt you're good at it.'

'I must be,' he said. 'They pay me enough.'

'And you go to parties like Erika's to make contact with the true believers?'

'I go to parties like Erika's because I don't have to think, and because I might meet a pretty girl there.'

'At Erika's?'

'Why the surprise?' Tim said. 'I met you there.'

Well well well, she thought. You've come a long way, Timmy my sweet.

'But I take my Socialism seriously,' he said. 'It's just that when I want to talk about it, really talk, I don't go to the Village.'

'Where then?'

'The Bronx,' he said, and moved on to the next topic. Very lawyerlike, thought Jane. 'Do you hear from the marquesa these days?'

The Marquesa de Antequera: perhaps the ugliest woman she had ever met and certainly the most remarkable. For her part she had thought Tim was remarkable too, and capable of great things: and sympathised with his young man's misery to the point where she had suggested Jane helped him to get over it.

'Young men were not born to be virgins,' she had said. 'Except the priests, of course, and for them too it is often difficult.'

She wanted me to play candy bar to his weeping child, thought Jane, and how close she came to doing it. Remarkable wasn't the word.

'Not for ages,' she said. 'Nor the marqués. Do you?'

'Not any more. I met them through Luis, their son. When he left Princeton we sort of lost touch.'

130

'Is he a Socialist too?' Jane asked.

'He was then, but I don't think it will last. He's got an awful lot of money – or he will have.' Suddenly he shook his head and laughed. 'Oh come on Jordan,' he said. 'You really are cynical tonight.'

She could almost hear Canon Messeter quote St Matthew: 'For he had great possessions.'

'I still think it's realism,' said Jane. 'No bad thing in a lawyer.'

'How about in a politician?'

'They need it too,' said Jane. 'It helps to keep their ideals close to the ground.'

'Ideals should soar,' said Tim.

'Not beyond the reach of the rest of us.'

He smiled at her then, and she remembered why it was that she had so nearly agreed to the marquesa's plans.

'I'd like to use that,' he said.

'You flatter me.'

'That would be an easy thing to do,' he said. 'To try to do, anyway.' He drank the last of his wine. 'I was in love with you, you know.'

'Indeed I do,' she said. 'You told me so.'

'I don't remember that,' he said. 'I thought I remembered everything, but I don't remember that.'

'When we took our ride together – and we stopped on the heathland by that Celtic Cross.'

'I remember that,' he said. 'I behaved like a lout.'

'You behaved like a young man in love,' she said, 'which is what you were.'

He stared at her. 'You haven't changed at all,' he said at last.

'You have.'

Careful, she admonished herself. None of that shrinking violet stuff. Besides, you may be quite wrong. But she knew she wasn't.

He stared at her again, as if he were committing her to memory, then sighed. 'I'm sorry,' he said. 'I'm more sorry than I can say, but I have to go to the Bronx. Will I see you again?'

'I'll call you,' she said, 'at Perkiss, Maberley, Bronstein and Fitt.'

131

He signalled for the bill, and Jane hoped there'd be a pretty girl among the Bronx's revolutionaries.

Andy had brought marigolds: a great armful of them, wrapped in sheets of the *Felston Echo*. From Billy Caffrey's brother's allotment, thought Norah. Got them for pennies. But that was all right. Pennies was all he had to spare. Walked a mile and a half to get them, then carried them through the town, through Felston, where a man carrying flowers was a man no more. Not that Andy would care, she thought, and not that anybody would laugh at him either: not to his face.

'Thanks, pet,' she said, and he bent to kiss her. Another thing men didn't do in Felston, she thought. Kiss their wives where other folks can see. All the same her lips welcomed his. She looked at where the marigolds gleamed against the whiteness of the sheets.

'They're lovely,' she said, and looked about her. 'I'll just see if there's a jug somewhere.'

But already a probationer nurse was coming to them, a vase in her hands. 'Here we are, Councillor Patterson,' she said.

Well well, thought Norah. At least he's got something for all those meetings of the Health and General Services Committee.

Deftly the nurse arranged the flowers, and put them on the table by Norah's bed. 'They're lovely,' she said, and walked away with her brisk, rat-tat nurse's walk.

'How are you, lass?' said Andy.

'Canny.'

'Canny' could mean anything from not too bad to really awful, as they both knew. This time Norah was saying 'It might be worse but I can't see how.'

'Does it hurt?'

She shook her head. 'Not like a pain,' she said.

'What then?' Being Andy he would have to know.

'I've lost the bairn,' she said.

'Aye,' Andy said. 'So they told me.'

The anger welled up in her: not against him, never against him: but who else was near?

'Don't you care?' she said.

132

'Of course I care,' Andy said. 'But I've still got you.'

Suddenly her body relaxed, like a clenched fist becoming a hand once more. 'I'm sorry,' she said. 'I had no right to say that. Only – ' She broke off. She had been about to say 'Only this is the fourth time it's happened. Maybe I'll never have any bairns.' But this was not the time to tell her husband she'd carried another man's children too. Perhaps there never would be a time.

'Only what, pet?' he said.

'Only I wanted it so,' she said.

'Aye. Me an' all,' said Andy. 'We'll just have to remember the proverb.'

'What proverb?'

'If at first you don't succeed,' said Andy, and winked at her.

She laughed then, and that did hurt, but all the same it was worth it. Andy making jokes, at such a time, in such a place. This was her Andy, the one that nobody else even knew existed.

'Dirty bugger,' she said, and despite the pain she smiled. His hand covered hers.

'Are they looking after you all right?' he said.

'Oh yes,' she said. 'Dr Stobbs was marvellous. The nurses an' all.' She looked about her at the long row of beds: identical white sheets, identical red blankets. 'It's just – ' she said.

'Just what?'

'Well it's not like being at home, is it?'

'All the same you'll stay here,' he said, and his hand squeezed hers. 'Stay till you're properly better, I mean. Don't worry about the money. We'll manage.'

'Dr Stobbs said the money's taken care of,' Norah said.

'Did he?' said Andy.

'Aye,' Norah said. 'He did. And seeing that's the case I've made up my mind to stay here till I'm well. On account of the proverb, as you might say.'

He chuckled, then bent over to kiss her once more. In a ward full of folk, too.

Norah said, 'There's just one thing.' He waited. 'Somebody'll have to let my mother know – and there's only you.'

'Then I'll tell her,' said Andy.

'You're a good chap, Andy.'

'I'm the chap that loves you,' Andy Patterson said.

They flew to California in a Lockheed Electra. Night flying was a novelty to them both, and so was the speed of the journey: New York to Los Angeles in twenty-four hours; one day out of her life. By train it had been more like a week. It was cold up in the air of course, but there had been plenty of hot soup and coffee, as well as picnic meals. In Los Angeles the sun was shining and Charles being Charles there was a limousine waiting to take her to Georgie's house, then on to his hotel. Georgie's house was worth seeing, at that. Nothing Georgian or Tudor about it, no home sickness for the Cotswolds, but a cool California–Mexican hacienda in gleaming white. As the car pulled up at the door Georgie raced out to meet them and embraced them both.

'Darlings what bliss to see you,' she said. 'But you must be worn out.'

'It is a little exhausting,' said Jane. 'I never could sleep sitting down.'

'Then I don't feel too bad about leaving you,' said Georgie. 'There's a photo call and darling Myrna's new movie's opening tonight and so there's a party as well, so you'll be able to get lots of sleep, and tomorrow we'll do things. 'Bye, darlings.'

She went to where the studio Cadillac was waiting.

'Thoughtful girl, our Georgie,' said Jane.

They were in bed in his suite at the Beverly Wilshire, and goodness what a fuss he'd made about that. They'd even had to take different lifts. Still, it was all for her sake.

'If only she wasn't so damn obvious about it,' Charles said.

'It isn't that she's being obvious,' said Jane. 'It's just that she didn't see that there was anything to be subtle about.'

'Like you?' he said.

'Well, yes,' said Jane. 'Though I must say I love it when you make such a fuss about my reputation. It makes me believe I still have one.'

He held her in the way she specially liked.

'I've missed all this,' he said, and indeed, she thought, New York had been devoted far more to the making of money than the making of love.

134

'Me too,' she said. 'Will there be lots of it in California?'

'My God yes,' said Charles.

Over dinner she told him about meeting Tim. Charles was always jealous of any man she had spent more than five minutes with, but he was slightly better if she told him first. Not that she mentioned the schemings of that nobly born female pander in Santiago de Compostela.

'A lawyer, is he?' said Charles.

'With Perkiss, Maberley, Bronstein and Fitt.'

'Then he's a good one.'

She said again, 'Perkiss, Maberley, Bronstein and Fitt.'

'What about them?'

'Nothing about them,' she said. 'It's just such a satisfying thing to say. Nice ring to it.'

He looked at her glass. It was still half full. Suddenly it occurred to him that she was happy, and that the happiness was because they were together. The thought pleased him so much that he forgot to be jealous.

'We must try it as a duet some time,' he said.

'Did I tell you Tim was a Red?' asked Jane.

'You did when you came back from Spain,' he said.

'That was all shining idealism and stuff he'd read in books,' said Jane. 'Some of them were rather good books, perhaps, but not too close to reality.'

'And now?'

'Now I rather suspect it's real,' she said. 'What people say, not what books say. He's decided that Socialism will work, and he's going to be one of those who sees it does.'

'Sort of mirror image of Creepy Crawley?'

'I doubt if he's as ruthless as Creepers.'

'If he's going to make Socialism work here he's going to have to be. – Or anywhere else for that matter.'

'You're thinking of Russia?' He nodded. 'But things can't be that bad over there, surely? I mean look at all those duchesses and archdeacons, who come back and say it's all marvellous?'

'None so blind as those who will not see,' said Charles. 'Other people have a different story to tell.'

'I've never read it.'

'I doubt if you ever will,' said Charles. 'Not so long as Russia's fashionable. – Talking of fashionables, the wedding went off all right. Not that I was there, of course.'

'So Brenda's Mrs Hugo Meldrum?' Charles nodded. 'Who was best man?'

'*Not* Piers Hilyard.'

'Thank God for that.'

'Some chap he was at school with. The only people Meldrum seems to know are the ones he was at school with – and his wife of course.'

'Was Piers there?'

'Salisbury Plain,' said Charles. 'And just as well. She spent most of the reception dancing with Lionel. Not that Meldrum gave a damn. He was at school with him, too. . . . You remember how Brenda used to go on about the Prince of Wales?'

'The Little Man,' said Jane.

'There's some quite juicy stuff going the rounds about him, too,' said Charles.

'He's got a new lady?'

'This one's an American,' said Charles.

'A lot of them are.'

'Oh are they?' said Charles, who had little flair for gossip. 'I can't say I can remember them, but I'll remember this one.'

'A stunner, is she?'

'Never set eyes on her. It's her name. She's called Wallis. Wallis Simpson.'

Jane laughed aloud. 'Darling, you can't be serious,' she said.

'So you really think I'm capable of making it up?' said Charles.

Next morning she found that he hadn't invented a word. The *Los Angeles Times* speculated freely on the chances of an American divorcée (two so far, and a Mr Simpson still to be shed) becoming Queen of England. Georgie, when she finally left her bed, said she was already bored by it all. 'It's been going on for absolute ages,' she said. 'It's time the newspapers found something else to bore us with.'

Yet there had been not a hint of it in the English papers. Not to be expected in *The Times*, perhaps, being above such things, but Jay Bower wasn't above anything that would sell, and the *Daily*

World hadn't uttered a word, not even a hint. Jane turned over the page to be told that the end of the Great Depression was approaching. It hadn't looked like that in New York.

Lazy days with Georgie. Shopping for the most part, though she didn't buy all that much. Georgie bought everything in sight.

'Darling,' she said, when Jane turned down a pair of Cartier ear-rings, 'you're not hard up or anything are you?'

'No no,' said Jane. 'It's just that everything I like I can buy in Paris for about half the price.'

'In the *Depression*?'

'The French are having one, too,' said Jane.

Still there were lunches at the Brown Derby and parties, and never any lack of partners. Friend of Georgie Payne, successful script writer, how could she lack partners? – and long, lovely afternoons with Charles that alternated between frantic activity and lazy contentment. Altogether, she thought, a happy time and place to be. True, when he wasn't bedding her, Charles was making even more money, Depression or not, but Charles was born to make money, as a bee is born to gather pollen. He was a banker, after all. She swam a lot, too, which was good for her. At least she wasn't getting any fatter. Georgie swam, too, but more and more it seemed that she had to rely on her steam bath.

'You could diet,' said Jane.

'No I couldn't,' Georgie said. 'I'm much too fond of food. What I could do is quit the movies, then nobody would give a damn if I weighed two hundred pounds.'

'But you couldn't do that,' said Jane.

'Why couldn't I? With what I made and what Dan left me I've got even more than I can spend. Besides – '

'Yes?'

Georgie looked at her. For once she was less than certain about what she wanted to say.

'Not for publication,' she said at last, 'but I think I may have found myself a nice chap too.'

'Anyone I know?'

'Darling, forgive me,' said Georgie. 'I'd rather not say who till I'm absolutely sure.'

'Quite right,' said Jane.

The butler was making his way to the poolside. He was a very Hollywood butler: tall and lean, with what he imagined to be the distinction of a diplomat, and a frantic need to be in the movies. He carried a portable phone.

'A telephone call for Miss Whitcomb,' he said, 'from England,' and plugged the phone into a socket by the pool bar. 'A Lady Catherine Bower.'

From the look on his face Jane had hit the bull's eye. A call from England, and from a Lady no less.

Jane took the phone. There was a sound like a storm at sea.

'Hello?' she said.

'Darling,' said Catherine through the storm, 'do forgive me but I simply have to speak to you.'

'But how did you know where I was?'

'I asked Jay.' Catherine sounded impatient at having to state the obvious, and indeed Jay always knew where everyone was, provided they might be newsworthy.

'How are you, darling?' Jane asked.

'Bloody.' Even through the howling of the storm, Jane began to hear the hysteria in Catherine's voice. 'I wanted to ask you for the name of that detective of yours – '

'Mr Pinner? Why on earth – '

'Some Irishmen have tried to murder Piers,' Catherine said. 'I want to make sure they're caught – and if he dies I want them to hang.'

. 16 .

He had got leave to come up to town to see his grandmother. There had been time to have his hair cut at Trumper's and take Mrs Hendry to lunch, first. She liked the Caprice and so they ate there. No harm in that provided his colonel didn't hear of it. The colonel considered the Caprice fast: the haunt of bad hats. Piers doubted if his colonel had ever been there, but he read the gossip columns.

Sybil was perfectly willing to be given lunch. She rattled away about life in the country and kept watching the door in case Noël Coward came in, and altogether treated him in a far too sisterly fashion. Hence lunch. He had suggested dinner and a nightclub and she'd turned him down flat, which was a bore. He'd rather looked forward to holding her in his arms while they danced, and you couldn't do that at lunch. Somebody else was making the running it seemed, and he rather suspected Bob. Too bad if it was. Bob was a chum of his – and the sort of competition he could do without. All the same he couldn't spend his entire love-life trailing after Brenda Thingummy – Meldrum, that was it. Besides, it embarrassed him dreadfully to go on meeting Meldrum in a social sort of way, and the fact that he suspected Meldrum knew all about it and didn't mind in the least embarrassed him more than anything else. I'll have to give her up, he thought. Soon. If only she wasn't so good in bed.

'You're not listening,' Sybil Hendry said.

'Of course I am,' said Piers, scrabbling frantically through his memory as he spoke. 'You were saying what fun it is to have your own place in the country.'

Her face relaxed. The half-heard words must have been the right ones.

'Well it is,' she said. 'I miss Tony, of course – '

'Of course.'

She looked up then, but there had been no hint of irony.

'But I love being there on my own. Making decisions. Telling people to do things. Didn't you ever live in the country?'

'We had a house in Ireland,' he said. 'In County Meath.'

'Don't you miss it at all?'

'Not any more,' said Piers. 'The IRA burnt it down.'

'Oh my God!' Sybil Hendry said, then added: 'Yes, of course. I remember reading about it. Mangan Castle. Your father's place.'

' I suppose it was,' said Piers, 'but we always thought of it as Granny's place. She was the one who ran it. Just like you.'

'What happened to her?'

'After the fire? She had a stroke, and then another. She can hardly speak now. The next one may kill her, the doctors say.'

'Did they ever catch the ones who caused the fire?'

'No,' said Piers. 'They never did.'

'My dear, what a terrible story,' she said. 'Quite ghastly for you.'

'You'd need to know Granny to realise just how ghastly,' he said. 'Know her as she was, I mean.'

He was doing his best to look impassive, but the pain he felt was all too apparent.

'Forgive me,' she said. 'I had no business to question you like that.'

'Quite all right,' he said. 'You weren't to know. I'm going to take tea with her this afternoon. She likes that – God knows why. I sit beside her and chatter away about the first thing that comes into my head, and she nods and smiles till her nurse chucks me out.'

'What sort of things?'

'Salisbury Plain, racing, India.'

'Did you enjoy India?'

'Some of it,' he said. 'The polo, and shikar – '

'Shikar?'

'Shooting things,' he said. 'You know: tiger, leopard, deer, wildfowl.' Pathans too, he thought, and a couple of IRA men, but I won't tell you about that, not even to lure you to my bed.

'It all sounds fearfully hearty,' she said.

'Well so it is,' said Piers. 'The army's a hearty profession.'

'Were there never any ladies in your part of India?' she asked.

140

'Sometimes.'

'Pretty ones?'

'Occasionally,' said Piers, 'but none so pretty as you.'

'You are sweet,' she said.

Piers thought, I haven't a hope, and signalled for the bill.

He put her into a taxi and set off to walk. It was a fair old stroll to Eaton Square, but there was time to kill before tea with Granny and he was full of restless energy that set him striding out as if Arlington Street were the beginning of a route march. Best forget about Sybil Hendry, he told himself. Think about India instead. Shikar. The kind he went in for was still dangerous: tiger, leopard, bear, and pig-sticking even more so. You could say you gambled your life: your skill and dexterity with rifle or spear against a charging beast that would rip you apart if you missed. That concentrated your mind as wonderfully as knowing you were about to be hanged, he thought, and believe me, Dr Johnson, I know what I'm talking about. If your quarry was man, the concentration intensified, or else you died.

The two IRA men now: that had been straightforward enough. They had to be destroyed and that's all there was to it. Mice to be trapped, foxes for the hounds to tear. Vermin. It had cost money of course, but then he had money, so that was no problem, and informers were no problem either, not in Ireland. Getting in and out had been the tricky part. The rest was pure text-book stuff. They'd gone sneaking off into the countryside for a little pistol practice. Mausers, he remembered. Old fashioned, but bloody accurate. All he'd had to do was appear in front of the pair of them, shoot them, and chuck them and their pistols into the nearest bog. A lot easier than shooting tiger, thanks to his informer. He'd got away with it, too, even after the bodies were found, years later. The only one to suspect him had been Jane, and she wouldn't tell. Simple. Easy. A job well done.

The Pathans were another matter. They had known their business far better than he did, but he'd been seconded for training to a Gurkha company who knew their business at least as well as the Pathans, and he'd been sent on patrol with a half section of them. The fiction was that he was the officer commanding: the fact that

141

they shepherded him about like so many nannies: up there north of Quetta, in what the locals called the hills, that anywhere else in the world would have been mountains; even in Switzerland. A dead place: arid, dusty, deserted: a sloping desert of rock with no hint of a path, and yet the Gurkhas crossed it as if they were walking along Shaftesbury Avenue to Piccadilly Circus: cheerful, smiling, and yet all the time with an intensity of concentration he'd never seen before. If those IRA men had possessed a tenth of it he would have been dead.

He'd had the sense to let them get on with it, and their relief was such that they couldn't hide it, though they were polite little men, but when at last they saw that he meant it they relaxed, and he went where he was pushed, and settled down to learn. By the end, the havildar, their sergeant, was as pleased with him as if he'd just won his colours for the junior school first eleven. That was after they'd killed the Pathans: five of them. Two and a half brace, you might say. He'd had a share in one of them, and the havildar had looked more pleased than ever. . . . The Pathans had wounded one of the Gurkhas, and the others had carried him down a slope that seemed more precipice than track. Going down was far, far worse than going up, but what could he do but get on with it? The others got on with it, even when it was their turn to carry the wounded man, who giggled whenever he was conscious. The giggling, the havildar explained, was because he was embarrassed. He'd had no business to get himself wounded in such an easy encounter. . . .

He arrived at Eaton Square at last, a long way from the Afghan border: just about as far away as one could get, and yet if there was nothing doing with Sybil Hendry he'd sooner be back with the Gurkhas, he thought, because that was where one learned one's trade, but he mustn't tell Granny that. He rang the bell, and the butler, Belling, admitted him, relieved him of his bowler and umbrella. Piers made for the stairs.

'If you please, Mr Piers,' said Belling. 'Your parcel's here.'

'Parcel?'

'From Harrods,' said Belling. 'The delivery man said I was to make sure I gave it to you as soon as you arrived.'

He went to a table in the hallway and took up a package wrapped in Harrod's paper: square in section, big enough to contain a coffee pot say, but who on earth would send him a coffee pot? Not all that well wrapped either, considering it came from Harrods. *It was ticking.*

'Throw it away,' said Piers, and dropped flat behind the massive oak chest that dominated the hall.

'I beg your pardon, sir?' said Belling, and the thing exploded, and did terrible things to Belling's body, though his face continued to wear an expression of mild outrage because Mr Piers was drunk at teatime while on his way to visit Lady Mangan.

Piers felt a tremendous and yet numbing blow on his left leg; the only part of him the chest failed to protect. There was another, sharper blow on the side of his thigh, and he observed that something sharp had pierced the artery there. He watched its rhythmic spouting for a second, then said aloud 'This won't do', and pressed hard with his thumbs above the wound. The spouting diminished, but blood still seeped through, then almost at once the first footman appeared, took one look, ran off and came back again with a long-handled clothes brush.

'Idiot,' said Piers. 'This suit is ruined.' Though whether he spoke aloud or not, he had no idea.

'Keep pressing, sir,' said the footman, and ripped off Piers's tie, wound it round his leg, and used the clothes-brush handle to make a tourniquet. Quick and deft and sure of what he did. Piers let him get on with it. The first footman – what was his name? James? Of course it was. The first footman was always James – had obviously done all this before.

'Good man,' Piers said aloud.

'Thank you, sir. William's phoned for the ambulance.'

William? Yes of course. The second footman. The second footman was always William.

'You did that well.'

'I was in the RAMC, sir.'

Medical Corps, thought Piers. My one bit of good luck today.

'If I may ask – '

'You shouldn't try to speak, sir,' said James. 'Not just at the moment.'

'Just one question,' said Piers. 'If you'd be so kind.'

'Sir?'

'The sight of Belling doesn't bother you?'

'I was at the Somme, sir,' said James.

There was the sound of the ambulance bell, shrill and malevolent, as if angry at being called out at teatime.

'Make sure Granny knows I'm all right,' said Piers.

'Of course, sir,' said James, but Piers didn't hear him. He was unconscious. The first footman looked at his leg.

But you're not all right, are you? he thought. You'll be lucky if you're ever all right again.

He waited till the ambulance took Piers away. Soon it would be the coppers, and somebody to remove what was left of poor old Belling. That just left him time to sprint upstairs and tell the nurse on duty what had happened.

'I couldn't come down,' she said. 'I'm sorry. There'd have been no one to look after Lady Mangan.'

The old girl's dying, he thought. Leave her or not she'd still be dying, but she's the one that pays you.

'That's all right, miss,' he said.

'Was it a gas main?' the nurse asked.

'No gas in the hall, miss.'

'What then?'

'A bomb, miss.'

'Don't be absurd,' said the nurse. 'How could it possibly be a bomb?'

You could go downstairs and see for yourself, he thought. But I wouldn't advise it. Not till they move old Belling.

'If you'll excuse me, miss,' he said, 'I'd better let Lady Catherine know her brother's been hurt.'

'Yes, of course,' said the nurse. 'Is there anything I can do?'

'Not just now, miss. You stay and take care of Lady Mangan.'

She looked up at him then, quick and questioning, but his face was impassive. On his way to the telephone he thought: Not Lady Catherine. Her old man. If I phone Mr Bower and I'm first with the news there'll be a fiver in it for me. A fiver at least.

Charles said, 'Jane, believe me. There isn't any point in going home.'

'Charles is absolutely right,' said Georgie.

'But he's so frightfully ill,' said Jane.

Charles looked at the telegram Bower had sent her: hundreds and hundreds of words. 'He doesn't say he's dying,' he said. 'He'd have told you if he were.'

'Yes, but – ' Jane began, then her hands fluttered: for once she had no words.

'He's got Catherine and Bower and his brother and his parents,' said Charles. 'What could you do, my dear, except get in the way?'

'Lady Mangan – ' she said.

'Doesn't even know, according to that cable,' said Charles. 'And just as well. Would you like to be the one to tell her?'

Jane's hands went to her face, but she didn't cry. It was a gesture her ayah would have remembered: an attempt to shut out the world when the world was too cruel to be borne.

'I'm so fond of Piers,' she said.

'Me too,' said Georgie.

'I like him too,' said Charles. 'Very much. If there was anything we could do we'd be on the next plane for New York. But there's not.'

Jane took her hands away. 'Must you always be so right?' she said, but somehow she managed to smile.

'Like your kid brother, isn't he?' said Georgie.

'Like David,' said Jane. 'Like Guy. A long time ago.'

'The ones who were killed?' Jane nodded. 'At least this one's still alive.'

'I ought to phone my mother,' said Jane.

'Be my guest,' Georgie said.

'Darling, she's in London,' said Jane.

'World Wide picks up my phone bills,' said Georgie. 'It'll be nice to hear Murray Fisch scream again.'

'Bless you,' said Jane, and went to the phone.

'You know about us, I take it?' said Charles.

'You take it correctly. You're not awfully good at hiding things.'

'I do my best,' said Charles. 'My wife's still alive, you see. Only she's desperately ill. Has been for years.'

Your wife's been mad for years, you mean, thought Georgie. But why should I tell you I know? Things are hard enough without that.

'I see,' she said.

145

'I don't want Jane hurt,' Charles said. 'Not ever.'

'Jane's tough,' said Georgie. 'In the nicest possible way – but she is. Sooner or later she could break, but she'd never bend.'

'I've never talked to anybody else about her like this,' said Charles. 'I never thought I could. I'm most frightfully grateful.'

Does that make me a big sister too? Georgie wondered. Well well well, Georgina Payne, you *are* getting on in years.

. 17 .

Mr Pinner said, 'This is really a matter for the police, Lady Catherine.'

'Well of course it is,' Lady Catherine said. 'They're all over the place. I suppose they have to be – but I want them caught – whoever did it – and somehow I don't think the police will catch them, but I rather think you might. I mean Miss Whitcomb says you're the best there is.'

'That's very kind of Miss Whitcomb,' said Mr Pinner, 'but this could be a tricky one. It could take months.'

She looked at him: not nearly tall enough to be a policeman, Old Bill moustache, the kind that sergeants grew in the Great War, neat suit, hard white collar, quiet tie: he looked like an undertaker, or the sort of person who managed a suburban branch of a bank: except for the eyes. Grey eyes, Mr Pinner's, that at first looked guileless, then suddenly weren't guileless at all, just patient and clever: not at all the same thing.

'You say you suspect the IRA,' Mr Pinner said.

'Well of course.'

'They didn't say they did it,' said Mr Pinner. 'They do, usually.'

'They killed the wrong man,' Catherine said.

'But they damaged the right one,' said Mr Pinner. 'Rather badly, I hear.'

'Yes, damn them,' Catherine said.

'He may never be fit enough to go back to the army, according to *The Times*,' said Mr Pinner.

'Then that's as good as killing him,' said Catherine. 'I hope to God they don't know that.'

'I'd like to talk to your brother, if it's possible,' said Mr Pinner.

'I'll find out,' Catherine said, 'and I'll telephone as soon as I know. – But you'll take the job?'

'I'll let you know, Lady Catherine,' said Mr Pinner. 'After I've talked with your brother.'

They had dined together at a new place on the way to Bel Air, French and really very good, she and Charles and Georgie and a rising young actor Georgie had summoned by telephone like ordering pastrami from a delicatessen: a most handsome young actor who didn't look homosexual, but then they never did in Hollywood. The poor chap – Chuck was it? Hal? – had spent the entire evening being overawed: an entire evening in the presence of the highest-paid female star in Hollywood, as World Wide Publicity Department never tired of saying, and of the Britisher who owned vast amounts of the studio that paid her, and for whom he longed to work far, far more than he longed for salvation. In the presence of Jane Whitcomb too, who seemed to have overawed him even more than the others had. And that was strange: odd, even.

She stared at her reflection in the mirror as she removed her make-up. She didn't look like the sort of person who overawed people, she thought, and she certainly hadn't harangued him or anything. Odd . . . Then Charles came in. Because of some process of logic known only to himself he had decided that as Georgie knew all about them that was OK, so long as they didn't actually share a room for other than carnal purposes. Why was not made clear. As for Georgie's servants, they knew as well as Chuck or Hal – no, Bart that was it – exactly how much of World Wide Charles owned, and they hoped to work for World Wide every bit as much as Bart did. Their goings-on would never reach the gossip columnists: not even Hedda; not even Louella.

'Explain something to me,' she said.

'Money?' said Charles, and took off his robe.

'Bart,' said Jane, then added helpfully: 'Georgie's young man for tonight.'

'What's to explain?' said Charles. 'Couldn't he dance properly?'

'Adequately,' said Jane. 'Not like Lionel, but competent. It isn't that. Why was he afraid of me? Perhaps that's overstating it, but he acted as though he were afraid of me.'

'Not overstating it at all,' said Charles. 'If Georgie and I didn't know you so well, we'd have been afraid of you too.'

'But why on earth – '

'You were thinking of Piers all night.'

'Oh dear,' said Jane. 'I suppose I was. I must have been very poor company.'

'Appalling,' said Charles, 'if company's a word one can use to describe you.'

'But you know how fond I am of – '

'Let me finish,' said Charles. 'Yes I do know. And Georgie knows. But that poor young chap had no idea. What was going on in your mind? Memories of Ireland? Sadness? Compassion for Catherine and Lady Mangan?'

'Well of course.'

'And nothing else? Just pain and anguish wringing the brow so to speak?'

She put down the bottle of cleansing lotion with a bang.

'You know far too damn much about me,' she said. 'I spent most of the night thinking about what I'd like to do to the ones who hurt Piers.'

'Ah,' said Charles.

Jane said, 'I've told you before, Charles, being right all the time is not endearing.' She reached for the night cream.

'It's how you looked, you see,' said Charles. 'It was all there on your face – as if you were shouting it aloud.'

'Oh God,' said Jane. 'Like Madame Defarge at the guillotine? Is that how I looked?'

'You looked beautiful,' said Charles, 'because you are, and there's nothing you can do about that – but it was a very cruel beauty tonight. Like that Hindu goddess – the one who destroys – '

'Kali,' she said. 'Oh God. Was I really like that?'

'No,' said Charles, 'but Bart thought you were. It was all love really, but how was he to know?'

She took off her robe, went to where he sat on the bed, and sat beside him. 'You've told me something tonight,' she said. 'Something beyond even the emeralds you gave me.'

'What did I tell you?'

'How much you love me,' said Jane.

149

'And how did I do that?'

'You spent the entire evening with Georgina Payne and then told me I was beautiful. Only a man who loved me could do that.'

His arm went round her waist. In his hotel there was a telegram even longer than Bower's. He had phoned London as soon as he'd heard about Piers, and demanded all the information possible. When successful merchant bankers demand information they tend to get it: over a thousand words of it. Except it wasn't information, not really. Flannel was what it was. 'It may well be' and 'Informed sources suggest', but no names, not even an organisation. All the same, who else could it be?

'Never mind Georgie,' he said. 'It's bedtime.'

She laughed then, that rich gurgle of laughter that was all the aphrodisiac he needed.

'There you go again,' she said.

Bower said, 'You're sure you've got all you need?'

'Rather more than I need,' said Piers, and then he flushed and said, 'Forgive me, Jay. That was inept, wasn't it? The trouble is I've been brooding too much, and there's nobody to take it out on but one's nearest and dearest.'

'Caged-up tight,' said his twin, 'and lashing your tail.'

'Give me half a chance and I'll lash yours,' said Piers, and then he and Catherine burst out laughing. Simultaneously, thought Bower: at the touch of the same button.

Catherine looked at the basket-work shield that kept the weight of sheets and blankets from his leg.

'Does it hurt a lot?' she asked.

'From time to time.'

She nodded. 'I thought as much,' she said.

Telepathy again, thought Bower. Each with their own telephone direct to the other's brain, and nobody else on the extension. Not ever. Nobody.

Catherine looked around at the room in St George's Hospital. Quite decent prints on the walls, Liberty curtains, furniture from Heal's. 'At least they torture you in style,' she said.

'They don't torture me at all,' said Piers. 'They chloroform me first.' But it wasn't true, he thought. Sooner or later he came out

150

of the chloroform and the torture began. Always the same torture, and always just within the limits of what he could endure.

'Lovely flowers,' said his twin.

'Mostly the family and Jane and Georgie,' Piers said. 'The Mess sent claret.'

'Georgina Payne sends you flowers?' Bower asked.

'Twice a week,' said Piers. 'It's frightfully good for my prestige. Even the surgeon's impressed.'

'Do you mind if I use that?' Bower asked. 'For the "Wicked World" column?'

Catherine bridled.

'Not at all,' Piers said. 'It'll be even better for my prestige.'

'So it will,' Catherine said. 'Some of the nurses here are rather pretty.'

'Ass,' said her brother. 'What use is that to me with one leg in half a basket chair?'

'Just as well,' said Catherine, and then: 'Piers.'

'Oh Lord,' Piers said. 'I know that voice. Let's have it.'

'You remember Jane's Mr Pinner?'

'The detective who traced her horse to Mangan Castle? What about him?'

'I went to see him. It was when people were saying you might die.'

'But I didn't die, thanks to James.' He moved slightly, and at once the pain attacked. He waited till it subsided and said, 'On balance I still think he did me a favour.'

'He did,' said Bower. 'He did us all a favour. I've tried to show our gratitude.'

Piers looked at him, and said at last, 'Thank you, Jay,' then to his sister: 'Tell me about Mr Pinner.'

'I asked him to find out who did it,' she said. 'Not just the IRA. The names.'

Piers looked at her, and again Bower was conscious of the telepathy. At last Piers said, 'And what did he say?'

'He said he'd have to talk to you first.'

'Then I'll talk to him,' said Piers. 'Then we'll see what I say, too.'

'Shall I send him in?'

'You've brought him with you?'

151

'Well of course,' his sister said. 'We don't want to waste any time.'

Don't we? Piers thought. I'm not so sure about that. Jane reckons Mr Pinner is hot stuff.

'I'll get him,' said Bower, and went out.

'It hurts, doesn't it?' Catherine said.

'Hurts like hell,' said Piers. 'But I can put up with that so long as it heals. – Heals properly, I mean. So I can get back to the regiment.'

'It's so important?'

'It's everything,' said Piers. 'It's what I'm for.'

His sister looked at him, and knew he meant every word.

Piers liked Mr Pinner: his spruce neatness, his relaxed yet deferential air; very much the senior NCO with a young officer, and the matter-of-fact acceptance of what persons unknown had done to him. All the same he knew at once that Mr Pinner was clever, perhaps even brilliant, though he did his best to hide it. Part of his technique, Piers thought.

'What rank were you?' he asked.

Mr Pinner chuckled. 'Still shows, does it?' he said. 'Company sergeant major by the armistice. Middlesex Regiment.'

'You saw action, no doubt?'

'I joined in 1915,' Mr Pinner said, 'and that was action enough. Lucky I'm here, really.'

'You ever get anything like this?' He gestured at his injured leg.

'Got hit by a shell cap,' Mr Pinner said. 'Only mine was the left hip.'

'But you healed up?' said Piers. 'You went back to your battalion?'

'Yes, sir,' said Mr Pinner, 'though mind you that was 1917. By then they used to say, "If you can walk, you're in" – and I could just about manage to walk.'

First he gives, thought Piers, then he grabs it back, but he's honest as well as clever.

'Shall we talk about your bit of bother, sir?' Mr Pinner said.

'That's one phrase for it I suppose,' Piers said, and told yet again the story of the Harrods parcel. It wasn't difficult. He'd told it often enough to the police. Mr Pinner listened in silence, though he gave a grunt of approval when Piers told him about James's efficiency.

When Piers had done, he said, 'I've been through all the newspapers. Checked with the BBC news as well. The IRA hasn't said they've done it.'

'Who else could it be?'

'That's a question I asked myself, sir.'

'Get any answers?'

'None that made sense, sir. And even if I did, we've got to take account of Mangan Castle, wouldn't you say?'

'The two *have* to be connected?'

'Anything else would be like the pictures,' said Mr Pinner. 'Very exciting at the time, but not much sense once you started to think about it.'

'But I wasn't even there,' said Piers.

'No sir, but Lady Catherine did mention that your grandmother used to find jobs in her factory for the villagers. – And after the bomb there were no more jobs. – Maybe this is their way of getting back at you all.'

'But why me?' said Piers. 'I'm just a soldier. My father and my brother Desmond are the ones on the board.'

'Maybe that wouldn't bother them,' said Mr Pinner. 'They mightn't be too fussy so long as they got one of you.'

'Only they didn't – and so they didn't make an announcement, either?'

'It's a possibility, sir.'

'Indeed it is.'

There was a silence. Mr Pinner, it seemed, had said all he intended to say.

'Are you going to have a shot at my spot of bother?' Piers asked.

'I'd like to, sir,' said Mr Pinner. 'I explained to Lady Catherine what my terms are.'

'So she told me,' said Piers. 'No problem there. Only you'll be reporting to me, Mr Pinner. Lady Catherine's out of it now.'

'Yes of course, sir.'

Piers grinned. 'No of course about it. She may not see it that way – and she's rather headstrong.'

153

Mr Pinner thought: Look who's talking, but said nothing except, 'I'd better get started,' and rose to his feet, his movements as neat and precise as everything else about him.

'Good luck, Mr Pinner,' said Piers, but after the other man had gone he thought: I wonder if I really meant that? It would be nice to know who did this to me, – I might even do something about it – on the other hand Mr Pinner really is clever. I did my best to act the gallant but stupid officer, well meaning and bewildered, but did Mr Pinner swallow it? If he didn't I risk being taken over to Ireland and charged with murder. But let him get on with it for a while, at any rate, thought Piers, and see what he digs up. After all I can call it off whenever I want to. That was part of the agreement.

He looked at the wall opposite him. On every other wall there was a picture, but this one contained only a notice in a frame. In bold red letters it proclaimed: 'What To Do In Case Of Fire'. I'd better have a look at that, he thought.

Charles Lovell came out from the house and joined Jane by the pool. 'New York was on the phone,' he said.

Together they watched Georgie swim: an eminently satisfying sight, thought Jane, and yet I doubt if he's even seeing her.

'Bad news?' she asked.

'Almost certainly not,' he said, 'except that I may have to go there for a while.'

'Mexico's off?'

'By no means,' Lovell said. 'This should take a day – two at the most. If I fly both ways I should be back by the end of the week.'

'All that way for a couple of days?' said Jane. 'Couldn't you just write a letter?'

Charles Lovell said, 'No,' and nothing else, and suddenly became aware of Georgie in the glittering blue water.

It seems that one thing's certain, thought Jane. Darling Charles is about to make rather a lot of money, Depression or no Depression.

And no doubt he did, she thought, but of course he didn't get back to Hollywood in four days. Money's like a pretty woman, she thought, who can be had if you work at it, but it's never as easy as you think it will be: and she went to Mexico with Georgie. Charles had promised he would join them later....

Mexico began with Acapulco. They flew there because much as Georgie hated flying, she hated long car journeys even more. Acapulco was ocean and sand, she discovered; even more ocean, more sand, than could be had in California. Tropical fruits, too; the kind she hadn't eaten since India: mangoes and papayas and mangosteens. There was a headland too, perched high above the water like a huge diving board, and beneath it a lagoon like a swimming pool surrounded by rocks, scores of feet below. For a dollar or two young men would dive from there, down and down into the water that slapped against the rocks that were only feet away from them as they entered the water.

'Nothing to it,' another tourist told them. 'I mean it. Anyone can do it once they learn the trick.'

A middle-aged man with a red face and greedy eyes, thin rather than lean. A man, Jane noticed, who stayed well away from the cliff from which they watched. I know darling Georgie can no more help attracting men than a dog can help attracting fleas, she thought, but I do wish she'd switch it off sometimes, whatever it is. But all Georgie did was look at him, as if she couldn't believe what she saw. He never came back.

The rest of the time they spent mostly by the hotel pool, Jane in the sun, Georgie in the shade, (because her contract stipulated that she must not get a suntan) and gossiped, about Hollywood and Mayfair, the Prince of Wales and Cap d'Antibes and Paris. Georgie was a gossip virtuoso, ready to talk about anything at all except her own nice chap to be, for though they were travelling hopefully they had not yet arrived, Jane was certain. Instead, Georgie talked about her husband.

'Not just a pretty face,' said Georgie, 'though Dan's face was very pretty. You must have seen it.'

'Well of course,' said Jane. She had seen Dan Corless in at least a dozen pictures, including her own.

'Clever too,' said Georgie. 'Or do I mean cunning? Yes, I do. Like Murray Fisch – only much nicer of course. Like when my last contract came up.' She waved her hand as if she had made a strong but rather obvious point.

155

'What about your last contract?' Jane asked at last.

'Options,' said Georgie. 'The studio always asks for options. Like you work for them for five years with an option on another five. That's OK. I'd just as soon work for World Wide as anybody else. But Dan had said I should have an option too – like not to work at all. The Front Office didn't like it because what they want to do is own you till you lose your looks, but then they figured they were paying me these insane amounts of money, and if I wasn't a star I was nothing. Just a Cheshire Cat's smile. And anyway I started getting these headaches.'

'Martinis?'

'Anxiety neurosis,' Georgie said repressively. 'Dan found me this psychiatrist and he explained how my identity crisis fuelled my obsession about my artistic integrity – '

'You're making this up,' said Jane.

'Girl Guide's Honour,' said Georgie. 'Anyway he explained that these headaches were so excruciating I simply couldn't go to work – and we were just about to start shooting *The Angel of No Man's Land*, so they signed, and Dan showed the contract to his lawyer and then I signed, which is yet another reason why Murray detested poor Dan.'

'He knew it was Dan's doing?'

'Well of course. He knew I couldn't work it out for myself.' She turned, careful to stay in the shade, and looked at Jane, easy as a cat in the sun's heat. 'So World Wide didn't own me, and Murray didn't own even my little finger. It was a lovely feeling. Like a galley slave having his chains struck off. . . . Don't get too brown, darling. Blondes should never get too brown.'

'Quite right,' said Jane. 'I'll swim instead. Only horses look good when they're piebald.'

. 18 .

It was good to have her home. The place had been empty without
her. He'd read that in a book once and thought how daft that was.
Now he knew it wasn't. She wasn't a hundred per cent of course,
not yet. How could she be after all she's been through? and no
shenanigans, not for a week or two anyway. Dr Stobbs had been
very firm about that, and very embarrassed too, thought Andy, and
grinned. There was a time he'd have been even more embarrassed
than Dr Stobbs, but not any more. This was important. They were
talking about his Norah. So he held her in his arms and kissed her
every chance he got, and lit the fire every morning and humped the
coals up from the coal house in the backyard, and took her tea in
bed on Sundays. She wouldn't let him cook for her, and just as well,
he thought.

One night she told him about the other miscarriages she'd had,
when she'd been married to Marty. He heard her out in silence.

'You don't mind?' she said at last.

'How can I mind?' Andy said. 'I didn't even know you existed.'
He looked at her face; troubled, anxious. 'You didn't have to tell
me, you know.'

'Oh but I did,' she said. 'I won't have secrets between us, Andy.'

They were sitting on either side of the kitchen fire, and she
reached out to touch his hand.

'I'm no good at hiding things. Never was,' she said. 'And anyway
– me mam would be bound to tell you one of these days. I'm not
saying it would be out of spite, but she'd tell you.'

Andy thought, I don't care. It doesn't matter. How could it? You
weren't the virgin, I was. All the same I'm glad you didn't have his
bairns.

'No secrets?' he said at last.

'I hate things being kept in the dark,' she said.

'Me an' all, ' said Andy. 'So I've got one for you.'

'What, pet?'

'One of these fine days you're going to be mayoress, even if I never get to be an MP,' he said. 'Not next year, and probably not the year after. But the year after that ... How do you fancy yourself with a gold chain round your neck?'

'It'll be like you told me, won't it?' she said. 'Me sitting on a platform – '

' – Listening to me spout,' he said. 'Dead easy that should be. You do it all the time.'

'I can do it if you're beside me,' said Norah.

'Where else would I be?' he said.

'Do you want me to tell Mam?'

'Not yet,' Andy said. 'We'll let it come as a surprise.'

Bob read Andy's letter again. Norah poorly, it said, but safely home from hospital. No more details. Miscarriage more than likely, he thought. When it came to women's problems there was no bigger prude than Andy. All the same, it just goes to show you. Our Andy married and in bed with a woman. Pretty woman too. Good luck to him.

He was folding the letter up to put in his pocket when Sybil Hendry came in. Not always dead on time, not Sybil, not even in her own flat. On the other hand being late wasn't time wasted, not on her. She looked really lovely, he thought. Ah, well. I deserve a treat, the way I work.

'Not more business?' she said.

'This?' He held up the letter. 'No no. Just a few lines from my brother. His wife hasn't been well. Miscarriage by the sound of it.'

'By the sound of it? Doesn't he say so?'

'Andy? Of course not. Female business, a miscarriage.'

'But that's bizarre.'

'So's Felston,' said Bob.

'Are you going to do anything for him? I mean, send money or something?'

'I would if he would take it,' said Bob. 'Chances are he wouldn't. Still – I could try.'

158

'You're fond of your brother, aren't you?'

'Yes I am,' he said. 'And it's funny. I mean we're such opposites. Him a Socialist that wants to nationalise everything in sight, and me a capitalist that won't even employ union labour.'

'Why won't you?'

'No need,' said Bob. 'Chaps queue up to work for me.'

'Because you're so sweet?'

'Because I pay above the going rate,' said Bob. 'Proper Jekyll and Hyde, me and Andy, but which is which depends on your point of view.'

Her gown was of some silver stuff that glittered, cut to show a lot of shoulder and back.

'Come here,' he said.

She looked at him warily. 'Later,' she said. 'There isn't time for me to make up again.'

'I'll not spoil your make-up,' he said. 'I promise.'

She went to him not because she had to, but because it was what she wanted. He was so good at it, good for both of them. Deftly his fingers touched her, like a small boy unwrapping a sweet she thought, but even so his fingers were as eloquent as an epigram. You're beautiful, his fingers told her, and it's marvellous. She moved away only just in time.

'It's bed or it's the theatre,' she said. 'There isn't time for both.'

'Whichever you want,' said Bob.

What a sunny disposition, she thought, but that's because he knows he'll get me anyway. Darling Printer – how I'd love to see you suffer just once.

'Theatre and supper, and then we'll see,' she said.

Shakespeare, which had surprised her, even though he told her that a printer would read anything. This one it seemed would watch anything too, including *Romeo and Juliet*. He watched with the intensity of a child. If he's adding Juliet to his list I'll really hurt him, she thought. But it wasn't that. He was simply devouring the play as if it were food and he was starving. When Mercutio died she thought he would cry out loud.

They took a cab then to the Café de Paris, and he kept his hands to himself, as he always did. Making grabs in taxis was boring. Clumsy, too, and no fun at all for the girl. Bob was far too cunning to waste his time in such an awkward and uncomfortable venue. What was it debs' mammas used to say? NSIT. Not Safe In Taxis. Their way of saying that certain debs' escorts were notorious grabbers. Not Bob. CSIT. That was Bob. Completely Safe In Taxis. Bed was his arena.

She'd chosen the Café de Paris because she wanted to dance, and Bob was good at dancing: far better than the well-born grabbers she'd met when she made her come-out, and far, far better than poor Tony.

Over supper she said, 'You enjoyed the play, didn't you?'

'Aye,' said Bob, 'I did.'

Aye instead of yes. Usually that was part of the love-game they played sometimes: the princess and the peasant, but this time, she was sure, it was because the play was still so close he couldn't even be bothered to choose between the language of his childhood and that of the West End.

'But you wouldn't do that,' she said. 'Die for love, I mean. The way you go on, you'd need more lives than a cat.'

He chuckled. 'Not me, no,' he said, 'but our Andy might.'

'Die for a woman? Wouldn't he be more likely to die for the Workers?'

'He very nearly did, once,' said Bob. 'But he could die for a woman, too.'

'What a tragic figure you make him.'

'Well he is,' said Bob. 'That's because he feels things so deeply. What's the word – vulnerable, that's Andy.'

'That hardly makes you Jekyll and Hyde,' she said.

'Not that part of him. No,' said Bob. 'But there's another side to Andy that isn't tragic at all, and that's the part that makes sense to me, because I've got it too.'

'Do tell,' she said.

'We both have to get on, even if it kills us,' said Bob, 'but more likely it'll kill other people.'

She'd always had money, it was true, and he was still busy making his, so he was entitled to be serious from time to time, but not in the Café de Paris for God's sake. He could have read her thoughts.

'This isn't the place to analyse me,' he said, 'and it isn't the place for the works of Shakespeare either. Let's have another dance.'

The band played 'Stardust', which could have been the very tune he was waiting for, she thought. By the time he'd finished, the battle was over and he knew it, but still he smiled, signalled for champagne to be poured, lit her cigarette. I'm falling in love, she thought. Like the girl in *HMS Pinafore* I'm falling in love with a member of the lower classes, but unlike the girl in *HMS Pinafore* I don't give a damn.

Bob said, 'To your right. Take your time looking,' and she half turned to reach the ashtray. Crawley was there, with Lady Catherine Bower, and a woman in an unfortunate dress that had almost certainly made its début for somebody else. On the other hand the rubies she wore were large and almost certainly real. Stingy-rich, she thought, but since she looks as she does I can hardly blame her. Half a stone overweight and a disastrous coiffure, and so far Crawley hasn't even looked at her. Abruptly Crawley rose and took Catherine off to dance. The woman on her own began to eat ice cream.

'Poor thing,' Sybil Hendry said, and then: 'I think I'd like to leave soon.'

'South Molton Street?' said Bob.

'Why not Bruton Street, for a change?'

'What about your servants?'

'In bed and asleep if they've got any sense,' she said, 'and if they haven't we'll tuck them up.'

Out of the corner of her eye she saw Lady Catherine break away from Crawley and hurry towards the ladies' cloakroom. She rose.

'I'll just powder my nose first,' she said.

'None of your business,' said Bob. It seemed that he had seen Lady Catherine too.

'I know,' she said, 'but Crawley's ghastly. I won't be long. Promise.'

Catherine stared at herself in the mirror and thought, I can't go on being nice to him. I can't. And then: But if you leave Jay you must. Granny can't help you. Not this time. A woman in a silver lamé dress sat down at the dressing table next to hers. Silver lamé should appear vulgar, actressy, tarty even. But not on this woman. On her it looks simply elegant. Sybil Hendry.

'Hello,' she said.

'Hello, Catherine. This place is packed tonight. Whatever happened to the Depression?'

Catherine shrugged. 'It's still about,' she said. 'You're here with Bob?'

Sharp eyes, thought Sybil. But then you would have, for Bob.

'And you're with Mr Crawley?' she said.

'Well yes,' said Catherine, 'though Jay's supposed to be joining us for the last hour and a half.'

'I don't think much of your chaperon.'

Catherine smiled. 'What a lovely name for her. She's Crawley's sister – and just about as ghastly as he is.' Her hand went to her mouth. 'Sybil, please. Forget I said that.'

'Certainly. Though you're absolutely right. He is ghastly.'

'And rich?'

'Stinking.'

'Yes,' said Catherine. 'Everyone's agreed on that.'

It occurred to Sybil that Lady Catherine was not entirely sober.

'You find that interesting?'

'Yes,' said Catherine. 'At least – well – yes . . . Do you suppose Bob's rich too?'

'Decidedly,' said Sybil. 'And getting richer.'

'I'll give you a piece of advice,' said Catherine. 'Of course you don't want it, but I'll give it anyway. It's lovely with Bob. Gorgeous. But you have to be careful. You see with Bob it's tears *after* bedtime.'

Bob didn't mind being on his own. The Café de Paris was like one vast cabaret put on specially for him. Not Shakespeare by any means, but fascinating even so. Men with the wrong sort of girl, girls with the wrong sort of man – and at least three of them he wouldn't mind rescuing, if he wasn't waiting for Sybil. Then there was Crawley, charging off to have a word with the manager, the maître fluttering after him like a bewildered moth. Something to do with the wrong sort of champagne. Much too sweet, it seemed. That left the woman who looked like Crawley in a nightgown looking at her rubies, trying to work out if they'd gone up in value since she took them out of the safe, thought Bob.

162

'Been stood up?'

Bob turned back from the Crawley table to look at Jay Bower. Immaculate as ever, he thought, but a little weary. Sober too, but that mightn't last.

'She'll be back,' he said.

'She?' Bower looked about him, saw the lady with the rubies, and turned away.

'Sybil Hendry,' said Bob. 'She's in the Powder Room. Sit down and have a glass.' Bower sat, and Bob poured champagne. Bower gulped at it.

'Meetings,' he said. 'Meetings all day and half the night.'

'I know how you feel,' said Bob, and then: 'Your wife's in the Powder Room too.'

'And Crawley?'

'Gone off to put the manager on the rack. He got the wrong sort of champagne.'

'Yeah,' said Bower. 'Yeah. I wish to God –' He broke off, sipped at the champagne this time, then said: 'What do you think of Fascism?'

'I don't,' said Bob.

'One of these days you'll have to, and you won't enjoy it, I promise you.'

Crawley came back, teeth bared in a smile that spoke of nothing but rage.

'My genial host,' said Bower. 'Nice talking to you, Bob.' He went over to Crawley, then Catherine appeared, and Sybil, and it was time to go.

Overture and beginners, she thought, and very nice too. Never a frantic hurry, not with Bob, and she bent her body helpfully, moving it always nearer, making it more vulnerable because with Bob there was never a threat of pain: only delight. And then the knocking began: a steady tapping at first, swelling in volume to a pounding fist.

'Who on earth –' she said.

'Not Santa Claus,' said Bob. 'It's too early.' He reached out for his trousers. 'You want me to go?'

'No, me,' she said. 'Only stay close, will you. Apart from you I

163

don't know any raging sex maniacs, but one can't be too careful.'

She put on a nightgown and a negligée on top of that, and still looked – wanton, that was the word. Not ready to deliver, not with all that silk and lace on her, but the promise was there. He put on trousers and dress shirt and shoes – he had never felt less wanton in his life – and followed her down the corridor. She moved briskly to the drawing room and on to the hall, not showing a trace of fear because, Bob was sure, she felt none. A remarkable woman. As she opened the door it was booming like a bass drum.

'Why Daddy,' she said. 'What an extraordinary time of night to call. Are you ill?'

Bob retreated back to the corridor.

'Worried about you,' said her father. 'Passed by half an hour ago. Thought I saw you with some gigolo or other.'

There could be no doubt about it. The general was as tight as a tick, thought Bob. Not that I can object to being called a gigolo, because that's what I am, really, except I don't get paid for it.

'Oh him,' said Sybil. 'Sweet boy, wasn't he? Insisted on seeing me to my door. There aren't many like him these days.'

'Who is he?' said the general, and then, more pertinently, 'Where is he?'

'Nobody you know,' said his daughter. 'Nobody you'd want to know, come to that. If I'd known you were going to spy on me I'd have found someone much more exciting. As to where he is, I've no idea. Probably in his flat, in bed and asleep and I wish to God I were. Please go home, Daddy.'

'I've lost my key,' said the general. 'I'll have to sleep in the spare room.'

'No,' said his daughter. 'I told you. This is not your flat.'

'But I can't sleep in the street. I tell you I've lost my key.'

'No you haven't,' she said. 'And even if you had you're not staying here. Go to your club.'

'The club's a ghastly place to stay,' said her father, and then: 'Are you sure that gigolo left? I didn't see him leave.'

'How sweet you are,' said his daughter. 'Spying on me to count my lovers.'

'I'd like a drink,' said her father.

To Bob's surprise Sybil fetched the whisky decanter. The general poured himself about half a glassful, settled in an armchair, drained it as if it were water, said 'Goodnight, old girl,' and fell asleep.

Sybil stared at him for a moment, took the glass from his hand, then returned to where Bob waited in the corridor.

'Let's go back to bed,' she said.

'What, now?' For once she had shocked him.

'He does this perhaps twice a year. Gets really tight, I mean, and it always takes him the same way. I doubt if even cavalry could wake him.'

The general snored. It seemed as though his daughter were telling the truth, and so they went back to bed.

Eminently satisfactory, she thought, as it always was with Bob, though from time to time she'd found him just a shade preoccupied. Really, Daddy could be a most dreadful nuisance. Lost his key indeed. If he persisted with that story tomorrow she'd send him home with a locksmith. In the meantime she yawned, and watched Bob dress.

'See you tomorrow?' she asked.

'Not tomorrow,' said Bob. 'I have to go to Birmingham.'

'Good God. Why?'

'There's some chap there with some shops to sell.'

'Don't you ever stop making money?'

'I will when I've got enough.'

'And when will that be?'

'Not for years,' said Bob. 'You can't beat it for excitement.'

'What about me?'

'You're not for excitement,' he said, then used one of what she thought of as his printer's words. 'You're for delight.'

He kissed her then, and left her. I bet there's a girl in Birmingham getting her beauty sleep even now, she thought, and snuggled down among the pillows.

Sybil had left one light burning in the drawing room and Bob tiptoed warily, the general's snores like gun-fire. Suddenly the bombardment ceased, and Bob looked to where the general stared at him, round-eyed. Bob put a finger to his lips and tiptoed on.

'Sorry,' said the general, and the gun-fire began once more.

. 19 .

They had left Acapulco and gone on to Mexico City. Just as well, really. Charles would have loathed Acapulco. He didn't really care that much for the South of France. But Mexico City was different, at least the part where they stayed was. Bustling and fashionable, and by Mexican standards expensive, but with a sense of foreignness that no European city could match. There was the sunshine of course, and the altitude that made one move warily for the first two or three days, and there were the Indian faces of so many of the servants, the cathedral, the Virgin of Guadalupe, that looked like no other cathedral she had ever seen, and the worshippers who moved towards it on their knees; there were the mariachi bands too, that one could hire by the hour or the day, or presumably the year: white trousers, glittering waistcoats, sombreros and guitars, and voices treacle sweet. Even the beggars in their part of the city looked picturesque, as if they had been chosen by Central Casting.

In other parts of the town they looked like beggars. She had hired a car – an elderly but still game Cadillac – and she and Georgie had driven around to see for themselves. They soon gave up. It would have taken a Dr Stobbs or a Canon Messeter to persist in looking at what they saw: tattered whores, diseased children, beggars at every corner: shanty town after shanty town, their only sewage disposal an open drain. It was far worse than Spain. Only India could match it.

'No wonder they have revolutions,' she said.

'I told you,' said Georgie.

'So you did,' said Jane, 'but if you knew it was so ghastly why on earth did you come with me?'

'If I'd let you loose on your own you'd have been looking around for an ambulance to drive.'

'Not here,' said Jane. 'God forgive me. To do that sort of thing here one would need to be a saint.'

'Let's go back to the hotel and drink martinis instead,' said Georgie.

Their suite at the Presidente was dark and cool, with a swirling fan on the ceiling that reminded her of punkahs in Indian bungalows. It had a balcony that looked on a garden ablaze with flowers, where the cool sound of fountains was a sort of continuo to the birdsong. Light years away from the nearest shanty town, or twenty minutes in the Cadillac.

Georgie said, 'Drinking martinis isn't nearly so much fun here.'

'They taste all right to me,' said Jane.

'They taste fine. It isn't that. The point is that here one's allowed to drink martinis – drink anything in sight, come to that. Where's the thrill of defying the law? All one does is get mildly sloshed.'

'Fat chance you ever had of being arrested,' said Jane.

'Now that's where you're wrong,' Georgie said. 'I was gathered in once in a joint near San Diego. Some man or other I was with thought it might be fun to go slumming, I can't think why. It was ghastly. Anyway some simply enormous policemen arrived, all guns and nightsticks, and swept me off to durance vile. Then one of them said I looked like Georgina Payne and I said I was Georgina Payne, so of course they had to let me go.'

'Had to?'

'They were California State Police, so of course World Wide was bribing them – to take care of little problems like mine.'

'Do all the studios bribe the police?'

'Well of course,' said Georgie. 'Some of the cops make absolute fortunes. Murray Fisch was furious.'

'One of the police might have refused a bribe, you mean?'

'I suppose it's possible,' Georgie said doubtfully. 'But it wasn't that. His big worry was that a reporter might have seen us, and that would have cost even more money. And the other niggle was he had to pay the cops a bonus, just to be on the safe side. Murray Fisch hates parting with money.'

'But it wasn't his money, was it?'

'Doesn't matter,' Georgie said. 'He just hates to see it go. Anyway he sometimes gets the idea the studio really does belong to him – or it should. Delusions of grandeur.' She filled their glasses from the pitcher. 'Did I tell you he's coming to Mexico City?'

'No,' said Jane.

'Some big distribution deal. Buying up theatres.'

'When's he coming?'

'About the time your nice chap gets back. After all Charles really does own World Wide. Or quite a lot of it anyway. Should be fun.'

'Georgie, what are you up to?' said Jane.

'I – ' Georgie hesitated. 'No,' she said at last. 'I think I'll keep this as a surprise. But I'll tell you this. Wherever Dan is, he'll be laughing. Murray hates queers, but he smarmed all over Dan, because Dan was money. Murray Fisch would smarm all over a goat if it was money.'

Charles flew from New York to Los Angeles, spent the night there – more meetings, no doubt – then flew on next day to Mexico City. He looked tired, as if there had been far too many meetings, but fit and well. He hadn't offered Murray Fisch a lift, no matter how many theatres Mexico had for sale. He's far too pleased with life to be shut up in a plane with his Head of Studio, thought Jane, and I must say I don't blame him.

'Nice flight?' she asked him.

'Hardly a bump,' said Charles.

She thought of the flight to Acapulco; beneath them nothing but desert: earth hard baked in brown and red, flecked here and there with cactus. To her amazement it had seemed beautiful.

'What did you think of the view?' she asked.

'Didn't have time to notice. I had papers to go through.'

She laughed, and kissed him.

After that it was holiday: trips to the Saturday Market, and Oaxaca where they made things in silver and turquoise, and Georgie and she bought rather a lot, and a day and night at the ranch of a very rich Mexican, a ranch about the size of an English village; but she drew the line at the bullfight, though Georgie went. It had been a good one, she said, and packed out. Like Jane she marvelled that there could be even five thousand Mexicans who could afford the price of a bullfight ticket.

It was while they waited, lazy and relaxed under the ceiling fan, for Georgie to come back from the Corrida, that Charles told her that Murray Fisch had arrived.

'Not that he'll bother you,' Charles said. 'He's harmless.'

'*Harmless?*'

'He is while I'm here,' said Charles. 'He likes his job.

'I adore masterful men,' she said.

He squeezed her waist. 'Thank you,' he said, 'but what I meant was we'll be at rather a lot of meetings over the next couple of days before I boot him back to Hollywood.'

'Masterful isn't the word.'

Another squeeze, a little harder, but not nearly hard enough to hurt. Darling Charles.

'It means leaving you and Georgie on your own till Friday,' he said. 'I hope you don't mind.'

'Georgie's never on her own unless she wants to be,' said Jane. 'Even I get offers, in my demure way. I can't think what comes over the men here. It must be the heat.'

'Demure be damned,' said Charles. 'All the same, that reminds me. World Wide's giving a cocktail party on Thursday night. I suppose I should go – '

'Well of course you should,' said Jane. 'You're a major share-holder.'

'The thing is the president's giving a dinner that night,' said Charles. 'I do wish I could take you.'

'No irregular attachments?'

'None. And it's bound to be frightfully pompous. – But would you mind awfully if you went to the cocktail party with Georgie?'

'Not at all,' said Jane. 'But it's far too late for me to be her chaperon. Or anyone else, for that matter.'

'I should think it is,' said Charles. 'And anyway it's equally late for her to chaperon you.' He considered what he had said, then added: 'That was clumsy and inept, as you'd be the first to tell me, but it was meant as a compliment.'

'And taken as such.'

Another squeeze, the best one of all.

'There's a bribe,' said Charles. 'To get you to the party, I mean. Rather an odd sort of bribe.'

'Do tell.'

'First you have to give me ten thousand pounds.'

'I don't call that much of a bribe,' said Jane. 'Unless – ' she turned on the bed to face him. 'You haven't lost all your money, have you?'

He laughed aloud. 'Oh I do love you,' he said. 'Of course I haven't lost all my money.'

'Then why come rattling your begging bowl at me?'

'It's about New York.'

'I thought perhaps it might be.'

'When we were first there I heard talk, but that's all it was. Talk. Wishful thinking, you might say. But I put some people on it, just in case.'

'What sort of people?'

'Not the sort you'd invite to dinner. Nosy people. Sly. Under-hand. Good at finding out secrets. *Damn* good, one of them. I took what they gave me and put it all together with what I already knew, and then a chap called Roosevelt made a speech – '

'The one who's going to be President?'

'That's the one. The reaction was quite extraordinary. People were happy. It was like the first warm day of spring. No reason for it. No reason in logic, I mean, and yet it was there. So I went back to my Nosy Parker's reports. . . . I'm sure I'm right. I have to be. God help me if I'm not.'

'You mean you really will lose your money?'

'Not all of it. Not by any means. But a fair slice, except that I'm right. I'm sure I am.'

'Charles, darling,' said Jane, 'please tell me what you're right about, and why I have to give you ten thousand pounds.'

'I'm right about the Depression,' said Charles. 'There's going to be an upturn.'

'*What?*'

'Quiet please,' said Charles. 'This is the most tremendous secret.'

The nearest human being was a gardener, and he spoke only Spanish, but she waited meekly.

'It'll be slow,' said Charles, 'unless something else happens, but I won't go into that now. But the point is we've reached the bottom. The market's ready to go up again. Not like the Twenties. That madness is over. All the same the market's about to climb again.

A dollar now will get you two next year. – Maybe three the year after.'

'And that's why you want my ten thousand pounds?'

'That's why.'

'Mr Medlicott said I wasn't to risk the stock market,' said Jane. 'So did Mr Rubens.' Her face took on the stubborn look he knew and dreaded. Medlicott and Rubens were her lawyers, and her last-ditch defence.

'You could spend that much on a new necklace and a bad night in Monte Carlo.' He kissed her shoulder. 'Idiot,' he said lovingly. 'This wouldn't be for you. I'm suggesting you do it for Felston.'

'Do what?'

'Give me the money,' he said. 'You can't just walk in on a broker, and plonk it down. We'll have to do it carefully, very carefully, if it's going to work.'

'What would you buy?' she asked.

'Industrials,' said Charles. 'Dupont, General Motors, United States Steel.'

'You really believe this will happen,' she said.

'I know it,' said Charles, 'and the beauty of it is you don't lose a penny. When you sell you take back your ten thousand, and Felston gets the rest.'

She turned to look at him. Robber baron, employer of spies and Protector of the Poor, all in one well-preserved, still elegant body.

'We're going to make love,' she said. 'We're going to make love as if tomorrow will be Judgement Day, and this time *you're* going to yell.'

Murray Fisch took over the party. It was, after all, a World Wide party, and he was Head of World Wide Studios, and so he took control. There wasn't on the face of it a great deal that he could do: food, drinks and music had all been arranged, and so Murray Fisch doubled or trebled every order. Three mariachi bands, so that they could look more like an orchestra, and a guitar, bass and drums as well as a jazz pianist: a piano on its own looked sort of cheap, he thought. More canapés too, and more, much more champagne, for obsessed as he was with saving World Wide's money he was even more obsessed with its image. World Wide

171

must never, never look cheap, and besides any unopened bottles could be sent back. Not that there would be many, he thought bitterly: not with a movie crowd. There would be politicians too, the ones who didn't get to go to the President's dinner, and politicians were all good drinkers. That left the rich guys and their wives. The wives couldn't take much, not in public, but the rich guys always drank a lot for free: that was how they stayed rich.

At least they'd enjoy themselves, the rich guys and the politicians. He'd brought in some broads, too: nobody in Georgie's class, but actresses every one. No hookers. They'd look good, too. They had to, that was why he'd brought them. Seemed like a lot of fuss for a dump like Mexico, but obviously Lovell didn't think so, and Lovell could smell money the way a bloodhound smells escaping convicts, so the party had to be a smash. . . .

Nice to know Lovell wouldn't be there, though. That would make *him* top man from World Wide: the host, greeting, gladhanding. Something really to enjoy: dispensing thousands of dollars worth of shareholders' booze. Cigars, he thought. Something really special for the ones with money. He made a note, then began to scribble another one to Georgie, telling her to wear something really nice, then tore it up. Everything Georgie owned was really nice, and if he started telling her what to wear she'd turn up in a sack. Best leave her alone. She knew how to look good, and so did the Whitcomb broad. A real class act, the two of them. The Whitcomb broad he wouldn't go near, except to see she was taken care of. From what he could see she belonged to Lovell, and even if she didn't, they were friends. Anyone could see that. Stay clear, he thought. After all he could have his pick of the supporting cast. He scurried off to harass an overworked kitchen staff.

'They go in for toasts,' said Charles.

'And speeches?'

'To start with. The President of the United States. The President of Mexico. His Majesty the King I suppose, since I'm there. But after that it's just toasts, and a staggering amount of brandy. Don't be surprised if you get a message that says come at once and bring your ambulance.'

She turned from the mirror to face him. He wears his evening dress really well, she thought: almost in Lionel's class, and really

172

it is rather cosy having him here while I dress. Like an old married couple ... Not now, Jane dear, she thought. Leave that for now. Just be thankful he's still got that look in his eye because you're wearing only knickers and bra.

'Medals too,' she said. 'Men do love dressing up to get tight.'

He stood up. 'Got to leave you I'm afraid.' He went to her and bent to kiss her shoulder, then her mouth. 'Be nice to the Second Eleven, won't you?'

'Second Eleven?'

'The ones who didn't get asked to the President's banquet.'

'Do my best,' she said. 'All right if I co-opt Georgie?'

'Marvellous idea.'

'She says she's planning some kind of a surprise tonight.'

'Does it involve Murray Fisch?' She nodded. 'I wonder if it's what I think it is. – Have a nice party.'

Then he was gone. Really he could be annoyingly cryptic sometimes.

A Fortuny dress because it was her oldest favourite. It was what the great man called a Delphos, a long, pleated dress of silk that hung from the shoulders to the ground like the chiton of the bronze charioteer statue at Delphi, each pleat kept in place by a bead of Venetian glass at its base. Its colour was an almost unbelievable pink, pale yet strong, and it clung to the figure in a way that made her glad she could still get into it, with rather a lot of help from the chambermaid: the perfect setting for her emeralds. Velvet shoes and a Fortuny mantle stencilled in gold and silver, and she was ready. The mantle really is necessary, she thought. It could be cold in the garden later on, but furs in Mexico seemed ridiculous.

She went to pick up Georgie, a Schiaparelli snow queen in blue and white, diamonds at her neck and wrist. Even by Georgie's standards she had gone to great pains to look her best. All part of the surprise no doubt, thought Jane, but took care not to say it aloud. Georgie could be quite as cryptic as Charles.

'Darling, you look gorgeous,' Georgie said.

'Hark who's talking,' said Jane.

Georgie grinned. 'Not bad, are we?' she said. 'It's indecent to look like us when we consider how much fun we have.'

173

The party was being given in the hotel's ballroom, and was clearly audible as they stepped out of the lift: mariachis in full flight, conversation, clinking glasses, champagne corks that popped so loudly and so often that Jane thought of grouse moors. Yet when they arrived at the doors to the ballroom there was a silence. The mariachis still played, but for a little while the voices ceased to shrill, the champagne corks ceased fire. That of course is Georgie, thought Jane. That woman could stop the stars in their courses, not least because she's one of the them. On the other hand I'm a blonde too, and gowned and bejewelled appropriately, and if I'm not the one they stare at, at least I'm at her side.

Georgie looked about her. The ballroom had flowers everywhere: roses, carnations, hibiscus, azaleas: and very nice too, thought Jane. But Murray Fisch was not the man to stop at flowers. On the walls, where there weren't flowers, serapes hung. Above each refreshment table hung a sombrero six feet in diameter. This, the ballroom bellowed, is Mexico, but in fact it wasn't. It was Hollywood.

Georgie spotted it at once. 'Dear God,' she said, 'it's the front lot at World Wide.' Hers was an actress's voice, clear and carrying. Too bad that Murray Fisch should be scampering up to them as she said it, but he never faltered.

'Georgie, Jane,' he said. 'It's great to see you.'

'Murray,' said Georgie. 'So glad you could come.'

Please God, thought Jane, let the surprise come soon, before I start longing for a fireside and a mug of cocoa.

But Murray took even that in his stride, or perhaps didn't even hear. Mercifully the uproar had resumed.

'Come in, come in,' he said. Maids appeared and took their wraps, and Murray Fisch eyed them critically. Nothing salacious, Jane noted. Just a quick glance to assess the value of their jewellery. Apparently it was adequate.

'This way,' he said, and conducted them to the big centre table reserved for the really important: snowy cloths, the flags of the United States and Mexico intertwined, and as a centre piece a waterfall of champagne, or at least sparkling wine, and on either side of it a sort of iceberg, pitted with little caves, and in each cave a tin of caviar.

'Murray baby,' said Georgie, 'you've certainly surpassed yourself this time.'

'Why thank you,' said Fisch, and signalled to a waiter for champagne, but out of a bottle rather than a waterfall. Pol Roger, Jane noticed. There was a lot to be said for being the boss's moll.

'I'll get a waiter to bring you caviar,' said Fisch.

'Oh please don't bother,' said Georgie. 'They've got far too much to do as it is.' She found a spoon, and Melba toast, and dug deep into the nearest tin, passed the result to Jane, and went back to dig again. Murray Fisch winced. What those two women were eating would have paid a waiter for weeks.

'I adore caviar,' Georgie said, and then playfully, reproachfully, 'but aren't you going to introduce us to people, Murray? We're not here to enjoy ourselves. We're flying the flag for World Wide.' She turned back to the caviar, and Murray Fisch sped off to find them partners.

'Bitch,' said Jane.

'I know,' said Georgie. 'Isn't it fun?'

In fact it *was* fun. There were lots of men to dance with, including several who looked like Ramon Navarro and one who looked even better. The food was good too, and the champagne unending. What with that and the décor it was rather like having a bit part in a World Wide film.

She and Georgie met again at the champagne waterfall, and Georgie went to the caviar with a spoon the size of a child's seaside spade.

'Have you been asked to look at the moon yet?'

Georgie, her mouth full, nodded and swallowed. 'You too?'

'Mm.' Jane too was eating caviar.

'Now I think they're drawing lots for it,' said Georgie, 'and a fat lot of good it'll do them. I'm not the first prize in a raffle.' She brooded darkly. 'I'll tell you something else,' she said. 'There isn't a moon tonight.' She looked at the miniature icebergs. 'And not a hell of a lot of caviar left either.'

Murray Fisch came over to them, eyes averted from Georgie's spoon. 'You ladies having fun?' he asked.

'Oh it's great,' Georgie said, 'but you know something, Murray? I think it will get even better.'

175

Here it comes, thought Jane.

'Terrific,' said Murray. 'Oh before I forget – I'd like to set up a meeting with you tomorrow.'

'Why Murray,' Georgie said. 'Now you just stop that.'

'No no,' said Murray. 'I have some papers for you to sign.'

'What papers?'

'Well you know we start shooting your new movie next week,' Murray Fisch said. 'Best part for you yet.' He looked into blue eyes as cold as the ice that chills caviar.

'Apart from the one Jane wrote for you.' At once the blue eyes melted.

'But I don't have to sign papers for that,' Georgie said.

'Well no,' said Murray. 'But your contract's up for renewal. You can't make a movie without a contract.'

'Oh the contract,' said Georgie. She signalled to a waiter for more champagne, and considerately saw that Murray got one too. Or maybe it's medicinal, thought Jane.

'I've been thinking about the contract, Murray,' she said, 'and if it's all the same to you, I don't think I'll sign it.'

He was a cunning and devious man, but at first her words made no sense. 'But you've got to sign it,' he said.

'Why, Murray?'

He sighed. The bitch was drunk – there could be no other explanation – but she was also Georgina Payne. He had to be *nice.*

He said patiently, 'Because sweetie, if you don't sign the contract you can't make the picture.'

'I don't want to make the picture,' Georgie said.

'*What?*' His voice was louder, but still under control.

'I don't want to make the picture.'

'Why not, for Chrissake? What's wrong with it? It's a great picture.'

'No,' Georgie said. 'It's not. It's a perfectly adequate script and the director's never less than competent. Never more, either. I might help it along a bit, if I did it. But I'm not going to do it. Don't drop by with any more contracts, sweetie. I'm going to sleep late tomorrow. I've retired.'

It was then that Murray Fisch screamed, and a virtuoso performance it was too. Even gunfire couldn't have silenced the party more quickly. Jane had heard him scream before, of course, from another room in Cap d'Antibes, over the telephone in Madrid, but in the flesh it was even more satisfying. More resonance, and much, much more volume. From the look on Georgie's face she found it even better than caviar. His colour was interesting too, thought Jane: a rather dirty crimson splotched here and there with plum.

Then, quite suddenly, the scream stopped, as if someone had switched off a wireless set, and at the same time the colour changed, first to white, and then to a shade that was almost green as he stared at the ballroom's doors. Within them, surrounded by attendants, Charles Lovell at his side, stood the President of Mexico. At once the musicians played the Mexican national anthem, and when it was done, Charles led the President across the room to Georgie and Jane. Murray Fisch, Jane noticed, had contrived to disappear during the anthem, no doubt through a gap in the floorboards.

Charles said, 'Your Excellency, may I present Miss Georgina Payne?' and Georgina curtsied. The President looked at once astonished and gratified.

'May I also present Miss Jane Whitcomb?' said Charles, and Jane too curtsied, a feat she hadn't attempted since her come-out. Somehow she contrived to regain the vertical without disaster.

'Charming, charming,' said the President, and took Georgie off to dance.

'It was what he'd come for,' Charles explained.

'That and the caviar,' said Jane. 'He's rather a greedy president.'

'Not nearly so greedy as some of his staff,' Charles said.

That was obviously another topic, but one that Charles would deal with in his own good time.

. 20 .

They were sitting in her drawing room in their dressing gowns, drinking coffee, which was a good idea after all that champagne.

'What made him come to the party?' she asked.

'I happened to mention after dinner that Georgie would be there,' said Charles. 'He cut the speeches, got through the business in fifteen minutes flat, and left the rest of the gang to get on with the toasts without him.'

'Georgie can still pull them,' said Jane.

'Yes, thank God. He adored dancing with her.'

'What on earth did he make of Murray Fisch?' asked Jane.

'Now that *is* interesting,' said Charles. 'He took it in his stride so to speak.'

'But he can't have done.'

'But he did. Let me explain. What did that ballroom remind you of?'

'Hollywood, of course.'

'Exactly. And Georgie was Hollywood and all those pretty actresses were Hollywood. And even you were Hollywood as far as he was concerned. Well Murray was Hollywood too, and so the President *expected* him to act like that. And remember he's a Mexican, and he has enormous power. For all we know he may scream a bit himself.'

'Oh how gorgeous,' said Jane. 'I'm so glad we curtsied to him.'

'What on earth made you do it?'

'Georgie said she thought it might help to relieve the tension,' said Jane. 'And it did.'

'It was the most Hollywood thing of the lot,' said Charles. 'He loved it.'

'Have you spoken to Murray?'

178

'He was waiting outside my door when I came up.'

'Did you put him out of his misery?'

'Certainly not,' said Charles. 'He's still got a lot of misery to come. What he did was disgraceful. Suppose the President hadn't appeared – what would the other guests have made of it? Or suppose he had appeared and decided he'd been insulted? Mr Fisch has worked damn hard for his misery. It's only fair he should get it.' He frowned at her. 'So don't you start feeling sorry for him.'

'I don't think I could,' said Jane. 'Not for Murray Fisch.'

'Just as well. Why on earth does he do it?'

'I think he enjoys it,' said Jane. 'Well – not enjoys, exactly, but it does relieve his tension. And then there's the fact that he *can* do it. I mean when you or the other owners aren't around, he's the big boss. What the comedians call the top banana. The star.'

'But tonight?'

'You said yourself the place was pure Hollywood. I think for the moment he forgot he was playing away, so to speak. And then there's Georgie.'

'What about her?'

'Georgie doesn't like him.'

'Georgie detests him,' said Charles.

That's my nice chap, she thought. Always does his homework. Even in Mexico.

'One of the ways she shows it is by making him scream,' said Jane. 'She's awfully good at it.'

'Obviously.'

'Though I don't think she expected him to do it tonight. You see he behaves as if he owns her. She works for World Wide, and he runs World Wide, and so – l'état cest moi.'

'Fool,' said Charles. 'Nobody owns Georgie. Nobody could.'

'Then there was some kind of sex thing at one point. On his part, at any rate. Georgie sent him packing. And so – this is all confidential, Charles.'

'Of course.'

'And so he dreamed up her marriage to Dan Corless. To punish her. Only she rather liked Dan Corless. They were happy together. They went their own ways sexually, of course, but they were content. Murray Fisch hated that. Also he hates queers.'

179

'Then he's in the wrong business,' said Charles.

My nice chap's really done his homework, she thought, then said aloud: 'Not because of what they get up to, and if they didn't work for World Wide he couldn't care less about them, but the ones who do work for World Wide might get caught and sent for trial you see, and that would be bad for the studio.'

'And until Georgie came along Dan Corless was the biggest name we owned.'

'Exactly.'

'Well well,' said Charles. 'What a nasty little mess he is, to be sure. I doubt if even Jabber Lockhart could straighten him out. You know what she said to make him scream?'

'I was there, remember?' said Jane. 'It was not signing the contract. She's resigning.'

He nodded, which surprised her. Somehow she'd expected something more dramatic. His biggest star, after all.

'Doesn't it bother you?' she said.

'I could wish for another year,' he said. 'But if she doesn't want to – what would be the point?'

'You could try more money,' she said. 'And why just one more year?'

'She isn't worth more money,' said Charles. 'She's got maybe three more good pictures in her, – a year's work, give or take.'

'Who told you this?' said Jane.

'Her fans,' said Lovell. 'Their letters aren't as many as they used to be – and when they're analysed – ' he shrugged. 'Three more pictures. But it's better for her to – what's that expression they use?'

'Quit while she's ahead?'

'Exactly,' said Charles.

For a moment her nice chap didn't seem quite so nice, and then he said: 'I think she knows it.'

'That she's slipping?'

'Mm.' Charles nodded. 'She's a realist, you know. And she's rich. No reason why she shouldn't get out now.'

'But who would take her place?'

'From what I hear,' Charles said, 'nobody. By that I don't mean she's irreplaceable – though of course she is. From what I'm told she's also the last of her line.'

'You have something else instead?' Jane asked.

'We're all going to be cheerful,' said Charles. 'And so we have new songs, modern songs, and new, pretty people to sing them in bright and cheerful surroundings. It was tactful of Georgie to retire now. Clever too.'

'You mean she also knew she was losing her appeal?'

'That's my guess.'

'You're a hard pair, aren't you?' said Jane. 'I'd better be careful – an old softy like me between the pair of you.'

'You'd always be safe,' said Charles, 'and you know it.'

'Nice of you to say so,' she said, 'and I know you mean it. All the same – '

'Yes?'

'You feel a fool being vulnerable,' she said, 'especially when you thought you weren't.'

'Not you,' he said. 'Believe me, never you. So long as it's within my power.'

'I do believe you,' she said, 'but – '

'But what?'

'Damned if I know,' said Jane. 'Shall we go to bed?' And then, 'To sleep?'

'Nothing I'd like better,' said Charles.

It was a queer business, Norah being the way she was. So near and yet so far. All that. He knew if he'd made a fuss about it she'd do it – might even be glad to do it – but it might be the worst thing possible for her. Like a policeman's, he thought: A woman's lot is not a happy one. But that was ridiculous. Norah was so happy she glowed, and maybe he did too. He could hold her; they could still do things to each other. They were happy.

And then Bob appeared. Out of the blue, you might say: on the doorstep, the big Yankee car behind him blocking off half the street.

'How are you, kidder?' said Bob.

'Canny.' Andy's voice was cautious: with Bob it never paid to be too enthusiastic; so often there was a catch.

'All right if I come in?'

'Of course,' Andy said.

Bob hefted the bag he carried. 'After you then,' he said.

Andy looked at the bag. 'That's not for us, is it?' he said. 'We can manage.'

'Oh get on with it,' said Bob. 'A party, that's all this is. We could all do with a party.'

After Bob had kissed Norah he felt better, and that was a funny thing. Bob kissed his wife and he felt better. To begin with chaps in Felston didn't kiss other chaps' wives, but Bob had walked straight up to Norah and kissed her on both cheeks, and all Norah had done was smile, as if Bob were her favourite nephew, and all Bob did was smile back as if she were his favourite aunt.

'What brings you here?' she said.

'Business,' said Bob. 'And my favourite sister-in-law.'

'I'm the only one you've got,' Norah said.

'I'm lucky, then. Sorry to hear about your trouble.'

'What trouble?' said Norah. She grinned at him, teasing. Andy watched it and thought, There's hardly a woman alive who wouldn't tease Bob. But Norah was his.

'Your time in hospital,' said Bob. 'I never did hear the details.'

'Miscarriage,' Norah said. 'But I'm fine now.'

'Course you are,' said Bob. 'Just need building up a bit, that's all.' He opened his bag. Tins, packets, jars cascaded on to the table, and then the bottles appeared. Port, for the most part. Not vintage, his wine merchant had said. Vintage would go off far too quickly, and in any case women liked something even sweeter. A fine ruby, perhaps. So a fine ruby it was. Bob tapped the tins and bottles one by one. 'Beef tea, chicken soup, lobster, asparagus,' he said. 'And I don't want any fuss about the asparagus. It's no worse than cabbage, and from what the doctor said it's good for the blood an' all.' He looked at the bottles. 'Port, this is. A glass every night before bedtime – and pull all the faces you like because it's medicine. And I mean that. It *is* medicine. So just you drink it.'

Norah said, 'I don't know what to say. You're far too kind.'

'No,' said Bob. 'I'll never be that. But you're family now, pet, and the Pattersons always take care of their own. Right, Andy?'

And there was Bob for you, Andy thought. Clever as a box of monkeys. How could he ever say no when Norah was family?

'That's right,' he said. There was a knock at the front door below.

'I'll answer it,' said Bob. 'It'll be the lad from number thirty-eight. I sent him off to get fish and chips three times. Save you the bother of cooking, Norah.'

He's right there, thought Andy. Norah could never have sent Bob away without a meal. Crafty bugger. But all the same he smiled.

Bob came back, his hands wincing at the heat of their supper, wrapped in the sports pages of the *Felston Echo*.

'Let's have some plates, then,' he said, 'and three glasses an' all.'

'Glasses?' Andy said.

'Well of course glasses,' said Bob. 'We're going to have this lot with champagne – see how the other half lives. Though the way things are these days it's more like the other ten per cent.'

He'd got ice from the Eldon Arms so the champagne was chilled, the cork came out discreetly. Norah gasped as Bob poured and the wine foamed into the glasses.

'Just like the pictures, she said, 'Who'd ever believe it?'

Bob passed her a glass, then one to Andy. 'Enjoy it,' he said. 'That's what it's for.' He raised his own glass. 'Your very good health, Mrs Patterson,' he said and drank. He'd bought a demi-sec, far too sweet for his taste, but Norah and Andy weren't ready for a brut yet, and probably never would be. But they enjoyed what he'd given them, which didn't surprise him. It was Mumm after all.

'We had a card from Jane,' Norah said.

'Oh aye?' said Bob. 'Where from?'

'New York,' said Andy. He went to the mantelshelf and passed the card to Bob. Picture of the Statue of Liberty they all made such a fuss about, though he could never understand why. Face that could stop clocks; even Big Ben, the size she was.

'Read it if you want to,' said Andy. Bob read it.

'Things is going to get better, she reckons,' said Bob, 'on account of this Roosevelt.'

'Their next President,' said Andy.

'That's all very well,' Norah said. 'But will things get better round here?'

'If they do in the States,' Andy said.

'You mean things only go right for us after they've gone right

183

for the Yanks?'

'The way things are in the world just now – yes, I do,' Andy said.

'It doesn't seem right,' said Norah.

'It's not right,' said Andy. 'But it'll be made right one of these days.'

'By your friend Joe Stalin no doubt,' said Bob, then wished he'd kept his mouth shut. The one sure way to start a fight with Andy was to make game of the Reds. But he hadn't allowed for the effects of marriage.

Andy said mildly, 'Now that's where you're wrong, our Bob. The Russians have their own way, and we have ours. Same destination you might say, but a different road entirely.' Bob willed his jaw not to drop.

Then Norah went to bed.

'On the mend, is she?' Bob asked.

'I think so,' Andy said. 'But it's taking its time.'

'Make sure she takes the stuff I brought,' said Bob. 'I asked a doctor what to get. One that knows his stuff.'

'I'll see she does,' said Andy. 'Though she'll want to give me half of it. Not that I'll take it.'

'The trials of married life,' said Bob.

'Fat lot you know about married life,' said Andy. 'I don't suppose you ever will. But it suits me.'

'It does an' all,' said Bob. 'You look years younger. And you've put a bit of weight on.'

'Aye, I'm flourishing,' said Andy. 'Even if she's not.'

'She'll get better, man,' said Bob. 'Just give it time.'

'I'd give her the sun and moon if I could reach them,' said Andy, and again Bob marvelled.

'Can we talk?' Andy said.

'We are talking.'

'I mean – personal things,' said Andy. 'Private.'

'If you want to,' said Bob. 'It'll go no further. You know that.'

'I never could talk about personal things before,' said Andy.

'Maybe that's because you were never married before.'

'Never in love,' said Andy. 'Never had a woman.'

'Andy, man – ' said Bob and thought, I didn't think he'd tell me that.

184

'No, listen,' Andy said. 'Never had a woman. Never had a man, either. But a man had me.'

'*What?*'

'Not so loud,' said Andy. 'Norah'll hear you.'

Bob thought: It can't be the champagne. He's only had two glasses.

'In gaol it was,' Andy said. 'Two chaps held me down while the third one had me. They took turns.'

'They did that to *you?*'

'Aye. Mind you it took three of them. But they had me in the end, so to speak.'

Dear God, thought Bob. He can even joke about it.

'But you're not like that,' he said. 'Couldn't they see you weren't like that?'

'Well of course they could,' said Andy. 'I wasn't a nance they could buy for tobacco. That wasn't what they were after.'

'What were they after then?' Bob asked.

'Rape,' said Andy. 'They fancied a bit of rape.'

'And wouldn't anybody help you?'

'Help me?' said Andy. 'Me? I was a bloody conchie, man. The lowest of the low. A few watched, I think. But nobody helped. Just left me to get on with it. Afterwards.' He hesitated. 'Do you mind me telling you all this?'

'You're my brother,' said Bob. 'Of course I don't mind.'

'It finished me,' said Andy. 'At least I thought it had. Sex. All that. I thought I'd never feel like that again. Not need it, even. Manage without.' He grinned at Bob, and suddenly he looked very like John. 'But I found out I was wrong, thank God,' Andy said.

'Happy ending,' said Bob.

'Aye,' Andy said. 'Happy ending. Except – '

'The miscarriage?' Andy nodded. 'You wouldn't touch her before she's better,' said Bob, 'any more than I would, but after – she doesn't have to get pregnant, man, not these days.'

'French letters, you mean?'

'Mebbe. There's other ways an' all.'

'She wants a bairn,' said Andy. 'So do I, come to that.' The smile came again, then vanished. 'But from what Stobbs said she might never have one. She could be ill every time.'

185

'Look kidder,' said Bob. 'Stobbs is a good doctor, we all know that. But he's not a what d'you call it? – you know. Sort of a specialist.'

'Gynaecologist,' said Andy.

'The very chap. Take her to one. It's what she needs.'

'She could mebbe do with a week in the Bahamas as well.'

'She can have both if you want them.'

'You're saying you'd pay?'

'Well of course,' said Bob. 'It's only money – and you're the only brother I've got.'

'It would cost pounds,' Andy said.

'I've got pounds. Look – it's dead easy. Have you had your holidays yet?'

'They're due in a couple of weeks,' said Andy.

'Come and stay with us in London. Nobody'll get too excited about that. She can pop in and see some chap in Harley Street when you're down. Nobody need be any the wiser. What d'you say?'

He looked at his brother on the other side of the fireplace: still worried, still troubled, because what he was being offered was a favour, not a right.

'I didn't tell you for that,' Andy said at last.

'Course you didn't,' Bob said, 'but it's the least I can do. Me own brother . . . What d'you say?'

'Thanks kidder,' Andy said at last. 'If I can talk her round, we'll do it. Thanks.'

To himself he was thinking, And maybe I did tell you for that.

. 21 .

There was a ball in Hexham: a grand one. A Hunt Ball in fact. He'd never been to one before. Interesting that would be, and Sybil had asked him to take her. And why not? He'd done all the business he'd come up for, and Norah had said she'd come with Andy to London and look in at Harley Street – and wouldn't his doctor's eyebrows go up when he asked him to recommend a good gynaecologist – so why not a little fun in the meantime? It would get a bit boisterous towards the end, so Sybil reckoned. Champagne bottles squirting like fire extinguishers. Still he could afford to have his dress suit cleaned. He picked her up at her flat in Gosforth. Green and silver this time: dress, handbag, evening coat, shoes: all green and silver. He looked at her, taking his time.

'Will I do?' she asked.

'Don't rush me,' he said. 'It's coming.' Hair so black on top of that silver and green, and face so white. Put it all together.

'Like another Shakespeare play,' he said. 'We did bits at school. I thought it was awful in those days. But it's not.'

'Which one?'

'*A Midsummer Night's Dream*,' he said. 'That's you.'

Bull's eye, Printer, she thought. If I don't watch it I'll be blushing. Aloud she said, 'I'm real enough. You'll see,' and went to the car. 'Still the Buick?' she said.

'Don't you like it?'

'I love it,' she said, 'but I thought you were going to get a Bentley.'

'So I am,' he said, 'when I've got time to go shopping.'

'The Buick's better for this dance,' she said. 'Half the cars there will be Bentleys.'

'And the other half?'

'The pompous ones will come in Rolls-Royces,' she said. 'Pompous

187

people think Bentleys are fast. God knows what they'll make of a Buick.'

'Rich lot are they?'

'No richer than you, I don't suppose.' She looked out of the window. Soon they'd be in the country. 'Excuse the question,' she said, 'but are you going to do your honest working-class-lad act? Ha'way the lads and all that?'

'No no,' said Bob. 'Just the usual self-made-man stuff. Bringing joy to the masses by letting them tune in – and money to me as a result.'

'Much better,' she said. 'Some of them will be the most colossal snobs.'

'Tell me about the place we're going to.'

'Garston Hall? Owned by Sir Timothy Brent – he's the MFH. Master of Fox Hounds to you.'

'I know all about that,' he said. 'It's all in Surtees.'

'You've read Surtees?' Then before he could say it himself she said, 'Yes, I know. A printer'll read anything.'

'He has to,' said Bob. 'Will they all be fox-hunters?'

'Mostly. And debs and debs' delights. Probably a duke. Almost certainly a duchess.'

'Well well,' said Bob. 'I am going up in the world.'

'Now you just stop that,' she said.

'Which duchess?' he asked.

'Duchess of Derwent,' she said. 'Rather a tartar, so you be careful.'

Will her younger son be with her? Sybil Hendry wondered. He really is awfully keen on me. I wonder what the printer will do if Roddy tries to cut him out?

'Just one more thing,' she said. 'These little affairs get a little bit rowdy towards the end.'

'So you told me. Fizz all over the place.'

'And some of the chaps get tight, and then there's horseplay. You know. I want you to promise me you won't treat them as you do Cambridge dons.'

'Up to them,' said Bob. 'But I won't start anything. I promise you that.'

They were in the country now, and the moon was up, turning

the colour of the grass to the green of a champagne bottle, the green of her dress. Clever printer to notice such things, but then he was clever in so many ways, and she was growing far too fond of him.

He drew up before the house at last. Garston Hall was a jumble of so many styles it looked like a potted history of English architecture: everything from a peel tower to a Victorian ballroom hitched on to the back of a house like a waggon hitched to a mixed team of horses. I do hope it will be fun, Sybil Hendry thought, but had little doubt that it would be, now that Bob was there. A chauffeur in uniform appeared to park the car, and she took Bob's arm and led him inside. He waited by the ballroom door while she got rid of her coat, and looked at the dancers. A lot of the men wore red coats – hunting pink that would be – and some of the older women wore tiaras. Very grand, he thought. I wonder what our Andy would make of it? He seems to be going off the guillotine these days.

Some pretty girls if you looked hard, but none in Sybil's class that he could see – no matter what you were after. He'd stick with what he'd got. Then the dance ended, the dancers applauded, and the band began again. 'I'm In The Mood For Love' it played. Me an' all, thought Bob, but then I always am. Then Sybil Hendry appeared, they said hello to their host and hostess, and the Midsummer Night's Dream moved into his arms, they danced and he smelled her perfume. He sniffed.

'I never could understand why women said they *wore* a perfume,' he said. 'But I do now. The one thing they can't take off.'

'That will do,' she said. 'There'll be none of that for hours. No jolly romps in the back of a Buick.'

'No fear,' said Bob, and concentrated on his dancing, not turning it on, she noticed. Not yet. Just dancing, though he did that well too.

The dance ended, and she looked about her. The duchess was there, but not the duke, and Roddy too, looking really rather sweet in his hunting coat. A few girls had made the trip from London, because the Garston Ball was rather a good one, but most of the crowd were those who lived their lives here, the people one knew: who talked of come-outs and death duties and the diminishing value of land. It was as if they had only one conversation, and they

189

used it every night of the week like a favourite gramophone record. The band played 'Love Is The Sweetest Thing', and they danced again.

When the dance finished she could see Roddy moving towards them, even before they'd had a chance to sit down.

'Hello Sybil,' he said. 'I'm so glad you were able to come.'

'Roddy, this is a friend of mine,' she said. 'Lord Roderick Strang, Bob Patterson.'

Roddy gave a nod that could have been measured in millimetres, and made no attempt to shake hands. No more did Bob, but his 'How d'you do?' was affable enough. Too damned affable, she thought. He looked as if he might burst out laughing at any minute.

'I'll go and talk with your mother,' she said. 'Do take Bob for a drink or something.'

The affable look didn't even shimmer. Instead Bob turned to Roddy. 'Lead on, old chap,' he said.

Sybil Hendry went over to the duchess, wondering as she did so whether it was a good idea to leave Roddy alone with Bob. At least, she thought, there won't be a poker school here.

Lord Roderick Strang said, 'Drinks over here.'

A long table covered with a glittering white cloth, a series of vast punch bowls, and a lot of champagne. Bob picked up a glass and sipped. Good champagne.

'Have you known Mrs Hendry long?' asked Lord Roderick.

'Not awfully.'

The other man blinked. Was there a hint of mockery, perhaps even insolence?

'May one ask where you met?' he said at last.

'Of course,' Bob said. 'At a party of Brenda Coupland's. She's Mrs Hugo Meldrum now. Do you know her?'

'We've met.'

'Didn't see you at the wedding,' said Bob.

Lord Roderick changed topics. 'Do you hunt at all?'

'No,' said Bob.

'Ride, perhaps?'

'Oh, yes,' said Bob. 'I ride. Every chance I get.' Still with that affable, grateful-to-be-amused look.

'May one ask where?'

'Anywhere,' said Bob. 'Anywhere I can find a mount.'

'Jolly good,' said Lord Roderick, and for the first time Bob thought he might be formidable, if it weren't for Sybil Hendry.

Lord Roderick looked down the bar to where a group of his fellows were clustered: young men in hunting coats, young men with loud, high-pitched voices, and the utter self-assurance which comes from never once in all their lives having to worry about where the next half crown was coming from, thought Bob. Or the next fifty quid come to that.

'Come and meet a few of the chaps,' Lord Roderick said.

He took Bob's arm and led him down the bar, and Bob went with him, still affable. It was far too early for what had Sybil called it? – horseplay?

'I say chaps,' Lord Roderick said, 'I'd like you to meet a new arrival.'

The group turned to look at him, red coated to a man.

'This is Mr Matheson,' Lord Roderick said. 'Mr Bob Matheson.'

They looked at him as hounds might look at a fox with nowhere left to run.

'*Patterson*,' Bob said. 'Bob *Patterson*. I'm afraid you got that wrong, Noddy.' But already he was looking at the two men further down the bar that the pack had obscured. 'Why Dr Pardoe,' he said. 'How are you?'

For Pardoe it was, and with him Jane's brother – what was his name? Francis.

'It's been absolute ages,' said Bob, and offered his hand. Pardoe began to gobble like a turkey, but Bob's hand was ignored.

'What the blazes are you doing here?' Francis said.

'Small world, isn't it?' said Bob. 'Same as you, I suppose. Drinking champagne, taking a look at the talent. Well well. I haven't seen you since that Cambridge May Ball.' He turned to Pardoe, his look reproachful. 'You weren't very nice to me that night,' he said. 'Coming the old upper-class toff on the poor working lad trying to make a living. Ah well, all forgiven and forgotten, eh? But where are my manners? Have you met Lord Noddy Strang?' He turned to the man in the red coat. 'That can't be right, surely?'

'I'm afraid not,' Lord Roderick said. 'It's Roddy, Mr Matheson.'

'Jolly good.' Bob's eyes looked past Francis to where a woman in a red dress sipped punch.

'I think I'll have a dance,' he said, 'if you chaps will excuse me.'

'But you can't,' said Pardoe. 'Not until you've been introduced.'

'How cruel you are,' said Bob, 'to make me seem so uncouth. Of course we've been introduced. That's Annabel Lane.'

The lady in red put down her punch glass. Tall, willowy, elegant, with brown hair and emerald eyes, and a reputation for plain speaking.

'Bob Patterson,' she said. 'My dear! I do hope you've come to ask me to dance.'

'Of course,' said Bob.

'Oh thank God. Do you know I honestly believe you're the only man here who can – dance, I mean. But what brings you here?'

'Sybil Hendry.'

'Yes,' Annabel Lane said. 'She could make you. I doubt whether any of the others could.'

'You did.'

'Hardly a gentlemanly remark,' she said, and smiled at him. 'Thank God you're not a gentleman.'

'Hear hear,' said Bob.

They danced on. She was too tall to be an ideal partner, but her body was supple and pleasant to hold.

'And what brings you here?' he said.

'My husband.'

'I didn't see him,' said Bob.

'How can you, ass?' said Annabel Lane. 'He's in the card room playing bridge. As always. Don't you remember anything?' They danced on in silence for a while. 'Why were you talking to Laurel and Hardy?' she asked at last.

'You mean Whitcomb and Pardoe?' She nodded. 'You know it's a funny thing,' said Bob, 'but about once every other year I run into Pardoe and he wants to hit me. Me! You know how loveable I am.'

'I should,' said Annabel Lane. 'But surely Francis Whitcomb doesn't want to hit you? Such a pretty little thing. He just isn't built for hitting people, though I suppose Pardoe is. But why? Why you, I mean?'

Bob thought for a moment. He wasn't going to bring Andy into this.

'Class struggle,' he said at last. 'Dr Pardoe's got the idea that chaps like me should be in the dole queue in Tyneside waiting for him to come riding to the rescue.'

'Instead of attending hunt balls in your Savile Row evening clothes?'

'Got it in one,' said Bob. 'But what's he doing here?'

'He and Francis are friends of Geoffrey.'

'Geoffrey who?'

'Geoffrey Brent. Sir Timothy's heir. Another Cambridge don. Not queer by the way. Just rather far to the Left. It won't last.'

'Why won't it?'

'He'll be too rich.' She looked over Bob's shoulder. 'He's quite large, that sparring partner of yours.'

'He's a boxer too.'

'Good gracious,' said Annabel Lane. 'Why aren't you terrified?'

'He's a gentleman,' said Bob.

Annabel Lane thought about that for a moment, then began to giggle. 'My grandfather used words that were completely out of fashion,' she said. 'One of them was bounder. It suits you perfectly.'

'I prefer it to cad,' said Bob.

The music stopped and he thanked her for the dance, and offered to fetch more punch.

'No thank you,' she said. 'I think I'd better take a look in the card room and see if we have any money left.'

He watched her go as Sybil Hendry came over to join him.

'It didn't take you long to find consolation in the arms of another,' she said.

'Old pal,' said Bob. 'Did you enjoy your chat with the duchess?'

'Not much,' said Sybil Hendry. 'She spent most of the time warning me of the dangers of a mésalliance.'

'I never did learn Italian,' said Bob. 'Blest if I know why.'

'It's French,' she said, then added hastily: 'as well you know.'

'Let me guess,' said Bob. 'It means chaps like me marrying girls like you.'

'That's exactly what it means.'

'What did you tell her?'

193

'I told her I wasn't planning any more matrimony just for the moment. That didn't go down too well either.'

'On account of Lord Roderick?'

'Yes. How did the two of you get on?'

'I was my usual cheerful self,' said Bob. 'Didn't work, for some reason. He doesn't like me at all.'

Because he suspects I sleep with you, thought Bob, and the thought is torture to him. It's not just your money he's after: it's that luscious little body of yours as well.

'Are you telling me he's jealous?' she asked.

''Course he is. Like half the chaps here tonight.'

The band played, and they began to dance once more.

'Only half?' she asked.

'Don't be too greedy,' he said. 'I reckon the runner-up could only manage ten per cent.'

'Roddy's watching us,' she said, and smiled up at Bob.

Bitch, he thought. Knife twister. Still it was Roddy's own fault. Fail with a girl? Then go and look for another. Common sense, that was. But Roddy continued to watch until the dance ended, then his mother summoned him, and reminded him that there were such things as duty dances.

By the stairs, Pardoe and Francis were talking with an earnest-looking young man and an equally earnest young woman, a pretty one. Makes a nice change, thought Bob. Most of the earnest ones are plain. But why go to a dance then just stand about and talk? Made no sense. Especially when his sister had gone to all that trouble to get him a reputation as a dancing man. But then nothing about queers made sense.

'You're looking very thoughtful,' Sybil Hendry said.

And that would never do, he thought. I was about to remember the things Andy had told me, and that would never do either.

'I was thinking about the time I duffed-up Dr Pardoe,' he said.

'When was that? What is it, come to that?'

'The General Strike,' Bob said. 'And what it is is giving somebody a belting.'

'Nineteen twenty-six,' she said. 'I wasn't even out, then.'

But Andy was, thought Bob, and risking going back inside with every speech he made.

'What did you do to him?'

'I'll show you later on,' he said.

'Oh dear,' Sybil Hendry said. 'I think I can guess.'

Bouches à la reine and cold lobster, and last night it had been fish and chips. But the champagne he'd brought to go with the fish and chips was better.

'I think we could reasonably leave quite soon,' Sybil Hendry said.

'Not before the horseplay,' said Bob.

'Idiot,' Sybil Hendry said, then went off to do some running repairs.

When she'd gone a group of Noddy's red-coated pals came in, and Bob reached for the champagne bottle. He hadn't expected the horseplay to start quite so early. They came up to his table, and he rose to greet them. Much better to be on his feet, especially when the odds were four to one.

'I say,' one of them said, 'Mrs Lane was telling me you're a friend of Piers Hilyard.'

Bob nodded.

'He and my brother are in the same regiment,' said the red coat. 'Or they were until that ghastly bomb – '

'The Rifle Brigade,' said Bob. 'Why do you say were? – '

'Because – according to my brother – he's hurt so badly he'll never walk properly again.'

I could bet you a pony you're wrong, thought Bob, but I don't take money from babies. The combined ages of all four would be about eighty.

'He told my brother – Lieutenant Calthrop by the way – I'm Toby Calthrop – he told him about that business at Cambridge when you made that cad stand up for the National Anthem.'

'Oh yes?'

'I don't wish to be nosey or anything,' said Toby Calthrop, 'but was it Dr Pardoe?'

'No,' said Bob. 'It was an obnoxious little sod called Burrowes. Pardoe was later.'

'Could you possibly go on a bit further?' said Calthrop.

One of his chums said, 'I rather think that champagne bottle is empty,' and signalled to a waiter for another. Bob motioned for them to be seated. The horseplay it seemed, was for later.

'Next day Pardoe came round to demand an apology,' said Bob. 'Either that or fight. It was a bit like a duel, I suppose.'

'But the man's a Red,' said one of the others.

Bob shrugged. 'Whatever he is he was going to belt me, but somebody reminded him of what happened the last time he'd tried it.'

'Somebody' had been Andy, but that was none of their business.

'What did happen?' Calthrop asked.

'I won.'

'But – excuse me – Pardoe used to be a heavyweight boxer. University half blue. All that. I mean – please don't take offence – but wasn't it a bit surprising you won?'

'Not surprising at all,' said Bob. 'I cheated.'

The others looked grave, even stern. One did not cheat at sport, he gathered: not even when one was giving away a couple of stone and three inches in height.

'I had to, you see,' said Bob.

'Had to?' Calthrop again. Counsel for the prosecution.

'He was bashing Piers at the time, and Piers was just about unconscious,' said Bob. 'I had to stop him the quickest way I could. So I did.'

'You were absolutely right,' said Calthrop, appearing for the defence this time. 'Wasn't yours rather a distinguished party?'

Bob grinned. 'Not with me in it,' he said, 'though mind you, Lady Catherine Hilyard was there – Piers's twin sister – and her fiancée, Jay Bower. He's her husband now. And Lionel Warley, who used to be a fighter pilot. And Jane Whitcomb.' He thought for a moment. 'I suppose it was distinguished.'

'Jane Whitcomb,' another red coat said. 'Isn't she the lady who drove the ambulance in the war?'

Bob nodded. The way the young chap had said 'lady' put Jane in a Bath chair.

'Georgina Payne played her in that film. *The Angel of No Man's Land.*'

'Was she there too?' Toby Calthrop asked.

'Not that time,' said Bob.

Toby Calthrop pounced. 'But you've met her,' he said sternly.

'Well yes,' said Bob. 'Now and again.'

196

The remaining red coat said, 'You've met Georgina Payne?' His voice was deep and very loud, and it boomed round the dining room. His face became as red as his coat.

'In Hollywood?' said Calthrop.

'Among other places.'

'Just one more question if I may,' Calthrop said. Definitely a career at the bar, thought Bob. All upper-class deference, and all the time asking bloody rude questions.

'We'll see,' he said.

'You see Larry and I – ' he looked at the boomer, ' – are at Cambridge, too, though not at that particular college. There are still rumours about that May Ball. Legends, even. I've heard all sorts of stories,' said Calthrop, 'but at least if you tell us we'll know whether they're true or not.' He gulped then. It was going to take all his courage to ask the question, but at last he got it out. 'Who was your partner?'

'A girl called Lilian Dunn,' said Bob.

'Not Josephine Baker?' the boomer asked.

'You think I'd have forgotten?' said Bob. 'Don't be daft. Lilian's a blonde.'

'Is she the one called Tiger Lily? At the Folies Bergère?' Calthrop asked.

'That's the one,' said Bob. 'They usually put her next to Josephine Baker. Nice contrast.'

'I saw her last vacation,' said another red coat. 'She didn't wear much.' Then he too went scarlet.

'Two or three ostrich feathers, said Bob. 'Sort of dungarees, you might say.' The others looked bewildered. 'Work clothes,' said Bob. 'Uniform.'

'And you took her to a May Ball at Cambridge?' said Calthrop.

Awestruck wasn't in it, thought Bob. I'm the chap who slew the dragon and brought home the lady fair.

'One of the best nights of my life,' he said.

'I should just about think it would be,' said the boomer, but this time his voice was a whisper.

'We're really very grateful to you,' said Calthrop. 'As I say, Cambridge is full of rumours. It's marvellous to know the truth.'

197

'Been a pleasure,' said Bob, and thought: And I'm most grateful to Annabel Lane. *And* her big mouth.

The other three looked at Calthrop, not quite nudging him, and Calthrop said: 'Oh yes. The Gallop.'

'I don't think I follow,' said Bob.

'The Post Horn Gallop,' Calthrop said. 'Later on the band will play it and the hunting chaps line up in two teams and dance. Nothing queer, you understand – '

'Certainly not,' said Bob.

'More like folk dancing,' said Calthrop.

'More like a cavalry charge,' said the boomer.

'Well yes,' Calthrop said. 'The point is that we go round the room from the centre to the periphery, so to speak – to begin with at any rate. And to keep us apart there's a chap we call the Pivot. At least that's what he's called officially. Between ourselves he's known as the Stag at Bay. Of course we have to find a chap who doesn't know the dance.'

' – And who isn't awfully nice,' another red coat said.

Calthrop said carefully, 'There was a suggestion that you might do. Self-made man and all that, but who cares about the right sort of school these days? I mean look at the things you've done, – I mean apart from Dr Pardoe. I mean Mrs Hendry told the duchess – '

'Told her what?'

'About all the people you know. I mean in London you go everywhere.' He put down his glass. 'We'd better be off. Sorry to ask so many questions.'

'Not at all,' said Bob, and the young men left.

What a bodyguard, he thought. Jane and Georgie, Catherine and Lily and Sybil. The most unlikely Amazons imaginable, and yet they'd routed the red coats.

'No need to look smug,' Sybil Hendry said.

'There's every need,' said Bob. 'I'm having the time of my life.'

'Just as well,' she said. 'I'd hate to think I was doing all this for nothing.'

His hand stroked her thigh. Like silk, he thought. Like satin. Like a woman's skin.

'What do you mean for nothing?' said Bob. 'Didn't I show you where I kicked Cud Pardoe?'

'Cud?'

'It's what we say for Cuthbert.'

'Oh what bliss,' she said. 'Cud. But it isn't that.'

'What then?'

'How the hell did you get yourself off the hook for the Post Horn Gallop?'

'You knew I was on it then?'

'I knew Roddy had it in mind.' She turned closer to him. 'A little higher please.'

His hand moved upwards.

'And you were just going to let it happen?'

'What could I do against all those big strong men except warn you? And I did do that. But you were determined to show how brave you are.'

'Brave?' he said. 'I didn't even climb into the ring.'

'Poor old Pardoe did,' she said. 'He looked as if a horse had rolled on him.'

'Aye,' said Bob. 'Did me the world of good that did.'

'Yes,' she said. 'It was fun, wasn't it? But even so – '

'What, pet?'

'It might have been you.'

'No,' said Bob. 'It mightn't. No chance.'

'You weren't to know those young apes had heard about your goings-on at Cambridge. Suppose they hadn't?'

'I'd have had to think of something else,' he said. 'You learn all sorts of tricks in the wireless business.'

They flew back to New York via Los Angeles, and the noise of the motors made conversation, if not impossible, then very public. Instead she lay back with her eyes closed, and tried to sleep. There hadn't been much chance of sleep in Mexico City. Parties every night: partly because of Georgie with a president in hot pursuit, and partly because Charles's business was doing well enough for Mexican politicians to start celebrating. She opened her eyes and looked at Charles, deep in papers as usual: graphs, reports, figures, reading them as easily as she could read a novel. Enjoying them, too. She closed her eyes once more, and huddled into her rug.

Georgie had once described Charles as looking like a very nice lion trying to decide which of two awful bull terriers he would eat for breakfast. Murray Fisch had been one of the bull terriers. Well, Charles had certainly had him for breakfast. She had never seen a man so crushed, or so scared. No doubt Charles had read *his* papers, too. The odd thing was that Charles hadn't fired him. It seemed he was too good at his job. He'd even been given a rise in salary, but it was obvious that Charles owned him now: a slave in golden shackles.

They had parted with Georgie in Los Angeles: all very amicable; no Murray Fisch stuff, but then Charles had told her why. Georgie's career was just about over, and it seemed she knew it, so there was no talk of suing or injunctions or lawyers, but Charles being Charles he'd had to have something back in return, and being Charles he'd got it. Georgie would make one last picture, which was not only a triumph for Charles but another humiliation for Murray Fisch. Even the nicest of chaps weren't nice all the time.

He was shaking her. They had arrived to a grey day in September, but already she felt warmer as the doors were opened. There would be a car waiting too, because Charles had arranged it, and cars were always waiting when Charles arranged it, but there would be no Manhattan apartment, no George and Martha. Somebody else had moved in while she was at the Coast. She would have to rough it at the Plaza instead. But not in the same room of course. She'd had to fight to get him on the same floor. Not that it mattered that night. Coffee and sandwiches and a bath and bed. That was her programme for that night, and she stuck to it, so that she felt rested at last: but next morning was different.

Charles had meetings all day of course, but he too looked rested: he could cope with meetings all day, and at least he'd promised her dinner, and so she went shopping. Saks Fifth Avenue, Van Cleef and Arpels, some of the boutiques in and around Park Avenue: all expensive of course, but not nearly so much as they had been a few years ago. Before the slump, she thought, but that really wasn't quite right, because even in New York the slump was beginning to loosen its grip. Charles was right about money, as usual.

The hotel servants, for instance. They didn't just say 'Yes mam, no mam', they were relaxed about it, as if the terror of losing their jobs had diminished to an occasional worry. The doorman had saluted when he opened the door of her taxi, but he had smiled, too. Vacant taxis weren't quite so numerous either, and some of the people in the shops were actually buying things. She thought of Timothy Jordan, beavering away at Perkiss, Maberley, Bronstein and Fitt. Maybe things were still ghastly in the Bronx, but at least in Manhattan they had made a start.

She lunched at the hotel, clam chowder and a glass of wine and nothing furtive about the wine, then went out shopping again. Not much of a haul at the end of the day: a silver cigarette case with a lighter attached, for Lionel, a really rather beautiful cameo brooch for her mother, and a tie from Sulka for Charles. Perfume for herself, but not too much. It was time she went to Paris again, and she would buy it there. Back to her room, where she fell asleep without meaning to. Really Mexico had taken its toll, or was it just that the old girl was getting on a bit? At least she woke in time to bathe and change before Charles came for her. Chanel, pale blue, and sapphires, and the Fortuny mantle because she loved it so and it was September after all.

'I thought Ciro's,' said Charles. 'I know it's a bit pompous, but I'm a banker, after all.'

'And we can always go to the Cotton Club later,' said Jane.

'Must we?'

'It's good for you,' said Jane. 'All the best saints agree.'

'What is?'

'Suffering,' said Jane, 'and anyway I bought you a present.'

'Jolly good,' said Charles. 'Where is it?'

'When we get back,' she said.

Ciro's was very grand: all black and white and silver and an excellent setting for sapphires and Chanel. The waiter poured champagne that had somehow found its way from Epernay to New York.

'Busy day?'

'Brisk,' he said. 'And you?'

'No, thank God. All I did all day was buy four presents and eat clam chowder.'

'The idle rich,' said Charles, and then: 'I invested your cheque.'

'Bless you.'

'You're not worried?' he asked.

'No,' she said. 'I'm not. I think you're right. Things *are* getting better. People are even beginning to look happy. To quote Lionel's old school chum, Roosevelt's been and gone and done it.'

'Not Roosevelt,' said Charles. 'At least I don't think so.'

'You don't like Roosevelt?'

He shrugged. 'I doubt if you'll meet a banker who does,' he said. 'All the same, it's happening.' He thought for a moment. 'It's just a hurricane that's blown itself out.'

Then the band played 'Happy Days Are Here Again' and they danced. Really he was dancing very much better, though he'd never be a Lionel. But then Lionel would never be a Charles.

'I've got a sort of present for you,' said Charles. 'In a way.'

'Gracious, how cryptic.'

'After I get mine,' he said, and held her a little closer: a very little, because he was a banker, but it was all she wanted.

'Are we in New York for much longer?' she asked.

'Not unless you specially want to be,' said Charles. 'I'll be finished here in a couple of days, then I'd rather like to go home. First boat we can manage.'

'I'll leave it to you then,' said Jane. 'I'd like to go home too.'

She made him take her to the Cotton Club because it really *was*

202

good for him, and because I want to go, she thought, and nowadays there's nobody else to take me. And he really did endure the ordeal rather well. Perhaps it was because its cheerful noisiness was in such contrast to the austere elegance of Ciro's, or perhaps it was just the chorus girls. There seemed to be about a battalion of them: every colour from coffee with double cream to coffee with just a dash of milk, and every one a beauty, but none so black as to offend white susceptibilities. . . . Now now, she thought. Don't start writing an article for Erika's magazine. You're here to enjoy yourself. Then Duke Ellington's band began to play, and she did.

He liked his tie. It had nothing to do with Winchester, the Rifle Brigade, or New College, Oxford, but even so he liked it.

'Now you,' she said.

'Mine's more a secret than a present,' he said, 'but in a way it's both.' He looked at her, grave as a priest in his black suit, white shirt.

'I'll keep both,' she said. 'You know that.'

'Of course.' He took a deep breath, like a man about to lead a charge. 'I need just one more telegram to make it a hundred per cent,' he said, 'but if I don't tell you soon I'll burst. . . . Mexico intends to expand its navy.'

'How interesting,' she said.

'To the extent of one destroyer. Which means, so far as I can gather, that Mexico will then have two destroyers that work.'

'But that's ridiculous,' she said. 'What on earth does Mexico want with warships? You should have *seen* the poverty –' she broke off. 'But you haven't finished, have you?'

'No,' he said, 'though I agree with what you say. The point is they want Harris and Croft to build it.'

'Harris and Croft?' she said. 'The Felston shipyard?'

'The very same,' he said. 'When I say they *want* Harris and Croft –'

'A lot of rich Mexicans became a little bit richer,' she said.

'Just so,' said Charles. 'But they'd have become richer whoever got it: Germany, France, the United States.'

'And that's why there were all those parties?'

Charles nodded. 'Georgie was a tremendous help.'

'Does she know?'

'Of course not.' Charles sounded outraged.

'So all those poor Mexicans go on being poor, and a few poor people in Felston will be a little better off – until they've finished building a destroyer.'

'That's the way your friend Andy would look at it,' he said.

'And you?'

'The contract was bound to go somewhere,' he said. 'Why shouldn't it be Felston?' Then being Charles he added, 'I'm on the board of Harris and Croft, but I swear to you that's not why I did it.'

'I know that, silly,' she said, and then: 'That's why you were looking so tired before we left?'

'It took a bit of doing,' he said. 'Without Georgie I don't think we could have done it.'

'You should get her to launch the ship.'

'What a marvellous idea,' said Charles. 'I'll get on to it tomorrow. El Presidente would love it.'

'You said you needed one more telegram.'

'If Georgie can't bring it, nothing will,' said Charles.

Next morning she telephoned Timothy Jordan at his office.

'Lunch?' he said. 'Yeah, I guess so. Had you anywhere special in mind?'

'Here if you like,' said Jane.

'The Plaza would be fine, except – is it OK if I bring a friend? – What I mean is, I promised this guy lunch, and – '

'Well of course not,' she said. 'Any friend of yours – ' She hung up, thinking how odd, and then, but keep it informal: Tim did have some rather odd friends. She ordered a buffet lunch for three.

They arrived prompt to the hour: two men in dark suits, white shirts with button-down collars, discreet ties, but one of them was as black as the other was white.

'Jane,' Tim Jordan said, 'this is – '

'Don't tell me. Let me guess,' said Jane. 'You're Booker T. Stanton.' There could be no doubting it. His face was just like his photograph, which should be silly, she thought, except that so often it isn't the case.

204

'That's right,' Stanton said. 'But how – '

'Your mother showed me your photograph. Come in, please. Make the drinks, will you Tim?'

Stanton came in as if the room might be booby-trapped, but all Tim did was mix martinis, and Stanton began to relax.

'My parents work for you?' he said.

'Whenever they're available,' said Jane. 'There's quite a queue, usually. That's why I'm here.'

Tim passed round the cocktails.

'I wish you'd seen us come in here,' he said. 'We did you proud.'

'Come in?'

'Well I didn't want to send Booker round to the service elevator, so I made him carry my briefcase for me and hand me a file on the way in. That's all it took.'

'I guess I should have said "Yassuh" now and again,' Stanton said, 'but I can't do the accent.' Jane laughed aloud.

It was a good lunch: two bright young men competing for the attention of an older but still attractive woman. What made it fascinating, she thought, was that Stanton, politically speaking, was far to the Right of Tim Jordan. Tim wanted a classless society: Stanton preferred a middle class with lots more blacks in it.

'But what are you doing in New York?' she asked at last, and then: 'Oh, of course. You're on vacation.'

'That's right,' said Stanton. 'I'm staying at my parents' place.' He looked at Tim. 'As a matter of fact I've got a vacation job. With Perkiss, Maberley, Bronstein and Fitt.'

'Good heavens,' said Jane. 'What's a medical student doing there?'

'He cleans,' said Tim. 'Floors, walls, bathrooms, windows. That's what he does. He cleans.'

'Ah come on,' Stanton said. 'I get paid, too. It pays pretty well.'

'Even so,' said Tim, but Stanton interrupted.

'Look,' he said. 'A lot of guys would like my job. White guys even. But I've got it. And next year – ' he knocked on the wood of his chair with a gesture that reminded her at once of his mother ' – next year maybe I'll be a doctor and somebody else will clean.'

'But – forgive me – ' said Jane, 'but surely you don't clean for Perkiss and so on dressed like that.'

'My day off,' Stanton said. 'After lunch my sister's giving a recital.'

'Oh I wish I could come,' said Jane.

'You'd be very welcome,' said Stanton.

'Then I will.'

After that they talked about the possible end of the Depression, which Booker Stanton thought was a good idea, though Tim, bless him, wasn't quite so sure. How could you have a revolution if poverty somehow managed to cure itself? At last the lunch ended, and Tim had to go back to work.

'Where's your sister's recital?' Jane asked.

'Harlem,' Booker said. 'Where else?'

'I'll phone for a taxi.'

'Good idea,' Booker said. 'Here's an invitation card. The address is on it.' He got to his feet. 'I'll go and catch a bus,' he said.

'But – ' said Jane, and then it hit her. She understood. 'Oh sod it,' she said.

'Yes mam,' said Booker. 'The sooner the better.'

He left at once, so that by the time the taxi pulled up at the First Baptist Hall of Harmony he was there to meet her. She had wondered if she would be the only white person there, but she wasn't. Not by any means. The others were mostly poor, mostly immigrant, and by the look of them musicians to a man and woman. The accompanist was white, too. This was to be a recital beyond race, or even politics.

Lucille Stanton appeared in a day dress which Jane remembered giving to the girl's mother years ago, and which had been cunningly adapted to the younger woman's figure and the passage of time. There was no introduction, no speech by a chairman of a Committee for the Promotion of Song in Harlem. The accompanist struck an introductory chord, Lucille Stanton sang, and that was it. Schubert, Brahms, Mozart, Debussy: and all apparently effortless, which was another way of saying with the greatest effort of all: a true, rich mezzo soprano that some idiot one day soon would compare to the song of the nightingale or the lark: as if birds could spend years practising scales or reading music, never mind interpreting some of the greatest music ever written for the human voice. When the recital was done the applause thundered on and on, and flowers appeared. Jane looked about her. At the back of the hall, Martha and George, late arrivals, sat in a daze of happiness.

Jane said to Booker, 'She's wonderful,' and all the young man could do was nod. Happiness had dazed him too. When the applause died at last Jane left her seat and rushed to Martha and George.

'Why Miss Whitcomb,' Martha began, but Jane threw her arms around her and hugged her hard.

'She's wonderful,' she said. 'She's absolutely wonderful. Oh I do congratulate you. Two marvellous children.'

'That good?' said Charles.

'Young,' said Jane. 'Still some things to learn. Still a student. But that good most certainly.'

'Pretty?'

'Not like the Cotton Club,' said Jane. 'She's too black and too positive for that. But my God she's attractive.'

'I know a man she should see.'

'Because she's attractive?'

'Because she's talented,' said Charles. 'This is a man who arranges concerts. You want me to talk to him?'

'Yes please.'

Charles suddenly assumed what she had come to know as his furtive look, the one that warned her he was about to ask her to do something she wouldn't like. 'I have to go out to dinner tonight,' he said.

'Oh yes?'

'Rather short notice I agree, but we'll be setting off for home in a couple of days.'

'Which ship?'

'The *Mauretania* – if that's all right?'

'Quite acceptable,' said Jane.

Charles threw a cushion at her. 'Don't start ragging,' he said. 'Not yet. It sort of ties in with this deal I made. General Motors, US Steel. All that. His bank is handling it for us. Will you come? Besides, he and Mrs Forest saw your picture.'

'You're not talking about Selwood Forest?' she said. Charles nodded. 'But he's even richer than you are.'

Charles looked smug. 'It's possible,' he said at last.

'Golly,' said Jane. 'Of course I'll come. Is he awful?'

'Not particularly,' said Charles. 'He's got an ulcer, so the food won't be particularly brilliant.'

Just as well, Jane thought, with the *Mauretania* in the offing. 'No champagne?' she said.

'Not for him, and his wife doesn't drink, but I said you and I would take a glass – if you come, that is.'

'Of course,' she said. 'I might even pass the hat for Felston if that's all right?'

Charles grinned. 'I warned him you would,' he said.

'And afterwards we could have a night on the town.'

'Where?' Charles said warily.

'Well I thought the Stork Club – ' Charles looked relieved, ' – and then maybe the Hotsy-Totsy and the Onyx and the Sligo Slasher's.'

'What in God's name are they?' he said.

'Speakeasies,' said Jane. 'It's probably our last chance. The way your Mr Roosevelt's going on they'll probably be done away with next time we're here.' She quoted Georgie. 'If we want a drink all we'll have to do is go to a bar, and where's the fun in that?'

Rose and Selwood Forest had been excellent hosts, and the food had turned out to be much better than Charles had feared. Their liking for her was evident too, though as Charles said, admiration was a better word. All his life Selwood Forest had done nothing but make money, and Rose Forest had done nothing but be married to it. Tim's friends in the Bronx, Andy, Dr Stobbs's patients, were to them as remote as African pygmies. All the same she'd received a cheque for five thousand dollars just for trundling out her old party pieces about Felston's poverty. She found that she liked them, too. They were lonely, not avaricious: sad, even pitiable. Grinders of the faces of the poor were never that. Lonely in a Park Avenue mansion with only half a dozen servants for company, or else in a house in Cape Cod with rather more. Yet they *were* lonely, and pitiable, perhaps because there was more wrong with him than ulcers. Cancer? she wondered. There had seemed to be no flesh on him at all. Whatever strength left to him was in his mind, and that

208

was still sharp and questing, but all it thought about was money. Even so, five thousand dollars . . .

Charles drank more champagne at the Stork Club, fortifying himself for the ordeal ahead. It wouldn't be champagne in the other places. In fact it was whisky, and not bad whisky at all, for Charles, and a very little gin for her: out of cups at the Hotsy-Totsy and the Sligo Slasher's, though there were glasses at the Onyx, but as Jane explained, the Onyx had class. In every place there was music: band, or trio or piano on its own, and in every place they heard 'Happy Days Are Here Again', and saw people react as if they believed it. Charles got drunk, just a little: not nearly enough to start singing, as so many of the Hotsy-Totsy's clientèle did. Instead he looked about him with a sort of bewildered delight.

'Amazing,' he said. 'Like seeing life put back into a corpse.'

'The end of an era, too,' said Jane.

'You should do one of your little pieces for Bower about it.'

'I've learned to wait till I'm asked.'

He looked up, then. Drunk or not, he could still read signs.

'You and Bower fallen out?' he asked. 'You didn't tell me.'

'We haven't fallen out,' said Jane, 'but you know what my "Dearest Daisy" pieces were like. All gush and frivolity. Well Jay's decided that frivolity belonged to the Twenties. The Thirties is all earnestness and good intentions.'

'Even so – ' he said.

'If you're about to say I could do that, too, you're probably right,' she said. 'But Daisy was different. Tricky, if you like. Combining a feather-headed chatterbox with serious information – it wasn't easy, but I adored doing it.'

'I wasn't going to say that at all,' said Charles.

'What then?'

'You talked so much I've forgotten. No I haven't.' He looked at her in triumph. Charles drunk was far more expressive than Charles sober. 'We still own quite a bit of Bower's paper.'

'No doubt we do, but – '

'Please,' said Charles, and held up his hand like a traffic policeman. 'My turn.'

Jane concentrated on not giggling.

209

'We own enough to make him publish whatever we wanted,' said Charles.

Suddenly the need for giggling was over. It was an appalling suggestion, and then suddenly perhaps it wasn't.

'Charles darling,' she said. 'Please don't drink any more whisky until you've answered one question.'

'Very well.' At once his face assumed a look of heroic self-sacrifice.

'Would you make Jay print an article by any other writer but me?'

'Certainly not,' said Charles.

'Why not?'

'Because I don't love any other writer but you,' said Charles. 'I don't love anybody but you. I thought I had made my position absolutely clear on that.'

Charles darling, she thought, how sweet you are when you're drunk.

'Furthermore I should like to add a rider,' said Charles.

'I should love you to add a rider.'

'I am not specially sober at the moment. – Not drunk, you understand, but not particularly sober.'

'I will accept that,' said Jane, 'as a working hypothesis.'

'Thank you,' said Charles, smiled his Chairman of the Board smile and reached for his glass. The meeting, it seemed, was adjourned.

'Charles, darling,' she said, 'you can't possibly have finished.'

'Can't I?' He put his glass down again. 'By jove you're right,' he said. 'What I should have gone on to say – the point I urgently needed to make – was this. Tomorrow morning I shall be sober. My word on that, and I would not have it otherwise.'

'Quite so,' said Jane.

'And that being so,' said Charles, 'it may very well transpire that I shall be obliged to withdraw my offer.' He blinked at her. 'Though just at the moment I'm damned if I can remember what my offer was. Shall we go back to our hotel?'

'Yes please,' said Jane. 'One way and another it's been a remark-able evening. Thank you.'

They got out of the Hotsy-Totsy and into a taxi without

complications. Charles seemed to be capable of competence at most things he attempted, including being drunk. Their taxi driver whistled as he drove, the same tune over and over. It was probably 'Happy Days Are Here Again', she thought, but he whistled so badly it was impossible to tell, and it was no good at all asking Charles. He was asleep with his head on her shoulder, and he did that competently too: no snoring. When the taxi drew up at the Plaza he awoke at once, and smiled at her.

'You always smell so *nice*,' he said, and gave the taxi driver far too much money. Even so he walked well into the Plaza, his back straight, no hint of a stagger: a Rifle Brigade officer and a gentleman.

When they left the elevator he said, 'Would you mind looking into my place for a moment? There may be some news for us.'

'Of course,' she said.

There were two messages, both from Western Union. He opened the first one. 'Mexico,' he said, and read intently, then passed it to her. The jumble of letters and figures it contained meant nothing at all, and she said so.

'Of course not,' said Charles. 'Forgive me please. I'll make more sense in the morning. But in a nutshell what it says is that Harris and Croft have got the contract.'

'For the destroyer?' He nodded. 'Oh thank God,' she said, and kissed him.

He looked at the other telegram. 'Two,' he said. 'Wasn't expecting a second one. If you don't mind I think a little cold water on the face might be in order.'

'Of course,' she said.

He left her, and she fiddled with the room's vast and elegant radio. It would take a Bob Patterson, she thought, to tell her whether or not the reception was worth all that fuss. News. Advertisements. Laughter more emphatic than sincere. Then, at last, music. A big band, the kind that was beginning to be known as an orchestra. Paul Whiteman, could it be? Guy Lombardo? Smooth, refined and syrup sweet, whoever it was. Not what she liked at all. Charles came back. His dress shirt was already wilting with the water he had splashed, but he looked a little more sober.

'I'll just take a look at this,' he said, 'then I'll turn in if you don't mind.' He tore open the other Western Union envelope and began to read, and as he did so the orchestra began on 'Happy Days Are Here Again', the crooner sang:

> Happy days are here again,
> The skies above are clear again.
> Let us sing a song of cheer again.
> Happy days –

Suddenly Charles shouted, 'Turn it off, for God's sake. Turn the bloody thing off.'

Her hand went at once to the switch.

In the silence he said, 'From Switzerland.'

'Your wife?'

'She's dead,' said Charles.

. 23 .

Somehow it created a sort of limbo. It was impossible for them to share a bed that night, even to sleep, and from then on Charles's life seemed to consist of the sending and receiving of very long cables: that, or telephone calls to Zurich. Then the morning after that he came to her room and asked for coffee. She ordered it at once.

'I've been neglecting you,' he said.

'Not by choice.'

'No no. She left rather a lot of money you see. It's – complicated. I shall have to go to Switzerland.'

'The funeral?'

'Rather late for that. Her affairs. Bankers and lawyers and so on. I wish I could take you with me.'

'My dear,' she said, 'it's out of the question.'

'I know,' he said, 'but all the same – I can't help wishing. It's because I've grown so used to you. Like a drug. When I don't have you with me it's just awful.'

She kissed him quickly and tenderly, and just as well, she thought. He was bound to ask her soon, but she couldn't give him an answer because she didn't know. She had no idea of what she wanted: none at all.

But love had made him perceptive.

'There are things we must discuss,' he said.

'I know that,' she said. 'I – ' He put his finger to her lips.

'Sh,' he said. 'Let me finish. I have to know,' he continued. 'But not yet. Not before I – when I get back from Switzerland.'

'Very well, Charles.'

'But if you don't mind – I'd like to go on sleeping with you. Not to make love – not if you'd rather not – but please let me be beside you.'

She had to embrace him then, because how could she not? and afterwards he shared her bed at the Plaza, on the *Mauretania*, and for one night at his flat before he set off for the boat train. For the most part he simply held her, not clutching or grabbing, but with a familiar ease that made her comfortable, content: but for him, she knew, it wasn't like that at all. For all his considerate gentleness he was clinging to her as to the one thing in the world he needed. She remembered Canon Messeter's quoting St Matthew about the rich man. 'For he had great possessions.' Well Charles had those, all right: a bank full of money, and large chunks of a movie studio, half a shipyard, a ranch in Canada, a railway in Brazil. The list was almost endless, and yet she was the only thing he really wanted, and it had taken the death of his wife to show how desperate the need was.

The one she really needed to talk to was her mother, but she and the major were away at Wetherby in Yorkshire. There was a horse there the major needed to see.

She hadn't felt so alone for ages. Decency, let alone friendship, decreed that she should phone Lionel, but when she did Pott told her that he'd been called away to Liverpool and he hadn't said when he'd be back. Liverpool meant sailors and sailors meant love, and probably troubled love at that, she thought. She would have to face her problem and try to think on her own. Think it through, Vinney, her governess, used to say. It was good advice, and besides there was no one else she was obliged to see, whereas she was obliged to think. Not like the saddhu who had once forecast greatness for her, his legs crossed in the Lotus position, while he meditated. When she thought she had to be on the move, and Kensington Gardens was a useful place for that. No risk of traffic. She had gone there often with Foch, but not since he died. As she walked towards the Round Pond alone she realised how much she missed the sturdy, self-assured little body moving beside her, red lead and collar glowing against the harsh black fur. She had missed him terribly, and then the loss had mellowed into a memory: she had thought it was all over, until her walk in the Gardens brought him back. But even Foch's ghost must wait: she had to think.

There wasn't on the face of it all that much to think about. To marry, or not? What could be simpler? Simple question, certainly, but by no means a simple answer. She was very fond of Charles. He found no difficulty in telling her he loved her, and meaning it, that was the point. Whether she loved him or not she didn't know. She'd loved John, no doubt about that, and there was equally no doubt that she'd never loved Jay Bower, and she very much doubted whether he had ever loved her, even though he'd asked her to marry him: but with Charles she simply didn't know.

Then there was her freedom, the gift of her darling Aunt Pen: the gift that freed her from thraldom to her mother, as she had been before she met the major, from the most boring kind of genteel poverty, perhaps, in part at least, even from her madness. A gift beyond price, in fact, except that it hadn't been beyond price at all: it was half a million pounds. Jewellery, Paris clothes, a rather splendid but unpompous house. Charles of course could give her all of that and more – no doubt he had dozens of half millions – but the point was that South Terrace was *her* house, and when she shut its door she need please nobody but herself, and that she found was important to her; perhaps the most important thing of all. . . . And yet Charles had the knack of making her life so pleasant. Head waiters always had good tables, taxis popped up like genies out of bottles, Presidents of Mexico appeared at parties. As the papers said about Mussolini, Charles made the trains run on time. Hardly a reason for matrimony, she thought, but was Charles's love for her a better one? On and on she walked, until she reached the Round Pond, and all she could think was, Oh dear God, why isn't Foch with me? He would have known what to do. It was a relief to go back to South Terrace and learn that her mother had phoned: that she was invited to dine.

'George is on the Downs,' her mother said. 'There's another horse there he considers should be looked at, and afterwards he's dining at White's. Such a nuisance having to take a dinner jacket out for the day, but a member there insisted on giving him dinner. He also has a horse he wishes to discuss, and as he owns the horse and he's a duke George found it impossible to decline. George dearly loves a duke.'

Jane refused to pick up the gauntlet her mother had flung down so determinedly. The major's snobbery was a sin so harmless as to be endearing.

215

'My stepfather's in great demand,' she said.

'Gratifyingly so,' said her mother. 'By us, not least. But he has promised to be with us in time for coffee. You enjoyed your time in America?'

'Quite a lot of it,' said Jane.

'And the rest?'

'Never less than fascinating,' said Jane. 'Especially Mexico.'

She began to talk about Mexico: the poverty, Murray Fisch's party, the President, the destroyer. Now that the moment had come she found it difficult to talk about Charles.

'Fascinating indeed,' said her mother. 'And the United States?'

'Hollywood's never a yardstick for anything but itself,' said Jane. 'Even if one talks about Los Angeles, they're bewildered. But New York . . . There really is optimism there, Mummy.'

'That has to be good news,' her mother said. 'Unfortunate that Mexico finds it necessary to buy another destroyer – but you did not call on me to discuss Mexican politics.'

'No Mummy,' said Jane, and told her about Charles, and the Hotsy-Totsy Club, 'Happy Days Are Here Again' and a Western Union cable. Her mother heard her out in silence.

When her daughter had done, she said: 'What fools atheists are. Only a fool could suppose such an irony to be possible without divine intervention.' She paused for a moment, then added: 'There is dry sherry on the drinks table. Pour me a glass, if you please. There is also gin, – and vermouth, and ice.' She produced a smile which, compared with her smiles of yore, was almost a grin. 'You see how I sacrifice my principles to indulge my daughter. Mix yourself a cocktail, child, and for heaven's sake light a cigarette. You are obviously overwrought, and we must find out why before dinner.'

Jane obeyed at once, because when Mummy issued the orders what else could you do?

Her mother sipped her sherry. 'Gratifying,' she said at last. 'Extremely gratifying.'

'Charles?'

'Of course Charles,' said her mother. 'On the few occasions when I have met him he has seemed both charming and intelligent. Very intelligent.'

'Very charming too,' said Jane. 'At least I think so.'

'Doubtless you are in a better position to make such a judgement than I,' said her mother.

Darling Mummy, thought Jane. She's been rapping me over the knuckles since I was three, and she still hasn't lost her touch.

'He is anxious to marry you, you say?' her mother asked. 'It isn't just – forgive me – it isn't just a sense of obligation because his wife has died?'

'No,' said Jane. 'It's not. Believe me Mummy, I know.'

'Of course.'

'To marry me is the one thing he wants. Please don't think I'm being a show off, and heaven knows why it should be, but it is.'

'He's a very lucky man even to have a chance,' said her mother. 'Goose ... Don't you see that? No of course you don't, which is one of the reasons why he loves you so.'

'Thank you Mummy,' said Jane, 'and I hope what you say is true. But – '

'But what, child?'

'The most ghastly things are happening all over the world,' said Jane. 'I saw them in Mexico. The most dreadful things. Even worse than Spain, and I didn't believe that was possible. Felston, too. Just three hundred miles away. I saw it, and I promise you I felt it – but now all I can think of is me. I know you'll say it's selfish, but I can't help that. It's true.'

'I shall say nothing of the kind,' said her mother. 'Why should I? You are caught up in one of those events which happen to all of us on occasion. For however short a time you are the centre of your world, and rightly so. It won't last, child, not with you, but while it does, accept it.' Then her mother smiled again, shyly this time. Jane had not thought it possible that her mother could be shy.

'Believe me,' her mother said, 'what you are undergoing does not make you unique. Do you intend to visit Felston?'

Jane thought of that other Jane, her godchild. Now was certainly not the time to tell Mummy about her.

'No reason,' she said.

'Canon Messeter's death has not been recorded in *The Times*,' said her mother. 'He would be glad of the opportunity to take one more glass of champagne with you.' Then she added surprisingly,

'Any man in his right mind would.' She paused for a moment. 'Being in motion is good when one has a problem like yours,' she said at last. 'At least I found it so.'

From the plains to the hills in the hot weather, she thought. From a hundred and ten degrees to seventy. All her children in England except the one still in her womb, leaving her husband behind with Posy Sanderson. The parlourmaid announced dinner.

The major, when he joined them for coffee, was surprisingly sober for a man who had dined at White's, which meant the major had been on his best behaviour.

'You know Derwent by any chance?' he asked.

'We've met,' said Jane.

'Kept boring on about a horse he'd bought that was going to win the National,' said the major. 'Well it's not. Not if you enter Bridget's Boy.'

'George, how often have you told me that in racing there is no such thing as a certainty?' his wife asked.

The major sought for, and to his delight remembered, a phrase of his wife's. 'In an ideal world,' he said at last. 'As it is Bridget's Boy could lick that horse of his over any distance you care to name. Time he was raced, my dear. He's developing a bit of a temper.'

'You went to see him?' Jane asked.

'Derwent's horse was in the same stable,' the major said. 'I couldn't resist. Had a word with your trainer. He agrees with me. Your horse needs work.'

'Hunting?'

'You mustn't dream of hunting him,' said the major. 'Not any more. Look what happened when Catherine Bower tried. He threw her so hard she damaged her knee. Nearly made her late for her own wedding. Not that she would – ' The major paused, aware that his wife's eye was upon him.

'Forgot what I was going to say,' he said.

The Bower marital rift must be common knowledge indeed if my stepfather's on to it, thought Jane.

'Perhaps you could take care of him for me,' she said.

'Delighted,' the major said. 'Soon as the jumping season starts. You've neglected him, young lady.'

'I've been away,' said Jane.

'Damn it you're always away,' the major said. 'How can we talk when you're away?'

'We?' said Jane.

'George is speaking on my behalf too,' her mother said. 'We talk about you often, but it's much more pleasant to talk with you.'

Jane found that she was blushing. It was the nicest thing that her mother and the major had ever said to her, but she still funked telling them about the small person in Felston she wished to adopt.

Lionel gave a party, choosing Pott's day off as being the most appropriate, in fact the only one possible. Pott hated parties. A crowd, far too big for dancing in a small mews house: barely room in fact to eat and drink. Bob was there, and Sybil Hendry, and Catherine, mercifully without either Crawley or Bower. Jane wondered if Lionel had invited Crawley and decided that the answer was probably yes. No doubt he had dangled Catherine's presence as bait. Not too many pansies – Lionel was always tactful about what he called his fellow sufferers – and no sailors at all. Which reminds me, thought Jane, that I must remember to ask about Liverpool, but first things first. She went at once to Catherine, and they kissed. Catherine was in her best looks, and that particular shade of blue just right for her.

'How's Piers?' she asked.

'Darling, how lovely to see you,' Catherine said. 'Later I want to hear all about Hollywood. Piers is quite well physically. I mean they didn't have to amputate or anything.'

'It was a possibility?'

'At the beginning,' said Catherine. 'But Piers wouldn't hear of it. The surgeon told him that he might die if he didn't.'

'What did Piers say?'

'He said we all have to die some time, even surgeons, and that if the surgeon took his leg off he'd hop back to the hospital and kill him personally.' Jane smiled. 'Honestly he's my twin and all that and I adore him, but I'm beginning to wonder if he's going mad. Violence can do that, can't it?'

Easy, Jane told herself. Easy, girl. She doesn't know about you. Nobody in this room knows, except Lionel.

'I dare say it's possible,' she said. 'But you're not telling me Piers is raving.'

'Well no,' said Catherine. 'Not that, thank God. But he's absolutely potty about exercise. I mean in the state he's in.'

'Physical jerks, you mean? Knees bend, arms upward stretch?'

'All that. And he wants one of those exercise bicycles. He even talks about riding. Riding! He can hardly stand.'

'He wants to strengthen his leg,' said Jane.

'Well of course,' said Catherine. 'And quite right too. But isn't it far too early?'

'He obviously doesn't think so.'

'No indeed. And he's got this weird instructor – sort of an expert on exercise – physiotherapist, that's it. She's a German refugee called Blumfeld. Renate Blumfeld. They spend absolute hours together.'

'You're afraid of an engagement?'

'Of course not,' said Catherine. 'She's Jewish. When Justin Crawley found out he nearly had a fit.'

Time to move on: more than time, but there were still things she needed to know.

'No doubt,' said Jane, 'but is she any good?'

'He can stand,' said Catherine. 'He can even walk a little.'

'But not enough,' said Jane. 'For the Rifle Brigade I mean.'

'That's right,' said Catherine. 'Piers would put up with anything for that – even that Jewess mauling him about. It's an idée fixe. He *can't* be right in the head.'

Lionel was talking to a tall and rather tousled young man without the least pretension to prettiness. Moreover the young man wore a day suit, a strident affirmation of Leftwing views when every other man there wore a dinner jacket or tails.

'Never in high summer,' Lionel was saying. 'Not the Uffizi. I don't care how many Tintorettos they've got. Darling, how marvellous to see you.'

He reached out to Jane, took her hand, then kissed her cheek, and said to the tousled man, 'May I introduce you to Jane Whitcomb? Darling, this is Geoffrey Brent, who is shortly to set out for Tuscany in hot pursuit of the visual arts. Jane,' he told the tousled man, 'is just back from Hollywood.'

'*The* Jane Whitcomb,' said Geoffrey Brent. 'I know your brother – but only in term time.'

'You're at Cambridge too?'

'Yet another economics don,' said Lionel. 'They will do it.'

'It keeps us off the streets,' Brent said. 'And how was Hollywood, Miss Whitcomb?'

'That's rather like saying "Describe the state of the universe. Write on one side of the paper only",' said Jane. 'In fact it's the same madhouse it always is. But quite happy about it. Being mad, I mean.'

'Psychotics often are, so I'm told,' said Brent. 'I'd love to talk to you about it some time. I'm doing a study – '

His voice became silent. It seemed he had suddenly become aware of Bob Patterson.

'Give me a ring,' said Jane. 'I'm in the book.'

'You're very kind.'

He nodded to them both, moved away, and stopped to speak to Sybil Hendry, the surest way to reach Bob Patterson.

'Nice chap,' Lionel said. 'Awfully Red of course, but nice with it. He and la belle Hendry are neighbours in the wilds of Northumberland.'

'Never mind that,' said Jane. 'What's all this about Liverpool?'

'One of my sailors got arrested,' said Lionel.

'Men's lavatories and coppers' narks?' said Jane.

'Certainly not,' said Lionel. 'My sailors do have certain standards. They wouldn't stoop so low. – Do please stop giggling. You know I didn't mean that.'

'Of course I do darling,' said Jane. 'But do tell. – What had your sailor done?'

'Drunk and disorderly and assault,' said Lionel. 'One policeman's helmet irretrievably ruined, and a blackshirt with a broken jaw.'

'Blackshirt? A Fascist you mean?'

'I do indeed. My dear, I simply flew to his defence. Hired a KC at vast expense, though I must say it was worth it. Between us we made up a simply splendid story.'

'I'm dying to hear a splendid story.'

'My sailor boy told the magistrate that the blackshirt offered him

221

money to commit an act of – what was the magistrate's phrase? – gross indecency. And of course he produced half the crew to swear they'd heard the blackshirt do it.'

'He got off?'

'Hero of the hour. Virtuous Jack Tar, spurning the vicious blackshirt's gold. – Well silver, actually. We called it five bob, just to keep it in the bounds of possibility. It really was worth a couple of nights in Liverpool, and almost worth the KC's fee. America was fun?'

'Not yet,' said Jane. 'But it will be soon.' She gave him his present and he unwrapped it at once.

'Oh what bliss,' Lionel said. 'No one can match the Americans for gadgets, can they?' He filled the cigarette case, offered her a cigarette, took one for himself, and lit them with the lighter, which worked first time. 'You see?' he said, and then more softly: 'Charles couldn't come?'

'No doubt you know why,' said Jane. Lionel always knew everything.

'His wife?' Jane nodded. 'Dead? . . . Poor Charles. Not because she's dead, that has to be a blessing, for her more than anyone – but the complications death leaves. – I assume there are complications?'

'I simply don't know,' said Jane, 'and that's the hell of it.'

'My poor love,' Lionel said. 'If you ever wish to talk in a less strident atmosphere – '

'I'll be round like a shot,' said Jane. 'Just one thing. Charles's wife. What was her first name?'

'Angela, poor darling.'

'Beautiful?'

'As if Botticelli had painted her,' Lionel said. 'Not meant for this world at all. Forgive me, my love. I simply must mingle.'

A hired waiter offered champagne, and she moved towards Bob. Brent was still talking to him.

'Of course I accept that you were entitled to look after yourself,' he was saying. 'I'd have done the same myself. But what they did to poor old Pardoe was barbaric.'

Jane pushed on determinedly. This was something she had to hear.

'Jane,' Bob called. 'Come and join us. We were talking about an old sparring partner of ours.'

It was hard not to laugh aloud, and Bob knew it.

222

'Dr Pardoe,' said Brent.

'Really?' said Jane. 'How is dear Cuthbert? And darling Marigold?'

'Marigold?' said Brent.

'Marigold Ledbitter,' said Jane. 'I always thought they would make a go of it. They looked so right together.'

'I thought it was you he was after,' said Bob. 'Not that I'd blame him.'

Brent looked bewildered. 'I hardly know him,' he said, 'except at meetings of a Cambridge society we both belong to. Your brother and he were staying with us – they're interested in the working conditions of the North East – perhaps disgusted by them would be more accurate – and my parents gave a ball for the local hunt. There was rather a lot of ragging at the end – '

'There usually is,' said Jane.

'Yes. Well . . . Some young hooligans persuaded him to join in a sort of dance. More like tribal warfare, really.'

'They flattened him,' said Bob, and smiled. Even remembering it was pleasure. 'Mind you, he flattened one or two of them as well. He punches his weight, that lad.'

'It was the most enormous fun,' Sybil Hendry said.

Really, thought Jane, she's as bad as Brenda Coupland.

Brent looked at Bob, who knew at once that Brent had been told that he, Bob, would be the prime target, and one that he no doubt had approved of, given Bob's background and politics. Now that isn't very logical, Bob admonished himself, but logic isn't exactly the first thing you look for when you're selecting a candidate for a belting, not even if you're a don at Cambridge. All the same he couldn't help liking the feller.

Brent said to Jane, 'You wrote a book about the General Strike.'

'Hardly your sort of book,' said Jane.

'Not at all. I enjoyed it very much. You should write more.'

'My brother seems to have taken over in that department,' said Jane.

'He's doing awfully well,' Brent agreed, but he was staring at Catherine, who was smiling at something Lionel was saying to her.

'Have you met Lady Catherine Bower?' said Jane.

'Alas not,' said Brent, without the slightest hint of whimsy in his voice.

'Then you must allow me to introduce you.'

Brent looked down at his clothes.

'I should have changed my suit,' he said. 'I thought there wasn't time. I could have made time, – but I didn't. Damn fool.'

'You're perfectly presentable,' said Jane. 'Come along.' She led him away.

'Well!' Sybil Hendry said.

'Smitten, d'you think?' said Bob.

'Bowled over,' said Sybil Hendry. 'Positively bouleversé.'

'You're talking Italian again,' said Bob.

But Brent had pulled himself together by the time they reached Catherine, and was able to make the right conversational noises while his eyes learned all they could about her, from the all too obvious wedding ring to the subtle magnificence of her Mainbocher gown. Jane and Lionel left them to it.

'I invited Jay, too,' Lionel said. 'His secretary told me he'd try.'

'He does work extremely hard,' said Jane.

Lionel looked at Catherine. Really, in full war paint she could look quite lovely. 'Harder than he need?' he asked.

'It's possible.'

Lionel smiled. 'You're a very loyal friend,' he said, 'which is a great comfort when one considers how many of my girlish secrets I've told you. But I know that Catherine and Jay are not exactly a model of nuptial bliss. . . . I know about Bob Patterson, too.'

'How on earth did you find that out?' asked Jane.

'People tell me things,' Lionel said. 'Don't ask me why. They just do. Catherine gave what I can only describe as a dire warning to Sybil Hendry in the Ladies of some nightclub or other. Not that I was using it. I hate dragging up, as you know.'

'But somebody else was?'

'Precisely. The perfect place to eavesdrop when one thinks about it. And so I was told. In strictest confidence, of course. She's in rather a mess, wouldn't you say?'

'Of her own making.'

'No doubt,' said Lionel, 'but even so – '

'Her enchanted castle was dynamited,' said Jane, 'her adored granny is all but dead and her adored brother may yet end his days as a cripple. Fate rather overdid things when it demonstrated to her that happy endings aren't part of the contract.'

'Exactly,' said Lionel. 'So – '

'But her life wasn't all bad,' said Jane. 'Now she lives in another enchanted castle, her brother didn't lose his leg, and Jay loves her. He may not be an easy man, but he's a damn sight better than that bastard Crawley.'

Lionel blinked, – Jane rarely used language like that – then looked to where Brent in his turn was making Catherine smile.

'It looks as if old Creepers has a rival,' he said.

'Oh damn the girl,' said Jane. 'Why can't she make do with Jay?'

But when Bower arrived it was obvious that his wife had no intention of doing so, and made no move to greet him. Brent, far too astute to try to talk economics to her, was telling her about a mare he owned that she might like to try some day. When Bower came in she waved to him, politely, as to a half-remembered acquaintance, and went on listening to Brent. Bower came up to Jane and she offered her cheek and he kissed it as Lionel bustled off to find him champagne.

'Charles not here?' said Bower.

'In Switzerland,' said Jane.

'Oh yes. Of course. Sorry. That was tactless of me.'

'You didn't use it?'

'We don't print such things about our proprietors.' His voice neither mocked nor jeered; simply stated a fact. Lionel came back to them and a waiter followed with champagne.

'Tell me,' said Bower, 'who's that improperly dressed young man who's got the hots for my wife?'

'Geoffrey Brent,' said Lionel. 'He's a don at Cambridge.'

'Jesus,' said Bower. 'Which candy bar will she unwrap next?'

'Jay, my sweet,' said Jane. 'Life may be getting you down, but you shouldn't say such things to us.'

'And especially not at one of my parties,' said Lionel.

Bower went without another word to talk to Bob. Perhaps it was because Bob bought a lot of advertising space in the *Daily World*, thought Jane: perhaps because Sybil Hendry was a very pretty girl. Whatever the reason, his wife made no move to join them.

225

. 24 .

'Good of you to come,' said Piers.

He says it as if St George's Hospital is a hotel full of boring people, she thought, and I've come to partner him at the most dreary dinner dance. What an attractive young man he is, even now.

'Not good at all,' she said. 'I wanted to see you.'

He rummaged happily through the Fortnum's hamper she had brought him: plovers' eggs, asparagus, caviar.

'They do feed me here,' he said, 'but not like this.'

She bent to kiss his cheek. Pushing forty, he thought, and she smells and acts like spring, and with good reason.

'I'll ask you now,' she said, 'a) because convention demands it, and b) because I must. Then it'll be out of the way and we can gossip like Christians. How are you?'

'Better,' he said. 'Really quite a lot better.'

She looked at the exercise bicycle that seemed to dominate the room.

'You go for a spin from time to time?'

'Through rather boring country,' said Piers. 'It was Renate's idea originally. Have you heard about her?'

'Renate Blumfeld? Yes . . . Catherine mentioned her.'

'Catherine doesn't like her,' said Piers. 'I'm blest if I know why.'

And I'm blest if I'm going to tell you, thought Jane.

'I think she's afraid Renate might make me overdo it,' said Piers, 'but she doesn't. Honestly. She holds me back.'

And a good thing too, thought Jane. In a thin silk dressing gown and pyjamas, seated in a vast leather chair, he looked about eight inches wide, but the fire inside him had just been stoked.

'Don't rush it,' she said. 'Do it right.'

'That's what Renate says. . . . But Catherine doesn't want me to do it at all.'

'Whyever not?'

'Because it mightn't work, and if it doesn't I'd be snookered,' said Piers.

Well there's truth in that, Jane thought. She's still your loving twin when she remembers.

'And would you be?' she asked.

'Well of course,' said Piers. 'But it will work. You'll see.' He paused for a moment. 'I can't be a cripple,' he said at last. 'It just isn't on. And please don't tell me a lot of people are and still manage to live useful, happy lives.'

'I had no intention of doing so,' said Jane.

Piers grinned. 'No,' he said. 'Not you. Usually when they talk such tosh I invite them to name three living examples, which cuts out Nelson. All they can manage is Roosevelt, and then they're stuck. You do understand why I mustn't be a cripple?'

'Of course,' she said. 'The army.'

'Of course.' He said it as if the army were the choice between life and death, which no doubt it was.

'You need two sound legs to be in the infantry,' said Piers.

He talks as if there's going to be another war, thought Jane. Is that why his sister thinks he's going mad?

'It's never boring to see someone take their profession seriously,' she said.

He looked at the rest of the books by his bed.

'Clausewitz, Wellington, Gustavus Adolphus, Hannibal,' he said. 'That madman Lloyd and his passion for the pike. At least I can learn from the masters when I can't do anything else.' He turned back to her. 'You haven't asked the other question.'

'What other question?'

'How well can I walk.'

'If you want to tell me you will,' said Jane. 'You were never tongue tied.'

He lay back in his chair then and shouted with laughter.

'Oh I do love you,' he said. 'Deferentially, of course.'

'Of course,' she said. 'Do you want to tell me?'

'I do, rather,' he said. 'It's beginning to work, you see. The treatment's hell, as a matter of fact, but it's effective.'

'You'll be back with your company?'

He put his finger to his lips. 'I pray rather a lot these days,' he said, 'but I don't despair.'

'Not you,' she said, then, 'If I may ask, how is your grandmother?'

'Does she know, do you mean? About me?' Jane nodded. 'The medicos can't say, but my guess is not. I pray not anyway.'

'Any point in my going to see her?'

'None,' said Piers. 'Excuse the cliché, but much better for you to remember her as she was.'

'I'll always do that,' said Jane.

'She thought the world of you,' said Piers, and smiled. For such a stern young man he had a beautiful smile.

The door opened and a young woman came in. Not beautiful at all, thought Jane. Not ugly, like the marquesa: just plain. What a dismissive word that was. Hair mouse colour, nose that the poor girl couldn't help, but there it was, and mouth too thin. Fine eyes, though; big and wide, the colour of oloroso sherry. She wore a white coat, and her shoulders were heavy, too heavy, no doubt because of the work she did, for this must be Renate Blumfeld, whose business it was to put Piers back on his feet. She looked quickly from Jane to Piers, and Jane thought: Oh dear, not another one, because the one look was enough to betray her.

'I am sorry,' Miss Blumfeld said. 'I didn't realise you had a visitor. It is three o'clock.'

'And time for your treatment,' said Jane, 'which I mustn't interrupt.'

Piers said, 'Miss Whitcomb, this is Miss Blumfeld,' and Jane received a short and rather clumsy bow, but there was no war between them. She could leave that sort of thing to Brenda Coupland now Meldrum. She offered her hand.

'How do you do?' she said. Miss Blumfeld grasped her hand cautiously, as something she could all too easily crush, and no doubt she could, thought Jane.

'How do you do?'

Jane went over to Piers and kissed his cheek.

'I'll leave you to it then,' she said. Piers made no effort to detain her. Walking out of that hospital was the only thought in his head.

She drove the Bentley up to Felston, knowing perfectly well it was bait: the most powerful bribe she could offer young Jane, but when she went to John Bright Street, to see Norah and Andy and find out how the land lay, she took a taxi. A Bentley would still be an irresistible challenge to the young of that area, and perhaps the not so young, too. The inhabitants of John Bright Street had no reason to cherish the rich.

It was Norah who tugged at the cord looped round the banisters, and so opened the door.

'Why, Jane,' she said. 'Come on up, hinny. Why didn't you tell us you were coming?'

Jane climbed the stairs, babbling about impulses and spurs of the moment. The brass rods that held the worn stair carpet in place gleamed like gold, but then the whole place gleamed. Norah couldn't live in it if it didn't. Jane reached the top, put her arms round Norah, and hugged her. Norah stiffened for a moment, as she always did – all the other women she knew were chary of embraces – then her arms came round Jane.

'By it's grand to see you,' she said. 'Andy's not back from work yet but he won't be long. Come in and have a drink of tea.'

Just like Grandma used to make, thought Jane, stewed to a mahogany brown no matter how much milk you put in it, but this wasn't refreshment after all, this was a ritual.

'How are you, darling?' she asked, and again Norah stiffened, then relaxed.

'Canny,' she said. 'You heard I had a miscarriage?'

'Bob told me. That was one of the reasons I decided to come here.' *Liar, Jane Whitcomb, but you mean it for the best.*

'I'd better tell you before Andy comes,' said Norah. 'He gets that embarrassed – about women, you know. The way we are. Miscarriages and that.' She was blushing herself as she said it.

'What about miscarriages?' Really, extracting information was like pulling teeth, but she must take care not to play the inquisitor, not with this woman she liked so much.

'Dr Stobbs said there's something wrong with me. I could

miscarry every time I – ' Her colour deepened. 'I might never have a bairn. Only Bob happened to come by a couple of weeks ago.' Sybil Hendry, thought Jane, and shops to buy. ' – and he said there were specialists in London – '

'Gynaecologists,' said Jane.

'That's right. In a place called Harley Street.'

'There are indeed.'

'It's Andy's holidays on Saturday – after he's finished his half shift, and we're going to London to stay with Bob and I'm going to see this specialist feller.' Then she added almost defiantly, 'Bob's paying.'

'Well of course,' said Jane.

'You don't think it's wrong?'

'Don't talk daft.' Jane's accent so exactly mimicked her own that Norah jumped, and the two women giggled.

'How can it be wrong?' said Jane. 'He's family, and the money won't bother him. I'd have suggested it myself if I'd known about your trouble.'

'Would you?'

'It would have been a pleasure. But you still haven't explained how you're going to go to London.'

Norah looked puzzled. 'By bus. That's how we're going to London.'

'Three hundred miles in a bus?' said Jane. She'd had no idea it was possible.

'It takes hours and hours,' said Norah. 'That's why I'm dreading it.'

'Why not take the train?'

'The bus is cheaper. A lot cheaper,' Norah said, then before Jane could speak she hurried on, 'Please don't say you'll pay for the train fare. It was bad enough taking from Bob – but I'm desperate for a bairn. We both are – but if we take the bus we can pay our own way. We won't be obligated. Do you understand what I mean?'

'I wasn't going to offer to pay for the tickets,' said Jane.

'Oh,' Norah said. 'I'm sorry. I don't want you to think – '

'I was going to suggest I gave you a lift in my car – and that isn't being obligated. I have to go to London anyway.'

'All the way to London,' said Norah, 'in that car?'

'Well it'll be quicker than the bus,' said Jane, 'and more comfortable.'

'Well of course it will,' Norah said. 'You drove me to the chapel in it, don't you remember? When I was married. So I know what it's like. Oh Jane, it'll be wonderful.'

Andy came up the back stairs and into the kitchen to find his wife embracing Jane. Norah's face seemed to glow with happiness, and she said, 'Andy, pet. Guess what?'

He smiled. 'Eight hours in the fettling shop's no training for guessing games. Just tell us,' he said.

'Jane's going to drive us to London in the Bentley.'

His face hardened for a moment. Worried about charity, thought Jane.

'Don't get the idea that I came here just for that,' said Jane. 'I've one or two things to attend to here, but I want to be back in town for Monday.'

'Town?' Andy said, then remembered Cambridge dons and their need to visit the British Museum. 'Oh, London. Aye. Well if you're sure – '

'I'll be glad of your company,' said Jane. 'It's boring – all that distance on my own.'

'Well,' said Andy, 'I don't know what to say. Except thanks very much.'

'That's settled then,' she said. ' And do forgive me, Andy. I haven't even said hello.' She moved towards him, but he backed away.

'Let me get out of this boiler suit and have a wash first,' he said.

Lying in bed that night, she reviewed the gleanings of her espionage. Bet and her husband Frank were well, and Frank might yet progress from tram driver to tram inspector, a height so Empyrean that Bet still crossed her fingers whenever she mentioned it. Little Frank was also well, which was gratifying if uninteresting, and young Jane still talked about the Bentley, and as an afterthought, about the lady who owned it, 'the one with the pretty clothes.' It wasn't much to build on, but it was all she would get: it would have to do.

There had been other news, too: news she had not wanted to hear. Canon Messeter, Andy was quite sure, was dying. She would call on him as soon as she had seen young Jane, she thought. No more champagne by the sound of it, but at least the chance of gossip and a blessing. No problems about going to the clinic either: not with a five-thousand-dollar cheque in her handbag.

Next day she took a taxi to Bet's house, where a Bentley would be just as much a challenge as in John Bright Street. She had prepared for the expedition with care: an unobtrusive suit, plain shoes, a hat that would have moved Lionel to protest. There were presents, too, but only for the children: she dared not risk too obvious a bribe. A toy car for Frank, and for Jane a couple of Beatrix Potter books: nothing too luxurious; again no hint of bribery. No money. Young Jane's money was already taken care of, in the trust fund that Jane and Bob had set up for her. No one could say – could they? – that she was trying to buy the child?

Bet received her with that mixture of resentment and awe which she always showed to Jane. Of all the Pattersons, she was the only one who could never be at ease with her. Because we're both women? Jane wondered, or is it because she senses I'm a threat to her, even when she doesn't know what the threat will be?

Frank was at work; – late shift, said Bet. He got that tired on late shift. Young Jane had taken young Frank to the shops in his push chair. Now or never, thought Jane.

'They're both well?' she asked.

'Never better.'

'And Jane's doing well at school?'

'A great one for her books, our Jane. The teachers is that pleased.'

'I'm delighted to hear it,' said Jane.

'Aye,' said Bet. 'Me an' all.' For a moment both resentment and awe were forgotten. 'I'll tell you something – if you don't mind.'

'Of course not.'

'All my brothers was clever. Well you know that. John an officer, and Andy making speeches, and our Bob that rich. – ' She paused, then continued. 'I wasn't clever. Not at school. Not now. Never will be. It doesn't matter all that much if you're a woman, not if you know how to run a home. – Not the way we live, anyhow. I manage.

'Young Frank's not brilliant either. He's not daft mind you – but he'll finish up driving a tram like his da. But I'll tell you a funny thing – '

Jane waited.

'Our Jane, *my* Jane, she's not just good at her books. Her teacher says she's brilliant. Now I know I said that's not important if you're a woman, but I was talking about me. Not her. Not our Jane. Being clever's as much a part of her as having two legs. I've watched her and I know. And watching her set me thinking – and I've talked it over with Frank and he agrees. It took a bit of doing mind you, but he sees it my way now.'

'Sees what, Bet?'

'Thanks to you and Bob my Jane's got money put by. That money's going to help her.' She leaned closer to Jane. 'That money and her brains is going to take her to the grammar school. Maybe even university. I don't care what it costs Frank and me. We'll do it for her. She's our bairn, but she's as good as any of them.'

'Of course she is,' said Jane. 'I knew that as soon as I'd spent five minutes with her.' She rose. 'Will you excuse me? I simply must go.'

'You'll take a cup of tea, surely?' said Bet. 'And our Jane'll be that disappointed if she doesn't see you. Frank an' all.'

'I'm sorry,' said Jane, 'but I simply must go to the clinic. I hear that Canon Messeter may not last much longer.'

'It's a miracle he's still here,' said Bet, 'but he's the one would know about miracles, wouldn't you say? Ah well. I won't press you, Jane. I know how you feel about him and it does you credit. You've got a real feeling heart.'

Jane walked to the clinic, and as she did so she played back the scene in Bet's house as if it were film on those editing machines she'd seen in Hollywood. Had Bet sensed what she was after? Had the talk about the grammar school been simply that – talk? She walked on for a while. Perhaps to the first question, she decided at last: a definite no to the second. Young Jane was Bet's child, and Bet was determined to do everything in her power to make her successful, to get on: but she would always be Bet's child. Consciously or instinctively, thought Jane, Bet's beaten you fair and square. No more taking that enchanting small person for a ride in the Bentley: no buying her clothes at Harrods, or teaching her French. No point in repining about it either. Bet was the child's mother, and she not only loved her daughter, not only intended to

233

make sacrifices for her, she intended the tram driver to make sacrifices also, and there was devotion indeed. I should like to cry, thought Jane, but the clinic is just round the corner. I'll have to wait till I get there and make do with a cigarette instead.

·The clinic was as busy as it always was: patients, helpers, nurses, packed into the utterly decayed grandeur of what had once been a handsome Georgian drawing room, but one of the nurses, those socially superior nurses whom Stobbs somehow bullied and black-mailed into working there for nothing, recognised her at once.

'Miss Whitcomb,' she said. 'What a surprise. Does the doctor know you're coming?'

Again Jane heard herself babble about being in the neighbourhood and spur of the moment.

'Of course,' said the nurse. 'You'll want to see the doctor?'

'And Canon Messeter – if it's possible.'

'I'll just take you to the office,' said the nurse. 'You'll be more comfortable there. Dr Stobbs will come to you as soon as he's free, I'm sure.'

The office was a grim little room with a desk, a filing cabinet, three chairs, a calendar advertising laxatives on one wall, and a print of a Mantegna Madonna and Child on another. Nothing else, not even a carpet, just well-scrubbed boards. Very much Canon Messeter's room, Jane remembered, when she had worked there. She lit a cigarette: it was still not possible to cry.

The door opened and Dr Stobbs came in, walking slowly for once, and yet again she began her recitation.

'I'm so sorry to bother you,' she said, 'but I had business in Felston and I – '

'You hadn't heard then?' said Stobbs.

Interrupting again, thought Jane, but then he does it so well. Stobbs could interrupt a charging rhino.

'Heard?' she said.

'Messeter's dead.'

'No,' she said. 'I hadn't heard.'

'He died at ten to seven this morning. No pain. Nothing like that. He just fell asleep. At Rest, as it says on the tombstones.'

Dr Stobbs, an atheist, did not approve of tombstones. The money they cost could be put to better use at his clinic.

'Would you like to see him?' he asked, and she nodded. It was unlikely that the Canon had seen a priest, not if he were asleep. Stobbs wouldn't have sent for one, he would be too busy fighting for the canon's life: but he had lost, and someone had to pray by him.

'In a moment,' she said. 'I'd better give you this first, in case I forget.' She handed over Forest's cheque. Stobbs took it and read the figures, then glowered at Jane, incredulous that anyone could possibly forget five thousand dollars donated to *his* clinic.

'I'll take you up,' he said.

'No,' said Jane. 'You're busy. I know the way.' She went to the door.

'Just a minute. Please,' said Stobbs, and she turned. Even then, at the beginning of her grief, that 'Please' had surprised her.

'He was my friend, too, you know,' said Stobbs.

'I know,' Jane said at last, 'but your business is with the living. It's what you always say, and it's true.'

As she went to Messeter's room she thought that what Stobbs had said was as close as he could ever come to affection. Was there perhaps a hint of jealousy as well? No jokes and laughter and champagne for Dr Stobbs. Only work, hard and unrelenting, and in the end, failure, because we all die. She went into the room. Stobbs was right. Almost the canon could have been asleep, except for that utter stillness. Like a creature made out of precious things, she thought: face and hands like ivory; hair like silver. Well, he had been precious. One of the rare ones; perhaps even beyond price.

She knelt by the bedside and began to pray: the Lord's Prayer and a Hail Mary because the canon had been 'High', then her own prayer for the soul of the departed. After that she knelt for a little longer, and remembered scraps from the Bible and the Prayer Book: 'As in Adam all die, even so in Christ shall all be made alive.' . . . 'I am the resurrection and the life, saith the Lord.' . . . 'in sure and certain hope of the resurrection to eternal life.' . . . No one she had ever known had more sure, more certain hope, she thought, and got to her feet. By his bedside was a clutter of objects: a Bible, a clock that appeared to have stopped, and a crucifix on a chain. She took the crucifix and inserted it between Messeter's clasped hands.

As she did so, the door opened, and the nurse who had found Stobbs for her came in.

'This way, my lord,' she said, and seemed hardly aware that Jane was there.

A man came in, tall, heavily built, strong featured: grey eyes and yellow hair rigorously clipped. In his thirties, thought Jane, and used to his own way every year of his life. He stopped at the sight of Jane.

'I beg your pardon,' he said.

'Oh I'm sorry,' said the nurse. 'Miss Whitcomb – this is the Marquis of Alston.' As she pronounced the title her voice was a fanfare: then she looked about her rather wildly and was gone.

'How d'you do?' said Jane, and offered her hand.

As he took it he said, 'Miss Jane Whitcomb?'

'Yes,' she said.

'You knew him rather well,' said Alston. 'As a matter of fact I did, too. He was my godfather. The doctor called us last night – my mother and father are away, but I set off first thing. – Still too late, alas.'

'He died just before seven,' said Jane. 'Just fell asleep and died.'

'He was the most remarkable man I ever met,' said Alston, and stood looking down at the body, his hands clasped in front of him.

No doubt he's praying too, thought Jane, and waited in silence.

At last Alston said, 'Forgive me. I really had the most tremendous affection for him but I find I can't stay in this room. I wonder – please don't think me impertinent, – but may I give you lunch somewhere? It would be a relief to talk to you, and you do know my father, after all.'

'Do I?'

'The Duke of Derwent,' said Alston. 'The canon bullied him into a public appearance when you organised the Felston Hunger March.'

'Yes of course,' said Jane, and remembered the duke's look of overwhelming dismay whenever politics was mentioned, and on a Hunger March politics is mentioned all the time. Canon Messeter had found it a cause for laughter which he assured Jane was perfectly innocent.

'I should like to lunch with you very much,' said Jane.

. 25 .

They drove to Newcastle, to the one hotel Alston considered reliable, and on the way they talked about the canon incessantly, as if reminiscence could at least keep something of him back on earth.

'He was a clipping rider,' said Alston. 'Took some fearful tosses in his day. Good soldier, too. Commanded his battalion in the Rifle Brigade just before the end.'

'Like St Francis,' said Jane. 'All worldly pleasures and soldiering – then suddenly he gave it all up to come here.'

'Not at first,' said Alston. 'When he first started out as a parson he was even more successful than he'd been as a soldier. He said to me once, "Do you know, I very nearly became a bishop. Near as dammit. What a narrow squeak." '

'And so it was, for him,' said Jane. 'What he wanted was what he finally got. In Felston.'

'Self-sacrifice?'

'More service, really,' said Jane. 'He wanted it as a miser wants gold.'

'And he got it and it killed him.'

For the second time that day Jane thought: But we all have to die of something. Then why not service?

Aloud she said, 'I would bet a very large sum that he died happy.'

'I wouldn't take you,' Alston said. 'I'm perfectly sure it's true.'

Then the chauffeur pulled up in front of the hotel, and the head porter scurried to open the car door. Suddenly it was a long way from the Felston Clinic and Canon Messeter.

He was a good host, attentive without overdoing it, and his memories of Canon Messeter fitted exactly with her own, until when the pudding arrived he touched his lips with his napkin,

237

sipped his claret and said: 'My mother and father saw that film about you. The one about the war.'

It was a change of subject so abrupt as to remind her at once of Charles doing his Chairman of the Board piece.

'Here at the Royal, I think it was,' said Alston. 'I saw it too. In California. Hollywood, actually.'

'Which theatre?' Jane asked.

'Not exactly a theatre,' said Alston. 'You see my father owns land there – in California – and he'd asked me to pop across and see how things were, and after I'd done it a friend of mine suggested I take a look at Hollywood, and as a result I went to a party given by a man called Murray Fisch. I gather you know him.'

'Not to say "know",' said Jane. 'We meet from time to time.'

'Ah,' said Alston, and Jane thought that he might well be a rather perceptive young man.

'He had a private screening of the film,' said Alston. 'What's more he persisted in calling it "my film", which made it worse, if anything.'

'Worse?' said Jane. 'You thought it all in bad taste?'

'Execrable,' Alston said. 'Who on earth shows off the family treasures to people one invites for drinks?'

Jane said, 'I never looked at it like that.'

'Why on earth should you?' Alston said. 'It's your life. And a most remarkable life too, if I may say so.'

'It wasn't quite like that,' said Jane.

'No dashing American heroes?'

'Not one.'

'All the same,' Alston said, 'a lot of it was true, or so I was told.'

'About half,' said Jane, 'except that it was noisier and far more frightening than anything in the movie. Smellier, too. Who told you?'

'Georgina Payne,' Alston said.

'She was at the party?'

'Not for the screening. Seeing her own films always depressed her, she said.'

'Really? Why?'

'When she sees the bad bits she wants to do the whole thing again, or else set fire to the film.'

That did indeed sound like Georgie.

'But she looked in later?'

'Yes she did,' said Alston. 'This Fisch didn't seem altogether pleased. In fact I rather got the idea she hadn't been invited. But that's ridiculous of course.'

'Not ridiculous at all,' said Jane. 'If Georgie wanted to go to a party she would go; invitation or not.'

'But how could she?'

'She's got an Academy Award,' said Jane.

'What's that?'

What bliss, thought Jane. He really doesn't know. Oh why isn't Murray Fisch here?

'The keys of the kingdom,' she said.

'Yes,' said Alston. 'Now that you mention it, the others did rather treat her like royalty. She's awfully nice, wouldn't you say?'

'Awfully.'

'And thinks highly of you, too.'

'Too kind.'

Can you be Georgie's very own nice chap? she wondered. She's really not the type to meet the heir to a dukedom and not say so without good reason, and what better reason could there be?

'We've known each other for ages,' she said. 'As a matter of fact she marched with us – for Felston I mean.'

'I'd no idea,' Alston said. 'I was away at the time you see, and my father never said a word.'

Of course he didn't, thought Jane. All that political stuff. All the duke wanted to do was forget it. Once again she heard the canon chuckle.

'It was just before she began work on the picture,' said Jane. 'She was over here in London and I asked her, and she said yes at once.'

She told Alston then how Georgie had marched all day, walking with each rank in turn, so that every man there could say that he had marched beside Georgina Payne: and at the end of the day she had sung for them too.

'How marvellous,' Alston said, 'but forgive me – from what you said do I gather that you walked the whole way?'

'Well yes,' said Jane, 'but I had to. It was my idea.'

'She's awfully sweet, wouldn't you say?' said Alston.

Quite the wrong word, thought Jane. Wonderful, delicious, exciting, maddening, gorgeous, hell on earth, but never, never sweet.

'Awfully,' she said.

There could be no doubt about it. This was Georgie's nice chap.

'That nurse said the funeral will be on Friday,' said Alston. 'Will you be there?'

'Certainly,' said Jane. 'The whole of Felston will be there.'

'I too,' Alston said. 'My mother and father will be devastated. Especially my mother. She and the canon were great friends years ago.'

St Francis too had been one for the ladies, she remembered, before he fell in love with God instead.

The service was held in the little church like a tram shed that the canon had made his own. The place was packed, but Dr Stobbs had warned her it would be, and kept a place for her among the chief mourners, most of whom were the canon's relatives, and all of whom were rich, and hopelessly at a loss to cope with a situation for which there were no rules, since everyone else in the church was poor. Men in blue serge suits and black ties, women in the blacks carefully preserved for death: all shiny with age, and all spotlessly clean, for the canon's sake as well as their own.

A church all black, a church full of crows, thought Jane, except that the hymns were played, at the canon's request, by the St Oswald Colliery Band, resplendent in scarlet and blue, their instruments golden in the soft murmuring gaslight. A bishop too, majestic in mitre and cope, and another priest only slightly less majestic – an archdeacon perhaps? – to take the service. Then off at last to the cemetery. Norah and Andy were in the church, she noticed, and they too were at the graveside. Like all the men there who had work, Andy had lost half a shift's pay to be present, but not to be there was unthinkable. So two atheists at least had disregarded their principles and entered a church when Canon Messeter beckoned.

The last time she had visited that cemetery it had been in a carriage drawn by two black horses, for the burial of Andy's father, Stan Patterson. Sharing it with her were a trade union Branch

Secretary and a Primitive Methodist. This time she went in a Rolls-Royce and her companion was a marquis. The cortège was enormous; there were cars, dozens of them, and even more people on foot, headed by the St Oswald Colliery Band playing, inevitably, the Tchaikovsky Funeral March, and the trade union banners that had cost so much skill and effort in the making. The pavements were lined, too, and from distant doorways men and women came running to be there when the coffin passed: to show the canon that they had not forgotten.

'Remarkable,' said Alston. 'All the women were crying. A lot of the men, too.'

'I shall cry myself quite soon,' said Jane, and then: 'Did many of his family come?'

'Everyone that was fit to travel,' said Alston. 'Brother officers too.'

Not Charles, she thought, and just as well. He has enough deaths to worry about.

They arrived at last, and Stobbs led them through the crowd to take their places by the grave.

'Man that is born of a woman hath but a short time to live, and is full of misery,' the possible archdeacon boomed, but Canon Messeter had never been that. Angry sometimes, sometimes despairing, but always lurking in the background the faith, hope and charity in which St Paul set such store, and laughter too. 'In the midst of life, we are in death: of whom may we seek succour but of thee, O Lord. . . ?'

That was more like it. The canon had seen death at the Somme, as well as in Felston, and in the end he too sought succour in God, but he still went on fighting until the fight killed him, and what better way to die?

'Forasmuch as it hath pleased Almighty God of his great mercy to take unto himself the soul of our dear brother here departed. . . .'

The clods of earth rained down on the coffin then, and as Jane cast hers she said silently: 'Goodbye my dear. We shall miss you; every one of us.'

Three trumpeters of the St Oswald Colliery band moved forward, marching, rhythmic and slow, the trumpets raised to their lips in unison. Company buglers, every one, thought Jane, and the older men stiffened to attention, knowing what was to come, as one trumpeter clicked his fingers, and the sound of the Last Post sounded: pure and soaring and heart-lifting, and yet unbearably sad. Jane realised that she was crying at last.

They had one suitcase between them, a scuffed and battered piece that cowered in awe behind Jane's elegant luggage, but they were cheerful, there could be no doubt about it. To ride to London in a Bentley was a rare treat indeed: perhaps unique. Jane made only one proviso: that they should stop for lunch, and that it should be on her. She had no wish to arrive in London starving. To her astonishment, Andy offered almost no resistance. Another treat for Norah, she thought, and he doesn't want to spoil it, but he acts as if it would be a treat for him, too, and once the Bentley left Felston he began whispering to Norah and made her giggle in a way that even Bob might have envied. Jane found herself praying that Bob's gynaecologist would turn out to be a good one.

She gave them lunch in a hotel in Nottinghamshire. It was just off the Great North Road, and the food, Bob had told her, was good. The head waiter checked for a moment at the sight of Norah and Andy in their best, but they'd arrived in a Bentley after all, and there was a hint of frost in Jane's eye that was as menacing as a pointed pistol. 'I have money,' the frosty look said, 'and if you try to be snooty with me by God you'll know about it.' He led her to the best table he had.

Vichyssoise and poached salmon and peaches and cream, and just one glass of hock because she was driving. Norah and Andy had roast duck: something else to enjoy for the first time together.

'It's just like the pictures,' said Norah, but then to her everything splendid was like the pictures: the only place for her where splendour existed.

Jane began to talk about the Brown Derby and the Garden of Allah in Hollywood: Twenty-One and El Morocco in New York, and Norah listened, wide eyed. Andy ate on doggedly.

Time to smoke just one cigarette, and then back on the road, and soon Andy had Norah giggling again. I have never in my life seen a man so changed she thought, as the Bentley nosed its way into the sort of countryside Norah had never even read about: green

242

fields, sleek cattle, expensive horses, and the first of the hay being forked into a cart drawn by Clydesdales the size of elephants. Farm houses, too, and manor houses, and pretty villages: neat brick, gleaming stone, and all of it saying money, not in a loud and vulgar way, but softly, behind the hand. Norah gaped: this was even more incredible than Hollywood, because this was real.

London at first was a disappointment: just the sort of trams and houses and shops you saw in Felston. More of them, that was all. Then Hampstead appeared with its slightly dotty grandeur, and Norah began to gape again, and Jane headed westwards, determined to take in all the sights she could think of. Norah might not have much time for sightseeing; and so she drove past the Houses of Parliament and Buckingham Palace and Piccadilly Circus, and Mayfair with its vast hotels, and Norah cried out aloud that such things could be, and Andy said not a word except 'By lad, there's nothing like that in Felston.' Marriage was indeed a remarkable institution, thought Jane.

Even South Molton Street delighted Norah. It was all right, Jane supposed, but nothing especially exciting. Late Georgian brick for the most part, and most of the houses done over into flats. Still, there were window boxes and the door knobs gleamed. It was pleasant, but hard to believe that it could inspire such ecstasies, and then she realised why. A piece of one of those houses belonged to Norah's brother-in-law.

Bob was waiting for them, easy and relaxed in his business suit. He took them at once on a tour of inspection: drawing room, study, dining room, two bedrooms, two bathrooms, and Norah loved it all, but she was puzzled, too.

'All this,' she said. 'Just for you? All by yourself?'

Jane busied herself in lighting a cigarette. Definitely not a time to look at Bob. She looked at Andy instead. Andy was doing his best not to laugh. It wasn't a very good best.

'All by myself,' said Bob.

'But who looks after it for you?' said Norah. 'The place is spotless.'

'The firm who own the house supply cleaners.'

'No maids?' She sounded disappointed.

'I'm away too much,' he said, 'and anyway a bachelor would be

243

more likely to have a valet. Can you see me with a valet?'

'No,' said Norah, and smiled. 'But I can see you with a maid.'

'Cheeky,' he said, and turned to his brother. 'I'm surprised at you, kidder. You should keep her in order.'

'I'm not that daft,' said Andy, and winked at his wife.

Bob went to the ice bucket and touched the champagne bottle. It must have been cold enough, for he opened it at once, and poured, then raised his glass. 'Good to have you here, the pair of you,' he said. 'Here's to a happy visit, and a successful one.'

Please God yes, thought Jane. She needs a baby so.

'An army with banners,' said Charles. 'Doesn't sound much like poor old Rupert, does it?'

'Yes, but they were such happy banners,' said Jane. 'All gold and scarlet and sky-blue. And they were carried by people who loved him. The whole army loved him.'

'And the Last Post too?'

'Three trumpeters.'

'Rupert would have liked that,' said Charles. 'Priest or no priest, he was very proud of being in the army, and so he should have been. He was a damn good soldier.'

She turned on her pillow to look at him. More lines, she thought, and more grey hairs, and goodness how tired he looked.

'He loved the good things too,' she said. 'The very last time I saw him he opened a bottle of champagne he kept in Stobbs's refrigerator. Stobbs was furious, I remember. He said it was for keeping medicines in. The canon said that champagne was a medicine too.'

Charles smiled. 'He could be tough when he had to be.'

'Well of course. He was a successful soldier. But it wasn't just toughness. He could be ruthless – if it was in a good cause. Remember when he asked me to do my grande horizontale turn to persuade you to keep that Felston shipyard open?'

'And you turned him down?'

'I can be ruthless too,' she said. It was meant as a joke, but Charles said at once: 'Don't I know it.'

'Not that it wouldn't have been a labour of love. It wasn't that. It just seemed to me that it was wrong.'

'How, wrong?'

'To use you,' she said. 'To use me come to that. We didn't come to be like this to exploit each other.'

But really good people never give a thought for such things. Look at that ugly marquesa, who tried to get her into bed with Timothy Jordan for no other reason than that it would be good for him. A work of charity, in fact. But Charles didn't know all the details yet, and there was no reason why he should. His demon of jealousy hurt him enough without that. . . . She reached out and touched his face.

'Was Zurich so very bad?' she asked.

'Shows, does it?' said Charles. 'Zurich was ghastly.'

'But how – '

'To begin with, they hadn't buried her. They'd kept her in some sort of ice-box contraption till I got there.'

'Good God, why?'

'They thought I'd want to look at her for the last time. It was the head quack himself who said that; Herr Doktor Kampfer. He had the most awful pious look on his face when he said it, and I'm pretty sure I know why.' He hesitated, then continued: 'I didn't visit her all that often.'

'Well of course you didn't,' she said. 'She didn't even know who you were.'

'Yes, but he was with her all the time, trying to cure her.'

'You paid him money for that,' said Jane. 'As he's the best of his kind, no doubt it was a great deal of money.'

'The Herr Doktor never talks about money,' said Charles. 'He talks about dedication, compassion, even love.'

'Oily little pig,' said Jane, and Charles laughed aloud.

'Thank you for being on my side,' he said.

'It isn't that at all,' said Jane. 'There are no sides. Look – Jabber Lockhart was all those things. He had to be to cure me. – But he didn't run around telling people so. It wouldn't ever occur to him. – Was he after more money?'

'Kampfer?'

'Well of course Kampfer,' she said.

'Don't get angry with me,' he said. 'I'm the one he was putting through the wringer.'

'Sorry,' she said, and kissed him.

'I keep reminding myself how quick you are,' said Charles, 'and I'd better not forget. Compassion, dedication, love, it was all money, really. My wife's money. He had the sense to see straight off that he wouldn't get any of mine. But Angela's – did I tell you her name was Angela?'

'No,' said Jane. 'You never did.' I asked Lionel instead, she thought, because I'm nosey.

'He'd got the idea that my wife was rich – and of course she was – so he suggested that I gave him enough of her cash to do research into what he called her unfortunate affliction. And this was just after the funeral. Me and the nursing staff drinking terrible Swiss wine and stuffing down cream cakes – them, not me – and he suddenly started yelping for baksheesh.'

'It must have been dreadful,' said Jane.

'Not quite as much as viewing the body, but dreadful enough,' he said. 'The body was –' he hesitated. 'God knows I saw enough bodies in the war, and you know as well as I do what they were like. And I never turned a hair. There was never time. We were always doing things. Anyway you daren't be upset.'

'I remember that, too,' she said, and it was true. The grotesque ugliness of a broken body had to be ignored, for the sake of the still living: the ones who might yet be saved. It was the sight of the tormented horses that had finally driven her mad.

'When I saw Angela I wanted to cry,' said Charles, 'but I couldn't. Not with Kampfer there. He was watching me, waiting for me to cry. But I wouldn't give him money, and I wouldn't give him that, either.' He hesitated, fumbling for words. 'She had been beautiful,' he said at last. 'Really very beautiful – but the creature in the ice box – I hadn't seen her for years. As you said, there was no point. She was fat – grotesquely fat, like the fat lady at the circus. She'd had hair like Georgie's, and now it was a sort of dirty grey. She lay there in a nightgown like a tent and I was looking at a stranger, and all I could do was think: I should have gone to see her. And then: But what good would it have done? And then again: But I should have gone. Over and over. In my head. Kampfer should have asked me for money then. I'd have given him anything he wanted, just to take me away from her.'

'Poor darling,' she said, and put her arms about him. He lay passive, like a child, but she had no doubt of his need of her.

At last she said, 'Were you the only one there – apart from the staff?'

'They dug up an Anglican parson from somewhere,' said Charles, 'but otherwise there was only the bereaved husband. God what a mess.'

Jane cradled his head on her breast, and he lay there, still passive, and still needing her.

She said at last, 'We've done it again, haven't we? Talked about important things lying down instead of sitting up.' But he made no answer: he was asleep.

'Is she all right?' Bob asked.

'Bit worried,' Andy said.

'Bound to be,' said Bob. 'The operation's tomorrow after all.'
He looked again at his brother. Worried sick. 'She'll be all right,
kidder. You'll see.'

'Can I have that in writing?'

Bob went to the drinks tray, poured out whisky for them both,
and added water. 'Here,' he said. 'Drink your nasty medicine.'

Andy sipped, grimaced, then sipped again. 'I never said thank
you – not properly.'

'Then for heaven's sake don't start now,' said Bob. 'You'd do
the same for me, wouldn't you?'

'Well yes, of course,' said Andy. 'But – '

'But nothing,' said Bob. 'She's a fine woman, and she loves you,
God help her. 'I'm glad I was able to help.'

'Thanks Bob,' Andy said, and struggled once more with his
whisky.

'Fancy going to the pictures?' Bob said. 'We could have a bite of
supper afterwards.'

'In a restaurant?'

'You wouldn't enjoy my cooking,' said Bob. 'And I certainly
wouldn't. Somewhere quiet. There's lots of little places round here.'

'How can I?' Andy said.

'Because I'll bloody well pay,' said Bob. 'I'll pay because you're
my brother. I'm entitled. Don't let's start that again.'

'I hate this,' said Andy.

'Being obligated? I don't blame you,' said Bob. 'It's a damn sight
worse than giving.' The doorbell rang. 'Who in the world is that?'
said Bob. 'I'm not expecting anybody.'

'Shall I go to the bedroom?' Andy asked.

'Of course not,' said Bob. 'You're my guest. If it's business I'll take them to the study.' The doorbell rang again. It wasn't business: it was Sybil Hendry.

'You haven't changed,' she said.

'Changed for what?'

'Bunty Fairweather's party. I thought we'd have a drink here first.' By the look of her she'd had a couple already.

'I haven't been invited,' said Bob.

'She told me to invite you,' Sybil Hendry said, then her hand went to her mouth. 'But I forgot, didn't I?'

'Come in and we'll talk about it,' he said, and escorted her to the drawing room.

Andy found himself looking at a girl wearing the sort of clothes that Jane wore at night: dark furs over a gown of pink and gold. When Bob took the furs from her, Andy saw that the dress was held up by a single strap, and there wasn't all that much to hold up either. Still, she was a very pretty girl. Trust Bob for that. Not that he was bothered – he had a pretty girl of his own now, if only she would be all right.

'Mrs Hendry,' said Bob. 'My brother Andy.'

'Call me Sybil,' the pretty girl said, and offered her hand. 'We can't possibly be formal. I've heard so much about you.'

Andy took her hand and said, 'Have you? Who from?'

'Bob,' she said. 'Who else? He talks about you all the time. My clever brother.'

So clever that I live in John Bright Street and he lives here, thought Andy. Not that I'm bothered about that, either.

'Are you here for long?' Sybil Hendry asked.

'Just two weeks,' said Andy. 'Just visiting.'

'His wife had to see a specialist,' said Bob.

'Oh dear,' Sybil Hendry said, 'I do hope it isn't serious.'

'No no,' said Andy. 'Just one of those women's problems.'

Really, she thought, are all the poor such prudes?

'About the party – ' she said.

'You're going to a party?' Andy asked.

'Well that was the idea,' she said, 'but like a fool I forgot to give Bob his invitation. I'd no idea he had a guest – '

'We were going to the pictures,' said Bob.

'I'll toddle off then,' she said.

'No no.' Bob had no difficulty in reading the expression on his brother's face. He wanted to be alone and now he could be. So much for brotherly love.

'You go to your party,' Andy said. 'I'll take myself for a walk. I could just do with a breath of fresh air. See you later, kidder.'

'Aye,' said Bob. 'See you later.'

'Goodnight, Mrs Hendry,' Andy said, and then he was gone.

'Kidder?' Sybil Hendry said. 'Were you both being tribal again?'

'Just affectionate,' said Bob. 'Who else is going to this party?'

'The same dreary crowd that goes to all the others,' she said. 'We don't have to go if you'd rather not.'

'A bit tricky staying here.'

'We could go to my flat. No fear of interruptions. Daddy's in Deauville.'

'The servants,' said Bob, and thought: She always forgets the servants. It's probably because to her they aren't quite real.

'Oh sod it,' she said, and then she smiled. 'I know what. We'll go to Daddy's flat.'

'No thank you,' said Bob, and she pounced at once.

'I've shocked you,' she said. 'Oh very well. Lock the door and hope your brother stays out and do it here.'

'Do what?'

'Whatever you want. I'm feeling generous tonight.'

There'd been a big piece about it in the *Evening News*: the Fascists were holding a meeting in Stepney. As soon as he'd read it he knew that he ought to go, but he couldn't as long as Bob was there. Then that luscious little piece turned up and let him off the hook. She and Bob had their party: he could go to one of his own. Not that he wanted to take part, not with Norah the way she was, but he wanted to *see*: had to, really. The Felston market place had been no more than a skirmish, or so he'd been told. London was where the war was, and tonight was the Battle of Stepney. At least if he couldn't fight he'd be a war reporter: tell them back in Felston what was going on.

A ride on a tube then a ride on a tram: a lot cheaper than the pictures – the pictures in London cost a fortune – then walk. Bethnal Green, the *Evening News* had said. No need to ask directions or look at his street map. All he had to do was follow the crowd. They were in pairs and groups for the most part, like chaps going to a football match, and nearly all of them were chaps. Not many on their own though, like him. Like chaps going to a football match they wanted to share the excitement, be part of a group. There was safety that way too. In numbers. Stay at the back, he warned himself, and keep your hands to yourself when the fighting starts. You owe it to Norah. Some of the men looked nervous, he thought, and some were fairly leaping with excitement, but they all looked determined. The opposition. His lot. Cloth cap and muffler, boots and blue serge: the uniform of the poor. He was wearing it himself apart from the muffler. In Bob's honour he'd put on a tie.

The men around him were moving grimly, purposefully, like troops approaching a battlefield, and he forced himself to slow down as the first policemen appeared. All in twos, he noticed, never one on his own, and all looking at his comrades as if they were the enemy. From a distance there came the sound of smashing glass, and then a shout of triumph. A man in the group nearest to him said, 'Synagogue?' and the man next to him said, 'More than likely.' Andy cut off down a side street and fumbled his way to where he had heard the sound, and found himself once more among hurrying men: more serge and caps and mufflers and boots, but these were the enemy. Scattered among them were young, tough men in black shirts and trousers, and they laughed together as they walked, and again Andy thought of football. They too were off to the match, and they knew beyond doubt that their team would win. Andy turned down another side street and fumbled his way back to where the crowd had already been, emerging at last to a wider road, still more police, and a pavement showered with broken glass.

It had been a synagogue. It had also been a tailor's shop and a restaurant of the kind the Jews called kosher. None of them looked worth much: the neighbourhood was too poor for that – but now they all looked desecrated. Broken glass was just the beginning. There were paint smears everywhere, and painted words: the routine filth of unimaginative hate and hastily scrawled swastikas

251

to underline the point. In the doorway of the synagogue somebody had deposited a pig's head; a real one, still dripping blood. It must have taken a lot of effort to get that, thought Andy, unless there was an abattoir near by. Two bodies lay on the pavement, covered by policemen's capes. Two men, one bearded and old, the other clean shaven and young. The old man moaned from time to time: the young one Andy guessed to be unconscious rather than dead.

Suddenly three young men appeared, surrounded him, and eased him into a doorway: three young men in black shirts.

'Going to say your prayers, were you, Jew?' said the one facing him.

'Jew?' said Andy. 'What the hell are you talking about?'

He sounded at once bewildered and afraid, which was precisely how he felt. The blackshirt on his right produced a large torch covered in some kind of synthetic rubber, a torch that might also serve as a club, and shone it into Andy's face. His eyes hurt, and he shut them.

'Open your eyes,' said the blackshirt facing him and he opened them at once, not because they put so much as a hand on him: because he was afraid.

'Fair,' said the blackshirt on his left. 'Eyes grey. Small nose. He's no Jew.'

'Then what's he doing here?' said the blackshirt on his right.

'I was going to the meeting,' said Andy. 'Only I got lost.'

'To the meeting?' said the blackshirt facing him. 'To make trouble?'

'To listen,' said Andy. 'Just to listen. No trouble. Honest.' He despised himself even as he spoke, then suddenly another man appeared, taller, heavier than any of them. A policeman: a sergeant.

'Time you lads were off,' he said. 'You wouldn't want to be late.'

The three blackshirts went at once, and Andy tried to follow, but the sergeant grasped his arm. It didn't hurt, but Andy remembered Durham Gaol and knew how easily it could.

'Want to tell me what you're doing here?' the sergeant said.

'I was just telling them other fellers. I was going to the meeting – only I lost my way,' said Andy. 'I'm a stranger here.'

'A Red, are you?' the sergeant asked.

'Of course not,' said Andy.

'Then why go to the rally? You're not trying to tell me you're a Fascist?'

'I was going to watch,' said Andy. 'To listen. Maybe to learn. We do that at political meetings where I come from.'

'What on earth for?'

'Like I said, sometimes you might learn something. And even if you don't it costs you nowt.'

The sergeant said, 'Not a penny,' then his glance flicked to the two Jews on the pavement, and back to Andy. 'Geordie aren't you?'

'That's right,' said Andy.

The sergeant looked pleased, as if he'd just solved the problem that had baffled Sherlock Holmes, Andy thought.

'I knew it,' the sergeant said. 'You talk just like a pal of mine. He's from Newcastle. That where you're from?'

'Aye,' said Andy. 'It is.' Felston was ten miles from Newcastle, but with the police it was best to keep things simple, especially if you'd done time in Durham Gaol for being a conscientious objector, and almost gone back there for incitement to riot.

'I knew it,' said the sergeant. 'But you're a bit far from home, aren't you?'

'I'm on me holidays,' said Andy. 'Visiting me brother. He works here.'

The sergeant took his hand from Andy's arm.

'That's all right then,' he said. 'But if I was you I'd go to the pictures. This rally tonight – they're not holding it so you can learn things.' He struggled for words, and dim memories of the Sunday School of thirty years ago came back to him. 'They're not trying to convert the heathen, not the Fascists,' he said. 'They're preaching to the converted. Now you get on back to your brother.'

'Thanks sergeant,' Andy said. 'Thanks very much,' and walked away from the direction of the rally. As he did so, an ambulance clattered, bell clanging, and braked beside the synagogue. The sergeant took his eyes from Andy, and moved to where the injured men lay, not hurrying, thought Andy, because there wasn't any kudos in hurrying: not for Jews. He turned off at a corner, and once more followed the road that would take him to the rally. Half an hour for an ambulance to get there, he thought, and no sign at all of blackshirts under arrest. But then why should there be? The

253

sergeant had had three of them right where he wanted them, harassing a member of the public, and all he'd done was send them on their way: high-spirited lads, maybe a bit exuberant, but no harm to anybody. Football crowds again, Andy thought. And all I did was say thank you. Thank you for not arresting me sergeant, thank you for letting me go, when my crime was such a wicked one: watching wounded Jews lying on the pavement, their buildings wrecked, and their attackers sent on their way with indulgent headshakes. . . . I was afraid, he thought. Well of course I was, but all the same I feel ashamed. Not because of the police sergeant: no one with my record would argue with him – but with that Fascist scum.. Don't talk daft, he told himself. There were three of them, all younger than you, and better fed. What chance would you have had? Even so, the shame remained.

They hadn't held the rally on the Green itself. That was tactics, so he learned later. Bethnal Green offered too much space: too many opportunities for victims to run and hide. The rally was held in a square close by: the crowd packed in tight, and the side streets guarded by what the Fascists called marshals: fit-looking young men armed with knuckle dusters they took no trouble to hide. A big crowd, Andy thought: far far bigger than Felston. There must have been thousands. Well I've talked to crowds as big as this and bigger, from a rostrum just like the one at the other end of the square. Just like it, except that this one had flags all over it: the jagged lightning flash that British Fascists used instead of a swastika, interspersed with Union Jacks. For some reason the Union Jacks disgusted Andy. He had never thought of himself as a patriot before.

The crowd was making that strange noise, part buzz, part hum, that Andy knew so well, when at last the platform began to fill: tough, arrogant men in black shirts, all of them young except the one in the centre: the one he'd seen before. Crawley. On one side of him was a small man, no bigger than a jockey, but he looked as hard as any of them, his face scarred by what Andy was sure was a razor slash. But it was the one on the other side of Crawley who Andy looked at. He wore the regulation blackshirt uniform, and looked as arrogant as any of them, but he lacked their toughness. It was Burrowes.

Suddenly Crawley rose to his feet, and his companions followed.

They began to sing the National Anthem, and here and there pockets of the crowd joined in, until at last they all were singing. Even me, Andy thought, and just as well. No sense in being the odd man out. Not in this mob. But he still felt shame. When it was done the little scar-faced man walked up to the microphone.

'We are here tonight,' he began, 'to dedicate ourselves to the welfare of our country: to make it great again. To rescue it from the defilement of those interlopers who have dragged Great Britain into the mire.'

No attempt at reason, thought Andy. No 'In my view' or 'Don't you think', or 'Comrades let us consider'. None of that. Just: These are your instructions and you will obey.

The interlopers were the Jews of course, with the Communists and Socialists a very poor second. The Jews romped home by a mile. Robbers of the widows and orphans, defilers of our women, unnatural perverts, world conspirators. Every evil in the country began with the Jews. Look at Marx. Look at Engels. Our great country had to be purged of the poison it had swallowed. Could it be done? Of course it could. Look at what Germany had already achieved. He paused for breath, and the blackshirts before the platform began to chant: Yids! Yids! We got to get rid of the Yids!

Then someone threw something – Andy thought it was a stone – at the platform. It was followed almost at once by other missiles: fire crackers, bottles, tomatoes, eggs. Crawley sat unmoved, staring rigidly ahead as the rubbish rained down, and his companions had no choice but to stay there with him, as press photographers worked frantically to record the scene. Then someone threw a stink bomb and Crawley reacted at once. Nobody could remain un-moved when confronted by such an appalling stench. A whisper of it drifted back even as far as Andy. Crawley barked out an order and the marshals went at once into action, swinging boots and knuckle-dustered fists, and the crowd heaved like a sea. Andy eased back further. It was time to go and he knew it was, but he had to see – just a little bit more. I'm like a child sitting up late, reading *Treasure Island*, he thought. Just one more chapter. Suddenly the crowd split apart to show Crawley's thugs in combat with a bunch of young men as hard and fit as they were. Our side, Andy thought, and we're winning for once. Partly it was because there were more of them, and partly because they were every bit as ruthless. But of course it didn't last: the workers weren't allowed to win. That was Rule One.

From the side streets the policemen came flooding in, formed up on either side of an inspector, truncheons in hand, then went into action. The Fascists they ignored completely. It was their opponents they were after, whether they fought back or not. Andy's sergeant in particular seemed happy in his work. In his element, you might say. Not only allowed to crack heads but being paid to do it. Andy could take no more. He turned and moved away, and a policeman posted in the side street yelled at him. Andy fled.

There were police posted at every approach to the Green, and Andy twisted and turned and wriggled his way like a demented hare with the pack closing in. But this time the hounds didn't try too hard: there was other, juicier prey to be had. Andy found the tram stop at last and became no more than a passenger who had run rather too fast to catch his tram, as anyone could see. But they couldn't see the shame.

It was midnight when Bob got back, and Andy was still sitting there, a glass by his side.

'Still up, kidder?' he said. 'I thought you were one for your beauty sleep.'

'I took a drink,' Andy said, his voice not quite steady.

Bob looked at the decanter. The whisky level was down by a good two inches. Dear God, he thought. Not two in one night.

'Help yourself,' he said.

'No,' Andy said. 'I've done.'

'Tea? Coffee?'

'I just want to talk,' Andy said, 'if you're not too tired.'

Bob sat. 'Not tired at all,' he said.

Andy said, 'You've changed your clothes.'

'I went to the party,' Bob said.

'Party? Oh – aye.'

'You didn't sit up till this hour to talk about a party you didn't even go to.'

'I thought *I* was going to a party – in a way,' said Andy. 'But it turned out to be a bloody massacre.'

Then out it all came. The synagogue, the wounded Jews, the menacing Fascists and equally menacing policemen, and then the rally and the riot.

'Somebody threw a stink bomb at Crawley?' Bob said.

'I don't know if he was the target,' said Andy, 'but he got it all right.'

'I met him once,' said Bob, 'at a house-party at Charles Lovell's. He was the nastiest piece of work I ever came across, and that's saying something.'

'What was he doing at Lovell's?' Andy asked.

'Pestering Jane,' said Bob. 'Not that it got him anywhere.'

Andy ignored it. 'Surely to God Lovell's not a friend of Crawley's?'

'Course not. He was trying to raise money for Felston. So was I.'

'You never told me about it,' Andy said.

'We never raised the money. Get on with your story.'

'Not much more to tell,' said Andy, 'except I ran off home.'

It was what they used to say when they were kids, and some other kid refused to fight. 'He ran off home.'

'Course you did,' said Bob. 'Not your fight.'

'But it was,' Andy said. 'It was my fight as much as any man's there. But the others stood up for themselves and I didn't. I'm ashamed of meself if you want to know.'

'I can see you are,' said Bob. 'But I can't see the sense in it. You can be a class warrior or you can be a married man. You can't be both.' It was not what Andy wanted to hear. Give it another try, Bob thought. He needs it by the look of him and you're his brother after all.

'You do your share,' said Bob. 'You know you do. Union work. Town councillor. Making speeches. All to get rid of the likes of me. You'll be mayor soon, so I hear.'

'No,' said Andy. 'That's out.'

'I thought you were set on it.'

'So did I,' said Andy. 'But where's the sense? A mayor's nowt, and a councillor's less than nowt when it comes to standing up for my class. Like watching those poor fellers being clouted by the coppers till their heads broke, then giving them an aspirin. Mayors are for tramcars and road repairs and drains, and that's about it. They're not where the power is.'

257

'Where is it then?'

'In the House of Commons,' Andy said, 'and if I can't get there then I might as well quit.'

He's drunk of course, thought Bob. He's had the hell of a lot of whisky for a chap that never touches the stuff. All the same I think he means it.

'What do you reckon your chances are?' he asked.

'Of me being an MP? Any odds you like,' Andy said. 'All the same –

> A man's reach should exceed his grasp,
> Or what's a heaven for?

The poet Browning said that – He must have done. They told me so at Cambridge. And that's another thing.' He lapsed into silence. Even drunker than he looks, thought Bob.

'What is?' he said at last.

'What's what?' said Andy. 'Oh – Cambridge. There was a chap from Cambridge on the platform next to Crawley. – What do you make of that?'

'It takes all sorts,' said Bob.

'Not like him it doesn't. At least I hope not. But what I mean is – this chap's a Communist. Now how can that be?'

'Perhaps he's changed his mind.'

'It wouldn't be the first time,' Andy said. 'I tried to kill him once.'

'We all do,' said Bob. 'It's a family failing. But you're not the only one with problems.'

'God knows that's true,' said Andy. 'Yours would be a woman no doubt?'

Drunk or sober he's got brains, thought Bob, and maybe that's a family failing too.

'Aye,' he said. 'The lady who came calling just before you went to your rally. The enchanting Mrs Hendry. That's what they call her in Bower's paper.'

'Call me Sybil,' said Andy.

'The very same. She was half cut when she got here – '

'Cut?'

'Drunk. Only she's good at hiding it. We're what they call lovers. I suppose you guessed that?'

258

'Well of course.'

'And she fancied a bit. Women can manage that when they've had a few. Men can't. Something you should bear in mind mebbe.'

'Mebbe,' said Andy. 'Get on with your tale. It's good up to now.'

'Well I fancied a bit an' all, only I thought it might be a bit tricky here. I mean you might have changed your mind and come home.'

'Not me,' said Andy. 'You should know that by now. Where the banana skins are – that's where I belong. And so I went to Bethnal Green. They grow like weeds there.'

'So I said it would have to be somewhere else, and it couldn't be her place on account of the servants.'

'Quite so,' said Andy. 'And yet they say the rich don't know hardship.'

'So then she said we should go to her father's flat on account of he's in Deauville. Only I said no.'

'Why not?'

'Because I didn't like the idea,' said Bob. 'I thought it was nasty.'

'Well so it was,' Andy said. 'So what did you do?'

'I put the chain on the door and we went to bed here.'

'Quite right,' Andy said. 'Nothing wrong with that – apart from fornication. Is that the end of your story?'

'Of course not,' said Bob. 'Just getting into bed – that's never been something I tell about. Not even to my own brother. Maybe him least of all. But when we'd done I got dressed and we went to Bunty Fairweather's party – '

'*Whose?*' Andy said.

'Never mind,' said Bob. 'The point is she had a lot more to drink and I had to take her home.'

'Noblesse oblige,' Andy said. 'I learned that at Cambridge an' all.'

'I dare say. Only in the taxi she told me her father wasn't in Deauville at all. He was at his club playing bridge. He could have walked in on us at any minute. Now I don't care how drunk she was. Where the hell is the sense in that?'

'Well it's obvious,' Andy said.

'Not to me,' said Bob.

'She wants to get married,' said Andy. 'To you, God help her.'

He tried to get up and found that he couldn't. In the end Bob had to help him to his room. They both had a lot to think about.

. 27 .

Mr Pinner stared at Piers Hilyard and could scarcely believe what he saw. The young man, elegant in silk pyjamas and dressing gown, was walking towards him, hand outstretched. He was limping, but he didn't use a stick – and not that long ago there'd been talk of amputation.

'Mr Pinner,' said Piers, and took his hand. 'It's good to see you.'

I hope you'll think so when I've done, thought Mr Pinner.

'I got back from Dublin last night,' Mr Pinner said. 'I thought it best to come here straightaway.'

'Of course,' said Piers. 'Do sit down – and smoke if you want to.'

'Thank you.' Mr Pinner began to fill his pipe. 'You're looking well if I may say so, sir.'

'Discharged next week,' said Piers. 'I'm not so easy to stop as some people think.'

'Back to the regiment, sir?'

'Not yet,' said Piers. 'But I will be. Now – what's your news?'

'I'd like to tell it in sequence if you don't mind, sir,' said Mr Pinner. 'It'll save time in the long run.'

'Fine,' said Piers.

'Usually what I do in a case like this is hire a local man,' said Mr Pinner. 'On account of my accent. Now there are some good local men in Dublin, but not for your problem.'

'You mean they'd be too afraid,' said Piers.

'Indeed they would,' Mr Pinner said, 'and far be it from me to blame them. But my business is like so many others. It's not what you know it's who you know. That and favours – given and received. Well there's a chap in Special Branch I've helped a couple of times, and I went to see him just before I left London.'

'A bit risky, surely?'

'Not at all, sir.' Mr Pinner was courteous still, but firm in his rebuke. 'Just you think about it. I was after a couple of terrorists – maybe more than two – who'd killed one man and wounded another and right in the middle of London, what's more. His own patch. And to make it worse they'd got clean away. They might even come back and do an encore.'

'Rather unlikely, surely?'

'Extremely unlikely,' said Mr Pinner, 'but my Special Branch chap wasn't to know that.'

Piers looked up at that, took out and lit a cigarette.

'Quite so,' he said. 'Do go on.'

'Well all things considered Special Branch are more keen to catch them than anybody else. Except perhaps yourself, sir. So naturally he said he'd do what he could, which meant he might consider bending the rules but he couldn't actually break them. But there was only one thing I wanted, so that was no problem.' Mr Pinner applied another match to his pipe.

'And what did you want?'

'An informer,' Mr Pinner said. 'They tend to be expensive, but there wasn't any other way – and you'd told me what your cash limit is.'

'An informer?' said Piers. 'But damn it man, everybody's afraid of the IRA – even your own colleagues. You said so yourself.'

'The informer I got wasn't,' said Mr Pinner. 'Perhaps that's because he's in it himself.'

'*What?*'

'Makes sense wouldn't you say, sir? Who else would know about a job like that – unless they were in the organisation?'

'But why didn't your Special Branch chum use the informer himself?'

'He'd have had to go to Dublin, just like me,' Mr Pinner said, 'and the odds are he'd have been recognised, and someone would kill him. Maybe even my informer. Just because he'd talk to me doesn't mean he'd talk to a London copper, especially Special Branch. So he told me no trouble at all, because with a bit of luck I might close his case for him, and I took the packet to Kingstown.'

'You're not trying to tell me you just walked in on the feller and said how much?'

'No indeed, sir,' Mr Pinner said. 'Very nervous creatures, informers. It goes with the job as you might say. I had a few cards printed.' He took out his wallet, extracted a card and gave it to Piers.

'Redpath and Snelgrove,' Piers read. 'Solicitors. Falcon Court. Middle Temple Lane. E.C.4.' Then printed neatly in ink at the bottom: 'G.A. Pinner. Clerk to the above.'

'I suppose I paid for this card?' said Piers.

'It's all on my account, sir.'

'Then I'll keep it if you don't mind. Sort of a souvenir.'

'I'd rather you didn't, sir,' said Mr Pinner. Piers looked at him, shrugged, and gave it back. 'Thank you, sir. The address is my own, sir, and I gave my lady secretary instructions about what to do if she had a call from Dublin.'

'And did she?'

'No, sir. But she'd have coped. She's very capable. I'd made up a story, you see. Redpath and Snelgrove had a client of Irish extraction. I won't give you the proper name, sir, but let's say it was Rafferty. Well the poor feller had died and in his will he'd left a couple of hundred to a cousin called Rafferty in Dublin, which is why I was there. I took a room in a hotel and put a notice in the *Irish Times*. I must have had a thousand replies. Thank God I used a box number. Then I started interviewing some of them, just for the look of the thing. I'd said he was T. Rafferty. About forty years old. I got old age pensioners and mothers writing on behalf of five year olds. I even got women called T. Rafferty. The only thing they had in common was they all remembered their rich cousin in England. So as I say, I interviewed the most promising – and a damn difficult job I had to get rid of them. And then at last my nervous friend wrote to the box number and I invited him to call.'

'And did he?' Mr Pinner, busy with his pipe, nodded. 'Taking a bit of a risk, wasn't he?'

'He didn't think so,' Mr Pinner said, 'and when he got to know me better he told me why. It was one of his terrorist pals who told him about the legacy. As a matter of fact – ' He hesitated.

'Go on, Mr Pinner,' said Piers.

'It was one of the ones who tried to kill you.'

'Go on,' Piers said again.

'Well the way he looked at it, it all worked out splendidly. This time he'd got two hundred pounds and he didn't have to worry about hiding it.'

'You mean he'd done it before?'

'Three or four times, so he said. We'd had quite a bit of Irish whiskey when he said it, but all the same I think it's true.'

'So he's – what's the word – disillusioned, is he?'

'Not at all,' Mr Pinner said. 'He'd die for Ireland tomorrow. For the IRA, anyway.'

'But he betrays his own comrades.'

'I thought about that on the packet coming home,' said Mr Pinner. 'From what he told me it's like this. Imagine a married man. Happily married. No problems. Loves his wife. But every so often he has to visit a prostitute. Not wants to. Has to. That's Mr Rafferty.'

'I see,' said Piers. 'And is Rafferty married?'

'No, sir.'

'He's mad, of course.'

You would think that, Mr Pinner thought, because you would no more betray a comrade than put your hand in the fire. And anyway it's such a neat solution. Ties up all the loose ends.

'I suppose he must be, sir,' he said.

'But you're satisfied he gave you the right names?'

'Quite satisfied,' said Mr Pinner.

'Do you mind telling me what they are?'

Mr Pinner took a sheet of paper from his pocket. For the first time he looked unsure of himself. He said at last: 'Do you mind if I ask what you intend doing with them, sir?'

'Hardly your business, wouldn't you say?'

'Well yes and no, sir. I mean – if they ever find out what Rafferty's done they might have another pop at you. And maybe me as well.'

'Yes,' said Piers. 'I should have thought of that. I'm sorry.'

'I didn't have to go, sir,' Mr Pinner said. 'A job like that has its own fascination, – like being an informer. But there's something else.'

263

'Yes?'

'Most people think – here and in Ireland – that your house took that bomb because your granny refused to employ any more Irishmen in that car components works of hers. Seems a likely enough reason after all. Created a lot of hardship, your family sacking all those Paddies. But you and I know that's not the reason at all.'

'Do we?'

'Of course we do, sir.' Mr Pinner's voice was steady. 'Found yourself an informer of your own, didn't you, sir? Not long after the IRA burnt down your castle in Ireland and your granny had her first stroke. Then two of the men who were responsible disappeared and were found years later in a peat bog. . . . Well now *your* informer's in a peat bog too.'

'Oh God,' said Piers. 'Are you telling me they'll try again?'

'They think you're a cripple,' Mr Pinner said. 'They know all about you. Soldiering, fox hunting, dancing. Now they think you can't do any of those things. To them that's better than killing you. Stay out of the limelight, sir, and they won't bother you.'

'Suppose they find out anyway?'

Mr Pinner said in the same steady voice: 'You knew the risks the first time, sir. They're the same risks now.'

'True,' said Piers. 'Pass me my cheque book will you? It's over there on the dressing table.'

Mr Pinner handed Piers Hilyard the cheque book, and then the sheet of paper: the names of those who had tried to kill him. What he did with it now was his business.

'How are you, pet?' said Andy.

'Awful,' said Norah. 'I've never felt pain like it if you must know.'

Andy flinched, and she said at once: 'Take no notice. It's the pain talking, not me. But what do I look like?'

'Like my wife,' Andy said, and she smiled then, a fleeting whisper of the smile he knew, but it was there.

'They think,' she said, 'at least the doctor thinks – '

'What?' said Andy.

'I'll be all right,' she said. 'We can have our bairns.'

It was the first thing the sister had told him when he'd come to the ward, but she had earned the right to tell him herself.

'That's marvellous,' he said.

'Isn't it though?' she said, and moved slowly, cautiously in the bed, seeking ease for her pain. The costliest bed, the softest pillows she had ever known, and all she felt was pain.

'What do you think of my room?' she said.

'Fit for a queen,' said Andy, 'and it's got one.'

Again the faint whisper of a smile. 'Oh you,' she said, and then: 'It must be costing Bob a fortune.'

'He's got a fortune,' said Andy. 'I don't mean I'm not grateful, but he's glad to do it. He told me himself.'

'Give us a kiss, bonny lad,' she said. Carefully, tenderly he kissed her, and she looked at him. 'You don't look all that grand yourself,' she said.

'I had a bit too much to drink last night.'

'You never!' But she was delighted. There could be only one reason why Andy would drink like that, and that was worry about her.

'There's better ways than drink to take your mind off things,' she said. 'Just wait till I'm out of here and I'll show you.'

'I remember Scarborough,' he said. 'That first time. And when it was over I looked at you and I said "Well I'm blest." Remember?'

'Well of course,' she said.

'And then I thought: What a daft thing to say, after what we'd just done. But it wasn't so daft now I come to think of it. I am blest.'

Her hand moved towards his and he took it and smiled, but he had no business smiling. He had not lied to her, not outright, but neither had he told her all the truth.

'Where are you off to, looking so authoritative?' said Charles.

'Do I? I was aiming more at something gentle and kind,' she said. 'You know, charitable, but without the Lady Bountiful overtones.'

They were lunching in a Soho restaurant, and really she thought she had hit it just right: grey coat and skirt, blue blouse, blue hat with a ribbon of darker blue.

'I don't *feel* authoritative,' she said.

'Quite the wrong word,' said Charles. 'Where are you off to, looking so gentle and kind?'

'St George's Hospital. Norah's still there.'

'Norah?'

She managed not to sigh, but really Charles seemed incapable of concentrating on anything apart from banking and sharing her bed.

'Andy's wife,' she said. 'Andy is Bob's brother. You've met him on several occasions. Bob owns Patterson's Wireless Rentals, in which you have shares.'

'Of course,' he said, with a look of mild triumph. 'She's here for some operation or other, isn't she?'

'She wants children. Now it seems she can have them.'

'I want children too,' he said. 'Jane darling – '

She interrupted at once. 'Is this a proposal?'

'Certainly,' he said. 'Wouldn't you agree I've waited long enough?'

'Of course,' she said. 'But not here. Not now.' He opened his mouth. 'And not lying down, either. The bedroom is not the place for a proposal of marriage. That you must do either sitting up or on one knee.'

Jay Bower had once got out of bed to ask her to marry him, she remembered, stark naked and kneeling on the floor. It mustn't happen again.

'Where then?' Charles asked.

'Dine with me tonight. You can do it after you've had your port.'

'Dutch courage,' said Charles. 'Let's hope I don't need it.'

She took a taxi to the hospital. Norah first, she thought. Piers would still be battling it out with his female wrestler. A probationer took her to Norah's ward, and Jane had a word with the sister on the way. Blue and grey might whisper of gentleness and kindness, but the little Cartier leopardess in her lapel screamed opulence. The sister eyed it covetously as she answered Jane's questions, then led her to Norah's room, and Jane went to her at once and kissed her, to the sister's bewilderment. She had thought Norah to be one of Jane's servants.

She looks – battered, thought Jane, and yet somehow she looks pretty too. Maybe she's pretty because of happiness. Let's hope so.

'How are you, darling?' she asked.

Norah smiled, and said, 'It worked,' and the happiness became a grin. It was happiness then.

'How marvellous,' said Jane. 'So it was worth it.'

'Just about,' said Norah. 'It hurt, you know. My God did it hurt.'

'And now?'

'Aches a bit,' Norah said, 'but it's going. I'll be out in a few days.'

'Don't rush it,' said Jane. 'Get well.'

'But it costs so much. I've seen some of the bills. Oh I know Bob can afford it – but there's Andy as well. He's only got a fortnight's holiday. I can't send him back to Felston on his own.'

Too many explanations, Jane thought. Too many Nosey Parkers.

'Stay longer then,' she said.

'We can't,' said Norah. 'Don't you realise – Andy would lose his job.'

'No he won't,' said Jane. 'That's something I can take care of. Promise.'

'You can talk to Andy's boss?'

'I should just think I can,' said Jane.

Norah looked at her, awed. It was like being friends with a fairy godmother. 'Did you send me a parcel?' she asked. 'A big one? With Harrods on the box?'

'Didn't you open it?' said Jane.

'I thought it might be a mistake,' said Norah. 'I've heard about Harrods. Nobody'd send me stuff from Harrods except you – so I thought I'd best make sure.'

'Open it now,' said Jane.

Norah was a picker: no ripping and tearing. String, wrapping paper, ribbon, cardboard box and tissue paper all taken off and folded with care, but then she might never get a parcel from Harrods again. When the last layer of tissue paper had been removed she examined her treasures: nightgown and dressing gown of blue silk, decorated with white flowers, her wedding dress pattern in reverse.

'Oh I can't take this,' she said.

'Whyever not?'

'People like me, women from Felston, we just don't have things like this.'

267

'Who's to know,' said Jane, 'apart from Andy?'

Norah, the old Norah, blushed, but the new one chuckled, then: 'Oh please don't make me laugh,' she said. 'It'll bring the pain on again.'

'You haven't finished,' said Jane, and Norah rummaged happily: blue-and-white silk slippers, and a blue-and-white case filled with make-up: lipstick, powder, rouge, perfume. The old Norah made one last try, looking wildly at Jane: the very glance asking, What will people say?

'Now don't say you can't do it, not after all the hours I spent teaching you,' said Jane.

'I'll put some on now,' the new Norah said.

She was just finishing when the sister came in, carrying a vast bucket of roses. How bewildered the sister looks, thought Jane, and no wonder. A bed strewn with French silk nighties and expensive make-up, Chanel perfume, and enough roses for a Battle of Flowers, and all for the woman with the funny accent. Perhaps she thinks Norah's married to a self-made millionaire: an old-fashioned robber of widows and orphans. How furious Andy would be if he knew.

When the sister had gone Jane took out the card and gave it to Norah.

' "I hope you're soon fully recovered", ' she read. ' "Best wishes, Charles Lovell." Who in the world's Charles Lovell?'

'He's a banker.'

'I don't know any bankers.'

'Andy does. Charles owns the house where the men stayed when they were on training for the Hunger March.'

'But that was Blagdon Hall.' Jane nodded. 'And this Mr Lovell owns it?' Another nod. 'He must be very rich,' said Norah.

'Oh frightfully,' said Jane.

'And Andy knows him?'

'Very well,' said Jane. 'They worked together on the Hunger March Committee.'

Norah could only echo her husband: 'Well I'm blest,' she said.

. 28 .

'How was young Hilyard?' asked Charles.

They had reached the dessert of a truly memorable meal. Mrs Barrow, her cook, was never less than splendid, but tonight she had really surpassed even her own exacting standards. Truett too had achieved rare heights: not even one long-suffering sigh. What her mother said must be true. Servants always knew when something was 'up', as the major said. And just as well. Charles might not enjoy what she had to tell him; might even hate it. It was only fair that he should enjoy what he ate. Drank, too. Lionel himself had chosen the burgundy. Suddenly she remembered Canon Messeter, the night he had dined with her. 'Comfort me with apples,' he had said (though Mrs Barrow had done rather better than that) and there was something about 'Stay me with flagons', but he had omitted the next bit: For I am sick of love. Charles might be that, too, before the night was over.

'Piers?' she said at last. 'He seems to be making a remarkable recovery. Walks with a limp, but at least he walks. He's even talking about hunting when the season starts.'

'Good man.'

'The only thing is,' said Jane, 'he seems to be obsessed with Mr Pinner. The detective, you remember? The one who tracked down the Pattersons for me.'

'What on earth for?'

'Catherine phoned me at Georgie's. In Hollywood. Surely you remember *that*? Just after the bomb. They wanted Mr Pinner to find out who had done it.'

'And did he?'

'He didn't say,' said Jane. 'Should I have asked him?'

'Certainly not,' said Charles. 'Hiring a detective's a private matter.'

269

And being blown up, she thought. Is that a private matter too? But she had no doubt that Charles was right. If there was a code of conduct in such things Charles would know exactly what it was.

'And your chum? Mrs Patterson?'

So far they had talked about Hollywood, Mexico, her mother, and her horse Bridget's Boy. Piers was a reminder that an agenda existed: Mrs Patterson a move towards the board room.

'Doing well,' said Jane, 'and most grateful for the roses. She wanted to write to you but I told her no. She isn't up to it. Not yet. But they really were lovely. And so many. They used up every spare vase in the ward.'

'Good,' said Charles, and chased the last of his chocolate mousse round his plate, then said, 'That they were a success, I mean. . . . This has been a marvellous meal.'

'I'll tell Mrs Barrow you said so.'

'No,' Charles said. 'I'll do that. . . . If you don't mind.'

'She'll be delighted. If I may ask – why did you send Norah those roses?'

'I have a great regard for Andy Patterson.'

'I thought it must be that,' said Jane. 'And now he knows it – in the nicest possible way.'

'She'll be good for him?'

'The best thing possible. Even Bob thinks so.'

'Bob,' said Charles, and paused. 'He behaved very well over this.'

He seems surprised, thought Jane, but then he's never seen the brothers together.

'He keeps pressing me to let him buy his shares in the business,' said Charles.

'And will you?'

'Yes,' said Charles. 'I rather think I will.'

Truett came in then, cleared the table, put the port decanter before Charles, and left. Jane rose, and Charles went at once to open the door.

'Don't be long,' she said.

'No bloody fear,' said Charles.

She had time to fit a cigarette into her holder, light it, and that was about it, when Charles appeared. He carried the decanter and two glasses.

'Forgive me,' he said, 'but I remembered that time when we lunched at Blagdon Hall before I bought it, and that oaf Blagdon set us at either end of a table the length of a cricket pitch. We drank port together then, so why not now?'

'Good idea,' said Jane. He poured out two glasses.

'You said I had to do this sitting up, but I'll stand if you don't mind. I'm nervous, you see. No, that's a lie. I haven't been so scared since I followed Rupert Messeter over the top at Second Ypres.' She willed herself to silence.

'Marriage isn't just about love,' he said, 'so we'll get the other stuff out of the way first. I can give you my word I'm healthy– I had a check-up on Monday– and God knows I have enough to support a wife.'

'Never mind that,' said Jane.

'But I do mind,' said Charles. 'It's my business to mind. I know you're rich too, and in a week or two you'll be even richer, but I have to know I'll be able to keep you in the same style if you lost every penny, and I can. So that's that.

'Now. Love . . . Not something I can talk about. I tried to write it once.'

'You did write it,' said Jane, but he hurried on as if he really were leading a charge.

'It doesn't mean I can't feel it,' he said. 'I do. Most profoundly. From the moment I wake up till I fall asleep, and even then you're waiting in my dreams, as often as not.

'You're a wonderful woman, Jane. To say you've changed my life is the sort of nonsense you read in books, except it's true. You have changed it, and I want you to go on changing it. More than anything in the world I want to marry you, but if I can't, please let us go on as we are. I don't think I could cope without you. In fact I know I couldn't.'

He raised his glass to his lips and found that it was empty.

'That's it,' he said. 'I've finished.'

'And a good thing too,' said Jane. 'I'd have been crying in a minute.'

'*Tell me*,' said Charles.

'It isn't easy,' she said, 'and I don't want to hurt you.' His face became impassive, and she hurried on. 'What I mean is, in your own language, what you're proposing is a merger, and I agree with that – except that there are a couple of assets I want to keep after we've merged.'

'Go on,' he said.

'First of all, no children,' she said. 'I'm too old to start that now, and anyway – ' She hesitated, but he deserved the whole truth. 'Hasn't it struck you that we've been extraordinarily lucky, when you consider what our shared hobby is? I went to Harriet Watson, and she sent me to what she called a gynae man. I rather suspect that he's Norah's gynae man too. I'm barren, it seems. Something might be done, but there'd be no guarantees and it would hurt.' She remembered Norah. 'Hurt like hell. I don't want that, Charles. I'm sorry. And anyway I was born to be an aunt. Don't you see? I seem to collect nephews and nieces like cigarette cards.'

'No children,' he said. 'Well I didn't expect there would be. But now that you've told me why – of course I agree. My poor darling.'

'We could adopt, I suppose,' said Jane. 'I mean somebody's got to inherit your vast wealth. And mine, come to that. I mean you haven't any close relatives, have you?'

'No one closer than Dodo,' he said. 'And she's taken care of.'

'I don't exactly see her running a bank,' said Jane. 'Or even this house.'

'Never mind that,' said Charles. 'What other assets do you want to keep?'

'My right to do what I want, even if it conflicts with your ideas. – And vice-versa of course.'

'Certainly,' said Charles. 'You wouldn't have it any other way. I know that.'

Oh Charles, she thought, you haven't taken Vinney's advice. You haven't thought it through. But how can I tell you that when you've given me what I wanted?

'Anything else?'

'I want us to keep this house.'

'Well of course,' said Charles. 'I love this house. And you in it.'

'That's all,' she said, and offered her hand. 'Shake on it?'

Solemnly they shook hands, and then he took her in his arms. After a while she became aware that Truett was in the room, and desperately trying to get out. Jane indicated as much to Charles, who turned, stared at Truett bemused, then said at last: 'It's all right. Honestly. We've just got engaged.'

'Heartiest congratulations, sir, madam,' said Truett. 'I wasn't trying to intrude.'

'Of course not,' said Jane.

'It's just that Lady Catherine's on the phone, miss. She says it's urgent.'

Suddenly Truett's face changed, so that she looked anxious, apprehensive. 'If I may ask, miss – '

'We're keeping the house on,' said Jane. 'Nothing will change except that it'll have a man in it.'

'Thank you, miss,' said Truett, 'and I'm sure we all wish you very happy.'

Catherine said, 'That maid of yours took her time finding you.'

'I was busy,' said Jane.

'My God you must have been.'

'Getting engaged,' said Jane.

'Oh,' said Catherine, then rather cautiously: 'Charles Lovell?'

'Of course, you ass.'

'Well I do wish you happy and all that,' said Catherine, 'but I did rather want to talk to you.'

'Not tonight,' said Jane. 'Not possibly. Tonight I expect to go on being busy.'

'Yes,' Catherine said. 'I dare say you will. How about tomorrow? May I come for coffee? In the garden?'

She wants to tell me a secret away from the servants, thought Jane.

'Not the garden,' said Jane. 'Truett's had enough shocks as it is, and she hates parlourmaiding in the garden. We'll go to my office. No one will disturb us there.'

'Fine,' Catherine said. 'Will eleven o'clock suit?'

'Perfectly.'

'Then I'll be there,' Catherine said, 'and I really do wish you happy, darling.'

But she says it as if happiness is impossible to achieve, thought Jane.

It was not so for Charles, who looked as if happiness were the only possible condition. In his hand was a jewel box. 'Unfinished business,' he said, and opened it. Inside was a diamond ring, a solitaire, and a whopper, too. Heaven knew how many carats. Nothing fancy or clever-clever, just a large and perfect diamond in a hoop of gold. He took her left hand, and slipped on the ring. Thank God that I never wear John's when I'm with Charles, she thought. Dear John. All so long ago it might have belonged to another life.

'Now we're engaged,' said Charles, and kissed her once more.

At last she said, 'We ought to tell people.'

'Who?'

'Lionel. Mummy. The major. All sorts of people. Even Brenda Coupland.'

'We'll make a list and I'll get my secretary to telephone them tomorrow,' he said. 'We'll have to give some sort of a party, too, I suppose.'

'Well of course,' said Jane, 'but we can't leave it to your secretary. Not to Lionel, and certainly not to Mummy. We'll have to tell them ourselves. Now.'

'But I want you to myself,' said Charles, which was all very gratifying, but even so they had to phone. Lionel was just on his way out.

'To a party,' he told her. 'Cynthia Townsend. You remember – that cousin of mine who screeches like a macaw. Married to the chap who makes agricultural machinery. We stayed with them at Cap d'Antibes.'

'Of course I remember,' said Jane. 'But I didn't ring up for a girlish chat.'

'What then?'

'To tell you I'm engaged.'

'But that's absolutely splendid,' said Lionel. 'Put the lucky man on at once.'

She did so, and then made Charles telephone her mother. While he did so, she took another look at the ring, and its box. Van Cleef and Arpels, the box proclaimed, so Charles must have bought the ring in New York soon after he'd heard of Angela's death. It was wonderful, but somehow rather frightening, to be loved as much as that. He'd bought it without even knowing she would say yes to him, and there could be only one reason: because the ring would be perfect for her if she did. At last her mother let him go.

'If she ever wants to take charge of our Bombay subsidiary she can name her own salary,' he said.

'She'd sooner go racing with the major,' said Jane.

'So long as she's happy. What do we do now?'

'Send for Mrs Barrow and tell her how well she feeds us.'

'A labour of love,' said Charles. 'And then?'

'Blest if I know,' said Jane. 'Unless we do what most engaged couples do. – Indulge in a little slap and tickle on the couch.'

'No hanky panky?'

'Certainly not,' said Jane. 'Not in this house anyway.'

So slap and tickle it was until Jane twisted in his arms and said, 'We should phone Bob. And Andy.'

'To tell Bob he can buy back his interest in the business?'

'That too,' said Jane. 'If you want to. But I was thinking of our engagement. After all I was engaged to their brother. I wouldn't want them just to read about this in *The Times* or the *Daily World*.'

'Oh,' Charles said, then, 'Yes. Of course. You're absolutely right.' No hint of jealousy this time, but then John was safely dead. Jay Bower, she thought, would be quite another matter.

Bob answered the telephone. 'I was just about to call you,' he said.

'So I've saved you tuppence. What about?'

'No no,' said Bob. 'You first.' She told him. 'By lad, that's marvellous,' he said.

'You think so?'

'Well of course. But then it's what you want to do, isn't it?'

A bit cryptic, she thought, but his delight in her news was real enough, and she passed him on to Charles. When he had finished it was time to talk to Andy, that model for every husband, and by the time Andy had finished telling them how wise and fortunate and lucky they were, Jane had forgotten that Bob, too, had things to say. Besides, it was getting late, and engaged couples unchaperoned should not be alone too long.

She pushed Charles out, protesting to the last. 'I'd no idea being engaged would turn out to be like this,' he said.

'Rectitude,' said Jane. 'Morality. All the penalties of marriage and none of the pleasures. Don't worry. We'll find the pleasures

275

soon enough. But not tonight, my darling. Tonight let's play it by the rules.'

'I've got pleasure enough for one night,' said Charles. 'Almost too much. Do you know I never dreamed – not till the moment you said yes?'

'But I did say yes,' she said, 'and I meant it. Call me early tomorrow, darling. Please.'

He embraced her once more, neither pulling nor urging: simply holding something beautiful and infinitely precious that somehow, magically, belonged to him.

Catherine said, 'Of course I'm delighted for you. I really am. I mean you and Charles Lovell – I've often wondered – I mean a lot of people did.'

'And now you know,' said Jane.

'Yes indeed.' Her eyes went to Jane's engagement ring. 'He's very rich, isn't he?'

'Immensely.' Jane held up her left hand. 'Do you like it?'

'My God,' Catherine said. 'It's even bigger than the one Jay Bower gave me.'

Jay Bower? To his wife? Jane looked at Catherine's left hand. No engagement ring, and no wedding ring either.

'You see,' Catherine began, but Jane held up her hand as Truett came into the small, book-lined room, and found space for the coffee tray between the typewriter and the extension telephone. Usually Truett detested Jane's office, where she could neither dust nor eavesdrop, but this time she could irradiate nothing but good-will, like the good fairy in a pantomime. When she had gone, Catherine fidgeted with cigarettes and coffee cup, then began to talk about Piers.

'I'm glad he's better,' said Jane, 'of course. But quite soon I have to go to lunch with my mother, so whatever it is you'd better tell me – unless you've changed your mind.'

'No I haven't,' said Catherine. 'It's just so damn difficult. I know it shouldn't be, but it is.' She drew a deep breath. 'The night before last my husband raped me,' she said.

She looks at once valiant and despairing, thought Jane: the plucky little woman almost – but not quite – at the end of her tether.

She also looks as if she's waiting for a round of applause, but that still doesn't mean that it isn't true. On the contrary.

'I swear to God it's true,' said Catherine.

'I believe you of *course*,' said Jane. 'It's not something you would lie about.'

Define rape, that was the problem. Somehow Jay Bower hadn't seemed that sort. He had slapped her bottom once rather too hard, and spent the rest of the night apologising, but that wasn't rape. . . . Define rape. Or rather don't. It's none of your damn business.

'It doesn't seem to bother you much,' Catherine said.

'On the contrary,' said Jane. 'It bothers me a great deal, but – '

'But what?'

'I honestly don't see what you expect me to do about it.'

From the look on her face it was obvious that Catherine hadn't the faintest idea either.

'We sleep apart these days,' said Catherine. 'In separate rooms. He came in – it was early morning and he was – not drunk, because then he couldn't have – but he'd been drinking. He just grabbed me and did it. No talk. No kisses. Just it. And when he'd done he just got off me and left me. The phone was ringing in his room and I could hear him answer. His bloody paper. An earthquake in Turkey. "How big?" he said, and then: "Oh great." As if I'd vanished from his mind – which no doubt I had. I lay awake all night. I couldn't think what to do. No. That's not right. I couldn't *think*. I knew I had to tell someone – someone in the family. But who? Not Piers, because God knows what Piers would do. In the old days it would have been Granny, but she isn't even there any more. Not really.'

'Your mother,' said Jane.

'Mummy's in the Bahamas,' said Catherine, 'or is it Barbados? Anyway she and Daddy are on one of their bloody boats. And even if she wasn't off cruising she'd probably just say, "Oh darling, I'm sure you're exaggerating. Men do get impatient sometimes, even the nicest of them. They simply can't help it, poor things. It's their nature." ' The mockery in her voice was far from affectionate. 'Well it bloody well isn't mine.' Then she sighed. Soon it would be time for tears, thought Jane.

'So I came to you. Jolly awkward, I know. You just getting

engaged and sex rearing its ugly head. – But I always come to you, don't I? I expect it's because you're so good at it. Advice to the lovelorn, I mean.'

'Hardly that,' said Jane.

'Right as usual. Advice to the ravished, then.' The tears came closer still. 'What on earth am I going to do?'

'Where's Jay now?'

'In Switzerland,' said Catherine. 'Geneva. There's a conference at the League of Nations. The Rôle of the Newspaper in Mass Education or something. He sent me flowers this morning, would you believe.'

'*Jay?*' It was impossible to keep the incredulity from her voice.

'Well of course Jay,' said Catherine. 'Who else do you suppose has raped me recently?'

Then the crying began: loud and ugly and shameful to watch, so that Jane reached out to the younger woman and held her as much to blot out the sight as to offer her body's comfort. Those tears were neither shame, nor rage, nor despair, she thought, but a mixture of all three; the lament for a Catherine who no longer existed. At last the ebb began, and Catherine shuddered and groped for her handkerchief.

'Sorry,' she said.

'Don't be,' said Jane.

'It's just – I've done this before, haven't I? And in this very room. After Bob left me.'

'I remember. . . . Bob isn't part of all this, is he?'

'Of course not. Bob's never raped anybody. He's never had to. Or do you mean do I still want him back?'

'That's what I meant,' said Jane.

Catherine's head was on her breast, and she stroked her dark and tousled coiffure.

'Spilled milk,' said Catherine. 'That's Bob. Or rather spilled champagne. No sense in crying for him, whatever he is. It's Jay I'm crying for. Not because of what he is. It's what he did.' Her body shook once more.

'When's he back in London?'

'Next week,' said Catherine. 'Oh my God – what am I going to do?'

'Take a holiday,' said Jane.

'On my own?' said Catherine. 'Oh I know you suggested Bunty Fairweather once, but I honestly don't think I could.'

Jane considered Bunty Fairweather. 'I don't blame you,' she said at last. 'But people do go on their own, you know. To resorts and plages and places like that. Or you could do one of those culture tours. You know – French cathedrals or the ruins of Greece or something. It doesn't really matter what. Just give yourself time to think.'

'And would you talk to him while I'm away?'

'If he asks me,' Jane said firmly. 'Only if he asks me.'

'He'll ask you,' said Catherine. 'I'll leave him a note.' She took her powder compact from her handbag and looked in its mirror.

'Dear God I'm a mess,' she said. 'May I use the bathroom?'

Jane waited. That the Bower marriage was over seemed obvious, and yet marriages survived the most extraordinary batterings if the need to stay together were strong enough. Consider the marriage of her own parents. But that was different: they had four children living then. The Bowers had none. . . . Jane dreaded the idea of talking to Jay Bower, not least because they had been lovers. What could she possibly say to him? But how could she refuse if she were asked? Catherine came back to her, make-up and coiffure immaculately repaired.

'Culture it shall be,' she said. 'After all, I should be able to cope. I did go to Oxford.'

. 29 .

Her mother said, 'I cannot tell you how happy you have made me. Not because Charles has made an honest woman of you – wed or unwed you were always that – but because I am confident that you will be happy. Hence the champagne.'

Krug, no less. Mummy must be thinking more of ecstasy than happiness, though Jane didn't think it would be like that. Stable and enduring, her marriage would be, with just enough laughter to keep dullness at bay.

'I'm glad you're pleased, Mummy,' she said. 'I mean it.'

Her mother smiled then: one of her rarest; without even a hint of malice, until: 'How upset Gwendoline Gwatkin will be,' she said.

'What on earth has poor Charles ever done to her?'

'Remained anonymous,' her mother said. 'You know how obsessively Gwendoline has followed your career – and she doesn't know that Charles even exists. Poor thing. Your good news on top of everything else.'

'Still obese?' said Jane.

'Vast,' said her mother. 'She's even barred from those hydro places these days.'

'Why on earth – ?'

'It discourages the others,' her mother said, then changed the subject firmly. 'George too sends his congratulations,' she said, 'and regrets that he couldn't lunch. Kempton Park,' she added by way of explanation. 'There's a filly there he wants to see.' Then almost shyly she added, 'I'm a little worried about George.'

'Good gracious. Why?' said Jane, and again her mother smiled. The reply it seemed had been a good one.

'You had observed nothing,' she said, 'and indeed perhaps

there's nothing to observe. But I'm concerned – just a little – about his health.'

'Mummy, what's wrong?' said Jane.

'He had a very strenuous war, both in France and India,' said her mother. 'And the work he does for the *Daily World* is really quite demanding.' She hesitated. 'You see why, of course.'

'He worries that he may tip the wrong horses?'

'Precisely,' her mother said. 'And it *is* a worry you know. Almost an obsession.'

'Tummy upsets? That sort of thing?'

'Among others,' said her mother. 'I have suggested he visits his doctor for a check-up, but he utterly refuses.'

Jane found it hard to keep her jaw in place. Not only had the major defied her mother, but her mother seemed proud of him for doing so.

'His reasoning may not be logical,' her mother said, 'but it is sincere. As George sees it, his business is to forecast what will win the four thirty at Epsom so that he can continue to support me in the style – ' she looked at the Krug ' – to which I have become all too accustomed. A doctor telling him to rest would inhibit any such business – and so George refuses to see a doctor. A gallant and foolish attitude, and one which explains precisely why I love him so much.'

Once again she eyed her daughter, but this time as if preparing herself for an onslaught of logic which would culminate in a demand for the major's instant hospitalisation.

'Does any of that make any sense to you?' she asked at last.

'All of it,' said Jane. 'You lost so many times, Mummy, but you won in the end.'

'I think we should go into the dining room,' her mother said. 'It would be too lowering for me to shed tears before lunch.'

From her mother's she went to St George's Hospital, to where Norah and Andy sat looking not in the least like a wife who's just had an operation and a husband who's relieved to know it. Norah if anything looked smug, and Andy looked furtive. But of course, thought Jane. Norah was wearing the negligée. They had been flirting. Perhaps even a little cautious slap and tickle.

'How are you, darling?' she asked.

281

'On the mend,' said Norah, and turned to Andy. 'Wouldn't you say?' Andy promptly blushed to a colour she could only describe as weather-worn brick.

'Charles's flowers look nice,' she said, and indeed the room was full of them.

'There's more,' said Andy.

'Flowers?'

'No,' said Andy. 'Fruit.' He held up a basket filled with peaches, pears, nectarines and grapes.

'How lovely,' said Jane.

'Yes, isn't it?' said Andy, and his voice sounded savage.

'Who sent them?'

'Sybil Hendry,' said Andy. 'What the hell is Sybil Hendry doing sending fruit to my wife?'

'Now, pet,' his Norah said.

'Being polite,' said Jane.

'Polite? She's never even met Norah.'

'She's met you,' said Jane. 'And she's met Bob many times. No doubt she considers herself a good friend of Bob's and so – '

'She considers herself a bit more than that,' said Andy, and then: 'Oh my God. You'll forget I ever said that. The pair of you.'

'I don't even know what you're talking about,' Norah said. 'And what's more you're forgetting your manners. Giving your orders like Lord Muck.'

'I mean,' Andy began, but Norah interrupted him.

'Heaven knows what you mean,' she said, 'but whatever it is we've forgotten it. Haven't we, Jane?'

'Yes, of course,' said Jane. What it meant was that Bob was under siege again, and the cryptic remark quite clear. 'But then it's what you want, isn't it?' It wasn't what Bob wanted.

'Now tell Jane you're sorry,' Norah said.

'Well I am,' said Andy. 'Believe me I am. I got myself in a bit of a state, but it was no fault of yours.'

'No harm done,' said Jane, 'but I'm surprised at you, Andy. The great male boss issuing his orders to mere females. Not exactly what you believe in, is it?'

'It makes it worse,' Andy said. 'I'm sorry for that, too.'

*

282

The guest list for the engagement party grew longer and longer, so that when the question of venue came up, Charles suggested the Albert Hall.

'How on earth do we know so many people?' he asked.

'Just luck,' said Jane.

'Good or bad?'

'Bit of both.' Charles's hand went to his breast pocket, and he pulled out a cable. 'By the way – before I forget – you remember the night when you made me the happiest man in the world?'

'Certainly I remember.'

'I told you that soon you'd be even richer than you are.'

'Did you?' said Jane. 'But I don't need your money, Charles. I've got enough.'

'I didn't mean mine. Though of course that's yours too.'

'Then what did you mean?'

'Dupont, General Motors, United States Steel,' he said.

'That nice Mr Forest?'

'The very same. He managed to buy all three, very quietly. And they've started to go up already.'

'But you said two years, maybe three.'

'Before they doubled or even trebled. But I also said unless something else happened. And something else did.' She waited. 'Hitler is Chancellor of Germany.'

'Charles, darling,' she said. 'You can't possibly be saying that there's going to be another war.'

'Not for certain,' he said. 'I'm not a crystal ball merchant. But what I do say is that the possibility has increased enormously, which is why your shares are doing so well.'

'I could wish they weren't,' she said. 'Are you sure?'

'Sure about the odds shortening,' he said. 'But no more than that.' He looked at her. He had never seen her quite so close to despair.

'There's better news,' he said. 'Georgie's coming over in time for our party.'

'To launch that destroyer?'

'They don't build them quite so quickly as that, not even in Felston,' said Charles. 'Just a private visit.' The private business would be Lord Alston, thought Jane. Georgie's very own nice chap.

283

'I suppose we'd better get back to this damn party,' said Charles.

'I've got a better idea,' said Jane. 'We'll get Lionel to do it.'

'We can't possibly,' Charles said. 'He's a friend of ours.'

'He'll love it,' said Jane. 'Designing decorations and bossing all and sundry. Of course we'll ask Lionel.'

Norah and Andy went home by train. Jane arranged it. She neither argued nor cajoled, simply presented Norah with tickets and reservations when they came to dinner at her house the night before they left. All Norah said was, 'Bless you, pet. Between you and me I was praying you would. I was dreading that bus.'

As she spoke, Andy was in the dining room, sipping at his port and listening hard.

'So that's where it is,' Charles Lovell was saying. 'There's an order for a destroyer for the Mexican Navy and Felston's got it.'

'Harris and Croft?'

'Of course,' said Lovell. 'Work for up to a thousand men – so long as it lasts.'

'And after?'

Lovell shrugged. 'Lap of the gods,' he said. 'If Harris and Croft do a good enough job – ' He left it at that. 'It's up to them – and you. I can't pull any more rabbits out of that particular hat.'

'When you say me – ' Andy began.

'I mean two lots of people,' said Lovell. 'One is the Felston shipyard workers. The other is you. You personally.' Andy tried to speak, but Lovell held up his hand. 'Let me finish,' he said, then topped up his glass.

'Everyone wanted that order,' he said. 'The Germans, the French, the Italians. Even the Japanese. But Felston got it. Can you guess why?'

'You?' said Andy.

'Me,' said Lovell. 'Good man. A company I have an interest in has guaranteed the ship will be finished on time. If it is – they'll make a little money. Not much, but enough to make it worthwhile. I personally won't make a cent either way.'

'Then why – ?'

'Because I want Felston to have it,' said Lovell. 'Ever since the march I've wanted to do something, because they deserve it.

284

They're good craftsmen. Good men. And so I've done it. But they have a weakness.'

'You mean they're Socialists. Union men,' Andy said.

'That's all taken care of,' said Lovell. 'Union rules. Union rates. But that's all. No unofficial strikes. No bending the rules.'

'Well of course not,' said Andy. 'I – '

'Because if there are,' Lovell said, 'I'll close down Harris and Croft, and God knows when it will open again.'

And there speaks the Boss, Andy thought; in all his glory.

'Because I'd have no choice,' Lovell said. 'If you mess up this job Felston, maybe the whole of British shipbuilding, will have even less of a future than they do now.'

'You keep talking about me,' Andy said. 'I don't even work there.'

'Sorry,' said Lovell. 'I should have explained. You're going to work there.'

'As a fitter? Not a foreman?'

'Of course,' said Lovell. 'Not all the saints in heaven could turn you into a foreman. But to get this ship done on time we'll need a works committee – problems of demarcation and so on. A committee of management and workers.'

'You want me to be in on it?'

'I want you to be chairman,' Lovell said. Andy sat in silence. 'There's a sweet after the nasty medicine,' said Lovell. 'A bribe if you like. My – Jane is setting up a trust fund for Felston. Ten thousand pounds in shares. She – we – want you to be its administrator.'

'What makes that a bribe?' Andy asked.

'Politics,' Lovell said. 'You're still interested in politics, I take it. As the head of a fund like that – '

'Folks would say I sold out my principles to get it.'

'Not at all,' said Lovell. 'Folks will say you were clever enough to gouge it out of the bosses.' He finished his port. 'We really ought to join the ladies. Do you want to sleep on it?'

'And lie awake all night? No thanks,' Andy said. 'The answer's yes to both. It has to be. But do you realise what you'll be putting me through?'

'I wasn't thinking of you,' said Lovell. 'I was thinking of Felston.'

What Lovell had offered him, what he had taken, was power, far more than that of a councillor, or perhaps even a mayor, so long as it lasted. The trust fund meant money, quite a lot of it, and him holding the purse strings, and money was always power. Chairman of the Works Committee? There was no money in that: it was just power in action. Him, Andy Patterson, showing the bosses how to get things done, and curbing the ardour of the hotheads, the kind that lost elections and strikes and even orders for ships because they couldn't see the point of compromise: didn't even know what it meant.

On the train going North they ate in the dining car, (Jane had insisted, and Norah had to keep her strength up, so how could he refuse?). Andy told her what his new job would mean, and she listened attentively, as she always did when Andy talked, but all she could think of was the other job, his job as a fitter at Harris and Croft. A year's work at least, and the chance of another ship after that, and a bairn on the way mebbes, and no more talk of being an MP. No more meals like this, she thought: gleaming glass, fine china, linen napkins: not for a long time, maybe never: unless Jane or Bob invites us. Not that she cared. Andy liked her cooking, and the place was always clean. It would be good to get back to it.

'I thought the Dorchester. I mean the Savoy's so obvious,' said Lionel.

'Mustn't be obvious,' said Jane.

'Exactly.' Lionel seemed pleased by her ready understanding. 'Usual band, usual food, usual champagne. That's quite obvious too, but it's expected. Should you like a cabaret?'

'My dear, it's an engagement party, not a charity ball,' said Jane.

'I adore cabaret these days. It gives me a chance to rest my feet. Anno domini – the enemy that never sleeps – except in your case may I say? You've never looked better.'

'I've always thought happiness made one rather smug,' said Jane.

'Not in your case,' Lionel said again. 'As for that man of yours he positively exudes goodwill to all. It's pretty to watch.' He produced the cigarette case with the lighter attached.

'You do spoil me,' he said. 'Every camp thing in London has plagued me for it. Such fun when I refuse. Have you a date in mind?'

'Rather up to the Dorchester,' said Jane. 'Whenever they can fit us in.'

'Impatient bridegroom?'

'Well he is, bless him,' said Jane. 'And after all these years, too.'

'He adores you,' said Lionel.

I was adored once. Piers had said that and it was true. Brenda Coupland had adored him, probably still did, but Piers had adored Sybil Hendry, who adored Bob, who adored nobody but himself, but was jolly nice to everybody who didn't happen to love him. Perhaps that was the best way to be. She had been jolly nice to Charles, as much and as often as possible, because he deserved it. But love? She rather doubted it. One couldn't turn it on and off like niceness.

'Fifty people, you said?' Jane smiled. 'Really my dear,' Lionel said, 'I've no doubt you're as blissful as the next bride to be, but you must pay attention.'

'Sorry, miss,' said Jane, and sat up straight.

'And that's quite enough of that. Now, for the third time – did you say fifty people?'

'Give or take,' said Jane. 'There's a list. I'll get it for you.'

'I'll get a quote for fifty four,' said Lionel. 'Just in case. And would you like me to do the placements?'

'Darling, would you?'

'Of course,' Lionel said. '*And* the decorations.'

There was a tap at the door, and Truett came in.

'Mr Bower,' she said. 'On the telephone.'

Oh dear, thought Jane, and said aloud, 'I'll be with him in a moment.'

'You run along,' Lionel said, 'and I'll put a few martinis together. But mind you watch what you're up to. His lady's in foreign parts, and brides to be must be careful.'

How on earth does he know? she thought, but the question was futile. Lionel always knew everything.

Bower said, 'I have to talk to you, it seems.'

'Not if you don't want to,' said Jane. 'I made that perfectly clear. In fact – '

'You'd rather I didn't want to? But I do. The trouble is where. Charles isn't exactly a mari complaisant yet. I doubt he ever will

287

be. You can't come to my club and a bar's out of the question. So's a restaurant. Somebody would be bound to recognise us. The *World* building?'

'No,' said Jane. 'Not there.' The *World* building was far too full of memories of Bower and her working together, loving together.

'Come to tea,' she said. 'Today.' Much better to get it over with.

'I'll have to put off a cabinet minister.'

'It'll be a new experience for him. Shall we say four thirty?'

'I'll be there,' Bower said, and hung up. Jay Bower had transformed hanging up first into an art form, just as Lionel had transformed the pouring of martinis into a rite. She sipped and said, 'Delicious as always.'

'One tries to maintain a standard,' Lionel said, and then his expression changed. He seemed almost embarrassed, or at least as embarrassed as it was possible for Lionel to be.

'We do exchange girlish secrets from time to time,' he said.

'I know you keep mine, and I think you know I keep yours.'

'Of course I do,' he said. 'That's why I'm about to give you another one. I doubt whether you'll want it, but I rather think I must. . . . Catherine Bower.'

'What about her?'

'You knew she was abroad?'

'A holiday. Yes.'

'But you don't know where?'

'No. I don't. Lionel what – '

'She went on her own, no doubt?'

'Yes she did, as a matter of fact. She couldn't face Bunty Fairweather. Not even on a culture tour.'

'Who could? But she didn't stay on her own. She went to Tuscany solo, I grant you, but there she acquired a tour conductor, as you might say. Geoffrey Brent.'

'The silly little bitch,' said Jane, then after a pause: 'Thank you for telling me.'

'Good of you to see me,' Jay Bower said. 'I mean that.'

'Well yes,' said Jane. 'Except that not to see you might lead to an even bigger mess.'

She waved him to silence then, as Truett brought in cucumber sandwiches, Battenberg cake and Indian tea.

'No sugar, as I remember?' she said.

'Who needs it?' Bower selected a cucumber sandwich and bit into it as she poured.

'Catherine came to see you,' he said at last. It was like an accusation of betrayal.

'She always does,' said Jane.

'What the hell does that mean?'

'Whenever she's in a mess. Try not to swear. It will only complicate matters.'

'Sorry,' said Bower. 'You're right. In a mess, you said?'

'Not necessarily of her making.'

'Mine, perhaps?'

'Perhaps.' Jane sipped at her tea. 'Please try to understand this. What she told me I had no wish to hear. On the other hand I had no means of preventing her from telling me.'

'Telling you what?'

'That you raped her.'

'Jesus,' said Bower.

'Whether you did or not is not my business,' said Jane, 'nor do I wish to hear your side of the affair. She said it and I heard it. I neither believe nor disbelieve.'

'Then what am I doing here?' said Bower.

'Up to you,' said Jane. 'You asked to come.'

'Yeah,' Bower said. 'Sure.'

He was thinking hard. That night he had finished early. Gone out of his way to leave a dinner, a very important dinner, long before he should. Gone back home to make love to his wife: take her by surprise. Lead her back to the old familiar paths when they had both been happy together: perhaps even give her a child. Well he'd taken her by surprise, all right. She'd taken him by surprise come to that.

'I didn't rape her,' he said. Define rape, thought Jane.

'*I didn't rape her.*'

'No need to tell the servants,' said Jane.

'Don't you believe me?'

'I neither believe nor disbelieve. I told you. She had no business to tell it to me, but – '

289

'I've never raped a woman,' Bower said. 'Never. We were happy once, you and I. Don't you know that's true?'

'I know about us,' said Jane. 'You never did that to me. You never had to. But that's all I know. All I want to know. Leave it at that.'

'What else is there?'

'Whatever you choose,' said Jane. 'All I can do is listen.'

Bower ate the last sandwich. 'You know she's left me?' he said.

'I know nothing of the sort,' said Jane. 'I know she talked of taking a holiday.'

'A holiday,' said Bower. 'Yeah. Sure. From married life.'

'A bit cryptic, Jay,' she said.

He looked at her and smiled. Perhaps the words had reminded him of the old days; the days before Catherine. Then the smile died.

'Cryptic? Sure. It's all a bit cryptic. What I meant was – did she tell you where she was going on this holiday of hers?'

'No,' said Jane. 'I don't think she knew herself.'

'She knew,' Bower said. 'Believe me. She was off to see her boyfriend. Her latest.'

Jane said nothing because there was nothing to say, but oh how grateful she was to Lionel.

'Want to hear about him?' Bower asked.

'No.'

'Can't say I blame you,' said Bower. 'There's nothing to say except he's rich – and a lot younger than me.'

'Leave it at that then,' said Jane. 'It won't do any good. Honestly.'

'I guess not,' Bower said. 'Just let me say this. He's a nice guy from what I hear. To me that doesn't matter a damn. He could be a prime bastard.' He broke off. 'Sorry,' he said. 'That's just the way I speak. The way I *am*. What I mean is – I don't care about him. I just want her back.' Jane waited. 'But I don't think that's what she wants,' said Bower. 'Just what in hell am I going to do?'

Before she could even begin to think of a reply he said, 'Sorry. That's the most damn fool question you'll be asked this year. You don't know the answer to it any more than she does. Am I right?'

'I'm afraid you are,' said Jane.

'But at least you listened. You're the best listener I ever met in my life.'

'It wasn't any help,' said Jane.

'Maybe not. But at least I could talk. I'm grateful for that. All I can do is wait, is that what you think? Get set for the punch?'

'I'm afraid so.'

'Well at least I'm used to it. I've gone twelve rounds so far. At least.' He got to his feet. 'Thanks for an unbiased hearing.'

'Happy to do it,' said Jane. 'Useless though it was.'

'You don't know that any more than I do.' He offered a hand then said, 'Oh boy. How selfish can you get. Congratulations.'

'Thank you.'

'I mean it,' said Bower. 'Not all marriages end up like mine. I wish you happy my dear, and my guess is you will be.'

He left then, and Jane looked at the tea tray. Every scrap of food had been eaten.

. 30 .

'Hard day?' Norah said.

'First days back is always hard,' said Andy. He had taken off his work boots in the yard and padded up the stairs in his socks. She had his slippers waiting for him, and there were sausages ready to be fried. An egg, too.

'What's your mates like?'

'Early days yet,' said Andy. 'They seem canny enough.'

Glad to be working, he thought. The lot of them. Though with some it might wear off after a while.

'I nearly forgot,' said Norah. 'There's a letter for you.' She took it from the mantelshelf and gave it to him.

Posh envelope, he noticed, with a House of Commons crest. Who in the world – ? He checked to see that it was addressed to him, but there had been no mistake. He tore it open, and looked at the signature. Burrowes. He might have known.

Dear Andy, [he read]
What a very long time and no see. You were in London, I'm told, and yet we didn't meet. Not so much as a glimmer. [You're wrong there, thought Andy. I saw you all right.] Yet you weren't idle, or so I hear. Got yourself three new jobs, they tell me. Only one that pays, alas, but the other two confer other benefits, as I'm sure you realised at once, for whatever your shortcomings you're by no means a fool.

Power is what those other two jobs give you, isn't it Andy? Rather a lot of power if you use it correctly – enough to make you an MP perhaps, and send out your letters in envelopes like this one?

I'm afraid not. You're a good speaker, and people like you, but you've become unreliable Andy, and that will never do. Beaver away as much as you like, but Parliament is not for you

292

– and please don't tell me you'll do better in future. You have no future.

    You shit, do you think I'll ever forget that railway bridge? You're not only unreliable, you're unstable too. Far too big a risk for us to take, and so we open our fingers and let you fall.

J de G Burrowes

I hope she gives you the pox.

'Not bad news, is it?' said Norah.

'What makes you think that?'

'You look so serious.'

He forced himself to smile. This mustn't touch her. 'Just a chap I used to know at Cambridge,' he said.

She smiled at him. 'Not many shipyard fitters get their education at Cambridge,' she said. 'What's this chap do? Sort of a teacher?'

'Journalist,' said Andy. 'When he can be bothered.'

'Rich, is he?'

'He's got a lot of rich friends.'

'He doesn't sound very nice,' said Norah.

'He isn't very nice,' said Andy. 'But he's clever. Clever as a waggon load of monkeys.'

'I bet he's not more clever than you,' she said, and he smiled at her again. She valued him far too highly, but he still enjoyed it.

'Let's have them sausages,' he said. 'I'm starved.'

She reached for the frying pan. 'Are you going to answer it?' she asked.

'I might have done if he'd bothered to give me his address,' he said. 'But he didn't.' He screwed up the letter, threw it in the fire, and watched it burn. She mustn't see a word of it.

'Do you miss Cambridge?' Norah asked.

'No,' Andy said. 'It was good at the time and I learned a lot, but I didn't belong there. Never would.'

'Where do you belong then?'

'Here,' he said, and put his arm around her. The letter was gone, destroyed, and Norah was safe, because he'd seen Burrowes at a Fascist meeting with that bastard Crawley, and that was a weapon far more powerful than the hands that had suspended Burrowes from the bridge.

*

Georgie arrived in London and went at once to the suite she had reserved at the Savoy. 'Force of habit,' she explained over the phone to Jane. 'I clean forgot that this time I'm paying my own bills. Come and dine with me darling and bring your nice chap – or rather your nice, *respectable* chap. Engaged indeed. It makes you sound like a debutante. I tell you what – why don't you come early, and we'll get the girlish secrets out of the way?'

The two women embraced, then looked at each other as they always did when they had been apart for a while. Chanel looked at Schiaparelli, diamonds at sapphires; and both women seemed suddenly relieved that their friend still looked so good.

'It's been such ages,' said Georgie. 'Martini or champagne?'

'Oh champers, please,' said Jane, and Georgie picked up the phone. When she had done she said, 'You first.'

'But there's nothing for me to tell,' said Jane. 'All I did was get engaged.'

'All?' said Georgie. '*All?* Will you just look at that monstrous lump of ice on your finger?'

Jane held out her left hand. 'I must say it is rather fetching,' she said.

'No more than you deserve,' Georgie said. 'You deserve your nice chap too, even if he is so shatteringly rich.'

'Now you,' said Jane.

'After the champagne arrives,' said Georgie. 'Mine's rather a saga, and I don't want us to be interrupted.'

When the drinks were poured and the waiter had gone, she said: 'You remember my husband?'

'We never met,' said Jane.

'I mean you remember I had one?'

'Well of course,' said Jane.

'Dear, delicious Dan,' said Georgie. 'The biggest Fairy Queen on the Christmas tree. But such a pal. No chance of his being a nice chap, but he was an awfully nice girl. And such a chum. Like your Lionel. What those two bastards did to him – ' She drank more champagne, shuddered, and said: 'Never mind that. The thing is, maybe I owe your nice chap an apology.'

'Charles? Whatever for?'

'Murray Fisch knew all about it. Knew who they were, I mean.

The ones who did those terrible things to Dan. He'd known for absolute ages. Though he never bothered to tell me – or anybody else, come to that.'

'But whyever not?'

'He thought it would be bad for World Wide Pictures, which means bad for Murray Fisch. Anyway, my gumshoes – '

'Your what?'

'Detectives,' said Georgie. 'Just like in *Black Mask* magazine. Golly, we stars of the silver screen do live. Anyway, they found out the names of those two swine and phoned me in Mexico City. They also found out that Murray knew who they were. That's why I made Murray make a fool of himself by turning down his lousy contract. I was absolutely certain he'd start screaming in front of hundreds of people and I was right. El Presidente was a bonus I maybe didn't deserve – but wasn't it bliss? All the same, maybe I do owe Charles an apology.'

'No,' said Jane. 'This wasn't the silver screen. This was real life. You did what you thought was right. I think it was, too, and I know Charles would. – And he got another picture out of you anyway.'

'And gave Murray hell,' said Georgie. 'I've never seen a man so – so – diminished.'

'What about the two murderers?' said Jane.

'They've been in Puerto Rico,' Georgie said. 'Now they're on their way home. When their boat docks they'll be arrested.'

'By your gumshoes?'

'They're private,' said Georgie. 'The LAPD will do it. Los Angeles Police Department. All my boys will do is hand over the evidence and collect a bonus from me.'

'What will happen to them?'

'Dan's killers? The electric chair.'

'Oh,' said Jane.

'Yes I know,' said Georgie, 'but think what they did to poor Dan.'

Gumshoes, thought Jane. Probably nice men, off duty. Solid and respectable. Like Mr Pinner. He's good at seeking out killers too.

'There was a time I thought I'd just have them killed,' said Georgie.

'Georgie, for God's sake,' said Jane, for it was obvious that Georgie meant it.

'It looked like there mightn't be enough evidence,' Georgie said, 'and I couldn't let them live, not after what they did to poor darling Dan. It wasn't just a murder. They had quite a lot of boyish fun before they – ' She shuddered. 'But then the evidence turned up and I thought it best to let them burn. – Didn't St Paul go on about burning?'

'He said better to be married than burn,' said Jane.

'Much better. But those two won't get the choice.'

'But how could you have them killed?' said Jane.

'It would have been difficult,' Georgie said, 'and expensive, but not impossible. Not in the United States. I could have had Murray beaten up, too. Or do you mean how could I bring myself to do it?'

'Just that.'

'You've never had somebody you cared for done to death the way Dan was,' Georgie said. 'Until you have there's no saying what you'll do. Anyway I let them live. For a while, anyway.'

'And Murray Fisch escaped his beating?'

'He got worse,' said Georgie. 'Much worse. I wrote a letter to Magda.'

'Magda?'

'Magda Fisch. Murray's wife. I gave her a list of all the women Murray had cavorted with down the years, including the three in Mexico City. Chapter and verse I gave her, and signed it "A Friend". I detest anonymous letters and I dare say you do too, but I couldn't get involved, for World Wide's sake. Murray would be the first to agree with that.'

'What did she do?' Jane asked. 'Do you know?'

'Moved out of the house and went straight to her cousin,' Georgie said. 'Her cousin's a lawyer. Murray is in deep deep trouble.' She wriggled luxuriously in her chair. 'Do you think I did the right thing?'

'Absolutely,' said Jane. 'But not if you'd hired gangsters to kill other gangsters.'

'I'm glad I didn't have to,' Georgie said. Jane left it at that. 'I have other news,' said Georgie. 'Better news. Concerning my marital status.'

'You've met your nice chap?'

'Indeed I have,' said Georgie. 'And not before time. I'm hardly in the first blush of maidenhood.'

'Any more than I was,' said Jane. 'But we both brought it off. Now yours – don't tell me. Let me guess.' She made passes over a non-existent crystal ball. 'A man in his prime,' she said. 'Tall. Distinguished. Of impeccable breeding.'

'Well of course,' said Georgie.

'Heir to great estates and an ancient title,' said Jane. 'At present he holds the rank of marquis. The letter "A" is there. Definitely an "A". And an "L". Could it be Alston?'

For the first time since she had known her, Georgie's elegant control had gone. She was gaping like an idiot.

'Who the hell told you?' she yelled.

'I met him at Felston,' said Jane. 'At a funeral. Canon Messeter's. You remember him – at the March?'

'Yes of course,' Georgie said. 'The sweetest man.'

'He was your nice chap's godfather. After the funeral he took me to lunch.'

'Did he tell you about us?'

'Just that he'd met you in Hollywood,' said Jane. 'Nothing personal. But it's quite obvious that he adores you, which is very right and proper. It's what you were put on this earth for, after all. To be adored by a nice chap.'

Georgie got up from her chair and kissed her. 'If it's true that makes two of us,' she said. 'Thank you, darling.'

Then Charles arrived and with him was Lord Alston, who went at once to Georgie and kissed her on the cheek before turning to Jane.

'Nice to see you again,' he said.

'We met downstairs,' said Charles. 'Had one in the bar as a matter of fact.' He went to Jane then and kissed her. 'Hello, darling. Have you had a lovely gossip?' he said. 'Have all the reputations gone?'

'One or two survived,' said Georgie. 'You and Ned know each other, do you?'

Jane looked puzzled.

'I'm Ned,' Lord Alston said. 'Christened Edward, you see. But I prefer Ned – among friends. Charles and I aren't precisely neigh-bours in the wilds of Northumbria – but I've been to Blagdon on a shooting party or two.'

'Nice that we should all know each other,' Georgie said, 'but darling, why are you looking so furtive?'

To Jane, Alston didn't look in the least furtive, but then he wasn't her nice chap.

'We've been asked to a party,' he said. 'Rather short notice. After dinner as a matter of fact.'

'*Tonight?*'

'I did explain that I had a dinner engagement,' said Alston, 'but when I said who they were she said you should all come too.'

'Who did?'

'Annabel Lane,' said Alston. 'She and George are giving what I believe is called a bit of a do in that great barn of theirs in Pont Street.'

'No more than a couple of hundred,' said Charles.

'Not counting the band and the waiters,' Alston said. Suddenly he seemed sunk in gloom as profound as his father's when con-fronted by politics. 'It's you she's after of course.'

'*Me?*' said Georgie.

'Well you and Jane,' Alston said. 'She's potty about the cinema. I do wish she wasn't.'

'You'll get used to it,' said Lovell. 'One has to.'

'You poor martyred thing,' said Jane.

'Yes, but I was looking forward to an evening on our own,' Alston said. 'Only you know how persuasive Annabel can be. – Oh my God! I've just remembered.'

'You mean there's worse?' Georgie said.

'HRH is going to be there,' said Alston, who seemed on the verge of despair. 'The Little Man.'

'You mean the Prince of Wales?' said Georgie. 'Remember I'm a bit out of touch.'

'I'm afraid I do,' Alston said.

'Is he so ghastly?' Georgie asked.

'He plays the bagpipes sometimes,' Alston said. 'Ukulele too.'

'He's hardly likely to play either at Annabel Lane's party,' said Charles.

'It's not just that,' said Alston. 'He's so boring. Forever doing the gracious. And he'll bring his latest. He always does.'

'Mrs Simpson?' said Jane.

'The Baltimore Belle,' said Alston. 'She'll hate you two.'

'Why on earth should she?' asked Jane.

'Better looking,' said Alston, and Georgie kissed him.

'I suppose we'll have to go,' she said, 'even if we do end up in the Tower.'

'Oh he'll like you,' said Alston. 'After all he's got eyes in his head. But it'll be so frightfully dull.' Suddenly he brightened. 'He probably won't stay late,' he said. 'He's always dashing off to the Embassy Club. We can always skedaddle as soon as they've gone.'

'What a charming guest you are,' Lovell said. 'Is there a Mr Simpson?'

'Used to be,' said Alston. 'He used to go about with her all over the place. Regular threesome. He seems to have disappeared just recently.'

'The headsman's axe?' asked Lovell.

'Back to the United States,' said Alston. 'Surplus to requirement, as you might say.'

'And to think men have the nerve to call us bitchy,' Georgie said, and then: 'Isn't Simpson her third?'

'He is indeed,' Alston said.

'We simply must go to this awful party,' said Georgie.

Quite a lot of people seemed to have had the same idea. The house was filled with gossiping groups and the ballroom too was gratifyingly filled. Mrs Simpson was very good box office indeed, said Georgie. Even so, Annabel Lane was effusive in her greeting to them, too. A world-famous star and the heir to a dukedom, and even their companions were lesser luminaries; not stars, perhaps, but satellites of substance: a famous writer and a man of great wealth. Her husband too greeted them warmly, especially Charles, Jane noticed. They moved further on and into the ballroom. No sign of HRH yet, nor his enterprising divorcée. Jane and Charles began to dance.

'Do you mind awfully coming here?' he asked.

'Not a bit,' she said. 'Your chum Ned made it sound like a wake.'

'He's in love,' said Charles. 'If he can't have Georgie all to himself he can just about cope with another couple who feel as they do, but he doesn't want a crowd and I can't say I blame him.'

'Would you rather go?'

'You forget,' said Charles, 'that I've been the luckiest man in the world far longer than he has.' She moved a little closer to him.

'Mr Lane,' she said. 'Are you and he old chums?'

'We sometimes do business together. Just at the moment I've got something he wants.'

'Me?'

'Money,' said Charles. 'I may give him some. I wouldn't give him you in a thousand years.'

'He might not want me.'

'More fool he,' said Charles. 'And a bigger fool if he did.'

'Why does he want money?'

'He owns an engineering firm,' said Charles. 'They're developing an engine for an aeroplane that's turning out to be expensive. On the other hand it could also turn out to be a winner.'

'Is HRH interested in aero engines?'

'He's interested in horses,' said Charles, 'and Lane owns rather a lot.'

'No wonder he needs money,' said Jane. 'Oh look. There's Jay Bower.'

Charles looked. 'Who's he dancing with? It isn't Catherine,' he said.

'Catherine's in Tuscany, acquiring culture,' said Jane.

'While her husband's in Mayfair, acquiring a blonde,' said Charles. The idea seemed to please him if anything. Jane allowed herself to be steered across the room. She had no desire to talk to Bower.

They were in the drawing room with Georgie and Ned when the prince arrived. There was a stir and silence rather like that in a theatre when the curtain goes up at the beginning of the first act, she thought, and then he came in, the compulsive divorcée at his side, Annabel and George Lane hovering near by. Bad construction, she thought, to send the star on at the beginning of Act One, but this wasn't Ruritania, after all. He was a real prince, and always came first wherever he went. A lane opened for him automatically

300

like the parting of the Red Sea, and his hostess singled out the fortunate few to be introduced. When it came to their group she didn't hesitate.

'I expect you've seen Miss Georgina Payne on the screen many times, sir,' she said.

'Good Lord yes,' said the heir to the throne.

'And Miss Jane Whitcomb? Miss Payne played her in *The Angel of No Man's Land.*'

'Good Lord,' said His Royal Highness. 'So she did.'

Georgie and Jane dipped in curtsies, but with none of the bravura they had shown the President of Mexico.

'Mr Charles Lovell,' said Mrs Lane. Charles bowed. 'And the Marquis of Alston.'

'Ned,' said HRH. 'What on earth are you doing here? Nothing left to shoot in Northumberland?'

'Ran out of ammunition, sir,' said Alston, and the prince laughed. It was obvious that the two of them detested each other. All the same it gave Jane a chance to take a better look at the Baltimore Belle.

But Alston was wrong there. She was by no means a beauty: not even what the French called a jolie laide. A plain woman if anything, and by no means young, but rigorously, even ruthlessly, groomed. Every hair in place, finger nails at once neat and gleaming, make-up unobtrusive and yet perfect, with a kind of majestic assurance that would have reminded Jane of no one so much as The Little Man's mother, were it not for the bare and gleaming shoulders and discreet décolletage.

'Well well,' The Little Man said. 'Enjoy yourselves,' and moved off suddenly, without warning, so that the Lanes had to scamper to keep up.

'Does he think we couldn't do that without his permission?' said Alston.

'Taking a chance, isn't he, towing her around like that?' said Georgie, and then: 'Good Lord. He isn't going to marry her, is he?'

'That's rather up to Mr Simpson,' said Alston, 'and anyway if you look you'll see they've also got Fruity Metcalf and his wife in tow. Sort of chaperons.'

'Fruity Metcalf?' said Georgie.

'His secretary. Now Mrs S. has stopped to talk to an old chum, see? She's got a lot more sense than he has.'

Mrs Simpson had indeed stopped to talk to a large woman in an unfortunate dress and rubies that needed cleaning.

'Thank God that's over,' said Alston.

'Hardly the way to talk of your future king,' said Georgie.

'It's an extraordinary thing to say about the heir to the throne,' Alston said, 'but in my opinion he's not a gentleman. I mean that accent of his – '

'He could use a voice coach certainly,' Georgie said, 'but so could lots of people. He struck me as being a bit sad, if anything. Didn't you think so, Jane?'

But Jane was staring at The Little Man once more. He had just finished flirting in an avuncular sort of way with Sybil Hendry, and now Bob Patterson was bowing to him. If only Andy had been there to see it.

'I said he seemed a bit sad,' said Georgie. 'Didn't you think so?'

'More pathetic really,' said Jane.

'There's a difference?'

'There are all kinds of reasons for sadness,' said Jane. 'Your dog dies, or your engagement's broken off. Things like that. But to be pathetic means that you're faced with something you're just not up to – and no matter how hard you try, it shows.'

They finished their drinks and went back to the dancing. Really it turned out to be rather a nice party, and Alston danced at least adequately. Bower had disappeared soon after The Little Man had spoken to him, which was just as well. Bob on the other hand pushed his way to them the next time they left the dance floor, and brought Sybil Hendry with him. Georgie's smile, Jane noticed, was wary to say the least, but she introduced Bob to Alston, and relaxed as Sybil Hendry babbled adulation.

'Do you see anything of my brother these days?' Alston asked her.

'Roderick? How can I? He thinks one needs a passport to go south of Newcastle.'

'Do him good to get out and about a bit, I agree. Are you from those parts, Mr Patterson?'

'No hiding that accent, is there?' said Bob. 'I was born in Felston

– but I agree with you. There's no harm in getting out and about a bit, is there Jane?'

'It certainly did you no harm,' she said. 'I bet you're the only one in John Bright Street who's been introduced to the Prince of Wales.'

'Grandma would have loved that,' said Bob, then echoed her own thought. 'But whatever would our Andy say?'

'Did you know Canon Messeter too?' Alston asked.

'Know him? He conned me into buying a new hot-water system for that clinic him and Stobbs had. He'd have made a marvellous salesman if he hadn't been a parson. He'll be missed up in Felston, I can tell you. . . . Well, mustn't keep you. Are you in London for a while, Charles? I'd like a word if I could.'

'Tomorrow,' said Lovell. 'Phone me. Afternoon would be best.'

. 31 .

'Charles?' said Jane. 'Are you and Bob chums now?'

'We're partners,' said Charles. 'Doesn't pay to be pompous.'

Jane unhooked her dress. Marriage couldn't come too soon, she decided. Once she was married she wouldn't have to undress then dress again every time they made love.

'That young man has some really good ideas. I'd let him call me Charles even if I didn't like him, and as it happens I do.'

'He seems very entangled with Sybil Hendry.'

'He'll get free if and when he wants to,' said Charles. 'A born survivor, that young man.' He took her in his arms.

Later she said, 'What did you make of The Little Man's new lady?'

'Not a patch on you,' he said. 'But elegant in her way. They say she bullies him.'

'Good Lord.'

'Some chaps have a taste for humiliation,' said Charles. 'Blowed if I know why.'

'She didn't try it tonight.'

'Too big an audience,' said Charles. 'On her best behaviour. Or so she thought.'

'Hardly discreet though, were they?'

'At least she called him "sir" all the time.'

'You're not suggesting she's going to shed Mr Simpson and wed our monarch-to-be?'

'To be quite soon,' said Charles, 'from what I hear. The king's far from well. But to answer your question – how can she marry him? Apart from everything else The Little Man will be head of the Church of England. How can he marry a divorced woman?'

'Depends how much he wants her,' said Jane, 'and how much

she wants to be queen.' She got out of bed. 'Come along, old man. Time to take your missus home.'

'I hate this bit,' he said. 'I like to be beside you when we sleep.'

'You're lucky I don't snore,' she said.

Tea and ginger bikkies and just as well, thought Bob. Far too early for whisky and soda, and he was going to need a clear head for this one. Charles's office was a bit overpowering too. Usually places didn't bother him; he'd been in all sorts: country houses, grand hotels, suite on a liner, Hollywood bedrooms, and none of them had been a problem. But Charles's office, that was something else again. Partly it was Charles. Very much the gentleman of course, like a more worldly Canon Messeter, amiable, easy-going – and as clever as they come. Only he didn't show it. Not ever. Too clever by half was Charles Lovell – for other people.

He looked around the room. Victorian, so he'd been told. Mahogany panelling, Turkey carpet, desk the size of a cricket field – and nothing on it except a telephone, a diary, and a blotting pad. Unbelievable, thought Bob. I couldn't even exist without clutter, never mind work. Leather everywhere on chairs and desk and the books in their gleaming bookcase. Typical banker's office in fact, if the banker happened to be a millionaire, except for the pictures. Bankers' offices nearly always had pictures, but usually it was some chap in a wig or a frock coat, or maybe a ship in full sail if the banker was in shipping. Lovell's pictures weren't like that. One was a woman with no clothes on. A bit on the fat side for his taste, but not bad looking. The other was a café in what he took to be Paris, about fifty years ago, and not much of a café at that. Chaps smoking clay pipes, women in cheap dresses. Not at all what you'd expect in a banker's office, any more than you'd expect a naked woman. Maybe that was why Charles had put them there, he thought. To put visitors off their stride. Or maybe he just liked the painter – a chap called Renoir. More than likely it was both. He heard Lovell's voice in the outer office, and swallowed the last of his biscuit.

'I'm glad to see Miss Blair looked after you,' said Lovell. 'Take your time and finish your tea. We won't be disturbed.'

'I've done, thanks,' said Bob, and reached for his cigarette case, offered it to Lovell.

'Thank you,' said Lovell. 'Oh, before we start I'd better tell you I agree to your request to buy me out.'

'Why that's marvellous,' said Bob.

'At a price,' Lovell said, and named a figure. Spot on, thought Bob. Neither soft nor greedy. Just right.

'That's fine,' he said aloud. 'It may take a bit of time – '

'I should hope so,' said Lovell. 'Otherwise you'd be buying me out.'

'Do you mind if I ask why you're doing it?'

'Glad to. The Patterson family seems to have adopted Jane, or maybe it's the other way about – and it occurred to me it would be a good idea for you to be independent now that we're going to be married.'

And there you had him, thought Bob. As long as Jane was free he wasn't sure of me, and his money in my business was like a gun at my head. Behave or else. But now he's got her he doesn't have to worry – and just as well for me.

'Now let's hear whatever it is you've brought me,' said Lovell.

'It was something I thought of at the party,' said Bob. 'Smart move, George Lane getting the Prince of Wales there – but then Annabel Lane's a friend of Mrs Simpson.'

'Who on earth told you that?'

'She did. Usually George Lane doesn't give a damn about parties. His idea of a good night out is bridge at a pound a point. Yet there he goes, lashing out all over the place. Champagne, caterers, a band, hired waiters. A lot of money that.'

'He's got a lot of money.'

'Not just at the moment he hasn't,' said Bob.

And who on earth told you *that*? Lovell wondered, but this time he didn't ask the question aloud.

'He's a born gambler, George Lane,' said Bob, 'and last night was just another gamble. One of his biggest. Spend a lot of money, show your rich friends how you're pally with the Prince of Wales and his lady friend, then borrow ten times as much as you spent.'

'His rich friends would lend it just because he's the friend of the prince?'

'They would if they wanted to be the prince's friend, too.' Lovell waited. 'Besides, he's got good security. That aero engine of his.'

306

'He did tell me it's a winner,' Lovell said.

'He told the truth – according to an engineer I know.'

'Forgive me,' said Lovell, 'but didn't you say you got this idea at the party?'

'The idea, yes,' said Bob. 'This is all background stuff.'

'You seem very good at it.'

'I should be,' said Bob. 'I made my living at it one time. When I worked for Jay Bower.'

'Go on,' said Lovell.

'There was an American at the party last night,' said Bob. 'Our future king's rather partial to Americans – and I don't just mean women in bed. He likes to play golf and poker, and so do Americans, and they don't have the bad taste to beat him.' He smiled. 'Not like Lord Alston,' he said. 'Last year he thrashed His Royal Highness over eighteen holes at Sunningdale, then took five hundred quid from him at poker the same night.'

'I did think I detected a touch of frost at the party,' said Lovell.

'More like the bloody Arctic from what I hear,' said Bob.

'And you do manage to hear rather a lot,' said Lovell, but he was smiling as he said it. 'Go on.'

'It's simple, really. George Lane really does need money, and the less people who want to lend it the better deal we can get.'

'But if he's such a chum of HRH – '

'He's not,' said Bob. 'I told you. It's Annabel who's a chum of Wallis Simpson.'

'Same thing, surely?'

'Suppose they were to fall out?'

'But why on earth should they?'

'Money,' said Bob, and hitched his chair forward. 'Lane really has lost a hell of a lot. Not so much here – though his horses haven't overworked themselves recently – '

'Where then?'

'Deauville,' said Bob. 'Monte Carlo. Sybil's father goes to both of them. He and Lane sit at the same roulette wheel. Born losers the pair of them. I rather think Annabel's had enough. In fact I know she has. Also she has a pretty fair chunk of Lane Engineering shares in her own right. She'd sell them like a shot if she got a good enough offer.'

'Is she leaving Lane?'

Bob shrugged. 'It's possible,' he said. 'But she isn't going to keep him in roulette money.'

'What you're saying is we'll do that?'

'Not at all,' said Bob. 'I'm saying we'll take over Lane Engineering.'

'I thought that's where we'd get to in the end,' said Lovell, and looked at his café full of poor Parisians, which meant that Bob had to look at the naked woman. No novelty in that, he thought. All the same he'd have given an awful lot of money to know what Lovell was thinking.

At last Lovell said, 'There's just one thing wrong with your scheme – supposing you and the fair Annabel bring it off – and that is that I finish up lending you even more money.'

'I can put up security,' said Bob.

'Patterson's Wireless Rentals?' Bob nodded. 'You really must think you can do it,' said Lovell. 'Very well. Let me have some figures. If they're not too exorbitant we can start work.'

'Doing what?'

'Robbing George Lane blind. Isn't that the idea? I take it you don't like him much.'

'I don't like him at all,' Bob said. 'In the first place he's treated his wife pretty badly – and in the second place he's a pal of Crawley's.'

'Ah,' said Lovell.

'So long as Annabel's all right I don't care what we do to her husband.'

What a dedicated Romantic Bob Patterson was, thought Lovell, yet somehow he managed to make money out of it.

'Get to work,' he said. 'If things go as you predict and you're not too greedy – I'm in. By the way – talking of HRH – he and Bower seemed like chums.'

'Another American,' said Bob. 'A good loser.'

'Just so,' said Lovell. 'He left the party rather early, didn't he?'

'Straight after His Nibs. Him and that blonde he had with him. They went to the Embassy.'

'A little relaxation?'

'That's what the blonde was for, but Bower was probably working. His Nibs needs advice.'

'On what?'

Again Bob shrugged. 'Just about everything. But what Bower does is tell him about getting his name in the papers – and even more about keeping it out.'

'Bower does that?' Bob nodded. 'Well, would you say?'

'Very well. Pictures, and articles too. Visits to Welsh Miners, day at Ascot, British Legion rallies. All that. He gets all the space that's going. – And not a word about Wallis Simpson. Name never mentioned. Not even a cut off of her photograph in the background. Bower's doing a good job all right.'

'Any idea why?'

'It never hurts to have the king on your side,' said Bob.

The engagement party was proving something of a pest. It was true that Lionel was doing all the hard work, and loving every minute of it, but it was left to Jane to worry about wounded susceptibilities, and damn heavy going it was. Dodo, still worried about her house in Maidenhead; Sybil Hendry, desperate to know a) that she'd be invited; and b) that she'd be placed next to Bob; and now this business of Bower.

Of course she'd asked him – not to ask him was unthinkable – and of course she'd asked Catherine too, and the first thing Catherine had done when she got back from Siena or Pisa or wherever it was, was to ask if it was absolutely vital for her to sit next to her husband. Couldn't she be with Piers instead?

'A little out of the ordinary, surely?' said Jane.

'So's my marriage,' said Catherine. 'Can I come to see you and talk about it?'

'Where are you?' said Jane.

'Staying with a friend. Place called Trumpington. Full of old-world charm. Believe me I could do with some. Can I come to see you?'

Jane temporised and looked up Trumpington in her atlas. Just outside Cambridge. It would be, she thought. Nothing good out of Cambridge.

Francis was for once living there, Long Vacation or not. Berlin it seemed was no longer acceptable, what with storm troopers and brownshirts. Much better to get down to serious work. The Left had a duty. These were not frivolous times. Bourgeois frivolity in the current political climate was unthinkable. By bourgeois frivolity, Jane gathered, her brother meant her engagement party. It had taken pleadings, blandishments, and finally the threat that she would drive to his college and fetch him by force to make him agree to be there. Why do I bother? she wondered, but the answer was obvious. She bothered for the sake of Mummy, and quite right too. All the same it would have been nice just to pop into a registry office somewhere with a couple of strangers for witnesses.

No place like home, thought Bob, and for him his office just about was home. After all he spent most of his working life there. Nice part, too. Off Kensington High Street, just round the corner from Ponting's, with a pub near by that could do you a good sandwich, when you weren't lunching a client. An office that really was an office. Miss Spicer outside trying to answer both phones at once, and a desk so covered in papers you couldn't tell what it was made of. No Renoirs on the wall, just a calendar from a firm that made wireless valves, and no cathedral-like calm, either. Usually he had a wireless going in the office, too: a new one from a firm that wanted his trade. It was only fair to give it a trial.

In short, he thought, a place where a man could work. He grinned, but it was true, for him. Maybe it was a reversal to his days as a printer, with presses banging, typesetters clicking away and everybody yelling if they wanted to be heard. He burrowed into the stack of papers in front of him and came out with an envelope and a pencil. Time to make a few notes. Things to do. Talk to Annabel, first and foremost. Without her they hadn't a prayer. On the other hand when he'd sounded her out, she hadn't been that unwilling. Then he'd got to get a look at that engine: get a copy of the machine drawings for preference. Tricky, that would be, but not impossible, not with Lovell's money. Not that Lovell would want to know. He'd be on his own on that, and quite right too. He was only just starting out, after all, and beginners had to take the risks if they were after big money. Lovell already had big money: enormous money.

How much to take over Lane's business? Not all of it; just enough to get him off the board. There was a broker he knew would tell him. Keep his mouth shut, too. He had to. He had a rich wife and a chorus girl he was potty about, and Bob knew them both. . . . Be nice to be there when Annabel let that Simpson woman have it. No trouble for Annabel, that. She enjoyed a good scene in public. It was the only thing that had kept her married to Lane for so long.

His affaire with her hadn't lasted long, though they'd both enjoyed it. The trouble was that Lane had found out and given her a black eye. Kept well away from me, though, thought Bob. I know all that pistols-at-dawn stuff finished ages ago, but at least if I'd done that in Felston the bloke would have given me a belting, or tried to. All he'd done was hammer his wife. That wasn't the Felston way at all. In Felston he'd have had to hammer me *and* his wife. He even let me stay when I went to the prince's party with Sybil, but that might have been because he didn't dare risk a scene.

So maybe my motives are pure, he thought. Maybe I'm doing this to avenge Annabel's black eye. – And maybe pigs can fly. I'm doing this for the money. Come to think of it, I'm even risking prison for the money. The orchestra on the wireless began to play 'In A Monastery Garden', and Bob turned it up. It was one of his favourites.

Miss Spicer put her head round the door and yelled, just like the print shop. 'Mrs Lane on one, Mrs Hendry on two,' she said, and looked at him as she might have looked at a small boy stealing sweets. He'd never tried to make love to Miss Spicer, nor did she want him to. What she liked was to see him at work: to know who was his latest. Gave her a real thrill, that, and it didn't cost him a penny.

'Tell Mrs Hendry I'll call her back,' said Bob. 'Put Mrs Lane on.'

Miss Spicer's eyebrows lifted. That wasn't how she saw the plot at all, but she put Mrs Lane through.

'Annabel, how nice,' said Bob.

'I thought we should have a talk,' she said. 'Lunch?'

'Usual place? One o'clock?'

'Super,' she said, and hung up. Not much in that for Miss Spicer, but then Lane's house had a hell of a lot of servants and a hell of a lot of extensions, too. Miss Spicer buzzed him.

'Shall I get Mrs Hendry for you?' she asked.

'In a while.'

He had to think about Sybil. Ditching her was not the answer. Not yet, anyway. Her late husband had left her a lot of shares in Lane Engineering. On the other hand he didn't want any more jolly japes like the one she'd tried when Andy was staying with him. A high-spirited girl, he thought. What an old-fashioned novelist would call a mettlesome female. If he'd belonged to the black-eye school of thought he'd have belted her one ages ago. Good in bed, though, and that was part of the trouble. You didn't get rid of talent like that till you'd found a replacement.

He didn't want to cause any uproar, either, not just at the moment, thanks, and Sybil was very, very good at uproar, and wouldn't take kindly to being dropped. There didn't seem to be any sign of a successor, either. He'd had hopes of Piers at one time, and that Lord Roderick feller was very keen, but she wasn't: not on either of them. What little Sybil liked was her freedom – and her fancy man. Bob faced the fact that he was the male equivalent of his stockbroker's chorus girl. He found it appalling, but it had to be endured if he wanted to take Lane's business from him. He buzzed Miss Spicer. Time for her treat.

'Get me Mrs Hendry,' he said. Be nice, he told himself. Forget about chorus girls. Her maid answered, and then there was a pause.

'Forgive me, darling,' Sybil Hendry said at last. 'Daddy's just arrived. He's taking me to lunch. Soho. Nice and cheap.' And then: 'I've missed you,' she said.

'Me too.'

'Do you know,' she said, 'I never thought I'd hear you say that? Not you.'

Careful lad, he told himself. Remember she's clever, too.

'Must be one of my good days,' he said.

'Oh I do hope so, because I'm rather hoping you'll come and see me tonight.'

'My pleasure,' he said.

'Could be. After we've dined somewhere. And I swear to you there'll be no sign of Daddy. I can't think how I came to be so confused last time.'

Last two times, he thought. Once when I left your bed to find him plastered in your drawing room, and once – he hated to think of it. She'd actually tried to get him into her father's bed while

Daddy was dining at his club and planning an early night. Apart from anything else, thought Bob, it isn't nice.

'So long as you're sure,' he said.

'Oh I promise,' she said. 'What time will you come for me?'

'Seven thirty?'

'Lovely,' she said. 'Darling, I must go. Daddy keeps shouting how hungry he is. I expect that means I'll have to pay.'

Bob hung up, retrieved the envelope he'd used for his notes, and wrote 'Andy' on it. After a pause he added the words, 'and Norah'. They'd never take his money, either of them, but they'd have bairns, no question, and they'd take money for their bairns. Norah would see to that. If this caper with Lane Engineering came off, he'd give them some. Quite a bit, in fact.

. 32 .

She had thought about doing it at the Molyneux Collection: all the rich bitches in London would be there, and the news would get around in no time at all – but in the end she decided against it. There were two reasons. One was that she liked Molyneux's clothes and quite often bought some: the other was that the day after the Molyneux display George was off to Ripon to watch one of his horses lose, and she didn't fancy going another twelve rounds with George for a long, long time. Then she had a bit of luck. Brenda Meldrum rang her up to ask if she could make up a four at the Embassy on the night of George's departure: a Thursday. The Little Man always went to the Embassy on a Thursday, as Brenda well knew. She wants a closer look at Wallis Simpson, Annabel Lane thought. Well now she's going to get one.

They dined first at L'Apéritif: Brenda and sweet, fat Hugo and a charming young soldier: Piers Hilyard. Of course everybody knew that he and Brenda had been rather a pair, including sweet, fat Hugo, until the IRA had done their best to kill the young man, but they hadn't succeeded, and he walked with the merest suggestion of a limp. She congratulated him on the fact.

'Doing very well,' he said. 'The battalion's still struggling on without me as best they can, but the quack says it won't be long now, and then God help them. The battalion I mean.' He looked away for a moment. 'Trouble is I can't dance yet – but Brenda tells me there'll be lots of dashing young men who can.' He prodded warily at his chicken Kiev.

'You must miss it dreadfully,' Mrs Lane said. 'Dancing, I mean.'

'I do, rather. But it won't be for too long, I hope.'

After all, he had started riding again, but he wasn't going to tell

314

her that, charming and attractive though she was. No point in asking for another bomb. But she *was* charming – and attractive. Bit of luck his being asked to squire her. A little tense, though. Not in any crazy kind of way, he thought. Just wound up tight like a spring, rather as he must have been with the Gurkhas just before things started to get interesting. All the same she was a delightful companion, and if Brenda didn't like it she shouldn't have asked her. What was the point in looking at HRH's latest anyway? All the same, Hugo had a jolly good taste in claret. He smiled at Mrs Lane, and talked of hunting in Ireland.

At last Brenda insisted that Hugo do his duty and he sighed, heaved himself to his feet and pushed his wife round the dance floor, oblivious to rhythm and other dancers alike.

'You must find this very frustrating,' Mrs Lane said.

'Depends on the company. At the moment I'm not bored at all.' She smiled. Still wound up tight, he thought, but enjoying it, whatever it was.

Then the music stopped and HRH came in with his chums. Mrs Simpson, *of course*, that equerry of his, Fruity Metcalf, and his wife, and half a dozen more of the same. The maître showed them to their table as if even being allowed to breathe the same air were a privilege, and the rest of the people there talked rather too loudly, pretending not to look and still staring very hard.

'Do you think she's pretty?' Mrs Lane asked.

'Not very.' Mrs Lane smiled. It seemed that he had given the right answer.

The problem was to get to her, Annabel Lane thought. If it came to the worst she would simply have to walk across the room and say it. She wasn't afraid to do it: it wasn't that. It would just look obvious, and she didn't want that. At last Wallis Simpson solved her problem for her. The prince was dancing with someone else, and she looked across at Annabel Lane and waved, or maybe beckoned. Let's call it beckoned, Annabel Lane thought, and got up to cross the floor.

'Annabel, my dear,' Wallis Simpson said. 'I'd no idea you'd be here tonight. I'd have asked you to join us.'

Elegant as ever, thought Annabel Lane. Not a hair out of place. Polished and gleaming and totally secure. Well, let's see.

'Last-minute decision,' she said. 'I just turned out to make the numbers up.'

Mrs Simpson looked at Piers. 'George not with you?' she asked.

'He has a horse running at Ripon,' Annabel Lane said, and Mrs Simpson sighed. The Little Man, too, often felt the urge to watch horses run.

'I haven't had the chance to thank you both for your lovely party,' she said.

Then Annabel Lane had a stroke of luck. The band had been playing 'Love Walked In', and now it stopped. Couples were returning to their tables. To have let it slip to Wallis would have been good enough, but to have her Prince Charming as a witness was perfect. She rose and curtsied as the Prince of Wales came back to his table.

'Annabel, how nice to see you,' he said.

'Thank you, sir.'

'I was just saying how much we enjoyed our evening at her house,' Mrs Simpson said.

'We did indeed.'

'It's very kind of you to say so, sir. Indeed I can't tell you how relieved I am that you're not too annoyed.'

'Annoyed?'

'With George, sir. I'd meant to write to Wallis about it, but when I sat down to do it I couldn't find the words. I think he must have been drunk, sir.'

Always a pretty woman, when agitated Mrs Lane looked very pretty indeed. The prince was fascinated.

'I haven't the faintest idea what you're talking about,' he said, and smiled.

'I can't tell you how grateful I am to you for taking it like this,' she said.

And then his curiosity became too much for him as she was quite sure it would.

'Tell me what it was your husband did,' said the prince. 'I insist.'

'It was just something he said, sir.'

'Tell me what he said then.' Still smiling, he added: 'Come now, Annabel. It's dashed bad form to disobey a royal command.'

'I expect he thought he was being funny,' said Annabel Lane. 'As I say, he had been drinking rather a lot.'

'*What did he say?*'

'It was the way he referred to Wallis. Not that it made any sense.'

'What did he call me?' Wallis Simpson said.

'Shanghai Lil.'

That was all it took. Both the prince and his lady swore quite dreadfully, and the prince told her that George must never again approach his future monarch, though she of course was always welcome. That was because I said the name didn't make any sense, she thought. Though of course it did.

There was a naughty rumour, a malicious and quite unsubstantiated rumour, that Mrs Simpson had paid several visits to a whorehouse in Shanghai, (some said Singapore, others Hong Kong) and while there had learned some very spectacular tricks, which explained her success with the prince. Still babbling apologies, she left them to their rage, and a few minutes later they were gone.

At her table, Brenda and Hugo Meldrum were sitting out, and Piers was chatting with friends near by. Hugo eyed her warily, and asked if she would like to dance, but she declined. What she wanted most in the world was a drink. It was true that she had brought it off, but the strain on her nerves had been considerable. As Meldrum poured, Brenda Meldrum said, 'What on earth did Wallis Simpson say to upset The Little Man so?'

This was far too good an opportunity to be missed.

'It wasn't her,' Annabel Lane said. 'She overheard what George called her at our party and she's simply furious.'

'What did George call her?' Brenda Meldrum asked.

'Well it makes no sense at all to me, but he called her Shanghai Lil.'

Hugo Meldrum snorted, and his wife giggled, told her friend exactly why poor Wallis had been so annoyed, and giggled once more.

'Oh my God!' Annabel Lane said. 'No wonder HRH said he never wanted to see George again.'

'If you ask me,' said Hugo Meldrum, 'old George is for it. He'd better stick to bridge in future.' Then he snorted again as one of his wife's young men took her off to dance. By the look of him, Annabel thought, he'd enjoyed his evening enormously, but then George had taken vast sums at cards from him in his time.

Piers came back to the table, and asked her to dance.

'Are you sure?' he said.

'I'll risk it if you will.'

She went with him to the dance floor. Hugo Meldrum seemed perfectly happy on his own, sipping his wine and snorting occasionally. The band played a slow foxtrot, which was just as well, she thought. Anything fast would be too much for him.

'His Nibs didn't look too happy,' said Piers.

'He didn't, did he?' Annabel Lane said. Piers was far too nice to be dragged into her murky schemes. They danced on for a while, then Piers said, 'I'm afraid I'm not too happy, either.'

'Whyever not?' she said. 'I thought I was dancing rather well.'

'So you are,' said Piers, 'but I'm not. Or rather I won't be very shortly. I can walk on the damn thing, I can even play a few holes at golf, but it absolutely refuses to dance, which is what I want to do more than anything else.'

'May one ask why?'

'So that I can hold you in my arms,' he said.

'We don't have to dance for you to do that,' she said.

She had never known Bob laugh so much. They were in his flat in South Molton Street, sharing a picnic hamper while she told him what she had done, and the name Shanghai Lil enchanted him as much as it had Brenda Meldrum, though he didn't know why it had such a power to annoy. When she told him the laughter began.

'By that's marvellous,' he said. 'Two words. That's all it took.'

'And the beauty of it is he can't even go to The Little Man and ask what he's supposed to have done. If he even tries to he'll be thrown out.'

Bob's laughter died. 'You realise you've just about destroyed him,' he said.

'George will recover. He always does. – And why should you worry?'

'Seems rather a high price to pay for one black eye.'

'What makes you think there was only one?' she said.

'Ah,' said Bob, and left it at that. There was absolutely no need

318

to feel badly about George Lane. Even so: 'Why didn't you leave him before?' he asked.

'Not enough mun. – Whereas if you bring off your dirty work at the crossroads I'll be rolling in it.'

'What about a few bob to keep you going till then?'

'No thanks,' she said. 'I'll manage. Sweet of you to offer though.' She smiled at him: 'You can be rather nice, sometimes.'

Which was a bit much, he thought, considering what we got up to in our time.

'So we've fixed your old man good and proper,' he said. 'That being so I wouldn't be around to welcome him when he gets back from the races.'

'No jolly fear,' she said. 'He'll have to find himself another sparring partner.'

'What will you do?'

'I've taken a flat in Baron's Court.'

Actually someone's taken it for me, she thought, but that's my secret. I'm a kept woman – and oh it is the most tremendous fun. For now, at any rate.

Jimmy Wagstaff decided to pack it in at last. Not that he'd grown tired of being Felston's MP – the best talking shop in the world, and where else would you get good booze at those prices? It was that last fall that had done it. Elderly men do have falls; uneven pavements, dog shit, banana skins: the risks were everywhere, – but this last one had been one too many. Trouble was it happened just outside the Palace of Westminster, and there'd been a press photographer handy to take a picture of a veteran back bencher going arse over tip, his hand still firmly clutching a bottle of Scotch from which the wrapper had fallen away. So there was nothing for it but resign: apply for the Chiltern Hundreds before the Whips made him do it anyway.

Andy got the news the next day, but he was well prepared: a stack of well wishers to back him, and what Cambridge called his curriculum vitae already typed by a solicitor's secretary who was much further to the Left than he was. All he had to do then was break the news to Norah.

She had no doubt at all that he'd be selected, and the thought

319

warmed him, though it terrified her. Harris and Croft it seemed would have to manage without him.

'All that time away in London,' she said.

'You'll be down an' all.'

'How can I be – with a bairn?'

'You don't mean –' he said and started to get to his feet. She pushed him back in his chair.

'Not yet,' she said. 'But it won't be long now, surely? Stands to reason.' Despite her terror she grinned at him, and he loved her more than ever. 'Eat your tea,' she said.

Liver and onions, done just the way he liked them, and he told her some of the more respectable stories about Jimmy Wagstaff until the ice-cream man called out in the back lane, and she went down with a basin to buy some.

Andy took out the *Daily Herald* he hadn't had a chance to read all day. A strike in Scotland, a lock-out in Wales, England a hundred and eight for two: nothing had changed much, it seemed. Then suddenly he saw something new. It was the picture of another anti-Fascist riot in the East End, and inset another picture of four young men whom the *Herald* described as victims. The police on the charge sheet had called them rioters. It all looked very much like the time he'd gone to the East End to see for himself, except that one of the alleged rioters, he was almost certain, was Manny Mendel. This was something he'd have to think about, but not now, not when Norah was coming up the back stairs with a basin full of ice cream. He turned the page and read about the Prince of Wales, who had gone racing at Newmarket. He didn't look all that pleased about it. Maybe his horse had lost.

'Poor Ned Alston can't come,' said Jane. 'Car smash. Nothing serious and not his fault, but his ankle's in plaster, and he's up in Newcastle, poor love. Georgie's absolutely frantic.'

'So I should imagine,' said Charles. 'Has she gone to him?'

'No,' said Jane. 'She'll be at the party. It's tricky for her. They're not engaged, you know. Not yet.'

'They jolly well ought to be,' said Charles.

'What *do* you mean?'

'No no,' said Charles. 'That's their business after all. What I meant was – they *look* engaged, somehow. I can't think why they're not.'

'Georgie's fault, if it is a fault,' said Jane. 'Her problem's the same as mine. She's become so used to her independence she finds it hard to let go. – Even when she wants to.'

He looked at her anxiously. 'Not having second thoughts are you?' he asked.

'Of course not,' said Jane. 'Would I be here if I had? – Darling, do mind my make-up. It took me absolute hours.'

He put her down. 'Any more non-starters?' he asked.

'Catherine,' she said. 'Frightfully sorry, but something urgent's come up. Something urgent in the shape of a Cambridge don called Brent, no doubt.'

'She and Bower are finished then?'

'I rather think so. He's coming, so at least we'll be mentioned in the *Daily World*.'

'I suppose I'll have to get used to it,' said Charles. 'Anybody else scratched?'

'George Lane isn't coming.'

'I'll try to bear it,' said Charles.

'There's the oddest story going the rounds,' said Jane, 'about Lane insulting Wallis Simpson at that party he gave.'

'I've heard it too,' said Charles.

'Can it be true do you suppose?' Charles thought for a moment.

'A friend of Crawley's could be capable of anything,' he said at last.

'Oh God is he? No wonder I thought his wife looked ruthless. She'd have to be.'

Charles said, 'Lane and I are involved in a business thing at the moment.'

'You said you might be. As partners?'

'More like enemies,' said Charles.

'Go in and win then,' said Jane. 'I know you will anyway.'

'It's rather a secret just for now.'

'I can keep secrets,' she said. 'Especially yours.'

They looked at each other. She was wearing the Fortuny gown, because it was his favourite as well as hers, and the emeralds set by Fabergé that had once belonged to a Russian countess.

'How lovely you are,' he said.

'And you – how handsome.' And it was true. Evening clothes still suited Charles, who somehow contrived to stay slim no matter how often he lunched in the City. 'Shall we send Truett to fetch a taxi?' she asked.

'Taxi be damned,' said Charles. 'There's a Rolls-Royce outside, and a chauffeur.'

. 33 .

The engagement party was a great success. She knew it was because she read about it in the *Daily World* next day, but for Charles and herself it was unrelenting hard work, though Lionel seemed to enjoy every minute of it while working harder than either of them. The flowers bloomed, the band was in tune, the waiters were deft, and Lionel bossed everybody in sight.

Jane looked long and hard at the major, when he and her mother arrived, but he seemed to be fine. A little red in the face perhaps, but he'd probably had a couple of chota pegs before he left, and not so chota either. The major didn't believe in stinting good whisky, and why should he? He worked hard enough to pay for it.

'You're a lucky young feller,' he told Charles.

'I'm aware of that, sir,' said Charles, who hadn't been called young for many a long year, though he seemed to enjoy it, she thought.

'All the same I'm glad the Rifle Brigade got her,' said the major. 'She's far too good for the Guards.'

Her mother kissed her. 'How stunning you look,' she said, then turned an ironic eye on Charles. 'Well my boy,' she said, but Charles had been ready for that, and asked her for the first available waltz, and Mrs Routledge beamed on him.

Francis had taken his time, but at least he'd got there, and looked quite passably smart as he held out his hand and congratulated Charles. No doubt about it, my brother detests Charles, she thought, because he epitomises all the aspects of capitalism that Francis hates most, but I rather think he's a little bit afraid of him too, which perhaps is just as well.

'You might have brought a girl with you,' she said.

'I don't know any girls,' he told her, so she introduced him to

Bunty Fairweather and sent them off to dance.

At last she and Charles were free to dance too. It was their only means of escape. No speeches, she had told Lionel, we'll save them for the wedding, so that was one embarrassment avoided, but people would insist on coming up to them and saying very sweet things, even if they couldn't quite hide their astonishment that they'd decided to do it at last. . . . Supper, and rather a lot of laughter, no doubt because Lionel had been firm about the quality of the champagne. More dancing then, and Charles got his waltz. Mummy looked quite devastating in black and silver, she thought, and her movement in the dance, though stately, was graceful still. The major, fortified by a couple more pegs, had approached Georgie and acquitted himself nimbly, at the same time looking ready to burst with pride at the thought of what he held in his arms.

Another dance, and one of Charles's relatives came up to her and asked her to dance. Tom, was it? The closest male by blood tie anyway. The one who'd had the highest hopes of inheriting, till Charles had lobbed his bomb – and indeed he holds me as if I were a bomb, terrified I might explode.

'How well you dance, Mr Lovell,' she said.

'Oh please call me Tim,' he said. So at least she knew what his name was. 'Have you settled on a date for the wedding?' he asked.

'Not precisely, but quite soon,' she said.

'And where will the reception be?'

That too would be up to Lionel, but she couldn't say so.

'Somewhere nice.'

'And the honeymoon?'

Somewhere even nicer, she thought, but she couldn't say that, either. What a man he was for questions, but then she remembered that Charles had told her he was a barrister. It was a great relief to dance with Lionel after that. Then Georgie signalled to her, and they retired to the Ladies' Room, sat before the mirror and repaired their make-up.

'What a busy night for Cupid,' Georgie said.

'Not my stepfather?' said Jane.

'Of course not,' said Georgie. 'He's an absolute poppet *and* he knows how to waltz.' She applied a little lipstick. 'Jay Bower,' she said.

324

'Jay made an improper proposal?'

'Well he's done it before,' said Georgie. 'To both of us. But there wasn't anything improper about this one. He asked me to marry him.'

'It had escaped his memory that he's married already?'

'He seems to think it won't be long before he's single again.'

'He could well be right,' said Jane, 'but even so – '

'He was rather sweet about it really,' said Georgie. 'He said that with a girl like me it was best to get to the head of the queue.'

'Did you tell him he wasn't – at the head of the queue I mean?'

'Certainly I did. I told him I was promised to another and when he asked me who and I wouldn't tell him, he got quite miffed.'

'That's the reporter in him,' said Jane.

'I dare say,' Georgie said, 'but we'll tell the newspapers when we're both ready, and not before.'

'Are there complications?'

'Ned's worried that there could be. I'm not exactly your typical duchess, am I?'

'Any more than Wallis Simpson's your typical princess?'

Georgie put a hand to her bosom, opened her eyes wide and declaimed: 'What, oh what, is happening to our noblesse?'

Jane's mother said, 'A most agreeable evening.'

'It was too bad that Francis couldn't stay to the end.'

'He stayed rather longer than I would have expected,' said her mother. 'But there is one other absentee, surely? The twin of that handsome young rifleman; the one who married our proprietor.'

'She's visiting in Cambridgeshire,' said Jane.

'Indeed?' said her mother. 'She'd have been much better advised to attend your delightful party.'

It was a relief when Bob came to ask her to dance, just ahead of Tim Lovell. It occurred to her that any girl who danced with him should be sworn in first by the court usher.

In the car she and Charles sat decorously together like an old married couple.

'I enjoyed dancing with your mother.'

'I've never doubted your courage, Charles.'

'Or the major's? But seriously, she really is the most enormous fun – once you know how to get on the right side of her.'

Jane goggled at him, but he appeared to mean it. At least their marriage wouldn't have in-law trouble.

The chauffeur turned the car into South Terrace.

'Want to come in for a nightcap?' she asked.

'Don't take it amiss if I say no,' he said. 'It's been a formal sort of night, and I'd like to end it like that. Formally. You don't mind?'

'Of course not,' she said. 'There'll be lots of times.'

'Indeed there will.'

The Rolls came to a halt, the chauffeur got out to open its door, and Charles walked with her to her house, and waited while she took out her key.

'Goodnight, my darling,' he said, and kissed her.

'Goodnight, my dear.'

She climbed the stairs to her bedroom, took off the Fortuny dress and hung it up carefully, because Truett loved it too and would sulk if she creased it, then took off her make-up and wished, for the hundredth time, that Foch was there so that she could tell him what had happened. Wearily she took off the rest of her clothes and put on her nightdress, got into bed. Sleep engulfed her at once, as soothing as a hot shower, and no remembered dreams, not until she heard the gunfire. A nervous sentry, she thought, or a bored machine gunner loosing off a few rounds. But she was miles behind the lines, and Sarah and Louise were on duty that night. It was her turn to sleep late, and wish that John was asleep beside her.

Someone was shaking her, and it jolly well wasn't fair. It wasn't her night to drive the ambulance, and anyway the gunfire had stopped: but the shaking went on.

'Miss!' Truett was saying. 'Please, miss.' The Western Front receded: Jane opened her eyes. Truett stood beside her, overcoat on top of her nightgown, hair in a net. 'There's a doctor downstairs,' said Truett. 'Says it's urgent.'

'What is?' said Jane. 'Has there been an accident?'

'He didn't say, miss.'

Jane thought of her mother, worried about her major: of Charles in that vast car. 'Does the doctor have a name?'

'Sounded like Pardoe, miss.'

Jane looked at the bedside clock: a quarter to four. It must be

326

serious. Even Cuthbert Pardoe wouldn't call at that hour to lecture her on the merits of the collective farm. She reached for her dressing gown.

'Tell him I'll be down at once,' she said.

'Do you want me to wait up, miss? Make tea or anything?'

'No,' said Jane. 'You go back to bed. – I'm sorry you were disturbed like this.'

'Quite all right, miss. I'll tell the doctor you're coming.'

'Doctor' was the word that intrigued her, thought Jane. A doctor in the middle of the night could only mean disaster. Maybe it would be true of a Doctor of Philosophy too, but she didn't want Truett there when she found out. Wearily she put on her slippers, ran a comb through her hair, and found her cigarettes and lighter. She'd have felt much better if she'd had Foch with her.

Pardoe said, 'I'm sorry to disturb you at this time of night. I assure you it's not without reason.'

'Yes, of course,' said Jane. He was looking at her dressing gown, not the thickest of garments, and enjoying what he saw. Jane lit a cigarette and fitted it into the Cartier holder. Pardoe had always detested that, and did so now.

'I can only hope I didn't wake the entire street,' he said. 'You seem to be very sound sleepers in this house.'

'Given the opportunity I've no doubt we are,' said Jane. 'Would you like to tell me what brings you here?'

'It's a matter of some delicacy,' Pardoe said.

Delicacy. Surely that couldn't mean death, or even injury?

'I promise to be discreet,' she said.

His big body wriggled in his chair. He's growing fat, she thought, and needs a shave, but then all men do at this hour.

'Your brother,' he said.

'What about him?'

'Please,' Pardoe said. 'This is a difficult matter. Let me tell it in my own way.'

It was a reasonable enough request. She willed herself to listen.

'There was a meeting of physicists at Imperial College,' he said. 'Rather a vital one from my point of view. I had a paper to deliver – quite successfully as it happened, but its exposition was exhausting.'

For the love of God get on.

327

'The result was that, like you, I slept heavily. It must have been some time before the telephone woke me. It was your brother.'

'Where was he?'

Pardoe looked at her reproachfully. 'I'm coming to that,' he said. 'He was at Vine Street police station charged with some kind of disorderly conduct.'

'Drunk?' she said, and thought: If I sound incredulous it's because I am.

Pardoe said, 'These interruptions serve no useful purpose. He was by no means drunk, but he had been attending some sort of party.'

'I know that,' she said. 'My engagement party at the Dorchester.'

'All very grand and splendid, I've no doubt,' said Pardoe, 'and criminally wasteful too in these depressed times, if I may say so.'

'You already have,' said Jane. 'Do get on.'

Pardoe flushed. 'After your party he went to another. A gathering of like-minded young men.'

'Oh God,' said Jane, and Pardoe smiled. He was beginning to enjoy himself.

'Some of them were paid to attend,' said Pardoe, 'and known to the police. One of them I gather betrayed all the others. The police – what is the expression? – raided the party: asserted in fact that it was a male brothel.'

'Was it?'

'I'm in no position to judge,' said Pardoe, 'but even if it were it's a private matter surely? In any decently run society the police would leave well alone.' He rose. 'That concludes my share of the business. The next move must inevitably be yours.'

'Did Francis suggest what the next move should be?'

'Bail, I gather. He is most reluctant to spend the night in a cell.'

'Naturally enough.'

'Bail for himself – and for his friend.'

'Which friend?' Jane asked.

'You won't like this,' Pardoe said.

'I don't like any part of it,' said Jane. 'Just tell me.'

'Burrowes is with him,' Pardoe said.

It needed but that. Suddenly Pardoe seemed inclined to continue his lecture on the need for reform to the laws concerning deviant sex, but she showed him firmly to the door, and phoned Lionel.

Mercifully he had a phone by his bed and woke very quickly. She told him what had happened.

'I'll come at once,' he said. 'Get ready and bring all the spare money you have. One never knows.'

Lionel too was unshaven, but somehow he got away with it in a way that Pardoe never could. In the cab on the way to the police station she explained what had happened.

'Oh dear,' he said. 'Aunty Pardoe on top of everything else.'

'He's not homosexual,' she said. 'Believe me I know.'

'But he goes around being so caring and understanding,' said Lionel. 'A fellow traveller in homosexuality as in everything else.'

'What must we do?'

'All you must do is look upset, tragic even, and leave everything else to me. Don't be surprised if I'm all booming and hearty, by the way. I've no wish to share a cell with Burrowes.'

'I'm looking forward to seeing you all booming and hearty,' said Jane, but in fact she saw very little. When they went into the station Francis was restoring his possessions to his pockets, watched by a baffled-looking sergeant, who came towards them with what seemed like relief that he was escaping Francis. 'Yes, sir?' he said.

'Captain Warley,' said Lionel, in clipped and martial tones. 'This is Miss Whitcomb, the sister of that man there. We were told he was in some sort of trouble.'

'If he was, he's out of it now,' said the sergeant. He sounded regretful.

'Jane!' Francis said. 'What the devil are you doing here?'

'I could well ask you the same thing,' she said. She was furious, and the sergeant looked at her with approval. Sensible, the look said, and pretty too, and she's landed with a brother like that. Aloud he said, 'Not in here if you don't mind, sir. Since you're lucky enough not to be staying with us, I suggest you go home.'

'Lucky!' said Francis.

'All charges have been dropped sir, your friends have all gone home, and you're free to go, too. If you'll just check your valuables.'

'I've done that,' said Francis, 'and I must say I resent – '

'Francis, come along,' said Jane, and dragged him to the door.

'Sorry you've had all this bother, sergeant,' said Lionel, and offered his hand. There was a pound note in it, and the sergeant palmed it deftly. 'Have a drink on me when you're off duty.'

'Thank you, sir.'

'What happened? Are you allowed to say?'

'The young lady your fiancée, sir?'

'Friend of the family,' Lionel said. 'Though as a matter of fact the young lady did announce her engagement tonight. No doubt you'll read it in tomorrow's papers. Shocking thing to happen. This night of all nights.'

'Yes indeed, sir,' said the sergeant. 'She has my sympathy. If I might speak in confidence – '

'Of course, of course.'

'I take it you know what the charge would have been.'

'Disgusting,' said Lionel, who was enjoying himself hugely.

'Couldn't agree more, sir. Well we'd got them, sir. All seven.'

'Seven, sergeant? Odd number – what?'

'There's pairs, sir, with them chaps, but sometimes there's what you might call a threesome.'

'Good God,' Lionel said. 'The times we live in.'

'Open-and-shut case,' said the sergeant, 'and we let them make a phone call, which is what brought you here – only your lady's brother's friend made one I can't specify – but very high up if you follow me, very high indeed, and the long and the short of it is, sir, all charges is dropped.'

Lionel felt that he'd had his quid's worth. 'Too bad, sergeant,' he said. 'You have my sympathy. Well . . . Better leave you to it, I suppose. Goodnight, sergeant. Carry on.'

The sergeant stiffened to attention as Lionel left. Nice bloke, the sergeant thought. If there were more like him, the country wouldn't be in the mess it is. He stowed the pound note in his wallet.

Outside brother and sister were quarrelling, which was scarcely surprising. They fell silent as Lionel walked up to them.

'You owe me a pound,' he said to Francis.

'There was absolutely no need to bribe that Fascist brute.'

'Bless you,' said Lionel. 'You couldn't bribe a member of the Force with a quid. Not these days. Not even the lowliest constable, never mind a sergeant. The pound was just a pour boire.' He turned to Jane. 'There was no room to manoeuvre with the cash we'd brought anyway. Not after they'd been charged.'

'You seem to know the devil of a lot about it,' Francis said.

'Well of course I do,' said Lionel. 'You don't suppose this is the first time I've been sent for, do you?' He turned to Jane. 'Not that I was needed. Burrowes had got them off.'

'Burrowes?' she said.

'I know you don't like him,' said Francis, 'but he was magnificent tonight.'

'There's a taxi,' Lionel said. 'We can't stand here praising Burrowes's excellences at four thirty am. Certainly I can't.' He called and waved, and the taxi came to them. 'Where are you staying?'

'My club,' said Francis, and for the first time looked worried. 'It might be tricky getting in at this time of night.'

Thank God he didn't stay with Mummy, thought Jane. Thank God, in other words, that the major can't stand him.

'You can't add cat burgling to your other escapades,' said Lionel. 'You'd better stay with me.'

'No,' said Jane. 'You've done more than enough already, darling. He'll stay with me. South Terrace, driver.' They got into the cab.

Francis said, 'It's all very well pointing out how righteous and self-sacrificing you both are, but Burrowes and I managed very well on our own. All you've done is find me a place to sleep.'

Lionel said, 'It must be absolute ages since I biffed anyone. You know. A good old-fashioned sock on the jaw. I wonder if I can still remember how to do it?'

Francis sulked in silence until they reached South Terrace, and in silence Jane showed him to his room, then went downstairs and left a note for Truett. She had made up her mind to sleep late. How Francis contrived to explain away the absence of luggage, day clothes, even a razor, was entirely his own affair. He'd already made it clear that he could manage on his own.

They met again at teatime, when Jane was calmer and more rested, if not more charitable. By then Francis had phoned his club and had the porter send his suitcase to South Terrace in a taxi, so perhaps there was some truth in his claim that he could take care of himself. When he joined Jane he was shaved, bathed, and dressed in a dark blue suit: every inch the respectable don.

'I didn't behave terribly well last night,' he said.

331

'No,' said Jane. 'You didn't.'

Francis sighed. 'I'm trying to say I'm sorry.'

'Then get on with it.'

'I'm sorry,' he said. 'Honestly I am.'

'You should say it to Lionel, too.'

'I will,' he said. 'I promise. Am I forgiven?'

'This time, yes,' she said. 'But next time – I wouldn't rely on it.'

'You seem very sure there'll be a next time.'

'Not sure,' she said. 'Afraid.'

He sighed once more. His martyr's smile, she thought: his why must the whole world be against me smile.

'Do you want me to explain it to you?' he said.

'If you can,' she said.

'I can try.' That was better. It sounded waspish, but it was better than martyrdom. 'To begin with,' he said, 'I don't think this is any of your business.'

'Nor do I,' she said, 'and yet you sent Pardoe of all people to fetch me.'

'I was thinking of Mummy,' he said.

This was the worst yet. The only thing she could do other than throw things was wait, and so she waited.

'Your party was pleasant enough,' he said at last, 'but not an adequate reason to leave Cambridge. I'd been working hard there, you know. All through the Long Vacation.'

Pardoe too claimed to have been working hard. Did they really think that Cambridge had cornered the market in hard labour?

' ... a serious study,' he was saying. 'Not like that piece of nonsense I did for the Socialist Book Club.' He thought for a moment, savouring the eminence of the height he had climbed. 'The chances are it will be regarded as something rather important in academic circles, if I may say so.' Still she waited, and he sighed once more.

'Then you forced me to come to your party,' he said. 'Oh I know it was a milestone in your life, and arguably in Mummy's also, but it never occurred to you that mine might have other priorities. You weren't even aware of the work I had done or what I had achieved. You will say that you couldn't possibly know, but my response is that you didn't even ask.

'Anyway I came to your party, and stayed till a reasonable hour. I even danced several times. In short I did all that was expected of me, then left to relax at a party that Burrowes had arranged: one that I would really enjoy.'

'In a brothel,' she said.

'You have absolutely no right to say that.'

'I didn't. Pardoe did.' In fact it was what Pardoe said the police had said, but it was up to Francis to work that out.

'In fact some of the people there weren't all that well off,' said Francis, 'and so naturally one was inclined to help them. They like nice things, but then we all do.'

'Quite young, were they?'

'Not adults in the legal sense,' said Francis. 'But by no means children. They knew what they were doing. They enjoyed what they were doing.'

'Even so – one of them betrayed you.'

'Boys – young chaps like that, are constantly at the mercy of the police,' said Francis. 'It isn't like Berlin as it used to be – a love affaire without stigma, either social or legal.'

And which was the more fun for that? she wondered.

'So one of them was got at by those damned Cossacks,' Francis said. 'Threatened. Perhaps even beaten. Anyway the house was raided. It was the most terrifying thing that ever happened to me.'

By the look of you it's absolutely true, she thought. Big, nasty, uniformed men bursting in on you, and how were you dressed, brother dear? Full evening dress, your underclothes, your birthday suit? I bet you were terrified.

'I take it you don't want me to go into details,' he said.

'Of course not.'

He seemed relieved: perhaps the teeniest bit disappointed too.

'We were carted off like criminals,' he said.

'You were criminals.'

The martyr's sigh again. 'In any half-way civilised society – ' he began.

'Not that again,' she said. 'I had all that from Pardoe.'

He let it go. 'We were charged,' he said. 'The police made it clear that we could go to prison for some time – seemed to take pleasure from it in fact. They also went into detail about what other prisoners would do to us.' He shuddered at that. Visibly. Jane felt that she should pity him and found that she couldn't. Once more she waited.

'I was allowed to make a telephone call,' he said. 'I knew it would be difficult to make contact with you after your – late night, and so I asked Pardoe to do it for me. The rest you know.'

'I don't know how you got off scot free,' she said.

'Burrowes,' said Francis. 'He knows vast amounts of people, some of them in rather – sensitive appointments. Perhaps he holds one himself. I never ask. All I know is that he phoned one such person, and here I am.'

Really, she thought, he makes Burrowes seem like the Scarlet Pimpernel.

'And what will you do now?' she asked.

'Back to Cambridge,' he said. 'I should never have left it, but you insisted.'

'I didn't send you to a male brothel.'

'I told you it wasn't that,' he said, 'but the human male has certain needs you wouldn't understand.'

'Of course I would,' she said. 'The human female has them too.'

The idea seemed to outrage him.

'Does Mummy know?' she asked at last.

'About last night? Not unless you've told her.'

'Don't talk like a bloody fool,' said Jane. 'I meant does she know you were going on after my party?' He shook his head. 'Then it's best we don't tell her.'

'Well of course,' he said, and got to his feet. 'I'd better be off. There's a fast train to Cambridge if I leave now.'

'Don't let me keep you. Did you leave Lionel his quid?'

'In an envelope on the dressing table.'

'Tip for my servants?'

'That's so bourgeois,' he said.

'That's what I am,' she said. 'It's what they want to be, too.'

She held out her hand, and he gave her money. It wasn't nearly enough.

'I suppose I ought to say thank you,' he said.

'I'd much rather you didn't,' said Jane.

334

. 34 .

Billy Caffrey couldn't understand it at all. He'd felt honoured when Andy had asked him to act as his agent – still did come to that – and he hadn't expected it to be easy – getting your man nominated as MP was a lot harder in Felston than getting him into Parliament, if he was Labour – but he hadn't expected it to be bloody near impossible either.

Usually it was the sort of job he liked: a quiet word here and there, a bit of manipulation behind the scenes: he had a taste for that as well as making speeches. But this time the chaps that counted, the ones on the selection committee, just didn't want to listen. They heard him out for his sake, not Andy's, that was obvious – but when it came to pledging votes all he got was excuses. Early days, not fair to the other candidates, best to sleep on it: the usual slaver. Something was up: he'd known that from the first, but what it was he had no idea, and no bugger would tell him. In the end he'd had to get hold of Fred Green and just about choke it out of him.

Nervous little feller was Fred. Didn't much care for loud voices, and Billy's was the loudest for miles: didn't much care for hands clenched into fists, either, and Billy's fists were sizeable, so in the end he'd told him. Rumours. Dirt. Tittle-tattle. That's all it was, and nasty as well. Nobody minded that Andy had gone to prison for conscience's sake: it had taken real guts to do that; but the rumours were hinting that he'd *wanted* to go to prison, because that's where the perverts were, the chaps like himself. Look at him after he came out, the rumours said All those years and never once seen with a woman except his mam.

But he's a married man, Billy had argued. His wife had a miscarriage just a few months back. The rumours had an answer for that as well. Oh yes, he's married now. Now he's back in politics: chasing after the nomination. You just about have to get married once you're in politics, if only to show you're the same as everybody else. All the same, look at all that time he'd spent at Cambridge.

When poor little Fred trotted that one out Billy Caffrey nearly did hit him, if only to relieve his frustration. Nearly all public school chaps at Cambridge, Fred explained, that was the point. And everybody knew what public school chaps were like. And look at the way Andy used to go on about how happy he was at Cambridge. Fred Green took another look at Billy Caffrey's face and said it might well be no more than talk, but Billy had asked what folks were saying, and that was it. Willing himself to patience Billy Caffrey had said in that case why wouldn't Fred pledge his vote to Andy.

The little man's reply was unanswerable. 'Suppose it's true?' he'd said.

'You don't make him sound particularly loveable,' Charles said.

'In that mood he isn't loveable at all, except perhaps to Burrowes,' said Jane. 'But then Burrowes is even less loveable than he is.'

'You hit him once, didn't you?'

'One of the most satisfying moments of my life, but I've never hit Francis. He's usually too timid. Not like last night at all. Or this afternoon.'

'He could still be in a state of shock,' said Charles. 'It takes people in different ways – and he must have got the devil of a fright when the police burst in.'

'He must have been petrified,' said Jane.

'And perhaps the only way he could control it was to fight back.'

'But why fight me?'

'I don't for one moment assume that you hid your disapproval.'

'How could I?' said Jane. 'Especially as he was rude to Lionel too. And when you think of the risks Lionel ran – going to a police station about an affair like that, even if he did handle it beautifully.' She told Charles about Captain Warley.

Charles smiled. 'I bet he enjoyed that,' he said.

'Every minute. All the same it was a risk, and all Francis did was tell him he needn't have bothered. He was very off-hand about Mummy too. Not in the least worried. Just took it for granted I wouldn't tell her.'

'Shock,' said Charles. 'Reaction. By tomorrow he'll be petrified.'

'He jolly well deserves to be,' said Jane. 'Let's change the subject.'

'How soon can we get married?'

'Tomorrow if it was just up to me.'

'Even with a special licence we'd have to hold on till next week.'

'But it isn't just up to me. There's Mummy, too, and the major. He'll be the one to give me away. Mummy will be absolutely mortified if we don't marry in church.'

'Then that's what we'll do. We can't have Mummy mortified.'

For once Jane looked hesitant, even shy. 'If we do, I'll be the one to be mortified,' she said.

'But why on earth should you?'

'Brides wear bridal gowns,' she said. '*White* bridal gowns, and it's rather a long time since I was a virgin. Also brides in bridal gowns are girls in their twenties, and I'll be forty before you know it.'

'Why don't you talk it over with your mother?' said Charles. 'She knows all about us after all.'

'Darling,' she said. 'That's a brilliant idea.'

'Delegation,' he said smugly. 'We Chairmen of the Board are good at it.'

'When we merge,' said Jane, 'I'm going to be chairman too.'

Inevitably he was kissing her when Truett came in to tell her that she was wanted on the telephone. Interrupting Charles's embraces seemed to be another duty Truett had assumed, thought Jane.

'Somebody sent me a case of champagne,' said Lionel.

'Me,' said Jane. 'To say thank you. A card came with it.'

'The card seems to have dropped off. No thanks needed, my dear. Rescuing my fellow fairies from choky seems to be my mission in life – though I must say if I'd known how rude your brother was going to be I wouldn't have tried nearly so hard.'

'He was atrocious,' said Jane. 'I can't apologise enough.'

'You already have,' said Lionel. 'Why don't you and your young man come round soon and help me guzzle champers. It's high time I started planning your wedding.'

337

'Darling, would you?'

'Don't you even dare think of asking anybody else,' said Lionel. 'If you do, I'll be absolutely livid. So there.'

'As if I would,' said Jane. 'I'm only sorry I can't ask you to be a bridesmaid.'

'Matron of honour would be more appropriate,' said Lionel.

She went back to Charles, and told him that Lionel was determined to organise their nuptials, which were due to take place soon.

'So long as he doesn't superintend the honeymoon,' said Charles.

'I hope you don't object to a Sunday, but until the end of the Flat it's difficult to find a free day during the week,' said her mother.

'Sunday's fine,' said Jane.

'Charles has no objection?'

'We'll meet later,' said Jane. 'But in fact my coming to see you was his idea – that's to say he thought of it first. The major won't be with us?'

'He's lunching at his club,' said her mother. 'Under the circumstances I thought it best.

'His health is better, I hope?'

'I hope so too,' said her mother. 'There can be no doubt that he's happy. Now mix yourself one of your concoctions while I pour myself sherry, and tell me whatever it is you've come about.'

While Jane mixed gin and vermouth in the shaker her mother said, 'It isn't Francis?'

'What I've come about? Of course not. It's me.'

'I ask because he seems to have left London in rather a hurry.'

'Did he?' said Jane. 'But then he would. He doesn't like London.' This at least was true.

'Such a rush to get back to Cambridge. His alma mater. "Sweet mother", isn't that what it means?'

'Yes, Mummy.'

'I'd rather hoped that I would be that,' her mother said, 'but I'm not even in the race.' She sipped her sherry. 'Now . . . Tell me your problem.'

Jane did so, and her mother listened gravely. To her at least Jane's dilemma was neither frivolous nor petty. As usual, she went straight to the nub of the problem.

'Is your decision to be married in church because of me?' she asked.

'You, me, and Charles,' her daughter said. 'I couldn't be married in a registry office. I wouldn't feel married at all.'

Like Norah, she thought, and as with Norah, it's probably true.

Lunch was of the kind her mother called perfectly adequate for females: vichyssoise, salmon and strawberries: cold, because cooks too go to church on Sundays, but there was lots of hock which the major must have chosen. As they ate, her mother talked of Jay Bower.

'Things aren't well with him,' she said. 'I know it. A newspaper office is a positive hotbed of gossip. One can't avoid hearing things: and her absence at your engagement party was most marked. Friends at Cambridge, indeed. That town has a great deal to answer for.'

'Actually it was Trumpington, Mummy.'

'It might as well have been Timbuktu,' said her mother. 'In fact it was a young man called Geoffrey Brent, as I've no doubt you know. Will she leave Bower for him?'

'To say she's fallen out of love with Bower would be an understatement,' said Jane.

'I do not press for details,' said her mother, 'even if you have them. But Mr Bower's well being is naturally a matter of concern to us.'

'Yes, of course,' said Jane. 'But Catherine finds it difficult to be in the same house as Jay, let alone the same room, and Brent is young, and attractive – and heir to rather a lot of money.'

'You don't make her sound very likeable.'

'Sometimes she isn't,' said Jane, 'but at other times she is. Like most of us.'

Her mother rang the bell and rose. 'We'll take coffee in the drawing room,' she said. 'We can talk there undisturbed.'

After she had poured coffee Mrs Routledge said, 'Let me say at once that I fully concur in your objections to what is called a white wedding. Your point concerning your age is perfectly valid, though you are still a remarkably good looking woman.'

'It runs in the family,' said Jane.

Her mother smiled, but stuck to her thesis. 'Your point about

339

your virginity or lack of it, is also valid,' she said. 'Your liaison with Charles has become all too common knowledge.'

'It's lasted so long,' said Jane, 'and neither of us wanted to end it.'

'Just so,' said her mother, 'and I can't tell you how glad I am.'

'Are you, Mummy?'

'I've thanked God for it many times,' her mother said. 'You have a loving and caring man, and one who makes you happy. In that at least he resembles George, if in nothing else. Now you're to be married I'm even happier, but that doesn't solve your problem. Are you determined on a large wedding?'

'As small as we can get away with.'

'Good,' said her mother. 'Then may I suggest this? Go to Paris – that is never a chore for you, and doubtless Lionel will squire you since it would be inappropriate for Charles to do so – '

'Why, Mummy?'

'Because he mustn't see the dress. Don't interrupt, child. Go to Chanel. Or Schiaparelli. A woman would be best. Choose a dress – or coat and skirt if you prefer, – but whatever it is it must be the most elegant they can contrive, and have it made in cream. Not white. Cream. Perhaps with a suggestion of some other colour, too.'

Norah, Jane thought, can it really be that you're as wise as my mother? But there were other problems to be faced, that Norah didn't have.

'But how can Charles and I justify a quiet wedding? Well a small one, anyway?'

'You will say that you feel that it would be wrong to indulge in a large-scale celebration at such a time. If anyone should be ill-mannered enough to press for further reasons, you will refer them to me.'

'Such a time as what, Mummy?'

'The king is ill,' her mother said. 'He may even be dying, I hear. People will say it would be just like me to restrict your wedding for such a quibble.'

'But don't you mind?'

'Not in the least,' Mrs Routledge said. 'I shall see my daughter married, and that's all I care about. Only please invite Gwendoline Gwatkin, or I shall have no peace.'

'I shall reserve two seats for her personally,' said Jane.

It had been a traditional Felston working man's Sunday: newspapers, Sunday dinner, roast, two veg, two kinds of potatoes,
rhubarb and custard, then in bed with the wife. (No need to wait
till the bairns went off to Sunday School, seeing there weren't any:
not yet. But what would he do when there were? He kept telling
everybody he was an atheist, but Norah wasn't.) Typical Sunday
so far, and now he was completing the cycle by strolling to the pub
for a pint with his mate. Eat, drink and be merry, he thought, for
he and Norah had been merry enough, except that she suspected
something was worrying him and was biding her time to find out
what it was. He'd have to find out what it was himself first, which
explained the pint with Billy Caffrey.

Billy Caffrey had told him at once, because he was a good mate,
and because he could think of no convincing lies. It was quite a tale
when you came to think of it: Billy flexing his muscles and little
Fred Green shrinking littler by the minute.

'So I'm a pansy, am I?' he said at last.

'That's what they're saying.'

'Who's they – apart from Fred?'

'Tom Spalding, Joe Turnbull, Artie Sparks. All that crowd.'

The diehards, thought Andy. The men of the Left. It would have
to be them.

'They're passing it on an' all,' Billy Caffrey said.

'To the selection committee?' Billy nodded.

'No further than that,' he said.

'Did Fred say why not?'

'Wouldn't look good for the Labour Party if one of their best-
known men turned out to be one of them,' said Billy.

'So I'm a *well-known* pansy?'

'I didn't say that,' Billy said. 'You're well known on account of
the march – and the speech you made in Trafalgar Square. I was
proud of you then, Andy lad, and I still am. But the others – ' he
shrugged. 'They talk like they hate you.'

Maybe they do, thought Andy. I was their rising star, once:
Redder than any. Not any more.

'I reckon there's another reason they're trying to keep it from spreading,' Billy said. 'They're afraid you might sue them.'

'Their word against mine,' Andy said. 'What chance would I have?'

'Aye,' said Billy. 'There's that. But I'll tell you this. I've met your wife and I've seen the two of you together – and if you're a pansy then I'm a Tory. All the same the sort of mud they're throwing – it's beginning to stick.'

'You don't think I'll get the nomination?'

Billy signalled for two more halves. 'No,' he said. 'I don't.'

'You telling me to quit?'

Billy shook his head. 'I don't think that's in you,' he said. 'And that's as good a reason as any for telling you. So you'll get your disappointment over and done with now – and not when they tell you you've lost.'

'Disappointment!' The word came out like a moan.

'I know,' said Billy. 'You think your world's over, but it's not. It's still turning – and you've still got your wife.' He drank some beer. 'I lost mine. But the sun still rose.'

'I'm sorry,' Andy said. 'I shouldn't be taking it out on you.'

'I'm the only one here,' said Billy. 'And better me than that wife of yours.'

'I'm not that selfish,' Andy said, and drank. Finish off this second half and take the long way home, he thought. Give himself time to think.

'Any idea who Spalding's lot are running?'

'Pal of Artie Sparks,' Billy said. 'Lives in North Shields. Worked in the shipyards and then got some kind of scholarship to college at Newcastle.'

'Doesn't that make him a pansy too?'

'He went in by bus every day,' Billy Caffrey said. 'Came home every night to his mam.'

'Little Fred told you that?' Billy nodded. 'Was he serious?'

'Dead serious.'

'Dear God,' said Andy.

'Anyway he's a qualified naval architect now,' said Billy.

'Where does he work?'

'He doesn't,' Billy said. 'When did they last design a ship round here?'

'What about that destroyer for Mexico?'

'Five men for every job,' Billy said, ' – and him being a Socialist – he never had a chance.'

'Victimisation?'

'Aye,' Billy said. 'Just that.' He hesitated, but honesty to Billy was like a passion. 'I met him a few times,' he said. 'Delegations, rallies. Durham Miners' Gala. Struck me as being a canny sort of feller. Fair speaker. Good brain. But he's not you, Andy, and he never will be. Bloody *hell*! I could flatten that bugger Spalding.'

But it wasn't Spalding, Andy thought, or Turnbull, or Sparks. They were the ones to fire the ammunition, but they hadn't the brains to make it.

It could only have been Burrowes, he thought, as he walked. True, he'd told Bob about what had happened to him in prison, but Bob was incapable of betraying him, and even if he wasn't, what would be the point? He had no interest in the politics of Felston, or Great Britain, or the Union of Soviet Socialist Republics come to that. The only thing Bob cared deeply about was Patterson's Wireless Rentals. Even his women weren't as important to him as his business. Nothing like. So it had to be Burrowes.

It was true that Burrowes didn't know about what had been done to him in prison, but he'd heard him talk about what had been done to others: like that poor devil from Renshaw after the Market Place Riot: the one who'd killed himself. Burrowes had got himself all excited about that. Rotten bastard.

Never mind that. Burrowes was clever: that was the point: he'd taken a hint, no more, and turned it into a biography. The stuff about Cambridge, for instance. Downright laughable that would be – in Cambridge. Laugh so hard they'd spill their port. But not in Felston. Burrowes knew that Felston hated Cambridge: hated its wealth, its class distinction, its automatic assumption that privilege was its due. Just like they hated Oxford, he thought. The only way Felston would cheer at the Boat Race would be if both crews drowned in the Thames, and Burrowes knew it; knew too that Felston would believe anything nasty about either of them, so he'd used the nastiest thing of all to Felston's way of thinking, and Felston (or at least its leading Leftwingers) had been delighted to believe it.

Because they think I'm betraying my Leftwing principles, he thought. Never mind that the Party, in the person of Burrowes himself, told me to act like a moderate, be a good Labour man, a trade unionist, a councillor. Never mind even that I did it though it wasn't all that easy to do, especially at first – though maybe I found it easier later on, and maybe Norah had something to do with that, but that isn't the point. The point is that I served the Party as I served the people of Felston: gladly and freely, and honoured to do it. Then the Party decided that I wasn't needed after all, and threw me away, like a child that's thrown away a toy it broke because of its own carelessness. All the same, Andy thought, I can hit back. I can hit back hard. But the first thing was to tell Norah.

She listened like a child to what he had to tell her, hands folded in her lap, body still, as if she were back at school, he thought, and would get the cane if she didn't pay attention, but it wasn't the thought of pain that made her afraid, it was love. Yet she heard him out in silence while he told her of the rumours, but not what had been done to him in prison. To tell her that was impossible: probably always would be. Besides he'd told her more than enough as it was. The first thing she wanted to do was take the poker to Spalding, Turnbull and Sparks, and he had a right old time quieting her down.

'A good belting's all trash like that understand,' she said. 'I can see you can't do it, being what they call a public man. But I can – and I will.'

'I'm not a public man any more,' he said, and that shut her up as nothing else could.

'No,' she said at last. 'You're not, are you? Oh pet.'

She stood up and went to him, cradled his head to her breast, and prayed as she did so, Please God don't ever let him see how relieved I am.

Then he told her about Burrowes and she took off again.

'The bastard,' she said. 'The stinking bastard.' It was the first time he'd ever heard her use words like that and it shocked him.

'He wants shooting,' she said. 'If I could lay me hands on a gun I'd do it myself.' Then suddenly, incredibly, she laughed.

'Oh pet, I'm sorry,' she said. 'But if you could only see your face. You never knew I had a temper, did you?'

'I do now,' Andy said.

'All talk, that's me,' said Norah. 'I couldn't bring meself to hit anybody, not even when I was a bairn. But I could shout the length of the street.' The laughter died. 'What are you going to do, Andy?'

'Nowt I can do,' he said, 'except bide me time.'

She didn't like the sound of that. 'You should talk it over with someone else.'

'I have,' he said. 'Billy Caffrey. He reckons I've lost and I reckon he's right.'

'Somebody not so close to the thing.'

'Our Bob? He probably won't be up here for ages. And anyway – he wouldn't be much of a hand at this sort of thing.'

'He'd be hopeless,' she said, 'except for belting those three buggers.'

'Who then?'

'Isn't it obvious?'

'Not to me,' said Andy.

'Jane.'

He saw at once that she was right, but all the same there were problems.

'I can't take time off to go down to London again, and I can hardly ask her to come up here. – She'll be up to her eyes in wedding arrangements. And I doubt I could put it all down on paper. It's too complicated.'

'You could phone.'

'It would cost a fortune,' said Andy.

'Didn't you say there's a phone in the shipyard office you could use?'

'That's because I'm convenor of the conciliation committee. Official business.'

'And it wouldn't be official business to talk to Jane? The one who's going to marry the man who gave the order for that destroyer? The one who's put all those shares into the Felston fund?'

'Maybe you should be the one who runs for Parliament,' Andy said.

'Get away with you,' said his wife. 'Now I'll tell you what we'll

345

do. I'll make us both a bit of supper, then we'll have an early night.'

'Taking my mind off things, are you?'

'It's not your mind I'm after, bonny lad.'

He was lucky to have caught her, she told him. She was off to Paris in a couple of days to go shopping. When I first knew her I'd have hated her just for saying that, he thought. Young and daft I was in them days.

'You haven't called to tell me you've changed your mind about the wedding?' said Jane. 'I can always find a place for you two.'

'No,' Andy said. 'Thanks all the same. Our Bob'll represent the family at the wedding. Some of us have got a ship to build. . . . This is serious, Jane.'

'Let's have it.'

Andy looked round the office yet again, but he was alone. Dinner hour. Nobody stayed indoors during the dinner hour, not when the sun was shining, so he'd brought his sandwiches and his tea-can. He looked at the clock on the wall. Ten past twelve. She'd be having herself a martini, likely.

'It's about Burrowes,' he said.

'Oh God.'

He told her it all, and she listened without interruption. She was a good listener.

When he had done she said, 'It sounds very much like his sort of dirty work, but – '

'But what?'

'You say you saw him taking part in a Fascist rally?'

And yet he's still a friend of Francis's, she thought, and Francis would no more go to bed with a Fascist than go to bed with a woman.

'I know it sounds daft,' he said, 'but I've been thinking – could he be some sort of a spy? Sounds just like the pictures, doesn't it?'

'I've been thinking that, too,' she said and thought: Especially after he had all his cronies freed from Vine Street. Aloud she said, 'But that would make him some kind of a hero as well. I don't think I could bear that.'

'Me neither,' said Andy. 'Him a hero. It doesn't seem possible.'

'I tell you what,' said Jane. 'I'll put Mr Pinner on it.'

346

'Mr Who?'

'That detective who got you off the charge of inciting a riot years ago. Mr Pinner.'

'I can't aff – '

'And please don't start being boring about money, Andy,' she said. 'If Burrowes can be exposed I want to expose him. It's what you might call my mission in life.' Georgie and I aren't so far apart as I liked to believe, she thought. 'I know that vengeance is mine saith the Lord and all that, but he's done my family – *both* my families – a lot of damage and it's time somebody stopped him. It's time somebody stopped him anyway. He's no better than a rabid dog.'

'Go ahead and stop him then,' said Andy. 'I wish you luck.'

'Thank you,' said Jane.

'There is one more thing,' Andy said.

'Yes?'

He told her about Manny Mendel, and his fear that he'd been one of the victims of a blackshirt attack.

'But didn't I meet him in Felston?' said Jane. 'Wasn't he a Party worker there?'

'That's right, he was,' said Andy. 'Only he got married and went South.'

'Married a girl called Bernice,' said Jane. 'Rather a nice girl. What do you want me to do? Just find out if it was him?'

'And if he's all right,' said Andy. 'I was thinking you could get the *Daily World* to do it. That way it would cost you nothing.'

I'll get Mr Pinner to do it, she thought. He isn't cheap, but this is no time to owe Jay Bower a favour.

Paris was great fun. Well of course it was. Money to burn so to speak – after all how often was she likely to be married at her age? – and Mummy's solution to her problem so satisfying. Chanel had been difficult, no doubt because she had quantities of unsuitable garments she had to palm off on somebody, but Schiaparelli had been no problem at all. A dress of cream silk, with a rose-coloured thread running through it, and various other frivolities, too. After all, how often was she likely to be on her honeymoon?

Lionel of course had been marvellous. Knowledgeable, strong on detail, and standing up to Chanel's wrath as if he were one of the burghers of Calais. There was time for just one night on the town before they went back to London, and he plunged zestfully into the world of caterers and musicians, and enjoyed every minute of it. For her there was Mr Pinner.

With Manny Mendel there had been no problem. He was the one in the photograph. These days he lived in Weybridge, and commuted every day into London – the West End, just off Berkeley Square – where he made a more than adequate living with an advertising agency forecasting which brands of canned soup or beans or sardines the great British public would eat next year. He must have been good at it because they paid him well, and yet all his spare time seemed to be devoted to opposing the blackshirts as violently as possible. Still married, Mr Pinner had learned, and with two children still quite young. His wife supported him to the hilt, it seemed. So there was good news for Andy. Inevitably when it came to Burrowes things were more difficult, and Mr Pinner asked for more time. What could she do but agree? She had her wedding to think of after all.

Charles seemed to be as busy as ever, which in an odd way was a comfort. She didn't want Charles to stop being Charles, married or single, and so she left him to it, not least because he always found time to be with her, take her to the nicest places, and tell her that he loved her, when there was no risk of his being overheard.

Charles's preoccupation was George Lane. Bob sniffed after him like a terrier in front of a rat-hole, he thought, and with just as good effect. The more he sniffed, the more he brought to life. George Lane, it became clear, was not a nice man, which was just as well, thought Charles, though I was after his money anyway – or at least his business. Lane won't exactly have to sing in the streets to earn a crust, but he won't own Lane Engineering any more. I'll do that, together with Bob – and Mrs Lane. And if there isn't going to be the next war that all the experts say is bound to happen then God help us, he thought. But that's the least of my worries.

Bob's worry was Sybil Hendry. She was still as pretty and amorous as ever, and still determined to marry him. She hadn't yet proposed to him, but Leap Year was fast approaching, and she knew it. In the meantime she tried her hardest to be nice to him, doing her best to atone for her attempt to coax him into her father's bed. No sense in stirring up trouble long subsided. All the same he wished she wouldn't go on about how happy Jane and Charles looked together. Not that it wasn't true, he thought.

Georgie and Ned looked happy, too. And what a pity that Grandma wasn't still there, he thought, to hear me call a duke's son Ned. Not just for that. Of course not. But she was one of those women men wanted to show off to, in the nicest possible way, and if calling a marquis Ned wasn't showing off then what was? Relatives were Georgie's problem, too.

'Wedded bliss,' she told Jane. 'His lordship's decided he'll settle for nothing less, and at least it'll make a change from poor Dan.'

'Are you to provide an heir?' Jane asked.

'It's thought to be a good idea if I can fit it in,' said Georgie. 'But it's not exactly in the contract. Life's always lagging behind the movies, wouldn't you say?'

'Perhaps as well,' said Jane. 'Are you telling me his parents know?'

'He went up North to do it,' said Georgie. 'Got back last night.'

'And?'

'My dear, he's been all day with lawyers. God knows what that means. All I can do is cross my fingers. Though I do have one card – '

'The power of Hollywood?'

'The power of you,' said Georgie. 'The *Angel of No Man's Land* is their favourite film.'

'Anything I can do to help,' said Jane.

They were in South Terrace, waiting for Ned and Charles to take them to dine.

'Parents are hell, aren't they?' said Georgie.

'Not necessarily.' Jane was firm.

'Oh not yours, darling. Your mother's wonderful – though she does take one back to the third form sometimes – and the major's absolute bliss.'

'Yours?' Georgie nodded. 'Still in Kenya?'

'Still in the Happy Valley,' said Georgie. 'And goodness it must be, the way they keep on getting married, but not to each other. Not any more. Poor Ned.'

'What's it got to do with him?'

'It won't look very good if they turn up for the wedding with four attendant spouses apiece.'

'Current and ex, you mean?'

'Well of course.'

'Then don't ask them.'

Georgie considered this novel solution. 'They do it in the Happy Valley all the time,' she said. 'They do it in Hollywood too, come to that. Still, one can but try.' She yawned and stretched. 'Just one more movie,' she said, 'and then with luck I'll be one of the landed gentry.'

'You don't think you'll miss it?'

'Every dog has its day,' Georgie said. 'That goes for the bitches too. It was me for the character parts, and now I hope I've got one. Wife to the heir apparent. Bliss.' She stretched again.

'Where the hell are our nice chaps?' she said. 'I'm starving.'

When they arrived it was in Charles's company's Rolls. 'Like a liner on wheels,' according to Ned.

'A Rolls?' said Georgie. 'Are we going somewhere pompous?'

'After all it is a celebration, darling,' said Ned. 'I booked us in at the Savoy.'

'The Savoy? But I've just come from there,' said Georgie.

'Not in a liner on wheels,' said Ned.

'Celebration?' said Jane. 'Does that mean you've – ' she quoted Hugo Meldrum ' – been and gone and done it?' Georgie nodded. 'But why on earth didn't you tell me before?'

'I wanted us all to be together,' Georgie said, 'and anyway I'm not quite sure I believe it myself yet.' Jane rang for champagne.

'Situation a bit fraught?' asked Charles.

'Not nearly as much as I'd thought.' Ned's relief was obvious. 'As I've no doubt Georgie's already told you, she's not the most obvious duchess material you've ever seen. But my father's potty about her, especially since she played you,' he said to Jane. 'And once my mother learned that Georgie wasn't American she was so relieved she gave in at once. Her one regret was that being English you wouldn't have any money.'

'But I've got masses,' said Georgie.

'So I told her. She said it was probably because you'd lived in America for so long. It bucked her up no end. You know I'm quite old enough to marry without their consent, but I'm jolly glad I've got it. I mean apart from the fact that it makes it easier when it comes to inheritances and things, I do rather like them.'

The champagne arrived, and Charles opened it and poured.

'Oh, I almost forgot,' said Ned. 'My mother sent you this.' His hand went to his pocket, and he produced an old and rather battered little leather box. Inside it was a sapphire ring, set in white gold.

'Been in the family ever since the third duke bought it,' said Ned. '1820 or thereabouts. Of course it doesn't have to be your engagement ring, if you'd rather choose your own,' her fiancé said.

'Put it on at once,' said Georgie, and held out her left hand. To her delight it fitted. Ned kissed her. 'You're beginning to look more like duchess material already,' he said.

'No rush,' Georgie said. 'Being a marchioness will be quite enough for now.'

'I think it's time for a toast,' said Charles.

The Savoy was full, but the head waiter had kept his best table for them. Of course he had, thought Jane. A film star and a marquis – who could possibly compete? The entire room seemed to be looking at them, but Georgie was too used to it to let it bother her, Jane had got used to it through being so often with Georgie, Ned was too much in love to notice, and Charles was convinced that absolutely no one was looking at him, so that all was well.

They danced, ate, drank wine and were happy, and Jane wondered if they had reached some sort of watershed of happiness, a calm content that she wanted to last for ever.

As they danced Charles said to her: 'Our Georgie a marchioness.'

'By lad it makes you think,' said Jane, in her best Felston accent. She thought of Ned's mother's obsession with wealth.

'Is Ned's father hard up?' she asked.

'No dukes are hard up,' said Charles.

'Then why did his mother bother so much about Georgie's money?'

'Because most rich people would like to be richer.'

'Would you?'

'Of course,' said Charles, 'but then I'm a special case. Of course everyone's bound to say that rather than just call it avarice, but what I mean is this. Money's what I'm for. My métier, discipline, whatever – and we all like to do what we're good at. But that's quite enough seriousness for a dance floor.'

'I loved Georgie's ring,' said Jane. 'It's absolutely her. But I prefer mine.' He hugged her and smiled.

Later she and Ned danced. 'The epitome of a happy man,' she said.

'That's right,' said Ned. 'A lucky man, too.'

'You're both lucky,' said Jane. 'And not just because you're both so nice. You belong together. You match.'

'Like you and Charles,' he said.

'I like to think so. When will you marry?'

'First chance I get,' said Ned. 'That's as soon as Georgie's made her last picture.' His face clouded. 'She says she doesn't mind giving all that up – but I wonder if it's true? She's had a fascinating time in Hollywood.'

'It's true,' said Jane.

'You sound so sure.'

'It was last time I was in Hollywood,' said Jane. 'Before I even knew of your existence. She didn't think it fascinating in the least. Up at five in the morning: dieting: rationing her martinis because of her figure: churning out picture after picture. She said then she'd be glad to give it up, and I believed her. I still do. She still says it come to that.'

He brightened at once. 'Thank you for telling me,' he said. 'Did you find it like that?'

'Hollywood? I've never stayed there long enough to find out, but I should think it's a place where one could become bored very easily.'

The band finished their stint, and they went back to their table, and began the sort of lazy gossiping that flowed from love and friendship and contentment. No need to surprise or sparkle or score points: being the group they were was enough. – And if that makes us smug then that's what we are, thought Jane, but oh it's a pleasant thing to be. Then George Lane came up to them.

Neither she nor Charles had seen him come in. He just seemed to appear in front of them. Like an apparition, she thought, if an apparition can be somewhat drunk.

'I'm looking for that bastard Patterson,' said Lane. 'But you'll do as well.'

'Oh push off, Lane,' said Charles. 'You're tight.'

'Patterson's a thief,' said Lane. 'I'm not sure you're not a thief too.'

'*Bob?*' said Jane, and wished she'd kept her mouth shut. The important thing was to get Lane to go away, but the accusation was so ridiculous –

'Bob the Ram,' said Lane. 'Bob the Thief as well. He's trying to steal my business. Did you put him up to it?'

Jane looked at the other two. For the second time since she'd met him Ned's face wore the look of horror that reminded her of his father when politics was mentioned: Georgie merely looked like a beautiful woman watching a rude man make a fool of himself and finding it amusing, but then Georgie was an actress.

'I'm also looking for my wife,' said Lane. 'At one time she used to chase after Bob the Ram, till I blacked her eye for her.' His voice rose. 'I wonder who she's chasing after now? Whoever it is it'll mean another black eye I'm afraid.'

Piers, thought Jane. She'll be with Piers, and if he starts a brawl when Piers is present Piers will hurt him, and a good thing too.

Charles signalled to the head waiter, who looked at Lane and scurried over at once. As he did so he must have made a signal that Jane didn't see, and another waiter followed.

'This gentleman's forgotten where his table is,' said Charles. 'Perhaps you'd be good enough to take him back to it. He doesn't belong here.'

'Of course, Mr Lovell,' the head waiter said, and took Lane's arm. 'This way, sir.'

Lane braced himself, not moving. 'I don't like thieves,' Lane said. 'You'll find that out.'

'Black their eyes, do you?' said Charles.

The second waiter, a much larger man, took Lane's other arm.

'This way, sir,' the head waiter said again, and this time Lane went.

Whatever else he had done, Lane put an end to the party. Nobody wanted to dance any more, the wine was finished, the coffee drunk. It was time to go home, and Jane said so.

'Good Lord, yes,' said Ned. 'I expect it's quite late.' It was in fact twenty minutes to midnight.

Georgie was staying at the Savoy, and as her fiancé was determined to see her to her door, Jane and Charles left them to it. The chauffeur of the liner on wheels was well aware of their presence behind him, but that was not the reason why Jane sat apart from Charles.

When they reached South Terrace she said, 'I want to talk to you.'

'Of course,' he said.

'Come in for a nightcap.'

The chauffeur opened the door. 'Wait,' Charles said. 'I shan't be long,' then followed her into the house.

She poured him brandy, and he sniffed and savoured. He knows me so well, she thought. That's why he's determined to stay calm. No show of righteous anger, no demand for explanations, just a calm acceptance of their status quo as an engaged couple. All the same she had to ask questions: she couldn't not ask questions.

'Nice brandy,' he said.

'Bisquit,' said Jane. 'You chose it. What was all that about?'

'Business,' said Charles, and sipped once more.

'Don't you think I'm entitled to more than that?'

'No,' said Charles. 'Not entitled.'

'He made a scene before two of our closest friends,' she said. 'He insulted you and Bob and his wife.'

'He was drunk.'

'He still said it.'

'Supposing that Murray Fisch had insulted you in just such a way – in the middle of making your film, let us say. It's perfectly possible, after all – and in pretty well the same terms. Insults to friends, hints of malpractice. All that. Would you say that I was entitled to an explanation?'

'No,' said Jane, 'but I would give you one.'

'And I'll give you one,' said Charles.

End of Round One, she thought, and Charles well ahead on points.

'We talked about this while we danced, you remember,' said Charles. 'I told you that money was my métier, but the dance floor was hardly the place – '

'I remember.'

'Maybe this is the place,' he said. 'We'll know quite soon.' The words held a menace she could not ignore.

'Lane is a brute,' he continued. 'Not that that matters a damn. He could be a saint and I'd still have acted as I did – except that a saint would have more sense.'

'He said you were stealing his business.'

'He said Bob was stealing his business, and that I might be.'

'And is he? Bob I mean?'

'No,' said Charles. 'Stealing, no.'

'What is he doing?'

'Trying to buy it.'

'Buy it honestly?'

'Stealing means you give nothing,' said Charles. 'Buying is only for cash.'

'Perhaps not very much cash.'

'As little as possible,' said Charles. 'But in Lane's case that's rather a lot.'

355

'So you are involved?'

'Yes,' said Charles. 'I tell you this because I love you and for no other reason.' She flinched at that. 'It was Bob's idea, but he didn't have nearly enough money to do it on his own, so he came to me. I looked at the figures and liked what I saw and so, as you say, I became involved.'

'What will happen to Lane?'

'Perhaps nothing,' he said. 'We haven't got what we're after yet.'

'But suppose you do?'

'He'll still be rich,' he said, 'provided he sells his stable and gives up bridge.'

'But you'll be richer?'

'I told you on the dance floor,' he said. 'It's what I'm for.'

'A machine for making money?'

Even then he didn't explode. His voice stayed gentle, though he had sense enough not to touch her.

'You saw the waiters take him back to his table. Did you see who he was with?'

She shook her head.

'Crawley,' he said, 'and a couple of tarts with dress sense. If he survives it will be because of Crawley's money.'

'Even so – '

'Let me finish. If it's Crawley's money then it will be Crawley's business. That's point one. Lane couldn't go on as he was. He was grossly under-capitalised. On the other hand who wants Lane as a partner? Bob spotted that and it was a smart bit of work.'

'Bob was thinking of no one but himself. Greed and grab, that's all it was. Are you always like that, the pair of you?'

He took another sip of brandy, his voice stayed gentle.

'That isn't quite true,' he said. 'Lane Engineering is about to make a new aircraft engine, and it's going to be a winner, so I'm told. If that's so the demand for it will be enormous. As I've said, Lane simply hasn't the money to cope with that, so one of two things will happen.

'The first is that he'll sell it – possibly to a German, more likely an American. Either way a lot of people in the Midlands will be out of work. The second is that he'll be taken over, either by Crawley or by Bob and me. I don't think it would be a good idea for him to be taken over by Crawley, knowing his politics. It's an aircraft engine, remember.

'On the other hand if Bob and I move in there'll be no political problems and we'll expand the business at least as much as Creepy Crawley would. A lot more jobs, rather than closures, and when the country needs jobs desperately. Not just in Felston.'

'And you'd make more money?'

'A great deal more. So would Bob. So might Lane, incidentally. He certainly wouldn't lose.'

'Then why is he making such a fuss?'

'Because we're trying to take his toy away from him,' said Charles. 'I doubt if he can read a flight manual, or even a blueprint, or tell one end of a spanner from the other. But he can go to City dinners and Engineering Employers' cocktail parties and pontificate for all he's worth, and the people he's busy boring have to listen because they know the product's good. That doesn't seem to me to be a particularly good reason.'

He yawned politely, but not bothering to hide it, and she realised that he was exhausted by all that greed and grab or creation of jobs or whatever one chose to call it.

'Forgive me,' he said. 'It's been rather a long day. Are there any more points you'd like to raise?'

Still the chairman of the board she thought, and aloud: 'Nothing else.'

'I'll say goodnight then.' He rose to his feet.

'Goodnight.'

She found that it was impossible to go to him. He looked at her long and hard.

'Are we finished?' he asked.

'I need to think,' she said. 'Will you call me tomorrow?'

'Of course.'

She heard the car door shut as she went upstairs, then the murmur of its engine. At least Charles could be exhausted in style. Dry eyed she undressed and put on pyjamas, then lit a cigarette, and wished for the thousandth time that Foch was still alive.

Once again Bob looked at the plump, pretty girl with no clothes on, Lovell at the people in the café.

'So I'm Bob the Ram, am I?' he said.

'His words.' Lovell shrugged. 'Lothario or Don Juan would have been nicer, but he didn't want to be nice.'

'No more he did,' said Bob, 'since he called me a thief.'

'And wondered whether I was one too.'

'It's all because he was drunk,' said Bob. 'I don't mind being a Don Juan – or a ram come to that – though it's a bit crude – but I'm not a thief any more than you are. It happens in business every day. I mean to say it isn't even against the law.'

'One could argue that it might be considered unethical.'

'Not in this case,' said Bob.

'You care to tell me why?'

'We'll do it better,' said Bob.

'Which is to say we'll make more money.'

'More jobs as well.'

My argument of last night, Charles Lovell thought. It didn't appear to get me very far.

'You're not thinking of calling it off, are you?' said Bob.

'Eh? Oh, no, no. Nothing like that.'

'I'm in pretty deep as you know,' said Bob. 'If you were to pull out – '

'I'm not. It's just that seeing Lane last night set me thinking. Are you in touch with his wife, by the by?'

'Sort of.'

'You'd better warn her that he talked about black eyes. Done it before, one gathers.'

'Because of me,' said Bob.

'So he said.'

'Right there in the middle of the Savoy? He must be mad.' Bob brooded for a minute. 'Did he mention Mrs Simpson?'

'I think perhaps he was going to,' said Lovell, 'but a couple of waiters removed him just in time.' He looked at his desk. One small notebook and a gold pencil were all it contained.

'We slipped up badly,' he said, 'when we ignored the possibility of Crawley's intervention.'

'You mean I did,' said Bob. 'Trouble was Annabel didn't see much of Crawley. He and Lane used to play cards together, at their club mostly. He didn't often go to the house. All the same I should – '

'I knew about their card playing,' said Lovell. 'I belong to the same club, after all. I'm as much to blame as you are.'

'What it amounts to is that Crawley's been chasing shares as hard as we have. Harder, maybe. He started later. He's had to pay a lot for them. Too much when you consider what Lane Engineering's worth.'

'But surely Crawley isn't forking out money so he can give the business back to Lane?'

Lovell smiled. 'Hardly,' he said. 'He wants the business for himself. But there'll be a bonne bouche for Lane. Non-executive director, chairman of the entertainments committee perhaps. Just enough status to go on being a bore at City dinners.'

'If Crawley wins.'

'Quite so. If we win he's out. Drunk or sober the man's a bore.'

'And will we? Win, I mean?'

Bob struggled to keep his voice as matter of fact as Lovell's, and didn't quite succeed, but then he had far more to lose.

'Six to four would be a reasonable bet at the moment, on us, that is to say. We could improve on that – or rather you could.'

'Anything you say,' said Bob.

'Don't be so rash. Wait until you hear what it is, Señor Tenerio.'

'Who?'

'Don Juan,' said Lovell. 'I've been doing sums, or rather one sum. The only one that counts. How many we've got and how many they've got, which is why I offered six to four. We're a bit ahead, Señor Tenerio, but not quite enough. According to my information there's one block of shares outstanding. Whoever gets them will have won.'

'Oh,' said Bob.

'Mrs Hendry's,' said Lovell.

'I somehow thought they would be,' said Bob.

She had tried to telephone to her mother, but the parlourmaid had said Haydock Park, in a tone of voice that ended the matter. Nothing for it but to go for a walk, even without Foch. Walking was the only way she could think, and so she went to Kensington Gardens and slogged on past the Round Pond and the statue and the flower gardens, and wondered as she always did why parks like this should attract only the very young and the very old, before the rhythm of her movement took over, and the thinking began, haphazard at first, but merging gradually into a pattern until at last she found herself facing some very unpleasant facts indeed.

When she looked at her watch it was two o'clock, and she was hungry. She'd had no breakfast, and she must have covered miles, but going home to eat simply wasn't on. Georgie would phone to discuss last night's events – had probably phoned already – and she couldn't bear to talk to anybody until she faced up to Charles. Even trying to reach her mother had been a mistake, she realised. It was her burden: and it was up to her to carry it.

She found an ABC that provided her with a curious cheese sandwich and what the waitress claimed was coffee, then went into a news cinema to wait for time to pass: short film after short film, over and over. A duck in a sailor suit who appeared to be constantly losing his temper, a travel film about a place called fabulous Benares, which bore no resemblance whatever to the city where she had once lived, and newsreels, so many: Movietone, Pathé, Gaumont British. Wars and rumours of wars, in China, Abyssinia, Palestine. Battleships being launched (but not in Felston, not yet), bombers bombing, fighters fighting, and riots and lockouts and strikes in Chicago, Lyons, Madrid, and what looked like half the population of Germany marching past a man with a moustache. The world it seemed was in a far worse state than even the most pessimistic of prophets had foretold. When it was time to leave she went to a phone box and Charles's secretary put her through at once.

'Can you come to South Terrace?' she said. 'Straightaway?'

'Half an hour,' he said. It would take her almost that long to get back herself.

She had time to wash her face, renew her make-up, and that was about it, before his taxi appeared.

'Would you like a drink?' Jane asked.

'Later perhaps.'

Reluctantly Truett left. Something was definitely up, and now she might never know what it was. Jane went through the ritual of cigarettes, holder, lighter. She knew precisely what had to be said, but it was so difficult to say it. Then she looked him in the face:

360

beyond that impassive look she knew beyond question that the man was in agony.

'I want to say I'm sorry,' she said, but he made no answer, and why should he, she thought, you damn fool? Sorry for what?

'Sorry for being such a fool last night,' she said.

Still he made no answer, and indeed there was still a long way to go. She couldn't blame him for his silence: he was far too vulnerable to risk words until he knew what they would cost him. Well Jane, she thought, you made the wounds. Up to you to apply the bandages – if he'll let you.

'I'm not usually such an idiot,' she said. 'At least I don't think I am – but last night I could have won medals. I mean for stupidity. I had to walk about five miles round Kensington Gardens to find out what was wrong.'

'You want to call it off,' he said. 'Very well. I – '

'No,' she said. 'It isn't that at all.'

She found that she was shouting, angry because of his lack of comprehension, but that would never do, no matter how difficult explanations were.

'It isn't that,' she said. 'Honestly. All that's up to you now. The thing is – ' She dragged at her cigarette. 'Bear with me. This is – difficult.'

'Of course,' he said.

'We were happy last night,' she said, 'and Georgie's and Ned's news made us even happier.'

He nodded.

'I remember thinking: There probably aren't four happier people in London, and if that makes us smug, then smug is what we are.'

What I can't say, she thought, is that Georgie and Ned are happier than you and me, because they love each other fifty fifty, and try as I might all I can do is like you very much.

'I was smug too,' he said. 'I enjoyed it.'

'What was wrong with me is so complicated,' she said. 'I know words are my business, but even so – Bear with me, please. I really am doing my best.'

'Of course.'

And stop being so nice, she thought. I don't deserve it.

'I suppose it's partly because Aunt Pen left me all that money all

361

those years ago,' she said. 'I've been my own boss ever since. Made my own decisions, my own mistakes. The point is they were *mine*. Like this house. Like the Bentley.' Again he waited.

'There was this idea – sort of hiding,' she said. 'What the psychologists call sub-conscious. I mean I didn't know it was there at the time, but it was. I suppose it began when you gave me this?' She held up her engagement ring, still on her finger. ' – And it just grew bigger and bigger like a snowball rolling downhill and I still didn't know it was there. If I had it might have been different. But I didn't. What I'm saying is that I was afraid of losing my independence, and it terrified me – and so I made all that fuss about something that had nothing to do with me.'

'You wouldn't have lost your independence,' he said. 'I gave you my word.'

'Yes, but – I know you, Charles. I trust you. Love you.' Somehow she got that out, true or false. 'But what bothered me was I wouldn't be alone any more. It would never be me, ever again. Always us.'

He tried to speak, but she held up her hand, and again he waited.

'Nothing wrong with that, you'll say, and no doubt there isn't, but I've never done it before and you have. I got – stage fright, I suppose you could call it. I'm told it happens to brides quite often, but not too many brides are my age. Not first-time brides, anyway. It all amounts to this, Charles. Can you possibly forgive me?'

Still he didn't answer: he kissed her instead. When they came up for air she said, 'Do I take it I'm forgiven?'

'I've never thought I deserved you,' he said. 'You had it all without me. But as long as you're sure – '

'Oh I am,' she said. 'Believe me I am.'

She liked him very much, and he would always be there. The panic had been just that: a clamour that said, But are you sure? And in the end the answer had been, Yes. Absolutely.

'I'm even more smug than I was last night,' said Charles. 'Or is it smugger?'

He kissed her again, until Truett hammered on the door as if they were playing Postman's Knock.

'Miss Payne,' she said. 'On the telephone.'

'Bring the ice,' said Jane. 'Mr Lovell will make the drinks.'

'Yes, miss. Right away, miss,' said Truett. If it was possible for a Primitive Methodist to look arch, then Truett did.

'Sorry I didn't call before,' said Georgie. 'I seem to have spent all day talking to Northumberland.'

'Your in-laws to be?'

'Absolute baa-lambs,' said Georgie.

And there was her strength, thought Jane. Once you had won an Academy Award no one could over-awe you, not even a duke.

'Then I had to go to Harrods to buy brogues,' Georgie said.

'To buy what?'

'Brogues,' said Georgie. 'You know. Stout shoes. It's what you wear up there in the tundra. And tweeds and things. But not for underwear. Not mine, anyway. They're giving a ball – more regal than ducal, wouldn't you say? Any chance of you and Charles doing your attendant lord and lady routine?'

'When?' Georgie told her. 'Hold on.'

She went back to the drawing room, where Charles was drinking a very large whisky. 'Medicinal,' he said. 'My hands were shaking too much to worry about how much vermouth.'

She kissed him and asked about the ball. 'Love to,' he said.

'Ned says it will be ghastly unless we get a few of our crowd,' Georgie said. 'You know – the under-fifties.'

'Thanks awfully,' said Jane.

She went back to Charles and mixed her own martini. 'I was rotten to you,' she said, 'and I haven't even said sorry. Not properly.'

'You've done better than that,' he said. 'You've explained.'

'Where are we dining tonight?'

'Somewhere quiet I should think,' he said. 'We've neither of us changed.'

'The quietest place I know is your flat,' she said.

The best way to set about it, Bob thought, would be to see Piers. The trouble was finding him. He never seemed to be at his grandmother's in Eaton Square, and he couldn't very well ask Catherine, always supposing he knew where to find her. She'd done a bunk too, so he'd been told. Maybe it had something to do with being twins. In the end he'd had to ring Annabel in West Kensington, and she'd asked him to visit her. She had hay fever, she said, and anyway she couldn't meet him at any of his places in case they ran into George.

There was no doubt about the hay fever. Her nose was red, and her eyes watered, but she was still a pretty woman, and that's quite enough of that, he told himself. She gestured to her drawing-room window. The flats were built in the form of a quadrangle facing on to a garden of lawn and flower beds.

'Pretty, isn't it?' she said. 'But that's no compensation for what it's doing to me. Pour us a drink, darling.'

He did so and said, 'It's your husband I've come about.'

'What about him?'

'He ran into Jane and Charles Lovell at the Savoy the other night.'

'Georgina Payne's engagement to that devastating marquis,' she said. 'I read all about it in the *Daily World*. Some people are lucky.'

'He was drunk,' said Bob. 'Your husband I mean.'

'It has been known,' she said.

'He talked about black eyes,' said Bob.

'Oh,' she said.

'He also talked about me,' said Bob. 'Bob the Ram he called me.'

'Not very flattering,' said Annabel.

'The point is that he didn't bother to keep his voice down,' said Bob, 'which means that our little affaire must be all over town by now.'

'Doubtless,' she said, 'though I doubt if it's reached West Kensington yet.'

'Will it matter if it does?'

'Tricky one,' she said. 'Let me tell you about this place. It contains quite a few ladies like me – ladies conducting liaisons, that's to say. I don't mean on the batter – although I think I've spotted a couple who may be – in a high class sort of way.'

Bob blinked: her language had never been as coarse as that. She chuckled.

'Don't worry,' she said. 'I haven't been drinking all morning. It's the pills I have to take for this bloody hay fever – they make you go all peculiar. Where was I?'

'Ladies with liaisons,' said Bob.

'Amazing how quickly one can spot who has and who hasn't,' said Annabel. 'We spy on each other in a genteel sort of way. One of them – quite a pretty brunette if rather chubby – anyway her chap's really rather famous. I met him at Goodwood, which is rather different from West Kensington. Nevertheless my chap installed me here. Did it with great enterprise and dispatch let me tell you, which rather made me wonder whether Piers had done it before. Installation, I mean.' Her hand flew to her mouth. 'Oh my God,' she said. 'You did know it was Piers?'

'Yes,' said Bob.

'That's all right then. Except that now Piers will know that once upon a time you were the installer, and not all that long ago either. That could be tricky, too. In fact it's jolly well going to be.' She turned from the window.

'You think so?' said Bob.

'I know so,' she said. 'Piers has just got out of a taxi.' Bob sipped his drink. 'You're not going to scoot?' she asked.

'No point,' said Bob. 'I'd run straight into him. Anyway – scooting never solved anything.'

'I used to do rather a lot of it when George put his boxing gloves on,' she said. 'But I see what you mean.'

A key turned in the front door lock, then the door was shut.

'Darling,' Piers called, 'I know I said I'd phone, but I – ' He walked into the drawing room, and his voice faded.

'No,' said Bob.

'What the devil do you mean, no?' said Piers, and strode over to Bob. Hardly a trace of a limp, Bob noticed, even at that speed.

'Whatever you're thinking the answer's no,' said Bob.

'I knew about you both,' Piers said, and turned to Annabel. 'Knew about it before you and I ever – but I must say I never expected this.' He turned back to Bob. 'Get up,' he said.

'No rush,' said Bob.

'Taking pity on a poor cripple?' said Piers, but already the anger was fading, thought Bob. He's beginning to use his brains and a good thing, too. He's got the brains to use.

'Let's hear it,' Piers said.

'Sit down first,' said Bob. 'I can't think straight with you looming over me.' Piers sat. 'In the first place you're a mate of mine,' Bob said.

'I thought that, too.'

'Let me finish,' said Bob. 'Being a mate means fair and square and out in the open, or not at all. That's point one. Point two is – what you're implying – what does that make her?' He nodded at Annabel. 'She's a lady, Piers. Sort of a female gentleman as you might say. She plays the rules too.'

'Then what the blazes are you doing here?'

Bob told him. 'Of course if you knew already about Annabel and me it was a wasted journey for that, but the black-eye talk. That wasn't wasted.'

Piers turned to Annabel. 'He beats you?'

'From time to time,' she said.

'He won't any more.'

'Wait now,' said Bob. 'There's a bit more thinking to do – and before you start asking why I didn't do something about it – it's because Annabel never told me.'

'Why on earth not?' Piers asked her.

'Because Bob would have hurt him dreadfully,' she said, 'and I didn't want him sent to prison for hurting an ape like George.'

Suddenly Piers smiled at Bob, suspicion and anger all gone.

'We first met in a fight, do you remember?' he said. 'That heavyweight don – '

'Cuthbert Pardoe,' said Bob.

Piers turned to Annabel. 'Amateur boxer,' he said. 'We were on opposite sides during the General Strike, and he was giving me the biggest hiding I'm ever likely to get, then Bob popped up and did something I couldn't possible describe to a female gentleman, and it was all over.'

'Oh how I'd love you to have done it to George,' said Annabel, 'but I couldn't possibly risk it.'

'It would be worse for Piers,' said Bob.

'Worse than prison?'

'You'd better tell her, bonny lad,' said Bob.

Piers hesitated for a while, then: 'Oh damn it,' he said. 'It needn't come to prison – I could probably dodge that.'

'What then?' she asked.

'I'd have to resign my commission,' he said.

'But you can't possibly do that. It's your whole life,' she said.

'Better leave that to me,' said Bob. 'I owe him one anyway.'

Piers looked at him. 'There's no reason why you should,' he said.

'Didn't you hear what I just told you?' said Bob. And anyway, he thought, you're still a mate, and I'll do a better job, and I need Annabel's shares. I may not have to, but if I do, then I will.

'Oh that would be wonderful,' she said. 'Bless you, Bob.'

'Be a pleasure.' He hesitated, trying to think how best to break it, but there was no easy way.

'He'll be looking for you. Your husband I mean.'

'Complete with knuckle dusters no doubt,' she said.

'Complete with lawyers,' said Bob. 'Unless you think he'll want you back?'

'Not this time. Not after the Wallis Simpson thing.'

'What I thought. So he'll be after a divorce, only he'll have to find you first.'

'You're the only one who knows – ' she began.

'Maybe for now. But he needs to find you, whether it's for a divorce, or a belting. Or maybe both. So he'll hire private detectives, good ones. – He's still got a few bob. I wouldn't hang about here too long. Could be trouble.'

'Thanks Bob,' she said.

Bob rose. 'Better be off,' he said, and turned to Piers. 'Just one thing,' he said. 'If you don't mind my asking – who told you about me and Annabel?'

'Don't mind at all,' said Piers. 'It was – let me think. Why of course. It was Catherine.'

That just about makes up the set, thought Bob, and left them to it.

When he had gone, Piers said, 'You've been crying?'

'Can you wonder?' she said. No point in telling him it was hay fever.

Jane drove them up to Northumberland in the Bentley. Charles being Charles and business being business, they made far too late a start to do it in one day, and that meant a night in a hotel in South Yorkshire. Even that didn't worry him too much. It was when she told him that they couldn't have separate rooms that the trouble began.

'But we must,' he said.

'How can we, Charles? Unless we tell them you're my brother, and we don't look in the least related.'

'But the ring,' he said. 'They'll know you're not married if you're not wearing a wedding ring.'

'I bought one in Woolworth's last week,' she said. 'Just for practice.'

'*Woolworth's?*'

'Don't worry,' she said. 'The engagement ring will hide it.'

Unless they think that came from Woolworth's too, she thought, but there was no point in going into that. Charles was jumpy enough as it was. But he had his revenge when they signed the register. Mr and Mrs C. Pardoe, he wrote. At least it was an improvement on Smith, and Pardoe had been trying to get her into a hotel bedroom for years.

In bed that night she said, 'Admit I was right.'

'You're always right,' he said. 'What are you right about this time?'

'Practising being married. Aren't you glad you don't have to get up and go to your own cold bed? Well aren't you?' But this time he'd outfoxed her. He was asleep.

. 36 .

No shared room at Derwent Castle of course, just a long and draughty corridor in which Charles could prove his ardour, not that it wouldn't have cooled a bit by the time he reached her. The castle itself was superb. Not much of the original castle left in point of fact, apart from a wall or two and the ruin of a tower. Most of the building was Georgian, with a few 'improvements' by Nash: stables, a library, a ballroom; odds and ends of that kind. The house itself was stuffed with the loot of centuries, so that even Lady Mangan's burnt-out home was nothing to it: Spanish, Flemish, Italian, English pictures; a Gutenberg Bible, pieces of Cellini silver, a Graeco–Roman statue. A house like a museum, in fact, except that some of it looked lived in, far more so than Charles's castle near by, Blagdon, where every room looked as if the restorer had just left, which was just about true. But here there were rooms, a small dining room, the duchess's drawing room, the gun room which was largely out of bounds to females, which seemed to have been lived in, dusted and swept, since they were first built a hundred and seventy years before.

The house-party seemed largely to have come straight out of Debrett, she and Charles Georgie's only friends, but that wasn't surprising. Georgie's other friends were nearly all in California. Even so it was a pity Murray Fisch wasn't there. It would have been nice to hear him scream just once more. . . . Not that they weren't made welcome. The duke and duchess fussed over them most attentively. *The Angel of No Man's Land* she thought, feeling smug, then realised it wasn't just that. The duchess went out of her way to be sweet to Charles, who even if he did own most of a studio had never made a picture in his life. On the other hand, she realised, Charles must be far and away the richest person there, or anywhere else he happened to be, and so the duchess was sweet. Yet another complication to married life, she thought, if I let it become so, but I won't. We've been through all that, poor Charles and I, and now I'm going to be married and I'm going to be happy and that's all there is to it.

She had been loaned a maid who helped her to dress: not Fortuny this time, but a white and green gown by Worth, and the Fabergé emeralds Charles had given her, years ago. Dukes and duchesses must be used to such things, she thought, and if they're not it'll give the duchess something else to be sweet about. As she fastened the necklace Georgie knocked and came in: silver and sapphires, Jane saw, and devastatingly beautiful, but Georgie had eyes only for the emeralds.

'Golly,' she said. 'Charles?'

'He bought them from a Russian count,' said Jane.

'He must be absolutely rolling in it,' said Georgie. 'I'm sorry, darling. It's just that I hadn't quite realised – '

'You won't be short of a bob or two yourself,' said Jane.

'We've come a long way since Chelsea,' Georgie said. 'Do you remember that time when Mrs Browne tried to take the bread knife to that picture of me in the altogether?'

The picture had been painted by an artist called Martin Browne, with whom Georgie had been living when the bread knife came into play. There had been police and other complications.

'Nobody can say we haven't lived,' said Jane. 'Do you ever have any word of Martin?'

Georgie shrugged. 'Still making a fool of himself trying to paint like Picasso or Modigliani or whoever it is. He was doing so much better when he painted like himself.' She brooded.

'Sybil Hendry's here,' she said at last.

'Complete with father?' The general was notoriously one for the flesh pots.

'From what Ned tells me she won't let him in the house any more, which isn't too surprising. He does drink, rather.' She lit a cigarette. 'Not Bob, either.'

'I should think not,' said Jane.

'Wouldn't do to assemble all my ex-lovers at my engagement party. Not that I ever had anything like as many as people think.

370

Certainly not a whole football team like Clara Bow. At least that's what people say. Where was I?'

'Bob,' said Jane.

'He couldn't have come anyway. Even if I had asked him. He has to stay in London and make money.' She waited, but Jane said nothing. 'Catherine Bower's coming,' said Georgie.

'Staying here?'

'No,' Georgie said and lobbed her bomb. 'As a matter of fact she's staying with Geoffrey Brent. The chap she went to Tuscany with.'

'The idiot!' said Jane. The bomb was a direct hit, Georgie noticed.

'What on earth do his parents make of it?'

'Oh, young Brent isn't an entire fool. How can he be? He's a don. He's invited a whole crowd along and Catherine's just one of them. At least that's the theory.'

'Have they all come to your ball?'

'Just those two. And the parents of course. Young Brent's known Ned for absolute ages, and Catherine sneaked in because she knows me – dating back to when we did good works together for Felston. Rather amusing, really – so long as he remembers to take his hands off her from time to time.'

'Like that, is it?'

'Smitten,' said Georgie. 'Shouldn't be surprised if he's proposed already.'

'How can he?' said Jane.

'Jay Bower proposed to me.'

'Young Brent's not in the least like Jay.'

'She wouldn't want him if he were. What's he up to? In London peddling his papers, I suppose. You know there's one thing I can say about my chaps. They could all make money. Even Martin. They say he sells those monstrosities of his for hundreds of pounds.' She stubbed out her cigarette. 'Well I think I've just about talked you through the minefield.' She went to Jane and kissed her. 'Wish me luck.'

'As if you needed it,' said Jane. 'But I do, and happiness, too. You're going to enjoy being a marchioness, aren't you?'

'Not arf,' said Georgie.

*

371

Charles risked the draughts in the corridor, and they cuddled for a while in silence, then they lit cigarettes and talked over the night's events in voices little louder than whispers, which was nonsense, thought Jane. The walls of her room were thick enough to absorb any noise short of artillery fire.

'Enjoy yourself?' he asked.

'Well yes,' she said, 'but more as a spectator than anything, though there was a certain amount of under-fifties dancing to enjoy.'

He unbuttoned her pyjama coat. 'That friend of yours – '

'No,' she said. 'Either we do this or we talk. But not both together.'

'Just trying to find somewhere to put my hand,' he said.

'Well not there. Not yet, anyway. Hot cigarette ash could ruin my evening. Or yours.' She rested her head on his shoulder. 'Which friend?'

'Catherine Bower.'

'I hope you don't call her my friend just because you disapprove.'

'Of course not,' he said. 'I call her your friend because she is. I mean you seem to spend half your life following her about and picking up the bits of her latest disaster.'

'Somebody has to,' she said.

He stubbed out their cigarettes, and drew her to him.

'Just a minute,' she said. 'Sybil Hendry.'

'Oh God, what about her?'

'A little bit tight, wasn't she?'

'Was she?' he said. 'I didn't notice.'

'What on earth were you looking at?'

'You mostly,' he said. Darling Charles to say such things. If only they didn't make her feel so guilty.

'She virtually impaled a peach with a fruit knife and waved it about in a most suggestive manner – and she was making very free with Ned's young brother.'

'Tight, as you say. Family failing, no doubt. Still, that's Bob's problem.'

He found the place to put his hand.

'What's ours?' she asked.

'Haven't got one.'

372

'Yes we have,' she said. 'Suppose I yell?'

'Just do it quietly,' he said.

Piers came to see him at South Molton Street, having telephoned first to make the appointment. Frightened I might have a girl with me, thought Bob. Some hopes, the mood Sybil's in, but Piers had brought a bottle of whisky. He held it up and said, 'Peace offering.'

'Come on in, man,' said Bob. 'We were never at war.' He went to the drinks tray for glasses and syphon.

'Takes two, thank God,' said Piers, 'and you had more sense. Trouble is I'm on edge half the time.'

'Annabel?'

'She too of course,' said Piers, 'but it isn't Romeo and Juliet, you know. We're lovers of course, but we're loving friends more than the star-crossed kind. You know.'

'Well – yes,' said Bob, and Piers grinned at him.

'The thing is I had no idea about this black eye business – not until you brought it up, and being a friend she wouldn't hear of my staying to face him if he hit her.'

'Wouldn't have been fair, anyway,' said Bob.

'Because of my leg, you mean?'

'You'd have murdered him,' said Bob.

Piers took his time thinking about it. 'Well yes, I probably would,' he said at last. 'Not literally of course. Murder I mean. But a damn good hiding. And then he'd have called in the police and I'd have had to resign my commission.'

'He might have done more than that,' said Bob.

'I don't think I follow you.'

'No,' said Bob. 'You wouldn't. Not you. But he could have gone to his pal Crawley and hired a couple of his blackshirt bruisers to do what he couldn't do himself.'

'Good Lord,' said Piers, and once again took his time to think. 'What a shit Lane is to be sure.'

Which means you agree with me, thought Bob, and said aloud, 'So what have you decided to do, the pair of you?'

'Annabel's gone abroad,' said Piers. 'Catherine went off to Italy to make a fool of herself. I suppose you heard that?'

'She didn't try very hard to keep it a secret.'

373

'Well I'm going to make a fool of myself in the South of France. I'm joining Annabel there next week.'

'There's a difference,' said Bob. 'You're being discreet about it.'

Piers looked uncomfortable. 'Not just me,' he said. 'Annabel wants it that way too.'

'Well of course,' said Bob, and thought: Tell me when I'm rich. Her very last words to me. They weren't the words of a woman dying for another go at matrimony, but then after Lane could you wonder?

'If I may ask,' he said, 'has Catherine left Jay Bower? None of my business of course, but I can't help wondering.'

'Nor anybody else,' said Piers. 'Blest if I know, officially so to speak, but the answer is almost certainly yes.'

'How's Jay Bower taking it?'

'We don't meet all that often,' said Piers, 'but he'd better get used to the idea – of a break-up I mean. Just as well, really. Once she's hit her stride you can't stop Catherine. Waste of time trying.' He finished off his whisky. 'Best be off,' he said. 'Annabel said she'd write to you as soon as we've settled in case you have news. A bit cryptic, I thought.'

A gentleman to the last. 'Her shares in Lane Engineering,' said Bob. 'I may be able to dispose of them for her. Make her some money.'

'She'd like that,' said Piers.

'Too true,' said Bob.

On the way back to London they were to stop at Felston, then spend the night at another hotel. No shenanigans at Blagdon Hall they'd agreed, not until they were married shenanigans, so Mr and Mrs C. Pardoe would once again share a bed, but first she had to see Andy. There was rather a lot to tell him, and some of it would be difficult to explain on the phone. So Felston it had to be. Charles didn't mind. He'd enjoyed the ball, enjoyed even more their night together, and now he was enjoying being driven.

'There's something I want to ask you,' she said.

'Oh yes?' At once his voice was wary.

'I don't know whether it's a big thing or a small thing, but there's something I want to buy.' He waited. 'It's a dog.'

374

'Well of course,' he said.

'You don't mind?'

'Supposing I did, it would be your dog. But as it happens I don't. I think it's a wonderful idea.'

'You don't have a dog.'

'Not in London. Not in a service flat. But I do at Blagdon Hall.'

'Gun dogs,' she said.

'Oh I know, I know. Working dogs. But I'm still fond of them. I don't see them nearly often enough, but they're my dogs when I'm there. At least they pretend they are. They're soft-hearted little beggars. What sort are you after? Another Foch?'

'Sort of,' she said. 'There could never be precisely another Foch, as well you know, but along those lines.'

'I look forward to meeting him,' said Charles, then closed his eyes and dozed. I *suppose* that's a compliment, she thought. Another proof of our happiness together, not to mention his trust in my driving. . . . As they drew near Felston she prepared to nudge him awake, but he opened his eyes before she could do so. Another opportunity missed. Charles sat up, yawned, and looked about him.

'Good Lord,' he said.

Of course, she thought. He's never seen Felston. Time for the conducted tour, Mr Lovell.

She drove him past St Oswald's Colliery, and the miners' cottages that flanked it, Colliery Row, then down towards the river and the most terrible slums of all, the tenements that had decayed for so long that a blast from the Bentley's horn might send them tumbling, then on to Dr Stobbs's clinic where his friend Canon Messeter had laboured so long, where he finally gave up his life.

'Good God,' he said at last.

She looked at him, almost shyly. 'Well at least now you know what all the fuss is about,' she said.

'I do indeed,' he said. 'Now it's been put into context, getting the town that destroyer isn't all that much, but at least it's a start.'

'It's life,' she said. 'Not till old age, nothing like that, but at least another year or two. It's the chance to hang on.'

She drove towards the river, to where the shipyards stood, one after another, dirty, rusting, silent; engine sheds deserted, cranes

375

like exhausted birds, the slipways a battlefield deserted by soldiers after defeat: and then they came to Harris and Croft. Even before they reached it they could hear the rattle of rivet hammers, the shrill toot of the yard locomotive, the crash of steel plate allowed to fall into place, and then as they approached, the works' whistle screamed, the gates opened, and men poured out, men on bicycles, men on foot, heading to where the buses waited, but all of them talking hard, still with energy to spare, smiling beneath the shipyard grime.

'There,' she said. 'That's what you've done. I hope you're proud of yourself. I know I'm proud of you.'

'I never realised,' he said. 'I mean I listened to you, every word, and I read all you wrote, but until you see it – '

She turned the great car away from the river and towards the market place and the Eldon Arms, where they were to meet Norah and Andy for drinks.

'I remember when I first saw it,' she said. 'It was like a vision of hell. Even the war – at least that finished. I know it took four years, but then it was over. Felston's war just goes on and on.'

She turned into Queen Victoria Street, with its trams and shops, and the beggar with the gramophone mounted on a pram.

'Here we are,' she said. 'The posh part,' and turned into the courtyard of the Eldon Arms.

'Good God!' Charles said again.

She hadn't wanted to go. Of course she'd wanted to see Jane – she always wanted to see Jane – but the thought of meeting that man of hers, that terrified her. A chap who could just snap his fingers and bring an order for a destroyer to a shipyard – more like a god than a man, a chap like that. But Andy said they'd have to go and of course that was it, so she'd ironed her wedding dress and done her best with the make-up Jane had taught her to use. All the same she was terrified.

On the tram she said to him, 'Where'll we be with them?'

Andy, washed, shaved and changed, boots polished, looked at her wearily. It had been a hard shift that day, and the labourer they'd given him just wasn't up to it.

'I told you,' he said. 'The Eldon Arms.'

'I mean – up in their room like?'

'No, no,' he said, making his voice soothe. 'In the lounge. You know – like the big room at the hotel where we had our honeymoon.'

'You mean there'll be other folks there?'

'I hope so,' he said. 'You're looking that bonny. Other fellers deserves a treat an' all.'

'I don't think I can do it,' she said.

'Of course you can,' he said. 'All you'll have to do is sit there and have a drink of something.'

'Drink of what?' The panic intensified.

'Whatever you like,' he said. But even that terrified her. Suppose she made the wrong choice? It was a relief when Frank Metcalf came up and asked to see their tickets, with just a shade of condescension. Frank had the rank of inspector now, and inspectors were a cut above shipyard fitters. Anyway Andy had his tickets and that made him a paying customer, and he wasn't taking any nonsense from Frank, who retreated to harass the other passengers.

'Cheek,' said Norah, feeling better at once, but the panic returned as they went through the revolving doors of the hotel.

'He's a nice feller,' Andy said. 'Honest. He won't eat you.' By the look on her face Norah wasn't so sure.

Jane was waiting by the desk and went to Norah at once to kiss her. Brass all over the shop, Norah thought, and a lot of it could have done with a good polish. Then she drew in her breath and her head came up. She'd seen enough photographs of Lovell to spot him at once. He rose to his feet as they came towards him.

'Darling,' said Jane, 'this is Norah.'

His hand came out at once. 'How do you do?' he said.

'How do you do?' said Norah. To save her life she couldn't have said, 'Pleased to meet you.'

He was wearing tweeds of a cut so elegant they must have been made in London: handmade, like his shoes, and his shirt as well, probably. Stripy tie, real silk, and a watch that looked like gold because it was gold. Just what he stood up in could have bought their flat and all its contents. Downstairs as well, probably.

'You remember Andy of course?' said Jane.

'How could I ever forget him,' said Lovell, and turned to Norah.

377

'I thought I was used to hard work, but that husband of yours nearly killed me getting ready for the march.'

Norah looked at Andy in horror, but he was smiling, and so, more importantly, was Jane.

Charles offered a hand. 'How are you, Andy?' he said.

'Better than I was,' said Andy. 'Thanks to you.'

'They're working you hard?' said Lovell.

'All the overtime I want,' Andy said, then looked at Norah and smiled. 'And some I don't.'

'The Mexicans are in a hurry for once,' said Lovell, and beckoned to a waiter. Like a greyhound out of a trap, thought Norah. Polite, gentle, soft-spoken, but one wave from him and waiters came running.

'What'll it be?' said Lovell.

He was looking at Norah, but it was Jane who answered.

'I'm driving,' she said, 'so I think I'd better have lemonade. Care to join me, Norah?'

'Oh yes please,' said Norah.

'Beer, please,' said Andy.

'Only bottled, sir,' said the waiter, despising him.

'Bass?' said Lovell. 'That all right with you?' Andy nodded. 'Make that two bottles.' The waiter went off, not so much horrified as bewildered.

'You driven far?' said Andy.

'Derwent Castle,' said Jane. 'Georgie's engagement party. Rather pompous, but it had its moments.' Could the tweeded god be blushing, Norah wondered.

'Georgie sends you her best,' she said to Andy, 'and congratulations to you both.'

'Georgie?' said Norah.

'Georgina Payne,' said Jane.

'The film star?' Norah's voice was a squeak.

'Not for much longer,' Lovell said, 'now that she's joining the aristocracy.'

'You know her?' she said to Lovell.

'She's by way of being a chum of mine,' said Jane.

'Oh yes of course. Andy told me, but – '

But how could you be a chum of a film star? They live in light and we watch them from the dark. The waiter brought their drinks.

'Georgina Payne,' said Norah. 'Well I'm blest.'

'As a matter of fact she used to work for Charles,' said Jane, and the waiter almost dropped his tray.

'Well in a manner of speaking,' said Charles. 'My bank has rather a large holding in World Wide films, and of course Georgie was under contract to World Wide, so I suppose you could say she worked for me.'

'What's she like?'

'Georgie?' Lovell looked to Jane, but she was already deep in conversation with Andy, their chairs pulled away from his and Norah's.

'In many ways she's rather a darling,' he said, 'though mind you she's got the devil of a temper when she's roused.'

'But she's always so nice in her pictures,' Norah said.

'She's a good actress,' said Lovell, 'which isn't to say she's not nice in real life most of the time. She did a day's walk on that Hunger March I was teasing Andy about, *and* sang to the crowd in Trafalgar Square. Surely he must have told you?'

'Well yes,' said Norah. 'But a film star . . . I mean this is real life, and Andy's met her!'

'Maybe you will one day,' said Lovell.

'Me? How could I?'

'You've met Jane.'

'Jane's different,' said Norah, and Lovell smiled at her.

'I think that too,' he said.

'We had no trouble finding your friend Mendel,' said Jane, and passed over a sheet of paper. 'Name, address, telephone number, all there.'

'Thanks,' Andy said.

'Not badly hurt either,' said Jane. 'Just a bang on the head. He's fit and well and back to work. The only thing is he's not sure whether it was the blackshirts or the police.'

'Either way it's bad.'

'Yes of course, but you can't blame him for wondering about it, can you? As for our friend Burrowes, he gave poor Mr Pinner a devil of a time, and Mr Pinner is nobody's fool, believe me.'

'I remember,' Andy said.

'The thing is Burrowes has friends in all sorts of places,' said Jane. 'I suppose he's bound to, since among other things he's the male equivalent of a poule de luxe.' Andy looked bewildered. 'Sort of a high class tart,' she explained, and Andy winced. If only the rich wouldn't say things like that straight out.

'In many ways the little swine lives a fairly open life,' Jane said. 'Acts as if discretion's a word he'd never heard of. But only up to a point. After that whatever path Mr Pinner followed turned out to be a dead end. We've no proof of what he is now – politically speaking, and before we could get any Mr Pinner was warned off.'

'Who by?'

'He didn't want to say,' said Jane, 'and I saw no reason to press him, but it was somebody important, I gather.'

'Somebody connected with the government?'

'I should think so.'

She lit her cigarette. 'So it seems we've learned nothing, but at least we've confirmed what we know: that he has powerful friends, that he at least pretends to be a Fascist, and that he's still a Communist.'

'And there's nothing I can do about it.'

'Not a thing.' To be less than matter of fact would be to hurt him even more. 'His friends are very powerful indeed, Mr Pinner says.'

'So I'll never be an MP?'

'Not unless circumstances change,' she said, 'but they often do, you know. There was a time when I thought I'd never get married – any more than you did.'

He smiled. 'At least there's that,' he said.

'I think that's it,' she said, 'unless you have any more questions.' He shook his head. 'Then I must have a word with Norah.' She called out to her, 'Norah, darling. Do come and sit by me. We haven't gossiped at all.'

Norah and Andy changed places.

'I like your chap,' said Norah. 'Before I met him I was terrified, but that was daft. He's really nice.'

'Well I think so,' said Jane. 'What did you talk about?'

'You and Andy mostly,' Norah said, 'and Georgina Payne.' She hesitated. 'Andy took a knock,' she said. 'You know that.'

'About being an MP? He told me on the phone.'

'It was me made him do it.'

'I'm glad you did. I'm only sorry I couldn't help him – though I did try.'

'Well of course you did,' said Norah, 'but that Burrowes – he was too much, even for you.' The thought seemed to be as appalling as it was incredible, but then she recovered. 'Anyway there'll be something to take his mind off it before long.'

'You're pregnant?'

'I think so,' Norah said, and rapped her knuckles on the arm of her chair. 'It won't be long before I'm sure.'

'Does Andy know?'

'When I'm sure,' said Norah, 'if you don't mind.' Jane winked at her, and Norah giggled. 'That Bob,' she said.

'What about him?'

'All that money, just to bring another Patterson into the world.'

'The world can't have enough Pattersons.'

'Well you would say that,' said Norah, 'seeing you were nearly one yourself.' Then she looked at Charles Lovell, deep in conversation with Andy. 'Oh I'm sorry,' she said. 'I didn't mean – '

'Of course you didn't,' said Jane. 'It's true. And darling – if there's anything I can do – about the baby I mean – '

'No,' Norah said. 'Thanks, Jane, but this one'll be all right. I've got a feeling.'

'Just remember the offer's there,' said Jane. 'Don't ever suffer in silence when you can come to me. I'm nearly a Patterson, remember. You said so yourself.' She waited for a moment, then asked: 'How's my god-daughter?'

'Young Jane? She gets prettier by the day,' said Norah. 'And that furtherly.' Jane looked puzzled. 'You know. Advanced.'

'I'm glad,' said Jane. 'I'd hoped to see her while I was here, but Charles is in rather a rush – '

'Perhaps next time,' said Norah.

'Goodness I hope so.'

'I love your ring,' said Norah. 'Real Hollywood.'

Changing the subject, thought Jane, and oh so tactfully. The Pattersons always did take care of their own.

*

For the tenth time Bob went over his figures. It was part compulsion, part relief, but he did it anyway because he had to. Lovell was right. They were there, he thought. If Sybil co-operates. I can send Annabel that telegram and tell her she's rich. And why shouldn't Sybil co-operate? She'd like to be rich, too. Or richer, in her case. So would he, come to that. He yawned and stretched. An early night, he thought. You're knackered, man. That's what work does for you. Sex never takes you like that. The doorbell rang and he put the note book with the figures into a drawer and locked it. – The friends he had, each one nosier than the last. – The doorbell rang again and he went to answer. Sybil stood there and smiled at him. Talking of sex . . .

'I was just thinking about you,' he said. 'What a nice surprise.'

She walked past him and into the room. 'All on your own?' she said.

'Want to search the place?'

'No need,' she said. 'I trust you. For now.' She peeled off her gloves. 'I just suddenly thought I simply had to come and see you.'

'You didn't think of phoning first?'

'I thought I'd give you a surprise.' She went to the mirror and removed her hat, and laid it on the table beside her gloves.

'Darling Georgie's party was very dull,' she said, 'but at least we all know now that she's engaged. A sapphire almost as big as darling Jane's diamond. Put them together and they'd have sunk the *Titanic*.'

As she spoke she wriggled to reach the zipper of her dress and pulled it down, elegantly, yet demurely too. Good God, he thought, she's doing a strip.

'What is this?' he said.

'You mean I haven't brought any music?' she said. 'Darling, you must excuse me but it's such ages since we had a chat.'

Slowly, carefully, so as not to spoil her hair, she pulled her petticoat over her head and dropped it on top of her dress.

'You don't mind?' she said. 'Only it's rather warm in here.'

Bra and suspender belt, knickers, silk stockings, high-heeled shoes, and all of a kind Grandma hadn't even known existed.

'I don't mind,' he said. 'Need any help?'

'Certainly not,' she said. 'This is my act.' She pointed to a chair. 'You just sit down there and admire the view.'

One by one the remaining garments were added to the pile: suspenders unclipped, shoes kicked free, bra and knickers slowly, elegantly, removed, before she stretched languorously, a feline, elegant movement, and clasped her hands behind her head to tighten her breasts that were already firm, then turned and walked towards the couch, hips gently swaying, buttocks alternately clenching and unclenching in a kind of slow tick-tock, before lying on the sofa in a pose far more erotic than that of the fat girl in Lovell's office. Where on earth had she learned it all? He began to loosen his tie.

'Get me a drink,' she said.

'A *drink*?'

'We've an awful lot to talk about and I *am* rather thirsty. Any champers?'

There was a bottle in the fridge. He went out and came back to her. She didn't seem to have moved at all.

He poured out two glasses and took one to her. As she took it she reached out with her free hand and ran it down the front of his trousers.

'Goodness me you are in a state,' she said, 'but you'll have to go back to your chair, my poor lamb. Business before pleasure. Isn't that what you business men say?'

'Not always,' he said.

'Well it's what this business woman's saying,' she said. 'Go and sit down.'

He didn't enjoy being bossed about, but it was either that, or take her by force, and he didn't think he'd enjoy raping her either. Besides, this conversation was going to be crucial, and they both knew it. He sat.

'Lane Engineering,' she said. 'Agenda. Item One. Shares in same owned by Sybil Hendry.' She sipped her champagne. It was barmy; it was downright mad. There she lay, as naked and provocatively erotic as she could get, hiding nothing, and there he sat in a state of randiness as painful as it was obvious, and they were going to discuss share options.

'You want them, don't you?'

'At a fair price. Yes,' he said.

'I had a word with my broker when I got back from the North,' she said. 'By the way that silly little cow Catherine Bower's making an absolute idiot of herself with a man called Geoffrey Brent. Not that it's any of your business.'

'Not any more,' he said.

'I do believe you're beginning to get my message.'

'Finish it and we'll find out,' he said.

'At least you go down fighting,' she said. 'That's good.'

As if she were awarding marks out of ten, he thought, and she lifted her glass and sipped once more. Her hand wasn't quite steady, which somehow he took as a tiny victory for himself, his one and only, then a droplet of champagne rolled from the rim of her glass, and on to her right nipple.

'I expect you'd like to lick that off,' she said, 'but I'm afraid you can't.' Then she smiled at him in a kindly sort of way. She took another drink, and this time her hand shook not at all. 'Now here's the offer,' she said. 'I'll give you my shares, hand them over for nothing – provided you accept Item Two on the agenda. Well?'

'Let's hear it,' said Bob.

'That we get married,' she said. 'The shares will be my wedding present to you. You get what you want most in the world, and me as a bonus. A lot of chaps would say I was a pretty generous bonus,' she said, and looked down at her body, but went on without allowing him to comment. 'Well that's just about it,' she said, then, 'No it isn't. There's Any Other Business.'

'Is there any?'

'There has to be,' she told him earnestly. 'Daddy says it's on every agenda. Daddy's not part of the agreement, incidentally. I wouldn't allow him anywhere near you unless you wanted him to be, which I very much doubt. Now AOB – that's your reply to my offer. I'm not going to press you for a reply now. I'm giving you two whole days to think it over. You must admit that's pretty generous of me.'

He made no answer, and she rolled over on her stomach to display the small curve of her buttocks, the elegant length of her legs, then stared at his crotch.

'You know if you don't do something quickly,' she said, 'either your fly buttons are going to burst or you are.'

. 37 .

'There was a chap came looking for you,' said Norah. 'A Jewish chap.'

'Tally man?' Andy asked.

There weren't that many Jews in Felston, and a lot of those there were sold things from door to door – or tried to.

'He didn't look like a tally man,' said Norah. 'Too well dressed for one thing. Not bad looking, for a Jew. Nice clothes. Oh – he left a note for you.'

She took a page torn from a note book down from the mantelpiece with an air of such studied unconcern that he knew at once that she'd read it, and how could he blame her? Some wives steamed open envelopes. Andy opened the folded paper and read.

'Manny Mendel,' he said.

'I thought he looked Jewish,' said Norah.

'I told you about him, remember? The chap that used to be Party Secretary here before he married and went South. Took a belting from the Fascists.'

'Is that what did it?'

'Did what?' Andy asked.

'He had sort of a scar across here,' Norah said, and her hand went to her forehead.

'Likely,' said Andy. 'You know it's funny. He never struck me as much of a fighter.'

'Jews never are,' said Norah, but Andy continued, unheeding.

'More of a thinker. Not a coward, far from it, but more of a thinking man really. He must have changed. He says here he wants to see me.' As well you know, he thought, but there was no sense in hurting her feelings.

'When? You haven't even had your tea yet,' she said.

385

'No rush. He's staying with his mam and dad. They own that big house in Welford Village, the one on the corner.'

Welford Village was the only rich area in Felston, and Norah recognised the house at once. 'They must be posh then,' she said, then – 'Hold on. Is that the Mendels that have the clothes factory on the Trading Estate?'

'That's the ones.'

'Fancy them having a son that's a Socialist.'

'They didn't like it. Probably still don't. But he's married now. Got a steady job. It probably makes a difference.'

'Does he want you to go to Welford Village?'

She was still acting her unconcern, and yet at the same time looking as guilty as a bairn with her hand in the sweetie-jar, and he loved her so much he wanted to kiss her.

'I doubt I'd be welcome there,' he said. 'His mam and dad always reckoned I led Manny astray. It was more him led me as a matter of fact, but try telling them that. No – he says he takes the dog for a walk about nine o'clock at night, and he'll be in the Black Horse by nine thirty.' He looked at the note again. ' "Tonight and tomorrow," he says. After that he has to get back to London.'

'Make it tomorrow,' said Norah. 'I've got a bit of news for you meself.'

When she told him what it was Manny Mendel was forgotten. He seemed to spend the rest of the evening saying 'You're sure?' then hearing Norah say, 'Well of course'. All the same, the following night he went to the Black Horse.

It was a big, noisy, anonymous pub: a barn divided into three sections, saloon, snug, and bar, each erected for one purpose only. The consumption of beer. From time to time a man with a few bob in his pocket might ask for whisky, the sort of woman who used the place might have a port and lemon, but beer was what the Black Horse was for. Barrels of it; a cellar-full in fact.

Andy decided to try the saloon. Its décor was no different from that of the bar – dark green walls, tobacco browned ceiling, deal floors in need of a scrub, but there were tables and chairs, justified by the fact that the beer cost a ha'penny more per glass. Incredibly the only attempt at decoration was an out-of-date calendar. On it

386

was a picture of Georgina Payne dressed as Jane Whitcomb as an ambulance driver. He must remember to tell Norah.

Anyway he'd guessed right, and Manny was already there, a bitter in front of him, and a large and apparently amiable dog for company. He got up at once to shake hands, then buy Andy a beer, and Andy sat warily by the dog. He didn't trust dogs, no matter how amiable their appearance. The dog looked at him and yawned. Manny hadn't changed a bit, he thought, but no, that was daft. Of course he'd changed. He'd acquired a scar for a start, a scar still livid. He'd acquired a kind of smoothness, too. Of course his clothes had always been expensive – they came from his parents – but he'd worn them carelessly: trousers in need of a press; the odd food stain. Now his clothes were clean and smart, and perhaps not quite so expensive as those he'd worn before, though that didn't mean Norah was wrong. They were still far more expensive than what most people wore in Felston. Manny bustled back with the beer, then raised his own glass.

'Good health,' he said. 'It's good to see you again.'

'You too,' said Andy. 'Been in the wars, I see.'

'No more than you in 1926,' said Mendel. They grinned at each other. A couple of class warriors, thought Andy.

'I saw your picture in the paper and I was going to write, but you beat me to it,' Andy said.

'Glad I did,' Mendel said. 'Gave me a chance to meet your lady. You're a lucky man, Andy.'

My lady, Andy thought. That must be the way they talk in London. All the same I like the sound of it, even if my lady's not all that keen on you. She thinks you're trouble, bonny lad, and I wouldn't say she's far wrong either. The difference is I think it's about time we had a bit of trouble.

'Been up to see your parents?' he said.

'That's right. Naturally they were a bit worried when they heard what happened, so I came up to show them I'm still in one piece.'

'Things all right between you?'

'Things are fine,' Mendel said. 'We've got children, you see. Samuel and Leah. And every Jew wants to be a grandparent. Have you – '

'Norah's expecting,' Andy said, 'but it's early days.'

387

Mendel raised his glass. 'Maseltov,' he said.

'Hasn't stopped you being active though,' said Andy. 'I mean being a family man.'

'I should say not,' Mendel said. 'Nothing must. You've got only one thing to worry about – the class struggle. But I've got being a Jew to worry about as well.' He leaned across the table, lowered his voice. 'We hear things,' he said. 'Out of Germany. Things you wouldn't believe. I find it hard to believe them myself. But if even the half of it is true –' he shrugged. 'I've got to fight. That's all there is. Those blackshirt bastards want to go down the same road as Hitler.'

'I know,' said Andy. 'I was in London a few months back. I saw them in the East End.'

'Did they get you too?'

'No,' Andy said. 'I was lucky.'

A coward more like, but how could he tell Manny that?

'But you were there, that's the point,' said Mendel. 'There saying no. Because it isn't just us Jews, Andy. Not even in Germany. The entire Leftwing Movement's in danger, believe me, and it's going to get worse. If we don't fight, we're finished. Not that I have to tell you. You were always a fighter.' He took a pull at his beer, and suddenly his mood changed: the vitality, the passionate belief, faded and died. 'I hear you're a councillor now.'

'Better than nowt.'

'Oh yes. A lot better.' Mendel had sensed the bitterness in his voice. 'But wasn't there talk of you being an MP as well?'

'Who in the world told you that?'

'It was after Jimmy Wagstaff had his picture taken,' Mendel said. 'Falling down drunk and waving a bottle of whisky at the camera, you remember?' Andy nodded. 'Some comrades were having a drink with me and one of them knew Felston and asked me who your next MP would be. I said it ought to be you.'

'Go on,' said Andy.

'So another comrade said weren't you the one that went to prison as a conscientious objector and led the Felston Hunger March and I told him yes. That's all.'

'I don't think so,' Andy said. 'Let's hear the rest of it.'

'Andy,' said Mendel, 'it was just chaps having a drink and a chat.'

'You didn't say "Isn't there talk of you being an MP?" You said, "Wasn't there talk",' Andy said. 'Like you knew the talk was over.' Mendel sat silent, and Andy leaned towards him.

'Never mind worrying about my feelings,' he said. 'I have to know.'

'You can pick up a nuance so fast,' said Mendel. 'Like a lawyer. I should have remembered, watched my tongue.'

'Just tell me,' Andy said.

'The comrade who'd heard about you said you hadn't a hope of getting the nomination round here because you were – '

'A homo?'

Mendel nodded. 'You'd already heard then?' he sounded relieved.

'Did he say where he'd heard it?'

'I asked him,' Mendel said, 'but he wouldn't tell me. All he said was he was glad to hear it was nothing but talk.'

'Well so it is,' said Andy, 'but they believe it round here.'

'Dear God,' said Mendel, and the dog looked up as if surprised to hear the young master swear. 'You mean you don't think you'll get the nomination?'

'I know I won't,' Andy said.

'No chance at all?'

'Snowball in hell,' said Andy, and went off to fetch two more beers.

After that it was just remembering the old days: Saturday night speeches in the market place and the Sally Ann for opposition. Stuff like that, and pleasant enough the memory of the time when they'd worked together, shared the same hopes and plans, but that was all it was. Andy had the feeling that he'd been – not judged exactly. If Manny had thought he was a traitor to his class he'd have got up and left at once – assessed, that was it. Weighed in the balance; and the balance had said there wasn't enough in Andy Patterson to be the slightest use to Manny Mendel, because rightly or wrongly Andy had got the idea that Manny was recruiting, looking out for men with a bit of weight behind them, men who could do things, and Andy wasn't one of them.

'You're saying that it happened exactly as you told it?' said Lovell.

'I am,' said Bob.

389

He'd had to tell somebody, and there wasn't time to go up North and talk to Andy. Not that there would have been any point. Andy would have understood the situation even less than he did. That left Lovell: there was no one else, and anyway not only did Lovell have far more sense than most, he was also involved, and so Bob had invited him to lunch at l'Apéritif. He couldn't face Lovell's office with a naked woman on the wall.

'It's the most extraordinary thing I ever heard,' said Lovell.

'All of that,' said Bob, and grinned. 'Painful, too.'

'And she was good at it you say?'

'You could have charged a guinea a seat and packed the place out.'

'Well I'm damned,' said Lovell.

All very well for you, thought Bob, but I'm not forking out for asparagus and Dover sole and Pouilly Fuissé just so you can be amazed. What I want from you is a little serious thinking.

Lovell wiped his mouth on his napkin and sipped his wine. 'Of course the situation's obvious – but that doesn't necessarily mean it'll be easier for you.'

His face took on a kindly look, which at once recalled the look on Sybil's face when she said he couldn't lick the champagne from her nipple.

'I'm afraid she's got you.'

'By the balls, you mean?'

'Almost literally.' Really, Lovell thought, much more of this and I'll be giggling like a schoolboy, but it really is the most extraordinary – he forced his mind back to rational thought.

'It's a straightforward yes or no,' he said. 'Surely you can see that?'

'She's a lovely girl and all that,' said Bob, 'but she was still pointing a pistol at me.'

'Exactly so.'

'Either I marry her and I get the shares, or I don't and we're out of business.'

'I take it you're reducing this to its most basic terms in the hope that I'll produce some complication, some nuance – that will enable you to escape?' Again the kindly look. 'But I can't, old chap. There isn't one. Either you do what she wants, or the business goes to

Crawley. You can be sure that McIntosh told her that, too, just as you can be sure she'll sell to Crawley if you turn her down. Get a damn good price, too.'

'You think she'd do that?'

'Bob,' said Lovell, 'she made you the most extravagant gesture I've ever heard of from woman to man. If you turn her down she'll want revenge. Any woman would. – And for revenge, Crawley's the perfect instrument. I'm only surprised she gave you two days' grace. Most women would have demanded an answer at once.'

'Say yes or I'll pull the trigger?'

'Just that. It has to be your move,' Lovell said gently. 'As opposed to ours, I mean. In the first place she doesn't want to marry me – '

Aren't you the lucky one? thought Bob.

'In the second place I couldn't marry her even if she did, and in the third place I shan't lose by it if we lose Lane's Engineering.'

'Whereas I'll lose a packet.'

'Let me just say this,' said Lovell. 'If you say no to her I shall continue to support you. Patterson's Wireless Rentals is a damn good business and I'll stay with it till you're ready to buy me out. – And I don't have to tell you this has nothing to do with sentiment. You were born to make money Bob, and I want some of it, otherwise I wouldn't be sitting here now.'

'Thanks,' said Bob. 'Thanks very much.' It was what he had hoped for, (despite the 'I want some of it') but it was good to hear it said.

'This is the daftest question I'm ever going to ask,' said Bob, 'and I know it, but I'm going to ask it anyway.'

'You mean what would I do in your place?'

'That's the one.'

'Quite impossible to answer,' said Lovell. 'Believe me I don't say that because I don't want to answer it, but because I can't. To begin with I don't have the ineradicable objection to married life you seem to have.'

'Sybil isn't Jane,' said Bob.

Lovell smiled his pleasure. 'I'm a lucky man, certainly,' he said, 'but it's possible that you might be, too.'

'I'm good at women,' said Bob. 'Always have been. Ever since I was old enough to do something about it.'

' "Good at women",' Lovell quoted. 'You say that as a man might say "Good at sums" or "Good at fretwork".'

'But that's about it,' said Bob. 'What I'm good at is starting a love affaire, and ending it. *And* the bit in between. All right. I'm a sprinter if you like. I'd never do for the marathon.'

'Isn't that –' for a moment Lovell hesitated, but then he ploughed on. It had to be said. 'Isn't that a rather adolescent view?'

'Well of course it is,' said Bob, 'but with women I enjoy being an adolescent. I'm only grown up when it comes to making money.'

'So we're back where we started,' said Lovell

'Either or?'

'Whichever choice you make you're bound to lose as well as win.'

Bob signalled to the sommelier. He felt he deserved a brandy. He had made the right choice. This was his world all right. Elegant. Delightful. Rich . . . And now this.

'She told me once,' said Bob, 'at the beginning of the affaire, that she didn't consider us to be tied to each other. Either her to me or me to her.'

'Well then – '

'That was when we were just seeing each other now and again. When I wasn't making deals, and she wasn't in Paris being measured by Vionnet.'

'You think your married life would be different?'

'I bloody know it would,' said Bob. 'Where do you think you've been till this time of night? You spent far too long talking to that overdressed blonde in the corner . . . . She'd time me with a stop watch, that one. And you see why, don't you?'

'I'm afraid I do,' said Lovell. 'Because she's bought you.'

'With eight thousand shares of Lane Engineering Preferred.'

Lovell looked at his watch. 'I'm sorry,' he said, 'honestly I am, but I have to go.' Bob signalled for the bill as Lovell asked, 'You haven't decided yet, have you?'

'Not yet.'

'You'll let me know when you have?'

'You'll be the first to know,' said Bob. 'Well the second anyway.'

'Needless to say this is all completely confidential.'

'Just keep it in the family,' said Bob.

392

. 38 .

They met in the Mount Street flat. Nowadays, as a respectable, engaged couple they tended to spend most of their free time in the drawing room in South Terrace, kissing, cuddling, listening to the wireless, but for what he had to tell her somewhere far more abandoned seemed to be required, and Mount Street was as abandoned as anywhere in London so far as they were concerned. She heard him out in silence, and when he had done, said: 'But surely you can't be serious?' then almost at once added, 'No of course you are. Why would anyone make up such a story?'

'I said much the same thing when I first heard it,' said Charles. 'It's true all right. If you'd seen Bob's face you'd believe every word.'

'Bob,' she said, and then: 'Ought you to be telling me this, do you think?'

' "Keep it in the family",' he said.

'But why even hint that you could tell me?'

'Because you're the only one left who may have the answer to his problem.'

'But there isn't one.'

'Exactly,' said Charles. 'Poor chap.'

'Speaking on behalf of God knows how many of my fellow females, I'm not too sure about the "poor",' said Jane. 'All the same I must say I take your point about the loaded pistol.' She nestled against him, her head on his shoulder. 'I must say this makes a change from Henry Hall on the wireless.'

His arm squeezed her waist. 'What do you think he'll do?' he asked.

'Blest if I know. You told him you'd still support him?' He nodded. 'But even that cuts both ways. He may look on it as just one more debt.'

'Not if he's got any sense,' said Charles. 'He knows I'm not out to destroy him.'

'I should have said obligation,' said Jane. 'He doesn't like obligations – any more than you do.'

'Damn,' said Charles, and then: 'But how could I not say it? I had to let him know I'd support him.'

'So she had you in a cleft stick too,' said Jane. 'What an enterprising young lady she is to be sure.' He was peaceful beside her on the sofa, his arm about her, and very nice it was, and be damned to Sybil Hendry. All the same she had to know.

'Tell me,' she said, 'has anyone ever done that to you?'

'Take all their clothes off and then ask me to marry them?'

'No, silly,' she said. 'Do a what's it called? – Strip tease – Good word for it by the way – especially in dear Sybil's case.'

'Not once,' he said. He sounded relieved, but was there not a hint of regret, too? After all Charles was a rich man, an *extremely* rich man: a natural target for pretty and predatory females.

'Do you wish it had?' she said.

'After I saw the effect it had on Patterson, no I do not,' he said.

'Put it this way,' she said. 'Do you wish I'd ever done it for you?' She was going to add 'I would you know, if you wanted me to', but he answered her too quickly.

'Of course not,' he said.

'I don't know whether I should be flattered or not.'

'You should be,' he said. 'Look. A woman would do that for one of two reasons, or perhaps both of them. Either because she's good at it, or because it makes a man want her. I'm not saying you wouldn't be good at it, but why should you bother? I want you anyway.

'What I mean is – for me – I don't need that, any more than I need music by Debussy or the Rokeby Venus or Spanish fly for that matter. I've got *you*, and you can do all that just by being where you are now. A laugh, a look, that's all it needs.' He turned to look at her. 'As well you know.' She chuckled. 'You see?' he said.

'Yes, but – about Bob,' she said. 'Do you think he will?'

'Marry her? Six to four he will.'

My favourite odds, he thought, but so many reasons to edge towards even money, and what tilts the balance is usually instinct.

'I hope he'll be happy,' said Jane. ' – If we're right, that is. But somehow I doubt it.'

'He does too.'

'And who can blame him? Remember her at Georgie's party – swarming all over Roddy Derwent. And that extraordinary business with the peach on the end of the fruit knife? And now all this Mata Hari stuff.'

'Sally Rand,' said Charles. 'Or was it Gipsy Rose Lee? She was the one in the States who was always being arrested.'

'That's right,' said Jane. 'I remember. She was forever in the papers – complete with picture, half way through her act. But that was just for money. It may not have been very moral, but at least it made sense. Don't you agree? But the delectable Mrs Hendry – why on earth should she?'

'To go after Bob.'

'She could have done that with her clothes on.'

'Certainly,' said Charles, 'but if you could have seen the poor chap. He was still crushed. My guess is she wants to keep him that way.'

'Poor Bob,' she said, and then, 'Do you know, I never thought I'd utter those words? . . . Poor Bob. Either way he loses.' She leaned closer to him. 'It's wicked of me to ask, but I'm dying to know. . . . After all the Salome stuff did she – did they – ?'

'I don't know,' said Charles. 'He didn't tell me, and I couldn't possibly ask, but my guess is not.'

'The bitch,' said Jane.

'She wanted him in pain,' he said, 'and he was in pain. Why make it better?'

The telephone rang and he went to it. 'Lovell,' he said, and then, 'Yes, yes, I see. . . . Did she now? . . . Jolly good . . . let's talk tomorrow.' He hung up and came back to her. 'Six to four it was,' he said.

'He's proposed?'

'And been accepted. . . . Six to four she's ended his pain, too.'

'She's still a bitch,' said Jane. 'Let's go to bed. All this rude talk is making me randy. As you say – like looking at dirty pictures.'

'I'd hardly have called Velasquez a pornographer,' said Charles.

'Never mind Velasquez. It's you that's going to do the work.' On the way to the bedroom she said, 'I'm glad we met here. After what you had to tell me it would have been disaster if Truett had listened at the keyhole.'

Being out of things wasn't as bad as he thought it would be. To begin with Joe Turnbull and his pals had managed to put the lid on all that gossip about him – keep it in the cadre so to speak. All they wanted was sweetness and light while they set up Joe's cousin for the nomination. Martin Lowe his name was – and less of the Marty, thank you very much. Comrade Lowe wasn't going the same road as Jimmy Wagstaff – falling down drunk and waving a bottle. Comrade Lowe might be younger in years but he had dignity, judgement and – what was the Cambridge word? – gravitas. Comrade Lowe was already trying to be statesmanlike, and he wasn't even elected yet. And that's enough of that, Andy told himself. You'd have been the same in his shoes.

He'd gone to hear him speak. Not bad. Not bad at all. A bit light on the jokes, and not exactly a dab hand at knocking the Tories, but good on the New Jerusalem stuff, Together We Shall Build The Promised Land. Well so we shall, he thought, and if I'm a good bairn and do as I'm told they'll let me in an' all. Again he reminded himself that things weren't so bad. His body had toughened up nicely, he was fitter than he'd been in years, and Dr Stobbs could foresee no complications in Norah's pregnancy. Blessings counted, in fact, and Norah had made him corned-beef sandwiches the way he liked them, with tomato and mustard, and he could sit in the sunshine with his back to the wall of the fettling shop and think in peace. Chaps didn't come badgering him with their bit problems: not any more. He'd be due for re-election to the council soon – Joe Turnbull's lot would probably let him go that far – but he wasn't going to bother. It wasn't sulking: he just didn't care.

A charge-hand came up to him. Charge-hands had no business being on the prowl in the dinner hour, but then charge-hands never stopped being on the prowl.

'You're wanted on the telephone,' the charge-hand said. 'Yard Office. You'd better look sharp. It's Mr Lovell.'

Coming from him the tone at least was polite, even if the words weren't. . . .

'Andy Patterson here.'

396

'Nice to hear you,' Lovell said. 'How's the work going?'

'Bang on schedule.'

'That's good news.' Lovell hesitated. 'Are you alone?'

'I am,' Andy said. 'It's the dinner hour. They're all outside getting a bit of sun.'

'Yes,' Lovell said. 'Bob said they would be.'

'Bob?'

'He wants a word,' said Lovell. 'He's got a bit of news for you as it happens. He wanted to write, but as it's important I said he should phone. I'll put him on.'

'Hallo?' said Bob.

'What on earth's happening?' said Andy. 'Are you all right?'

'Never better,' said Bob, though he didn't sound it. 'Just thought I'd better let you know I'm engaged to be married.'

'You never,' said Andy, delighted. 'Who's the lucky lady? Do I know her?'

'You met her once – at my flat. Sybil Hendry.'

A dark, fiercely pretty girl in green. Quick temper by the look of her, but a lot of style. Rich, too, unless Bob had paid for the clothes.

'I thought she was Mrs Hendry,' said Andy.

'She's a widow.'

Three hundred miles apart both brothers were remembering their father, and his unshakeable belief that one partner was your ration, and when your spouse died you just had to manage without. The greatest crime Frank Metcalf had committed was to be a widower when he married Bet.

'When's the wedding?' Andy asked.

'Give us a chance, man,' said Bob. 'I've only just got engaged.'

'Can I tell Norah?'

'Go ahead. And Bet. It'll be in the *Felston Echo* soon enough.'

'Well – congratulations,' Andy said, and very nearly added good luck. But you don't wish a chap that, not when he's just got engaged. He's supposed to have it. Andy looked at the clock on the wall.

'I'll have to go now,' he said. 'It's nearly knocking-on time. Wish your lady well for me and Norah.'

'Is she well?'

'Champion,' Andy said. 'Give my best to Charles and Jane.'

'Will do,' said Bob. 'Ta-ra, bonny lad. Take care of yourself.'

Andy hung up and went to the dock-office window to watch a group of apprentices playing football on the waste ground by the slipway. Young and daft and eating regular. Not a care in the world. Bob was the one finding out about care, to judge by the sound of him. What on earth had made him do it? Suddenly Andy longed for the afternoon to be over, so that he could go home and tell Norah.

Charles Lovell said, 'Was he surprised?'

'Amazed,' said Bob. 'Like everybody else. Only he hid it better than most.'

'You're sure you can go through with it?' Lovell said. 'I mean – the longer you go on with this engagement, the harder it will be to break it.'

Bob looked at the naked fat girl. Far too much of her, but all in the right places.

'It's too late now,' he said. 'I've said I will and I meant it.'

'She's given you the shares?'

What a shrewd bugger you are, thought Bob.

'Handed them over as soon as I proposed,' said Bob.

Did she have any clothes on at the time? Lovell wondered, then thought really these prurient speculations are disgraceful. All the same –

'That was clever of her,' he said. 'She's obviously decided that you're the sort of man who abides by a contract. After all you could have got a deed of gift for the shares then reneged on the marriage. She took the gamble that you wouldn't – and it worked.'

'Like you say, I don't work like that,' said Bob, 'and anyway I don't think it would have been a good idea. Not with her.'

'Why her particularly?'

'She doesn't like being cheated, any more than I do.'

Lovell left it at that. Bob's opinions on women were always those of the expert.

'She asked me a funny thing,' said Bob. 'Would I feel any better if she sent her father to live abroad somewhere? Not France, she said. Somewhere where there weren't any casinos.'

'Could she do that?'

'She has the money,' said Bob.

'Might as well make the poor devil join the Foreign Legion and have done with it.'

. 39 .

Jane decided on a West Highland terrier. To get another Scottie would inevitably lead to comparisons with Foch, almost certainly to the other Scottie's disadvantage, whereas a Westie looked sufficiently different to be accepted on his own merits, whatever they might prove to be. Moreover tactful enquiry had elicited that both Truett and Mrs Barrow quite liked the idea of a Westie, and as they would have a large share in its welfare it would be best if they were on the Westie's side. She made an appointment to see the vet in Fulham who had looked after Foch, and explained her needs, and learned without surprise that he knew just the dog. With human beings Mr McPhee could be, and usually was, tongue tied and gauche, but with dogs he was as sound as Bob on women.

The dog he produced proved to be a charmer. A perfect little gentleman by the look of him, but by no means lacking in courage, despite the fact that he had had what Mr McPhee delicately referred to as 'the operation'. So much better for London dogs, unless you want them to breed. His hair was white just tinged with silver, and with a longer curl to it than Foch's: a cavalier, one might say, to Foch's Roundhead. Black button eyes might well have echoed Foch, except that this chap's were milder; far less censorious. And that too is just as well, she thought. I've reached the age when a confidant is what I want: not a Calvinistic confessor.

'But he's just about perfect,' she said.

'Well no,' said McPhee. 'Not quite that. He's a little too big for absolute purity.'

Somehow she contrived to remain grave, unsmiling: but it was a judgement she would cherish for the rest of her life.

There remained the delicate question of price. Somewhere in her mind there lurked the picture of this innocent charmer as the idol of a family of children, whose parents, fallen on hard times, unable to feed him, had been obliged to put him on the auction block for whatever he would fetch. Mr McPhee disabused her.

'Dogs' Home,' he said. 'One I do a little work for from time to time. He was picked up as a stray. A guinea would suit them nicely.'

She gave rather more. Mr McPhee's work for a Dogs' Home, she was quite sure, would be of the unpaid variety.

'Does he have a name?' she asked.

'At the home they called him "Mac",' said Mr McPhee. Neither he nor the Westie seemed to find the name appropriate.

She drove him back to South Terrace in the Bentley, which the Westie approved of at once. Really upper class in his way, she thought: definitely one of the nobs. One of the Scottish nobs of ancient lineage, she thought, so much beloved of Sir Walter Scott: not Ivanhoe, and certainly not young Lochinvar – the Westie after all had no need of saddle bows for maidens – but a Scot of breeding none the less. The Marquis of Montrose perhaps, or better still, the knight who had made Edward I's life a misery for so long. Sir William Wallace. 'William!' she said aloud and the Westie barked, aware at once of his identity.

Truett and Mrs Barrow were enslaved at once. Even 'the operation' was in his favour: no embarrassing moments when next door but two's poodle bitch was in heat.

That night Charles dined with her at South Terrace, and William had his first taste of côtelettes réforme.

'I like your dog,' said Charles. 'Gallant little chap.' It was exactly the word she had been looking for.

They were sitting on the drawing-room sofa and his arm was around her waist. William lay on a rug near by, replete.

'Any more news of Bob?' she asked. He told her about the shares.

'You're right,' she said when he had done. 'It *was* a clever move. What a year for marriages.'

But Charles's mind was still on Bob. 'I've told him he should pay her for them,' he said. 'Set up a fund if necessary. Pay by instalments.'

'But surely if they're married – ?'

'Things could still go wrong,' he said. 'If ever a woman was trouble it's Mrs Hendry.' He told Jane about Sybil Hendry's plans for her father.

'Good God,' said Jane.

'Exactly,' said Charles. 'One day she may decide to send Bob off to Fort Zinderneuf too. He'll feel a lot better footslogging across the Sahara if those shares are bought and paid for.'

'How right you are,' said Jane.

The next morning Sybil Hendry phoned. Could she come round? she asked. In fact she was due to lunch with Lionel, but there would be time for a cocktail first.

'Of course,' said Jane.

Sybil Hendry arrived prompt at midday, and William, a gentleman to the tips of his paws, stood up at once.

'What a charming fellow,' Sybil Hendry said, and Jane had no doubt that she meant it. What a bewildering creature she was.

'Name of William,' said Jane. 'The latest member of the household,' she continued as Truett came in with the ice, 'and totally spoiled by the rest of us.' Truett and William pretended not to hear, and Jane began to mix martinis.

'I came to see if you had a list,' Sybil Hendry said.

'List?'

'For wedding presents.'

'No list,' said Jane. 'Whatever you and Bob think we deserve.' She handed Mrs Hendry her glass and raised her own. 'Congratulations by the way.'

'Thank you,' Sybil Hendry said, and smiled the innocent smile of one to whom naked cavortings were unthinkable.

'The thing is we're not exactly setting up house,' said Jane. 'Charles and I both have places to live in.'

'That's our problem, too. I mean there's my flat in town and the house in Northumberland.'

'Not to mention Bob's flat in South Moulton Street.'

'He's giving that up,' said Sybil Hendry, in a voice that made Jane think of prison doors slamming shut.

'Good idea,' she said. 'There's such a thing as too many places to live, especially in this day and age.'

'Exactly,' Sybil Hendry said. 'Service flats are all very well for a

401

bachelor, but not for two people who love each other. They're far too impersonal.'

Jane was doing her best not to stare: to hide the fact that she wondered just how pretty a body there would be beneath the Lanvin suit. Very pretty indeed, she thought. And then: Bob and monogamy. It seemed incredible.

'Bob's been on his own for far too long,' Sybil Hendry said. 'He admits it himself. Until now his life has been nothing but work.' Jane did her best not to gape. 'But now we'll be together,' Sybil Hendry continued. 'Ours won't be one of those so-called modern marriages where people go their own way. We'll be part of a team. Whatever has to be done, we'll do it together.'

'His business?'

'He needs someone to discuss ideas with,' Sybil Hendry said. 'I could do that. Then there's rather a lot of entertaining to be done. You must know that. Well I can take care of that, too.'

'What will happen when he has to go away?' Jane asked.

'I'll go with him.'

'All those dreary places – Wolverhampton? Birmingham? Leeds?'

'It's not Bob's life any more,' Sybil Hendry said. 'It's ours. We share it. Of course I'll go.' The words came out with a snap, as if daring Jane to intervene.

Poor old Bob, Jane thought. His last escape route cut off.

'You see I know all about Bob and those obliging little friends of his. Catherine Bower, Annabel Lane, that actress Sarah something *and* that dancer. Tiger Lily. All of them – although I'm not absolutely certain about Georgina Payne.' She brooded on that for a moment. 'I don't mind telling you because you never were – were you? One of his friends, I mean?'

Jane said gently, 'I was Bob's brother's girl.'

'So you were. The one who was killed. He was in Daddy's brigade or division or whatever it was. Do you know I thought Daddy might turn out to be a problem, only I've solved it. I've solved Bob too, as a matter of fact.'

'Have you?' said Jane, startled.

Sybil Hendry said brightly, 'I've bought him.'

'Cash on the barrel.' It was a foolish thing to say, but Mrs Hendry did tend to make one blunt.

402

'I don't think I quite understand that.'

'It's what the Americans say when they pay for something outright,' said Jane.

'Well that's what I did, only it wasn't cash exactly, but as good as. I'm afraid I can't give you more details because I promised not to – no matter who it was.'

'No reason why you should,' said Jane.

The bright, aggressive manner faded, and Sybil Hendry smiled. She had a particularly charming smile when she chose to use it, thought Jane.

'How I do run on,' Sybil Hendry said. 'Chatter chatter. It's probably having Bob all to myself at last.'

'I wish you very happy,' said Jane.

'Oh I will be,' Sybil Hendry said, and added almost as an afterthought: 'Bob too.' She finished her martini and rose. William rose too.

'He is a nice dog,' Sybil Hendry said. 'I think I'll get Bob one. Something bigger, but well mannered like yours. Well ... I mustn't keep you from your lunch.'

There was no doubt about it, thought Jane. At best pretty little Mrs Hendry was barely sane.

. 40 .

The king got better, then worse again after he had celebrated his Silver Jubilee, 'the biggest and best-humoured party London ever threw', Bower wrote in his *Daily World* editorial, and not a bad description, thought Jane. Street parties and processions, flags and bunting, a mug of sweets for every child in the country, the jingling splendour of the Blues and Royals, and in the midst of it all, a man, old, bearded, tired, his wife beside him, in a coach more fitted for Cinderella, bewildered by the fact that his people loved him. That they did was obvious by the shouts that arose whenever he and the queen appeared.

Somehow Jane and Charles contrived to get married, which had turned out to be by no means an easy thing to do. The major had been unwell – 'heart' was all her mother would say – and as the major had longed to give her away, she and Charles had to wait until the major was well enough to do so. Then Charles had managed to irritate all his male relatives at once by asking Ned to be best man, and Ned had agreed, provided Charles would do the same for him. Georgie called it the suicide pact. But at last the day dawned.

She had not chosen one of the grand and fashionable churches. No St George's Hanover Square, or anything like it. Georgie would have to put up with it, but then Georgie, used to a supporting cast of thousands, might even have insisted on it. Jane chose St Thomas's, the little Victorian church close to her first London home, the one from which her father had been buried, a church so small that the fifty-odd people she and Charles had invited might be described as a swelling throng. Charles would have liked something even smaller, like a registry office, but Jane would have none of it. Apart from the fact that her mother would

404

never forgive her, she would never forgive herself.

In fact the church looked delightful, as Lionel said, in a Burne-Jones sort of way. Lionel had got up at what he called dawn to do the flowers, then later changed into the most perfectly cut morning coat Jane had ever seen, and was briskly efficient as usher, leaving Ned with nothing to do except worry about his speech. Jane's one regret was that Canon Messeter would not perform the ceremony, and it was Charles's, too.

The dress was about as close to perfection as one could get, which, given Schiaparelli's prices, was only fair, and her bouquet of red and cream roses complemented it perfectly. Truett, Brown and Mrs Barrow oohed and aahed in ecstasies, then dashed for the taxi that would take them to the church before the major arrived in the liner on wheels to collect her. Georgie was her only bridesmaid, looking almost demure in pink. Georgie hated pink, as Jane well knew, but she'd insisted that it was the only colour to complement Jane's dress. What she meant was that on this day of all days, she would play a supporting rôle, and given her temperament Jane called that pretty handsome of her.

'No time for a quick one?' she said.

'None,' said Jane. 'By the time I'd mixed it the major will arrive, and then we'd have to offer him one, and then he'd start remembering the Punjab in 1917. By the time I finally reeled down the aisle Charles would be married to someone else.'

'Bunty Fairweather no doubt,' said Georgie. 'I do hope the major's going to be well enough to waltz with me again.'

'He's been talking of nothing else for days, Mummy says. I hope he behaves himself.'

'Oh beautifully,' said Georgie.

'He'll be off to his club first chance he gets,' said Jane. 'Swanking like mad.' She smiled. 'Bless him,' she said.

'Is he very bad?'

'Mummy won't say,' said Jane, 'which makes me rather think he is.'

The Rolls-Royce tooted its very superior horn and the two women rose.

'I know it's expected,' said Jane, 'but I mustn't cry. There isn't time to renew my make-up.'

405

'Darling,' said Georgie, embracing her, 'you look positively edible. Go out there and knock 'em in the aisles.' She let Jane go and straightened her dress. 'You'll enjoy being Mrs Charles Lovell, won't you?' she said.

'Not arf,' said Jane.

As she walked down the aisle on the major's arm, Georgie decorously behind her, she looked anxiously for Francis, but he was there, beside her mother where he should be, and not, to her intense relief, in Vine Street police station. Moreover there was no sign of Burrowes. The happiest day of her life indeed. Then as she drew level, her mother turned, looked at her and smiled, and her eye closed and opened in a wink as quick as a lizard's blink, as Jane moved on to where Charles was waiting. Her rifleman, the major had called him, and a good thing too, he'd said. Jane was far too good for the Guards.

Another rifleman to pass first. Piers with his sister beside him. No sign of Annabel Lane or Geoffrey Brent. She had insisted on a tactful wedding, and Charles had agreed. No sign of Jay Bower either. Another conference in Switzerland. More tact. Her old ambulance-driving chum Harriet Watson was there though, and with her husband. Now there was a novelty. They were the ones who had first introduced her to Charles. All the other drivers were there too, the countess and Fred, the lesbian, and 'that actress Sarah'. Mercifully on the other side of the church Bob was with Sybil Hendry, complete with engagement ring. Emeralds. Just the thing when one wore so much green – if one wore anything at all. Now now, she admonished herself, remember you're in church; and then she reached Charles's side and the vicar began the service. 'Dearly beloved, we are gathered here together in the sight of God and of each other. . . .' He did it well, but then so he should: he and Georgie were the only pros in the building. On and on majestically (those bishops of more than three hundred years ago had been incapable of putting a foot wrong), until the final 'Whom God hath joined together let no man put asunder', and she was Mrs Charles Lovell at last.

Then Mendelssohn, more cheerful and far louder than Wagner, and the vestry, and the register to sign, and her mother and the major determined to be witnesses, as well as Georgie and Ned, though Francis had somehow managed to curb his ardour and stayed inside the church, which was odd when you came to think about it, since, like Marx, he saw religion as the opium of the masses. Best not to think about it. Better, far better, to go to the reception.

Here Lionel had rather spread himself. Since Charles was paying, and his wealth was vast, Lionel had avoided the obvious choices, the Savoy, the Dorchester, the Ritz, and settled for a suite of rooms in Chelsea and every caterer whose food he'd ever enjoyed, including a couple from Paris. Once again in his element, once again bossing everybody in sight, he made the party go. Jane and Charles stood at the door and received their guests, with time for no more than a greeting and 'How good of you to come' before the guests passed through to where the champagne was waiting. Later, after Lionel's delicious food, there would be time for talk.

For the food was delicious (yet another triumph for Lionel) and the wine superb. Speeches kept to a minimum, the major, Ned and Charles ('On behalf of my wife and myself') and then Lionel the conjurer this time produced a jazz quartet and there was dancing. Jane and Charles opened the dance as they were bound to do, then drifted from table to table, being congratulated, talking with friends.

Catherine said, 'I do congratulate you. It may sound a bit odd, coming from me, but I do, honestly. And thank you for inviting me.'

'What nonsense,' said Jane. 'We've been friends for years. Why shouldn't I invite you?'

'Jay,' said Catherine.

But this is my wedding, thought Jane, and I want no skeleton at my feast. Not even one so substantial as Jay.

'We must have a chat about him sometime,' she said, and moved on to Piers, who at once asked her to dance.

'If you're sure it's all right,' she said.

'Oh absolutely,' said Piers. 'Sea bathing, that's the thing, and lots of it. Horse riding too, of course. Fresh air and exercise. The quack reckons that in another few months I'll be back with the battalion.'

'My dear, that's wonderful,' she said. 'No wonder you look so happy.'

Bob did not. He was polite and smiling, and answered when spoken to, danced as well as ever, but one could not call him happy.

'Your turn soon,' she said.

'And Georgie's,' said Bob. 'Busy year for parsons.' Definitely not happy.

She moved on to the Watsons who sat gossiping over their wine. Like her mother and the major, these two had the air of appearing to be old friends as much as husband and wife, and very endearing it was.

'Whoever would have thought it,' Harriet said. 'Keith and me, responsible for all this.'

'What a clever pair of Cupids you were,' said Jane. 'And don't say after all these years. I'm far too happy to be reminded of my years.'

'You are, aren't you?' said Harriet. 'Happy I mean. And quite right, too. You deserve to be. Charles looks happy too.'

'He is,' said Keith.

'Lucky man,' said Harriet. 'That's what they usually say on these occasions. But if you're both happy then you're both lucky, and that's far and away the best way to be.'

Keith asked her to dance and she accepted at once. Next to Lionel, he was the best dancer she knew.

'I ran into an old chum of yours last week,' he said. 'Cuthbert Pardoe.'

Jane thought uneasily of Yorkshire hotels.

'You were in Cambridge?' she asked.

'He was in London. Briefly. He's off to the States. MIT.'

'Is that some sort of society?'

'Massachusetts Institute of Technology,' said Watson. 'Very high-powered stuff. He's gone to shatter a few more atoms.'

'Did he take his boxing gloves?'

Watson snorted. 'Given it up,' he said. 'Putting away childish things, though of course he didn't express it quite like that, being an atheist. The truth of the matter is he's too old.'

So's that oaf Lane, she thought, but all he does is find smaller opponents.

'He'll do well, do you think?' she said.

'He'll do brilliantly. Incredible, isn't it? Like a chimpanzee with a talent for trigonometry.'

As she went towards her mother the quartet played a waltz, and the major headed purposefully for Georgie.

'You look gorgeous, child,' her mother said.

'The credit's all yours,' said Jane.

'And Schiaparelli's,' her mother said. 'Did I tell you that Gwendoline Gwatkin was one of those who rebuked me for making a fuss about the king's illness? I knew she would be. . . . You saw her at the church no doubt?'

'She's rather difficult to miss,' said Jane, 'but why did she cut my party?'

'She positively wept,' her mother said, 'but her doctor's told her she must live for a month on boiled fish and biscuits. The thought of what she would have to refuse here was too much for her.'

'And is my brother living on boiled fish and biscuits too?'

Her mother winced. 'He had a meeting,' she said. 'No doubt you will tell me that he usually does, but it's very often true. The truth is that he finds George's company most uncongenial, and of course he disapproves of Charles.'

'But he hardly knows Charles.' Best to pretend ignorance for once.

'Of his wealth,' said her mother, 'and the way in which he makes it.'

This is the happiest day of your life, she told herself, according to all the story books. Forget about Francis. She looked at the major, busily twirling, Georgie laughing in his arms.

'I'm glad the major gave me away,' she said.

'He too,' said her mother. 'It was a rôle he was proud to play. He seems happy, wouldn't you say?'

'Very.'

'To dance with your friend is a treat for him. It would be for most men, and for me to be jealous would be ridiculous. Besides, he may never have that particular treat again.'

Before she could pursue this the music ended and the major escorted Georgie to her table and came back to them. The next foxtrot was Lionel's.

'Such a day,' he said. 'I'm beginning to wilt already.'

'You did a marvellous job, darling.'

'I had to,' Lionel said. 'Everything had to be designed as a setting

409

for that dress. The Italian surpassed herself. Chanel will be livid.'

The honeymoon wasn't due to begin until the following week, though not everyone knew why. That night would be spent in South Terrace, and Charles was looking forward to it enormously. . . . They escaped at last after another embrace from Georgie, (her mother had already taken the major home) and stepped out into the cool autumn night. There was a mist from the river that made the landscape pearl and silver and grey.

'I'd better unpack,' said Charles.

'Truett can do that for you.'

'She can do the trunk when it comes tomorrow,' said Charles, 'but I want to do the case myself.'

'What on earth for?'

'It will be the first time I ever got as far as your bedroom. Come with me.'

Together they went upstairs. Charles looked around him and was content. Bathroom en suite with shower and bath, elegant, unfussy furniture and a bed more than big enough for two.

'I think I'm going to be very happy here,' he said, and then in a tone that for him was almost shy, 'and I hope you will be too. I'll do my best to make you so, I promise.'

'Of course I'll be happy,' she said. 'So will you.'

He took her in his arms, but at last she had to break free.

'Do your unpacking while I repair the damage,' she said. 'Don't worry. We'll have an early night.'

'A very early night.'

'Yes well – first we'll have to go downstairs and be congratulated. And it can't be too early. They wouldn't approve.'

'Who wouldn't approve?'

'Truett. Mrs Barrow. Brown. All your harem. Do you realise you're the only man in the place?'

'There's William,' he said.

'Well there is and there isn't,' said Jane.

'I see what you mean,' said Charles. 'Still every harem should have its eunuch.'

'There's no need to be coarse,' said Jane.

They had a last drink together, seated on easy chairs on either side of the fire. Married life it seemed had no need of sofas. William lay between them, and yawned.

'I know exactly how you feel,' said Jane.

'Quite a day,' said Charles. 'I'd no idea matrimony could be so exhausting.'

'What about the first time? – if I'm allowed to ask.'

'Of course you are, but it's just a blur really. Forgotten. The way one forgets one's dreams.' He sipped his whisky and soda. 'Bob didn't look overjoyed exactly, did he?'

'No he didn't,' said Jane, 'but Sybil Hendry did.'

'Well behaved and fully clothed,' said Charles, 'as those about to be married should be. Bob gave me a piece of news. Two, in fact.' Jane waited. 'The first is that his Sybil doesn't want to be paid for her shares. I told him to open an account and do it anyway. He doesn't have to tell her till the time's right.'

'And the other?'

'It's about Mrs Lane. She and Piers have agreed to separate, perfectly amicably, one gathers.'

'She's found Another?'

'She'd better not,' said Charles. 'She's suing Lane for divorce. No more cavortings for Annabel till the decree absolute.'

'Mr Lane's cup of sorrows appears to be running over,' said Jane.

The next day was to be an Extraordinary General Meeting of Lane Engineering, which was why the honeymoon had been postponed.

'He deserves every drop,' said Charles. 'She won't be at the meeting, since Lane's bound to be there, but she's given me her proxy – though it's Bob she's grateful to.'

'I can see that not giving it to Bob is what is known as tact,' said Jane, 'but why does Bob deserve her gratitude? You'll be the one who'll do all the talking.'

'You remember the night Lane was so rude at the Savoy?' said Charles.

'Vividly.'

'And you remember who he was with?'

'Old Creepers,' said Jane, 'and a couple of high-class tarts.'

'Well I happened to mention that to Bob, and he put your Mr

411

Pinner on it, and Mr Pinner tracked them down – the tarts I mean, and she's citing one in the divorce suit.'

'How absolutely gorgeous,' said Jane.

'The first time Bob looked happy was when he told me,' said Charles. 'He feels it evens the score for Annabel's black eye.' He chuckled. 'It gets better,' he said. 'You see Crawley found out about it and he's absolutely furious. Hardly the correct behaviour for our Fascist-in-Chief, wouldn't you say?'

'But how on earth did Crawley find out?'

'Bob told him.' This time the two of them laughed aloud, and William sat up, indignant. He had just nodded off.

'Indirectly of course,' said Charles. 'Neither Lane nor Crawley could *prove* it was Bob, though I've no doubt Lane rather suspects. Anyway Creepy's demanded that Lane should not defend the divorce.'

'But how could Crawley force him?'

'Lane owes him rather a lot of money. He's been gambling very foolishly, even for him. Really he ought to be grateful to me tomorrow. His shares – if he's got any left – should increase in value quite soon.'

'And you'll be richer than ever?'

'*We'll* be richer.'

'Just how rich are you, Charles?' she asked. He told her, and she looked at him aghast. 'But you can't be,' she said. 'No that's ridiculous. Of course you can. But – so much?'

'When it's as much as that it isn't just money, it's power,' said Charles. 'That's why I have to work at it so hard.'

'Even on the first day of your marriage.'

'Call that work?' he said. 'It's nothing of the kind. All I'm doing tomorrow is taking candy from a baby.'

They made love more as a matter of form than anything else. The first night of their marriage? Not to do so was unthinkable, but afterwards Charles was asleep almost at once. She fell asleep and dreamed of Foch, who was miffed because she wouldn't take him to Egypt on their honeymoon.

Charles came back to her at lunchtime, which was just as well. Mrs Barrow had laboured long and hard.

'What time do you have to go back?' she asked.

'I don't,' he said. 'All done.'

'So quickly?'

'Just one item on the agenda, and almost no opposition. It took no time at all.'

'So now you own Lane Engineering as well?'

'I do, and you do, and Bob does too.'

'I don't like to think of your money as mine.'

'I don't like to think of your money as mine, either,' he said. 'We'll just have to get used to it. For better for worse. All that. What's for lunch?' She told him.

'After that lot I think I'd better take William for a walk. Do him good. No doubt he'll be eating the same as us.'

'I expect so,' said Jane. 'They spoil him dreadfully.' William, who also knew what was for lunch, sat up looking alert and reliable.

'Georgie phoned,' said Jane. 'She wanted to know if we'd like to go to a movie. Early show then a bite of supper. It's one of yours. "White Tie and Roses".'

'One of Fisch's, or rather his director's,' said Charles. 'All I do is count the ticket money, and I must say it isn't doing badly. Would you like to go?'

'So long as it's early,' she said. 'I have to go racing tomorrow with Mummy and the major at Cheltenham. My horse is running.'

'Good Lord, so he is,' said Charles, and then a wonderful thought struck him. There was nothing happening at the bank that somebody else couldn't handle. Married life really was marvellous. 'Mind if I come too?' he asked.

Sybil had wanted him to stay at Crag Fell when he came up North, but he'd told her that wasn't the way an engaged lady behaved, and she saw at once that he was right, so then she hadn't wanted him to go at all, but he wasn't having that. Once let her have a say in how he ran his business and he really would be a doormat. In the end they compromised: she stayed at Crag Fell and he went to the Newcastle hotel where he'd first bought her lunch: where his happiness ended, in fact – though it hadn't seemed like that at the time – and drove over to be with her as often as he could, which left him with no time at all to look for anybody else, or even *at* anybody else, and maybe it was just as well. He wasn't ready for it, not yet. When it happened, and knowing himself as he did he was quite sure it would happen, the row that followed would be like Armaggedon. All the same he made time to spend an evening with Andy and Norah. When he'd told her he'd expected uproar, though in fact she was pleased for all three of them, but then she approved of Andy.

'Shouldn't I see them too?' she asked.

'Of course. We'll give them lunch in Newcastle on Sunday.'

'I thought we'd spend Sunday at Crag Fell.'

'Look,' said Bob. 'Andy works. Every week day, from eight in the morning till five at night, and a half shift on Saturday. Eight till twelve.'

'We could give them dinner on Saturday night.'

'No we couldn't,' said Bob. 'Andy won't eat dinner – it's dead against his principles – and Norah would be terrified at the very idea. It'll have to be lunch on Sunday.'

Once again she gave way. For some reason he found it worrying.

Andy was delighted to see him, and so was Norah. Well on in her pregnancy, thought Bob, but no complications it seemed. They both looked very happy, which was what love does for people, he thought. Some people anyway. Then Andy being Andy, he found something to worry about.

'We should have asked Bet and Frank,' he said. 'They'll want

414

to hear about your engagement an' all.'

'I've already been,' said Bob. 'Frank's on late shift and she couldn't leave the bairns. Anyway I gave her a new wireless.'

Andy snorted. 'That's three to my knowledge. Has she one in each room?'

'Likely,' said Bob.

'Did you see the bairns?' Norah asked. 'A proper little picture, that Jane.'

'She is an' all,' said Bob. 'Little Frank's more like his dad.'

Andy snorted once again. 'How's our Jane?' he asked. 'Married life suiting her?'

'Down to the ground,' said Bob. 'Her horse was running at Cheltenham last week. It won. Six to one. I had a fiver on him. Very nice too.'

Norah had no time to waste on horses. 'What was her dress like?'

'At Cheltenham?'

'At the wedding, you daft ha'porth.'

Bob did his best to describe it.

'She must have looked lovely,' said Norah.

'She did,' said Bob. 'A credit to us all.'

'So long as she's happy,' Norah said, and rose to her feet. 'I'll be off and get the fish and chips.'

'Let Andy and me go,' said Bob. 'It's a fair step to the chip shop.'

'I'm pregnant,' Norah said. 'Not crippled. I can get as far as the chip shop. You and Andy sit and have a bit crack. But no sitting up late, mind. The hooter still goes at eight o'clock.'

At one time Norah or any other woman even saying the word pregnant would have sent Andy scarlet with embarrassment, but now all he did was grin.

'Just be careful down the back stairs,' was all he said, and produced a bottle and glasses. 'Amber Ale suit you?' he said.

This was Andy's house and Andy was in work. There was no question of Bob paying his share. 'Fine,' he said, and Andy poured.

'I saw you got your name in the paper the other day,' Andy said. 'Lane Engineering.'

'You started reading the *Financial Times* now?'

'The *Herald* still keeps an eye on what you capitalists are up to,

415

but what in the world do you want to get mixed up in engineering for?' Andy asked. 'You're in the wireless business.'

'Sybil has shares in Lane's,' said Bob. 'I've got a few myself come to that. So I went to keep an eye on them.'

'Charles Lovell has shares in it too,' said Andy. Bob nodded. 'A lot of shares. And now he's running the business.'

'Chairman of the Board,' said Bob. 'What Charles Lovell runs is the money. Other folks makes the engines.'

'This Lane,' said Andy. 'The way the *Herald* tells it Charles just walked into the meeting and took his company off him. Now you can't tell me that's right.'

'Lane's a bastard,' said Bob, 'and an incompetent bastard at that. If we'd let him alone he'd have ruined the company and sold it off to some Yank. As it is there's folks in the Midlands still got jobs.'

'You said "we",' said Andy. 'Who's "we"?'

'Charles, Sybil, me, the other shareholders.'

'So you capitalists are fairy godmothers nowadays,' Andy said. 'You wave your magic wands and make jobs for the workers?' But he was grinning as he said it.

'No,' said Bob. 'Your lot's the ones who believe in fairies. All the same my lot can't make money unless your lot have jobs.'

'My lot,' said Andy. 'I'm not too sure I've got a lot to belong to. Not any more. You heard I didn't get the nomination.'

'I heard,' said Bob. 'Man, it fair beats me. You must have been far and away the most outstanding bloke on the short list. How on earth could they justify turning you down?'

'Simple,' said Andy. 'You might even say beautifully simple. They didn't put me on the short list.'

Bob stared at him, then threw back his head and laughed, but there was no amusement in the laughter, only rage at what had been done to his brother.

'That one could have been thought up by that Cambridge pal of yours,' he said. 'That Burrowes.'

He finished his beer and Andy opened another bottle.

'What's all this about not belonging?' Bob asked. 'You're never telling me you've finished with politics?'

'I doubt I'll ever be that,' Andy said, 'but just now I've given up kicking the ball. I just go along to the match. And then there's

Norah. It's not an easy time after all she's been through. But she finds she feels better when I'm here with her.'

'Talking of the baby,' said Bob, 'if there's anything needed – '

'Now that'll do,' said Andy. 'I've already been into all that with Jane.'

'Just remember we both mean it,' said Bob, but Andy's mind was still on domestic bliss.

'I'm making canny money for a fitter,' Andy said. 'Wouldn't keep you in shoe leather I've no doubt, but Norah and me – we manage. Glass of beer when I feel like it, and she'll have a shandy with me. Then there's the pictures. We saw an old one of Jane's pal's the other day.'

'Georgie Payne?'

'That's right. All about Spain and a millionaire and some gypsies. She was sort of the gypsy princess. I never knew gypsies was blondes. It was funny, though – but I tell you what was funnier.'

'The cartoon?'

'The newsreel,' Andy said, and leaned back expansively. 'What at Cambridge we used to call "funny peculiar, not funny ha-ha".' Bob threw a cushion at him.

'Mind me beer,' Andy said. 'You see on the newsreel they had the real Spain – not a Hollywood picture postcard. And very nasty it looked. Barcelona it was. Riots . . . Now you and me've been in a riot.'

You more than me, thought Bob, but it was Andy's tale and he'd let him tell it.

'Mounted police,' Andy continued. 'One of them hit me on the head with a truncheon the size of a sabre. Cossacks I called them, when I got enough strength back to speak. Cossacks.' He shook his head. 'Bob man, compared with that lot in Barcelona they were more like Boy Scouts. Wolf Cubs even.'

'More like Crawley's lot?'

'Given the chance I dare say they could do it,' said Andy, 'but compared with the Spanish coppers they've still got an awful lot to learn.'

There was the sound of Norah's footsteps on the stairs, and Andy began to talk about Felston United's chances next season.

*

417

Andy found it strange that Norah didn't make anything like the fuss about having Sunday lunch with Sybil Hendry that she'd made about having a drink with Charles Lovell. Partly he thought it was because Sybil was unlikely to produce a destroyer the way other conjurers produce rabbits, but even more it was curiosity. She wanted a really good look at the woman who had finally put the handcuffs on Bob, so that later on she could speculate endlessly on how she had managed to do it. Then she'd successfully let out her wedding dress to meet the needs of her pregnancy, and what with that and the bits of jewellery Jane had given her, she didn't think she looked too bad. Even her pregnancy would be a weapon if one were needed. 'You may be young and pretty and rich, but I'm six months gone with my husband's child.' Let her start anything, Norah thought darkly, and me and the bairn inside me will jolly soon finish it.

To her relief it wasn't like that at all. Bob had sent a car to take them to Newcastle, so that they arrived in style. Her pregnancy had helped her there, too, because Andy was too relieved not to have to get her on a bus or a train to put up a fight, and when they did get there it was all plain sailing. Bob and his girl were already there to meet her, and she came at once to Norah, hand outstretched.

'How sweet of you to come,' she said.

A pretty one all right, Norah thought. Dark and luscious as a plum. 'A pleasure,' she said.

'Come and sit down,' said Bob's girl. 'I hope the journey wasn't too tiring?'

About five hundred times better than the bus, thought Norah, but how could she say so?

They went into a hotel lounge that was far lighter, and smarter, than the lounge of the Eldon Arms in Felston. Not nearly so much brass for a start, but what there was had been polished that morning.

'I expect you know my name's Sybil,' Bob's girl said, 'and that's what I'd like you to call me. And if you don't mind, I'd like to call you Norah. After all we'll be sisters-in-law soon.'

Norah sat in an armchair that seemed to have been built solely for her comfort.

'That's fine with me, Sybil,' she said.

Bob ordered champagne, knowing his brother's weakness, but Norah asked for lemonade.

'But surely – ' Sybil said, but Norah patted her stomach. 'Oh yes of course,' said Sybil. 'I can be an absolute bloody idiot sometimes.'

Somehow Norah managed not to blink.

But most of the time Sybil was the perfect hostess, deferential but not gushing, and charmingly aware of Norah's pregnancy: fanning away the cigarette smoke when it moved towards her. The movement of her hand made Norah look at her engagement ring, and very nice emeralds they were too, she thought, but our Jane's got better ones. All the same she did her best to be kind, and she was kind. Bob's relief at the fact was so obvious it was hard not to laugh.

As they sipped at their drinks Sybil said, 'I expect it was a surprise when Bob told you our news?'

'Well yes,' said Norah.

'He absolutely swept me off my feet,' said Sybil. 'Didn't you darling?'

'That's right,' said Bob.

'Men get so embarrassed when we give away our girlish secrets,' said Sybil, 'but since it's happened anyway, why not enjoy it? That's what I say. Don't you, Norah?'

'Every time,' said Norah.

It was easy really. All she had to do was agree, and remember the details: the lipstick that was just a shade too bright, the voice always on the attack, the cigarettes lit in endless succession, one after the other. Yet all the time what the other woman was saying was 'I'm doing my best to like you. Honestly I am. Please try to like me too.' And so Norah tried.

The lunch was the best Newcastle could offer: chicken soup, whitebait, saddle of lamb, fruit, cheese. And claret. A fair bit for Bob and Sybil, and a glass for Andy. She stuck with the lemonade, but she enjoyed the food. Through it all Sybil chattered about Jane, what a marvellous person she was, what a lovely wedding, and what a pity Norah and Andy had missed it.

'You know Jane's lucky,' Sybil continued. 'I honestly think I can say that because I admire her so.' She turned to Bob. 'Isn't that true, darling?'

'Yes,' said Bob. 'It's true.' It seemed he meant it.

'But surely,' said Andy, who really did admire Jane, 'you don't mean she's lucky because she's got a rich husband?'

Of course she doesn't, you daft un, Norah thought, but all the same I love you for asking.

'Certainly not,' said Sybil. 'That might not be luck at all. Not good luck, anyway. I should know, I've done it twice – or will have quite soon. That's beside the point,' she said severely. 'What I mean is her parents. That fabulous mother – and the major straight out of a story book. My father's a pig.'

She stabbed out her cigarette in the ashtray, and began to eat her lamb.

Norah said, 'When's your wedding to be?' Her voice was tranquil, or at least it sounded so.

'Soon,' said Bob. 'Before Christmas.'

'Of course you'll be coming,' said Sybil.

'Depends on the bairn,' said Norah.

'Forgive me. The little devils make their own rules, don't they?' said Sybil.

'That's right,' Norah said. 'The rest of us just have to do what we're told.'

'Bob says this is your first,' said Sybil.

'It is,' said Norah. 'We tried and tried and I kept miscarrying. Then Bob found out. If it hadn't been for him – '

'Oh yes of course,' said Sybil. 'That's when I met Andy. Bob's flat in London. What a bloody idiot I am. Still I did send you some fruit – didn't I?'

'The best I ever tasted,' Norah said.

Sybil turned to Bob. 'What you did for Norah,' she said. 'That was good. Wonderful in fact.'

Like she's giving him marks out of ten, thought Andy.

'Family,' said Bob. 'Nothing's too good if it's family.'

'Except my father,' she said, and turned to Norah. 'Jane and Charles are going to Egypt for their honeymoon.'

Potiphar's wife and Moses in the bulrushes and the Nile waters parting, thought Norah.

'It'll be hot likely,' she said.

'Oh extremely. But they'll have ice in their drinks and electric fans and the right sort of clothes. Not that one would need a lot of clothes in Egypt.'

Bob cleared his throat. 'Anybody fancy anything with their coffee?' he asked.

'No overcoats or scarves or gloves,' said Sybil. 'Just silk and cotton and a deck chair in the shade. Wouldn't you like that, Norah?'

'Sounds like heaven,' Norah said.

'Maybe one day we'll all go together,' said Sybil.

'Maybe,' Andy said, but at least he didn't laugh. Norah was grateful for that.

In the taxi on the way home Andy said, 'No need to start packing for Cairo. – Not just yet.'

'What did you make of her?' Norah said.

'She'll be a handful,' Andy said.

'All of that. I wouldn't want what Bob's got in store. Still, she spoke well of Jane.'

'And her mam. And her stepfather. Would you like to go to the wedding if we can manage it?'

'Your only brother? Of course I would. But could you get away?'

'Lose a bit pay, but I could manage a few days.'

'Then we'll do it,' Norah said.

'Thanks, pet.' Andy squeezed her carefully, mindful of the baby. 'It wasn't nice, her talking about her father like that,' he said. 'And the language. . . . And smoke smoke smoke all the time other folks was eating. Not like Jane at all.'

'And yet she was, you know,' said Norah. 'Like Jane, I mean. The way she wears her clothes, the way she talks. I don't just mean the accent. The words. The way she puts them together. You can tell they were both brought up to be ladies.'

'And half of them succeeded,' Andy said.

Norah giggled, but there was a part of her mind that worried. There was something wrong with that lass. Not that she could talk to Andy about it – his own brother's fiancée. But she could talk to Jane first chance she got, and she would, too, even if it meant getting her on the telephone when she came back from Egypt.

*

'She's nice,' said Sybil. 'Really awfully nice.'

'That's why Andy married her,' said Bob.

They too were in a taxi, bound for that mysterious flat in Gosforth that never seemed to have other occupants, not even servants, though it was always clean, the beds made, the refrigerator well stocked. One day soon he'd have to ask her about it, he thought. To put it off much longer would be cowardice, and it would never do to give Sybil the idea that he was afraid of her.

'Do you think she liked me?' Sybil asked. She sounded shy.

'Well of course she did,' said Bob. 'You could tell by the way she got on with you.'

'That could have been acting.'

'Norah's no actress,' said Bob. 'She wouldn't know where to start. If she likes you she shows it, and if she doesn't – well she can't hide that either.' Please God let that be the truth, he thought.

'She's so different,' said Sybil.

'She's poor,' said Bob. 'Always has been.'

'Do you really think that's all it is?'

'If she and Andy had money she'd still be simple and direct, but you wouldn't think she was so different.'

'Wouldn't I?' She thought about it. 'We could give them money. We've got masses. Or better still you could give him a job.'

'Do you think I haven't tried?'

'And he wouldn't take it? Whyever not?'

'I won't have the union in my business,' said Bob.

She burst out laughing. 'How perfectly priceless,' she said.

'Yes, isn't it?' said Bob. His voice was savage. 'The only proper work Andy could do for me would be craftsman's work, and for Andy craftsmen don't just have a duty to join the union, it's a sacred obligation.'

'You could make him a manager.'

'Show some sense,' said Bob. 'Andy doesn't know anything about being a manager. If I made him one I'd have to get somebody else to do the work, and Andy would never stand for that. And in any case – can you imagine Andy sacking people? Because if you can you've a damn sight more imagination than me.'

'I've annoyed you, haven't I?' she said. To Bob's surprise she seemed more contrite than proud.

422

'Not your fault,' he said.

'All the same I did,' said Sybil. 'I deserve a good smack.'

The taxi pulled up at the block of flats.

Straight into the bedroom. No novelty that, and he'd had enough to drink anyway. Gratefully Bob loosened his tie, unfastened his collar. He'd better start thinking of a bigger collar size. By the bed, Sybil was tearing off her clothes. As if there was a prize for who could do it fastest, he thought. No strip tease this time, no Gipsy Rose Hendry. Just tear them off, pull them down, throw them away. Women's clothes came off so easily that she was naked in no time. He unbuttoned his trousers and looked with pleasure still at the firm, familiar body. She moved towards him, then stopped, turned with her back to him and bent forward, her buttocks well within his reach.

'I *said* I deserve a good smack,' she said, 'but that isn't strictly true. I want one. Would you care to oblige?'

. 42 .

Egypt was mostly culture on a colossal scale; interspersed with dances, receptions, polo, even a cricket match; 'and rather a lot of pink gin in Alexandria,' she wrote to Georgie, 'because of the navy being there.' Within twenty-four hours of their arrival it became clear that Charles was not only immensely rich, he was immensely important, too. No doubt the one caused the other, but whatever the reason they were invited everywhere. Ambassadors, ministers, captains of battleships, battalion commanders, even the fat, pathetic king, all sent invitations to their suite at Shepherd's Hotel, where the servants treated her as once servants had treated her in India. And very nice too.

'All the same,' she grumbled, 'it's more like a goodwill tour than a honeymoon.'

'You don't suppose I'm enjoying it, do you?' grumbled Charles in his turn. 'Full evening dress in this heat? At least you have next to nothing on.'

She looked anxiously in the mirror. What Charles had said was accurate enough as to quantity, but what there was had been strategically placed.

'Poor darling,' she said. 'The sooner we get on that Nile boat the better.'

'Antony and Cleopatra,' said Charles. 'I can't wait.'

She had once played Cleopatra for Jay Bower, but he had preferred the rôle of Caesar. It seemed to belong to another life time.

They went to yet one more reception, to eat the same kind of food, drink the same kind of drinks, and discuss the same topics: was King George really going to die this time, and if so what about Mrs Simpson, whose divorce had been made absolute before they

424

left England? Jane discovered that Charles, and she too, achieved a certain mild notoriety because they had met America's most famous divorcée.

The boat down the Nile was much more fun. To begin with their suite was so big that they need see nobody else unless they wanted to, which meant that at last the trip became a honeymoon, and in the second place culture became an optional extra. It was true that they saw even more massive chunks of cultural heritage, but quite often they turned over and went to sleep instead.

There was a limit to the amount of gods, goddesses and Pharaohs that one could absorb. Moreover the Nile boat was a splendid venue for them to get used to each other. It was true that they had been lovers for years: that making love, while no longer a novelty, had a familiar rhythm and charm that were its own fulfilment, but that had been when chance was on their side; when time and place made love possible. Now they were together all the time, and the Nile boat was the perfect place for them to be aware of the fact.

They returned to Cairo easy and relaxed, and with an awareness of each other's presence so pleasing that they could face even the prospect of more parties, more receptions. Two things prevented it. One was the news that the king had died: the other a telegram from her mother to say that the major was dying. Jane read the words once more. A plain statement of fact, except for the word 'love' at the end.

'She doesn't ask me to,' she said, 'but I'll have to go back.'

'Of course,' said Charles. 'I'll have a word with the desk. They'll find out about aeroplanes.'

She went to him and his arms came round her. 'Bless you,' she said. 'Mummy must be devastated. She adores her major.'

Charles picked up the phone to find out what Imperial Airways could do.

They flew next day: the exact reverse of the flight out. From light to darkness, warmth to cold, and laughter to tears, she thought. Bitter tears indeed for Mummy. Huddled in warm coats they drove to South Terrace, left their luggage, and went on to the major's house in Kensington. They were shown in at once, and her mother embraced her.

'You came so quickly,' her mother said. Jane waited. 'He's still alive,' said her mother. 'Just alive. Upstairs in our bedroom. There was talk of hospital, but he said he'd much rather stay here, and why should I move him? He was so happy here – and I have a nurse to help me.'

'Can we see him?' asked Jane.

'Of course,' said her mother. 'It's what he's waiting for.' They followed her upstairs.

The major lay propped up among pillows, his coverlet strewn with newspapers, form books, pictures of horses. His appearance shocked Jane, not because he looked unwell, but because he was so obviously dying.

'Nice of you to look in,' he said. 'How brown you both look.'

'Egypt,' said Jane.

'Yes of course. A bit like India, as I remember.'

'Very,' said Jane.

'What I said to your mother.' He looked at Mrs Routledge and smiled, then his hand moved across the coverlet and pushed a newspaper towards Jane. The effort was such it could have been a load of bricks. 'Your horse won again,' he said.

Jane picked up the paper. It was open at the racing page. Bridget's Boy in the 3.30 at Plumpton. A hundred to eight.

'A lot of chaps said the heavy going wouldn't suit him, hence the odds,' the major said. 'But I knew better. Last horse I tipped. I'm glad it was yours.'

'Me too,' said Jane.

'The Gold Cup,' said the major. 'He's ready and he's full of frisk and he can do it even if the going's soft. Now promise me.'

'Word of honour,' said Jane.

'There's a good girl,' the major said. 'Nice honeymoon?' He chuckled then, a dry, rattling sound. 'What a question. Only a dying man would dare ask it.'

'Very nice,' said Jane. 'I brought my husband to say the same.' She drew Charles forward. The major looked at him.

'Ah yes, the rifleman,' he said. 'She was too good for the Brigade of Guards. Don't forget I told you that.'

'I won't,' said Charles, 'and whether she's too good for the Rifle Brigade or not, at least I'm the one that's got her.'

426

'Good man,' said the major. 'Mind you hang on to her.' He turned back to Jane. 'Give me a kiss,' he said. 'There'll be a nurse along in a minute.' He smiled at his wife. 'A pretty little thing, but bossy. Does things to me I thought I'd never put up with from a living soul. All the same I do.'

Jane bent to kiss him. 'Night night,' she said.

'Be a long one when it comes,' the major said.

'He simply collapsed,' said her mother. 'In the middle of getting ready to go to Haydock Park. I called the doctor at once. He told me George wouldn't last the night.' She smiled the old, ironic smile. 'So much for medical science. But now that he's seen you, I doubt he'll last much longer. I am not, I hope, addicted to hyperbole, but he does love you, and he has affection for Charles also, which was why I sent you that telegram. Forgive me.'

'Mummy please,' said Jane.

'You must forgive me,' her mother said. 'At a time like this one gives way to foolishness, I find.'

'Would you like me to stay with you?' Jane asked.

'Thank you, but no,' said her mother. 'You must stay with your husband.'

'I could stay here too,' said Charles.

Her mother blinked at him. 'What a very nice man you are,' she said. 'But no. It would upset George even more if he knew that you were here in the house. He's seen you together, which is what he wanted, and he knows you're happy.'

She hesitated. 'No doubt you are wondering where your brother is?'

'Well yes,' said Jane.

'I rang his college to acquaint him with the facts, and was told he was visiting friends in the Lake District, but no one was sure precisely where.' Mrs Routledge accepted sherry from Charles, and sipped. 'And you two flew back from Egypt,' she said. Suddenly she put down her glass, covered her face, and wept.

Two nights later the major died. It was very peaceful, her mother said.

'The night nurse was good enough to alert me before she

427

telephoned the doctor, and so we had a few minutes alone together. He talked for a while in Urdu and so of course I was able to answer him. He seemed to think he was still in what he called the Puffers – the Punjabi Frontier Force – but then I said to him, "Do let's talk English, George. So much nicer." – He came back to the present at once.'

'What did he say?' Jane asked.

'He said, "Hello old girl. I reckon I'm really for it this time." I said, "Please don't be morbid, my dear. You know how it upsets me." "Sorry old girl," he said, and lay quietly for a while. Then he said, "You'll be all right, you know. For money I mean. My horses will take care of you." Then he lay still again, and just before the nurse came in he said, as if there were someone else in the room, "I never thought I'd have the nerve to do it, but I did. Asked her to marry me straight out and straight out she said yes." The nurse came back in at that point, and told me the doctor was on his way. But George was dead.'

'Poor Mummy,' said Jane.

'There was of course no need for the doctor's presence,' said her mother. 'Nothing could have saved George. His heart was in a dreadful state, poor darling man.' Her voice broke. 'I'm dreadfully sorry,' she said, 'but I'm afraid I'm about to cry again.'

Jane held her as she wept. For my own father, she thought, my mother shed not a single tear, but then he had betrayed her, and George Routledge had loved her.

'There,' her mother said at last. 'I've done. For the time being, at least. A ridiculous spectacle at my age, I have no doubt, but I can't help it. Nor do I want to.'

'Of course not,' said Jane. 'I cried for John Patterson.'

'You went mad for him,' her mother said. 'Quite literally. I wasn't much help to you in those days, was I?'

'We're close now, and that's all I care about,' said Jane.

'Thank God,' her mother said.

Jane tried to persuade her mother to stay at South Terrace for a while, but her mother wouldn't hear of it, either then or after the funeral.

'This is where I belong and South Terrace is where you belong, you and Charles,' she said. 'Perhaps I may take a trip in a little while, but this is my home, mine and George's. I couldn't possibly live anywhere else.' She was adamant.

Francis turned up on the day before the funeral. The Lake District in fact had been swapped for the Yorkshire Dales, so that finding him would have been a task beyond even Mr Pinner's powers. His meeting with his mother was an awkward one: he had never even attempted to hide his dislike for the major, who in his turn was too often given to speculate why fate should have given him a pansy for a stepson.

But in the end he behaved well, thought Jane: gentle, sympathetic and loving to his mother, and polite at least to Jane, with none of the snarling petulance he had shown last time they met. Charles was right, she thought. He must have been in a state of shock.

When at last their mother went to lie down, Francis said, 'I owe you an apology.'

'People do go away without leaving an address,' she said, 'and anyway, how could you on a walking tour?'

'Oh that,' he said. 'I didn't mean that. – When you and Warley got me out of that mess. To be honest I haven't a very clear recollection of what happened, but I rather think I was rude to you, and if I was, I'm sorry.'

'That's all right,' she said. 'I'll tell Lionel you said so.'

'Thank you,' he said, then, still pleasantly: 'Please don't mind my asking, but why did you bring him?'

'He's not without experience in such matters, whereas I was.'

'Oh,' said Francis. 'I see.'

'Tell me,' she said, 'why do you dislike my friend so much?'

'You mean all we nancy boys should stick together?'

'Not at all,' she said. 'I just wondered.'

'He's so old fashioned,' he said. 'Ten years out of date. He has no concept of today's realities. He never will have. He's far too busy wallowing in nostalgia for the Twenties.'

Whereas Burrowes represents the hard-headed realism of today? Well perhaps he does – but she kept the thought to herself.

The funeral too was held in St Thomas's, as her father's had been, when Dr Dodd had been vicar. But Dr Dodd too was dead. The

429

penalty of the passing years, she thought: one by one they die, those whom one knows and loves; though with her the process had begun early. John had died on the 10th November, 1918, and she had gone mad because of it, and because of what she had seen and endured in the two years before, when she drove the ambulance. Then her father, her Aunt Pen, Grandma and her son Stan, Canon Messeter and now the major. The list was long and would grow longer. It was inevitable that it should. 'In the midst of life we are in death,' the clergyman was saying, and that just about summed it up.

Her mother had insisted on a quiet ceremony, so that the little church was far from full, not packed to the doors as it had been for her father's funeral, when all his surviving friends from the Indian Army and Civil Service had attended to stare at each other and wonder who would be next.

This time there were only her mother, Francis, Charles and herself, the major's surviving brother and cousins, all of whom disapproved of the way he earned his living, a few cronies from his club and the *Daily World* – and Georgie and Lionel. Two most unlikely birds of paradise among such a collection of crows she thought, and yet though their plumes too were black, birds of paradise they were. Her mother had been both pleased and astounded that they had asked to come, and agreed at once, for the major had adored Georgie in the nicest possible way, and as for Lionel, his personal life was his own affair he'd said, but he'd had a damned good war.

And so they stood there with the others, and heard the words those Anglican bishops had written in committee all those hundreds of years before: words that still had the power to console, to heal, or to make one gasp aloud at their splendour. The vicar finished at last, and it was time to go to the graveside.

Cousins and cronies came back for sherry and biscuits and the chance to say they'd had drinks with Georgina Payne, then scurried off to catch trains, finish an article, gossip in the club library. Georgie and Lionel rose too, but Mrs Routledge motioned them to stay.

'Nice to have people one likes at a time like this,' she said.

'It would be very difficult indeed to like some of the major's relatives,' said Charles.

'All relatives are ghastly,' said Lionel, and put down his sherry glass, which was almost full. 'If you like me, Mrs Routledge, please may I mix myself a martini? Sherry upsets me dreadfully.'

'Of course,' Mrs Routledge said. 'Jane will fetch the ingredients. Forgive me, but I did not care to produce them while George's people were present. You and Georgina have provided them with enough gossip without cocktails.'

'They seemed very much concerned about the will,' said Jane, hunting in a cupboard for gin.

'Top left behind the biscuit barrel,' said her mother. 'They hoped George had left them something.'

'And did he?' Jane asked.

'Not a sou. I did suggest it might be as well to leave them some sort of keepsake, but he refused to accept the idea. They all said very unkind things about his livelihood – and about me too I may say.'

'How dare they!' Georgie was furious. 'What gives those snivelling wretches the right to criticise you?'

Mrs Routledge rang for ice, and Lionel set to work.

'Genteel poverty,' Mrs Routledge said. 'George was the only Routledge who ever made any money. Actually he did rather well – but the rest of them aren't worth a penny.'

'Serves them right,' Georgie snapped. Lionel offered her a martini. 'What a gorgeous man you are,' she said. 'Always there when you're wanted.'

'Talking of appearances,' said Jane, 'why didn't Gwendoline Gwatkin make hers?'

'She is most unwilling to appear in public these days,' her mother said. 'People stare so.'

'I'm not surprised,' said Charles.

'Your wedding was her last appearance of what might be called a public nature,' said Mrs Routledge. 'She telephoned and asked to be excused, and I was happy to oblige her. I have sorrows enough without poor Gwendoline, though now of course she will regret her absence bitterly.'

'Why on earth should she?' Georgie asked.

431

'Because you were there,' Mrs Routledge said. 'At least he danced with you.'

'He waltzed beautifully,' Georgie said.

'He did indeed,' said Mrs Routledge, and began to cry again.

Well he'd asked her and she'd told him, and serve him bloody well right, he thought. Ask a stupid question and you get a stupid answer, but it hadn't been quite like that, not this time. Ask a painful question and the answer you get may turn out to be excruciating.

'The flat in Gosforth? It's mine,' she said. 'I thought you'd have guessed that much.'

'But why?' He'd even asked her that. Whatever brains he'd been born with, she was making short work of them.

'For my chaps, silly,' Sybil said. 'It's the stable where they cover the mare.'

That's when he should have hit her. It was what she wanted anyway, but that wasn't why he kept his hands to himself. He hated hurting her almost as much as she enjoyed it.

'Don't you want to know who the last one was?' He shook his head. 'It was you,' she said. 'Ever since I met you there's never been anybody else. Word of honour.'

Suddenly she was wiped clean of all the cruelty, and looked about sixteen years old. 'Does it bother you?'

'How can it?' he said. 'The life I led . . .'

'But now we're Beatrice and Benedick? Is that it?'

'I never saw that one,' he said, and thought: She's all right now. For the time being, anyway. Keep it light. 'Better make it Darby and Joan.'

She'd smiled, delighted, and flung herself on the vast bed that was all he could ever remember of the Gosforth flat, quite unaware of her nakedness. It wasn't an invitation, not even a hint. She wanted to sprawl so she sprawled. He found it endearing.

'Daddy doesn't know about this place.'

'Well of course not.'

'Golly,' she said. 'You sounded quite shocked. What I mean is he's quite sure there is a place, but I'm taking damn good care he won't find it. That would never do.' Suddenly she looked

432

sixteen again. 'Promise you won't tell him,' she said.

How to phone Jane had been an enormous problem, and then suddenly Norah had the answer. Maybe God had sent it to her, she thought. Andy would have found that ridiculous, perhaps – for reasons she could never understand – even shocking, and put it all down to the fact that she was pregnant, and so Norah kept it all to herself, but all the same, if it was God's doing, then she thanked Him for it.

'Sorry to hear about your mam's bereavement,' she said.

'You're very kind,' said Jane. 'It's hit her very hard. It was so sudden, you see. But how did you find out? I mean I meant to let you both know, *and* Bob, but honestly there just hasn't been time – '

'Of course not,' Norah said. 'After a death there's so much to do. I know that. But it was in the *Daily World* you see. Almost a full page. It mentioned you, too. Didn't you see it?'

'Yes,' said Jane. 'I saw it. But it's just as you say. After a death there's no time even to think. But it was sweet of you to call. Where are you calling from, by the way?'

'Harris and Croft's Dock Office,' said Norah. 'You and Charles arranged it so Andy could use the phone, if it was – what was the word they used – a relevant call? Andy thought this wasn't. Just family, he said. Though mind you that doesn't mean he doesn't sympathise. He does. A real caring chap is Andy.'

'Of course he is,' said Jane.

'But the way I looked at it this *was* relevant,' said Norah. 'Whatever that means. I mean it wasn't just a death. It was a death in your family, and that means Charles's family too, the way he thinks about you, so I spoke to the Yard Manager – '

'You did?' said Jane.

'Certainly,' Norah said. 'I told him who I was and who you were.'

'And?'

'He brought me here himself,' said Norah.

I should cheer, thought Jane, and perhaps I should cry, too. For Norah to approach a being so elevated as the Yard Manager was an act of courage so great as to warrant shouts of triumph, and that she should do it for me – that was cause for tears indeed.

'Good for him,' she said. 'Are you both well – you and the baby?'

'Canny,' said Norah, and this time it seemed that 'canny' meant pretty good. 'But that wasn't the only reason I called.' Her voice dropped a little. 'There's nobody else here,' she said. 'I can tell you straight out.'

'Norah, what is it?'

'Bob,' said Norah. 'Him and that Sybil.'

'What about them?'

'Did you hear they took us out to dinner? Only they called it lunch.'

'While we were in Egypt?'

'That's right. Posh hotel in Newcastle. No expense spared as they say.'

'Bob's very fond of you both,' said Jane.

'And so we are of him. No problems there. It was that Sybil of his.'

'Sybil? She was rude to you?'

'No she wasn't,' said Norah. 'As a matter of fact she was very nice. Really trying hard.' The fact seemed to surprise her. 'Only now and again she was well – funny.'

'Funny?'

'If you've got a bit of time to spare,' said Norah, 'I'd better tell you the whole story. It's the only way I can show what I mean.'

'Go ahead,' said Jane, and reached out for her cigarettes and lighter. At once William leaped into her lap. At least Foch would have waited to be asked, she thought, but then William wasn't Foch: he was William. She let him stay.

Norah told her story well. She had a sharp eye for detail, and a sense of drama that brought the whole thing to life without forcing her opinions on you.

When she had done, Jane said, 'Do you think she hates her father?'

'She called him a pig,' said Norah.

'There was another reference, too,' said Jane.

'Bob said "Nothing's too good if it's family", and she said "Except my father." Then she went straight on to talk about your honeymoon.'

'And she smoked and swore a lot?'

'You're thinking I'm a what's its name? A prude?'

'Not necessarily,' said Jane. 'But I've been known to swear, and I certainly smoke.'

'And a lot of us had fathers we didn't care for,' said Norah. 'But it wasn't like that, Jane.'

'Of course not,' said Jane, and puffed at the Cartier holder. 'If it had been you wouldn't have phoned me. Tell me what it *was* like.'

'It was like she was – ' Norah hesitated.

'Mad?' said Jane.

'It sounds terrible when you say it out loud like that.'

'It *is* terrible,' said Jane. 'For Bob it would be disastrous if you're right.'

She thought about Sybil Hendry, trying to see beyond the prettiness. A little selfish perhaps, and more than a little wilful: but good natured, even kind when it wasn't too much trouble. Prone to sudden rages, but then her own father had been that too, and whatever his faults he had been eminently sane. It was his daughter who had taken care of the mad department. . . .

'Jane?' Norah said.

'Sorry, I was thinking,' said Jane, and then, 'Did Andy notice anything?'

'Said she'd be a bit of a handful for Bob, but that was all.'

And so she will be, thought Jane, whatever her state of mind.

'I'm sorry to land you with this,' said Norah, 'but I couldn't think of anyone else to talk to.'

'Not even Andy?'

'If he couldn't see it for himself he'd think it was all on account of I'm expecting.'

Shrewd Norah, thought Jane. The idea had crossed my mind, too. And yet, and yet . . .

'If he couldn't see it when it was in front of his eyes, where was the sense in me telling him?' Norah continued. Shrewd again.

'My dear, has it never occurred to you that all men – even the nicest of them – think we actually are mad from time to time?'

'Well of course,' said Norah. 'It's what we think about them, after all. But not like this.'

It was the last four words that did it. Norah, Jane knew, was sure.

'Jane – what am I going to do?' Norah said.

'Nothing,' said Jane.

'*Nothing?*'

'Darling, what can you do? Suppose you're right? You don't want to tell Andy – and you don't want to tell Bob either.'

'I couldn't,' Norah said.

'Nor could I.' Silence at the other end. It seemed that Norah's fondest hope had been denied.

'But don't you see,' Jane continued, 'that if you're right Bob's going to find out for himself quite soon? From what you say it sounds as if it's only just beginning – '

'Well yes,' said Norah. 'I suppose it does.'

'So it'll either get worse or it won't. If it doesn't Bob'll think she's a bit highly strung. He's tough enough to cope with that.'

'And if it does?'

'That will be Bob's decision. There's nothing we can do about it.'

'Yes,' said Norah. 'You're right. Oh dear I'm sorry for wasting so much of your time.'

Georgie could take twice as long to describe a new hat, thought Jane. Aloud she said: 'But you didn't waste my time. You had to tell somebody, and I'm flattered it was me.'

'It was kind of you to listen,' Norah said, and then, 'I'd better be off, I suppose. The hooter'll go in a minute and Harris and Croft'll be wanting their phone back. Ta-ra, Jane.'

'Bye bye, Norah.'

Jane hung up, and stroked William in the way he particularly liked. He shivered.

'Yes I dare say,' said Jane, 'but we weren't born into this world for pleasure alone. Do you think Bob's about to find that out?'

William neither knew nor cared. It would have to be Charles after all.

He heard her out in silence. He had always been a good listener: one of the hundred reasons why she liked him so much, and really Norah's doubts and fears weren't easy things to convey at second hand. Yet when she had done all he said was 'Oh dear', and sat for a while with that frown on his face that showed that he was concentrating hard.

At last he said, 'You want to know what I think?'

'If it's fair to ask,' she said.

'Between us it is. We're married after all.' He paused and collected his thoughts, and at once his Chairman of the Board look came into place. And a good thing too, she thought. That look on his face meant that his mind was working flat out.

'I see a lot of Bob these days,' he said at last. 'The Lane Engineering take-over mostly – and the more I see him the more I like him. Respect him, too. He has his own set of rules, I grant you, but he sticks to them. One of them is he keeps his personal life just that: personal. All the same I get the feeling he's worried, and perhaps Norah's seen the reason why.'

'He hasn't mentioned Sybil's father?'

'Just once,' Charles said. 'When the take-over was ready I asked him if we should offer a few shares to Sybil's father, and he said no. Very crisp. Adamant, you might say. Then he said the old boy hadn't any head for business and not a hell of a lot of money either. We left it at that.'

'You think Sybil must have told him something about her father?'

'No,' said Charles. 'I think he knows there's something she could tell. Something pretty nasty – if Norah's right.'

'Oh dear,' said Jane in her turn. Charles looked at her, then came over to the sofa, sat beside her, put his arm about her.

'Who are you thinking of?' he asked. 'Angela or yourself?'

Clever Charles, to be so perceptive. Kind Charles, too.

'Both,' she said.

'You don't come into it,' he said. 'You were unwell, and Jabber Lockhart cured you. Poor Angela was incurable. We don't know nearly enough to say whether Bob's girl's even ill.'

'We have our doubts.'

'But that's all they are,' said Charles, 'and even when we do know all we can do is help if we're asked.'

'And if we're not?'

'One of us will think of something,' he said. 'We're both fond of

Bob.' He squeezed her waist. 'Did Norah say anything about Harris and Croft?'

'The destroyer do you mean? Not a word. It was all Bob. Hardly any Andy, even. But why do you ask? Is it finished?'

'Nothing like,' he said. 'There's all the fitting out to do. But it'll be ready for launching soon.'

'Who have you got for that?'

'I thought some royalty or other,' said Charles. 'You can always get one if you book early enough.'

He makes them sound like a suite at the Ritz, she thought.

'But you had another idea.'

'Did I?'

'Georgie,' said Charles.

'Yes of course,' said Jane. 'I remember. She'll do it beautifully.'

'She'll enjoy it too,' said Charles, and then, 'Would you care for a trip to Blagdon Hall?'

'More passing the hat?'

'Now's not the time,' said Charles. 'No. The thing is you told me Georgie's going up there to visit the Derwents. We could ask her over – and Ned of course. Tell her the good news and enjoy ourselves at the same time.'

'There's Mummy,' said Jane.

'I'd like her to see your country cottage,' said Charles. 'By all means bring her too. . . . And there's another reason. Bob's in the Midlands – sorting out Lane's, and his girl's at her place – what do you call it?'

'Crag Fell.'

'We could ask them over too.'

'If Norah's right she could ruin the party.'

'Indeed she could,' said Charles, 'but we rather owe it to Bob.'

They dined early and went to the cinema. Donald Duck, who was funny, and Greta Garbo, who wasn't, and another newsreel that was all disasters, in China, in Abyssinia, in Spain. Two wars already, and a third about to happen, said Charles.

'It's hard to be sure even who the sides are,' said Jane. 'Church and State?'

'More like Fascism and Socialism,' said Charles, 'but being Spain it won't be quite that simple. Would you like to dance somewhere?'

438

To her surprise she heard herself say that she wouldn't. 'Please forgive me,' she said, 'but Norah's theory's rather upset me. I'd much sooner have an early night.'

'Me too,' said Charles, 'but being a gentleman I was obliged to ask.'

And there was another reason why she liked him so much. The words had been phrased and spoken so deftly that she would never know if he'd lied or not. In the taxi she slipped her arm through his. She really did like him: liked him so much that it might be the beginning of love, but she wasn't ready to think about that. Not yet.

. 43 .

In two very different cinemas, Andy and Piers saw the newsreel too. Andy watched it in a sort of incredulous horror, and turned to Norah to tell her to close her eyes, but Norah's eyes, though open, hardly seemed to see the screen. Manchuria, Abyssinia, and Spain alike were all so far away as to have no meaning. Thinking of knitting patterns, thought Andy. Matinée coats most likely.

Piers watched closely, and analysed what he saw. Japanese who knew their business; Italians who didn't; Spanish mobs the size of battalions without the slightest idea of how to fight, but doing their damnedest to learn. Soon he'd have to go to see his MO, who would almost certainly pass him fit for duty. As he left the cinema he showed no trace of a limp. Perhaps he ought to think about that.

Bower looked at the woman who walked into his office, and scowled. She was a pretty woman, slender, dark and elegant, but the scowl stayed in place. She was also his wife.

'I told you not to come here,' he said.

'It's the only place I can ever find you,' she said.

Bower sighed, and put down the copy he had been reading, a little 'think' piece for the *Sunday Globe* that contained far too much thought for the *Globe*'s readers.

'Make it quick,' he said.

Catherine sat in the chair facing his desk and took out her cigarette case and lighter. Bower began to drum on the desk top with his fingers.

When the cigarette was lit she said, 'I want a divorce.'

'OK,' he said, and pulled the copy towards him. That Oxford don had been a mistake. He'd quoted Cicero. Twice.

'What do you mean, OK?' said Catherine.

'What I say,' said Bower. 'You want a divorce – you've got it.'

'I want to divorce you,' said Catherine. 'Not the other way round.'

'Well sure,' Bower said.

'You agree to that?'

'Why not? I divorce you and everybody says I'm too old for you. You divorce me and everybody says , Well what do you know? He can still get it up, even at his age.' She flinched, and Bower thought, Crude, Jay, but boy it was effective. It could even be the last one. I'm glad it got through. He dropped the copy once more.

'Just one thing,' he said. 'No settlement – and you pay your own costs.'

'Well of course,' said his wife.

'Geoffrey paying, humh?'

'He's delighted to do so.'

'Takes all sorts, I guess,' said Bower.

'You have a new secretary I see,' said Catherine. 'A new, young, blonde secretary.'

'It's like I told you,' said Bower. 'I can still get it up.'

Catherine left her chair and hurried from the room, leaving the door ajar. She had long since learned that it was not the kind that can be slammed effectively. Bower got up, closed the door, and went back to his copy, that oozed red from every sentence. The most fun I've had all day, he thought. Let's hope the evening's better.

Georgie stepped out of the elderly Daimler and ran up to the steps that led to the door, where Jane stood waiting. The two women kissed, then surveyed each other as they always did when they'd been apart for a while. Checking to make sure that all the pieces were still in place, thought Jane, and when they were sure they were they grinned because it was so.

'Mrs Lovell, you look well,' said Georgie.

'And you, Miss Payne,' said Jane. 'Charles sends his regrets, but he'll be back before lunch. The bailiff wanted him to look at some Gloucester Old Spots.'

'Some what?'

'Gloucester Old Spots. It's a sort of pig.'

'Not my idea of a party, I must say,' said Georgie. 'Ned's off on the same sort of caper, only with him it's Percherons. I had hopes of that. It sounded as if it might be claret, but it turned out to be horses. But he too will be here in time for cocktails. I take it there will be cocktails?'

'Well of course,' said Jane. 'Aren't there always?'

'Not at Derwent Castle,' said Georgie. 'Not unless you absolutely insist – and sometimes it's just too exhausting.' She looked about her at the vastness of the entrance hall. 'I say,' she said. 'You do live, don't you?'

'Charles calls it the weekend cottage,' said Jane.

'He's the only man I know who could say that and get away with it. Don't you ever get lost?'

'Not any more. Come and have coffee after I've shown you your room.'

'Can we have coffee in rather a small room where I won't have to whisper? I have a secret to tell.'

'Oh goody,' said Jane. 'We'll go to my sitting room.'

A small room, elegant rather than dainty, like its owner, thought Georgie, with early Victorian furniture that had been used and polished since the day it was installed.

'Such a splendid room you gave me,' said Georgie. 'Just my shade of blue. And its very own bathroom, too. Bliss.'

'But surely at the Derwents' they – '

'Baths at the Castle are in very short supply,' said Georgie. 'I'm not sure they don't wash the Percherons in mine.'

'About your secret,' said Jane firmly.

'Jay Bower,' Georgie said, 'and Mrs Bower.'

'What about them?'

'Divorce,' Georgie said.

'He's divorcing Catherine?'

'Vice versa actually.'

Jane thought about it. 'I must say that seems decent of him.'

'You forget that I was to be the consolation prize.'

'So I did,' said Jane. 'Where was this?'

'The Brompton Grill,' Georgie said. 'He was having lunch there – and lots of wine. At one point I thought he was going to propose to me again.'

442

'You were alone with him?'

'Except for twenty customers and ten waiters. All the same I told Ned.'

'And?'

'He said Bower had no business to get drunk at lunchtime. That was Ned being nice.' Georgie smiled. 'Bower made a little speech,' she said. 'He told me about his marriage, and what a mess it was. It was all funny and sad at the same time. I never thought I could pity Jay Bower.' She thought for a moment. 'You know it's weird, but he still doesn't really believe I'll marry Ned.'

'Whyever not?'

'Well I'm hardly of the noblesse, am I?'

'You will be soon,' said Jane.

'It took me ages to convince him,' Georgie said. 'And I hadn't even got the ring with me. It's being altered to fit my finger. All I could do was tell him to watch *The Times*. At first he thought I was kidding him, but when he saw I wasn't he started to get quite angry.'

'Why on earth – ?'

'He thought I should notify the *Daily World* as well.'

Jane chuckled. 'Dear Jay,' she said. 'As set as the stars in their courses.'

'If I may ask – ' Georgie said.

'Let's see.'

'Did Bower ever ask you to marry him?'

'Ages ago. Shortly after the Relief of Mafeking he made a proposal that wasn't indecent.'

'And you turned him down,' said Georgie. 'I'm so glad.'

'Me too,' said Jane. William got up and came to her. There weren't any biscuits, but at least they weren't laughing.

'We don't have to wait for our nice chaps, do we?' Georgie said. 'I'm dying for a martini.'

When Charles asked her to launch the destroyer she was overjoyed, and so, Jane noticed, was Ned. The Marquis of Alston it seemed had no problems in assuming the rôle of Mr Georgina Payne.

'But what bliss,' said Georgie. 'I wonder if Murray Fisch will scream when he hears?'

'I doubt it,' said Jane. 'You don't belong to World Wide any more.'

'No indeed,' said Georgie, and winked at her. 'I'm promised to Another.' She turned to Ned. 'You don't mind, do you darling?'

'Just as long as I get a fair whack of whatever champagne is going,' her fiancé said. 'You'll do it beautifully and I don't want to miss it.'

They went into lunch, and talked of Percherons and Gloucester Old Spots. In the middle of it all Ned suddenly put down his napkin.

'Oh good Lord,' he said.

'Darling, what's wrong?' said Georgie.

'I promised to phone Uncle Rollo at two.' He turned to Charles. 'May I?'

'Of course,' said Charles. And Ned left the room.

'Charles, what is this?' said Georgie.

'Better save it till Ned gets back,' said Charles. 'Do you know who Uncle Rollo is?'

'Ned's mother's younger brother,' Georgie said. 'Someone frightfully grand at the Foreign Office.'

'The very same.'

'But why should Ned want to talk to him?'

'He might not,' said Charles. 'All the same it's just as well to be sure.'

He signed to the butler to pour more claret, and Georgie realised that she would have to wait until the coffee at least.

When the four of them were alone Ned spoke at once.

'Not war,' he said. 'Not yet. But it could happen any minute.'

'War?' Jane sounded incredulous, and well she might, thought Charles.

'Spain,' he said.

'But that's impossible,' said Georgie. 'Spain's in Europe. I mean I suppose you're talking about revolution – and people don't have revolutions in Europe, surely?'

'Somebody forgot to tell the Spaniards,' said Ned. 'It's just about a hundred years since they had their last one. And very nasty it was. They'll be more than ready for another.'

'Oh my God,' said Georgie.

Jane turned to Charles. 'Fascists versus Communists?' she said. Charles nodded.

'And Church versus State,' said Ned, 'and Anarchists versus everybody.'

'What else did your Uncle Rollo tell you?' asked Charles.

'One of their top generals has done a bunk from Tenerife,' said Ned. 'Name of Franco. He wasn't exactly a prisoner, but the government thought him a nuisance so they sent him to command the armed forces there – say two platoons and a drummer boy – with strict instructions not to leave till asked. Only he was rescued by Englishmen – women too – in the best Scarlet Pimpernel tradition.'

'But how on earth did they do it?' Georgie asked. 'Tenerife's an island, isn't it? Nowhere near Spain.'

'Aeroplane,' said Ned. 'Uncle Rollo thinks there were four of them – two loving couples on the spree, and the pilot. They landed in Tenerife, the gallant general just happened to be passing the landing field, in he popped, and off they shot.'

'To Spain?'

'To North Africa,' said Ned. 'Spanish Morocco. The best fighting troops Spain's got are in Morocco, which is why Uncle Rollo's so sure it'll happen soon.'

The butler came in. 'Telephone, Mr Lovell,' he said. 'The London Office.' Charles went at once.

'But why did these English people do it?' said Georgie. 'It's like something out of a movie. The kind I used to make. Was it money?'

'No,' her fiancé said. 'They're Catholics – and they've become rather tired of reading about priests being murdered and nuns being raped.'

'You think this Franco will stop it?'

'His men will rape and murder the Reds instead,' said Jane.

'Almost certainly,' said Ned. 'The Spaniards take their revolutions very seriously.'

'Darling, it isn't funny,' said Georgie.

'No by God it's not.' The look Ned gave her was bewildered. 'It's just – I can't seem to be able to take it in,' he said.

'And will he really invade his own country with its own troops?'

'That's what makes it so hard to believe,' said Ned. 'The best troops Franco's got are of two kinds. The Spanish Foreign Legion is one of them – and they're mostly Spaniards, despite their name, so part of the answer to your question is yes. But the other first-rate troops are the Army of Africa, and they're not Spanish at all. They're Moors.'

'Good God!' said Jane.

'Exactly,' said Ned. 'It isn't even five hundred years since the Spaniards managed to get the Moors out of Spain, and now this Paladin proposes to bring them back again.'

Charles came back into the room. 'Your Uncle Rollo's remarkably well informed for a Foreign Office chap,' he said. 'My office has just been telling me the same thing. Pretty well all the troops in Morocco have gone over to him. Next stop Spain, I suppose. Crawley's already issued a press statement. "Spain has shown us the way", he said.'

'He would,' said Jane.

'The market's taken it well,' said Charles, and Ned looked a little more relaxed. Jane knew well that the only market with which Charles had the remotest acquaintance was the stock market, and had made it a rule never to discuss her husband's business affairs in public. Georgie had no such inhibitions.

'But this is a revolution,' she said. 'How can that be good for stocks and shares?'

'It's a revolution against Communism,' said Charles.

As they dressed for dinner Jane said, 'I can understand why this Spanish thing's so important to you – at least I *think* I can – but why is Ned so bothered?'

'He looks after the family money,' said Charles.

'Good gracious. And is he good at it?'

'Extremely.'

Jane thought of the Duchess of Derwent. 'Well that's a relief,' she said. 'But will this Spanish business affect their money? Or yours, come to that?'

'Ours,' said Charles, and examined his tie in the mirror. 'Well yes, it will. But not adversely.'

'How can what's happening in Spain make any difference to our enormous affluence?'

'They'll fight,' said Charles, 'and to fight in the modern world they'll need weapons.' He hesitated. 'Are you sure you want me to go on?'

'Yes please,' she said.

'So the arms manufacturers, heavy industry, steel, they'll all do well. And to a lesser degree the brokers and the finance houses.'

'Harris and Croft?'

'Not yet,' said Charles. 'At least I shouldn't think so. But Lane's certainly.'

'Don't you think it's beastly?'

'Well of course,' said Charles, 'and if I could stop it I would. But I can't. Nobody can.'

'When you bought Lane's – ' she said.

'Not all of it,' said Charles. 'Bob bought some too, remember? So did Ned.'

'You didn't know about this Civil War?'

'Of course not,' said Charles. 'But I knew a war was coming – not necessarily in Spain,' he added hastily.

'Where then?'

'Almost anywhere,' he said.

'And it turned out to be Spain.'

Charles went to her, and helped her to zip up her dress. It was of cream silk, designed by Maggy Rouff, and the perfect setting for Charles's sapphires. She looked over her shoulder at him as his fingers moved. It was the classic expression of love, or at least of sex, but what she said was: 'You think that's what will happen, don't you? It won't just be Spain?' His expression was answer enough. 'Us?'

'I think so,' he said.

'But darling, why?' said Jane. 'Why on earth should it be?'

'Because it's what the Germans want.'

The Germans?

'Well of course,' he said. 'They've already sent Franco a goodwill message – so has Mussolini for that matter – but Hitler's the one to worry about.' Before she could ask the question he said: 'The Germans have never forgiven us for the last war, you see, and Hitler's promised them he'll do something about it.'

'All politicians talk,' she said.

'Indeed they do,' said Charles, 'but Hitler acts as well.'

'And because he acts we'll make money?'

'We might even live to enjoy it,' said Charles, 'but I wouldn't want to guarantee that in writing.'

His fingers had done, and she turned to face him. His voice had been easy throughout, but his face betrayed him. This wasn't a man contemplating enormous profits: rather it was one staring at disaster.

'My poor darling,' she said. 'How patient you are. Can't we get you out of it?'

'Not possibly,' he said. 'When it happens chaps like me will have the devil of a lot of work to do.'

She kissed him, careful not to leave a lipstick mark.

'At least it'll be in a good cause,' she said, and then: 'Oh dear. I've never felt less like being hostess at a dinner party.'

'How many?' said Charles.

'Just six of us, thank God. – But one of them is Sybil Hendry.'

It began well, even though Sybil was the poorest lady present, something that she was not at all used to, but her dress and jewellery were a match for Georgie's and Jane's, and her man was much more than a match if they did but know. Not that they looked as if they had been deprived of that particular pleasure, she thought. They were as sleek as cats the pair of them, cats that had done their share of purring too, even if they weren't in what you might call the first flush of youth. But whatever it was called they still had it, she thought, and in quantities. Look at what they'd landed: a millionaire and the heir to a dukedom. *And their fathers were both dead.* Jane's stepfather had died too, not that stepfathers counted anyway, but she'd read about Georgie's a few weeks ago, in some newspaper. Died in Nairobi. Car crash. Some women had all the luck. . . .

It would be all right so long as nobody talked about fathers, she thought, but in fact they talked about Spain, and Alston and Charles Lovell seemed to know even more about it than Bob, who seemed to know a quite bewildering amount. Lovell commented on the fact.

'There was a piece in *The Times* two days ago,' said Bob. 'Set

448

me thinking. I was in Birmingham so I got a clerk at Patterson's Wireless Rentals to see if we had the right sort of customer. He came up with a chap who taught politics and economics at the university there, so I went to see him. Daft on classical music he was, and our new set's the best reception he's ever had. So I offered him a year's free rental if he'd answer a few questions.'

'Didn't he mind?' said Sybil.

'Not a scrap,' Bob said. 'Professors always like to talk. Remember that bunch at the Hunt Ball? They never stopped.'

'And what did he tell you?'

'The Reds are the established government, with the majority of the country behind them. They control the Treasury and the industry and a fair bit of the armed forces. The revolution will fizzle out in a fortnight.'

'Is that what you think?'

'No,' said Bob. 'It's what he thinks. A great one for facts, that lad, but not all that good at using them. Franco won't be got rid of that easily, if he's got rid of at all.'

'How can you say that?' Georgie asked.

'He may not have the most but he's got the best,' said Bob, 'and from what my Prof was saying he's got Hitler and Mussolini too if he needs them.'

All good stuff, thought Charles. Bob really had brains and knew how to use them. Time, more than time to put him on the board of the bank. All the same he was aware of the dismay on his wife's face. Firmly he began to talk about the prospects for grouse shooting that year.

When the women left them to their port the talk drifted back to Spain.

'What was the feeling in the Midlands?' Lovell asked.

'The factory workers were all for the Republic, as you'd expect,' said Bob. 'All except the Catholics. Their priests have been preaching about atrocities a fair bit.'

'Can you blame them?' said Ned. 'It's chaps like them the Reds are after.'

'But the ordinary chaps on the factory floor?' Lovell persisted. 'Are they very concerned about Spain?'

'No,' said Bob. 'It's a long way away to them, and they're never going to go there. Like I say, they hope the Republic wins, but not so much as they hope Aston Villa will win the Cup next season.' Ned looked bewildered.

'Football,' Bob said helpfully. 'Soccer. The Football Association Cup.'

'Quite so,' said Ned.

In the drawing room their three ladies chatted sedately about wedding plans: Vionnet and Paquin, St George's and St Margaret's and who should do the catering. How satisfying it was, thought Jane, to have all that behind one, to sit on the sidelines and say 'I know, I know', and try not to show relief because in her case at least it was over.

'It's a bloody awful time really,' Sybil Hendry said.

Jane blinked, but Georgie, who had spent so much of her life in Hollywood, did not.

'Except for the clothes,' she said. 'I adore clothes.'

'I suppose I do too,' said Sybil. The thought seemed to surprise her.

'Well of course you do,' said Jane. 'Bob loves to show you off.'

'Did he tell you so?'

She asks questions like a barrister with a hostile witness, Jane thought.

'Of course not,' she said. 'It's just obvious, that's all.'

'He'll have to wear a morning coat,' said Sybil. 'He hates all that top hat stuff.' The thought seemed to cheer her.

'Ned too,' said Georgie, and laughed aloud. 'That'll teach him to get out of the Coldstream. He looked absolutely marvellous in uniform.'

'Who'll give you away?' Jane asked.

'Not Murray Fisch,' said Georgie. 'I'll have to dredge up a relative of poor Daddy's from somewhere, if I can find one who hasn't been cashiered or struck off or unfrocked.' She turned to Sybil. 'Who'll give you away?'

'From what I gather it will have to be my father,' said Sybil. She stirred her coffee, then added, 'I know he's a rotten bastard, but it's sort of mandatory.' Then in the same breath she added, 'Didn't you two once go to Spain together?'

450

'Why yes,' said Jane. 'We did.'

'What did you think it was like? I don't mean Bob's bloody output and trade figures – I mean the place and the people.'

'Sometimes horrible, sometimes wonderful,' said Georgie. 'But never dull.'

'We saw a riot in Madrid,' said Jane. 'That was terrifying.'

'They say they screw a lot there,' Sybil Hendry said, and even Georgie froze. It was a relief when the gentlemen joined them.

'Swearing and what my mother used to call strong language and detestation of her father all over again,' said Charles as they lay in bed together.

'Just as Norah said. Though I must say she behaved better when you and Ned and Bob appeared.'

'She landed Bob a juicy one,' said Charles.

'That dig about you used to have just two thoughts in your head but now you've only got one?'

'A bit strong to one's fiancé, I thought. Even Georgie blushed.'

'Not without reason,' said Jane.

Charles thought for a moment. 'Oh,' he said.

'Oh is right,' said Jane. 'Our Bob was a busy little bee in his day.'

'And now his day is over?'

'That seemed to be the message. Making money is fine, but making advances to anyone but her is absolutely verboten.'

'Do you think she's mad?' Charles asked.

'Put it this way,' said Jane. 'A visit to Jabber Lockhart wouldn't hurt her.'

Charles put his arm about her, and yawned almost at once.

'Gracious how ardent,' she said.

'Been a long day,' said Charles, 'and another one tomorrow.'

'More Gloucester Old Spots?'

'Sheep,' he said. 'Cheviots. If there's anything more boring than sheep I don't want to meet it.'

His hand found the gap in her nightgown and began to stroke.

'No ardour,' he said. 'I just like touching you.'

'I adore being touched,' she said, but he was asleep.

. 44 .

His days were long in London, too, once they returned. Long hours at the bank, long meetings, long City dinners, and Spain as often as not the principal item on the agenda. Arms, sanctions, embargoes. Jane saw very little of her husband, and discovered that she missed him far more than she had imagined. There were compensations: shopping with Georgie took up a great deal of her time. Not only a trousseau but a launching – a warship outfit to be acquired, which of course meant Paris, and was so agreeable that she missed Charles hardly at all when she was there. If she wanted to dance there was always Lionel, still elegant, still amusing, still the best dancer in London, but the underlying melancholy that was so much a part of him was far more evident than it once had been. There was her mother too, adamant in her determination not to be a 'burden' as she called it, yet willing to be coaxed to a matinée or an exhibition if Jane was persistent enough, or even a day at the races. To Jane's astonishment Mrs Routledge had not abandoned racing once her major had died. It seemed that his passion had now become hers too, and Jane drove her to Ascot and Epsom and Goodwood in the Bentley, and they both waited impatiently for the flat season to end so that they might see Bridget's Boy in action. . . . A rut, she thought, but a comfortable one. Velvet lined compared with some: Andy for example. Up every morning except Sunday before daylight as the year went by, the shipyard grew colder.

Then Norah had her baby. Bob telephoned to tell her so, before he set off for Felston: a girl he said. Jane sent a cheque at once. It was true that Bob had said he'd see to all that but in this world girls needed all they could get, unless they had an aunt who left them half a million. No point in her going up when Bob was there: not when she'd be there soon anyway, to see Georgie launch her warship.

In the meantime she continued to go racing and watch plays and films: between yawns, she thought; but it wasn't that bad, not really, her velvet-lined rut. The trouble was that she had nothing to do. There was no longer a Jay Bower to ring her up and demand five hundred words on whatever his latest fad was by six o'clock at the latest. Almost invariably he had been rude, aggressive and all too demanding, but he had also been responsible for so much of the excitement in her life. Ah well, at forty one shouldn't expect too much excitement, though there had been her birthday party: a few friends to dine and dance at the Savoy: after a struggle, her mother among them. Charles gave her a painting done in secret of Bridget's Boy at pasture. Darling Charles. He was never too busy to think of the right present. Catherine sent a birthday card, but no hint of where she was staying. Piers turned up and danced for half the night.

'How well you look,' she said.

'All done by will power.' And a muscular German lady, thought Jane.

'You'll be going back to your regiment soon,' she said.

'Not quite yet,' said Piers, and ventured on a hesitation spin. 'The sawbones think there's one more course of treatment I should try first.'

'Good gracious, what?' she said.

'Blest if I know,' he said, 'but I'll let you know when I do.'

'Your young friend seems in spirits,' said her mother.

'He's almost fit,' said Jane.

'Just as well,' her mother said. 'He could never endure idleness. Has Francis communicated with you at all?'

'Not since my wedding,' said Jane. 'Has something happened to him?'

'He is most concerned about Spain.'

'Like everybody one knows.'

'I think we can say that he is rather more concerned than most. A prelude to disaster, he says.'

'Others too,' said Jane.

'Indeed. But do others say that Franco must be stopped by armed intervention?'

453

'By whom?' said Jane.

'England. France. It is the only possible answer, Francis says.'

'And what if the Germans and Italians intervene on behalf of Franco?'

'Francis has it on excellent authority that they will not.' Jane snorted.

'An understandable reaction,' said her mother, 'though unlady-like.'

'Sorry, Mummy.'

'Francis is of course upset because the Reds are not doing so well as they – and he – had hoped. It has seriously impaired his powers of rational thought, which are usually considerable. The rôle of Tiresias does not become him.'

Dimly Jane remembered that Tiresias had been a prophet in ancient Greece. Hadn't there been a suggestion of effeminacy too? Androgynous. That was the word. Francis must have annoyed Mummy considerably.

'He is involved with some petition or other,' her mother continued. 'You were not invited to sign it?' Jane shook her head. 'Doubtless he thinks that Charles would forbid you to do so.'

'If he does his powers of rational thought really are impaired,' said Jane. 'If he did ask me, I'd turn them down for my own reasons.'

'Which are?'

'That it wouldn't work, and even if it did it would bring another war even closer. He asked you to sign, I gather?'

'He did indeed, and I declined for much the same reasons as you. He was not pleased. He had the insolence to blame what he termed the malignant influence of George for my refusal.'

'Really Mummy,' said Jane, 'considering his chosen way of life he seems to set considerable store by the influence of husbands.'

Her mother, who had shown signs of distress, delighted Jane by laughing instead.

'Obviously I refine too much on it,' she said. 'But to be subjected to such malicious nonsense by Francis – '

Whom you love so much, thought Jane. Then the band played a waltz, and Lionel came to claim her mother for it. Mrs Routledge adored to waltz, especially with Lionel as her partner. Charles came over to her.

454

'May I?' he said. 'I've done all my duty dances. Surely I've earned a bit of pleasure?'

She rose at once. 'I too,' she said, 'though mind you it's been a giddy round of pleasure all day. This lovely party *and* that picture.'

'You really like it?'

'Love it,' she said.

'I'm glad. Munnings told me he was one of the likeliest jumpers he'd ever seen. He's going to risk a few bob on him himself.'

They danced in silence for a while. He dances so much better now, she thought. Smoothly, easily, without having to concentrate. If I've done nothing else, I've taught him how to relax.

'I'm sorry there weren't any more sapphires,' he said at last.

'That picture's better than sapphires or emeralds,' she said. 'It's exactly what I wanted.'

'I was going to give you both, but – '

'The count had no more sapphires or emeralds?'

'Oh he's got them,' said Charles. 'A bracelet and a brooch. But they're attached to his new wife apparently. He married a Vanderbilt.'

She gurgled with laughter then, and noticed that at once Charles was looking at her in a way that took her back to the days before they married.

'I'm sorry I can't wear the picture for you,' she said. 'Not like the sapphires.'

'We'll manage without them,' said Charles. 'We have before.'

Marital rights, she thought, and why not? He deserves a treat. Come to that so do I. If I know anything about it hubby's going to be late for work tomorrow.

They went to Newcastle by train, Georgie and Ned and Charles and she, and stayed once more at Blagdon Hall. The bank's Rolls-Royce had preceded them. Short of an elephant and howdah, she could think of no more blatant grandeur, but it was, Charles assured her, vital. The Mexican ambassador and his wife would be at the yard, examining every detail from transport to ladies' dresses. Everything must be of the best. Mexican honour demanded it, not to mention the Mexican money paid out for that sleek and menacing piece of grey steel that was obviously meant only for war, even before its engines were fitted. Even half finished it looked complicated and modern and difficult. Jane thought of the poor she had seen in Mexico City.

'Who on earth's going to teach the Mexicans to handle that?' she asked.

'We are,' said Charles. 'They'll send us some bright ones and we'll give them a few lessons. They'll soon pick it up.' Then he put on his chairman of the board smile. How glibly men refer to killing, even very nice men, she thought, then took her position slightly behind Georgie, whose turn it was to be Queen For A Day, or more aptly star of the show, for the Mexican ambassador made it clear that he had no yearnings for the aristocracy. It was Hollywood he craved.

It was Hollywood he got. Georgie wore a Nina Ricci creation of blue and white that somehow made her look like a very well-dressed mermaid. Pearls were its only embellishment, pearls and the Derwent engagement ring, but both were of a size and quality that made the ambassador's wife blink. Then it was Jane's turn, but she had no cause for alarm, she thought, not with the Schiaparelli wedding dress and the Fabergé sapphires. She too was awarded a blink.

The favoured few chatted and drank coffee that was good enough even for a Mexican to drink. Perhaps Charles brought over a Mexican to brew it. The Mexican ambassador's staff, Felston's mayor, the local Catholic bishop (for this would be a Catholic ship that must be blessed if it were to destroy its enemies with God's help), and designers, managers, accountants: all the management of the yard, who used the staff dining room and never started work before nine o'clock. And their wives. All dressed in their best, and staring at Georgie with hatred or envy or both. Staring at me too, thought Jane, wondered if it bothered her, and decided that it didn't. They all ate three meals a day after all, and the food was of their own choosing. Anything above that was simply the winning ticket in the lottery.

The favoured few formed up in procession and moved out to the platform prepared for the launch. The air from the river was cold, but Georgie hadn't put on a coat. It was the dress, the glamour, that the crowd were waiting for, because the platform was only a

456

stage after all, and Georgie above all else was a performer, so she wore no coat, and Jane didn't either, and assured herself that there was no risk of pneumonia: well only a very little.

The cheering began the instant Georgie appeared. Hollywood had come to Felston. It was true that Georgie had visited Felston once before, to sing at a Christmas concert, but then she hadn't been Hollywood, she'd been the BBC, but this time she was a star. The crowd roared on. Scattered among them would be men who had walked with Georgie when she'd joined, for a day, the Felston Hunger March on London. Now they really were the favoured few, thought Jane, and wouldn't they let their workmates know about it.

Speeches. Far too many speeches, considering the thinness of Schiaparelli's silk. The managing director, the mayor, the bishop, some politico or other who thanked Mexico for choosing an English yard, and the Mexican ambassador who thanked everybody in sight, until at last it was Charles's turn, and all he did was to invite Georgie to get on with it in the nicest possible way, and this Georgie did.

'I name this ship *Esperanza*,' she said. 'God bless her and all who sail in her.' *Esperanza*. Hope. An odd choice of name for a machine designed for destruction. All the same the world needed all the hope it could get.

Georgie let fly with the champagne bottle. Charles had told her that the bottle had been scored all over with an engraving tool to make sure that it shattered on impact, but even so it burst like a bomb, and for once the whole launching system worked, and the *Esperanza* began at once to glide down the slipway as if a blow from a champagne bottle was all that was needed to make it move. Slowly at first, then faster, faster, down to the river, feeling its first water, sending up a great bow wave, then riding easily as the weight of chains it towed became her anchor, attendant tugs came fussing, and the other ships in the river whistled and hooted to welcome the newcomer. And all the time the cheering continued, until at last, here and there, a rhythmic chant began: Georgina Payne. Georgina *Payne*, and Georgina, whose ideas of protocol were hazy at best, stepped forward and blew kisses in all directions, and the cheering grew louder.

'Dear God,' said Charles, awed. 'I've never seen anything like it.' Then, more practically, 'Let's get her back indoors before she bursts into song.'

The cream of the chosen few went to take champagne and then lunch in the boardroom, and the Mexican ambassador made a speech in his own version of English, then presented Georgie with a gift, an Aztec brooch in massive gold. There was only one other like it in Mexico, he said, but even so the President had insisted that Miss Payne should have it, because of the affection in which Mexico held her. Georgie then delighted the company and terrified Ned by delivering a brief speech in flawless Spanish, after which Charles put on his Chairman of the Board smile once more, and suggested that Jane get rid of the women. The time for brandy had arrived. Jane looked at Georgie who rose at once, and the other women followed as the Courvoisier appeared.

Coffee and more glances of hatred or envy or both, before one by one the women drifted away, and Georgie put her feet up and sighed. 'What now?' she said.

'Where on earth did you learn to speak Spanish?'

'I didn't.' Georgie sounded indignant. 'I got a chum of mine to write a few lines about what an honour it was, and learned it like a parrot. Was it all right?'

'It went well,' said Jane, and got to her feet.

'Where now?'

'Nursing home,' said Jane. 'To see Andy's wife's new baby.' There was a shout of laughter from the boardroom.

'Do you mind if I come too?' said Georgie. 'It'll be more fun than listening to men drinking brandy.'

Before they could leave, the door opened and Bob appeared. For once he looked harassed. Another shout of laughter from the boardroom did nothing to calm him.

'Oh Lord,' he said. 'Is it all over?'

'The *Esperanza* sank hours ago,' said Georgie. 'It was the most enormous fun.'

He looked at her for a moment, then smiled, and somehow the Bob they knew was back in control.

'Sybil,' he said. 'She hasn't been well. . . . Nerves, you know. I expect it's the wedding.'

'It often is,' said Jane.

'There wasn't any way I could leave her.'

'Well of course not,' said Jane.

'All the same I'm sorry I missed it,' said Bob. 'Was there a lot drowned when it sank?'

'As a matter of fact they refloated it,' Georgie said. 'That's what they're celebrating next door. If you hurry there'll be some brandy left.'

'Where are you two going?' he asked.

'To see Andy and Norah's new baby.'

'Andy,' said Bob.

It was his brother's name after all, but even so Jane said, 'He isn't ill, is he?'

'Potty more like,' said Bob.

'Potty?'

'Daft as a brush,' said Bob. 'A real nice wife and a bonny little daughter, and all he can talk about is Spain.'

'But why on earth should he do that?' Georgie asked.

'He wants to go there,' Bob said. 'Mind you that's confidential. Norah doesn't know. Not yet anyway.'

'Of course,' said Georgie. 'But why on earth does he want to go to Spain?'

'To fight,' said Bob. The harassed look showed signs of returning.

'If I were you I'd grab some of that brandy,' said Jane. 'We'll talk later on.'

Bob opened the door to the boardroom, to be greeted by the loudest laughter so far. A kind of irony? Jane wondered.

Their reception at the nursing home showed neither hatred nor envy: more like awe, Jane thought, but then the women at the nursing home were much worse off than the helpmeets of the middle management at Harris and Croft. Not the real rock-bottom poor – a nursing home attended by Dr Stobbs wouldn't charge much, but it had to charge something or else cease to be. . . . As they entered the ward Jane was aware of the old, familiar carbolic smell, as matron sailed ahead of them, two nurses in attendance (for these were important women, famous women, women who gave money to the clinic), but there were no lines of men in regulation pyjamas, no missing legs, or arms, or eyes. This ward was for life, not death, its inmates all women with their babies. Norah had finished feeding hers and it slept. She looked up at once when she saw Jane, and smiled. There hadn't been much sign of a smile before that, thought Jane.

'Jane, pet,' she said, and matron looked shocked, until she saw Jane bend to kiss Norah.

'You haven't met my friend Georgie, have you?' said Jane. 'Miss Payne. Mrs Patterson.'

'How do you do?' said Georgie.

'Pleased to meet you, miss,' said Norah. No smile for Georgie, only awe; but Georgie was used to that.

'I brought you these,' she said, and held out a vast bouquet. 'Compliments of me and the Mexican ambassador.'

'The Mex – ' Norah began, and the smile returned. 'You've launched her?'

Georgie nodded and Norah looked at the great mass of roses and carnations, violets and peonies. 'They're gorgeous,' she said.

'Nurse will put them in water for you,' said Matron, and nurse jumped to it at once. 'I'll send you all some tea,' Matron said. 'I'm sure you have lots to talk about.'

She left them, and Jane looked at the baby. 'She's lovely,' she said, and indeed she looked far more like Norah than Andy.

'Would you like to hold her?'

Jane took the baby warily, but the child slept on. 'What will you call her?'

'Dorothy Norah.'

'Very pretty,' said Jane. 'Is Dorothy a family name?'

'It was Andy's grandma's name.'

'Was it?' In all the years she had known her, she had never been anything else but Grandma.

'My turn,' said Georgie, and then to Norah: 'If I may?'

'Oh yes please,' said Norah, and Georgie handled the infant with ease, even skill. If she gave the Derwents an heir, thought Jane, at least the heir will be well nursed, if Georgie could ever fight her way through the serried ranks of nursemaids, nannies and governesses. Her money was on Georgie.

*

460

On the way back to Blagdon Hall she felt restless. Georgie chattered away happily enough, the old familiar prattle, but Jane could only think of Norah. The scene came back to her all too clearly.

'Andy's got something on his mind,' Norah said.

'Fatherhood.'

Norah smiled, but briefly. 'He's got that all right. But there's something else an' all. Something that makes him restless. Did Bob say anything?'

'I hardly spoke to him,' said Jane. 'He arrived late. Just time for a quick hallo and a dash for the brandy.'

How I hate myself for lying, she thought, but honestly God, what else could I do?

'If you find out what it is you'll tell us, won't you?' Norah said.

'Of course.' *God, please do I have to do this?*

'He's all the world to me is Andy,' Norah said.

Then Georgie came back from signing autographs for nurses, and they talked of other things. . . .

But it wasn't just Norah. She was unsettled, on edge, with a restlessness like an itch she needed to scratch. That launch, for instance. Write it properly and it was just the thing for the *Daily World*. She ached to write it properly. . . .

Out of the blue, Georgie said, 'Where are you? Mexico? Passchendaele? You're certainly not with me in a pompous car on its way to the Northumbrian wilds.'

'Darling, I'm so sorry,' said Jane, and told her about Norah, and the *Daily World* too. One of the many joys in having Georgie as a friend was that you could tell her things.

'About Norah you can do nothing, but then you know that, ' Georgie said. 'As for worrying about the *Daily World*, you're afraid of upsetting Charles, that's all. But husbands were made to be upset. So were wives. Tell him and have a row. It's high time you did.'

· 45 ·

She went to call on Bower in Fleet Street, and for once didn't telephone for an appointment. It was Monday morning and Bower was always in his office on Monday morning, ransacking whatever the stringers and foreign correspondents had sent him, like a child tearing open birthday presents.

'What name did you say?' the new, blonde secretary asked. 'He's awfully busy – '

'Mrs Lovell.'

'Oh,' said the new, blonde secretary, and Jane knew at once that she was on the 'A' list, side by side with Charles, but then between them they owned a goodish chunk of the *Daily World*. The Duke of Derwent was on the 'A' list, too, she remembered, acquired at the time of the Felston March. She wondered whether Ned Alston would be on it as heir apparent, and Georgie too, or would she have to wait until she was a marchioness? The new, blonde secretary came out of Jay's office.

'Please go in, Mrs Lovell,' she said. She sounded amazed that Jane hadn't been told to wait: resentful, too.

'Mrs Lovell,' said Bower, and put down the enormously long telegram he was reading.

'Am I not to be Jane any more?' she asked.

'Oh sure,' said Bower. 'I was just trying it for sound so to speak.'

'And how was it?'

'Good,' said Bower. 'It suits you. You're looking well.'

'You too.' It was true. He looked years younger than the last time she had seen him, and far more relaxed. Ego massage from the girl in the outer office, no doubt.

'Not bad considering my wife's divorcing me and your best friend turned me down.'

462

'Georgie?'

'Certainly Georgie. How many best friends have you got? Promised to another, she said. And quite another it turned out to be. Who can compete with a potential duke?'

'You could,' said Jane. 'You would too, if it was what you really wanted.'

He grinned, then: the old, what the hell grin she hadn't seen since his marriage.

'I'm glad you came,' he said. 'What can I do for you?'

She told him about the launch.

'Make a nice piece,' he said. 'Go ahead and do it.' He hesitated, then, 'How did Georgie look?' he asked.

'Like a potential duchess,' she said.

The grin came back. 'Leading with my chin, at my age,' he said. 'I'll never learn.'

The telephone rang and he scooped it up. 'I told you no interruptions,' he said, but the telephone squawked back and at last he said, 'OK. Put him on.' A pause and then the telephone squawked more deeply.

'Holy shit,' said Bower.

He doesn't even know he's said it, thought Jane: doesn't even know I'm here. Whatever he's got, it's a beauty. She prepared to leave, but her movement reminded him that she was there and he signalled to her to stay before rattling out more instructions, more demands. At last he put the phone down and said, 'Mrs Lovell, we're about to sell more newspapers. Hundreds of thousands more newspapers.'

'How nice,' said Jane. 'What's happened?'

'A bishop in the North of England – Bishop of Bradford would it be? – '

'Very possibly.'

'He preached a sermon yesterday.' Bishops usually did preach on Sundays. It was hardly epoch-making news.

'And get that look off your face,' said Bower.

'What look?'

'That Big Deal look. Because this is a big deal. The biggest. In the sermon the bishop said he hoped the king would remember his responsibilities as a Christian.'

'He said what?'

Bower grinned again. He had never looked happier.

'It's out now,' he said. 'The whole glorious mess. All the wraps are off. Yachting trips, nightclubs, weekends at Fort Belvedere, the lot.' In his face happiness intensified, became bliss. 'Special editions,' he said. 'Supplements. Court Correspondents. Legal Correspondents. Archbishops. What the Man in the Street Thinks. What Australia Thinks.'

'Australia?'

'He's their king too, isn't he?' said Bower. 'Oh boy oh boy oh boy.' The telephone rang again, and again he scooped it up at the first ring. 'Hold it,' he said, and then to Jane: 'If you don't mind. – There's a hell of a lot to do.'

'Of course not,' said Jane, and rose. 'I'll leave you to it. Do you still want my piece? Will there be room for it?'

'Sure,' he said. 'Good contrast stuff. Let me have it tomorrow. Bye, honey. Great to see you again.'

'Goodbye, Jay.' But he was already talking into the telephone, and so she left him. It required a great effort of will not to shake her head – ruefully, wasn't that it? The way heads were shaken on such occasions?

'You're absolutely right,' said Charles. 'The bishop did use those words. But my chaps seemed to think he was talking about dogma rather than a divorcée.'

'Whatever he was talking about it's let Jay off the leash, *and* Beaverbrook and Rothermere.'

'Uproar in Fleet Street?'

'Pandemonium,' said Jane, 'but of an absolutely blissful kind.'

'Has he – how shall I put it – declared allegiance yet?'

'As I left he was talking to someone, who I rather think was Churchill. He said he wanted to be one of the King's Friends. Like a mediaeval knight swearing fealty. Goodness he was enjoying himself.'

'Are you still doing your piece for him?'

'He insisted on it. Good contrast stuff, he said. And Georgie always sells.'

'Have you heard from her?'

464

'Not yet,' said Jane. 'She'll be livid she's missing it – the juiciest scandal in years, – and all to make one last movie. Still it might rumble on till she gets back.'

'I doubt it,' said Charles. 'Oh I know Baldwin's good at putting things off – sometimes it seems that's all Prime Ministers are for these days, and God knows he's dithered over this for months – but now it's out he'll have to resolve it.'

'The Prime Minister? Not the king?'

'Good God no. The monarch doesn't resolve things. Not any more. He declares things open, or launched, or well and truly laid or whatever. Not the same thing at all.'

'Poor little man,' said Jane. 'Not even Brenda Coupland as was to turn to.'

Andy wasn't bothered about Edward VIII. It was true all the papers were full of it, even a good Socialist one like the *Daily Herald*, but then they had no option, had they? It was just the sort of thing folks wanted to read about. Glamorous American divorced woman and the King-Emperor who ruled over the biggest empire the world had ever known. Straight out of Hollywood, that was. And just like Hollywood it was illusion and nothing more. It wasn't as if the King-Emperor had no relatives. He was surrounded by the buggers – and whatever Edward did or didn't do, the Empire would survive, for the time being at any rate. The *Daily Herald* had got it all wrong for once. What happened in England wasn't important. It was what was happening in Spain. . . .

Most folks weren't bothered, even good Labour men. Even the likes of Joe Turnbull and Artie Sparks. They hoped the Republicans would win of course, but pretty well the same way they hoped Newcastle United would beat Arsenal. No more than that. They just couldn't see it: that this might, just might, be the beginning of the Socialist millennium they were all so good at describing – if the Republicans won: on the other hand if Franco won it just might mean the beginning of the end of the world. But they couldn't see it: or wouldn't, more likely. They were old enough to remember the Great War: the thought that there might be another was too much for them to swallow: even seasoned class warriors like Artie Sparks.

All the same somebody had to take a bite and start chewing. Norah and the rest of the town could spend their spare time – when they weren't worried about their dole or their job or their rent or their bairns – worrying about whether a woman called Wallis would be queen of England – but not him. For Andy, Spain was worry enough.

It stood to reason, – but then maybe you had to put in a bit of time at Cambridge for reason to make any impact. All the same – they meant what they said, that was the point. Franco, Mussolini, Hitler, they meant what they said, and they weren't all that coy about saying it, either. No hints, no whispers. Not them. Up on their hind legs in front of a bank of microphones, and film cameras cranking away to make sure the world got the message, and thousands and thousands of idiots yelling to order, telling the world that they'd got it too. Democracy must go. The Jews must go. The Left must go. They meant it, every word, and all his country could think about, even the *Daily Herald*, was whether the head of the Church of England could marry a divorced woman. And poor bewildered Edward wasn't even that. It might say on the coins that bore his portrait he was, but for all practical purposes he was no more head of the Church than he was captain of Chelsea football club. It was plain daft – and yet folks went on about it. On and on. Take Norah for instance. Her tongue never stopped wagging. On the other hand it was an interest for her, a bit of excitement. She hadn't had so much to talk about since Jane got married. A king for gossip, a daughter for occupation, and a husband in work. You couldn't beat that.

Andy yawned and stretched in the shelter of the fettling shop wall. His daughter wasn't a great hand at sleeping: not yet. All the same there wasn't time for him to doze off: not now. Knocking on again in twenty minutes – and the *Esperanza* and Harris and Croft waited for no man. He drank what was left of the tea in his can and took Manny Mendel's letter out of his pocket once more. Not that he needed to; he almost had it by heart. His eyes went at once to the part he dreaded, yet had to read.

. . . seems to me there is no choice,' he read. 'Not any more. We kill them or they kill us. The Jews are used to being killed,

466

but it's a habit they're going to have to break. And not just the
Jews: the whole of the Left. When Hitler or Franco says we
must be destroyed, they're not going to let us die of old age. A
bullet if we're lucky. A bullet like the answer to a prayer. Well
we can get bullets too, and learn how to fire them. And that's
what I'm going to do. I'm off to Spain, Andy, to join the
International Brigade. . . .

Just like that, Andy thought. Bernice left behind, and his bairns
– Samuel was it? Leah? And Manny Mendel off to smash Franco
and the Army of Africa. You could say it was stupid, it was
downright daft, but for anyone who was Cambridge trained it was
logical, too.

Only how could he tell Norah that? And what did she care for
logic anyway? What Norah cared about was him and their home
– and that enchanting small person who gave them no rest. What
was Spain to her? It was miles away. And anyway, she would say,
the Republicans had soldiers too, didn't they? Let them do their
own fighting.

And indeed the Republic did have soldiers, and workers armed
by the government, and Anarchists and Communists who had
armed themselves. They had heroism and self-sacrifice and devotion, oratory without parallel, and a just and righteous cause – and
all the time Franco was winning. It was true he had Italian troops
and German planes to help him, but what did that matter? He was
winning. Day after day he was moving north, advancing on Madrid, and once Madrid fell the war would be over, the Fascists
would have won. – And Norah would say, Oh what a pity, and go
back to reading about Wallis and Edward, once Dorothy stopped
yelling.

He would have to go, he knew that. He was well into his thirties
and a family man, but Manny Mendel was a family man too, and
not all that much younger than he was, and he couldn't let Manny
fight his battles for him, because in the end that was what it boiled
down to. Men like him and Manny, they had to go. But telling
Norah – how in the world was he going to do that? And yet he had
no choice. Someone had to set an example.

Piers left the colonel's club with an urgent need for a drink. His colonel didn't exactly splash it about when entertaining junior officers: it was the duty of junior officers to be fit and alert, even when on sick leave, and fit and alert meant sober. . . . Piers turned into a cocktail bar off Piccadilly, and ordered champagne: half a bottle to be going on with – and then lunch at the Ritz. Too bad it would be on his own. He could have just done with a little female company: Annabel's say. But Annabel was still in France, counting her dividends and waiting for her decree absolute. Still, the day was young. And apart from the absence of female company, the day was perfect, thought Piers, because the colonel had been an absolute brick: heard him out, agreed with every word he'd said, and wished him luck. Even said he'd square the MO. What more could a convalescent subaltern ask?

'The real thing,' he'd said. 'No substitute for it. None. It'll make all the difference when you come back to us – if indeed you do.'

He'd meant if you don't get yourself killed. But that was what wars were for, and soldiers too: killing other soldiers. He hadn't done too badly the one chance he'd had; that little foray with the Gurkhas against the Afghans: hadn't done too badly against the IRA either, the two who'd destroyed his grandmother, even if their chums had got back at him. But Spain – that would be a much bigger thing – an altogether broader canvas, you might say, after those two miniatures. He finished his champagne: time to be off to the Ritz. He'd better buy a Hugo's Spanish Primer on the way.

He was still looking at the wine list when a girl came to the table next to his, the head waiter fussed: and no wonder, thought Piers: she was an absolute stunner. – And I know her by God! She's that girl of Bob's – the one who dances at the Folies Bergère. Lilian Dunn. Tiger Lily. He rose and went to her table.

'Good afternoon, Miss Dunn,' he said.

She looked at him appraisingly. Not worried, and certainly not embarrassed: he was just one more in an unending line of attempted pick-ups. It must happen to her three times a day, he thought. At least. Then the look of cool appraisal vanished.

'But I know you,' she said.

'Cambridge,' he said. 'A May Ball. You were there with Bob Patterson.'

'You're Piers Hilyard,' she said. 'You two made that nasty little poof stand up for God Save The King.' She frowned. 'One of you was going to fight a fat man, only it never happened.'

The absence of violence, it seemed, was to be regretted.

'It must have been Bob,' said Piers. 'I'd already fought that particular fat man.'

'Oh how super,' said Miss Dunn. 'Do sit down.'

'But isn't someone joining you?' Piers asked.

'I've been stood up,' she said.

'Impossible,' said Piers. 'Unless the poor chap's insane.'

'It's Bob,' said Miss Dunn. 'I phoned him and got his secretary. Meet me at the Ritz, I said, and phone my number if you can't make it. I *told* her to tell him that and she wouldn't lie. But the bloody man didn't ring and I'm only here till Thursday, so please sit down. I'm starving.'

She very often was, he remembered, and sat while she read the menu as a don reads a text, and the waiter brought cutlery, a napkin, glasses.

When her choice was made he said, 'You hadn't heard? About Bob, I mean?'

'What about him?'

'He's engaged to be married.'

'*Bob?*' She couldn't have been more surprised if he'd said Bob had grown another head. It had taken a lot of people that way, Piers remembered. 'Who to?'

'A lady called Sybil Hendry. A widow.'

'Pretty?'

'Extremely,' said Piers. 'Rich, too. And very much the jealous type, one gathers.'

'Not of me,' Miss Dunn said firmly. 'Once a chap's engaged that's the end of it. What is it the Italians say – finita la musica. You're not engaged, are you?'

'No,' said Piers, 'but how could you tell?'

'I don't know,' she said. 'I just can. You just don't look engaged. Too relaxed for one thing.' The food began to arrive, and Miss Dunn demonstrated that if she hadn't been starving, she had been very hungry indeed.

Between bites she said, 'Describe her,' and Piers did his best to describe Sybil Hendry: her looks, her taste in clothes, her house in Northumberland.

'About the jealousy,' said Miss Dunn.

'Pathological,' said Piers. 'So one gathers.'

'I know I went to Cambridge, but it was only for one night,' said Miss Dunn, 'so kindly keep it simple.'

'He's the only thought in her head,' said Piers. 'If he left her God knows what she'd do.'

'Kill him?'

'I honestly believe it's possible – from what I've heard.'

'You don't see him any more?'

'Not many of his old friends do.'

'Not lady friends either?'

'Absolutely not,' said Piers.

Miss Dunn carved reflectively into her tournedos Rossini. 'Poor old Bob,' she said.

They had reached the coffee when Bob appeared. Somehow it wasn't in the least surprising that Bob had appeared, because even with a jealousy as dangerous as Sybil Hendry's no normal male could let go of Lilian Dunn without even a goodbye: Tiger Lily, as fair as Sybil Hendry was dark, and even more ripe, more luscious. Bob checked at the sight of the two of them, then came over to their table. For the first time since Piers had known him he seemed nonplussed, dazed.

'Hello Bob,' said Piers. 'Sit down. Have a brandy or something.' He signalled to the sommelier, then said, 'We were both lunching alone, so we joined forces. Bit of luck for me.'

Bob gave no sign that he had heard him. To Miss Dunn he said, 'Hallo' and then just sat, as tongue tied as a child.

'Hallo Bob,' she said.

Bob made a terrific effort and spoke at last. 'I had to come and explain,' he said.

'No need,' said Lilian Dunn.

'Yes,' said Bob, and the word was a muted scream. The brandy came, and he gulped at it. 'I couldn't get away,' he said. 'I thought I might – but I couldn't. It would have been nice just to see you – here – but – ' He drank more brandy. 'Oh hell,' he said, 'what's the use of making up lies for you?' He turned to Piers. 'Or you either.

470

You were always a good friend. You deserve the truth, the pair of you.' He drank again. 'She'd bribed my secretary,' he said.

'Your fiancée has?' said Lilian Dunn.

'Who else? If a woman phones me my secretary has to listen in and report to Sybil in full. I found that out just a couple of hours ago.'

'How?' Piers asked.

'Sybil told me herself. "I know it's vulgar and distasteful and not cricket," she said, "but the alternative would be not knowing what you were up to, and we can't have that, now can we?" '

'What on earth did you say to her?' Piers asked.

'Nowt,' said Bob. 'Not a bloody thing. She hadn't finished, you see, and all I wanted was for her to get on with it. Get it over with. And so I waited. And at last she said, "You would have gone, wouldn't you? To the Ritz?" And I said, "Well of course I would. An old friend I haven't seen for years. . . . A bite of lunch . . . Where's the harm? And anyway, what do you mean, I *would* have gone?" '

' "Because you're not," she said. Well you didn't have to be a genius to see that coming. All the same she had that look in her eye and I waited again. She can't bear silence, not when she's like that.

' "All that's over," she said at last, "and don't tell me it was only lunch. You'd have enjoyed that too, so far as it went. But you're not going to. Forbidden my dear. Verboten. Unless I'm there too. . . ." She rather liked the sound of that. "Shall we both go?" she said, and I said no. God knows the scene she'd have made once she saw you.'

'Why me in particular?' said Lilian Dunn.

'Show some sense,' said Piers.

'Oh,' Lilian Dunn said, not displeased. 'So what did you do instead?'

'Went to her flat,' said Bob. 'Sent out for sandwiches. Opened a bottle of wine. She was as nice as pie. Then suddenly it hit me. She was nice because I was doing what she wanted. She's always nice when I do what *she* wants, but there has to be more to married life than that. And so I – '

'Told her you were coming here?' said Lilian Dunn.

The look Bob gave her was withering. 'What would be the point?' he said. 'She'd be here this minute if I'd done that. Yelling the place down.'

'So what did you do?' said Piers.

'Locked her in the bathroom and took a taxi,' said Bob. He looked at his watch. 'If you don't mind I think it's time I went back and let her out.'

'Of course,' said Piers.

Bob got to his feet and shook Lilian Dunn by the hand. 'It was good to see you again,' he said. Above everything else he still seemed bewildered.

After he'd gone Lilian Dunn said, 'Well!' And then: 'Why on earth does he put up with it? Is it the money?'

'That's the gossip,' said Piers.

'It must have been the hell of a lot.' She looked at him across the table: more like scowled than looked he thought, but he had the sense not to take it personally, because all her thoughts were of Bob, and how happy they once had been.

'I bet you wouldn't have put up with it,' she said, 'but then you've *got* money, haven't you?'

Not nearly so much as Bob, he could have told her, but he had the sense to let that pass, too.

'I'm sorry,' she said at last. 'I didn't mean – '

'Of course you didn't,' said Piers. 'Bob's an awfully nice chap. I feel for him too.' He signalled for the bill.

Smart London could talk of nothing else. In bars, in restaurants, at dances, the one topic was would they or wouldn't they? And if they did, what was it they would do anyway? All over Mayfair people seemed to be giving parties for the sole purpose of assessing the odds on Wallis being queen. Not that she went to any of them. She'd scooted off to France as soon as the Bishop of Bradford had said his piece, and HM hardly seemed to venture outside Fort Belvedere, and who could blame him?

'A dreary place at the best of times,' Brenda Meldrum told anybody who would listen, 'and even worse when he played the ukulele: not to mention the bagpipes.'

Her husband seemed to swell in the reflected glory of it all: a pineapple ready to burst.

Charles, on the other hand, listened politely when he had to, but

472

spoke wistfully of the charm of the theatre or the cinema, or even an evening at home, especially with such a cook as Mrs Barrow to do their bidding.

'But you said it would be over in no time,' she said.

'And so it will,' said Charles.

Next day she telephoned Lionel, and he too was bored with the crisis. 'When you've seen one queen you've seen them all,' he said, and took her to a matinée instead.

Bower on the other hand was beside himself. The longer it lasted, the greater his fervour. Of course like Wallis Simpson he was an American, but there was far more to it than that. He was like a Jacobite whose bonny prince was about to achieve his kingdom, *and* the bride of his dreams, and the more he declaimed it, the more the *Daily World*'s circulation soared, for the *Daily World* was now like a simplified version of Sir Walter Scott: all lace at the throat and swirling kilts (and even bagpipes), and a loyal sword cast down at the feet of the king.

'Do you suppose Jay Bower has any Scottish blood?' she asked William, but William, even if he knew, was too canny to say, and in any case the king's courtier in chief was Winston Churchill, and surely he didn't have any Scottish blood? On the other hand he was half American. . . .

And then there came the broadcast. National Anthem. This is London. All that. Visual pageantry transformed into sound, and whoever did the announcing solemn, portentous. The rumour was that announcers who read the evening news changed into dinner jackets. Would this one, she wondered, be wearing full evening dress, and medals, and orders?

But then the king began to speak, in that strangely accented voice that stated as clearly as anything could that he hadn't the faintest idea who he was: a bit of American, a bit of cockney, and a great deal of bewilderment. ' . . . without the support of the woman I love,' he was saying. In other words ladies and gentlemen of the British Empire you've had your chance and you muffed it. You turned my Wallis down, so sucks boo to you. Then rather touchingly he spoke of his brother, and ended with the words 'God save the king'.

'Well at least he finished nicely,' she said.

473

'I expect somebody else wrote that bit,' said Charles.

Almost overnight the whole thing was forgotten. Instead of a glamorous American queen the country was to have a pretty Scottish one, with two pretty daughters as a bonus. All in all it was agreed to be not a bad swap, and now the new king was to be a family man like his father before him, as all the newspapers pointed out, including the *Daily World*, now loud in its praise of The Family and Wholesome Moral Values. ('Well I'll say this for him,' said Charles. 'There's nobody can do a backward somersault like Bower.') King Edward VIII suddenly became the Duke of Windsor and sailed off in a destroyer, King George VI prepared to be crowned, and every child in the country was promised a Coronation Mug, filled with sweets and decorated with portraits of the Royal Family. It was all very English and very nice, thought Jane.

Except in Spain of course. There the slaughter continued with an enthusiasm as horrendous as it was enthusiastic. There were horror stories from both sides: nuns raped then strangled with their own rosary beads, priests crucified, Communist men, and women, dowsed in petrol and set alight. They were just rumours of course, but the newsreel pictures of bombing and shelling were real enough. Like the pictures of the horses, thought Jane. The Spanish armies still used cavalry, especially Franco's, and both sides had far too few lorries and far too many horses and mules, even donkeys. Deliberately Jane set herself to study them, in magazines, newspapers, cinemas, and found that she could endure it. Even the dead ones failed to make her scream, but then the dead ones the cameramen had chosen were intact: no missing heads or legs, no entrails visible. Even so it was good that she had felt no need to scream.

Then one day Bob telephoned her. He had to speak to her. Urgent, he said. She and Charles were going to a dinner in the City, but she could change early and still have time to talk to Bob. Charles, she knew, would dash in at the last minute, shower furiously, change with an actor's speed and appear looking immaculate, so she had jolly well better look immaculate too. The blue and white elegance of Balenciaga, as Georgie was safely in Hollywood, and the sapphires. The City was old fashioned and preferred diamonds, but she didn't. The sapphires were special.

She was mixing martinis as Bob's cab drew up, but she took one look at him and reached for the whisky instead.

'Bob, my dear,' she said, 'what's wrong?'

'Shows, does it?' he said, and looked in the mirror. He was very pale, and yet sweating as if he were running a temperature, and one cheek was scarred. 'Aye . . . it does.' He took the whisky she poured him. 'There's two things wrong,' he said. 'One's a mess of my own making, and it's up to me to get myself out of it. If I *can* get myself out of it. The other's our Andy's mess. There's nothing I can do about that one either – but I'll feel better if I talk about it. You don't mind, do you?'

'If it isn't a secret,' said Jane.

'It'll be in the *Felston Echo* next week. Andy's off to Spain. International Brigade.'

'But he can't,' said Jane. 'What about Norah and the baby?'

'Just what I said. But he'd had time to think about that on his way down. He made me a speech. I couldn't fathom half of it. Economics. Politics. Destiny. War. Give me wireless sets any day. You know where you are with them.'

'But what did he *say*?' said Jane.

'Spain's just the beginning,' said Bob. 'After that the Italians and the Germans will start on the rest of us – after they've used Spain for practice. Sort of a punching bag.'

'Dear God,' said Jane.

'And when that happens Norah and the bairn will be at risk anyway.'

'He thinks the Germans will come here?'

'He thinks the bombers will,' said Bob, 'and he could well be right.'

'But he knows nothing about soldiering, and he's far too old.'

'I told him that an' all. Manny Mendel's there already, he says. Only a couple of years younger than me, wife and two bairns, never fired a shot in his life, but he's there. Other comrades will teach him. They'll teach me an' all. I've got to go, he says. He was like a Crusader setting off for Jerusalem. "I love Norah," he says. "You know that. I love the bairn too. It's for them I'm doing it." '

She didn't believe that, not entirely. There had to be other reasons too, but now was not the time to look for them. She waited.

'I can't help it, he says. It's my duty,' said Bob.

'Stern daughter of the Voice of God,' said Jane.

'More Shakespeare?'

'Wordsworth,' said Jane.

'He got that one right,' said Bob. 'It sounds just the way Andy looked.'

'When does he go?' asked Jane.

'First chance he gets. He has to get a letter from Britain's chief Communist first.'

'Harry Pollitt?'

'That's the one. He's off trying to see him now. So's a lot of other chaps. Times like this there's always a pack of idiots that can't wait to get killed – but Andy reckons he'll be at the head of the queue.'

'Any idea why?'

'It sounds like some bloke in Cambridge is backing him, but he wouldn't say who.'

'And meantime he's your lodger?'

'He's a bit more than that,' said Bob. 'He's my pensioner so to speak. Or rather Norah is. I'm going to make her an allowance so long as Andy's away.'

'How much?'

'Fiver a week,' said Bob. 'He reckons she'll manage fine on that.'

'Send her another one from me,' said Jane.

'Ten quid a week?' said Bob. 'Not even charge-hands make that in Felston.'

'She'll be miserable,' said Jane. 'She'll think her heart is broken. Money won't mend it, but at least she'll be miserable in comfort. I'll send you a cheque tomorrow. When it's used up I'll send you another.'

'I could manage it on my own,' said Bob. 'Nothing easier. But I know you want to do it. OK. Send us your cheque.' He got to his feet. 'I'd better be off.'

'Please finish your drink,' said Jane, 'and tell me what else is wrong. Where did you get that scar for instance?'

'I was scratched,' said Bob. 'By a cat. Not that I'm complaining. This cat can't help scratching any more than the rest of them. Best leave it.'

476

'Isn't there anything I can do?'

He shook his head. 'If there was I'd ask you,' he said. 'You're family. But there's not. Best leave it,' he said again, then smiled: the ghost of that old familiar smile that acknowledged the presence of a pretty woman. 'You're looking bonnier than ever,' he said.

'It takes longer these days,' said Jane. 'Rather a waste, too. Nothing but aldermen and cordwainers and things.' She brooded. 'Does Andy know you came here?' she asked at last.

'He does,' said Bob, 'because I told him, but all he said was, "I'll not see her. Tell her that. Tell her it's nothing personal, but I don't want to see her." Frightened you'd make him change his mind, likely.'

Frightened I'd make him ashamed, thought Jane.

Bob stood up once more. 'Time I was off,' he said. 'Give Charles my regards.'

'Yes of course. And tell Andy I send my best wishes.' Bob looked surprised.

'I don't agree in the least with what he's done,' said Jane, 'but I do have an idea of what he's getting into. He'll need all the good wishes he can get.'

'Boots,' said Charles. 'Most important thing of the lot. Walking boots. Harrods do them. I'll phone Bob in the morning.'

They were in the liner on wheels, ploughing the waves of Fleet Street on their way to the City's harbour.

'Is that all?' said Jane. 'Just boots?'

'All I can think of,' said Charles. 'He's behaving like a bloody fool, but you don't need me to tell you that.'

'He'll be in a great deal of danger, won't he?'

'Well above average, I'd say. From what I hear they use the International Brigade as shock troops. First wave attack. All that. Not that the Spaniards are cowards, it seems. Too damn brave for their own good most of them. But a lot of the International Brigade are trained for it, you see. Trained by experts.'

'What experts?'

'Well a lot of them are German Communists, and while that means they're men of the Left, it also means they're Germans, and nobody trains you for war like the German Army. They're so damn good at it, you see.'

Suddenly she found she could take no more of Spain, efficient Germans, heroic Spaniards, or of Andy, hell-bent, so it would seem, on sacrifice.

'Tell me who else will be at this pompous dinner,' she said.

He'd got back first, made himself a sandwich, taken a bottle of beer from the fridge. It hadn't taken him long to appreciate a well-chilled beer. They'd have it in Spain, likely, he thought, the climate being what it was.

Harry Pollitt had been even more helpful than he'd hoped for, and there was a letter in his pocket to prove it. Knew a lot about him an' all, the hell of a lot, but then he'd got that don Antrobus to write to Comrade Pollitt from Cambridge, and what Antrobus didn't know about ex-Councillor A. Patterson wasn't worth knowing. All the same: doing time in Durham Gaol, the General Strike, the Market Place Riot, Comrade Pollitt knew the lot. He knew all about him pretending to be a moderate Labour man an' all, so he could become a power in the Labour Movement, maybe even Felston's next MP. 'The hardest job of the lot,' Comrade Pollitt had told him, and he wasn't far wrong either. But Comrade Pollitt hadn't told him why that particular plan had been dropped, why somebody else had been chosen. Still, his not to reason why, particularly now he was a soldier, because that was what he was, under orders to get himself to France and be smuggled into Spain, and maybe learn something about firing a rifle on the way.

The door opened and his brother came in, looking worse than ever, Andy thought. Best keep it light.

'What fettle, kidder?' he said. 'Can I get you a beer?' But Bob was already heading for the Scotch decanter.

'Bloody awful,' said Bob, and slouched in a chair, lit a cigarette. 'I went to see Jane like I said.'

'She was never rotten to you,' said Andy.

'Of course not,' Bob said. 'After that I went to the Lions' House at the zoo. – The Lionesses' anyway.'

'Sybil? You and she have a row?'

'We have nowt else,' said Bob, and drank. 'Wasn't like that with you and Norah, was it?'

478

'Never,' Andy said. 'At least not until I told her I was off to Spain. She gave me what for then, all right.'

'She was entitled to.'

'You said you wouldn't start on that again,' Andy said. 'You promised.' Bob shrugged. 'But that wasn't the worst of it,' said Andy. 'It was when she cried. I hated myself then. I hated the whole world for making me do what I have to do. All I loved was her.'

'You're still going,' said Bob.

'Soon as I get a passport,' Andy said.

Next morning Bower phoned her. 'I may have another job for you,' he said. He sounded uneasy, but then she thought it's bound to be tricky if the one you want to work for you also happens to own a sizeable chunk of your business.

In his office he said, 'It's good of you to come at such short notice,' and scowled at William. She had brought William to prove that concessions must not be unilateral: dogs were forbidden in the *Daily World* offices. She had brought Foch there too.

The scowl vanished. 'I've an idea that might interest you,' he said.

'An article?'

'A whole series. . . . . It's Spain, of course. Everything is Spain right now.'

'You want me to go there?'

'Just let me tell it,' he said, and did so. She lit a cigarette and listened. At the end he said, 'Not the War Correspondent stuff, obviously. That isn't you at all – and anyway I've got a guy on that already – but the human-interest stuff, the behind-the-lines stuff. You'd be perfect for that, Jane. You couldn't miss.'

Careful before you answer, she told herself. Be very careful indeed. 'Sounds good,' she said at last. 'Sounds excellent, in fact.' He looked disappointed. He'd expected her to turn cartwheels to express her joy, but she could only do that inside her head – so far.

'May I think it over?' she said. 'Let you know later?'

'It'll have to be soon,' said Bower.

'Tomorrow,' she said.

Telling Charles would be tricky, she thought. It was true that he had no control over her, had even agreed that that was so, but nevertheless she was his wife, and she was very fond of him. As they went down in the lift she said to William, 'Yes I know I'm fond of you too, but it isn't the same, let me tell you.' William, who was no doubt wondering what Mrs Barrow had cooked for lunch, wagged his tail anyway, to show goodwill. He was much much less censorious than Foch, she thought, and just as well. Now was not the time to be thinking of Andy, who was also married, and en route for Spain.

'You have something to tell me,' said Charles. 'Something I won't like.'

She handed him his martini. 'How on earth did you know?' she asked.

'Written all over you,' said Charles. 'For me to read anyway. You're hopeless at hiding things, so you don't try. I love that, too.'

The word 'too' made it all the more difficult, but the sooner she told it the better.

'I saw Jay Bower today,' she said. 'He wants me to go to France.'

'France?' said Charles. 'What's the point in going there – unless it's Paris and dresses?'

'It's Biarritz,' she said, 'and the war in Spain.'

'Great God alive,' said Charles, 'has he gone completely mad? Does he think I'll let you get yourself killed?'

'No,' she said, 'and I won't be. There's no fighting in France yet. The point is – '

'It's out of the question,' said Charles. 'You and trouble are like iron filings and a magnet. Tell him it isn't on.'

'Because you say so?'

He looked at her then, his Chairman of the Board look, while his mind raced through the relevant facts, for and against.

'You're about to remind me that I promised you should live your own life?' he said.

'Only if I must.'

'No,' he said. 'Never that. Tell me what Bower wants you to do.'

'Human interest,' she said. 'Stories about refugees, children, old people. I could do that well, Charles.'

'None better,' her husband said, 'but could you do it from Biarritz?'

'That's where a lot of the refugees are,' she said, 'but I'd have to go into Spain from time to time. Obviously. Only not where the fighting is.'

'Oh indeed,' said Charles.

'Indeed,' she said. 'Bower has a man to do that. He's called a war correspondent.'

'And what will you be called?'

'Jane Lovell,' she said. 'He wanted Jane Whitcomb, but I said she didn't exist any more. I meant it, too.'

The thought was dear to him, soothing, at a time when he had no desire to be soothed.

'If I may ask,' he said, 'did Bower do this to annoy me, do you think?'

At first the question seemed fantastic, but then she remembered how much the two men detested each other.

'I'm quite sure not,' she said. 'It's just that he thought I was the right person for this particular job.'

Again the Chairman of the Board look. 'He's right there,' he said. 'And you want to do it very much?' She nodded. 'Because you *can* do it?'

'It could be the best thing I've ever done,' she said. 'Please, Charles. Don't make it hard for me.'

'Never that,' he said, 'but I couldn't bear to lose you. I mean that. I couldn't bear it.'

She went to him, put her arms about him. 'I'll take care,' she said. 'I promise.'

'Care?' he said. 'You?' But he embraced her even so, then after a while, because he was human after all, 'Andy,' he said.

'You mean I'm like him?' she asked.

'Well of course.'

'But I'm not,' said Jane. 'I'll be behind the lines. I told you. I've no intention of being a shock trooper or whatever they call them.'

He kissed her. 'After all,' he said, 'I can always pop across to Biarritz to see how you're getting on.'

Too late, far too late, she tried to hide her dismay.

'Not that I will,' he said. 'You know how I hate being in the way.'

. 46 .

Getting there hadn't been too bad, Andy thought. Mostly it was by train, apart from the Dover–Calais ferry, and there had been a flat calm in the Channel: he wasn't sick. The thing was that he wasn't the only one off to join the International Brigade; there was half a dozen of them: three Welsh miners, a butcher, a Cambridge undergraduate who was also a poet, and himself. Each one there to keep an eye on the others maybe, but that didn't bother him. He wasn't going to move an inch from the Party line, even if he was down in the books as a fellow traveller: besides, he had his letter from Harry Pollitt. All the same he was glad he wasn't sick on the boat: degrading, that would have been, not to mention the implication that he might be scared.

By the time they were half way across, the miners were drunk, and he wasn't surprised. Dennis, the poet, was disgusted; the butcher, Albert, was both disapproving and drunk as well, but handling it better. The Welsh miners sang, Albert listened, Dennis read a book by a man called Auden, and Andy thought about Norah and the bairn.

The odds were he was finished with Norah, he thought: not that she would leave him, any more than he would leave her. It was just that they were finished as man and wife. Bed if you like. No more bed, no more bairns. One look into her eyes, that's all it needed. They were finished, all right. *And it wasn't his fault.* He'd gone off to Spain because there was no other way. The Fascists had to be stopped, and if nobody else would do it it was up to him and Manny Mendel – he smiled at the thought – and three Welsh miners and a poet and a butcher. The butcher would come in handy all right. . . . The Fascists had to be stopped. Smashed. Rooted out. Destroyed. It was the only way, and when it was all over he would go back to

Tyneside and tell the tale in the Labour halls, play on heartstrings like he was Fritz Kreisler, and get himself elected to Parliament, and why not? That was service, too. To the poor, the downtrodden, the oppressed: the ones that needed him.

He hated the Fascists. Once he had thought, like his father, that it was wrong to hate anybody, but the Fascists were different: they had put themselves beyond the pale of humanity. Antrobus had said that, and he was right. Shooting was too good for them, though shooting it would have to be. Not that he'd ever shot in his life except for a catapult when he was a lad, and once with an air rifle at a fairground. Never hit a thing, he remembered, but everybody knew the sights in those fairground air rifles was fixed. . . . John had shot a few, he thought. He must have done: he'd got medals for it. Well now he'd have to be like John, only this time some of the blokes on his side would be Germans. German Communists with even better reason to hate the Fascists than he had. Comrades.

The miners were singing a hymn tune. The Welsh always had to be singing something, he thought, but why did they have to bring religion into it?

Guide me O Thou Great Redeemer,
Pilgrim through this barren land [they sang].
I am weak but Thou art mighty
Hold me with Thy powerful Hand.

No chance of that, he thought. For what's coming to us we're on our own. They'd got a fair crowd round them, too, he noticed, and the crowd liked what they heard. Pretty soon Albert the butcher would be passing the hat round. . . . Then the lead tenor switched to Welsh, and the words became meaningless. Dennis closed his book and came over to sit beside him.

'I know it's the opium of the masses and all that,' he said, 'but they do sing beautifully, don't you think?'

'Very nice,' Andy said.

'It's their heritage, you see,' said Dennis. 'Their tradition. Something they grew up with. Nothing to do with bourgeois art or bourgeois education. Their own free, proletarian art form. That's why it's so beautiful.'

I'd forgotten the Cambridge need to explain things, Andy

483

thought. They always have to explain things, even when we're on our way to be shot at. And anyway Dennis was wrong. The miners didn't sing well because theirs was a proletarian art form: they sang well because they were good singers.

Albert the butcher came over then, hardly the hint of a lurch in his step. He carries his liquor almost as well as Burrowes, Andy thought.

'Be in soon,' Albert said. Liverpool, that accent, Andy thought – and he reckons mine is funny.

'You speak French, likely?' Albert said to Dennis.

'Pretty well.'

'I reckon you'd better see us through the Customs then,' said Albert.

He talks like a sergeant, thought Andy. Maybe he is one. There have to be sergeants, even among comrades. . . .

They had to report to the International Brigade recruiting office in the rue de Lafayette in Paris, and just as well they had Dennis with them, thought Andy. I'd have had a hell of a time finding it on my own. So would Albert. The miners probably wouldn't have bothered. They were far too used to being told what to do. At the office the staff checked his passport, and gave him a medical.

'You are in very good health,' the doctor said. He seemed surprised, but then the doctor didn't know he'd walked the three hundred miles from Felston to London. After that it was Socialist commitment, as was only right and proper. Raised eyebrows that he wasn't a Party member, but Comrade Pollitt's letter took care of that, as he'd known it would, and they spent the night in a doss house hotel and the miners got drunk all over again.

Next morning they took the train to Perpignan. The carriage seats seemed to have been stuffed with rivets, thought Andy, but he didn't want to sleep anyway. He stood in the corridor and watched France unwind past him, ate sandwiches of French bread and cheese, and drank wine that didn't taste nearly so nasty as he'd expected.

There was an awful lot of France. Biggest country in Western Europe. Antrobus had told him so, or was it Jane's brother Francis? Never mind that. Forget Jane Whitcomb. Forget Norah. Forget the bairn. . . . The train chugged on through countryside that could

484

have been anywhere: a bit of industry, a lot of agriculture, and every open space filled up with an unfamiliar kind of shrub that he took to be vines, until at last – it was as if they had crossed a frontier – the sun came out, and there were olive trees, and lemons, and oranges, and Andy saw what Spain would be like.

Dennis came along the corridor and joined him, and Andy offered him the wine bottle. Dennis shook his head.

'No thanks,' he said.

'You don't?'

'I do,' Dennis said. 'Indeed I do. But I don't think now's the time.'

Andy looked at him. Nineteen, he thought. Maybe twenty. At that age I was the same: the only one who was important was me. Even in Durham Gaol.

Suddenly Dennis blushed. He was a plain-looking lad with a constellation of spots on each cheek that became all too apparent when he blushed.

'I didn't mean that you shouldn't,' he said. 'It's just – '

'It's what?' Andy said.

'I've never done anything like this before, so it's best I keep my wits about me. Have you? – Done anything like this, I mean?'

Strikes, thought Andy. Lock-outs. Mounted police coming at you like Cossacks.

'Nothing like this,' he said.

'Do you think you'll be able to cope?' Dennis asked.

'I'll have to,' said Andy. 'We all will. I mean we're in it. What else can we do?'

Dennis looked as if he were about to explain that nothing was ever as simple as that, but in the end he smiled instead and looked at the landscape. And just as well, thought Andy. The poor kid's scared even worse than I am. No sense in telling him there's nothing to worry about. There's everything to worry about.

They left the train at Perpignan and Albert lined them up. Albert the sergeant. 'Almost there,' he said. 'We'll be across the frontier in an hour, so what I want to say to you is this. No more drinking. We don't want to disgrace the Party, do we?' Albert the Keeper of the Party Conscience, too. He turned to Dennis. 'Lead on, son,' he said. 'Find out which is our train.'

The Spanish train took them through Barcelona, and from there they went on to Albaceta, half way between Valencia and Madrid, where the barracks of the International Brigade was. It was a grim little town in the huge, grim plain of La Mancha, and the Brigade's barracks had been the barracks of the Guardia Civil, the armed police, when fighting began. They had been massacred to a man, and there were still bloodstains on the ground floor to prove it. Dennis and the Welsh miners at once went up to the next floor, to cram themselves in with the rest of the new arrivals. Andy stayed where he was, and unrolled his blankets: so did Albert.

'I'm a butcher,' said Albert. 'Blood doesn't bother me – and anyway I was in the last lot. I take it blood doesn't bother you, either?'

'It's dry,' Andy said. 'It won't stain. And anyway there's more room down here.'

Albert stared at him long and hard, then huddled into his blankets and rolled over on his side. 'Goodnight,' he said.

Next day they got their uniforms: scratchy corduroy that fitted where it touched, and a steel helmet, but Andy's boots were his own: bought and paid for by Bob at Harrods. He began training next day too: a whole week of training, because there was no more time to waste. Madrid needed them. All the training was concerned with weapons: marching they could learn as they went along, and there was no space for manoeuvres, not in Madrid, so weapons it was, and by weapons all the instructor really meant was the rifle: the bayonet was just something you stuck in the enemy if you got close enough – and if he let you.

Their instructor was an American, a tall and stringy Southerner, who, like Albert, had survived World War One. He lined them up and made a speech. 'This here rifle,' he told them, 'is a good one, just so long as you're good, too. If you ain't, your gun ain't worth shit, so hear what I tell you – eye, sights and target in line and this rifle's your friend. The only friend you got, but mess with the line and the rifle won't help you, because it can't. And just one more thing. Never mind what you seen in the movies. It ain't the one who fires first who survives – it's the one who fires straight. Eye, sights and target.'

One by one he went to them, showed them how to load, aim and fire: not even targets; the Fascists had captured the town where the targets were made: bottles on a wall.

When it came to Andy's turn the sergeant made a discovery: Andy was a very good shot indeed.

'You've done this before son,' the instructor said.

'Never in my life,' said Andy.

'Would you just oblige me by hitting what's left of the bottle on the left?' said the instructor, and Andy did so.

'Holy shit,' the instructor said. 'You remind me of my paw. Back in West Virginia at the turn of the century paw went out to shoot squirrels, and met this here New Yorker who said to him: "You'll never hit a squirrel with a gun like that."

'Well paw was a good old boy and he said straight off, "I'll shoot all I see, and what's more I'll hit them between the eyes. Bet you a dollar apiece."

' "Done," says the Yank and at the end of the day he owed paw fifteen dollars. Well sir he paid up like a gentleman, and anyway paw was the one with the gun. . . . As he was counting the money the Yank says, "You know something? It was *worth* fifteen dollars. That's the best damn shooting I've seen in my entire life."

' "Hell," said paw. " 'Tain't nothing. This job's got sights on it." '

He clapped Andy on the shoulder. 'If you'd been around in paw's time I reckon you could have given him a game.' He looked at Andy once more. 'You sure you ain't never shot anybody?'

'Certain,' said Andy.

'Well you just take my word for it. You will,' the instructor said.

That night Dennis and Andy listened to the news in a café by the barracks. The wireless's reception was bad, and Dennis's Spanish wasn't nearly so good as his French, but there was no mistaking what the announcer was saying. The Fascists were winning.

Of course it was all just a temporary setback and the government forces were rallying, but just at the moment, and because of circumstances that even Socialist planning could not have foreseen, the Fascists were winning. Not that the wireless announcer ever used the word. Nothing like that, but he did tell his listeners that somehow or other, more by good luck than good management and aided and abetted by German and Italian tanks and planes, Franco's forces, the heathen Moors, the ruthless Foreign Legion, the bewildered peasants conscripted into his army, had somehow advanced to the suburbs of Madrid.

'Dear God,' said Dennis.

'Surprised?' Andy said.

'Well of course. Aren't you?'

The cowboys, it seemed, were always supposed to beat the Indians. Always.

'No,' said Andy. 'I'm not. The Fascists are good at fighting.'

'How can you say that?' said Dennis.

Andy sighed. For a chap that went to Cambridge Dennis had a lot to learn. But then of course he did. Twenty years of age if that.

Gently he said, 'War's what they believe in. What they're for. Of course they're good at it. We'll be good at it too, once we've had time to learn. Stands to reason. We believe, don't we? The just society. The one thing worth fighting for. But learning takes time, so they're winning for now. But we'll learn quick – because we have to. And then we'll win.'

'You really believe that?' Dennis said.

'Well of course,' said Andy.

Else why would I be here? he thought. Wife and bairn abandoned to my brother's charity, job abandoned too. I didn't give up all that for a defeat. *And anyway, losers don't get to be MPs.*

He clamped down on the thought, went to the bar and bought two glasses of wine. It was a struggle to pay for them: that's how popular the Brigade was.

Dennis said, 'That Albert. Do you get the idea that he's our political commissar?'

'Well of course,' Andy said again.

'Does it bother you? What I mean is we're here to fight for what we believe, so why do we need any sort of moral tutor for our beliefs?'

Moral tutor, thought Andy. Cambridge again. All the same Dennis too was a damn good shot. Learned it on his father's grouse moors likely.

'We believe what's right,' he said, 'so Albert needn't bother us. – So long as he does his share of the fighting.'

'He'll have to,' Dennis said. 'We all will. Soon, too. In a week, they say.'

'After that news bulletin I should think that's all the time we've got,' said Andy.

Four days later the next contingent arrived: British, Germans, Italians, Americans. Almost all of them had come through France, but now the French wouldn't let them cross the frontier. They'd had to walk over the mountains. At least I was spared that, thought Andy. On the sixth day the buses arrived, and the newcomers abandoned their threadbare tents for the shelter of the barracks, and Andy wondered how many would choose to sleep among the bloodstains. Not that it mattered. Where he was going, bloodstains went with the job. He got into the ancient bus that coughed and wheezed its way towards Madrid. As they passed the rifle range he could see the instructor telling the next star pupil about his paw and the squirrels and the job with sights on it.

They could hear the war long, long before they saw it: the crash of gunfire, and as they drew nearer, the scream of the shells before they hit. The bus passengers stirred, like leaves rustled by the wind.

Not long now, Andy thought. Mind you do your best, bonny lad. You didn't come all this way to make a fool of yourself.

They began with a parade. At first it had sounded silly, holding a Victory Parade before they'd even fought a battle, except that this wasn't a Victory Parade. This was Propaganda, Solidarity, Comradeship, and the Spaniards took it as such. The Germans led off, because most of the Germans had been trained soldiers even before they left Germany, and they marched like it, the same as the Italians. Most of them were trained soldiers too. Sandwiched in between them was the tiny British contingent, the first thin trickle that would soon be a flood. Somehow they managed to get by; the ones who had been in the Scouts or the Boys' Brigade showing the others how it was done. The Welshmen of course wanted to sing, but Albert wouldn't let them. This was Party business.

Suddenly, four ranks ahead, Andy caught a glimpse of Manny Mendel. They had reached the Gran Via by then, a vast road dense with people who yelled and roared, and applauded the men who had come from the ends of the earth to show that Republican Spain did not fight alone. That's why we're marching, thought Andy. This is what we're for. It was hard to get a good look at Manny, but from what little he could see he didn't look well. He hadn't been out all that long. Surely he couldn't have been wounded already?

The Brigade marched on to the Plaza de España, where the crowd was denser still, so that militia men had to clear a path for them. Hands reached out to touch, to shake, throw flowers, and some of the women kissed him. Andy acted like the others, and twined a red carnation into a buttonhole of his uniform jacket. Then suddenly the crowd ended, and they were in a place of green trees and shade. The West Park, where people came in peacetime to look at the flowers, hear birdsong, but only the Brigade was there now, and not just because it was November. They were very near the Front Line. There was a hot meal waiting for them: stew, and Spanish bread, and the wine he had already learned to enjoy. He got a plateful of stew and looked about him. Manny sat in the shelter of a tree, trying to enjoy what he ate, then he looked up, saw Andy, and smiled.

'Didn't take you long to get here,' he said.

'Longer than you,' Andy said. 'Are you all right?'

'Shows does it?' Manny Mendel said.

'Were you wounded?'

'Dysentery,' said Mendel. 'First day I got here.' He prodded suspiciously at a piece of meat in the stew. 'You don't suppose this is pork, do you?'

'No pork I ever ate tasted like that,' said Andy. 'It's probably goat.'

'That's all right then,' said Mendel.

He means it, thought Andy. He really means it. And him an atheist.

'Seen any action yet?' he asked.

'Only been back three days,' Mendel said. From close by there came the rattle of small-arms fire, the thud of a field gun.

'Soon make up for it,' said Mendel.

Then whistles began to blow, and the Brigade began to assemble by companies, and they wished each other luck and parted. They never saw each other again.

The German who commanded the company to which they were attached came over to give them a briefing. He had once taught

490

languages, and his English was pedantically accurate, but heavily accented. The Welsh miners looked bored in three minutes, but fair do's thought Andy. They hadn't come here for a briefing: they'd come for a fight.

'The Fascists have captured part of the university building,' the German said, 'by the Casa de Campo. Their positions are strong and their troops are good. For us they are using only the best.' He paused for a moment, but the men said nothing. 'But then we also are the best.' Some of them smiled then.

'Our plan of attack is simple,' he said. 'After a bombardment, we advance on the Fascists. They have no deep trenches, just fortified positions. We advance on them and drive them back. Whenever possible, kill the machine gunners first. The Moors are very good with machine guns.

'However, they also like to fight in open ground – and where they are now, there is none. Good luck.' The whistles shrilled again, and they moved off by companies, and the nightmare began.

The bombardment did its best, but when it ended there were still an awful lot of the enemy left alive, and an awful lot of machine guns too. When the whistles blew for the last time that day Andy found himself facing a machine gun emplacement that was more a scratch in the earth than a trench, and ran obliquely from it as the others ran for it, dropped prone and did exactly as the man from West Virginia had told him, not rushing it, not fumbling, but easy, steady, bang and bang and bang, and the Moors around the machine gun ceased to fire.

He raced on, following the German officer, who was running into a pockmarked but still imposing building that he learned later was the university's Hall of Philosophy and Letters. Men rushed to the windows and looked out. Advancing on them was a group of Legionnaires. The officer called out in German, the Germans with him began firing and Andy joined in. That bit was all right. Nothing to it. He was under cover and the Legionnaires weren't. All he had to do was pull the trigger and down one would go, but of course it didn't last. The Legionnaires pulled back. Not a rout: even a novice like him could see that, but what they called a strategic withdrawal, and the Fascist artillery took over instead.

They took a bashing all right, but the place had cellars: they could even brew tea down there, and when the bombardment stopped and the Legion tried again all they had to do was knock them down again. Regular skittle alley.

The November night came early, and the infantry called it a day, but the artillery had enough light to work by, thanks to the buildings that still burned. Andy and the others slept on the floor, on cushions ripped from the seats in the hall. An hour before dawn they were relieved by a company of Spanish militia, and Andy shook Dennis and the miners awake.

'Relieved, are we?' a miner said. 'Glad I am to hear it. I could just do with a pint.'

In the darkness Albert said, 'You don't expect a day off after just one day's work, do you? Get yourself outside. The next shift starts at sunrise.'

He went out, and the Welshmen watched him go.

'Hardly what you would call likeable, is he?' said the thirsty one.

'Doesn't have the right attitude to singing,' said another. 'If he could sing he might be a bit more human,' Then all three picked up their rifles and left.

'Did you kill any?' Dennis asked.

'All I could,' said Andy.

'Does it bother you?'

'No reason why it should,' Andy said.

'They're human beings after all,' said Dennis.

'They're the enemy,' Andy said.

At dawn it was their turn to be on the outside trying to get in. Their objective was an unfinished building called the Clinical Hospital.

'Ironic that, in a way,' said Dennis.

'I won't say it's not,' said Andy, 'but it's not funny.'

Then the whistle blew, and it was the Moors' turn to play at skittles, but some of the Germans had grenades, small fragmentation bombs on sticks of the kind they'd used in John's war, the kind they called potato mashers, and they turned out to be a novelty the Moors weren't prepared for. With their help they fought their way inside, but it was inside the building that the fun really started.

To Andy it was simply unreal: something that just couldn't happen outside the cinema. Beau Geste, maybe: the capture of Fort

Zinderneuf. Inside the building most of the killing took place at a range of thirty feet or even less. A lot of it was hand to hand. Andy found himself using the rifle butt, even his boot. Not the bayonet, he'd forgotten it was there, and in any case he didn't know how to use the bayonet, but the rifle butt made an appallingly effective club.

At last the Moors broke, and fled to the next floor, and the Brigade followed, the whole thing began all over again. Some mechanically minded Germans even thought of a way of sending bombs up in the lift, to explode in the faces of Moors daft enough to open its doors, but mostly it was still hand to hand; the rifle fired at point blank range, or the butt swung at where it would do the most damage. Slowly but almost inevitably Dennis and the Welshmen began to stick close to Andy, until the Clinical Hospital was cleared. . . . A day off, then they were fed; a day's leave spent in the West Park. Andy slept for eighteen hours, and spent the rest of it eating, and drinking red wine, and watching the dog fights above the city. The Fascists dropped a hell of a lot of bombs, but the Republic's aircraft got better and better at shooting them down. Russian aircraft for the most part. Moscas and Katinskas, so Dennis told him. Katinska sounded like a girl's name. He liked it. With a name like that the girl should be pretty.

Back again to another university building, the Casa de Velazquez, where the Polish comrades defending it had died to the last man. The Spanish Foreign Legion held that one, and they had no inhibitions about fighting in confined spaces. . . . Once again Andy had the unreal sense of taking part in a film, though no producer would permit on the screen the kind of wounds he saw. At last the Casa de Velazquez was theirs because there were no more legionnaires left to kill. The ones that survived the Brigaders shot out of hand. Andy didn't help them, but he made no move to stop them either. He was asleep.

Two days on and one day off. Five times it happened, then at the end of a fortnight both General Staffs decided they'd had enough, and the troops began to dig in. Trenches, sandbags, saps: all the paraphernalia of a formal war. But the Brigade was granted leave. Three whole days. Three days in which to sleep, drink wine, perhaps even have a bath. Andy went outside with the others. One of the miners had a head wound but he could still walk with the help of his friends. Dennis was there too, but there was no sign of Albert.

'What happened to him then?' one of the miners asked.

'Got hit,' said another.

'We could have a song then,' the first miner said.

'Show some respect,' said the third one.

'A sad song,' said the first miner. 'Something with a bit of regret in it. "All Through The Night" maybe. There's regretful for you.'

'How do we go to our billets then?' the third miner asked.

'There's a tram,' said Dennis.

'Funny sort of a war by damn,' the third miner said.

On the tram they sang 'All Through The Night'.

'We sent for you,' the German company commander said, 'because Comrade Haggerty is dead.'

So it's true Albert the Butcher's gone, thought Andy. Nothing will stop the Welshmen singing now.

'He had an important rôle in your English – platoon, would it be?'

'Just about,' Andy said, 'but there'll be more of us soon. A lot more.'

'Indeed yes, and Comrade Haggerty's rôle would be so much more important. But he is dead.'

'So you said.'

'Yes.'

The German looked at the Englishman. No regret, but no exultation either. Simply the acceptance of a fact. He remembered how the other English had stayed with this one, not reluctant, fighting well, but waiting to see first where this one went, what he did – and then they would follow. This was a good one: one to be used.

'Comrade Haggerty was more than just a soldier,' he said at last. 'He had other duties. Ideological duties.'

'He was our political commissar,' Andy said.

'Yes – well, it is not an expression we use. Not yet, anyway. But between us, that was what he was.' He motioned to a chair. 'Please sit, Comrade Patterson,' he said, and Andy sat. 'Have a cigarette.'

'I don't smoke,' said Andy.

'You will excuse me,' said the German, 'but I do.' He lit a cigar, then said, 'Comrade Haggerty must be replaced. It is thought that you might replace him.'

Now there's an offer, thought Andy. Power, influence, position; all his for the taking. What would Manny Mendel say to that? Not to mention Antrobus, or Burrowes. All the same, he answered at once.

'No, Comrade Captain,' he said.

'But why not? You would do it well. Of this I am sure.'

'I'm not a member of the Party.'

Andy took Harry Pollitt's letter from his pocket, and passed it to the German, who read it once, then again. As he did so Andy thought, the kind of power you offer's all very well in its way, but it isn't enough: not nearly enough. You're offering me half crowns. I want five-pound notes. Carefully the German folded up the letter and handed it back.

'So,' he said. 'Why are you not a Party member?'

'It was thought I could be more useful outside,' Andy said.

'Sometimes it is a decision that has to be made,' said the German. 'It is never an easy decision – especially for the one who makes it.'

There was a time I would have agreed with you, Andy thought.

'But I regret, I very much regret, that I must withdraw my offer,' said the German. 'You may go, Comrade.'

He took the train into Madrid and had a bath. There was nothing to it. If you had money all you had to do was find a hotel with bathrooms, and Bob had seen to it that he had money. He went to a place near the Puerta del Sol, and came out clean and shaved. A maid had even sponged and pressed his uniform. Close by were the cafés and bars that the Brigaders used: the firstcomers – Manny Mendel's contingent. Andy asked for him in each of them, but no one had seen him; few even knew who he was, till at last a tall Frenchman said, 'Yes. I remember him. A little man. A Jew. He was very frightened.'

Andy bristled. Manny hadn't been a coward when he fought the Fascists in the East End, he thought. It was me that ran away at Bethnal Green.

The Frenchman said more gently, 'I mean even compared with the rest of us he seemed frightened. But he did not let that prevent him from fighting. He had great courage, as well as fear.'

'Where was this?'

'The university,' the Frenchman said. 'The Science building.'

'Did you see him afterwards?'

'He was not of our unit.' The Frenchman poured wine from a jug and offered Andy a glass. 'He was a friend?'

'A very good friend,' Andy said.

'You should go to the Ritz,' said the Frenchman, then looked at Andy's face and chuckled. 'Not a place for good Socialists like us, you are thinking. But you are wrong, my friend. The Ritz is a hospital now. All our wounded are there. – In fact if you're not a good Socialist you can't get in.'

Andy went to the Ritz, but they had no record of Comrade Mendel. Give it a day or two, he thought, but he knew already that Manny must be missing or dead. And he'd be dead anyway if he was missing and the Legion got him, or the Moors. They don't take Brigaders prisoner any more than we take them. Poor Manny, he thought. Travelled all the way from London to Madrid: learned to shoot: learned to fight. All that courage and fear mixed up together – and he'd been killed in his first engagement.

Then suddenly it hit him. And so could I be, he thought. Nothing easier. I could have been knocked off a dozen times. All that way for nothing. It mustn't happen. I've got to go through with it and I've got to survive, and it's no good asking God to help me because He doesn't exist, and even if He did He wouldn't have time for me. . . . All I can do is go on and hope, and stop at the next bar for a drink.

The next bar was near the Prado, nice and handy for the Ritz, and even a month ago he would have thought it far too posh for him, but here he had no time for that nonsense. Not any more. Literally, no time. He went in and ordered wine. He would have liked to order food, too, but the odds were there wouldn't be any. There wasn't much food anywhere in Madrid.

He drank his wine at the bar and listened to the wireless. Spanish music. Guitars and hand clapping, and a singer who sounded as if he smoked too much. – Wonder what Norah would make of him?

. . . She sneaked back into my mind when I wasn't looking, the way she always does, he thought, and so to speak took her by the shoulders and shoved her out again. It wasn't any *use*.

At the other end of the bar a man and woman were quarrelling. They were close, and they were having a row. He didn't have to eavesdrop: it was just obvious. Not that they were yelling or thumping each other. The hunch of a shoulder, the muttered insults, the carefully maintained distance between them: it was all there. The funny thing was they wore uniform – her an' all – and a damn sight better fit than the one he was wearing. Sort of a khaki colour, pressed that day. Very smart. Not a mark on it. The row continued. Married, would they be? Lovers? Whatever they were they knew how to hurt each other. Better try some-where else, Andy lad, he thought. You've seen enough fighting for the time being.

Then suddenly the man swung round and walked out, a man not tall, pushing forty, but lean and fit. He walked like an officer, but the uniform was like nothing Andy had seen in the Spanish Army. The door slammed, and Andy put down his glass, but before he could move the young woman came up to him, and spoke in a language he didn't understand. Sounds like French, he thought. I need Dennis to put me right.

'I'm sorry,' he said, 'I don't understand. I'm English, you see.'

'Indeed,' said the woman. She was almost as tall as her chap, elegant even in uniform, and it didn't hurt to look at her either. Probably had money too, which meant she was unlikely to be Spanish. All the rich Madrileños were in hiding, if they hadn't been shot.

'The man who left me so rudely is English too,' the woman said.

'We're not all rude like that,' said Andy. 'We'd be daft if we were.'

'Daft?'

'Foolish,' said Andy, and the woman smiled. It was a pretty smile, but it made Andy think of cats: the expensive kind. Siamese, say.

'I was asking you if you had just come from the fighting.'

'That's right,' Andy said.

'May I ask where? – Oh by the way I am not just an inquisitive

497

woman, though it is what I'm paid for. I'm a journalist with *Le Matin*. My name is Séverine Jannot.' She offered her hand.

'Andy Patterson,' said Andy, and took it.

'I want you to tell me about it, if you will,' Séverine said. 'If you like I can take you to a restaurant I know and you can tell me about it over dinner and the paper will pay.'

'I'd like that very much,' Andy said.

'But first we must have another drink.' She signalled to the barman and champagne appeared: Spanish champagne and very nice too. The woman took a cigarette case from her pocket, a case that looked like gold, and offered it to him. 'Cigarette?' she said.

'Why not?' said Andy and took one, and thought: You don't need Dennis this time, not for what she's after. Andy lad, you're being picked up.

. 47 .

'I can't believe it,' said Norah. 'You coming all this way to see me.'

'And Dorothy,' said Jane, and indeed Dorothy was a sight to see: not seven months old, but already very much her mother's daughter.

'I'll put the kettle on,' said Norah, inevitably, for in Felston the tea ceremony was as exigent as in Japan.

'Charles and I are at Blagdon Hall,' said Jane. 'Weekend break. I thought we might go through there – the three of us. There's nobody else there.'

'You mean take Dorothy too?' Jane nodded. 'In your car?' Another nod. 'I'd love to,' Norah said.

Jane looked at her. New dress, new hair-do, make-up applied as she, Jane, had taught her. This was a very pretty Norah indeed.

Norah knew at once what she was thinking.

'All that money,' she said. 'It's mebbe sinful to say it, but it does make a difference. Takes your mind off things. For a while anyway. If it wasn't for you and Bob – '

'Never mind that,' said Jane, and quoted Bob: 'You're family. So's Dorothy.'

'You wouldn't think so after what Andy did to us,' Norah said.

'Money won't cure that,' said Jane.

'Maybe nothing will,' said Norah. 'Would you mind if I told you – try to, anyway?'

'That's why I'm here,' said Jane.

'It was all of a sudden,' said Norah. 'I knew something was brewing of course, but I wasn't expecting *that*. We'd been so happy you see, after my operation. Him in work, and then the baby coming. Honeymoon wasn't in it.

'And then he started to change. When the other feller got the

499

nomination. Lowe, would it be? And then he got elected. Well of course he did. They'd vote for a pig in Felston, so long as it was a Labour pig. Anyway Andy went to a few of his meetings, just for old times' sake, he said – and every time he came back he was worse.'

'Bad tempered?'

'No,' Norah said. 'Never that. Just – not happy. Not the same.'

'Did you quarrel?'

'Not to say quarrel,' said Norah. 'I asked him what was wrong and he said nothing, what could there be? and I knew he was lying, but how could I say so?

'Then he started on about Spain, about how Barcelona could have been a Workers' Paradise, a model for the world, if the Fascists hadn't interfered. On and on. Reading every paper and borrowing books from the library, and still I didn't see it.

'Then one Sunday night he went out for a drink with Billy Caffrey. He very often does on a Sunday. – Did, I should say. And as soon as he came in I knew something was up. Not that he was drunk or anything. He was never a drinking man. Three gills instead of two, mebbe. But the extra one was to help him tell me. . . . He told me, all right.

'Jane, I couldn't believe it. Another woman I could understand. I'd have fought her for him and that would have been that – but a country. – Not even a country. A principle.'

Like a Crusader setting off for Jerusalem, Bob had said, and now Norah was saying the same thing, but there was more. There had to be.

'Just up sticks and away,' Norah said. 'Off to Spain to fight the good fight, and me and the bairn left to shift for ourselves. Bob'll take care of you, he says. I know he will. He'd never see you without. And he seemed to think it was the perfect answer. Leaving me depending on his brother's charity. Where was his self-respect?' The tears were in her voice then.

'The operation, yes,' she said, 'but that was because it was family, like you say. And the wedding presents the same, *and* the money you both sent for Dorothy, but to make you both fork out a pension like I was a bloody widow already –' She broke off then, and her hand went to her mouth. 'Oh Jane, hinny, I'm sorry,' she said. 'I had no right to swear at you.' Then the tears began, a great storm of weeping, on and on. Jane took her in her arms and held her. 'You had every right to swear,' she said, as the tears fell faster, and then, 'Hush now, hush. You'll wake Dorothy. I can't nurse you both, you know.' At last the sobbing eased.

'I'm that sorry,' Norah said. 'It's just – I've never been able to talk to anyone before.'

'Your mother?'

'All my mother said was, "What did you expect? Marrying a gaol bird." We haven't spoken since. And Bet's no better. All she can talk about is what folks will say. What do I care about what folks'll say? All I want is him back the way he was, and that's the one thing I'm never going to get.'

'You're going to leave him?'

Norah looked at her, bewildered. 'How can I?' she said. 'He's my husband.'

'He'll come back,' said Jane.

'His brother didn't,' said Norah, then, 'Oh my God, Jane pet, forgive me. I wasn't talking out of spite. Honestly.'

'Of course you weren't,' said Jane. 'And John did die. But he survived three years, you know. One more day and he would have lived.'

'Yes but – I know it sounds daft but it's like there was a curse on the Patterson brothers. One killed, one in a war, and the other tied to a mad woman.'

Not Sybil Hendry, thought Jane. Not now.

'More people lived than died, even in the war I was in,' said Jane. 'Andy will come back, you'll see.'

I have no right to say that, she thought, and yet it had to be said: a straw for Norah to clutch at. It was the wrong straw, it seemed.

'Even if he does,' said Norah, 'how will we manage?'

'There'll be lots of work in Felston soon,' said Jane. 'Charles is sure of it.'

Because there's going to be another war, she thought, but better not go into that, either.

'That's not what I mean.' Norah sounded impatient that one as bright as Jane Lovell should fail to see the obvious.

'Him and me, we loved each other. It's not a word we use a lot

501

round here, but we did,' said Norah. 'At least I did, and he seemed to. I mean he's not exactly an actor, is he? That's why I can't understand – ' She shook her head. 'I'm getting off the point.'

'Love,' said Jane.

'Well yes,' said Norah. 'And being young we – '

'Made love to each other? Well of course,' said Jane.

Norah flushed scarlet. 'It's not something I've talked about before. Never in my life,' Norah said. 'But I want to finish if you'll let me.'

'You can trust me,' said Jane. 'I keep all my secrets.'

'It was – like magic,' Norah said. 'I never knew it could be like that. Him neither, he said. Right until he went out for those three gills with Billy Caffrey. But after – I couldn't bear to let him touch me. I told him if he did I'd kill myself, and God forgive me, I think I meant it.' She looked dazed then, bewildered by an event so vast it was beyond her comprehension.

'I hope he does come back,' she said. 'Honestly I do. But he won't come back to the woman he left behind.'

It was time to go then, to renew make-up, change Dorothy into brand-new baby clothes bought the week before, while Jane went to collect the Bentley. It was good for Norah to get out of Felston, thought Jane, even if she would soon have to go back. Felston was now for her no more than a great, sprawling prison, where even her fellow inmates were hateful to her. Something must be found for Norah, she thought. She couldn't just be left to rot.

The car's motion lulled the baby to sleep, and Norah began to talk about the happy days, the days gone by, about Felston March, and the trip to London in the Bentley, and the time when she, Norah Patterson, had met Georgina Payne. On and on she talked, as if by reconstructing the past she could blot out the present.

At last she said, 'You should have told us to shut up miles back.'

'Why?' said Jane. 'It was interesting.'

'It was daft,' Norah said. 'Crying for what you can't have. There's nothing dafter.'

At last the Bentley rounded the curve of the drive and the house became visible.

'Oh my,' said Norah. 'Do you really live in that?'

'Every chance we get,' said Jane.

502

The Bentley stopped at last, and the butler appeared at the door, a footman scurried down the steps to meet them. Dorothy opened her eyes, looked at a man in outlandish costume and prepared to yell, but her mother's arms cuddled and soothed, Jane sent the footman to fetch the pram from the Bentley's boot, and Dorothy decided not to bother. Jane helped Norah extract Dorothy from the car, and together they climbed the steps.

The butler said, 'Mr Lovell left word he'd be back by twelve, miss.'

'Very good, Smith,' said Jane. 'Mrs Patterson and I will manage by ourselves till then.'

'Very good, Mrs Lovell,' said Smith, and moved away majestically like a man at the head of a great procession, as a good butler should. Norah gaped.

'Well I thought Bob's place was something,' she said. 'But this – it's like something you see on the pictures.'

'All the Americans who come here think so,' said Jane. 'It's a great help when Charles wants to do business with them. Would you like to see more?'

'Oh please,' said Norah. 'I want to see it all.'

They were still exploring when Charles came back at twelve and demanded martinis.

'What was it this time?' said Jane. 'More Gloucester Old Spots?'

'I got word that Hebden has a hunter that might suit you,' he said. 'He's bringing her round after lunch.' He went over to the pram, where Dorothy gurgled at him affably.

'Yet another pretty lady,' he said. 'This is my lucky day.'

After lunch Jane went to change into shirt and jodhpurs. Charles had seemed serious about the hunter; but she would have to ride it before she bought. Dear Charles. He'd been absolutely sweet to Norah, who had even survived the horrors of being waited on by a butler. But then Smith had been absolutely sweet, too. Perhaps like Charles he was fond of babies.

Charles Lovell said, 'It's impossible for a man to explain to a woman why men spend so much time killing each other – or trying to.'

'You were in the Last War?' Norah asked.

503

'Three years almost to the day,' said Lovell.

'Officer likely?'

'Captain,' said Lovell. 'Like my wife's then fiancé. Canon Messeter was my battalion commander at the end.'

'The canon was a soldier?'

'I think you mean that the canon was involved in killing people. Well so he was. He was good at it – just as he was good at caring for people, too.'

'I never knew that,' said Norah, but then Dorothy began to cry, though not without reason. It was her turn to be fed.

When Jane came down, Charles was alone. 'I hope you don't mind,' he said, 'but I've invited the other two ladies to stay the night.'

'Be a pleasure,' said Jane.

'The thing is she looked so miserable when I first saw her. Being here seems to do her good.'

'You should have seen her in Felston,' said Jane. 'The poor woman's so lonely where she lives.'

'Damned hell hole,' said Charles. 'Bless you for having her. We won't be able to change for dinner of course, but Smith will just have to put up with it.'

'What nonsense,' said Jane. 'Norah can borrow a dress of mine. We mustn't shock Smith.'

Hebden worked a farm that was part of the Blagdon estate, and traded in horses whenever he could. He had a good eye, and it hasn't let him down this time, thought Jane. The grey mare he had led over to the paddock was a beauty; not too heavy, elegant in movement, well ribbed up. Jane went to her at once, stroked her soft muzzle, offered the usual sugar-lump bribe, which was accepted at once.

'I'll try her,' she said, and mounted the mare, who snorted once, then waited warily. Now was the time when they would find out about each other, and they both knew it. Walk, trot, canter, a brief gallop: the mare took them all, so to speak, in her stride. There were hurdles in the paddock, and the mare tackled them too, then the post and rails of the paddock's fence. She was altogether a treasure thought Jane, and trotted her back to where Hebden and her own groom waited. Now was the time to show modified enthusiasm at best. Hebden had as good an eye for money as he did for horseflesh. She swung from the saddle, and turned to her groom.

'What do you think?' she asked.

'She seems to go quite nicely, mam.' The groom knew Hebden's reputation, too.

'Not too old?'

'She's got a year or two yet, mam.'

Hebden remained unmoved. The mare was in her prime, and all three of them knew it. Jane turned to Hebden. 'What are you asking for her?' she said.

'Mr Lovell said if you wanted her he'd settle himself,' Hebden said. 'She's to be a present, Mrs Lovell.'

'You'd better talk to Mr Lovell then,' said Jane. 'I like her rather a lot.'

The groom looked disgusted: a good haggle ruined.

'What's her name?' Jane asked.

'Mabel, mam,' Hebden said.

'We'll see about that,' said Jane.

She had no time to speak to Charles before dinner. All her time was taken up with changing, then coaxing Norah into a Hartnell dress that was far and away the most modest she possessed, but altogether too revealing for that stern moralist. Gracious what prudes the people of Felston were, she thought, except for poor Bob of course. No wonder he'd left it the first chance he got, *and* poor darling John.

Charles handled the whole thing beautifully, but then I've begun to expect that of Charles, she thought. He told them both how pretty they looked, and made not the slightest attempt to peer into Norah's décolletage, (or indeed her own). After that he told Smith to pour champagne, and Norah, who might have resisted Charles, had no defences against Smith, so she sipped instead, and found she liked it.

'We watched you ride,' said Charles. 'I drove Norah to the paddock. Dorothy too.'

'I was worried sick,' said Norah.

'But why?' Jane asked.

'That enormous great beast,' Norah said. 'It might have killed you.'

'No she wouldn't,' said Jane. 'She's a perfect lady.' She turned to Charles. 'Hebden says I should say thank you, kind sir, and so I do. . . . Thank you, kind sir.' Then to Norah she said, 'She's a present, you see.'

'A going-away-to-Biarritz present,' said Charles.

Norah had been told all about Jane's going to Spain, and the prospect appalled her, even though Jane had promised faithfully to keep a good look-out for Andy.

'Has she got a name?' Charles asked.

'Hebden says she's called Mabel, but that will never do.'

'What then?'

'I thought "Recuerdo", if you've no objection,' said Jane.

'My Spanish is rather rusty,' said Charles. 'If you would care to translate – '

'Sort of like "Souvenir",' said Jane.

Charles smiled. 'Perfect,' he said.

Norah enjoyed her evening, and it showed. Once or twice they even contrived to make her laugh, but it ended at last with coffee and petits fours, and the certain knowledge that in three hours' time Dorothy too would order supper.

As they undressed Charles said, 'She can't possibly go on living in Felston. She'd do much better here.'

'Well of course she would,' said Jane, 'but we can't invite her to stay here indefinitely.'

'Not in the house,' said Charles. 'But I've been thinking about the Holiday Homes.'

The Holiday Homes was his name for the little village of wooden huts on the estate. Built originally for the Felston Marchers to live in while they trained for the three-hundred-mile walk to London, it had then become a sort of holiday village for Felston's poor, where families could live, walk, fish, swim in the stream, take charabanc trips to the seaside. In term time there was even a school.

'What about them?' Jane asked.

'They're clean enough, and quite well maintained,' said Charles,

506

'but they're – I don't know – a bit dour perhaps. They need the woman's touch.'

'We can hardly ask Norah to scrub floors.'

'Of course not,' said Charles. 'Women from the village do that. They wouldn't be best pleased if we fired one to make room for Norah. No,' he said. 'What the Homes need is a supervisor.'

'Sort of a châtelaine,' said Jane.

'The gift of words,' said Charles. 'How often I've envied you that.' She threw a pillow at him.

'Sort of run the place,' he continued. 'Keep an eye on it. Work out meals and trips and things.'

'Do you think she could do that?'

'She used to run a fish and chip shop,' he said. 'If she could do that in her part of Felston she could do anything.'

'I never knew that,' she said. 'Who told you?'

'She did.'

'You know how to get round a girl,' she said.

'My winning ways, my boyish charm,' he said. 'But seriously – I know you tell me her nearest and dearest have treated her badly, but an awful lot of people in Felston must have enormous respect for her.'

'Must they?'

'Of course they must. She's Mrs Andy Patterson – wife of the local hero. Apart from anything else he's the man I consulted when we built the *Esperanza*.'

'She's also the woman Georgie went to visit in hospital,' said Jane.

'We'll lend her a cottage on the estate,' said Charles. 'Lots of people around her. People who work for us – and they're not a bad lot on the whole.'

'And they'll know by now she's our friend,' said Jane.

'Precisely,' said Charles. 'Of course we'd pay her. Châtelaines don't come cheap – '

'I already pay her.'

'That's a private arrangement,' said Charles. 'This is work. A contract. Two weeks' notice on either side. Not that I expect to invoke it, and I hope she won't either, because it will be money earned, money she can put by for Dorothy – in case Andy doesn't

507

come back. She'll have her independence. What do you think?'

'First Recuerdo, now this,' she said. 'Take your clothes off.'

Despite the vastness of the house he looked at the door as if Norah might hear, or even Smith.

'There isn't much I can give to the man who has everything,' she said. 'Only myself. Please accept.'

'The offer I can't refuse,' said Charles.

> She's really doing rather well. [Charles wrote] Settling in nicely. I went up at the weekend to keep an eye on her. Recuerdo, too. Both are well. Norah is still slightly dazed at what she sees as unbelievable good fortune, but she's well up to the job. Already the place is beginning to look more human, if you see what I mean.
>
> As for Recuerdo, if she's a lady's mount then all I can say is that all the gentlemen will envy you. I tried her out, just for a little, – don't worry, she's well up to my weight – and she's a joy. Bridget's Boy is the only one to match her – which reminds me, it will be time to enter him for the Gold Cup soon. I can attend to that if you like. . . .

And so on and so on. A good, old-fashioned gossipy letter, that must have taken him absolute hours to write.

She was reading it as she took coffee in the suite of her hotel in Biarritz, and I must say, she thought, Bower does one rather well given half a chance. Flight to Paris and a night at the Crillon, then Pullman to Biarritz, and a car waiting to take her to the Hôtel du Palais, and very nice too, for this one really had been a palace, built by Napoleon III for the Empress Eugénie. It still had that air about it, as if Palmerston would arrive by phaeton at any minute, though Bower had supplied her with a car, a very smart de Dion. He had also offered her something called a courier, but she'd turned that down flat. In the first place it would diminish her past redemption in the eyes of her fellow journalists, and in the second place she would never be quite sure that courier wasn't Bower's word for spy. She settled for Bower's local correspondent instead: her French was just about up to it – better than his English – and she needed him for his Spanish, if she was to do a good job, and she must. The de Dion and the Hôtel du Palais between them were a very satisfactory bribe.

508

Charles had used that word, too. She flicked through the pages. 'Blandishments', he had written. 'That's what you offered me. A bribe if you like. Or just what you called it then. The gift of yourself. How happy you make me, and how much I miss you, though that must not be construed as a plea for your return. A bargain's a bargain after all.' What a man, she thought. Still a super lover, though marriage had tended to diminish the amount of time spent heaving and gasping; the most generous of givers, and a gentleman to his fingertips, as that last sentence proved. I wish so much that I could love him, though if I did, she thought, I wouldn't be here.

Her telephone rang. 'A Mr Ellis is here,' the receptionist said.

'Send him up.'

'Of course, Mrs Lovell,' said the receptionist. 'At once.'

Probably take a whip to him if he doesn't move fast enough, thought Jane. When it came to having his cake and eating it there was nobody to touch Bower. Baulked of her by-line as Jane Whitcomb, he had taken to referring to her as Mrs Lovell, the former Jane Whitcomb, thereby establishing her both as wife to one of the richest men in the kingdom and a wartime heroine with a movie made in her honour. What chance had poor Ellis? He was only a war correspondent who had spent most of his time being bombed and shelled in Madrid, to the *Daily World*'s greater glory. There was a tap at the door, and she called, 'Come in.' Ellis, with only one flunkey for escort. At least he hadn't been frog-marched.

'Mr Ellis,' she said. 'How nice.'

She offered her hand and he took it at last, but it was obviously something he would rather not have done. Jane looked at her watch.

'Whisky or martini?' she said.

He started. 'Whisky please,' he said.

'Bring both,' said Jane, and the flunkey swept up the coffee tray and seemed to leave the room by a process of levitation.

'You have no wish to be here,' she said. Again he looked startled. 'I'm sorry for that, but believe me it isn't my fault that you are here. I didn't ask for you.'

'Or need me?'

'That I don't know, but I read your pieces for the *World*, and Spain is where you should be. Not here. Here is where I belong.

We're not in competition, Mr Ellis. Didn't Jay Bower tell you that?'

'No,' said Ellis. 'He didn't. Mind you, sending cables can be a bit tricky.'

'I expect it can. Did he tell you why you've been sent here?'

'Background,' he said.

Jane snorted. 'I could have got that from your articles,' she said. 'Or come into Spain.'

'I shall do that soon,' she said. 'But not Madrid. Not the battlefields. That's part of the deal. You cover the fighting and I cover the widows and the orphans. I'm what the Americans call the paper's sob sister. No fighting. Not this time.'

She's telling me she's done her share in that ambulance of hers, he thought, and maybe she has, and maybe she's telling me the truth. We'll just have to wait and see. But she did offer me a drink without being asked.

At that moment the drinks came. She motioned to Ellis to help himself, and mixed her own martini. It looked like a good one, too. Ellis lifted his glass to her, sipped, then turned to the drawing-room window.

'Nice view,' he said.

Formal gardens that led to a beach that was cleaned every day, with blue Atlantic rollers to match: the wedding-cake casino an easy stroll away.

'St Jean de Luz is that way,' she said, and pointed. 'The nearest refugee camp's about half way there.'

'When did you go?' he asked.

'This morning.'

'And when did you get here?'

'Last night.'

Ellis smiled. It was a wary, almost an unwilling smile, but he did it.

'Last night I was on a train out of Madrid,' he said. 'Got as far as San Sebastian. Met a chap there with a car. He dropped me at my hotel. I got here just in time to shave and change.'

'Haven't you had any sleep?'

'On the train,' he said. 'After a bit of practice you find you can sleep almost anywhere. Just like the war.'

'You were in it too?'

'Just the last year. The Oxford and Bucks.'

A light infantry regiment, but then he had the light infantry look about him: lean, not too tall, but with a whipcord toughness.

She motioned him towards a chair. 'Sit down and tell me all about it, Mr Ellis,' she said, 'then the *World* will buy us a spot of lunch.'

He took his time answering, which at least means he takes me seriously, she thought. At last he said, 'Franco will win. I'm not saying I'd bet the family silver on it, any more than I would on any other six-to-four favourite, but that's what I think.'

'But surely, so long as Madrid holds out – '

'The old chestnut,' said Ellis. 'What happens when the irresistible force meets the immovable object? Do you remember the answer?'

'It goes round it,' said Jane. 'But surely – '

'And sooner or later Franco will,' said Ellis, 'because he'll have to. He would have done it before, but he's rather a stupid man, the kind who confuses the symbol with the reality. The way he sees it he won't own Spain until he's conquered Madrid, and Madrid's right there in front of him, waiting to be conquered. Except that it's holding on.

'I agree it must be maddening for him. He's almost there, after all. The Moors and the Legion are on the very edge of the city – in the university itself. But so is the International Brigade, and for once the Moors and the Legion are up against men who know as much about weaponry as they do. Neither side can teach the other much about courage. . . . No wonder Spain's the land of the bull fight. Death's simply the last chapter of life, to them. It's not when you die but how you die. All the rest is of no importance.

'But the Germans and the Italians don't see it like that. They're in this war to win it, and if Madrid refuses to play Franco's rules then ignore it. Bypass it for now and starve it out later. They're on short rations as it is.

'The funny thing is I like the Spaniards. Apart from their obsession with death – killing, as well as being killed – they're a remarkable people. Brave of course, but generous too, compassionate, even gentle. I know that sounds nonsensical after what I've been saying, but they are. All the same I'm pretty certain Franco will win. We won't see much compassion then.'

511

'But the Russians,' said Jane. 'Surely they'll help the Republic?'

'Stalin doesn't want the Republic to win,' said Ellis. 'He wants the Communists to win. So he won't help the Republic all that much until the Reds are running it – and by that time it may be too late. . . . I'm sorry,' he said. 'I seem to be going on a bit. But you did ask.'

'Certainly I did,' said Jane. 'You can finish the lecture over lunch. This place is supposed to do the best one in town. Let's eat here.'

She knew what was going on, or at least she knew as much as Ellis knew of what was going on, but then she'd have known just as much if she'd simply read his articles. It was just Bower – going out of his way to be nice for once, going out of his way to show the rich, powerful and possibly still talented Mrs Lovell that when it came to loyal support nothing was too much trouble for Bower of the *World*, and indeed he and Pierre Aguirra, the local man, had done their damnedest to get her all the necessary identity cards, passes, visas, accreditations. The bribery involved must have been huge.

It was time to go to work, to take a closer look at the misery war creates as inevitably as a fire creates smoke. The other refugee camps near by, then a cautious foray into 'safe' Spain, which meant that part of Spain which had escaped so far: San Sebastian, an elegant resort town with hotels almost as smart as those of Biarritz, except that now they were full of Basque children, old people, wounded servicemen. The wounds hadn't changed all that much. They were every bit as nasty as those of her own war. There were wounded children and old people too: the bombing of San Sebastian had already begun, and people with deep cellars were envied almost as much as people who had food, because already there was hunger too. San Sebastian was a port, but neutral ship owners were nervous of Franco's navy, and not much food came in, not nearly enough for children big eyed and gaunt from the need to eat, old people apathetic with hunger.

At a hotel near the theatre a group of children had gathered in the garden and were singing Basque songs – to take their mind off food, she thought. Suddenly there was a blast of sound from a loud speaker. More meaningless words.

512

'Air-raid,' said Pierre. The helpers were already shepherding the children into the hotel. There was a buzzing, snarling sound, and Jane looked up. Three planes flying in formation, big, two-engined planes, bombers of the kind she had seen in so many newsreels. The small boy in front of her called out aloud, and Aguirra, a Basque speaker like the boy, translated.

'He says there's no need to hurry. They're only Italians. They never hit anything. If they were Germans he might run, but not for Italians.'

Even so they hustled the children inside, and then her companion hustled her into a sand-bagged room reckoned to be more safe than most.

In French she said, 'I can't stay here.'

'I promised Mr Bower,' he said.

'Look,' said Jane, 'you're a Basque too, aren't you? It's my job to write about these children, make the English want to help them. Don't you want that?'

'Of course,' he said.

'Well I can't write it if I can't see it,' she said. 'Let me do my job. We don't have to tell Mr Bower.'

Reluctantly he agreed. With the bombers overhead, he was far more a Basque than a Frenchman. The only concession he demanded was that she should wear a steel helmet, the property of his uncle, a former poilu, which fitted her rather like a coal scuttle, but at least the children enjoyed it. There was even some laughter, until the bombs sounded nearer and nearer still, and a priest appeared, the children knelt to pray. 'Ave Maria, gracia plena. . . .' The Mother of God, the only mother they had left to run to.

From the roof of the hotel a machine gun rattled.

'A little inadequate surely?' said Jane.

'Firing it will make him feel better,' said her companion, 'like prayer for the little ones.'

She went into the hotel foyer, and crouched by the door. The three aircraft were very close now, searching the sky for a target like hounds nosing after a scent. Once more the machine gun rattled, but Pierre doubted whether the planes' crews even knew they were being fired on.

Then suddenly there was another buzzing, snarling sound, even

513

more frantic than that of the bombers. Two small biplanes appeared, heading straight into action. God how worn out and frail they looked, the sort of fighters Lionel must have flown, like two old men about to tackle three bullying louts, but even so the bombers turned and ran for it, and the fighters followed. The children's prayers had been answered this time.

'Any more?' her companion asked.

'No,' said Jane, 'I've got enough for now. I'd better go back to Biarritz and write it.' Firmly she handed back the poilu's helmet.

There was a good line to London, and she read the piece over to the copy-taker.

'Sounds rough where you are, Mrs Lovell,' he said.

Jane looked at her room: imitation Louis Quinze furniture, enough flowers for a florist's, fruit and champagne supplied by the manager.

'Rough in parts,' she said.

Next morning when she woke she knew at once that she had dreamed, then suddenly she remembered what the dream was. She and Charles had been out riding, he on Bridie, she on Recuerdo, and in the distance they had seen John, still in his out-dated uniform, cantering away on Bridget's Boy.

'Let's hope he can hold him,' Charles had said.

'He's got nothing to worry about,' she'd said. 'Not these days.'

At least all three horses had been unmarked.

She was eating a croissant when the telephone rang.

'Great stuff,' said Bower. 'We'll get a lot of letters out of that one. In fact if it goes as well as I think, the *World* will start a fund.'

'Refugee Fund?'

'For the children,' said Bower. 'I'm sending a photographer.'

'Pierre takes pictures,' said Jane. 'Why don't I just use him?'

'We'll try him,' said Bower. 'Lots of children.'

'And old people,' said Jane. 'They're hungry too.'

'They don't sell papers like orphans.'

'Think of them as orphans' grandparents,' said Jane. 'At least let me have a try.'

'I'll hold the children's piece till I get the pictures – and follow it with the old people the day after. Phone it in tomorrow.'

Then he hung up. It was just like old times.

She broke the news to Pierre Aguirra that he'd been appointed official photographer and he took it well. After all, it merely meant that he'd be paid more money. There had been a rather unseemly haggle about that, but when she'd said very well, I'll pay Pierre myself, Bower had given way at once, and just as well, she thought. Pierre took some marvellous pictures.

In the end Bower liked her piece about the old people as much as the one about the orphans, not least because of the photographs, she thought, though of course she never told him so: but there was something heartrending about those old women welcoming death like a lover, those old men who faced him as they would a charging bull.

Her mother wrote: 'I cried for the children. I wept buckets for the old people, no doubt because I'm one myself. A fellow feeling. All that . . . The incredible old man who saved the bread for his grandson because the boy would soon be big enough to hold a rifle, and his own eyesight had gone long since. I thought at once of George.' And indeed, Jane thought, that simple acceptance of reality was something that Major Routledge would have recognised at once, and shared.

'What a talent you have,' her mother wrote, 'and how dreadful that you should be obliged to use it in such a cause.'

Lionel sent her a picture postcard of Frith's Derby Day. 'Please remember there's still some pleasure left,' he wrote, 'so do take care. I know you won't but at least I've said it.' Charles wrote her pages and pages, and sent even more red roses. Soon the hotel would run out of vases. . . . After delicate negotiation Pierre obtained permission for them to go to Barcelona to see more orphans. It's because Charles is a banker, she thought. Even the Republicans know they'll need money until they finally establish the Workers' Paradise. They drove across France in the de Dion, and crossed the frontier at Irun. On through Gerona, a bit battered, but not too bad, not yet, and on to Barcelona.

The city was a kind of joyous madhouse. Even Pierre who, being Basque, had no great opinion of Catalans, responded to the sheer zest for life that pervaded it everywhere. It was mad, of course. The Fascists were moving towards them: Pamplona, Huesca, Zaragoza:

515

and still pushing hard, drawing closer day by day, and yet Barcelona was en fête: a fiesta that went on day after day. Not much food, but lots of wine, and flowers everywhere: red carnations far and away the most popular, and scarlet geraniums in pots on every window ledge. Wherever they went people smiled at them, made them welcome: the policemen and soldiers who examined their passports, the waiters in the cafés, (no tips, the notices admonished them. Here we are all free men and women, all comrades) even passersby on foot, or on the trams that scurried across the city between the air-raids.

Barcelona knew a great deal about air-raids: more than San Sebastian, almost as much as Madrid, for in the early days there had been no laughter; only execution on a massive scale. Bourgeois men and women, even children, the inevitable priests and nuns, those who were traitors for sure, and those who might well be, and who therefore, however regrettably, had earned a bullet if the People's Republic was to be safe. Franco knew all about the killings, and the Balearic Islands were already his, and within easy flying distance of the city. The bombing began almost at once, and sometimes too a warship would appear, and lob shells very much at random, but more often than not with dreadful results.

And still the city rejoiced. Leftists of every kind, Socialists, Communists, Anarchists, (for at that point Barcelona was very much the Anarchists' city) held street parties between the raids, danced their national dance, the Sardana, even at night, even in the black-out, so long as there was enough moon for them to see by. Soldiers on leave pulled them in among the dancers, offered them cigarettes, goatskins filled with wine. Once Pierre met some French Anarchists, and once Jane was approached by an Englishman who was as mad as the rest.

'It won't last,' he told them. 'These poor chaps think it will, but it won't. I give it another year at best. But in the meantime – isn't it wonderful?' He wiped the sweat from his forehead. 'Where are you staying?'

'A hotel by the Cathedral,' said Jane. 'Where are you?'

'I'm a machine gunner,' he said, 'on the Lerìda Front – but I felt like a dance so I got a lift on a lorry. I go back at midnight – rather like Cinderella.'

The Catalan band, that sounded like oboes under stress, gave an admonitory squeal, and he pointed his toe, grave as any dancing master.

Next day she and Pierre visited a hospital, and here there was no laughter, yet cheerfulness persisted among the patients, though not, Jane noticed, among the doctors and nurses. There was also a quite appalling shortage of everything a hospital needs, she thought, from ambulances to aspirins, and yet the cheerfulness persists, even among the amputees.

Two more air-raids, and Pierre insisted that they must go back, and there was no doubt that he was right, she thought. One bomb had fallen in the next street. Pierre had got his photographs, and she had seen things last observed twenty years before, but air-raids were not in her brief and it was time to go. In a village near Gerona they were holding an impromptu bullfight to raise money for Catalan orphans, and Pierre photographed that, too: Jane got enough for another piece, then they drove back to Biarritz: to hot baths and the most heavenly food, and an impatient Bower screaming, 'More, more,' down the telephone: and a cable from Georgie aboard the *Queen Mary* that said, 'Darling, you haven't forgotten my nuptials, have you? I'll be in London Thursday.'

Of course the whole hotel knew about the cable, and Georgie, so that her prestige soared even higher until she told the manager that she would have to leave. She thought that the poor man would burst into tears. Pierre Aguirra did. Even so it would be nice to go to Georgie's wedding, and to see Charles again. And William.

Charles was absolutely sweet to her, though William, like Foch before him, was all too easily seduced by Mrs Barrow's largesse.

'I've missed you more than I can say,' said Charles that night. 'When we were lovers we were either together or not, and one simply had to accept it, but being married and you not there – it wasn't easy, my love.'

'It was in a good cause,' she said.

'And one I know all about. I lay in bed one night and it all came back to me – trench raids, mortars, air-raids, and a day on the Somme for a grand finale. I didn't want to do it – it just came into my head and refused to go. All your fault.'

'Charles!' she said.

'But it was. It was worrying about you. You in it and me not.'

'But I promised you I'd stay out of the dangerous places this time.'

'And I said I believed you, and we both lied.' She wanted to argue, but his arms came round her, friendly, gentle. 'Be fair,' he said. 'We've both been in it. We both know that any place can be dangerous. The Barcelona air-raid, for instance.'

'That – just happened,' she said. 'It was the orphans I'd gone to see.'

'I believe that. Of course I do,' he said. 'In wars air-raids always happen. All the same you might have been killed.'

'Not when I was wearing Pierre's uncle's helmet,' she said, and began to describe it. Soon she had him laughing and from laughter to kisses to love-making was easy and inevitable. All the same his words stayed with her: 'You might have been killed.' For Charles that was simply another way of saying, 'Without you my happiness is over,' and whether it's true or not, she thought, he certainly believes it.

. 48 .

Getting there hadn't been all that difficult, thought Piers. He'd been advised to go to see a man in Kensington, a Spaniard who was obviously a soldier, and that man had passed him on to another in Paris. Boat train and a nice calm day for the crossing, which was just as well: he was a rotten sailor, and being sick would have done nothing for his self-esteem; then on to Paris and a taxi to the Crillon in time to change for dinner. His only regret was that Lilian Dunn wasn't at the Folies Bergère that week, but he mustn't be greedy.

The Spaniard lived in the rue Pasquier in the eighth arrondissement, and what he had was a house, not an apartment, a house with a garden and trees and things, and that made him rich, maybe even in Granny's class, but even so he was another soldier in civilian clothes: Señor Ibañez. He walked with a limp, which probably explained why he was in Paris and not in Spain. Something in common, thought Piers, but he might be touchy. I won't mention it unless he does.

There was one other guest for dinner: a woman introduced as the Marquesa de Antequera: quite the ugliest woman he'd ever seen, and more than a little mad. As he was brought in to be introduced, the marquesa was talking in Spanish to Señora Ibañez, a woman still slim, still elegant, still, within limits, beautiful. The contrast did nothing for the marquesa.

'May I present Captain Hilyard,' Ibañez said. 'The Marquesa de Antequera.'

The marquesa changed languages as a good driver changes gears.

'Ah, the young man who is going to fight for Spain. I am delighted to meet you.'

'My pleasure,' said Piers.

'Perhaps not that,' the marquesa said. Mad or not she knows

519

exactly what I'm thinking about her, Piers thought, but no doubt she's had a lot of practice.

'But I can tell you about the task you have set yourself.'

'The marquesa was in Madrid when the war began,' said Señora Ibañez. 'She only just got out in time.'

'My husband did not,' the marquesa said. 'Nor did my son.'

'I'm very sorry to hear it,' said Piers.

'The irony of it is,' the marquesa said, 'that my son had a deep sympathy – one could call it even compassion – for those who shot him. My husband of course did not.'

'Please,' said Señora Ibañez, 'you mustn't upset yourself.'

'I am not upsetting myself,' said the marquesa. 'This young man must be told, but perhaps I should postpone my story until after dinner.' She paused for a moment, then said, 'Hilyard? Surely I have heard that name?'

Oh Lord, Piers thought, she must have read about me and the IRA. It had got into a lot of foreign papers because of daddy being a lord.

'Jane Whitcomb,' said the marquesa. 'She stayed with us in a house we had in Santiago de Compostela, a house which is now blown up.'

Snap, thought Piers.

'She was with the most beautiful woman I ever saw,' the marquesa said. 'Georgina Payne, the film star. You know them also?'

'Jane I know well,' said Piers. 'Miss Payne I met a couple of times.'

'There was something she said about you. What could it be? Oh yes. You were a most distinguished horseman and she had a horse you wanted but she would not sell.'

'I'm not surprised,' said Piers. 'It's going to win the Gold Cup.'

'You must give me its name,' said Ibañez. 'I shall have a bet on it.'

They ate well of course. The rich in Paris always ate well, except for the marquesa, who ate very little and drank even less. During the meal they talked of racing and the cinema and Georgina Payne, and was she really so beautiful as she appeared on the screen? Even more said the marquesa and Piers, which Ibañez and his wife found hard to believe.

Over coffee in the drawing room the marquesa said at once, 'I must tell the captain now. He must know.'

'Of course,' Señora Ibañez said, but she didn't sound all that enthusiastic, Piers thought.

The marquesa said at once, 'It began in the summer. First it was restlessness. People talking too loudly, drinking too much, shouting to be heard over the noise of the radio in cheap cafés, and on the radio nothing but speeches. The Left! The Left! Struggle. The masses. Liberation. The Left! The Left! . . . Then it was riots. At first quite small ones. Not many killed though many were – trampled, is that it? But at first the police were good at keeping them in check.

'My husband wished to go to San Sebastian for the summer. It would make a change from Santiago de Compostela, he said – but my brother and sister-in-law were in San Sebastian, and I am not fond of my sister-in-law, and so I – prevaricated? Surely that cannot be right.'

'Procrastinated,' said Piers.

'Exactly so. Procrastinated. It was a foolish thing to do, and of course God punishes foolishness. I think God was still in Madrid at that time.'

The others sat in silence, and the marquesa continued, unaware that she had said anything extraordinary.

'The riots got bigger – in all the main plazas. The cars of the rich were scratched, hit with stones, tyres let down – and the police began to lose control. I think in their hearts they still despised the crowd – those "masses" the radio speakers worshipped like saints – but the police began to be afraid of them. Even the Guardia Civil. First they did not try so hard, then they did not try at all. . . . Some of it, of course, was funny.'

'Funny?' said Piers.

'Certainly. In every tragedy there is a fool – like the picadors' horses at the bull-fight – but these were not horses. They were bourgeois, the ones who had so much to lose, but were not rich enough to run away. So they tried to look like the masses. Like Anti-Christ.'

Again the others waited in silence.

'The women wore their oldest clothes: the men left off hats, collars, ties. Some even put on dungarees. – But of course Anti-Christ knew who they were. And then the killings began.

'Young men with guns would seize a motor car and announce that it belonged to the state, then drive to an area where the bourgeois lived and seize one: usually a man. When one considers the fuss he makes about equality, Anti-Christ has little faith in women as effective creatures: which is of course why I am here.

'It was all done in what I can only think of as a Hollywood manner. Gangsters and pistols and being – taken for a ride? Is that it?'

'That's it,' said Piers.

'And in the morning a body would be found in the Casa de Campo. Or two bodies. Or even ten.' She turned to Ibañez. 'You remember the Casa de Campo? Just outside the city? Near the President's Palace?'

'Of course,' said Ibañez.

'That was where the bodies were left, but for the most part no one came to identify them. To do so would be to say "I am a bourgeois too." ' Inconsequently she added, 'It was very hot throughout that time.'

But was it inconsequential, Piers wondered, or was she talking about Hell?

'It was time to go, and I said so, but my husband by then was waiting for payment from someone who owed us money. "One more day," he said, and my son had got hold of a gun he swore he would use, – even against Anti-Christ for whom he felt such compassion, – and so we stayed.

'By then the martyrdom of the priests had begun also. Beating or whipping, and then the firing squad. That was the usual way. Nuns also – but they were not whipped. Or rarely. How Anti-Christ scorned them, as he scorns all women. . . .

'On the last day we were packing to leave my house. My husband had been paid what was owed to him, and we were happy because we were leaving. And then they came. Three young men who had seized a motor car because it belonged to the state. My son shot one of them, and the other two killed him, then began to drag my husband away. I said "Take me too," but they said No no. Not you. We don't need you. What they meant was you're much too

522

ugly. Just go away. I did not understand it then – I still do not – but I suspect that that was what they meant. I have often asked God what they did mean, but He will not tell me. Not yet . . . My husband too was found in the Casa de Campo. . . . It was then that I knew that God had left Madrid, and I left it too.' She turned to Piers.

'No doubt your newspapers are calling our nightmare a Civil War? But it is not that. Believe me it is not. It is a crusade. A crusade to bring Christ back to Spain.'

Ibañez said, 'I'm sorry about that.'

Piers said, 'Not at all,' because what else was there to say?

'I hadn't realised just how – unwell she is,' said Ibañez. 'Nor had my wife. If I had – ' He paused, then said again, 'I'm sorry.'

They were in what he called his library, which did indeed contain a lot of books, as well as some quite memorable cognac.

'If I may ask – ' said Piers, 'what will happen to her?'

'Some nuns have charge of her,' Ibañez said. 'For the moment. She has no money, you know. None at all.'

'But this brother and sister-in-law – '

'She said she was not fond of her sister-in-law, but in fact she detests her, and not without reason. I gather it is mutual.'

'They won't help her?'

'Not a centimo. They are very foolish.'

'Foolish?'

'When we have won this war – the marquesa will be rich again.'

It was nice to know that his side was going to win.

Ibañez sighed. 'Poor Spain,' he said. 'We deserved many things – but not this.'

'It really is that bad?'

'Oh yes,' Ibañez said. He hesitated for a moment, then added: 'On both sides. This is a Civil War, remember: a family quarrel. No one knows how to hurt each other like the members of a family. Are you sure you want to be involved in another family's quarrels?'

'Quite sure,' said Piers.

'May I ask why?'

'Because while I accept that what you say is true – of course I do – in the final analysis you are right and the Reds are wrong.'

And because I must, he thought. It's the only way I can learn my trade.

'Very well,' said Ibañez. 'I shall write to my friend Bolin who commands the Tercio of the Legion at Cadiz. I am quite sure he will find a use for you. To get there – the Reds are still strong in the North – it will be best if you go from here to Marseilles, then take a boat to Morocco, then another boat to Cadiz. You do not mind sea voyages?'

'Not in the least,' said Piers.

Cadiz looked like the wreck of what had once been a prosperous city, but Piers had no wish to examine it. For once the Mediterranean had been far less friendly than the English Channel. Instead he took a taxi to the Legion Barracks, and spoke in his incredible Spanish first to the guard, then the guard's sergeant, then the adjutant, and at last to Colonel Bolin. The legionnaires looked very much as Ibañez had described them: tough, hard bitten and smart, even by Rifle Brigade standards. And far more ruthless.

Bolin spoke even better English than Ibañez, to Piers's relief. He was fair haired, stocky, just beginning to be overweight. When he looked up from Ibañez's letter at last he said, 'It seems you'll do.' Piers waited.

'He says you dined with a friend of his wife's who told you exactly how bad things are here in Spain, but he still says you'll do.'

'I intend to try, sir,' said Piers, 'if you'll let me.'

'All any of us can do,' the colonel said. 'Naturally I can't make you a captain, but they're short of a lieutenant in the fourth bandera – a bandera is the nearest we have to one of your battalions. I can give you that – on trial of course. But you'll have to work at your Spanish.'

'Thank you, sir.'

'You're fit I take it?' Bolin said.

'Oh yes, sir.'

'Yes . . . All the same, you'd better see the doctor, just in case,' said Bolin. 'This is a very active regiment.'

Dr Serra examined Piers as if he were about to try for an Olympic Pentathlon. He spotted the leg at once, and tested it far more severely than he'd tested the other one, but his physiotherapist had done her work well: the leg passed. And so did the rest of him. Then he asked his questions, and Piers explained.

'The IRA did this?' Dr Serra said. Piers nodded. 'May I ask why?'

'My father is a peer with estates in Ireland.'

'Peer?' said Dr Serra.

'A lord,' said Piers. 'The Earl of Mangan. In Spain he would be a count.'

'Spain.' Dr Serra made a gesture that pushed the Spanish nobility to the back of the queue.

'I have always admired England,' said Dr Serra. 'Your noblemen especially. Such houses. Such elegance . . . Your noblewomen too. Before this war I used to read the *Tatler* as soon as it came out, but now it is impossible to get. You have a house in England?'

'Mostly we live in Mayfair,' said Piers.

'Mayfair.' Dr Serra was enchanted. 'How I long to visit there.' He offered Piers a cigarette. 'If there is anything you need my dear Hilyard, please do not hesitate to tell me.'

'You're very kind,' said Piers.

A bargain, it seemed, had been offered. Maybe even struck.

. 49 .

'On a vast scale,' said Georgie. 'Even MGM would be impressed. A cast of thousands. They've even rented a bishop.'

'Rented?'

'Well he's not under contract or anything. Just hired by the day I suppose, like those extras from Central Casting.'

Georgie had had two martinis before lunch, but the flippancy wasn't because of them. The wedding day was close and Georgie was beginning to feel the strain. No sign of regret, and certainly none of the panic she had felt before her own marriage: Georgie, like the actress she was, knew that her rôle was the starring one and would demand all her talent, and was preparing for it in her own way.

'Tell me about the cast of thousands,' said Jane.

'Well there's me above the credits,' said Georgie, 'and Ned close behind. And Charles and you, matron of honour in charge of bridesmaids. I must say I don't envy you that. There must be scores of them.' Jane snorted. 'Well a dozen anyway. Every existing young Derwent virgin – and they guard them well in Northumberland. Pull up the drawbridge every night.

'Then there's all Ned's brother officers and all the rest of the Derwents as well.'

'And on your side?'

'Just you,' said Georgie. 'All I want. All I need really. You fill a hall on your own. Script writer, journalist, tycoon's wife, heroine. . . . The Derwents won't know what's hit them. But it isn't that.'

'What is it then?'

'At a do like this one good chum's all that's needed – and I've got the best.' She lifted her glass and Jane found that she was blushing.

526

'I say,' Georgie said, 'your Mrs Barrow does do one rather well.'

'She knew you were coming,' said Jane, 'and she always puts herself out for you and Lionel because you appreciate her genius.'

'Well so we do,' said Georgie, 'which reminds me. There are two more from my side.'

'Two?'

'Lionel and your mother. Will she like the idea, do you think?'

'My God yes,' said Jane. 'She'll love it.'

Not least for the pleasure of telling Gwendoline Gwatkin about it afterwards.

'About the dress,' said Jane.

'Blue and white,' said Georgie. 'From Chanel. Try-on's tomorrow.'

'And the bridesmaids?'

'White with blue twiddly bits.'

'And the matron of honour?'

Georgie fidgeted, became almost clumsy. 'Darling, you could do me the most tremendous favour,' she said.

'Let's hear it.'

'Could you bear to wear your wedding dress?'

'Well of course I could,' said Jane, 'but won't Coco be furious? Schiaparelli at a Chanel wedding?'

'Oh balls to Coco Chanel,' said Georgie. 'It's me that's getting married. Me that's doing the whole production, come to that.'

'Production?'

'Lights, choreography, direction, costume, make-up. Everything except the fight arranger, and we may need one of them before it's over. When I married poor darling Dan it took about twenty minutes. This one's a two-hour epic.'

'You're loving it,' said Jane.

'Well of course,' said Georgie.

Over dinner that night she told Charles all about the lunchtime chat.

'Sounds more like *Quo Vadis* than a wedding,' said Charles. 'I hope I don't forget my lines.' Then his smile faded. 'Bob phoned me at the office,' he said. 'He wants to drop in here later for a chat. I said I didn't think you'd mind.'

527

'Of course not,' said Jane. 'Sybil?'

'It usually is,' said Charles, but it was of Andy they talked before Bob arrived. Norah had telephoned to say that she had received a letter, that he was well and safe, and sent his love.

'Did she say where from?'

'She said she'd no idea.'

'But surely the postmark – '

'She burnt the letter and its contents as soon as she'd read them.'

'Oh dear,' said Jane. 'And yet – '

'You're not really surprised?'

'During our first chat together, before I brought her and the baby to Blagdon, she never referred to him as Andy. Not once. It was always "him".' Charles nodded. Point taken.

'So we don't know where Andy is?' Jane asked.

'Norah doesn't,' Charles said, 'but that set me thinking. Surely somebody in Felston must know.'

'And do they?'

Charles refused to be hurried. What he was talking about they both considered important. It would be as well to have the facts in order.

'A man goes off to war,' he said at last, 'not because he's conscripted, but because it's a matter of conviction so intense he's willing to jeopardise his entire personal life for it. Surely he'd tell somebody.

'I have contacts up there, men who can ask questions without being conspicuous, and I set them to work. It didn't take long.'

'Billy Caffrey,' said Jane.

Charles looked astonished. 'Who on earth told you?' he said.

'Nobody,' said Jane, 'but he's the best friend Andy's got. The man he had three gills with the night he told Norah he was off to the war.'

'Smart girl,' said Charles, looking smug. Brains as well as beauty, and all were his. 'Billy Caffrey it was. Andy writes to him every chance he has – almost like a war diary, – and Billy Caffrey makes sure all his pals see it. I'm not sure he doesn't have it duplicated.'

'But why on earth – '

'Don't let's have any doubts about it, Andy's seen some pretty savage fighting. He's been with what's called the Clement Attlee

Battalion in Madrid for the most part, and it's been nasty.'

'Shock troops?'

'Just that. He doesn't go out of his way to say it, but reading between the lines Andy's turned out to be pretty good at it. And of course he enjoys his work.'

'Enjoys?'

'He's killing Fascists, after all. A terrier can enjoy killing rats, and yet leave the lambs in peace.'

'Yes, but even so – '

'Let me finish,' said Charles. 'Please.' She nodded. 'The upshot of it is that Andy's the local hero once again. The men who started those rumours about him – '

'Tom Spalding, Joe Turnbull, Artie Sparks.'

'Nothing wrong with your memory,' he said, more smug than ever. 'They've taken a knock in local opinion, and so's the new MP they pushed.'

'Lowe,' she said. 'But surely Felston had made up its mind that Andy was queer?'

'Felston's made up its mind that lies were told. Wicked, spiteful lies. How can their local hero be queer when he's killing the enemy?'

Jane thought of Lionel. Very easily, she thought.

'So all he's doing is looking for votes?' she said.

'Not all,' said Charles. 'By no means all. He's as likely as not to be killed after all. But at the end of the war – if he survives – Andy's making sure he'll get all the goodwill that's going. He won't be Felston's MP – like it or lump it, they opted for Lowe – but there'll be other seats near by.'

'Vaunting ambition,' she said.

'All of that. But also an over-riding impulse towards sacrifice: a feeling that evil must be stopped whatever the cost.'

'What you're saying is he's human.'

'Like the rest of us,' said Charles.

They were drinking coffee when Bob called, a third cup waiting. If Andy was in the wars then Bob was too, she thought, and gave him coffee as Charles poured brandy.

'I'm sorry to bother you like this,' said Bob.

'No,' said Charles. 'Just get on with it. By the look of you it won't wait much longer.'

'It won't,' said Bob. 'You're right. It's Sybil. Again.' But as he said it his face softened. 'I suppose you know she's mad?'

'Just tell it,' said Charles.

'Well she is. I couldn't believe it, didn't want to believe it, but in the end I had to.'

'And what was the end?'

'When she stuck a knife in me. Here.' He touched the flesh by his ribs. 'I had to tell a doctor all kinds of lies and I don't suppose he believed the half of them, but I paid him cash.'

'Why did she do it?' Still Charles asking the questions, but it wasn't her turn: not yet.

'I went to see Lilian Dunn. It was just to say goodbye. A social call. She ended up having lunch at the Ritz with Piers instead of me – but Sybil wouldn't see it like that. She said I wasn't to go, but I went anyway. And when I came back – ' He broke off for a moment. 'It wasn't serious,' he said at last, 'but it could have been. The doctor said it could have killed me.'

'Go on,' said Charles.

'For a while she wouldn't admit it,' said Bob, 'even though she'd scratched me, kicked me, hit me with a bottle. That was just girlish fun, the way she put it – but trying to kill me – how could she? She loves me.

'And she does,' he said. 'Far more than I ever loved her, even before she – but that's just the way I'm made. I liked her well enough.'

Oh please get on with it, thought Jane. I like Charles. *Well enough*.

'She was – what's the word? Fond of the chaps?'

'Promiscuous,' said Charles.

'That's it. But then I knew that. It didn't bother me. I mean how could it – the way I am? Then she got it into her head we should get married. – There was all that business with the shares.'

'I told Jane,' said Charles.

'Well of course,' said Bob. 'I said you could. But still I didn't see it. That she was mad, I mean. . . . High spirited. A bit wild. In love. Yes. But not crazy. It never dawned on me. Not for a minute. Not then.'

530

'When did it dawn?'

'After the knife,' said Bob. 'That's when.'

'You worked it out?'

'She told me herself,' said Bob. 'She said, "You mustn't let it upset you too much. It's just that I go mad sometimes and hurt people. People I'm fond of." '

'Did she say why?'

'She thinks people she's fond of are out to get her, so it's as well to warn them she can hit back. She can do that all right.'

'Out to get her?'

Really, thought Jane, when it comes to cross examination Charles is just like that KC cousin of his.

'She thinks there isn't a single human being who can love her for herself. We're all very good at pretending to, but it's always a screen for this need to hurt her. That's when she's crazy of course, but since she decided to marry me she's been crazy nearly all the time. Can you see why?'

'I think so,' said Charles. 'Because once you're married you'll be in a better position to hurt her than anybody else.'

'Anybody except her father.'

'Oh my God,' said Jane.

'She told me the hell of a lot about him, and in the end I took her to see a man in Harley Street. Name of Lockhart.'

'Jabber,' said Jane.

'You know him then?'

'I haven't seen much of him lately what with Mexico and New York and Spain, but we still bump into each other occasionally. He's awfully good.'

'I had the devil of a time coaxing her to go and see him,' said Bob. 'Now she can hardly keep away. She worships him. To hear her talk he's a sort of saint.'

'Perhaps he is,' said Jane.

'Anyway he sent for me – on the quiet. No chance of our marrying just yet, he says. This one's going to need a lot of work.'

'Are you still engaged?' said Charles.

'I could get out of it if I wanted to apparently, but it wouldn't do her any good, so I said we'd just leave things as they are. Lockhart was relieved. A bit surprised, too. Anyway I won't be seeing her for a while. There's a chap in Switzerland he wants her to see. Runs a sort of a clinic there.'

'Did Lockhart give you his name?' asked Charles.

'Plattner,' said Bob. 'Dr Heinrich Plattner.'

Not the one who treated Charles's first wife, thank God. That would have been altogether too much, thought Jane.

'I can see her from time to time before she goes,' said Bob, 'and pop across to Geneva on a visit now and again. But it's all got to be very quiet. No excitement. No – sex.'

'Has he given her anything?'

'Stuff to calm her down. He hates doing it, but he says it's too big a risk without the pills.'

'Where's her father?' Jane asked.

'Deauville,' said Bob. 'He practically lives there nowadays.'

'Does he know?'

'I haven't told him,' said Bob, 'and I doubt if she has.'

'Forgive the question,' said Jane, 'but he molested her, didn't he?'

'From the age of three,' said Bob. 'Things I didn't believe a man could do to any child, never mind his own.'

'No wonder she kept saying she hated him,' said Jane.

'She asked me once if I ever fancied little girls. I thought she was drunk.' He shook his head. 'When I said no, I don't think she believed me.'

'When did it stop?' Charles asked.

'It hasn't,' said Bob. 'Not the way she tells it. He hasn't – tried anything since Sybil and me started going out together, but that's only because she gave him enough money to go away.

'You know how tough she is? Well all the time I've known her there's only one thing she's afraid of – and it isn't her father. Not exactly. It was the fact that he could still get her into bed with him – that she wanted to go. So she sent him to Deauville. I wish to Christ it had been Australia.' He shook his head once more, like a boxer who has absorbed too much punishment. 'Not exactly the ideal way to start married life, is it? You know she once – ' He broke off. 'Maybe I shouldn't say this in front of you, Jane.'

'Oh for heaven's sake,' said Jane, 'I've been your big sister since the day I first met you in John Bright Street. Say it if you want to, but don't make me the excuse if you don't.'

'Fair enough,' said Bob, then, 'She once wanted us to – make love at her father's flat. Of course I said no. It sounded such a daft idea. But now I think I understand why. She wanted him – her father – to catch us at it. See us. It was the only way she could think of to tell him his day was over.'

His hands went to his face then, but when he removed them he was dry eyed. 'I'm sorry,' he said. 'I just don't seem able to get used to the idea.'

'I should think not,' said Charles.

'Because in a way you could say it was my fault,' said Bob.

'I wondered when we'd get to that part,' said Jane. 'Perhaps you'd better tell us why.'

Charles looked appalled, Bob outraged. She was trying to deprive him of his masochistic treat. But this flagellation had to be stopped: one lunatic was more than enough.

'Those shares,' said Bob. 'The ones in Lane Engineering.'

'The ones you sold your body for.'

'Damnit, Jane, this isn't funny,' said Charles.

'Indeed it's not,' said Jane, 'but by the look on Bob's face it isn't even going to make sense. All the same I apologise for what I said.'

He'd hardly heard what she'd said.

'It was a deal if you like,' said Bob. 'A straightforward business deal. A trade. The shares for marriage. Or put it another way – those shares were her dowry. – But I didn't have to go through with it, did I? If I'd turned her down – '

'Well?' said Jane.

'She'd have been all right, wouldn't she?'

'All right enough to go back to bed with her father?'

For a moment she thought that Bob would jump round and hit her, then somehow he controlled himself.

'Bob dear,' she said. 'This mess is none of your making, just as it's beyond your power to clear it up. That rests with Jabber and his Swiss friend. All you can do is carry on as usual, and see her when you can and be sweet to her. But you must do that.'

'Yes,' said Bob. 'I must.'

'Is he on your board?' she asked.

'He will be. Next board meeting.'

'It's weird,' she said.

'You mean the coincidence?' Suddenly he turned to her. Bob had gone long since, but they still continued to chew on the problem, as Foch had once chewed on a carpet.

'I didn't mean you,' he said.

'I know that, silly. Though Jabber was another coincidence I could have done without.'

'Like Switzerland,' said Charles, and then: 'She sounds pretty bad.'

'I think she is,' said Jane. 'She built a dam, but it burst.'

'Poor old Bob.'

'At least he's got his seat on your board,' she said, 'and he doesn't have to get married. Jabber would probably give it to him in writing.'

'You're a hard one,' he said, but even that was said smugly, lovingly.

'One of us has to be. . . . Those shares – '

'He paid for them. Paid her broker. They're his now, no question.'

'So when the bold general returns, breathing fire and brimstone – '

'You think he will?'

'Don't you?'

'Yes,' said Charles. 'I do. His daughter's out of her mind and he's next of kin. Apart from anything else he'll see it as a marvellous opportunity to get control of her money, including the shares, I have no doubt.'

'But if they belong to Bob – '

'If he goes to the right sort of lawyer they're bound to give it a try. Only if they do, they'll be taking on the bank as well.'

'I wouldn't give much for their chances,' she said.

'No more would I,' said Charles, and grinned.

William nudged open the drawing-room door, went to Jane and leaped on to her lap.

'Should he be allowed to do that?' said Charles.

'No,' said Jane, 'but we both enjoy it.'

'I know just how he feels.'

*

The wedding was a triumph for Georgie. She directed it with a steely precision that von Stroheim might have envied. Junior brides-maids imagined themselves back at school with the headmistress in constant attendance, older ones merely trembled and obeyed. All Jane had to do was make sure that they stayed in their correct pairs, as Georgie had graded them. There was absolutely nothing to it for her. Even the Schiaparelli dress still fitted perfectly, which was gratifying indeed.

The walk down the aisle took far longer than that at the little church in Kensington, Georgie's train, borrowed from a World Wide epic about Catherine the Great, stretched for what seemed like yards, two page boys holding its hem, then the matron of honour, and then the bridesmaids like a corps de ballet, all clutch-ing the bouquets that Lionel had designed. The organ played Wagner, Ned and Charles waited at the altar rails, and the bishop sailed forward on queue. Jane noticed without surprise that it was the same bishop who'd preached such a rotten sermon at Blagdon, ages ago. Well he wouldn't preach a rotten sermon today. Georgie had vetoed it. Half way down the aisle Jane passed Lionel and her mother. No lizard wink from Mummy this time, but then her daughter was safely married, and all Mummy's thoughts would be of her major.

'Dearly beloved,' the bishop began, trying to sound as if he meant it, and even if he was a little tense there could be no retakes, not for this epic. On and on he boomed, the choir sang, the congrega-tion stood and knelt by turns, and not one bridesmaid fidgeted or felt sick, the page boys stood rigid as guardsmen. Georgie's iron rod somehow contrived to be at once threatening and invisible.

Then suddenly it was all over, and they were in the vestry signing, kissing, then back to the aisle and the organ pealed out Mendels-sohn, a cascading joy like fountains of champagne. Ushers held back the doors and they were on to the next set, Hanover Square, with Coldstream officers forming a guard of honour, and for some reason a piper playing rather odd-looking pipes. Not Scots pipes, Ned explained later, Northumbrian pipes. Pipes and piper alike appeared to be the property of his father the duke.

The square itself appeared to be jammed with about half Lon-don. Studio photographers, press photographers and newsreel cameramen in the foreground, taking pictures like mad, and behind them just people with time enough for the best free show since the coronation, for how often could you hope to see a Hollywood star married to the heir to a dukedom? And she so beautiful and he so handsome? Police cleared the way to the cars, and Jane and Charles clambered into the liner on wheels, the chauffeur set course for the Savoy.

'Wasn't Georgie splendid?' said Jane.

'No one else could have played the part,' said Charles. 'All the same – '

'Yes, Charles?'

'Ours was better.'

She reached out and touched his hand. No other gesture was possible, not then.

'You noticed the bishop?' she asked.

'How could I miss him? He was only a foot away most of the time. Pompous old – '

'Charles!'

'Prelate,' he said. 'I was definitely going to say prelate. I could do with a drink.'

Champagne, if not in fountains, was ready and waiting: dozens and dozens of bottles lined up with rigid precision like Coldstream Guardsmen, but first there were more photographs and the bride and groom to be kissed.

'Happy, your ladyship?' said Jane, and thought: What a question. She looks absolutely radiant.

'Not arf,' said Georgie. This time it was Jane who winked, before she went to find her mother, who was drinking champagne with Lionel.

'What a grand affair,' her mother said. 'I cannot recall when I last saw so many good-looking young men.'

'My very thought,' said Lionel, and her mother tapped him, playfully the only word, on the cheek. Lionel knows exactly how to handle her, Jane thought: knows too how much she's missing her major. Once again Mrs Routledge showed that astonishing ability to read her daughter's mind.

'He'd have loved it, wouldn't he?' she said.

'Every minute,' said Jane, and went to be greeted by the duchess, who admired her greatly because she was a heroine, and even more because her husband was so rich, then more champagne, and lunch and speeches, and dancing, with Charles, with Ned, with Lionel, until at last it was time to go.

Outside the Savoy the press still waited. Georgie and Ned had declined to say where they would spend their honeymoon, a preoccupation with secrecy that newspaper editors considered unseemly in such newsworthy persons, so that when a blonde woman in elegant day clothes and a hat with a veil, accompanied by a man with a handkerchief held to his face made a bolt for it, in the ducal Daimler, the whole pack followed.

'Jay Bower isn't going to like this,' said Charles, and put his handkerchief back in his pocket.

'Talking of Bower,' said Jane, 'he wants to give me lunch tomorrow.'

'Somewhere nice, I hope?'

'The Savoy Grill.'

'How you do haunt the old pub,' said Charles. 'Is it Spain again?'

'Very likely,' said Jane, 'but I'm making no decisions till I hear what he's got to say.'

'Very wise,' said Charles.

The Daimler pulled up outside South Terrace, and the pack watched them get out, then milled about in a desperate effort to turn before racing back, snarling, to the Savoy.

'Much good may it do them,' said Charles. 'They'll be half way to Croydon Airport by now.'

'They'll go to Nice I suppose?' said Jane.

'And motor on from there.' They had rented a house deep in Provence, where nobody had ever heard of the English milord, though half the population would know about Georgie, but Georgie would know how to handle that.

Bower was displeased. They might be lunching at the Savoy Grill, but he was displeased even so.

'A disgraceful thing for a journalist to do,' he said.

Jane tucked into her chicken Kiev. Sinful, of course, but she would be off to the wars soon: of that she was almost certain.

'You killed that story,' said Bower.

He makes it sound far worse than killing a child, she thought. Even one's own. She sipped at her claret. A Pauillac, ten years old at least. Definitely she was off to the wars.

'I wasn't being a journalist at the time,' she said aloud.

'Then what the hell were you?' said Bower.

'A chum.'

'Oh come *on*,' said Bower.

'That's what Georgie called it,' said Jane. 'She had this weird impulse to spend her honeymoon just with her husband, and not half the press corps as well, so she asked me to help because we're chums. So I did.'

Bower looked at her in a way she had never been looked at before. Balefully, would it be? The trouble yet again was that he was simultaneously her employer and the person to whom he owed rather a lot of money. He owed her husband even more.

'Besides, you did get a story,' she said. ' "Our Jane Helps Georgie's Dash For Freedom". Really, Jay.'

'You didn't like it?'

'It was fair enough,' she said. 'I mean Charles was furious at first, but in the end I made him see that you had to print something.'

'Very kind of him,' said Bower.

'But he still doesn't like "Our Jane". If it comes to that, neither do I.'

'But you won't let us call you Jane Whitcomb,' said Bower. He sounded hurt, aggrieved even.

'Because it isn't my name. Not any more. I told you. Lovell's my name.'

'And that's the name we put on your by-line. All the same we have to remind our readers who you are, and to them you're *their* Jane, the one and only, the one who writes for the *Daily World*.'

Laying it on with a trowel, she thought, but he does it so well. No wonder I'm enjoying it. All the same I bet I'll be on my way home to pack as soon as we've finished the pudding.

'The Orphans and Aged Fund topped ten thousand last week,' he said.

'Quite a flood,' said Jane.

'It was,' said Bower. 'But it's slowing. It'll be down to a trickle, soon. People forget so damn quickly.'

Here it comes, she thought.

'I'd hoped for twenty thousand,' said Bower. 'God knows those kids and old people could use it.'

That at least was true. 'And more,' she said.

'There's only one way we'll get it,' said Bower, 'but you know that, don't you?'

'Jog their memories?'

'That's right. You do that and the tap could be turned on full. What do you say?'

'What can I say? I'll go, of course.'

'When will you tell your husband?'

'I've already told him,' said Jane.

It was more of the same. The luxury of the Hôtel du Palais, with every conceivable horror by way of contrast: horror that always attacked the innocent: children blinded, limbs blown off; old people burned or maimed or starved. Like a freak show, she thought, as she addressed the *World*'s readers. You thought the last one was bad, but look at this – and this – and this. But the money began to flow once more, and that was what she was there for, after all.

Then one day the telephone call came. She and Pierre were just back from a trip across the border, where they had been to see a little Basque town ripped apart by German aeroplanes, which as always had turned out to be very good at their job. Not one stone left upon another. . . . Jane had just finished wallowing in a bath, and then a shower, till no vestige of the dust and dirt remained, though the horror was still there, waiting to be turned into the kind of prose that would coax pound notes and cheques and postal orders from the readers of the *Daily World*. She yawned, but that would never do. Weariness must wait until the words were written. It was then that the phone rang.

'I've been phoning you all day,' said Bower.

'Forgive me,' said Jane. 'I took a day off. I went to Spain.'

'Where?'

'A place called Guernica.'

'Never heard of it.'

'You will,' said Jane.

'Why?'

'From all accounts it was a pleasant little place,' said Jane. 'The Basques looked on it as the centre of their world. Old churches, ancient trees, all that. Now it doesn't exist. The Germans bombed it to bits.'

'Wait a minute.' Even from that distance, she could hear him turning over papers. 'Yeah ... I've got it. Ellis filed a story on it. Why did you go there?'

'It was a *town*,' said Jane. 'A town full of people. Old people. Young people. Now most of them are dead, but the ones who survived – my God they need our help.'

'Give it all you've got,' said Bower, and then: 'There's something else.' For once he sounded almost furtive.

'Yes?'

'I want you to go to Madrid.'

'You what?' Jane knew that she was yelling, but after what she had seen that day this was too much.

'I know, I know,' said Bower, 'but I've had a tip-off. It's the story of a lifetime, and there isn't a living soul who could handle it like you can.'

Not a trowel this time, she thought. A damn great shovel.

Even so: 'What story?' she said.

'Andy Patterson,' said Bower. 'He's in Madrid.'

'Along with most of the rest of the International Brigade.'

'Yeah, I guess so, but I've just heard from Ellis. Patterson's done something pretty wonderful.'

'Let Ellis handle it. That's what he's there for.– The fighting.'

'Sure,' said Bower, 'but this wasn't fighting. A bomb fell on a Metro station. People use them as air-raid shelters, but this time a bomb got through. Killed a lot of people, including kids. Patterson helped pull out the survivors. Nearly got killed himself. Your late fiancé's brother. It's made for you, honey. Like I said, who else can do it? It's just the story the paper needs – and the fund.' She was silent. 'Jane, I'm serious,' said Bower. 'This is *big*. Will you do it?'

'All right,' said Jane.

'Great,' Bower said. 'I'll get on to Aguirra – he'll go with you – and talk to Ellis in Madrid. You phone in your story and get some rest. I want you on the road first thing tomorrow. Every paper in town will want this one,' he said, 'but the *World*'s the one that's got you.'

Our Jane, she thought, as Bower hung up.

It was vital that she speak to Charles, but when she tried she was told there was a fault on the line. All night she tried, and next morning too, but each time she tried, the fault was still there. In the end she had to settle for a telegram.

'For reasons that will soon be apparent I beg you to come to Biarritz soon,' she wrote. 'Impossible to explain except face to face. All love my darling. Jane.'

I could always pop across to see how you're getting on, he'd said, meaning if things got really out of hand. Well they couldn't get more out of hand than going to Madrid, but all the same, Bower was right. It was the story of a lifetime. Her story of a lifetime. And for that you'll risk Charles's happiness, comfort, love? she asked herself. But not just for that. For the children, the old people who've never even heard of me, and yet depend on what I can do for them. How very like Andy Patterson I sound, to be sure, she thought, but even so she wrote her story, phoned the copy-taker, then slept.

The journey down to Madrid had been dreadful. She had forgotten just how dreadful wartime journeys were, especially over a distance. They had gone by car, too, because the Germans had bombed a supply train and a stretch of line, and no trains could get through, perhaps for days. So they'd gone by car. The de Dion was a tough vehicle as well as an elegant one, which was just as well. Spanish roads were appalling even when they hadn't been shelled.

It was like her own war, she thought, when they finally got to Spain, and yet it wasn't. Troops on line of march, that was the same, and yet they didn't march the same. Some didn't march at all, just walked at their own pace. Their equipment was different, too. Each man had a blanket slung over one shoulder, and whatever they could carry in the way of food, as well as a rifle and ammunition – all kinds of rifles. In one battalion she counted three kinds at least. Yet the men marched cheerfully, even sang, and the ones Pierre said were the peasants among them moved with an easy slouch that would carry them, and their equipment, all day. The

541

townsmen found it more difficult, but they kept on, even so.

There were lorries, too, and guns pulled by more lorries, horses, even an ancient tractor, and a team of mules towed a gun so antique she began to think of Wellington's march on Madrid. He'd had trouble there, too, she remembered, though he'd been made far more welcome than Franco would ever be. . . . Not many ambulances, she noticed, not nearly enough considering the number of men on the march. Good natured, as cheerful as Tommies, and far less bashful when it came to noting the presence of a pretty woman driving a smart car. Pierre was a brick-red colour for half the journey.

But they were no trouble: the car had 'Press' and 'Prensa' notices stuck all over it, and the back seat was stacked with cartons of cigarettes. From time to time Pierre would toss one out to the marching men, and the shouts would grow louder. They had a laissez-passer too, signed by a general.

It was Barcelona all over again, she thought, only much, much further. Beyond San Sebastian was Fascist country, and so they had to drive east across France for a hundred miles (but at least the roads were good), before crossing the frontier and heading south at last. They had left at first light, but by nightfall they were still on the Castellón road, no more than two thirds of their journey completed. But the general had provided them with another laissez-passer, the address of the only decent hotel in the region still surviving, so that she had the luxury of a hot bath and a meal, before she went to bed and fell asleep at once, despite the fact that every guest in the place seemed to possess a wireless set which was turned on full blast. As her eyes closed she could hear the Internationale played in three different keys.

Next morning at first light they moved off again. Pierre had contrived a bath, a shave and a meal, though he had slept in the car, but he was happy: already he'd got some good pictures. They skirted Teruel, which was held by the Nationalists, and headed west towards Cuenca and the Madrid road at last. The first signs of all-out war began to appear; churches put to the torch, the rubble that bombers had made, roadside graves marked by no more than a home-made cross.

But still no horses. They buried them quickly, Ellis had told her, or cremated them if there was petrol to spare. They had to, he said. In the heat of a Spanish summer a dead horse could kill more than a live Moor. . . . She thanked God for what she had been spared, and Pierre tossed out a carton of cigarettes to a squad of soldiers struggling to set right an overturned lorry. The road sloped upwards and Jane picked her way among the potholes to the top of the crest, then pulled to a halt. Below them, Madrid lay waiting.

The sun shone and the air was clear, and yet the city had none of that precise quality of light that she remembered. It was like a city in a dust storm, she thought, and then, But of course it is. Bombs. Shells. Explosions. Small-arms fire for months on end. In her war there had been no cities under siege.

'Let's go to work,' she said, and let in the clutch.

The road blocks began, the spot checks, the random stoppages, but still the general's talisman worked its magic, and they reached the Puerta del Sol at last, and on to the Plaza Mayor, to the café where she was to meet Ellis, a café from which she had once seen a student activist shot dead. Ellis was there, waiting, and made no effort to hide his relief when they walked towards him, the de Dion parked near by. She introduced the two men and Ellis said, 'Let me order a drink. I doubt if they'll run to a snack as well. Tapas and things. Most places can't. Not any more.'

'Oh dear,' said Jane. 'All we brought was cigarettes.'

'Oh you'll eat,' said Ellis. 'Eat quite well.'

'Black market?'

'Press Club,' said Ellis.

'Last time I was here we ate at the Ritz.'

'You won't this time,' said Ellis. 'It's a military hospital nowadays.'

The waiter brought drinks: coffee for Jane, beer for the two men.

'Rough journey?' Ellis asked.

'Not rough exactly,' said Jane. 'Just dreadfully uncomfortable. Serves me right for saying I'd never come here.' Ellis ignored that. 'Tell me about Andy.'

Ellis looked surprised, then, 'Of course. You know him quite well,' he said.

'We worked together on the Felston March. He was very nearly my brother-in-law.'

'Good Lord,' said Ellis.

'My fiancé was a captain in the Royal Northumbrians. He was killed on the 10th of November, 1918.'

'Good *Lord*,' said Ellis again. 'What damnable luck.'

'Terrible,' said Pierre.

'Excuse the question, but did he serve for long?' Ellis asked.

'Three and a half years,' said Jane. 'He won a DSO and an MC.'

'Can I use that?' Ellis asked.

'Of course.' She would use it herself. She'd been proud of John.

'You see it sounds like a real fighting family,' Ellis explained. 'Of course the IB don't go round dishing out medals – '

'IB?' said Pierre.

'International Brigade – but from what I gather your friend Patterson's turned into a first-rate fighting man. Not every unit has one, but the ones that do should count themselves lucky. Chaps like that can do more damage on their own than all their pals put together.' He was silent for a moment, and Jane had no doubt that he was remembering his own war.

'What time can we see Andy?' she asked.

'About ten o'clock tonight,' said Ellis and grinned. 'When he's finished his shift.'

'His shift?'

'He's up at the Front all day,' Ellis said, 'but it's his company's turn to sleep in billets, and so they come back here at night. By tram, as a matter of fact.' He looked at Jane's face and grinned once more. 'I wonder what Earl Haig would have made of that,' he said, and finished his beer. 'I tell you what, since you've got the car, why don't we do a quick tour of the city, then I'll show you where the fighting goes on.' Pierre bridled. 'From a safe distance of course,' said Ellis.

Madrid hadn't changed all that much since her last visit, except that here and there chunks of it had been smashed, but it would take an enormous amount of explosive to make any lasting impression on a city the size of Madrid. It was just that sometimes, in one street or another, a house had been knocked out like a tooth from a jawbone. Occasionally there was larger damage; a cinema, a restaurant, a block of flats, but still the life of the city continued, its inhabitants tuned in to the sound of raids like wireless sets to a transmitter. Only when the aircraft were really close did they take shelter. It was the only way, Ellis said. If the enemy aircraft began to dictate their hours of work then the city would die. . . .

He guided them to the Metro station, which was still no more than a heap of rubble pushed to one side so that cars and trams could pass. Jane stopped the car and Pierre got out and began to take photographs. It was a spectacular heap of rubble, a crude, ugly gash in what had been an elegant street of shops. Knightsbridge Tube Station, thought Jane.

'Your friend had been to the cinema, just over there,' Ellis said, and pointed. The cinema appeared to be still intact, if pockmarked.

'He was coming out as the bomb hit and dived straight in. As I say, it's a rare gift to know precisely what to do in a crisis – but once he started doing it other people joined in.'

'The children?' Jane asked.

'A school over there.' Ellis pointed. 'The teachers thought the children would be safer in the Metro.' Jane looked at the school: it was unmarked. 'Shall we take a look at the war now?' said Ellis.

'He's been in Madrid far too long, thought Jane, and it's beginning to show.

'Why not?' she said.

Pierre was appalled once more. After all Mr Bower had said. But Jane insisted on going, and resolutely declined to wear the poilu coal scuttle. Pierre gave in at last. After all, there were bound to be pictures. . . .

. 50 .

The war zone, for civilians, even accredited correspondents, ended some distance from the university buildings where the early fighting had taken place.

'Franco had almost won,' Ellis said. 'One last heave, that's all he needed, but the IB turned up at the eleventh hour, so to speak. Not that they did it on their own, though a lot of the Lefties claim they did. The Spaniards themselves did most of it, but when the IB turned up they suddenly saw they weren't alone. Till then they'd been in despair, then all these young men appeared: the Germans who hated Hitler, the Italians who hated Mussolini, Frenchmen, Americans, British who simply believed that what they were doing was right.'

When it's over he's going to write a book, thought Jane, and just for now he's trying it out on me, and who am I to blame him?

She looked at the university buildings, sturdy by the look of them, still standing for the most part, but comprehensively shelled and blasted until now they were no more than fortified caves. As she watched a gun boomed in the distance and a shell landed on what had once been a part of the Science block, reducing rubble to smaller rubble.

'Waste of time and money,' said Ellis. 'Probably the Italians. They can't bear peace and quiet.'

Jane borrowed field glasses from Pierre. Dug deep into earthworks in front of the rubble were the university's defenders, clinging to the earth like a mother, and far safer, she thought, than in those battered buildings.

'First off it was all hand-to-hand fighting,' Ellis was saying. 'Floor by floor. Rifles and pistols. Bang bang you're dead. Like gangsters and G-men. Your chum was good at that, too.'

'Why don't you like him?' said Jane.

'You think I don't?'

'Yes,' said Jane. 'I do. From what you've told me he's done nothing but good things – as a man and a soldier – but every time you speak of him there's a sneer in your voice.'

'Oh my God,' said Ellis. 'It's got nothing to do with snobbery. I mean just because he's a working man – '

'What has it to do with then?'

'Envy,' said Ellis. It wasn't the whole truth but it was all she would get. Jane left it at that.

Part of the Nationalist line, a little in advance of the artillery, was the remains of what had a year ago been a pretty villa surrounded by fruit trees. Now it too was rubble, surrounded by matchwood. Captain Hilyard of the Spanish Foreign Legion looked through the Zeiss glasses his sister had sent him. They were very good glasses.

'Good Lord,' he said.

His sergeant, lighting a cigarette beside him, looked up.

'Capitan?'

Piers handed him the glasses and pointed.

'Over there,' he said in his extraordinary Spanish. 'Two men and a woman, going to that white car.'

The sergeant looked. 'Journalists,' he said.

'The woman's rather pretty, wouldn't you say?'

'I would indeed,' said the sergeant.

'She's rather a friend of mine,' said Piers. The sergeant looked impressed. 'Well dressed too, wouldn't you say?' said Piers. 'Paris if I'm any judge.'

'Chanel,' said the sergeant. 'Just what a woman should wear to walk around a battlefield. Schiaparelli would be far too fussy.'

Before the war the sergeant had owned a dress shop in Barcelona. It was only because he'd been on a buying trip to Paris when it started that he was still alive. . . .

Dinner at the Press Club wasn't bad at all. The Club was part of a hotel, relatively unmarked, with baths and showers that still worked, and it had almost anything you wanted to drink, even Scotch. Ellis ordered some at once, but Jane and Pierre drank red

547

wine. So did the American three tables away, but he drank by the bottle as everyone else drank by the glass, with an occasional brandy for a chaser. I've seen him before, thought Jane, and suddenly remembered where. In Paris. At the Café Deux Magots had it been? La Coupole? Anyway it was years ago. She'd gone there for the Quatr' Arts Ball with Bower, and that extraordinary cousin of his, the one who was quite sure the world would end at any minute, had suggested they go for a drink. She and Bower had been lovers then, and now she found it hard to remember, even to believe. Not like poor darling John at all. . . . The American drank yet another brandy, and the girl with him tried hard to be impressed.

Ellis looked at his watch and said, 'He's late,' but as he spoke, Andy appeared.

He looks good in uniform, even the clumsy odds and ends that were the best the Republican government could manage. But even that suited the lean height of his body, and he looked hard all through. He came over to them at once.

'I'm a bit late,' he said. 'Somebody I had to see. I know orders are orders, but this was a personal matter.'

'Orders?' said Ellis, and Jane cut in at once.

'What nonsense,' she said. 'How could we order you? We've absolutely no authority. It was a request, that's all. Aren't you glad to see me?'

He smiled then. 'A bit bewildered to tell you the truth,' he said.

Pierre stood up and offered his hand. 'My name is Pierre Aguirra,' he said. 'I'm Mrs Lovell's photographer. Let me say how much I admire what you did. Maybe later you will permit me some pictures of you. In the meantime Mr Ellis and I will leave you two old friends to talk.'

'Yes,' said Ellis. 'Yes of course.' He was reluctant to leave, but he'd already had one turn and Andy would talk better without him.

When they went over to the bar Jane said, 'Have you eaten?'

'Yes,' Andy said, 'but I could do with a beer.' Jane ordered one.

'It's about the kids, isn't it?' Andy said. 'The ones I pulled out of the Metro?'

'That's right.'

'You going to make me look like a hero?'

'You are a hero.'

'Mebbe.' Andy reached into his pockets and to her amazement produced cigarettes and matches.

Again he smiled. 'Surprised you, didn't I?' he said. 'Surprised myself an' all. You were up our way this afternoon, they tell me. The university.'

'That's right.'

'Never could learn to keep out of trouble, could you?' he said.

'Look who's talking,' said Jane.

'When you do your piece, will you mention the Brigade?' Andy asked.

'Don't you want me to?'

'Well yes,' he said. 'It wouldn't make sense if you didn't. Only don't go putting in anything about me being a Communist, will you? Because I'm not. Staunch Labour man, that's me.'

'Whatever you say,' said Jane.

'Thanks, pet.'

Jane looked at him warily. It could have been Bob speaking. Somewhere between Felston and Madrid, Andy had learned to be relaxed with women, even flirtatious. Poor Norah, she thought. Poor darling Norah.

'Ask your questions,' said Andy, 'then we'll have a proper talk.' And so she asked them, and the answers, she knew, would delight Bower and sell many newspapers. At last he said, 'That's it then?'

'Except to have your picture taken – but not here if you don't mind. Somewhere that looks more Madrid.'

'There's plenty of bars that do that,' said Andy, and again she had to force herself not to look startled.

'Before we do that though,' said Andy, 'there's a couple of things.'

'Norah?'

'And the bairn,' he said.

'When last seen they were both thriving,' Jane said. 'She's working for Charles now, at Blagdon. Supervising the holiday homes.'

'Aye, she wrote and told us. Used up very near half a sheet of paper.' He pulled at his cigarette. 'Sent a photo of Dorothy too.'

He brought out a battered wallet, and extracted a picture, handed it to her.

'Beautiful,' she said, and indeed it was almost true. Not in the class of that other Jane, her godchild, at that age, but pretty enough.

'Aye,' said Andy. 'Like her mam.'

'No photograph of Norah?' she said.

'Of course not,' Andy said. 'She must have told you how she feels about me.'

'Yes,' said Jane, 'I'm afraid she did.'

It seemed his marriage was something Andy didn't want to talk about.

'Our Bob wrote to me,' he said. 'Apparently his marriage isn't going to happen. Not yet, anyway.'

'Did he say why?'

'She's mad,' said Andy. 'Not surprising, is it? No lass could take on our Bob and stay sane.' But it was said with kindness, even affection.

'What's the other thing?' she said. 'You did say there were two.'

'Ellis,' he said.

'What about him?'

'It's not something I'm proud of,' said Andy, 'but it's something that happened, and if I don't tell you, he will.'

'Andy, for heaven's sake – '

'I went off with his girl,' said Andy.

This time she did not need to hide her surprise. She quoted Ellis instead. 'Good Lord,' she said, and then, 'Is she Spanish?'

'French,' said Andy. 'Her name's Séverine. Séverine Jannot. She works for a newspaper. *Le Matin*. As a matter of fact she'll probably be at the bar we're going to.'

'Do you want to leave now?'

'Just give me a minute.'

He got up and headed for a door which had once been labelled 'Caballeros' and was now called 'Hombres'. 'Bliss was it in that dawn to be alive,' she thought, but that was just dodging the issue. The issue without doubt was the new Andy, an alarming but somehow attractive amalgam of Bob and John. Then suddenly the issue became something else entirely, as the entrance door opened and Burrowes came into the room.

Whether he was drunk or not would take a more practised judge to decide, she thought, though she had no doubt that he hadn't been really sober in years. Even so he spotted her at once and came towards her, lurching just a little, but already yelling, 'Bourgeois bitch', 'Class enemy', 'Ball-cutting cow'. That last one was droll, she thought. He must have seen a few Americans lately. The odd thing was that few of the pressmen there even bothered to look up. This was a nightly event, it seemed, unpleasant but inevitable, like an air-raid. Jane motioned with her hand for Pierre and Ellis to stay where they were, as he came to the table and hung on to the chair in which Andy had just sat. The smell of garlic was worse than ever, but this was Spain, after all.

'Well cow,' he said, 'how do you justify your presence here? Madrid is for heroes, true believers, people of the Left who have dedicated their lives to the overthrow of people like you. Bourgeois exploiters. Blood suckers. Beasts.' The chair trembled under his hand. He's been hitting it hard, she thought.

'If it comes to that,' she said, 'how do you justify your presence here?'

Over Burrowes's shoulder she could see the wine-drinking American trying to get to his feet. He wasn't doing terribly well at it, but the girl he was with made no move to help him. Jane hoped he wasn't going to be sick.

'What are you babbling about, you silly bitch?' said Burrowes.

'The last I heard of you you weren't even a bourgeois, you were a Fascist,' said Jane. 'Black shirt and all. Sitting at the right hand of Crawley at an East End riot.'

Suddenly he went green, and Jane thought he might be sick on the American's behalf, but somehow he recovered.

'Lying cow,' he said. 'Who'd believe that?'

'Nobody, if it was a lie,' said Jane, 'but I've got a witness. A Leftwing, working class witness, an International Brigader no less, who actually saw you and could scarcely believe what he saw.'

'Who?' said Burrowes. 'Go on tell me. Who?'

Jane looked at the door marked 'Hombres'. Andy Patterson was just coming through it.

'Your old chum,' he said.

Slowly, moving like a man manoeuvring through an earthquake, the American came up to the table and tapped Burrowes on the shoulder. Burrowes turned and the American hit him, a good solid punch, all his weight behind it. Burrowes fell down flat.

'I'm sorry,' the American said. 'I shouldn't have done that.'

'Quite all right,' said Jane. 'I've done it myself in my time.'

He looked at her glassily. 'That isn't what I meant,' he said, then his eyes closed and he too began to fall, until Andy fielded him neatly and lowered him to the floor. The American's girl came over to them.

'Oh God,' she said. 'Why can't the age of chivalry be dead? No offence, honey, but you were doing fine on your own.'

'Well I thought so,' said Jane, 'but when you feel the need to hit Burrowes it's almost impossible to resist the urge. Believe me I know.'

She went to the bar and collected Pierre, and Ellis stayed where he was.

The Café Libertad had once been the Café Amor, as traces of the original gold paint still proved. It was a big and noisy place with a tiny dance floor, and a staircase in almost constant use by couples who looked sad, or in love, or simply randy. Pierre went to the bar for drinks.

'I don't bring Séverine here,' said Andy, as she watched the stairway. 'Not for that.'

'Well of course not,' said Jane.

He looked at her then, but she'd meant what she'd said, and he believed her.

'It's just – it's exciting. Life if you like.'

She looked about her. The place was packed with soldiers and girls. In a corner a group of International Brigaders were singing a song about the war; some in English, some in German. By the dance floor an enormous gramophone was playing a record of Irving Berlin's, 'What'll I Do?' It was scratched almost beyond audibility, but the couples who danced and embraced didn't even notice. When the air-raid warning sounded they still danced, the singers still sang. Andy listened, head cocked, to the faint rumble of gunfire.

'Miles away,' he said. 'We're all right here.' And then: 'Manny Mendel . . . You remember him?'

'Of course,' said Jane. 'He's the one who first directed me to Grandma's house.'

'He's dead,' said Andy.

It wasn't surprising. He was a soldier after all.

'The fight at the university,' Andy said. 'He was wounded and captured. When the Foreign Legion could find the time they would have shot him – '

'A wounded prisoner?'

'Well of course,' said Andy. 'We shoot theirs.' Not like her war at all. 'Only some German artillerymen got their hands on him.' She stared at him. 'Germans, Jane. Nazis. Manny was a Jew.' Still she waited. 'They killed him eventually,' Andy said, 'but they took their time.'

'You're sure of this?'

'We counter-attacked,' Andy said. 'We found his body. The thing is, folk should know about this. Can you write it?'

'Not me, no,' said Jane. 'I'm the Orphans and Aged Department. Tell it to Ellis.'

'How can I?' he said.

'Easily,' said Jane. 'It's a marvellous story.' It was too, but even so Bower might spike it. People in England weren't yet ready for that kind of horror. 'Write it out,' she said. 'You've written for the *Daily World* before. Send it to me and I'll see Bower gets it.'

'Thanks, pet,' said Andy, as Pierre came back with the drinks, and Séverine arrived.

She was tall, with a Parisian elegance that even the Café Libertad failed to subdue, and she was obviously potty about Andy, even going to the bar for more drinks because Andy was having his photograph taken.

'Surprised you, didn't I?' said Andy. He was getting more like Brother Bob by the minute, thought Jane, and said repressively, 'She seems jolly nice.'

This was nonsense. Séverine was elegant, good looking, with a kind of cool sexuality and enormous assurance, but she could never be nice. Even so, Andy sulked, which was what Jane wanted. Then another man came in and the sulks vanished, he was up on his feet, shouting a greeting. Jane turned to see the newcomer.

'Why Booker,' she said. 'What a wonderful surprise.'

'Jane!' the negro shouted. 'Jane Whitcomb.'

Jane went to him to shake his hand, and Pierre took a picture.

'How out of date you are,' she said. 'I'm Jane Lovell now. And you – you must be Dr Stanton now?'

'That's right,' Booker said. 'Patching up the IB heroes like Andy here.'

'He's got his own ambulance too,' Andy said. 'Given by the negro people of America.'

'Must be the world's busiest,' Booker said.

'But how do you come to know each other?' Andy asked.

'Mom and Dad used to work for Jane,' Booker said.

'Servants?' said Andy, and at that moment it was very much the old Andy speaking.

'Now just you lay off that,' said Booker. 'It wasn't the South before the Civil War. They were fond of Jane. Still are.'

'How are they?' Jane asked.

'Doing well,' Booker said. 'They must be. They're talking about retiring.'

'And your sister?'

'Lucille's doing just great. The main reason we've got an ambulance is the concert she gave to raise funds. There's talk of her singing at the Met soon. Saint Saëns. *Samson and Delilah*.'

'Oh I wish I could see it,' said Jane.

'All you've got to do is turn up,' said Booker. 'You and your husband. It was you two got her started, she tells me. Seats will be no problem.'

Séverine came back to them, followed by a waiter with Spanish champagne. No beer: not even for Andy. Jane moved closer to Booker.

'Do you ever see Tim these days?' she asked.

'Tim Jordan?' She nodded. 'You didn't hear then?'

Oh God, she thought, and aloud, 'What didn't I hear?'

'He joined the IB too,' said Booker. 'Abraham Lincoln battalion. He was killed in their first engagement.'

'No,' said Jane. 'I didn't hear. There was nobody to tell me.'

And yet I'm not surprised that he joined, she thought. I'm not surprised he was killed, either. There was always an innocence about him, and the need to trust too much. He would carry that

554

with him, even into battle, she was sure. He'd had no trace of Andy's brutal competence in combat, though they were equals in dedication.

Booker drank his champagne. 'He was a nice guy,' he said, 'but this war was too rough for him.' It might have been his epitaph.

'Men like him,' Booker continued, 'the thinking men, the intellectuals with a conscience, – a lot of them are like that. Their hearts and souls are in this war, but their bodies just aren't up to it. They're strong, but they're not tough. Not like the miners are tough, and the field hands and the factory hands. – Not like Andy's tough.'

Séverine came up to Booker then, and began to talk about the chance that some of the International Brigade might be moved to the Basque country, making it clear that Jane, as a new arrival, had no idea of the importance of what she, the old hand, understood so well. Not nice at all, thought Jane, but suddenly she was extremely tired. All she wanted to do was go back to the Press Club and sleep. She said goodnight to the others, and Booker and Andy offered to escort her, but she refused. It was very close, after all.

'Suppose you meet Burrowes?' Andy teased. 'You're not exactly his favourite reporter, now are you?'

'Well I should be,' she said. 'If it wasn't for me he wouldn't be able to go around boasting he'd been knocked out by Ernest Hemingway.'

'A metamorphosis in fact,' said Charles.

'Goodness what a splendid word.'

'That's because I had an Armagnac with my coffee. A quite enormous Armagnac.'

'I know,' said Jane. 'I watched you. I simply couldn't believe it.'

'That I would drink Armagnac?'

'That you would be so nice. I expected ranting and roaring, and at least the possibility of a black eye.'

It had not been an easy journey for him to make: he'd had to postpone meetings, travel at impossible hours, and yet as soon as he saw her he embraced her as if she'd just survived a shipwreck that wasn't her fault, and in the lobby of the hotel what's more, in front of a dozen people at least. . . .

'I'm glad I was nice,' he said. 'I can't tell you how happy I felt to see you.'

'I broke my word to you.'

'We've been into all that before,' he said. 'After Barcelona. It's a war. You're either in it or you're not – and God knows you're in it. So no sooner had Bower said "Andy Patterson" than our intrepid reporter was up and running. I worried about you of course, but there would have been no point in being angry.'

She leaned into his shoulder; for the first time in days she felt relaxed.

'Bless you for that,' she said.

'Metamorphosis,' said Charles, and kissed her forehead. 'That's what I want to hear.'

'Well it *is*,' said Jane. 'You never saw anything like it. I mean I've always known he didn't lack courage – or the ability to absorb punishment. Durham Gaol proved that, *and* the General Strike, but the ability to hit back – '

'That isn't what I meant,' said Charles.

'But – forgive me, darling – it's where it all comes from. I'm quite sure it is. You see Andy had persuaded himself long enough since that he wasn't a fighting man like John. Like Bob for that matter. Oh I know Bob's never gone to war, but he's been in a few fights. But Andy was a Conscientious Objector. A Pacifist. A man who couldn't fight – until he found out he could. And then the real Andy took over. He's having the time of his life.'

'He could die tomorrow – '

'If he does he'll die happy.'

'Or he could be wounded and live,' said Charles.

'Yes,' said Jane. 'So he could. And in the middle of the night I've no doubt it occurs to him – but the rest of the day's his own. Besides, he's discovered champagne.'

'What happens to Norah?'

Jane said firmly, 'That's up to him. And her. Let me tell you about Tim Jordan.' She did so.

'Good God,' said Charles. 'Him *and* Mendel. I'm glad your friend Booker survived.'

'Me too,' said Jane. 'He's the sort of survivor we're going to need.' Then she told him about his sister.

556

'So at least I do a bit of good sometimes,' said Charles.

'What about me?'

'You do good all the time,' said Charles. 'You're – what is it the Americans say? – you're a tough act to follow.'

They went back to London together. Her piece about Andy had been a success, so Bower said. Once more the money for the Orphans and Aged cascaded in. But for the time being at least Jane had had enough. She had survived the horrors and she thanked God for it, but she wasn't ready to see any more. Instead she gave little talks about Spain, as once she had about Felston, and went to concerts, theatres, parties, always with Charles, usually with Georgie and Ned too, and danced with Lionel as often as possible, and tried not to think how soon the next Great War would be. That there would be one she now had no doubt.

What to do about Norah? The only sane answer was nothing. It was up to Norah, and to Andy, as she'd said to Charles. On the other hand she couldn't be back in England and not see her. She talked it over with her mother when they next lunched together.

'Your decision is of course correct, inasmuch as it is a decision,' Mrs Routledge said. 'But what do you mean precisely by "up to them"?'

'No mention of Andy redivus,' said Jane, 'and especially no mention of any French ladies. I met Andy one night in Madrid for the sole purpose of writing about what a splendid thing he'd done – and it *was* splendid – and then he went back to the war and I went back to Charles and that's it.'

'Excellent,' said her mother. 'The only possible solution in fact,' then, after a moment: 'I read your piece about him in the *World*. Do you know if he has seen it?'

'Bower sent him a copy.'

'And?'

'Apparently he's delighted.'

'I wouldn't doubt it for a moment,' said her mother. Later she asked, 'Have you plans for Christmas?'

'We thought of going to Blagdon Hall,' said Jane.

'And Mrs Patterson?'

'I've written to her,' said Jane, 'but I'll have to see her of course.

But what we're after is a house party. Quite a small one. Just Charles and me, and you, and Lionel if he's free. And of course we'll pop across to see Ned and Georgie.'

'I should love to come, of course,' said Mrs Routledge, 'but – '

'But what?' said Jane.

'At my age wouldn't I be just a little de trop?'

'Darling Mummy,' said Jane, 'how could you ever be that?'

Lionel said much the same thing, but Jane was firm. If her big sister was available then of course he must come to Northumberland.

'I'm all too available these days,' said Lionel. 'Not that I've lost *all* my charm. – At least I hope not.'

'How could you possibly?' said Jane.

'It's just that the way the world is now there's just no *demand* for charm. Bless you, darling. Of course I'll come.'

At the last moment Charles invited Bob, too. It seemed that he had nowhere else to go. Given the way Bob had lived until then this was almost incredible, but Jane had no doubt that it was true.

She badgered Charles into taking two weeks off, which meant they could spend New Year's Eve in Northumberland as well. It was the first real break he'd had since their wedding, if one didn't count two days in Biarritz. The poor darling really did work awfully hard. What finally tipped the scale was her offer to drive him in the Bentley. He adored being driven in the Bentley. At the overnight stop he signed them in as Mr and Mrs C. Lovell. He'd almost made it Pardoe by force of habit, he said, then remembered just in time. She'd had her picture in the *Daily World* rather a lot just recently. Besides, they'd brought William with them, and he'd had his picture in the paper, too.

The very first day she went to visit Norah. Best to get the unpleasant task over before the fun began. Charles had very decently offered to go with her, but she vetoed that. There was no point: he hadn't been to Madrid, and so she took William instead. The walk to Norah's cottage took five minutes, and she hated every second. . . . It was a pretty cottage, stone-built, with a garden by no means at its best in mid December, but with space enough for Dorothy to play. The door opened at once and Norah stood facing her. Beside her, uneasily erect, was Dorothy.

'Why she's walking,' said Jane. 'How marvellous.'

'Come in,' Norah said, 'and I'll put the kettle on.'

Another tea ceremony, but first there was a gift to bestow; not Christmas, – those gifts would come later – but a teddy bear seen by Charles in Hamley's and bought at once.

'But she may have one,' Jane objected.

'A child can never have enough teddies,' said Charles, and to judge by Dorothy's reaction it was true. William was ignored, but not in the least upset by the fact.

'I've been thinking of getting a dog myself,' said Norah. 'Bit of company. – Not that I'm short of friends,' she said. 'Far from it. It's lovely here. But a dog's special. I've always wanted one, and now I can afford one.'

'I quite agree,' said Jane. 'A dog's always special.' William snorted modestly. 'But it's good to know you've got friends.'

'Oh yes,' Norah said, and indeed, she'd gained a little weight, looked more relaxed. 'It's just – it's just not the same, that's all.' She looked at Dorothy, who appeared to be teaching her new teddy some form of wrestling. 'Thank God I've got her.' Her hand shook and the tea slopped in her cup. She put it down. 'I read your piece in the paper.'

Jane took out cigarettes, lighter, holder.

'It didn't sound like him at all,' Norah said. Still not calling him by his name.

'He's changed a great deal,' said Jane.

'Being a soldier?'

'Well – yes.'

'You made out he's a good one.'

'Not my opinion,' Jane said. 'I'm not an expert after all.'

'But you must have looked after dozens.'

'Hundreds, by the time it was over,' said Jane. 'But by the time I got them they weren't proper soldiers any more.' Get off that, she told herself. No matter how she feels about Andy now, get off it. 'It was other soldiers who said he was good. – The judgement of his peers, so to speak.'

'Have they made him an officer?'

'He was offered some kind of promotion, but he refused.'

'That doesn't make sense,' said Norah. 'Not the way he's been acting since he left us. Showing off all the time – all those letters to Billy Caffrey. He writes to him more than he writes to me. All about defending the working man and how hardships have to be endured. All that.'

'But how do you know he writes to Billy Caffrey?' said Jane.

'They're a busy lot in Felston,' Norah said. 'Even my own mother – ' She broke off, and suddenly her fists clenched. Here it comes, thought Jane.

'He's got another woman, hasn't he?'

'How could I possibly know?' said Jane. 'It's not the sort of thing he'd tell *me*, now is it?'

'Some men would,' said Norah. 'My first for one. Not coming straight out with it – but making sure I got to know.'

Dear God, thought Jane. She's had it all before. How could Andy do it? But that wasn't the point. The point was that he had.

'We talked about his friends, and the place where he was fighting,' she said.

'Where was that? Where he was fighting?'

'The university,' said Jane. 'It's a ruin now. Smashed to bits.'

'Not like Cambridge,' said Norah. 'The stuff I could tell you about Cambridge. . . . He saved a lot of bairns, you say.'

'A bomb fell on an underground station,' said Jane. 'What they call the Metro. Andy happened to be near by and organised a rescue. A lot of the injured were children.'

'I thought he was in Spain to fight.'

'They get leave sometimes,' said Jane. 'He'd gone to the cinema.'

'Him and some lass,' Norah said, but there she left it, began to talk instead about how good the country air was for Dorothy, how much she enjoyed the work Charles had set her to do.

'The amount of organising you've no idea,' she said. 'I know I hadn't.'

'I hope we're not overworking you,' said Jane.

'No no,' said Norah. 'It's good to be busy. . . . And like I say, friends. I never knew there was so much to do in the country. Whist drives. Church socials. The lady next but one's got a bairn as well. We take turns minding them. Now and again I take Dorothy into Newcastle. There's times I can't believe how lucky I am.'

She looked away, and Jane sensed that she wanted to cry, but that this time she didn't want Jane to see, and indeed, soon it would be time to bathe, and change for dinner. She got to her feet.

'I must go,' she said. 'So much to do. My mother and a friend of ours are coming to stay with us tomorrow. – And Bob will be coming up later on.'

'Bob?'

'I forgot to tell you – or perhaps you knew,' said Jane. 'About his fiancée – '

'He wrote to me,' Norah said. 'She's gone mad it seems. It's a risk you have to run when you take up with a Patterson.'

She doesn't know, thought Jane. She can't possibly know what happened when John died. But it was even more necessary that she should leave. She embraced Norah, gave Dorothy a wary kiss, and set off for the hall. William too seemed glad to get away.

. 51 .

'She got it all wrong about Andy not accepting promotion,' said Charles when she told him. 'Of course he didn't. He wanted to stay with his friends, his comrades – and I bet he told Caffrey too. Otherwise she seems to have read him pretty well.'

'She's had a lot of practice,' said Jane.

'No wish to seem prurient,' said Charles, 'but do you think Norah's found somebody else?'

'Not yet,' said Jane, 'but I think she may be looking. – Not that she's aware of the fact.'

Next day her mother and Lionel arrived by train, and she drove to Newcastle to collect them. They approved of everything they saw.

'No wonder that dotty peer hated you so,' said Lionel.

Madness it seemed was to be the skeleton at what proved to be a memorable feast.

They were an unlikely but successful house-party. From time to time Charles invited neighbours, or they drove over to Derwent Castle, where Mummy was accepted at once, after the quality of her jewellery had been assessed. (Why doesn't the dear duchess buy a jeweller's loupe and have done with it? Jane wondered.) Lionel too went down well, but then Lionel knew everybody and could gossip by the hour about all the duchess's friends and enemies. The duke's too, for that matter.

Georgie drew Jane aside at the first opportunity.

'I want you to be the first to know,' she said. 'Apart from Ned that is.'

'You're not – ' said Jane.

'In the family way?' said Georgie, and added automatically: 'Not arf. Oh darling, do pray it's a boy. I don't think I could go through

562

it a second time. The doctor's already threatened to stop my martinis.'

Jane hugged her.

It was a good Christmas. The ground was too hard for hunting – there was even snow from time to time – but everything else was like pages out of Dickens. Holly and mistletoe and log fires, carol singers and parties and, when the time came, Santa Claus. Mrs Routledge and Lionel, townees both, even approved of the snow. In the country, as her mother said, it seemed somehow appropriate. Certainly it was beautiful: awesome too, accentuating the vastness of the moorland around them.

On Christmas Eve Bob arrived, just back from Switzerland, the strain of it still showing, but even he began to relax with good food, good wine, and carol singers sound on 'Good King Wenceslas' but not quite so at ease with 'The Holly and the Ivy'. On Christmas Day after breakfast they exchanged their presents, and Jane scored a bull's eye with her gift to Charles: a silver statuette of a rifleman of Wellington's day.

At teatime when the estate workers arrived there was more present-giving. Norah had brought Dorothy, who looked enchanting and elflike in white and green. Bob went to them at once. Oh dear, thought Jane, but it was the child he embraced, the child who smiled back at him. How very like Andy he looked at that moment.

When the presents were handed out Norah found that she owned a bottle of Chanel Number Five, and Dorothy a silver mug, from Jane and Charles. From Bob there was a gold bracelet for Norah, and another, tiny one for her daughter.

'But – but I can't,' Norah said.

'Of course you can,' said Bob. 'If you want to. It would make me happy, I know that.'

All around them people were tearing and unwrapping parcels, eating sandwiches and cake, helping themselves to drinks from the buffet set out in the hall.

Carefully Norah slipped the bracelet over Dorothy's fat little wrist. There wasn't a lot of room to spare.

'No bother,' said Bob. 'I'll have it enlarged till she stops growing. How's yours?'

Norah put it on 'Perfect,' she said.

The gramophone began to play. It was a Gershwin song, 'But Not For Me.'

> They're writing songs of love
> But not for me.

'Never did care for that one,' Bob said.

Jane and Charles began the dance, followed by Smith and the housekeeper, then one by one the tenants followed. Bob continued to play with Dorothy, until the child smiled, and showed him all her teeth.

'Seven!' said Bob. 'My you are a clever girl.'

The dance ended, and somebody re-wound the gramophone and turned the record. More Gershwin.

> It's very clear, [the crooner sang]
> Our love is here to stay.
> Not for a year, for ever and a day.

'That's more like it,' said Bob. 'Come and dance.'

'How can I?' said Norah. 'I've got the bairn.'

Bob picked up Dorothy, swung her high, then put her in her pram, turned to a woman sitting out.

'Keep an eye on her, would you please?' he said. 'My sister-in-law promised me this one.'

'Glad to,' the woman said, and Bob went to Norah, his arms came round her. Suddenly it really was Christmas.

Jane watched them dance, and told herself, It's none of your damn business. But she was fond of Norah. Bob too, come to that, if only he would stay away from women she was fond of.

In her dressing room that evening she told Charles what she had seen.

After a moment he said, 'Switzerland was rather hell for him I gather.'

'She didn't recognise him?'

'On the contrary,' he said, 'she recognised him all too well, and when he returned he found a letter from her father, demanding to be told where his daughter is and why.'

564

'Did Bob tell him?'

'She doesn't want her father to know. She told Lockhart so, *and* Plattner. Bob wrote back and told him so. The gallant general phoned Bob from Deauville just before Bob went to catch his train. Said he intends to institute legal proceedings. Bob wished him a Merry Christmas.'

'What will happen?'

'As I said, he's after his daughter's money,' said Charles, '*and* her shares. They've rather shot up in value just recently. No doubt he knows it. We'll have to fight him. I told you.'

But so much had happened. 'Will you win?' she asked.

'It may not come to court,' said Charles, 'but if it does we'll win all right. Any lawyer who knows his business would tell him so.'

'But how can you be so sure?'

'He's taking on one of the country's richest financial institutions. He'd be ruined before it got to the Court of Appeal.'

'The power of money,' she said.

'Just so,' said Charles, 'but don't go feeling too sorry for him. Those shares are better with Bob than on the chemmy table at Deauville Casino.'

'Yes,' she said. 'That's true, but it's all beginning to look like –'

'Like relatives haggling over a will before the poor girl's dead? That's not the way Bob sees it.'

'No?'

'Absolutely no,' said Charles. 'He misses her. Wants her back. It wasn't all just sex, you know.'

'What then?'

'They were mad on the theatre,' said Charles. 'Especially Shakespeare. We never did see *Hamlet*,' he said. 'Perhaps it's as well.'

'Ophelia, you mean?'

'Another one who did what Daddy told her,' said Charles.

'Oh damn it,' said Jane. 'Damn the whole bloody business.'

She began to cry, and Charles embraced her.

'All the same,' she said at last, 'I wish he hadn't gone to Norah for comfort.'

'I rather think the comfort's mutual,' said Charles.

'He walked back to the cottage with her,' said Jane. 'Did you know that?'

'He pushed the pram,' said Charles. 'Hardly Casanova, is it?'

She smiled then. 'Perhaps not,' she said. 'Ah well, time to change I suppose.' Charles left her. She began to undress, and was naked, hunting for a missing slipper, when William wandered in from the bedroom. She looked at him severely.

'Don't you ever knock?' she asked.

The meal that night was a buffet supper, and there were only the four of them there. Bob had discovered a dance at the next village, and persuaded Norah to go. At least he didn't ask to borrow the Bentley, she thought, not that she would have allowed him to take it, not in the state he was in.

He'd seemed all right until he'd met Norah: a little subdued perhaps – and who could wonder when one considered his trip to Switzerland? but coping, in control; but when he came back from Norah's cottage the control was slipping visibly.

'I know it's bad manners,' he said, 'and in the normal way I wouldn't dream of doing such a thing. But this isn't the normal way. I can't explain. Not yet. but take my word for it. Please.' He'd never begged before.

'Well of course,' she said, 'but how will you get there?'

'Where we're going there's a taxi service,' said Bob, and tried for a touch of his old manner. 'I've hired the entire fleet. It's a Morris.'

'That's all right then,' said Jane, and then: 'I'm sorry Bob, but I must say this. Norah's been through a bad time too. She's even more vulnerable than you are.'

'I know it,' said Bob. 'And believe it or not I respect her. It's just – we need each other just for now. We never thought we would – but we do.'

After supper Lionel wound up the gramophone, and they danced for a while. He was teaching Mrs Routledge to foxtrot, and an apt pupil she proved, but in the end they just sat, and listened to the music, and gossiped. Bob was inevitably first on the agenda.

'He's a rascal of course,' said her mother, 'and a likeable one, though God knows I'd never have admitted it if I'd been thirty years younger. And yet – it's odd that I never observed it before – how very vulnerable he is. I hope all goes well with him, but I have a dreadful feeling that it may not.'

'He was absolutely splendid when he and Piers Hilyard attended to Comrade Burrowes at the Cambridge ball,' said Lionel.

'That reminds me,' said Jane. 'Someone else attended to Comrade Burrowes in Madrid,' and related what Lionel instantly referred to as the Incident at the Press Club. He was enchanted.

'From what you say,' said her mother, 'the war is not going well for the Republican faction.'

'It's going very badly indeed,' said Jane. Mrs Routledge looked at Charles, who nodded in agreement.

'When a war goes badly, especially a civil war, it almost invariably means that it goes worst of all for the innocent,' said her mother, and turned to Jane. 'Your Orphans and Aged.'

'I'm afraid it does, Mummy.'

'There isn't enough spare cash in the kingdom to take care of those unfortunates,' said her mother, 'but one does what one can,' then appeared to change the subject. 'You remember the Bengal Famine before the war?'

'Yes, Mummy,' said Jane.

'And the typhoon three years later? It killed thousands. Just like an army.'

'I was in England with Aunt Pen and Uncle Walter for that one, but you wrote to tell me all about it,' said Jane.

'The point I wish to make,' said her mother, 'is that I was involved in both of them. Famine Relief. Organising distribution and medical aid.'

'Well of course you were,' said Jane. 'I remember. You got a letter of commendation from the viceroy, and wasn't there some sort of medal as well?'

'That is *not* the point,' said her mother, 'except for the fact that that foolish piece of parchment is written evidence that I was good at what I did. It is a talent that should not be wasted. I have offered my services to the Basque Refugee Committee and they have been accepted.'

'But that's wonderful,' said Charles, and Jane prayed, Please God don't let her be hurt. 'You'll take care, won't you, Mummy?' she said.

'At least as much as you do,' said her mother.

'I'll make sure she does,' said Lionel.

'You don't mean you're going too?' said Charles.

'It seems they have a plane,' said Lionel. 'A rather elderly machine – '

'You're never going to join their air force?' said Jane.

'At my age, you mean? Goodness how one feels one's years. . . . But my career as a fighter pilot ended in 1918. Far too late to renew it now. No. This is – or was – a Vimy bomber, but it's spent most of its working life transporting things – and people. I shall be doing the same.'

'Transporting what?' asked Charles.

'Orphans, aged, medicines, food.'

'Do you need any money?'

Always the banker's question, thought Jane, but it's kindly meant.

'All you can give us,' said her mother. 'Medicines never come cheap.'

'We'll talk before you go,' said Charles, and poured brandy for Lionel and himself and lifted his glass. 'Here's to you both,' he said, 'and a safe return.' Jane lifted her wine glass and sipped.

'Safe return,' she said.

'We shouldn't have done it,' Norah said.

'Maybe not,' said Bob, 'but we did. We couldn't help it.'

'More than that,' Norah said. 'It was like we had to. Both in the same boat, like. Helping each other. All the same – I hope I don't have another bairn.'

'You won't,' said Bob.

She made a face, then: 'It's hurt you, hasn't it – her being like that? Hurt you a lot.'

'More than I thought possible,' he said.

'Me too. Except I never thought it was possible. Him and me – we'd always be like we were, I thought. Maybe another bairn or two, but always the same. . . . Together. And as for – what d'you call it – what we did?'

'Adultery.'

'That's it. If you'd told me I'd have said you were kidding –. Not that it's anything to joke about. All the same – he started it.'

568

'*Andy?*' Bob seemed astounded. 'I admit he just upped and went – '

'And said you'd look after me. Well you looked after me all right. But he got himself another woman too.'

'You can't possibly know that,' said Bob. 'I mean who could tell you?'

'Your own sister for one,' said Norah.

Yes, he thought, Bet would tell you. But how could she know? She answered his question. 'There's others from Tyneside went to Spain as well as him,' she said. 'Chaps that have a friend – or maybe a relative – in Felston. They write home – some of them – and the friends and relatives spread the good word. There's no such thing as a secret in Felston.'

'And our Bet told you?'

' "I thought you should know," she said. "For your own good," she said.'

'Bloody bitch,' said Bob.

'No language,' said Norah. 'Whatever else she is, she's your sister.'

'Sorry.' His arms came round her.

'And less of that,' she said. She didn't mean it, and he knew it. His arms continued to hold her.

'Hurt,' she said. 'Hurt deep. Like you'd been stabbed. Is that how it is with you?'

'That's it all right.'

'I thought I'd be like a nun for the rest of me life. And just look at me. . . . Us.'

'I feel better,' he said. 'Thanks to you. And not just this.' He touched her, and she shivered. 'Talking. Being together. Sharing.'

'That's just it,' Norah said. 'That's exactly what it is.' Suddenly she chuckled, a rich and gurgling sound, the happiest he'd heard her make.

'I bet when you paid me that allowance you never thought I'd earn it like this,' she said.

The days dawdled on between the Castle and the Hall: dances, parties, a formal ball on New Year's Eve. Every day more grandeur as Lionel said, as he danced a foxtrot with Mrs Routledge.

'I must say I'm enjoying it far more than I'd anticipated,' she said.

'That may very well be so,' said Lionel, 'but I must ask you not to lead.'

'Some habits are hard to break,' said Mrs Routledge.

'Save it for Biarritz,' said Lionel. 'Lead like mad once you're there, but on the dance floor leave it to your devoted slave.'

Georgie sat out with Jane, and sneaked a glass of champagne when Ned wasn't looking. 'You see what it's come to?' she said. 'And his mother's even worse.' Her voice became a savage caricature of the duchess's. 'Are you sure you should be drinking that, my dear? You had half a glassful the day before yesterday.'

'I thought babies were supposed to prefer milk,' said Jane.

'And that's another thing,' Georgie said. 'What on earth's going to happen to my figure?' She looked across the dance floor. 'Friend Bob isn't exactly the life and soul tonight, is he?'

He was dancing with a pretty blonde, and making rather a hash of it, thought Jane.

'The Sybil Hendry business hit him rather harder than anyone expected,' she said.

'Oh God yes. Poor little Sybil. You mean everyone thought that with Sybil out of the way he'd be up to his old tricks?'

'Exactly.'

Georgie said, 'Surely you're not telling me that Bob was in love with her?'

'It's just about impossible to say what that sort of love is,' said Jane, 'unless you're one half of the people concerned. What I mean is he feels that he's responsible for her – not for her being the way she is – I don't mean that. But she's half of the pair, you see. He owes her that. He grieves for her, too.'

'Poor old Bob,' said Georgie. 'Fancy finding out what it's like to be human at his time of life. . . . So he hasn't found consolation in the Arms of Another?'

'If he has,' said Jane, 'he doesn't talk about it.' And neither will I, she thought. It was all too complicated to explain to Georgie, who left the emotional overtones to her scriptwriters.

London was more of the same, once her mother and Lionel had

gone: it was pleasant enough, but it was all marking time. Jane knew it, Charles knew it, perhaps even William knew it. Truett certainly did. She scurried to the phone every time it rang, simultaneously longing for and dreading the voice of her old enemy Bower.

It came on a Monday in February when Jane had just returned from a fitting for the suit she was to wear at Cheltenham for the Gold Cup.

'I've got news for you,' Bower said. 'Perhaps more than news. About Andy Patterson.'

'What about him?'

'He's been wounded,' Bower said. 'Badly.'

'Is he dying?'

'Ellis says not. . . . Hit in the leg. The telephone line was terrible. I didn't get it all.'

'Where did it happen?'

'A place called Jarama,' said Bower. 'On the road from Madrid to Valencia. The Nationalists attacked. Did you read about it?'

'A bit.'

'It was a big one. The Fascists threw in all they had, and so did the Republicans. A real, old-fashioned slaughter, just like 1916. Patterson was one of the ones who didn't get lucky.'

'Thanks for telling me.'

'I want you to go there,' said Bower. 'He's your story if he's anybody's.'

'He may be dead by now.'

'He'd still be your story. He belongs to the *Daily World*, Jane, just like you do. We took him up, featured him, printed stories under his by-line. Oh I know you ghosted it for him, but it was under his name. If he's dead he'll be a martyr: if he lives he'll be a hero, but either way he's your story.'

'All right,' she said, and hung up on him. As compensation it was less than adequate, but she enjoyed it.

'It'll make three times,' said Charles. 'Isn't that pushing your luck, rather?'

'Yes,' she said, 'but I can't help myself.'

'For Andy?'

'For John,' she said, 'and for Grandma too.'

571

He took his time thinking about it, but at last he said, 'Yes. I see what you mean. If it were me I'd do the same.'

William, timing his moment, scrambled into Charles's lap. He knows jolly well who goes and who stays, thought Jane.

Charles tickled him behind his ear, a process the little dog adored.

'Under the circumstances the question may seem ridiculous,' said Charles, 'but what about Cheltenham?'

'I'll be back for that,' said Jane. 'It isn't for another month.'

'You're sure?'

'Girl Guides' honour.' Charles said no more. Really he was too much.

'I'll make you another promise,' she said. 'This is the last time.'

'No!' Charles shouted the word, and William shot up, bewildered. More quietly he said, 'No promises. It's tempting fate rather more than I'd like.'

The next step was to tell Bob. There simply wasn't time to tell Norah, and she couldn't do it on the phone. Bob would have to attend to that. She telephoned him that night but he was out, and so she left word with the night porter at his block of flats, said it was urgent. He arrived next morning just as she'd finished her packing.

'I've been up North,' he said, and then: 'Is it about Andy?'

'How did you know?' she asked.

'Just a feeling. And anyway there's a lot about Andy these days.'

She told him what she knew. Andy had been wounded seriously but not fatally, at somewhere called Jarama – a valley, she had learned, rather than a town. The casualties had been forty thousand at least, and the International Brigade in particular had taken heavy punishment.

'And you're going there?' She nodded. 'Why?'

'I told Charles it was for John and Grandma,' she said. 'And so it is. But it's for the paper, too. He'll want that.'

'Aye,' said Bob. 'He likes his name in the paper these days.'

'I'm sorry,' said Jane, 'but you'll have to tell Norah. I leave for Paris in an hour.'

'Yes all right,' he said, and smiled. 'Funny. I just left her yesterday. Now I'll have to go back.'

'Then it wasn't just a – ' For once she couldn't find the word.
'One Night of Love?' She nodded.

'No,' said Bob. 'It's a bit more permanent than that. At least it was.'

The Paris papers too were full of the Jarama battle, and she read about it on the train down to Hendaye. 'Huge Slaughter,' she read, 'Enormous Death Toll'. Both sides claimed a victory. The Nationalists had advanced a few miles to no advantage, and the Republicans had retreated those same miles to no particular disadvantage that she could discover. The Nationalist artillery fire had been the heaviest yet, and the Moors had once again demonstrated their ability to move across country without being seen, then inflict appalling casualties, but they had been met and held. It was stalemate: both sides were exhausted. They clung to what they had: to renew the attack was impossible for both of them.

Pierre was waiting for her at Hendaye Station with a car, another de Dion. Really Bower thinks of everything, she thought, except the fact that I want to be at home in South Terrace with Charles, discussing Bridget's Boy's chances at Cheltenham. Pierre showed her the documents she would need: more press cards, creditations, another laissez-passer with another general's name. This de Dion too had Press and Prensa written all over it. Jane got behind the wheel, and she and Pierre looked at each other, unsmiling.

'This one,' said Jane, 'may turn out to be tricky.'

'It will be worse than that. It will be awful,' said Pierre.

. 52 .

Another overnight stop at the hotel on the Castellón road, but on the way no songs, no shouted compliments from the marching troops. Even the wireless sets in the hotel seemed more quiet, and the occupants listened to the news unsmiling. The proprietor was convinced that the only reason his hotel still stood was because the Nationalist officers intended to use it when they advanced that far. That they would advance that far he didn't doubt for a moment. They set off in the early morning chill, heading south, hooking round to the valley of the Jarama. It stayed cold, and then the rain began with a steady persistence that reduced visibility to yards, and just as well, thought Jane. No sane pilot would take off in such weather, and an insane one would never see them from a thousand feet up.

In the distance they heard shell-fire, a steady mutter like a snoring dog, and she headed towards it. One of the oldest military maxims of all, John had told her: when in doubt move towards the sound of the guns. Soldiers appeared, sheltering under rocks or trees, or in makeshift lean-tos. Nobody stopped them to ask for papers: they were too exhausted. . . . On to where the guns sounded quite loud, and Pierre shouted out to ask for directions, the car fumbled its way to a farmhouse half in ruins, surrounded by bell tents, and trenches dug close by for when the rain would clear and the enemy aircraft return. In an outhouse without a roof, camouflaged by branches, an ambulance was parked. On it was painted 'From the Negro People of America to the People of Republican Spain'. Jane pulled up.

'We're here,' she said.

From the farmhouse a man emerged.

'Hallo Jane,' he said.

'Hallo Booker.'

'We got word you were coming. Seems a long way to come for just one man. I've got fifty here you can have if you want them. Come tomorrow, I could have fifty more.'

He looked even more exhausted than the troops on the road.

'I'm sorry,' she said. 'One's all I can cope with.'

'Andy Patterson must be pretty important.'

'Not yet,' said Jane, 'but I've a feeling my editor thinks he will be.'

'Come inside out of all that rain,' said Booker, and took them to a room that was the only privacy he had: a child's bedroom with a bed too small for him, a table and two chairs, then called out 'Rita'. A black nurse came in.

'Bring some wine, honey,' he said, and when they had a drink, he leaned back and sighed. Jane offered him a cigarette. He looked at them hungrily, then shook his head.

'I can't,' he said. 'There isn't a cigarette in the place. I can't smoke if the others can't.'

'I've got a car-boot full you can have,' said Jane. 'Get some, would you please, Pierre?'

Pierre went at once, and Booker lit up.

'As I said, I got my instructions,' he said. 'I wasn't all that crazy about that. I'm in charge of this hospital such as it is – acting rank of major. I make the decisions. I take it, but I dish it out too.

'Then I get orders from a doctor who's a *general*, for God's sake. That sure as hell outranks me. One guy, one, is to be taken by plane to France and then on by train to London, and I'm to provide the ambulance to take him to the plane. Now we all know that generals are a mite crazy, but why would even a general who's a raving nut issue an order like that? What makes Andy Patterson so important to *him*?'

'My guess is that Jay Bower – the man who owns the *Daily World* – bought him.'

'*Bought* him? Are we back in New Orleans in 1860?'

'With medical supplies,' said Jane. 'A whole plane load.'

'Cash on the barrel,' said Booker. 'That's the capitalist system for you.'

'You don't approve of it?'

575

'It's terrible,' said Booker, 'but it works a sight better than the crazy theories my side want to put in its place. Besides – I need those supplies. When will the plane get here?'

'As soon as the rain eases. But the pilot can't come too close.'

'Yeah yeah. They told me. It's an old plane. Doesn't even carry a hand gun. A German fighter would eat it and we can't have that – not with my supplies aboard.'

'It's got an old friend of mine aboard too,' said Jane. 'The pilot.' Booker looked at her.

'My general said he'd send us a signal when your plane's on its way,' he said. 'As soon as we get it we'll get moving. Get him off to France as quick as we can. What do you want to do till then?' Pierre came in with a sack bulging with cartons of cigarettes, and again Booker called out 'Rita' and the black nurse appeared.

'It's Christmas,' Booker said, and held out the sack.

'Oh my,' Rita said. 'There really is a Santa Claus.'

'Before you resume that disgusting habit could you find out how Mr Patterson is?' Booker said.

'I know how he is,' said Rita. 'He's sleeping. I gave him his sedative three hours back.'

'He'll be awake in an hour,' Booker said. 'Why don't you folks go have a look at the war, take some nice pictures? There's a hill back of this farm here – you'll get a real good view from there. Tell you what – I'll come with you – the soldiers never stop me going anywhere.'

'Now you be careful,' said Rita.

They went on foot, but Jane was wearing trousers and a raincoat, and brogues bought, like Georgie's, at Harrods. From the hillside they looked down at a landscape that put her time clock back nineteen years, to the spring of 1918. Beneath her lay hastily dug trenches, the men in them crouching, wary of snipers, burned-out lorries, smashed artillery, the charred remains of horses burned into abstract shapes that now had no power to recall the sight she dreaded most. From time to time a gun banged beneath them, followed by a puffball explosion by the distant trenches, makeshift as those below her, where the Nationalist troops crouched, wary of snipers. . . .

'Backs to the wall,' she said. Booker looked puzzled.

'That's what Sir Douglas Haig said when the Germans drove us back to the Channel Ports in 1918, only there wasn't any wall, just the sea. But we hung on anyway until the Doughboys arrived, and we counter attacked and the war was over.'

'Don't quote me,' said Booker, 'but there's not going to be any counter attack here.'

'Then the Republic will lose.'

'We sure will,' said Booker.

All the time Pierre took pictures: single soldiers, living and dead, men cooking a meal under the shelter of an overturned lorry, trenches under a weeping sky. Maybe he too is going to publish a book, she thought: A Pictorial History of the War in Spain.

'Did a war correspondent called Ellis visit your hospital?' she asked.

'He did,' said Booker. 'So did a war correspondent called Séverine Jannot. They arrived separately and left together. Seemed to be your friend Andy's idea.'

'I like your Rita,' said Jane.

Booker chuckled. 'That's not changing the subject; it's association of ideas, right?'

'Right,' said Jane.

'She's not mine yet,' said Booker, 'but I'm working on it.'

When they went back Andy was awake, lying on a bed in what had been the farmhouse's living room. Booker had warned her of course, and she had prepared herself as best she could, but even so it was a shock. He had lost his left leg just below the knee, and the drape of the blanket made it as clear as a printed sign. Even so his face, if very pale, was alert and lively, with the look that said 'Where have you been? What kept you?' as he dragged on one of the *Daily World*'s cigarettes.

'Nice of you to look in,' he said.

'Not at all,' said Jane. 'I was in the neighbourhood anyway.'

Andy scowled. Wounded heroes, it seemed, should monopolise the irony.

'I gather you've come to take me home,' he said.

'To start you on your way, at least.'

'But not the others?'

Jane did her best not to sigh. He already knew the answer to this,

577

but then the other seven patients in the room could hear every word.

'Just you,' she said.

'You care to tell us why?'

'Because if I do you've a better chance of recovery.' He flinched, and so she added, 'And when you do you've got work to do.'

'That's true at least,' he said, and Jane risked a glance at the others: a man with an arm missing, a head wound, two with their eyes bandaged. Burns. She'd seen it all before but it was still appalling.

Andy said softly, 'It's all due to the *Daily World* then?' She nodded. 'What's it going to cost me?'

Jane shrugged. 'That's between you and Bower,' she said. 'My job's to get you on your way and tell your story.'

Andy said, 'I sent Séverine away, I don't know if you heard. I doubt she'd be the ideal mate for a one-legged shipyard worker.'

He really is over-doing this strong-man-who-knows-best performance, she thought. Séverine may well have come to the same conclusion on her own.

'She went back with Ellis,' said Andy.

'So all's well that ends well,' said Jane.

He glowered at her. 'To think I used to like you once,' he said.

'It's mutual,' she said, and got up to go.

'Wait,' he said. 'Ellis did give me one piece of news. About Burrowes. He gave a press conference.'

'*Burrowes?*'

'Told them how he'd infiltrated the British Fascists so he could denounce them for the villains they are.'

'Did he say he was a Communist?'

'Of course not,' said Andy. 'Just a free-born Englishman with a love of fair play and sympathy for the underdog.'

Jane thought about it. 'And in Madrid too,' she said. 'He's wriggled off the hook very cleverly.'

'Aye,' Andy said. 'He's a smart one, all right.' He even sounded admiring. Again Jane moved to go, but he said again, 'Wait . . .' Then more softly: 'Does Norah know what's happened?'

'Someone from the *World* will have told her.' Now was not the time to talk of Bob: perhaps there never would be such a time.

'Will she know where to meet me?' he asked.

'She'll have been told.'

'Do you think she'll be there?' Before she could think of an answer he said, 'What a bloody silly question. Forget I asked.'

This time she escaped. He wants her there because of the picture it will make in the *World*, she thought. Adoring wife meets caring hero. And even better if Dorothy's in it as well.

After dinner she and Booker sat together and drank another glass of his red wine. At least there seemed to be no shortage of that.

'We've got personnel problems too,' Booker said. 'My ambulance driver's got dysentry.'

'I can drive it.'

'You sure?'

'Certain.' Booker thought about it.

'That would be a help,' he said. 'A big help. And don't think I'm not grateful. But if we put Andy on that plane somebody's got to go with him, and I don't want to lose a nurse for two whole days.'

'You want me to do that too,' said Jane.

'If you think you could. I know it sounds like I'm all grab, but as I told you earlier, we'll have another batch of wounded along soon, and I'm so short-handed – '

'I can do it,' she said. 'Don't worry.'

'It's everything,' said Booker. 'Anaesthetic, medicine, bandages, even safety pins. I've got two ambulances and three drivers – and one of them is sick. I need ten times that. I need ten times everything. So all I can do is exploit what I've got. I'm grateful, Jane. I mean it.'

'Fiddlesticks,' said Jane. 'What's the point of being here if I don't make myself useful?'

Next morning Rita shook her awake at dawn.

'I'm sorry, honey,' she said, 'but the rain's stopped and the airplane's on its way.'

Somehow Jane lurched out of bed, washed her face, then drank American coffee as Booker gabbled last-minute instructions and Andy was loaded into the ambulance. A soldier from Castellón joined them as a sort of navigator, and in Castellón too they would pick up another driver to bring the ambulance back to the Jarama Valley.

579

The ambulance was a Buick with a big engine and softly sprung, the best conveyance available for a badly wounded man, but even so she knew how it must hurt; it was bound to hurt, but Andy made no sound. It took them six hours to reach the field outside Castellón where the aircraft waited, camouflaged with branches as the ambulance had been. Lionel and his navigator, a Frenchman, waited beside it in flying gear, smoking cigarettes, the plane's cargo neatly stacked, and Jane ran to him and kissed him, and the navigator blinked.

'How dashing you look,' she said.

'Ageing chorus boy,' said Lionel. 'And just look at that plane. Does it look like a piece of woodland? No, it does not. It looks like an ageing aircraft covered in branches. The whole damn war would be a musical comedy if it wasn't for the horrors.'

'That is true,' said the navigator.

Lionel looked up at the sky. 'Let's get your chum aboard and shove off,' he said. 'We can do without company.'

'I'm coming with you,' said Jane.

'So they tell me. There's some spare flying gear in the cabin. You can look dashing, too.'

Jane changed, then as gently as they could they eased Andy into the plane. On that cold morning sweat gleamed on his forehead, but still he made no sound. When they had finished the spare ambulance driver appeared, and he and the soldier began to load the medical supplies. At once Lionel motioned Jane into the plane, the navigator swung its propellors.

The plane moved over the rutted grass, and Andy sweated harder than ever, until at last they were airborne, climbing, and the pain eased. Jane saw that he was trying to speak to her, but the roar of the engines drowned his voice. She bent over him.

'How long?' he said. 'To France?' She held up four fingers. 'Four hours?' Jane nodded, and Andy lay back on the stretcher, she tucked more blankets round him, then incredibly, he slept. There was a sort of porthole by her seat, but nothing to see except a lot of grey sky, but that was all she wanted to see. No visitors. They might upset her patient. They would certainly upset her. After a while she slept too, then woke, at first bewildered by the aircraft's noise, then angry with herself because Andy might have needed her, but Andy slept on, the flight was easy. Once she saw another aircraft, a biplane, but they were over Republican territory, the plane was Russian. Jane yawned, and wished she could smoke, and drank the flask of coffee Lionel had brought, for in spite of the flying gear she was cold, then the plane's nose went down, and at once Andy was awake. Jane bent over him.

'We'll be landing soon,' she shouted. 'A few more bumps I'm afraid.' Andy nodded, but in fact the landing was far softer than the take-off had been, and Lionel taxied over to a group of waiting officials, the navigator was already producing papers. Jane left the plane clutching her own collection of documents as French ambulance men went in for Andy.

There were press men there, photographers, spectators. There was even the local mayor, who, being a politician, made a speech. 'Courage in the service of a wounded hero . . . Brave lady who serves humanity . . . Gallant airmen who risk their lives so that others may live.' Lionel lit a cigarette.

'For a moment I thought I was going to be called a brave lady too,' he said, 'then I turned out to be a gallant airman instead. Such a relief.'

Jane said, 'There's Mummy,' and set off at a run to where her mother stood waiting. Their arms came round each other, and they hugged and hugged.

'Nobody told me,' said her mother. 'Nobody dropped so much as a hint.'

'There was nobody else, that's why,' said Jane. 'Last-minute arrangement.'

'But wasn't it terribly dangerous?' said her mother. 'Lionel should never have permitted it.'

'He hadn't any choice,' said Jane. 'We couldn't let Andy fly unattended.' She hugged her mother again. 'Oh Mummy, it's wonderful to see you,' she said. 'And looking so well.' And indeed her mother did look well, surprisingly so.

'It's because I'm so busy,' said her mother. 'That and a certain talent for what Lionel calls my effortless ability to bend others to my will,' and smiled. 'I will show you my orphans –' she said as Lionel came up.

'Mind if I join you? They're my orphans too,' he said.

'Do by all means,' said her mother, 'but first Jane must change out of those ridiculous garments. She looks like a character in one of Georgie's films.'

'So you had to be a heroine after all,' said Charles. The line was good: she could hear the bitterness in his voice.

'Darling, I – '

But for once he interrupted her. 'Just as well I didn't let you make that promise,' he said.

'Darling, please listen,' said Jane.

She was in her suite at the Hôtel de Palais; champagne, chocolates, hothouse roses and all. Soon her mother and Lionel would arrive: they would dine together.

'I'm listening.'

'The only reason I did it was because there simply isn't anybody else. I couldn't let him fly alone – '

'You're not a nurse.'

'They taught me enough when I learned how to drive an ambulance. As it happened I didn't have to, but I could have coped.'

There was a long silence. He's thinking it through, she thought, as he thinks everything through. Please God let him believe me.

'Yes, all right,' he said at last. 'I've no doubt what you say is true.' Oh thank you God. 'But all the same I can't help worrying about you. You could have been shot down.'

'It's a neutral plane,' said Jane. 'Non-combatant.'

'Do you think a fighter pilot would make sure of that before he opened fire?'

She stayed silent. Lionel had told her that, too.

'When will you come home?' Charles asked.

'Soon,' she said. 'Very soon. Just one more story. Medical supplies in the Jarama Valley.'

'The ones Bower swapped for Andy Patterson.'

Charles's information service was at least as good as Bower's.

Keep it light, she thought. 'The very same,' she said. 'Yet another proof of what a splendid paper I write for. Then when that's done it's England, home and beauty I – '

'Don't say "I promise", ' said Charles. 'I don't think I could stand it.'

582

. 53 .

They had visited the orphans, and a heartrending sight it had been, and yet wonderful too, because of the way her mother and Lionel reached out to them. Of course in Lionel it was not surprising. Entertainment was his métier, so to speak. He sketched and drew cartoons, and made jokes in his terrible Spanish until they shrieked with laughter, but it was to her mother they turned when they needed comfort, reassurance, strength. Her mother gave all three as if she had an unending supply, and Jane remembered her as she had been thirty years ago, before she even knew of her major's existence. . . . Despite the heartaches, it had been a wonderful afternoon.

'You seem sad, child,' her mother said.

They were eating in Jane's suite, where there were no photographers. There had been far too many among the orphans.

'Missing Charles,' said Jane. 'He's missing me. . . . And those orphans of yours, how could I not be sad?'

'Some of them will do rather well,' her mother said. 'Quite a lot of them will go to Ireland. The Basques and the Irish have a lot in common.'

'Their Catholicism do you mean?'

'And their obstinacy,' said her mother.

'And even the least fortunate among them have one advantage,' said Lionel. 'Whatever else, they're out of Spain.' He hesitated, then said, 'I dropped in on Patterson on the way here. Just to make sure he had enough cigarettes and things.'

'And had he?' Jane asked. It should have been her business to find that out, but at the moment Andy had no wish for her company. Perhaps it was mutual.

'The *Daily World* had got there before me,' Lionel said. 'In that

583

sense he's got all he needs. But he did tell me something rather odd. About when he was wounded.'

'Yes?'

'He and his IB chums were up against a company or whatever it is of the Spanish Foreign Legion. Andy said that he thought his side were pretty good but the Legion crowd were brilliant. He also says that they were led by a young officer who supplied most of the brilliance, in his opinion. Outflanked them, forced them back, made them turn and run in fact, till a lump of shell hit him in the leg.

'But the point is this. He's not certain, he never can be, but he's got the idea that he'd met the officer before. . . . At Cambridge. He's pretty certain it was Piers Hilyard.'

'Good God,' said Jane.

'You see what that means, don't you?' said Lionel. 'For a young officer, no matter how promising, to get leave to fight in someone else's war he'd have to go pretty high up, and even then he'd only get it if the high-ups believed we were about due for a war of our own.'

'Your reasoning is sound, as usual,' said Mrs Routledge. 'Oh how I wish it weren't.' Then to Jane: 'When do you propose to return to Spain?'

'Train the day after tomorrow,' said Jane. 'After I've done my piece about Andy Patterson.'

'You will portray him as a hero?'

'That's what he is,' said Jane.

'As a virtue courage is by no means my favourite,' said her mother, and added, 'From what you tell me he has no intention of returning to the shipyards, always supposing they would employ a one-legged man.'

'He'll go straight into politics,' said Jane.

'For which one leg is perfectly adequate,' said her mother.

'He'll also need a wife,' said Lionel. 'Wasn't there some talk of an estrangement? Won't do him any good in politics.'

'He'll make it up,' said Mrs Routledge. 'He has no choice.'

It may not be so easy, thought Jane, but kept the thought to herself.

*

584

'You have been busy,' the copy-taker said.

'This isn't about me,' said Jane; and began to dictate. When she had done the copy-taker said, 'Blimey. That's as good as the pictures. Did they get a photograph of you in your flying gear?'

'Yes,' said Jane bitterly. 'They did.'

The way her mother and the copy-taker were talking, Georgie would be making a comeback to play Jane Whitcomb as soon as she'd had her baby.

'Oh by the way,' the copy-taker said, 'the boss says to tell you we're running a feature on you, too.'

'Tell him I don't want it.'

'I'd rather you did if you don't mind,' the copy-taker said. 'He seems sort of set on it.' He paused for a moment, then added: 'Our Jane.'

'That's quite enough of that,' said Jane.

Bower's new secretary said he wasn't available, a fact which appeared to give her pleasure. He wasn't available when she phoned from Hendaye either, so she sent a telegram instead, then went to where Pierre waited with the de Dion. Time to drive back to the war.

The wait at Victoria Station was dreadful for both of them. There were too many reporters, too many photographers, and the only way they could hide was to sit in the buffet behind a pillar. At least Norah hadn't brought Dorothy with her. That *would* have been a give-away. Instead she'd left her with the neighbour at Blagdon, and Bob had found her a room in a hotel in Paddington. No gossip, no scandal, though they'd gone to bed together that morning, and the day before.

'I can't see why they want to look for me,' said Norah. 'It's him they've come for.'

Bob had worked for Bower long enough to know how newspapers are sold. 'Because you're his wife,' he said, 'and if a wounded hero has a wife to come home to it makes a far better story. But I knew you'd hate it. That's why I kept you hidden. – Just as well they haven't got a picture of you.'

'You've done wonders,' she said. 'In all sorts of ways . . . What we had – you couldn't exactly call it love – '

'Couldn't I?'

'No,' she said. 'Not with Sybil the way she is. Any more than I could, with a husband in Spain and me and the bairn living off his brother. . . . No. Not love. But not lust either. Comfort, like we said. When we both needed it.'

'Will you ever tell him?'

'Not unless he asks. And even then I won't say who it was. How could I? But he won't ask.'

'Why not?'

'There's some truths it's better not to know, and us is one of them. No Bob. Even if he ever suspected, he wouldn't ask.'

'You're telling me it's over, aren't you?' said Bob.

'How could it be otherwise?' she said. 'We were happy. And that couldn't last, not the way things are.' For a moment he thought that she would cry, but she smiled instead.

'What is it it says in the Bible? A woman taken in adultery. Me. . . . Whatever would me mam say?'

The loudspeaker system, metallic, distorted, clicked into life. 'The train now arriving at Platform Three is the Golden Arrow Express from Dover. The train now arriving at Platform Three is the Golden Arrow Express – '

'Oh God,' said Norah.

'Shall I come with you?' said Bob.

'We said not,' Norah said, 'and we'll stay with that. You follow on after.'

'All right.' He handed her a platform ticket. 'Here. That'll get you through the barrier. Not that you'll need it. Just tell them who you are.'

'Thanks,' she said, and got to her feet. 'I'd better be off.'

'I'm sorry I can't kiss you,' said Bob.

'Me too,' said Norah, 'but you can't. Never again.'

She left him and he lit a cigarette, then walked out, taking his time. Ahead of him Norah walked to Platform Three, then moved more quickly as the Golden Arrow steamed in.

At the barrier a reporter came up to her. 'Excuse me,' he said. 'You're not Mrs Patterson by any chance?'

'That's right,' Norah said. 'I've come to meet my husband.'

More reporters joined them: the flash bulbs began to pop, and

Bob loitered by a tobacco stall to buy cigarettes he didn't need.

Andy appeared at last. The other passengers came out briskly, yelling for porters, but four of them were busy lowering his wheelchair from the guard's van, then helping down the pretty nurse who was to push it. The photographers saw him and sprinted through the barrier and Norah followed, still surrounded by reporters asking questions. Her voice seemed almost out of control, but that did not surprise them. This must be the most emotional moment of her life. On and on she walked, past figures as blurred as the images of a dream, and then at last she saw him plain: a thin man with a bone-white face, neatly dressed, clean shaven, sat in a wheelchair, a pretty girl to push him, smiling at the cameras. Smiling. He had a blanket round his legs, she noticed, or round one leg, anyway. It lay flat against the space where the other leg had been. That morning she had wondered if the sight of him, maimed like that, would make any difference to the way she now felt about him. It made no difference at all. Suddenly he saw her and began to wave, then spoke over his shoulder to the nurse. The wheelchair came towards her and Norah moved forward to meet it because what else could she do?

'Hallo, pet,' he said.

'Hallo.'

'I'm sorry I can't get up,' he said, and the reporters smiled. Norah thought: I bet you've been rehearsing that one all the way here.

'Haven't you got a kiss for us then?' he asked, and she bent over him because she had to, and the flash bulbs exploded around them, they walked on to where Bob stood, waiting.

'What fettle, kidder?' said Bob.

'What was that?' a reporter asked.

Andy said quickly, 'It's my brother. He's asking how I am.' Then to Bob, 'Canny, how's yoursel'?'

'Better than you by the look of you.'

'Don't you be too sure of that,' said Andy, and then: 'Thanks for taking care of Norah and the bairn.'

'My pleasure,' said Bob.

Andy turned once more to the reporters. 'My brother's a business man. Patterson's Wireless Rentals.– It never hurts to advertise, eh Bob? – If he hadn't helped me I'd never have been able to go to

Spain and get my leg blown off.' The reporters scribbled furiously.

'Where are you off to now?' Bob asked.

'St George's Hospital,' said Andy. 'Courtesy of the *Daily World*. There's a chap there going to fit me a new leg the Fascists can blow off any time they like – because there'll always be a new one waiting. Come and see me.'

'All right,' said Bob.

Andy reached under the blanket and came up with the late edition of the *Daily World*.

'Here,' he said. 'There's a piece there might interest you. Stop Press. Ta-ra, Bob.'

'Ta-ra,' said Bob. 'Ta-ra, Norah.'

The procession moved on, and Bob turned to the Stop Press.

'MP Killed in Car Crash,' he read. 'Mr Martin Lowe, the Member for Felston . . . Kingston By-pass . . . Icy Roads . . . Death Instantaneous . . .'

There's a saying about wanting something so much you'd give your right arm for it, thought Bob. Well Andy had wanted something so much he'd given his left leg for it, and now he'd got it.

Carefully they wheeled Andy into the ambulance, then Norah got in beside him, the nurse sat with the driver, and they set off for Knightsbridge.

'Too bad you couldn't bring the bairn,' Andy said.

'So she could get her picture in the paper an' all?'

'So I could see her.' Suddenly he began to sweat.

'Are you all right?' she asked.

'It hurts, that's all.'

'I dare say it does,' she said.

There was a great deal of fuss and delay, even more photographs, before he was finally left alone with his wife. A room to himself, Norah noticed. Flowers and fruit. All that. Ah well. The *Daily World* could afford it. She waited.

Andy lit a cigarette and said, 'You don't seem pleased to see me.'

'I'm not.'

'Well that's honest, anyway. Is it because I went to Spain?'

'It's because you left me,' she said. 'Used me an' all.'

'*Used you?*'

588

'You're still after a job in politics, aren't you?'

'And I'll get it. I'm bound to. Listen, Norah – '

'No, you listen,' she said. 'Just for once. That's why you married me, isn't it? To get on in politics. Till you left us I couldn't believe it, but that's what it was. To get on in politics you have to have a wife, and I was the nearest.'

Andy opened his mouth to shout a denial, to argue, to plead, but then the pain came back and he could do nothing. The Victory Parade at Victoria Station was being paid for at last.

'Well we're married,' said Norah, 'and there's nowt I can do about it. I'm stuck with you, and I'll just have to put up with it, but I'm telling you this. It's separate beds from now on. You lay a finger on me and I'll divorce you – and don't think I can't. – And then where will your job in politics be?'

Bob's taxi took him up Knightsbridge, past the hospital, to the restaurant where he would eat a solitary dinner. As they chugged past its vast bulk he thought: She'll still be in there, alone with him and hating it. Him too by now, but all the same he's stuck with her like she is with him. Brother Andy. The hero. And so he was a hero. Courage and endurance. The nightmare of Durham Gaol and homosexual rape and still he came back fighting. The General Strike. More fighting. Then Spain and a sizeable chunk of him buried on a battlefield there. Courage. Just like John. And a need for women. That wasn't so much John – Jane had been enough for him: would be enough for most men – but it's very much like me, he thought. Norah was right. There was a lot he owed Sybil: would always owe. Then he remembered the pretty nurse. All the same, he thought, the leopard doesn't really change his spots, not all of them, and when you think about it, it's hardly the leopard's fault.

. 54 .

Booker was pleased to see her, but so busy with his supplies he hardly had time to show it: the little boy with a train set for his birthday. Jane and Pierre went to work and took pictures and wrote words: black doctors and nurses with white patients, and the only thing that mattered was the pain, and the skill of the doctors and nurses, the administration of drugs, that kept the pain at bay. At last she confronted Booker in his room.

'We have to talk,' she said.

'What about?'

'This piece I'm writing. It's mostly you.'

He yawned. The man's still exhausted, she thought. I doubt if he can remember a time when he wasn't.

'Sorry about that,' he said. 'You just write whatever you want and say it's me. . . . I'm sure it'll be OK.'

'It doesn't work like that.'

'No, I guess not,' he said, and poured out wine, offered cigarettes. 'Ask your questions.'

'Will you stay till it's over?'

'If I have to,' Booker said. 'I'm not exactly anxious to be a guest of General Franco, being a person of my colour. And I know Rita isn't crazy about it, either. Or any of the others. Seems to me I have a duty to get them out – as well as an urgent personal need.'

'Is Franco anti-black?'

'His buddies the Germans are. He may not have much choice. I'd sooner take my chance in Alabama with the Ku Klux Klan.'

'When you go home, what will you do?'

'Pretty much what I'm doing here. Orthopaedic surgery. Only back home it'll be car crashes instead of gun-shot wounds. – Until the next one starts.'

'You too,' said Jane. 'You're that sure?'

'Aren't you?'

'Yes,' said Jane. 'But tell me what a wonderful gift those drugs and things were. Our readers have enough wars on their plate for now.'

'Well so they were a wonderful gift,' Booker said. 'I just wish I didn't have to use them.'

She finished her interview and Pierre took his last pictures. Next morning they said goodbye to Booker and his staff and Jane pointed the de Dion north, the only direction Charles cared about. Castellón overnight for the last time, and she wrote up notes to the sound of wireless sets. No rousing speeches, not any more; no more *Internationale* in three keys: just music: any kind of music. Any kind at all, she thought, so long as it's sad.

They were off again next morning at first light; fewer soldiers now, fewer lorries and guns, and the little car pushed on briskly. It was on the road to Tarragona that they saw the ambulance. It was an adaptation of a big Renault lorry, very like the kind she'd driven in France, twenty years ago, and it was pulled up at the side of the road while a woman wearing trousers peered into it suspiciously, resentfully even. Jane pulled up and called out, 'Can we help?'

The woman turned to face her. 'Why, Miss Whitcomb,' she said. 'What on earth are you doing here?'

It was Peggy Hawkins. Jane got out of the car.

'It was Jane last time,' she said, 'and anyway I'm Mrs Lovell now.'

'Congratulations,' Peggy said, and the two women embraced.

Jane turned to Pierre. There simply wasn't time to explain that at one time, when she was mad, Peggy had not been just a friend, she'd been her only friend, as well as her mother's housemaid. In those days Peggy had lied for her, protected her from her mother's wrath, for her mother as Lady Whitcomb had been far different from her mother as Mrs Routledge.

Later Jane discovered that Peggy had an aptitude for languages. Lionel had coached her and she had founded a scholarship to send Peggy to London University and from there she'd gone to Geneva and the League of Nations.

'Miss Hawkins is an old friend,' she told Pierre. It was woefully inadequate, but it would have to do. She turned back to Peggy.

'What on earth are you doing here on your own?' she said. 'Those brutes used to take two of us to handle them.'

'They still do,' Peggy told her. 'I'm just the apprentice really. They only let me come along because I speak Spanish. The proper driver's in hospital in Barcelona. Appendicitis.'

'And they let you tackle that on your own? Without even a proper lesson?'

'There wasn't anybody else,' Peggy said. The never-ending cry.

'Let's have a look,' said Jane.

It was only the plugs, thank God, and a good clean put them to rights.

'Thanks awfully,' said Peggy, and looked at the ambulance in that same suspicious, resentful way.

Oh God, thought Jane, I can't do it. I just can't. She turned to Pierre. 'Look,' she said. 'You'll have to go back without me.'

'But Mrs Lovell – ' Pierre began.

'I'll give you my notes. Let Mr Bower know at the *Daily World*, and let my mother know too. She'll take care of everything. Tell her I'm taking Miss Hawkins to – ' She turned to the other woman. 'Where are we going?'

'Guadalajara. It's a bit north-east of Madrid. The Fascists attacked there yesterday. It's pretty ghastly there.'

'Tell them that too,' said Jane, 'but don't overdo the ghastly bit. Not to my mother.'

Pierre went because he had to, but he hated to go.

Jane searched in her handbag, took from it the little Cartier leopardess that Aunt Pen had given her years and years ago, to commemorate the fact that when she was a child in India a holy man, a saddhu, had told her ayah that she would achieve great things.

Well I haven't, she thought, but all the same it's always been my lucky charm, and if ever I needed luck it's now.

'Best let me drive for a bit,' she said. 'When you think you've got the hang of it we'll swap.' They climbed into the cab. 'Didn't you once have a gentleman friend, too?' Jane asked.

'Mine got away,' Peggy Hawkins said. 'I didn't have enough money, you see.'

'How rotten,' said Jane. The other woman shrugged.

'I got over it,' she said, 'but then this nightmare started, and translating pompous platitudes from French to Spanish seemed rather irrelevant. So here I am.'

'Here we are,' said Jane, and let in the clutch. 'Tell me about Guadalajara.' Peggy told her.

'Italians, the Foreign Legion, Moors, Requetés – Franco's crack troops – and vast quantities of tanks, lorries, artillery, aircraft. The last big gamble for Madrid.' The Republic would need every ambulance it could get: even an ageing brute like the one she was wrestling with.

Beyond Tarragona they saw an air-raid. It wasn't much of an air-raid, just a single aircraft that dropped one solitary bomb on a road near a village. Lightening its load, thought Jane, the pilot anxious to get to base for a pre-dinner drink. She drove on down the road, and prepared to squeeze past the crater that the bomb had made. There had been a casualty it seemed. Just one. A mule had been dismembered every bit as messily as anything she had seen in France, but the thing was that she couldn't be bothered with that now. There was no time. They had to get on to Guadalajara, and Peggy Hawkins had to be reminded how vital it was to double de-clutch when you wanted the brute to change gears. . . .

In the back of her mind she wondered if she would ever see Bridget's Boy win the Gold Cup, or if Charles would ever forgive her.

. 55 .

The Guadalajara battle was quite unnecessary, said Ellis: it was achieving nothing for either side, but then Jane remembered being told that the Jarama Valley battle too had achieved nothing, and it simply wasn't true of either. Both battles had achieved a quite staggering loss of life. All the same she listened, because even if he did tend to treat Peggy Hawkins and herself as if they were a packed audience at a staff college lecture, at least he seemed to have some idea of what was going on. So far he'd been the only one who did.

They sat, the three of them, in the lee of the ambulance, which was protected in turn by the wall of a ruined farmhouse. Jane had found a bucket, and fuel, and so there was a fire, and more important, she and Peggy both wore fur coats. By then in Madrid one could buy anything: or even better, barter for it, particularly if one had cigarettes and food, and the fur coats were vital. For Guadalajara was cold: Guadalajara was bloody freezing in fact, and covered in snow, which was why at the moment the Republicans were winning. The Nationalist tanks and planes were grounded. . . . Jane remembered a photograph taken twenty years ago, perhaps even to the day: five girls in the lee of another ambulance; Sarah and Harriet and Bill-the-Lesbian and Louise and herself, all wearing fur coats, sables, mink, leopard skin, as protection against an equally freezing landscape. They had all been laughing, even she: but then she'd been twenty years younger.

'It won't last of course,' said Ellis. 'It can't.'

'What won't?'

Ellis sighed a God-give-me-patience sigh that even Bower might have envied. Perhaps it went with working for the *Daily World*, she thought. Perhaps I do it too. How awful if I do. But then just at the moment everything is awful.

'The weather,' said Ellis. 'There should be a thaw coming soon.'

'Thank God for that,' said Peggy, and huddled even more deeply into her silver fox; a totally unexpected garment for an ex-parlour-maid to wear.

'It'll alter the whole balance,' said Ellis. This was not the time for personal complaint it seemed, not when he was discussing tactics – or was it strategy? Charles would know, but how could she ever again ask Charles anything?

'It's all very well to say the Republicans are winning – '

'Don't you want them to win?' Peggy asked, in her best League of Nations, kindly-answer-the-question voice, which was more than a match for the God-give-me-patience sigh.

'Well of course,' said Ellis, 'but I honestly don't think they can.'

Jane huddled into her own coat, an ocelot she didn't much care for, but at least it was warm. For that moment she liked Ellis, because he wasn't lecturing, just telling the truth.

'Some of them are ghastly – I know that,' he said. 'I've seen it. But not nearly as ghastly as Franco's Merry Men. Those Moors of his – '

'Why can't they win?'

Peggy it seemed was in no mood for sensational journalism. What was required was facts: relevant facts and look sharp about it.

'They have almost no money left, and very little food. They're poorly armed and equipped – and nobody wants to help them.'

'The Russians help them.'

'Not enough. Stalin's tried out his tanks and aircraft and blooded his generals, and now he's done it I think he's decided Spain's too far away – and in any case, my guess is it's Germany he's worried about.'

The kettle on the bucket fire came to the boil, and Peggy took it off and began to make tea in a battered metal teapot.

'Mine too,' she said.

Ellis took from his greatcoat pocket a bottle of brandy. 'Care for a drop of this in it?' he asked.

'We can't,' Peggy said. 'We're driving.'

For once Ellis looked disconcerted. 'When?' he asked.

'As soon as you've finished your interview with Jane.'

'I'd better get on with it then,' said Ellis, and Peggy Hawkins rose.

595

'I'll leave you to it,' she said, then turned to Jane. 'I'll just check the equipment,' she said. 'What there is of it,' and offered Ellis her hand. 'So nice to have met you,' she said.

As she spoke an infantry company went past with the reluctant slouch of men who knew only too well what was waiting for them. They went past in silence, but their eyes said it all. Two pretty women. Two *rich* pretty women. The man must be a general at least.

Ellis said, 'Bower's very keen on this one.'

'I thought he might be,' said Jane.

'But you aren't?'

Jane shrugged. 'It might raise a few more quid for the orphans if he handles it right – and he usually does.'

'It's the wheel comes full circle effect he's after,' said Ellis. 'You know: this is where you started – behind the wheel of one of those.' He nodded at the ambulance. 'All those years ago.'

'Twenty.'

Ellis nodded, and inwardly marvelled at her looks. True she had money, and probably luck as well, but if he hadn't known better he'd have sworn that twenty years ago she'd have still been wearing pigtails.

'Then the glamour part,' he said. 'Hollywood and country-house parties and the Roaring Twenties. And the charity work too.'

'Charity?' she said.

'Felston Clinic, the Hunger March,' said Ellis.

'That wasn't charity.' The words rapped at him like bullets.

'What was it then?'

'Obligation. I could do it – and so I had to.'

'Just you?' Ellis asked. 'No one else?'

'I hadn't time to look.'

Somehow when she says it it doesn't sound like vanity, Ellis thought, and yet it has to be.

'Society life,' he said aloud. 'Film stars and aristocrats for friends, a rich and handsome husband, and you gave it all up to come back to this.' He gestured at the battered landscape around him. 'Shall I say that that's obligation too?'

'If you like,' said Jane. 'It – my being here – is a very complicated thing to explain, and I'm very tired. It's an exhausting job driving one of these.' Her hand touched the ambulance. 'In fact this one's an absolute pig to drive – but it's all there is. Obligation explains me as well as any other word.'

'Not duty?'

Jane thought of Bob then. 'Stern daughter of the voice of God?' she said. 'That's all right for Wordsworth – but a little bit pompous for me. No . . . Obligation will have to do. – And a good word for the orphans.' She thought of her mother then. 'And the aged,' she said. 'And a good word for Peggy Hawkins too. She's earned a good word, believe me.'

'Will do,' said Ellis, and got to his feet. 'I'd better be off. Our proprietor's in a hurry.'

He stood up and stretched, then walked back to a BSA motorcycle that had 'Press' and 'Prensa' notices plastered all over it. It looks about the same vintage as the ambulance, she thought, but it's a jolly sight easier to coax down narrow roads. Ellis kicked at the starter, and the BSA exploded like a mortar shell.

Needed an overhaul months ago, she thought, but we've all got the same problem. There just isn't enough time – even for essentials.

She opened her handbag, took out cigarettes, holder, lighter, and then the letter again.

> My dear, [she read]
> This isn't an ultimatum. Nothing like that. You and I have never pointed pistols at each other, and I've no intention of starting now. It's just – I honestly don't think I can take any more. If this makes me sound like a softy then I'm sorry for it, but a softy's what I am.
> No ultimatum, I promise you. Just the fact that I can't stand being married to you when your life is in danger. I mean that. I simply can't stand it because I love you so much. Love is a painful business, and I can't bear any more pain. Please come home.
>
> Charles

Love is a painful business. Jay Bower had said that once, when he was in love with Catherine, and now Charles had made the same discovery. But then obligation was a painful business too: obligation to wounded men, to Booker, to Peggy Hawkins. She folded the letter – if she kept on doing that much longer it would fall apart – and put it back in her bag, took out from it the little Cartier leopardess Aunt Pen had given her, and pinned it to her coat. She wasn't afraid, she thought – well no more than usual – but she was becoming much too apathetic for the job she had to do. She could do with a little of the leopardess's aggression.

The embers in the bucket began to die and she shivered inside the coat. Charles had sent the letter to her weeks ago, via a bank, the Banco de los Obreros de Madrid, and the bank had tracked her down at once, like a Mountie getting his man. But then even the Bank of the Working Men of Madrid would oblige Charles Lovell, and darling Charles had known it, love's pain notwithstanding. . . . The trouble was she couldn't go back yet. Love and Obligation. Obligation wasn't just a longer word: it was a stronger word, too. She got up and shovelled snow into the bucket, the embers sizzled and died, and she emptied them out as Peggy came out of the ambulance.

'Ready?' she said.

'Ready as I'll ever be.'

'Would you like me to drive? I need the practice.'

'Nonsense,' said Jane. 'You're doing splendidly.' And indeed it was true, when you considered what a bastard that pig of a vehicle was. I'm not making sense, she thought. Bastard pig indeed. If only I weren't so tired.

She waited as Peggy climbed aboard. Please God let the starter work. I don't think I'm up to swinging the handle. I should have made Ellis do it before he dashed off to write a newspaper story about a non-existent heroine. What would dear Séverine have to say about it all? she wondered. The starter worked, and she too scrambled aboard, Peggy let in the clutch. Time to visit her doctor.

'They've moved the forward dressing station,' Booker said, 'on account of we seem to be winning for a change. Same road, but a few miles further up. The Buick's up there loading now. I want you to try to bring back the rest.'

'In one trip?' Peggy asked.

'If you can. The weather's beginning to clear, and the Rebs' artillery's feeling the need of exercise – and when it comes to Red Crosses, those boys are a mite colour-blind. The less trips you make the better – and in and out fast.'

598

'Off we go then,' said Jane.

Despite his tiredness Booker grinned at them. 'May I say how much we appreciate you ladies dropping in on us like this,' he said. 'You bring distinction to an otherwise squalid environment, – and it's appreciated, believe me.'

'Just because you haven't got a fur coat,' said Jane. 'Jealousy. That's all it is.'

'No it isn't,' said Booker. 'It's Rita. . . . She wants a fur coat too. She gives me no peace.'

They left the field hospital, another shattered farmhouse, almost indistinguishable from the one in Jarama. In Spain there must be thousands of them. . . . Peggy coaxed the pig on to the main road and they drove, wary of shell holes, towards the sound of the gunfire. Half way there they met the Buick ambulance coming the other way, and squeezed aside to let it pass, then jolted on again. The sound of the guns grew louder.

Jane looked out of the cab window. Dark soon, she thought. No chance of a return trip tonight, no matter how many clients we have. Peggy swerved round a shell hole, and the sound of the guns was louder still.

'We must be almost there,' she said, but there was no answer. Peggy risked a glance to her right, and saw that Jane was asleep.

'Jane,' she said. No answer. 'Jane please.' Still no answer, but when Peggy touched her Jane was awake at once.

'Are we here?' she said.

'I think so.'

Peggy looked about her at a landscape that had been systematically smashed, gutted, set on fire. Dead horses and mules burned into abstract shapes, dead men half buried in snow, a machine gun broken apart like the toy of a gigantic child.

From a shell hole a soldier appeared and waved to them. Peggy edged the ambulance forward and the soldier shouted.

'Two hundred metres,' Peggy said. 'There's a dip in the road there. Some sort of cover.' They sidled on.

There was a tent pitched in a hollow, and all the rest was bare ground, snow, and icy wind. Peggy pulled up by the tent, and she and Jane looked down. Five of them, thought Jane. One too many for the pig, but they'd manage if one of them lay on the floor. An army medic stood up as they approached, and saluted, but it's not for us, thought Jane. It's the coats. They're irresistible. Peggy spoke to him in Spanish and as she did so, the other medic appeared, the one who had given them directions.

'Tell them we'll take all five,' said Jane, and Peggy did so. The medics shrugged.

They had a point, thought Jane. One of their clients had an arm missing, one had bled so much his uniform looked red, even in the lamplight. The others – she looked away. Even if they survived, the others had achieved an ugliness that they would be ashamed of for the rest of their lives. The medics picked up the first stretcher. They did their best not to hurt, but they were as impersonal as porters at Smithfield Market. They've been at it too long, thought Jane. We all have. . . . Three young Spanish Republicans – the one who had lost an arm looked about fifteen – and two men from the International Brigade. Yanks. The Abraham Lincoln battalion. Not that it made any difference. They were all entitled to a ride, whoever they were, even if they turned out to be Moors. Except that if they had been Moors the International Brigade would have shot them. And, of course, vice versa.

'I'll drive back,' she said.

'Darling, are you sure?'

Hawkins calling me darling, she thought, and to the manner born. Lionel would be proud of her. I know I am.

'I promise I won't fall asleep,' she said.

No wonder I call it the pig, she thought. Obstinate: hating to be driven, always seeking the easiest way no matter where it led to. . . . Why didn't that nice Mr Bentley make ambulances?

From the back of hers a voice began to sing. The tune was *Red River Valley*, but the words were different, though she'd heard them before.

> There's a valley in Spain called Jarama, [the voice sang]
> It's a place that we all know too well,
> For 'tis there that we wasted our manhood,
> And most of our old age as well.

One of the Yanks. Homesick for the battle he'd survived, and

600

who could blame him for that? She slowed down for a shell hole, and the singer started again, the same four lines, over and over. He had a nice voice, she thought, but she wished he knew more words.

'Should we try to shut him up?' Peggy asked.

'Why?'

'He's disturbing the others.'

'I doubt if it bothers them,' said Jane, 'and anyway we can't stop now. It's almost sunset.' The Yank sang on:

> For 'tis there that we wasted our manhood,
> And most of our old age –

And there he ended: he and the song both. Dead, she thought, and was grateful for the silence. It had been difficult for her to concentrate on her driving while he sang so sweetly.

Booker was waiting as he always was, and Rita, and the orderlies. The singer, it seemed, had been the blood-soaked man. Booker muttered something and the stretcher bearers pushed him aside, and none too gently either, but then she was right: the singer was dead, and Booker and his hospital had time only for the living. Jane yawned and stretched.

'You won't need us any more tonight,' she said.

He looked up from the one-armed militia man. 'Go and eat and get some rest,' he said, and she nodded.

'We'll see you in the morning,' she said.

'Maybe before that.' Booker looked furtive. 'The moon will be up later. If the sky's clear – there are still some guys waiting for you.'

It was downright incredible, she thought. Booker, Dr Stanton, was tall and black: Dr Stobbs in Felston was stocky and white; yet when they asked her to do something unreasonable they both had the same furtive look.

'There's soup,' Rita said, 'and bread. The soup's not bad. Make sure you both have some before you sleep.'

Peggy grinned at her. 'Yes madam,' she said, and for a second she was a housemaid again.

After the soup they went to the room they shared, and lay down without undressing. The more comfortable they were the harder it would be to wake up.

'I had no idea it would be possible to be as weary as this,' Peggy said. 'Not even when I was in service.'

A few seconds later an aircraft snarled past. 'One of ours,' said Jane, and Peggy sighed. She was asleep.

Time to think about Charles's letter. She thought about it every night, but never seemed to get any closer to an answer, because her mind was exhausted too. She huddled in the ocelot coat, covered her feet with a blanket and admonished herself, 'Think, woman, for heaven's sake. You're supposed to be good at it.'

He had said the letter wasn't an ultimatum; he'd even meant it: but an ultimatum was what it was. Come back or else. But it wasn't Charles being the masterful male: he had never sounded less masterful. What he was saying was: Either we're married or we're not. If we are, come back to South Terrace and be my wife, and if we're not – separation? Divorce? One or the other, she thought, because what he'd written was the truth. He simply couldn't stand life as it was, and if he had to exist without her, being the man he was he'd sooner get it over with.

How to tell him that she couldn't go back; that what she did was too important for her ever to weaken, even though to weaken was what she longed, craved, ached to do? And not just to rest, either; bathe in a hot bath, sleep in a familiar bed, but to be the half of that entity she and Charles had become, to touch and respond, or just to lie and feel his warmth beside her. Soon I'll be hating those Brigaders and militiamen, she thought, for keeping us apart.

But they sang about the Jarama valley and died, or forgot to duck until it was too late and paid an arm as a forfeit, that was the point. She should write and tell Charles so. He'd fought his war, too: he knew what it was like. Besides, he was a good man, even compassionate. He would see it. . . . Only she couldn't write. She'd picked up a pen two days ago, and the words just wouldn't come. She who had always been so fluent, and now she couldn't find the words. Like a worked-out mine. . . . In Felston the mines still had coal in them, but they didn't dig it any more. And besides, John Patterson was dead, which was why she was still here. He wouldn't have put up with her nonsense. He'd have come and fetched her. Taken her back home.

Somebody was shaking her. It was cruel. Unfair, too. She worked hard, as hard as any of them. She was entitled to her rest. But the shaking went on and she opened her eyes, looked at Rita.

'If I had a gun I'd shoot you,' she said.

'That's my girl,' said Rita.

Jane looked across at Peggy who was already awake, drinking the coffee Rita had brought. Jane reached out for her own mug of the stuff: thin and far too sweet, but at least it was hot.

'Moonlight?' she said.

'Just enough,' said Rita. 'You won't need headlights.'

'I should think not,' said Jane. 'With headlights we'd be a better target than daylight.'

'Oh,' said Rita, and then: 'I'm sorry, honey. I'm sort of new at this game.'

Jane got to her feet, sought and found cigarettes.

'Same place?' she said.

'Yes,' said Rita. 'The Buick's acting up and Booker reckons it's serious. Cylinder head. So there's only you.'

'How many?'

'Nine,' said Rita.

'Two trips,' Peggy Hawkins said.

'I'm sorry, honey,' Rita said again.

Peggy shrugged. 'It's what I signed on for, after all,' she said.

Jane thought: I don't think I can manage two. Not with only three hours' sleep.

The first one was easy. The moon gave them adequate light, and Peggy drove there without trouble. Her driving got better every day. Soon she would be able to cope on her own – or at least with a learner assistant, which means they'll find me a different ambulance – and a different learner, which will be a pity, she thought, because I like Peggy Hawkins. . . .

Five on the first one, and she drove back because she was better at avoiding the jolts that could hurt or even kill the men behind. Yet again Booker was waiting for them, and got to work at once. Look at him, she thought. Look at all that energy, that need to heal, and he's even more tired than you are. All the same I don't think I can manage a second trip.

'Shall I drive out again?' Peggy asked. Jane made no answer.

'Jane,' said Peggy, and Jane looked at her. 'Do you want me to drive out – same as before?'

'Yes please, darling, you drive out,' said Jane. 'What a long way it is to be sure.'

Peggy opened her mouth as if about to speak, then shut it again and got into the cab, and Jane followed.

Getting there wasn't too bad, and the four soldiers, when they saw them, a pretty average collection of horrors: another almost certain amputee, a shattered face, a pierced lung, and a man whose groin would never be the same again. The stretcher bearers pushed them on to their bunks like postmen pushing letters into slots, then scurried for their billets, while Jane cautiously, gently, manoeuvred the pig round in the road and set off for home. The moon shone more brightly as more clouds disappeared and Jane set off down the road, the pig grumbled on its way in bottom gear. A healthy man could have strode past them without breaking into a trot, she thought, but that was just the point. She wasn't transporting healthy men.

The landscape before her was like something out of a nightmare. Peggy had said that, and Booker and Rita, so it must be true, but the point was that to her it was beautiful, too. It cried out for a painter. Perhaps it was the moon and the snow: silver and white and the blackness of shadow; no bright colours at all. Georgie could have worn a dress made of what she saw and looked absolutely stunning. Georgie in moonbeams . . . But then Georgie always looked stunning.

She eased the brake down further for a shell hole that covered half the road, and coaxed the pig round it, crawled forward once more. A moonscape, she thought. That was what it was. A moon desert. Tundra, was it? A place abandoned even by God: pocked and splintered and frozen with two more or less healthy women and four desperately sick men the only life left, crawling across its surface inside a mechanical pig.

It was the Italians who proved her wrong – or so they told her later. Italians who should have stuck to Verdi and spaghetti carbonara and the Uffizi. Instead they pointed a field gun from a distant hillside, aimed and fired. And a very good gun it must have been, she thought. Its shell exploded ten yards behind the pig, which moved perhaps another ten yards at forty miles an hour, then stopped. Jane switched off the engine and waited, but the next shell didn't come. They were in a patch of moon shadow, the only piece of luck they'd had so far.

'How are the clients?' she said.

Peggy looked behind her, but that wouldn't do. She got out, taking a torch from a side pocket, careful not to switch it on until she was inside the pig. Really, thought Jane, I do like Peggy Hawkins.

Behind her Peggy said, 'Three are pretty much the same. The chap who got one in the you know whats is dead. I don't suppose it bothers him too much.'

'No,' said Jane. 'I don't suppose it does.'

Peggy climbed back into the cab. Getting on was going to be tricky. The shadow extended for yards in front of them, and the last bank of cloud obscured the moon, making it grow dimmer.

Jane said, 'If we had any sense we would stay here, but it wouldn't do the clients any good.'

'It would probably kill them,' Peggy said. 'That hospital's the only chance they've got. Just as well we haven't any sense.'

'I'll have to put the headlights on,' said Jane.

'Let me say a prayer first,' Peggy said. Jane tried to pray too, but she was too tired even for that. God help me was all she could manage, and hoped that it would be enough.

'Whenever you're ready,' Peggy Hawkins said.

Jane switched on the lights. They flashed like swords in the darkness, and in their beams was the remains of a horse that had not been there on the way out: the front half of a horse, or perhaps a little more, propped on its front legs, mouth still open in an unfinished scream, frozen upright: the rest of it spilling out behind it like the stuffing of a broken doll.

'Oh my God,' said Peggy. Jane let in the clutch.

'What?' she said.

'The horse,' Peggy said.

'Watch the road,' said Jane. 'I can't leave these lights on much longer.' She eased the pig forward and the Italians fired again, again the shell fell short, but once again was close. She shut off the lights. Better some of us dead than all of us, she thought, and eased the pig into second.

605

. 56 .

'The other three may make it,' Booker said. 'Two of them anyway.'
She nodded. The funny thing was that she felt all right, sitting there
in what Booker called his office. She felt quite well in fact, except
that she was cold. Stove going full blast, fur coat buttoned to her
throat, sloshing down a mixture of hot tea and brandy, and she
was freezing.

'Where's Peggy?' Booker asked.

'In bed,' said Jane. 'Asleep.'

'Where you should be. Do you want a sedative?'

'No,' she said. 'I want to talk to you.'

At once he looked wary. This woman, the look said, is about to
tell me she's had enough. Jane offered cigarettes and he took one.

'First a question,' she said. 'Are you my doctor?'

'More like your CO,' he said, 'if we're being formal.'

'I don't mean that.' The words were close to a scream. 'I mean
are you my *doctor*, for God's sake. If I'm ill. Hippocratic Oath. All
that.'

Easy boy, Booker told himself. This one's had just about all she
can take. 'I'm your doctor,' he said.

She nodded. 'I can't go on,' she said. 'You knew I was going to
say that – but the point is you're entitled to know why. Only I can't
tell you unless you're my doctor.'

'The Hippocratic Oath?'

'Exactly.'

'Go right ahead,' he told her. 'There's nothing leaves this room.'

'And nothing on paper?'

'No mam.'

She drew on her cigarette. At last she said, 'We were in the
darkness and I switched on the headlights because I had no choice

606

– and when I did, half a dead horse was looking at me. The last time that happened was nearly nineteen years ago. . . . I must have seen dozens. It didn't bother me – at least I didn't think it did. I was too busy for it to bother me – just like now. And then – and then –'

She told it all because she trusted him, and because he had a right to know. John's death, the nightmares, the craziness, and the long, hard climb back to sanity, Jabber Lockhart her only guide. When her hand reached out for her tea and brandy it was perfectly steady, but she hunched into the fur coat as if it held no heat at all.

'Well that's it,' she said at last. 'I'm sorry, Booker. I know what you must think of me, but that really is it. I'm sorry.'

'You haven't the remotest idea what I think of you,' Booker said.

'Well?'

'I think you're wonderful,' he said, and all she could do was stare at him: gawk.

'You carried all that inside your head all these weeks and said *nothing*. You risked all Lockhart had done for you, all you'd done for yourself, because the soldiers needed you, I needed you – and everybody here, and you never said a word. Yes sir, you're wonderful, all right.'

He says it with the same certainty he'd have used to say 'You've got appendicitis,' she thought.

Booker drew on his cigarette, and continued: 'Peggy told Rita about the leopardess and the holy man, how you would do great things – and Rita told me. I hope that's OK?'

'Of course.' She gestured. 'It's a good story, but that's all it is.'

'For a real smart cookie you can be awful dumb,' said Booker. She tried to speak. 'No wait,' he said. 'Let me finish.'

'I read your book about your General Strike,' he continued. 'Tim lent it to me. The things you did. . . . For that place Felston. That clinic. Andy Patterson told me about that, too.'

'Andy did?'

'Seemed like he couldn't talk enough about you. The things you did. That Hunger March.'

'That was his.'

'Don't lie to me,' said Booker, and grinned. 'I'm your doctor. That march was yours. He told me so himself.'

607

'But he detested me – ever since Jarama. Maybe even Madrid.'

'He envied you,' Booker said.

'He had no reason to. He's a born organiser. He'll make a brilliant politician.'

'He has one quality you lack, and oh how he wishes you had it.'

'What quality?'

'Ambition ... Selfishness. But that isn't the point.' She waited. 'The point is that your holy man was right,' said Booker. 'You have achieved great things – and a bitter price you've paid for them. But once is enough, Jane. You mustn't pay that price again. Even Dr Lockhart couldn't help you a second time.'

'You know him?'

'I've read him,' Booker said. 'What a man. Fifteen years ago he was the one piece of good luck you had.' He hesitated, then: 'I'd like to ask a favour.'

'Yes?'

'About the holy man and the prophecy. Not your illness – that's doctor and patient stuff. Just the leopardess. I'd like your permission to tell it to my parents.'

'Of course,' she said. 'Except please don't tell it when I'm there. I might start blushing.'

'It's more than I can do,' Booker said. 'Now about you – '

'You're going to fire me?'

'I'm about to give you an honourable discharge.' She nodded. The soldiers' lives were important. If she wasn't up to the job any more then Booker mustn't risk them.

'Now you better get some sleep,' he said. 'You sure you don't want a sedative?'

She shook her head. 'I don't even want to sleep,' she said. 'I'm scared of what I might dream.'

'Sleeping's one thing I can't cure you of,' said Booker. 'You've got to face that one on your own, honey.'

Jane finished her tea and brandy. 'I'd better get on with it then,' she said.

In fact she dreamed only of Aunt Pen, waking up in her bed in her house in Mount Street when Jane came in, a dream within a dream. Aunt Pen looking flushed and girlish and delighted as she always did when she thought of her husband.

'I was dreaming of Walter,' she had said. 'So naughty.'

The dream was all right: she had adored Aunt Pen, and Uncle Walter. It was the cold that bothered her. It woke her up three times.

They were in billets near the Ibarra Palace: not that it was a palace; more of a country house, and nothing like Chatsworth – or even Blagdon Hall, but a nice enough place before the heavy artillery and the Russian tanks had had a go at it. Now it was as big a shambles as the rest of the Guadalajara battle. That had been the Italians' fault. They might choose to give themselves melodramatic names – Black Arrows: Black Flames – names that Puccini should have set to music – but they were rotten soldiers. Still, it wasn't all their fault. They were conscripts for the most part, and that made them reluctant soldiers, too, and half of them were in tropical kit when the snow began to fall. But even so . . . Good transport, good equipment, and the International Brigade had eaten them for dinner – and damn near had us for dessert, but in the end we held them. At a cost ... Piers turned from the window that still had glass in it, and went back to the letter he was writing to Catherine, though God knows when she'll get it, he thought. I don't even know where she is – except that she'll be with that don of hers.

A lorry rattled into what was left of the courtyard, and he looked up. Oh dear God, he thought. Another lot. Poor devils.

The lorry was crowded with young men in civilian clothes, and behind it was a car with a machine gun mounted, manned by legionnaires, men he knew. Men of his own bandera, rifles slung, went over to join them. Nice chaps for the most part, clean, cheerful, good soldiers, good fighters, but all the same they could do this without a blink. His sergeant barked a command and the young men jumped down from the lorry. Aged seventeen to thirty-five, he thought. The entire young manhood of the village of Brihuega. As they lined up they shivered. The snow had ceased to fall but the cold was intense. They'll be colder soon, thought Piers.

His sergeant walked down the line and pushed two of them aside: a cripple and an obvious idiot, then snarled at the legionnaires in the car for bringing them, and ordered the men from Brihuega to strip to the waist, walked down the line again, and examined each right shoulder. Looking for a bruise or a callous, Piers knew. The mark a rifle makes when you squeeze the trigger and the butt recoils against your shoulder. Three more men joined the cripple and the idiot: the rest were marched away. They didn't even try to pick up their clothes: they knew there was no need. Behind them went the men of his bandera.

The Brihuega men could claim that they were deserters, or conscripts on leave who didn't want to fight anyway, but they didn't. The Legion wouldn't listen. The Brihuega men knew that, too. They rounded a corner, and when the shots came there was nothing to see. Piers was grateful for that, but really it made little difference, he thought. He'd seen it all before a dozen times. The villagers wouldn't even have received the dubious dignity of a firing squad: just be told to keep on walking, then shot in the back of the head. . . . His men came back, casual, unconcerned, as if they had had a good day at the partridge. Colonel Bolin appeared and his men stiffened to attention.

The colonel said something to the sergeant, who said, 'Eleven, colonel.'

'Excellent,' the colonel said. 'That's eleven less for us to worry about.'

And this was the man who yesterday had asked him when he'd last written home. Christ has not returned to Spain, he thought. Not yet.

Then he remembered that morning, just before dawn. He'd been with his bandera on the hillside by the road to Madrid, waiting for the lorries to bring them here, when those *bloody* ice-cream sellers had started shelling an ambulance. Piers tore up the letter he was writing. Suddenly he knew he'd had enough. Both sides were murderers, and both sides would go on being murderers, though they preferred the word 'executioner'. They could prefer what the devil they liked, he thought. I joined to be a soldier, not a bloody hangman. Time he went to see Dr Serra, he thought, and remembered to limp as he left the room.

. 57 .

'I called you both in,' Booker said, 'because I've had to make a decision and it affects you both.'

Very formal and serious was Booker, and Jane and Peggy sat prim and serious before him.

'I'm disbanding the unit,' Booker said, and Peggy gasped. 'The patients you brought in last night were the last ones.'

'Are we allowed to ask why?' Peggy asked.

'Sure. The organisation that raised the money to send us here, they're not fools, thank God. They know what Fascists are – but then every half-smart black in America knows what Fascists are.

'So before they shipped us over we talked it through, and the decision we made was this: when the time came I would turn over all the equipment and supplies to the Republican Medical Corps and take my little flock of black sheep back to the States, and I would be the one to decide when the time had come.' He smiled. 'At that time I didn't figure on acquiring a couple of white sheep, too, but I guess the same rules apply.' Peggy tried to speak. 'Because they're the only rules we can play.' Peggy waited.

'I managed to make a couple of phone calls last night,' Booker said. 'The weather's about to break and the uproar's going to start again. Götterdämmerung. They'll be coming in close, the Foreign Legion and the army of Africa and the Requetés, the best men they've got.'

Peggy nodded agreement then. She had first told Jane about it after all.

'And the worst,' said Booker. 'They'll come in close because it's what they're good at – and maybe the Italians will come with them. In fact it's almost certain. And maybe some Germans will come along too, – just so they won't miss the fun. Well I'm not having

611

my little black sheep barbecued by any of them, especially the Germans, and so like I say, the decision is mine and I made it. I hereby declare you honourably discharged.'

Peggy said, 'I don't know. . . . What do you say, Jane? I mean we could always go back to Madrid and drive for the Medical Corps.'

Booker said, 'Last night I asked Jane a favour. I made her promise she'd go back to England the first chance she got and write about what we've done here. The unit isn't functioning any more, but we still have to raise money for Spain any way we can.'

Oh Booker, she thought, what a kind man you are, but these days I can't even write a letter to my husband.

Peggy still looked undecided.

'You want to go to Madrid I can't stop you,' Booker said, 'but I learned something else last night. . . . The big one is coming.'

'Another war? Bigger than Spain?' Peggy sounded incredulous.

'This is just the rehearsal,' Booker said. 'Once it's squared away – maybe even next year – then it'll be time for the really big one, and all those clever mechanical toys they invented for hurting people here – they'll multiply the order a thousand per cent and people like you will really be busy. They'll need you, Peggy, I promise you, because you're one of those who knows what it's all about. Spain's finished, believe me. Back home's where you're needed.'

Back home wasn't all that easy to get to, but they arrived eventually; bus to Valencia, ship to Marseilles, and then civilisation took over: train to Paris, and shops to buy new clothes; the Golden Arrow, train and ferry, then London at last, where she and Peggy kissed and vowed to keep in touch. This time, thought Jane, they would do it.

A taxi then to South Terrace through a London that was as busy and self-centred as always. Cold, too, but not nearly as cold as Guadalajara. On the boat she had almost stopped feeling cold, but as she drew near South Terrace the shivering started again. . . . She had sent a telegram from Paris, so that Truett and the rest of the harem knew that she was coming. William even managed to wag his tail, though his eyes were on the kitchen, where Mrs Barrow was. And the food. Only the pasha was missing.

'Telegram arrived yesterday,' Truett was saying. 'Such a relief, madam. Bad news, telegrams, nine times out of ten . . . I thought it was best to open it, seeing the master isn't here. I hope I did right.'

'Yes of course,' said Jane. 'Where is he?'

'Called away, madam. Urgent business. – Said he'd written to you,' she added carefully.

'I've no doubt he did,' said Jane, 'but the post in Spain is terrible, just at the moment. . . . I did get one letter,' she added, and Truett relaxed a little. 'He said he might be going away, but he wasn't quite sure when. How long has Mr Lovell been gone?'

'Two weeks, madam.'

'Then he ought to be home soon,' she said aloud, and thought though whether he will be or not's another matter, but now is not the time to go into that. 'I expect there are lots of letters,' she said.

'Oh heaps, madam. They're all in the study.'

'They'll keep till tomorrow,' said Jane. 'I'm far too tired to worry about them now.'

'I'm not surprised, madam,' Truett said. 'After all you've been through.' Jane turned to her.

'It was all in the *Daily World*,' said Truett. 'A whole page about you. And a photograph. Only you weren't wearing that coat.'

'Don't you like it?'

'Not much, madam.'

'I can't stand it,' said Jane, 'but it did keep me warm.' *Well, some of the time.*

'I thought Spain was supposed to be hot,' said Truett, another illusion shattered.

'Quite often it was,' said Jane. 'Did you keep that piece in the *Daily World*?'

'Oh yes, madam.'

'May I see it please?' Truett went to get it, and Jane turned to where gin, vermouth and ice were waiting, and mixed a dry martini. Charles should have been waiting too, she thought, or Lionel at least, but there was no one. She sat down with her drink, and at once William scrambled into her lap.

'At least there's you,' she said, 'and oh I am grateful for your company.' She scratched the place between his shoulders that he could never reach, and the little dog shivered.

The piece in the *World* was what she had expected: our Jane, heroine extraordinary, a cross between Joan of Arc and Edith Cavell: and look what happened to them, she thought. Still the photograph was a good one. Pierre had taken it when Jane had repaired the pig, the first day she'd met Peggy. Nothing glamorous: there never was in Pierre's pictures. Her forehead was smudged with oil. Even so, Charles had bolted the very next day. Bolted where? That was the problem. She could hardly write to him at his bank, now that she was back in England, – always supposing she could remember how to write. Supper and then bed, she thought, and I'll see what I can do tomorrow.

She phoned her mother first, but Mrs Routledge was still in St Jean de Luz. So was Lionel, according to Pott, who seemed surprised that Jane wasn't in Spain. Disapproving, even. Heroines, it seemed, should not frequent South Kensington. . . . Blagdon Hall was unlikely, she thought, and anyway, she could hardly ring up Smith and ask if he'd seen her husband, and Charles had given up his service flat as soon as they were married. Phone the bank and risk being snubbed by that snooty secretary of his? Only if she had to, she decided.

In the end she sent a telegram, and spent the morning reading about what was happening in the rest of the world. All she knew about was Spain. . . . What was happening was mostly Hitler, and the going at Plumpton was firm, which would have been good news if Bridget's Boy had been running. She threw aside *The Times* and started on the *Telegraph*. More Hitler. But in the *Telegraph* Mussolini was at it too, and there was a long article about 'Why Franco Is Bound to Win'. She found herself agreeing with every word, and looked at her watch. Much too early to mix a martini, though God knew she needed one.

When Truett came in she was on her feet at once, ready to rush to the phone, but it was only a message from Mrs Barrow, asking what she wanted for lunch.

'Anything,' she said, and Truett left, William snorted in disgust. 'I know,' she said, 'but it's the way I feel. I love him, you see.' Then, oh my God it's true, she thought.

Think it through, Vinney, her governess, had told her, whatever it is, but how do you think love through? It's simply there. Charles had loved her from the start. It had been what the French called a coup de foudre, a thunder clap, and that was how it had been with her when she met John. But it hadn't been like that with Charles, not at all like that. She had liked him of course, once she discovered that his brusqueness was no more than fear of a rebuff, liked him better than anyone else she had known since Aunt Pen died, and he was nice to sleep with. A sort of more refined Jay Bower, she thought, though she'd liked Charles far more, and she could never have married Bower, but once he'd agreed to her terms she'd married Charles like a shot.

Did that mean she'd always loved him, if only a little at first, and that little had increased day by day without her knowing it, because Charles was always there – whenever he was needed? What a rotten way to treat him. . . . Great oaks from little acorns grow. That was another one of Vinney's, and in this case Vinney was absolutely right. Her love wasn't an acorn any more, it was a thumping great tree – now that Charles wasn't there to bask in its shade – and serve you jolly well right, she thought, but I don't want to be served right, I want to love Charles, and oh please God I want him to love me.

It was teatime when he phoned, and she was in despair till Truett summoned her, so that she had to force herself not to run to the phone, yet when she held it she could hardly speak.

'Hello?' said Charles.

'You got my telegram?' she said. What a stupid, what an asinine thing to say. 'I didn't know where you were, you see.'

'I'm sorry it took so long,' he said. 'I've been to Birmingham. Just got back.'

'Business?'

Another stupidity. Why else would Charles go to Birmingham? Why else would he go anywhere, now that she wasn't there to coax him into having fun?

'That's right.'

This won't do, she thought. He's becoming as tongue-tied as I am.

'I want to talk to you,' she said.

'We're talking.'

'Not on the phone.'

'I could give you dinner somewhere.'

'No.' She almost screamed the word.

'What then?'

'I want to talk to you here.'

'I don't think I can do that,' said Charles.

'Oh,' she said.

'I honestly think a restaurant is best. Somewhere quiet.'

But she couldn't talk to him where other people could see her. I'll cry, she thought. I'm bound to cry. And I can't do that where people are watching.

'Please Charles,' she said. 'I accept that you can't come here – honestly I do, but I need to talk to you on your own. Isn't there anywhere we can go?'

A hotel, she thought. I should have suggested a hotel, but that would have meant luggage, signing a register, even if they were married, and a room with a bed they wouldn't share.

He said at last, 'There's the flat in Park Street.'

'What flat?'

'The bank's. We keep it for emergencies. I gather this is an emergency?'

'It is, rather,' she said.

'Eight o'clock?' he said. 'I have to change first, then look in at the club. There's a chap there I absolutely must have a word with.'

'Eight o'clock,' she said.

'See you then.'

They both hung up, then she had to call him back in a panic, minutes later. She had forgotten to ask the number of the Park Street flat, and Charles had forgotten to tell her. She went back to the drawing room, and William stood up politely.

'I don't deserve it,' she told him. 'I behaved like an absolute idiot. You'd have been ashamed of me.'

If he was going to his club he'd change, she thought, which was reason enough for her to change too. Considering what was to come she'd need every advantage she could grab. First a long, hot bath, because it was supposed to soothe you, and even if it didn't quite do that it helped you to relax, then the Chanel perfume he liked so much, the underwear he liked even more, and the Fortuny dress and emeralds by Fabergé. Look at me, take notice, it would all say. Would I go to all this trouble if I didn't love you? Not that she had much hope of the underwear. . . .

Not the ocelot coat (the sooner that went to charity the better) and not the Fortuny mantle, either. It was still much too cold. Sables, that was the thing: the ones he'd bought her. Then she sent Truett to fetch a taxi, and looked down at William.

'Wish me luck,' she said, and went downstairs. That she needed all the luck going was obvious. In the taxi she shivered all the way to Park Street, in spite of the sables.

The entrance to the block of flats reeked of opulence, which was only right and proper. Its sole function was to impress the richest of Charles's clients, and it did it very well, in an impersonal kind of way. Nothing ostentatious, nothing overdone, not with Charles paying the bills, but as elegant as a stage set for a Noël Coward play, if a great deal more comfortable. . . .

Charles opened the door at its first ring, and they looked at each other. Neither made the slightest attempt at a kiss.

'Hello,' she said.

'Please come in,' said Charles, and stood aside. She walked past him, undoing her gloves, and suddenly thought of Sybil Hendry. I could do a strip, she thought, but what would be the point? All I've got to sell is me, and I'm too old now to stand in the footlights in the altogether. . . .

The flat's interior was more Noël Coward, and very nice too: white leather and plate glass, and all the paintings real.

'There's gin and vermouth,' said Charles, 'if you'd like a martini.'

'Yes please,' she said.

'You do it,' said Charles. 'You're far better at it than I am.'

A gentleman to his fingertips, like William. Why can't he swear and knock me about, she thought. I just can't cope with all this niceness, but she made the martinis and poured them out even so, and they sat on either side of an electric fire as the curtain slowly rose.

'I got your letter,' she said.

'Is that why you came back?'

'I was going to write to you and explain,' she said, 'only I found I couldn't.'

'You were ill?'

'No,' she said. 'Not ill. Tired. Please – may I just tell it to you? Afterwards you can ask all the questions you want – but may I just tell it first?'

'Of course,' he said. The Chairman of the Board look had never been more apparent, but whose fault was that?

She told him everything, from the first encounter with Peggy and the broken-down ambulance. Booker and the hospital unit and their mind-numbing weariness, the endless succession of smashed and mutilated men. No time to think, let alone argue. Just fetch and carry, day after day. Legs missing, arms missing, 'There's A Valley Called Jarama': out it all came.

'It was my whole life,' she said. 'Not that I wanted it to be. It just was. Those men – there was nothing saintly in the way I felt about them. Most of the time I hated them – inside my mind. But they were there. They had to be fetched. And then I saw the horse.'

She took a sip of her drink, and he waited, but said nothing. Still the gentleman.

She told him about the horse, and her talk with Booker, and the decision Booker had made, and her journey home with Peggy Hawkins, who still didn't know that anything was wrong.

'So it amounts to this,' she said. 'What I did wasn't a problem in moral philosophy; it was just life – and rather messy life at that. Because I was there I did what I had to do – mostly because I was one of the very few who could do it. If I'd been here in London with you, I'd have stayed.'

'Despite Jay Bower's pleading?'

'Of course,' she said. 'He could have sent somebody else to write it all up for the *World*. He couldn't have sent an ambulance driver. But I was there, Charles, and I drove because I was good at it, drove until I couldn't do it any more.'

'The horse?'

She nodded. 'I'd got your letter before that,' she said, 'and I should have written, I know I should, and oh my dear I'm sorry. But I was so tired I ached all over, and my mind was even more tired than the rest of me. That's no excuse. It's just the truth. I wanted so much to write to you. I love you, you see.'

'You don't have to say that,' said Charles.

'Of course I don't, especially now. But the fact that I love you – that's the truth, too.'

He looked at her, but for once his face told her nothing. 'Why did you say "Especially now"?' he said.

'Because it's too late,' she said.

'No by God it's not,' said Charles. 'Not unless you want it to be.'

'It's the last thing I want,' she said.

'That letter of mine,' he said. 'That stupid bloody letter. The trouble is I meant every word. Still do.'

'It's a beautiful letter,' she said.

'Beautiful?'

'Of course,' she said. 'To be needed as much as that – of course it's beautiful.'

'What you did – that was beautiful,' he said. 'What I did was just – '

She got up as he spoke and came to him. He stood up at once and his arms came round her and they kissed. Chanel and silk underwear, Fortuny and Fabergé had done their work. 'Especially now' had helped too, and the hint of a catch in her voice. Inspired by Mr Coward, she thought as they kissed, but I don't care. Why on earth should I? I've got him back.

When they came up for air he said, 'Are you hungry? The thing is I haven't eaten all day – '

'Nor I,' she said. 'Apart from a bowl of soup. Mrs Barrow's worried sick.'

'Then let's go back to South Terrace,' he said. 'Mrs Barrow can make us an omelette or something, and we can have an early night.'

'An early night's exactly what I need,' she said, and he kissed her again.

In the cab on the way home, his arm firmly round her, no matter what the taxi driver might think, Charles said, 'I'll tell you something else.'

'Yes darling?' said Jane.

'It's the Gold Cup next week.'